CONQUEST

THE CHRONICLES OF THE INVADERS

JOHN CONNOLLY + JENNIFER RIDYARD

CONQUEST

headline

First published in 2013 by
HEADLINE PUBLISHING GROUP

1

Cataloguing in Publication Data is available from the British Library

Hardback ISBN 978 1 4722 0963 4
Trade paperback ISBN 978 1 4722 0962 7

Typeset in Bembo by Avon DataSet Ltd, Bidford-on-Avon, Warwickshire

Printed and bound in Great Britain by
Clays Ltd, St Ives plc

Headline's policy is to use papers that are natural, renewable and recyclable products and
made from wood grown in sustainable forests. The logging and manufacturing processes are
expected to conform to the environmental regulations of the country of origin.

HEADLINE PUBLISHING GROUP
An Hachette UK Company
338 Euston Road
London NW1 3BH

www.headline.co.uk
www.hachette.co.uk

For Geoffrey and Vivienne Ridyard

CHAPTER 1

In the beginning was the wormhole. It bloomed like a strange flower at the edge of the solar system, dwarfing Pluto in size and majesty. It was beautiful: theory become real. Once it was discovered, the eyes of the Earth turned upon it, and the space telescope *Walton* was redirected to examine it more closely. Within days, images were being sent back to Earth.

What *Walton* revealed was a kind of blister in space, a lens-like swelling in the fabric of the universe. As one scientist remarked, to the discomfort of her peers, it looked almost as if humanity were being examined in turn. The stars behind it were distorted, and slightly off-kilter, an effect explained by the huge amount of negative energy necessary to keep the wormhole open. An intense light at its rim dimmed to a dark centre like an unblinking pupil, and so the newspapers began to refer to it as 'The Eye in Space'.

Once the initial thrill of its discovery had worn off, disturbing questions were raised. Had it always been there, and if so, why had it not been seen before? The answer, it seemed, was that the Eye had not been open before. Why, then, had it opened now? Was it a natural phenomenon, or something more sinister?

The early years of the twenty-first century had yet to offer any proof that mankind was not alone in the universe. Shortly after the discovery of the wormhole, mankind received conclusive evidence that the universe was more crowded than it had ever imagined.

A fleet emerged from the Eye, a great armada of silver ships, graceful and elegant, moving unstoppably towards the small blue planet in the distance at speeds beyond human comprehension.

And the people of Earth watched them come: steadily, silently. Efforts were made to contact the craft, but there was no reply . . .

Fear and panic spread. There was talk of the end of the world, of imminent destruction. Riots crippled the great cities, and mass suicides occurred among the more extreme religious cults, convinced that their souls would be magicked up to the approaching starships.

But wherever it was that their souls ended up, it was not on those ships.

The fleet stopped somewhere near Mars, and the Earth braced itself for attack. Some people fled to bunkers, others sought shelter in underground stations and subway systems, or retreated into caves. They waited for explosions and devastation, but none came. Instead, the Earth's technological systems began to collapse: electricity, gas, water, communications, all were hit simultaneously, sabotaged by their own computers, but in a deliberate and targeted way – national defence systems shut down, but hospitals did not, and warplanes fell from the sky while commercial jets landed safely. All control had been seized by an outside force, but one that appeared careful to avoid more fatalities than were necessary. Still, fatalities there were.

Now, the Earth's generals warned, the real assault would come, but there was no further attack. The silver ships sat silently above, while below, society fell apart. There was looting, and murder. Mass exoduses from the cities began. Cattle and livestock were stolen and slaughtered for food, so farmers began to shoot trespassers. Men turned against men, and so great was their fury that, at times, they forgot the fact of the aliens' existence. After a mere three days, armies were firing on their own citizens. All that mattered was survival.

Then, on the fourth day, power was restored selectively to the hearts of nine capital cities across the world: Washington, London, Beijing, New Delhi, Abuja, Moscow, Brasilia, Canberra and Berlin. A single word was sent to every computer in every government office. That word was:

SURRENDER

And the Earth did indeed surrender, for what choice did it have?

When the planet's new overlords eventually made themselves known, they were not what anyone on Earth had anticipated, for the Illyri were not unlike themselves. In their grace and beauty they resembled their ships. They were tall – the smallest of them was no less than six feet – with slightly elongated limbs, and their skin had the faintest of gold hues. Some had glossy, metallic manes of hair, whereas others kept their perfect skulls smooth and bald. They lacked eyelids, so their eyes were permanently open, and a clear membrane protected their retinas. When they slept, their coloured irises simply closed over their pupils, leaving their resting eyes like vivid, eerie marbles set in their fine features.

The Illyri spoke of a 'gentle conquest'. They wished to avoid further bloodshed, and all necessities and creature comforts were restored to the people. However, modern weapons systems remained disabled. Air travel was initially forbidden. Telecommunication ceased, and for a time, the Internet no longer functioned. There was a period of adjustment that was difficult, but eventually something approaching normal life resumed.

The Illyri knew what mattered to the planet they had colonised, for their technology had been hidden on Earth for many decades, ever since the earliest human radio signals were detected by probes at the mouths of wormholes, and the first quiet infiltration of the planet began. Tiny clusters of Illyri androids, most no bigger than insects, had entered the atmosphere in the late 1950s, hidden in meteor showers, and began sending back details of Earth's climate, atmosphere, population. The Illyri followed the progress of wars and famines, exposed to the best – and the worst – of what the human race had to offer. The Internet had been a particular bonus. Nanobots embedded themselves in the system; not only were they capable of transmitting the sum total of mankind's accumulated knowledge back to the drones, but they became part of the technology itself. As humanity embraced the Internet, and computers became an integral part of life, so too mankind unwittingly welcomed the Illyri into their lives and sowed the seeds for their arrival.

After the initial shock of the invasion, the human resistance commenced. There were shootings and bombings. Illyri were kidnapped and killed, or held as hostages in a vain attempt to force a retreat from the planet. World leaders conspired to fight back.

In response, the citizens of Rome were given twenty-four hours to evacuate their city, and it was then wiped from the map in a massive explosion that sent dust and debris over all of Western Europe, a reminder that the Earth's empires were as nothing before the invaders. Then the Illyri announced that one tenth of the population between the ages of fifteen and twenty-one in every city and town would be conscripted into the Illyri Military brigades for five years. Essentially the youths would be hostages: each family from which a young adult was removed had a responsibility to report saboteurs, or face the consequences. If violence was committed against the invaders, the townsfolk were informed that they would never see their young people again. It was a charter for informers, designed to sow distrust and crush cooperation among those who would challenge Illyri rule.

But the Illyri also offered hope. They erected great condensers in arid climates, transforming deserts to fields. They genetically modified fruits, and grains, and vegetables, making them more abundant and resistant to disease. Within two years, hunger was virtually eliminated on Earth, as were many communicable diseases. Geoengineering – the use of giant reflectors to send sunlight back into space before it struck the planet – tackled the problem of global warming, reducing the Earth's temperatures to levels not seen since the start of the nineteenth century.

The Illyri did all that was possible to change the Earth for the better.

And still the humans fought us at every turn . . .

CHAPTER 2

Syl Hellais, the first of her kind to be born on Earth, jumped from her desk and rushed to the bedroom window. Below stretched the grey stone walls and cobbled courtyards of Edinburgh Castle: her fortress, her home and, she sometimes felt, her prison. Beyond the castle lay the city itself, brooding beneath the dark Scottish skies.

There! A column of smoke rose to the east, the aftermath of the explosion that had caused Syl to abandon her schoolwork. Faintly she could hear sirens, and Illyri patrol craft shone spotlights from the sky on the streets beneath. The humans were attacking again. They liked bombs. Bombs were easy to plant. They could be hidden in bags, in cars, even under dead cats and dogs. If it wasn't bombs, it was snipers. All Illyri were potential targets, although the human Resistance preferred to kill those in uniform. They were more tolerant of young Illyri, and females in particular, although they were not above targeting them for kidnapping. Syl put herself at risk every time she walked the streets of Edinburgh, but that knowledge served only to add a thrill to her explorations. Still, she had learned to conceal her alien nature from prying eyes, and with a little make-up, and the right glasses and clothing, she could sometimes pass for human.

And after all, was she not also of this planet? She was Syl the Earth-born, the first Illyri to be born on the conquered world in the early months of the invasion. In her way, she was as much its citizen as the humans. She was a child of two realms: born on one, loyal to another. She loathed the Earth, and yet she loved it too, even if she rarely admitted this love to anyone, even herself.

Shaking her head, Syl turned away from the window, from the

smoke and the unseen carnage. There would be more of it. It never ended, and it never would, not as long as the Illyri remained on Earth.

She was Syl the Firstborn, Syl the Earthborn.

Syl the Invader.

But Edinburgh was not the only target to be hit that night. Further south, another attack was about to commence, and it would change the life of Syl Hellais for ever.

The Illyri Military had established many of its bases on the sites of great fortresses from Earth's past. Those still standing – among them the Tower of London and Edinburgh Castle in the United Kingdom, the Stockholm Palace in Sweden, Prague Castle in the Czech Republic, and the Forbidden City in Beijing, China – were simply adapted for Illyri use. Where nothing of the original forts remained, replacements were either built offworld and lowered into place from ships, or constructed from materials found on Earth.

The fort at Birdoswald had been erected by the Roman Empire as part of Hadrian's Wall, which originally stretched across the width of northern England to protect the south from Scottish marauders. Before the coming of the Illyri, only the lower parts of its buildings and walls had remained standing, the pattern and logic of them apparent when viewed from the hills above or the slopes below. Danis, the head of the Illyri Military in Britain, was particularly fascinated by the Romans, and had made some efforts to ensure that the old fort was not completely spoiled by its new additions. He had used local stone to rebuild walls, and the living quarters were also faced with stone so that they blended into the landscape.

Danis had garrisoned the fort with a small force of amphibian-like Galatean conscripts commanded by an Illyri officer named Thaios. Not that Thaois was Danis's first choice, for he was not a member of the Illyri Military. Instead he was a member of the Diplomatic Corps; the Military and the Diplomats were always at one another's throats, each constantly seeking to increase its power at the expense of the other. Nevertheless, Danis had been ordered to give Thaios command, for Thaios was a favourite of the Diplomats, and was being groomed for leadership. It was also accepted that, at some point in the future, administration of the Earth would pass to the Corps, and the Military would move on to other campaigns. Giving command positions to Diplomats was a first step towards that end.

Still, as far as Danis was concerned, Thaios was a spoiled brat, and Danis, an old soldier, wouldn't have trusted the boy to command a fish to swim. Thaios, meanwhile, viewed the command of a small garrison fort in the middle of nowhere as beneath him.

However, the garrison was considered necessary. The smuggling of weapons was commonplace in the area, and the local population was regarded as particularly hostile, as is often the case at contested borders. The threat of permanent exile for their children seemed only to have antagonised many of the Scots, and not far from Birdoswald a primitive Improvised Explosive Device had recently destroyed two vehicles in a Military convoy. Among the casualties had been Aeron, Thaios's predecessor, who had been blown into so many pieces that his head had never been found. Since then, most Illyri travel to and from Birdoswald was conducted by air. Where once cars and coaches had parked, bringing parties of tourists to view the fort and the wall, a pair of lightly armed interceptors – small, agile craft that were used for short-range sorties and patrols – now rested on a landing pad.

Otherwise, the garrison at Birdoswald was defended largely by the conscripted Galateans, rugged, grey beings, their skin leathery in texture, their bodies narrowing to a head without the intervention of a neck, their eyes bulbous, their mouths wide. The humans called them 'Toads'. They communicated through a system of clicks and croaks, and the strangeness of their features made their emotions impossible to read: they ate, fought and killed with the same impassive stare.

The conquest of the Galatean system had been one of the Illyri's more profitable campaigns. It yielded a ready source of troops, for the Galateans were natural soldiers, used to being commanded and genetically seasoned for combat by millennia of inter-tribal warfare over scarce resources. Also, since their homeworlds were little more than barren rocks inhabited by an array of predators – with the

Galateans themselves trapped somewhere in the middle of this natural cycle of killing and being killed – they were more than willing to enter the service of the Illyri. They provided far more than one in ten of their young to conscription, and most went voluntarily.

Eight Galateans stood on the walls of the fortress, and one occupied the observation tower. All were equipped with night-vision lenses and high-velocity weapons. Each also wore a curved knife, like the claw of some great reptile rendered in steel.

A vehicle was detected on the garrison's radar while it was still a mile away. It was coming from the west at about forty miles an hour, following the road that ran parallel to the remains of the wall. The Galatean monitoring the screen summoned Thaios.

While the movement of vehicles along the road was not forbidden, the Illyri had imposed a standard curfew in certain areas. Motorised travel was not permitted between the hours of sunset and sunrise unless cleared in advance through the proper channels. No such communication had been received that night by the garrison at Birdoswald.

Thaios watched the dot moving on the screen. He was a muscular figure, and prided himself on his physical strength, although he had yet to be tested in battle. His head was shaved, even though this style was traditionally adopted by more senior members of the Corps. Thaios aspired to join their number, and shaving his head was a means of demonstrating his ambition.

Thaios was always angry, as many secretly frightened people frequently are. The Galateans did not respect him because he did not respect them. The local population hated him because he had taken to ordering searches of vehicles and raids on houses, which interfered with daily life and resulted in damage to property, as well as the occasional arrest. The Military hated him because he was a member of the Corps; much of the Corps distrusted him because he was the nephew of Grand Consul Gradus, one of the Corps' leading figures, and it was believed that he relayed negative comments back to his uncle – which was true. It was also felt that he was being groomed for leadership only because of his uncle's influence, which was, again, true.

'Alert the guards,' ordered Thaios. 'Reinforce the detail at the main gate.'

A siren blared. Six Galateans emerged from their guardhouse, weapons at the ready, and loped towards the entrance. They were halfway across the central square when there was a whistling sound from the night sky, and moments later the first mortar shell landed among them, killing three of them instantly. Another shell followed while the garrison was still reeling from the shock of the first, and the Galateans who had survived the initial blast were killed by the second.

The two guards above the main gate were caught between trying to find the location of the mortar and monitoring the approach of the truck, which was now visible to the naked eye. It was travelling without lights, but the Galateans' night-vision lenses picked up its shape, and the shadowy outlines of two people in the cab. Without waiting for further orders, the guards concentrated on the most immediate visible threat, and commenced firing on the truck. It crossed the central line of the road as the first bullets struck, then accelerated, heading straight for the gates. The doors on either side of the truck opened and the two humans jumped to safety as the vehicle struck the gates.

The force of the impact knocked one of the guards from the wall beside the gate. He lay sprawled on the ground, one leg twisted at a grotesque angle, his damaged skull leaking fluid through his nostrils and earholes. His companion had managed to hold on to a metal support strut, and although shaken and driven to his knees was otherwise unharmed.

He was still rising to his feet when the truck, packed with fertiliser, exploded.

The massive gates were blown from their hinges, one of them landing on the nearest interceptor, crushing its cockpit. The second gate landed on the roof of the main guardhouse, cutting through the tin like the blade of a knife, trapping inside the building those that it did not kill.

Gunfire erupted from the surrounding fields. Thaios's eardrums had burst as a result of the explosion at the gates and he was in agony as he tried to organise his surviving troops, shouting orders that he himself could hear only as distorted noise. The guards on the walls returned fire, but now there were humans moving past the burning wreckage of the truck, and a concentrated burst of automatic fire knocked the guard from the watchtower. A human was standing at the door of the ruined guardhouse, spraying the interior with bullets. Thaios drew a bead on him and fired a single round. The man twisted and fell, but before Thaios could pick another target, he felt a hammer blow to his shoulder, and a great burning followed. The bullet had passed straight through his upper body, and the wound was already pumping red Illyri blood. He retreated to a corner by the ruined guardhouse. There was a dull explosion behind him as the trapped guards used a grenade to blow a hole in the rear of the building. Thaios summoned them to him, and from behind the ruined walls of the old fort they fought the insurgents, dark figures that darted and weaved and were only occasionally illuminated by the flames of the burning truck. A second great explosion rent the air as the remaining interceptor was blown up, and Thaios and his soldiers found themselves under heavy fire. One of the Galateans fell, then another and another, until at last only Thaios remained standing.

The shooting stopped. All was quiet for moment, until a voice called out to Thaios, 'Surrender! Surrender and you won't be hurt.'

Thaios examined the digital read on his pulse pistol. The charge was almost empty: only one shot left. He could have attempted to pick up another weapon from one of the fallen Galateans, but he could see the insurgents working their way around him. If he moved, he would be exposed.

'Throw out your weapon,' said the same voice. 'Then stand up and show us your hands.'

Thaios was suddenly very tired. He had been so ambitious, so anxious to progress. This was all such a waste.

The order to surrender came again. The humans were drawing closer. One of their shadows almost touched his boot.

Thaios put his gun in his mouth.

'I'm sorry,' he said. The human nearest him frowned, but it had not been to him that Thaios was speaking.

'Stop him!' someone yelled.

It was the last thing Thaios heard before his head exploded.

CHAPTER 3

The following morning, Syl walked quickly through the hallways of Edinburgh Castle, the soft silk of her trousers swishing against her legs, her face set in an expression that she thought of as determined but those who were responsible for her would have wearily described as 'obstinate'. It was a word used often to describe Syl. Perhaps, the young Illyri told herself privately (and rather hopefully), she took after her mother, the beautiful Lady Orianne, who had been both wilful and charming, a combination that made her quite impossible to resist.

Syl, by contrast, was still working on the charm component. And beauty? Well, her father told her beauty was in the eye of the beholder, and to him she was the most beautiful creature in the world, indeed in all worlds. Of course he would say that! The truth was that she was not unpretty, but her features still held the unformed softness of youth, coupled with an unnerving intensity in her eyes and a sharpness in her manner. The effect wasn't helped by the fact that Syl wasn't given to smiling just to please people, because smiles could be much better employed than that, and she only laughed on occasions that truly merited it. And how else was she to behave? she asked herself, for she had no intention of smiling for no reason, or wasting time laughing at stupid jokes. Anyway, Syl took the view that laughing at something just to be kind usually meant the joker would plague you with another attempt at humour, and you'd have to laugh again, and so the cycle would continue until she either died of boredom or killed someone. Frankly she couldn't be sure which might happen first.

And yet much tolerance was shown to Syl, for she had been conceived among the stars, and as the first Illyri child born on Earth, she was a living link between the homeworld of Illyr and the conquered planet. Of course, it helped that her father was Lord Andrus, governor of the islands of Britain and Ireland, and by extension all of Europe. Like all Illyri females, though, Syl bore the name of her mother's family. She liked being Syl Hellais. Syl Andrus sounded, well, ugly.

Britain had been the obvious base for Illyri operations in Europe: even before the invasion, it had been a country obsessed with surveillance, both obvious and secret. Its streets were infested with security cameras, many of them with facial-recognition capacity, and the actions of its citizens were constantly being monitored by government departments. The Illyri had hardly needed to change anything upon their arrival. The same was true for the other most powerful nations: China, Russia, the United States. The governments of Earth, aided by populations too lazy or trusting to care, and obsessed with putting every detail of their lives on the Internet, had helped to give the Illyri control of the planet.

Andrus was also responsible for the overall administration of Europe, and the governors of the other European nations deferred to him. Technically, he enjoyed equal status with the administrators of similar large territories, including Africa, China, Russia, Australasia and the Americas, but he chaired the Ruling Council, which gave him a deciding vote on every important decision. Effectively, Governor Andrus was the most powerful man on Earth, although Syl knew better than to use the words 'Do you know who my father is?' to get herself out of trouble. Well, she knew better than to try it a second time . . .

And then there was the fact that the Lady Orianne had died when Syl was only a year old, succumbing to an attack of malaria while the Illyri were still coming to terms with the diseases of the new world. There is no substitute for a mother and so there was a sadness that lingered around Syl, coupled with an anger that she found difficult to suppress. Recently Andrus had begun to despair of her behaviour, but as Althea, Syl's childhood governess, would gently point out to him, he was not the first father to have been rendered speechless with frustration by a daughter approaching adulthood.

'Even were her mother here, my lord, I suspect Syl would still be a difficult proposition,' she would murmur. Althea had been entrusted with Syl's care since the death of Lady Orianne, mothering her as best she could, and she loved the girl as a daughter. Her own child, a son, had died shortly after birth, another victim of disease, and she had become Syl's milk-mother. A special bond had formed between Syl and Althea, but the teenage years were proving trying for the governess too. Still, she had high hopes for the girl. Syl would do well in life, assuming her father didn't throttle her first.

Now Althea hurried to catch up with her charge as Syl rushed through the corridors.

'Why aren't you in school, Syl?' said Althea.

Like all children of the Illyri, Syl attended classes each day: science, mathematics, history, languages. They were taught of Illyr and its empire, but they learned too of the cultures of Earth and the other principal conquered worlds.

'Leave me be, Althea,' said Syl, as the older woman fell into step beside her. To amuse herself, Syl varied her pace, slowing down and speeding up, so that Althea was alternately left behind or stranded a foot or two ahead of her charge. Either way, she ended up talking to empty air, but she had an idea of where Syl was going, and was determined to stop her.

'Your father is not to be disturbed,' said Althea. 'He arrived back in the early hours, and has barely slept.'

'It is my birthday, Althea. I'm entitled to ask a favour of him.'

It was a tradition among the Illyri that on the anniversary of their birth they could make a single request of a loved one that had to be granted. It was a relic of an older time, but still fondly regarded. Husbands would ask for a kiss from their wives, mothers a meal cooked by their sons' hands: small gestures, but no less meaningful for that.

'You may talk to him after your classes,' said Althea.

Syl had already tired of her earlier game, and was now determined to leave Althea in her wake, so the frustrated governess was forced to scamper to keep up with Syl's long strides. Althea was short for an

Illyri; today, on Syl's sixteenth birthday, the girl was already much the taller of the two.

'My request is that I should not have to attend classes,' said Syl. 'I would like a day to myself in the city.'

As if Althea was unaware of what that might involve, Syl stopped by one of the castle windows and gestured dramatically at the streets of Edinburgh below. Edinburgh and London provided twin administrative bases for Andrus, but he preferred Edinburgh, and its great castle perched above the city, to the confines of the Tower of London. London was a difficult city to like: overcrowded, smelly and increasingly violent. Three months earlier, the Tower itself had come under attack from a suicide bomber piloting a small plane packed with explosives. The assault was thwarted, but secretly Andrus would have been quite happy if the Tower had been blasted to smithereens. He would have loved an excuse to spend more time in Scotland, with its harsh but beautiful landscape that reminded him of the northern wilds of Illyr itself, where he had spent his youth. Syl, too, was happier in Edinburgh, and so it remained her home when her father was absent in the south for weeks, or even months.

'So,' Syl continued, 'how can my father grant my birthday wish if, by the time I ask it, my birthday will be over?'

Althea had to admit that the girl's logic was unarguable. Unfortunately, she also knew that Andrus had given strict orders that he should not be disturbed. There had been two attacks the previous night, and the dead were still being counted, leaving Andrus under pressure from his offworld superiors to provide an appropriate response to the latest outrages. He already trod a delicate line between those who advocated gentleness and understanding in their dealings with the humans, and those who called for harsher discipline. As with the humans, so with his daughter, thought Althea.

'Syl, this is not a good time. There were killings last night . . .'

'Oh, there are always killings, Althea,' said Syl. 'Every day, every week. If we're not killing them in firefights, then they're killing us with guns and bombs. Maybe we shouldn't be here at all.'

'Hush!' said Althea, grabbing Syl's arm. 'That's all very well for classroom debates, but it's not to be said within earshot of your father's chambers. There are those who would take great pleasure in whispering that Lord Andrus's daughter speaks treason in the governor's castle.'

Syl wasn't so sure that even the classroom was the place to debate the rights and wrongs of the Illyri's conquests. She was one of twenty students, the youngest of whom was only seven. They were all taught by the same tutor, Toris, who was so ancient that Ani, Syl's closest friend, said there was no such thing as history for him: it was all personal experience. Toris did not encourage independent thought. His purpose was to tell them things, and his students' purpose was to remember them.

'Since when did expressing an opinion become treason?' asked Syl.

'Don't be so naive. Suggesting to someone that the weather might change is an opinion. Stirring up dissent is treasonous.'

'Why, do you feel stirred, Althea?' said Syl, and even while being mocked, Althea loved the spirit that dwelt within this one. 'Will you take to the streets in protest if the weather holds?'

Althea took the girl by the hands and held her there, looking up into her eyes. They were reddish gold, like her mother's. She had her mother's voice too, low yet musical. What she had inherited from her father was not so clear. She had certainly not acquired his diplomacy, nor his ability to refrain from speaking his every thought aloud. Despite that, she had an uncanny way of winding others around her little finger, of gently bending them to her will. Even Althea was not entirely immune to Syl's manipulations.

'You must be careful, Syl,' said Althea. 'Your father's position is not secure. There has been talk of recalling governors because of the escalating levels of violence. Already the Diplomats have increased their presence here. Washington is now a Diplomat city, and the Diplomats have just been granted a special order excluding the Military from Iceland, effective from next month. As the senior Military commander on Earth, your father is furious.'

Syl's obvious surprise made it clear that she had not heard any of this, and Althea instantly knew that she had said too much.

'A recall?' said Syl. 'Then we could return to Illyr?'

Althea noted the use of the word 'return'. Like many Illyri now marooned far from home, Syl longed to see her homeworld. Althea had no such illusions. Illyr was not what it once was. It had changed. The conquests had changed it.

'Perhaps,' said Althea. 'Your father could return, but it would be in disgrace, possibly even in chains. And remember, Syl, your father loves it here. He does not want to go back. All his life he dreamed of seeing new worlds, and he has spent more time away from the homeworld than he has living on it. He wants to be buried on this alien world with alien sun warming his grave. If your mother had lived, things might have been different. She was bound deeply to Illyr. She loved the homeworld, but she loved your father more.'

'And she died for it,' said Syl, bitterly. 'Died for the sake of a planet that hated her, and all like her.'

Althea did not argue. She had heard all of this before, and there was some truth to it.

'I am not my father,' continued Syl. 'I want to live on Illyr. It is my true home.'

Illyr: she had seen it only in books and on screens – projections of forests that towered ten times higher than any vegetation on Earth, and oceans deeper and cleaner than the polluted waters of the Atlantic or the Pacific; of the creatures that walked and swam and crawled and flew through its environs, so much more noble and striking and beautiful than the denizens of this planet, the greatest of which – tigers and blue whales, gorillas and polar bears – were already close to extinction. Most of all, Syl wanted to see its cities: Olos, the Gem of the North; Arayyis, part of it built beneath the ocean and part above; and great Tannis itself, the City of Spires, the most beautiful city in the Illyri Empire, the place in which her mother had been born. True, she had walked on Illyr by activating the virtual-reality programs in the wired rooms of the castle, but she was always aware that they were an illusion. She wanted to breathe Illyri air, not some computer's pumped-in imitation of it. It was only during Toris's discussions of Illyr that Syl showed any patience with her tutor, for the old fool was as besotted with the planet as she was.

'Illyr is not as it was,' said Althea. 'Do not believe all that Toris shows or tells you. That old man will drown in his own nostalgia.'

Syl freed her hands. 'Nothing pleases you, Althea. You are as sour as an unripe apple.'

Then, just as Althea seemed set to take offence, Syl planted a big kiss on the older woman's cheek, and sprang away, smiling. That was another of her talents: the ability to recognise when she had gone too far, and to act to prevent any further harm being done. If only, Althea thought, she could stop herself *before* she went too far.

'Now you're distracting me,' said Syl, 'and I have a favour to request.'

'Syl! I told you, he's busy.'

'Don't worry, I won't disturb him. I'll just wait outside until he's finished. And please stop running after me. You know you can't keep up.'

Syl darted down the hallway, waved from around the corner and was gone. Althea sighed deeply and leaned against the nearest wall. Below her, the city went about its business, the bomb of the night before already forgotten. In the distance loomed the crag known as Arthur's Seat. There was a grandeur to Edinburgh, thought Althea, but its beauty was stern and austere. Summer was at an end, and the first hint of a cold, damp winter was already blowing through the laneways. Althea hated the cold. She wished Andrus had become governor of Spain and Portugal, or Central America, somewhere with a little heat and light. These northern territories oppressed her with their gloom.

But now someone was coming. She looked up to see the tutor, Toris. He was a scowling, wrinkled figure who walked with a pronounced stoop. There was no harm to him, but Althea, like Syl, regarded him as an old bore. Unlike Syl, though, she did not have to listen to him unless she chose to do so.

'I seek Syl,' said Toris. 'Class has commenced.'

'Feel free to chase her, if you can run fast enough. She has no mind for classes today. It is the anniversary of her birth. She will spend the day in her own way, whether permitted to or not.'

Toris seemed about to protest, then gave up and contented himself with a resigned shrug. 'Well, let her roam, then, and much good may it bring her.'

Althea was surprised. Toris was not usually one to allow such leniencies. Ani, Syl's best friend and partner in crime, was regularly reported to her parents for even the slightest of infractions, and Toris would have beaten a similarly frequent path to Lord Andrus's door to complain of Syl's behavior if Andrus were not the governor, or if Althea had not done her best to soothe Toris's wrath. Old books seemed to calm him, she found. So did wine. Speaking of which . . .

'Have you been drinking?' asked Althea. 'It's not like you to give up so easily.'

'I was young once,' Toris replied stiffly.

'Were you now?' Althea sniffed. 'I wonder that you can remember back so far.'

'It is my task to remember,' Toris reminded her, with some dignity. 'I remember, so that others will not forget.'

'You fill her head with talk of the glories of Illyr, her and the other children. They dream of returning to a place they have never known, and meanwhile the life that they have passes them by.'

'Illyr is great,' said Toris.

'Perhaps it was, once,' said Althea. 'But they will never see it, not as it was. Never.'

'You do not know that,' said Toris.

'I do,' said Althea. 'And you know it too.'

Toris did not bother to continue the argument. He and Althea had had this discussion before, and would have it again, but not this morning. Toris was tired, and he felt old. He always felt old on the birthdays of his students. He left Althea, and shuffled off to bore those of his charges who had not, so far, managed to escape.

CHAPTER 4

The two young men walking towards the little restaurant near Edinburgh's London Road were no different in appearance from any of the other youths who still viewed Edinburgh as 'their' city, despite the presence of aliens, police and anyone else who might have been of another opinion. One was taller and older than the other, but the similarities between the two were too obvious for them to be anything but brothers. Their names were Paul and Steven Kerr, and they were members of the Resistance.

Paul had been born not long after the initial Illyri invasion. Now he was just a few weeks short of his seventeenth birthday, but he carried himself with the authority of an older man, as befitted someone who had risked his life in the fight against the Illyri occupation. His brother Steven had just turned fifteen, and was less certain of himself. So far he had only been involved in minor operations, mostly as a lookout. Steven suspected that it was Paul who had been responsible for keeping him away from the action, although Paul had always denied it. Steven now felt that he was old enough to fight; after all, young men and women his own age had already died at the hands of the Illyri and their servant races, and it wasn't right that he should be stopped from playing his part in the Resistance. Paul gradually seemed to have come to terms with this, at least in some small way, which was why he had agreed that Steven should accompany him on this particular mission. School would have to do without them for a day.

Despite his relative youth, Paul was one of the Resistance's best intelligence officers. He was good at listening, and skilled at slotting himself into places and situations that might yield useful information.

The Resistance had young spies all over the city, and many of them reported, either directly or indirectly, to Paul. There was little that went on among the Illyri about which the Resistance did not know, or so they had long believed.

Recent events, though, had caused them to reconsider this view. Whispers had reached them of possible secret tunnels beneath Edinburgh, constructed without their knowledge. There were darker rumours too: the sick and old disappearing from hospitals, and corpses sent for cremation becoming lost in the system. And all that was even before the attack on Birdoswald: Paul had not known of it in advance, and he was usually entrusted with prior notice of such operations. This troubled him, which was why he was glad that a meeting had been called. He wanted to know more.

'Hurry up,' he said to Steven. 'We're going to be late.'

Steven obediently sped up. Although there were sometimes tensions between them, as there were between any brothers, Steven adored Paul. Paul was a fighter.

Paul had killed.

As the restaurant came in sight, Paul halted.

'Remember,' he told Steven. 'Stay quiet. Don't say anything unless someone asks you a question first. If I tell you to leave, do it, okay? No objections.'

'You won't even know I'm there, honest,' said Steven.

Paul had been told to bring Steven along. He would not have done so otherwise. He knew what was going to happen. It was time: the Resistance had decided that his little brother was ready for major operations.

Danny's Diner was a typical greasy spoon. It offered breakfast all day, put batter on anything from sausages to Mars bars, and served chips with everything. It was even possible to order a plate of double chips, which was basically chips with chips. Danny's Diner was the unhealthiest restaurant in Scotland, and it was sometimes whispered that it had killed more Scots than the Illyri. Nobody looked at the boys as they entered. Everyone in there was a friend of the Resistance, but they still knew that it was best to mind their own business. Only Danny, who was working behind the counter, gave them the smallest of nods.

Two young women, both of them only a few years older than Paul, sat in a booth at the back of the restaurant. Their names were Jean and Nessa Trask, and their father was one of the most important Resistance leaders in Scotland. They had cups of greyish tea before them, and the remains of some toast, with the mandatory chips now shrivelled and cold.

'I thought your dad might be here,' said Paul as he slid on to the plastic bench.

'He's busy,' said Nessa, the older of the girls, 'but we'll pay for your tea anyway.' She signalled to the waitress, who scurried off looking nervous, and with good reason. Nessa was bigger and broader than her sister. Some of the boys called her Nessy, after the Loch Ness monster, but only behind her back; she'd broken the nose of the last person she'd heard calling her by that nickname. Her sister Jean was prettier, and not as smart, but she was much more dangerous. She had a way with knives.

'Lot of activity last night,' said Paul, referring discreetly to Birdoswald.

'We were as surprised as you were,' said Nessa.

'It wasn't us?'

Nessa shook her head. 'The fireworks in the city were ours, but not the business at the fort. Dad's looking into it. That's why he's not here.'

Their tea arrived, and the older teenagers watched in cool amusement as Steven took a tentative sip. It was horrible, as always. The boy immediately poured several sachets of sugar into his cup and stirred it vigorously before trying again. The sweetness helped, but not much.

'So,' said Nessa, still looking at Steven, who tried not to appear uncomfortable under her scrutiny, 'this is the new little soldier.'

Jean snickered. She picked up her butter knife and began playing with it, balancing it on the tip of her finger. It was a neat trick.

'He's been on jobs before,' said Paul, springing instinctively to his brother's defence.

'He's stood on street corners watching for patrols,' said Nessa. 'My dog could do that.'

'Then why isn't your dog here?' said Steven, which surprised Nessa, even as Paul raised his eyes to heaven and gave his brother a sharp kick on the right ankle.

'He even barks like my dog,' said Nessa, but she seemed amused by Steven. 'My dad says he's ready. What do you say?'

She levelled her gaze at Paul. Jean might have been prettier, but Nessa had something special, a kind of charisma. Paul might even have found her attractive if she hadn't been so terrifying.

'He's ready,' said Paul, after only a moment's hesitation. Beside him, Steven's cheeks glowed with pride.

'What do I know?' said Nessa. 'I'm only a girl,' but she said it in the same way that a heavyweight champion of the world might have said he was only a boxer.

'What's the job?' said Paul.

Nessa leaned in closer to him, and lowered her voice.

'We think we've found one of the tunnels . . .'

CHAPTER 5

Syl could hear her father shouting as she neared his office. She
paused while she was still out of sight of Balen, his secretary, who
carefully controlled access to the governor from his desk outside the
door. Syl rather liked Balen, and his affection for her was obvious, but
she could tell as she peered around the corner that he was unlikely to
be welcoming this morning. He was staring at his vidscreen, his fingers
rapidly manipulating the display. The screen was a projection created
by the castle's artificial intelligence system: a similar one could be
summoned at any time, in any room. As a child, Syl had thought it
magical. Balen was simultaneously fielding calls to his communications
console, adjusting his tone according to the importance of the caller,
though each received roughly the same response: no, it would *not* be
possible to talk to Governor Andrus . . .

The door to the office stood ajar. Syl could not see her father, but
she glimpsed a short, balding human wearing a suit that was two sizes
too small for him. It was McGill, the First Minister of the Scottish
Parliament, who served as the main channel of communication
between the Scottish humans and the Illyri. The Illyri had allowed
most local councils, and even national parliaments, to remain active,
although they offered only the illusion of self-government, since no
major decisions could be made without the Illyri approval. Governor
Andrus was often heard to remark that given how poorly human
governments performed even the simplest of tasks, they might have
found it preferable to hand all power to the Illyri, and at least see the
job done right.

As Syl listened, her father's voice rose again.

'Greater freedom of movement?' he shouted. 'Are you insane? Do you have any idea what is happening in this damned country of yours? Shootings, bombings, acts of sabotage and murder. We had an explosion in the city last night, and then the garrison at Birdoswald was attacked. We lost twenty Galateans, and the captain of the garrison, not to mention two interceptors reduced to charred metal, and you're asking me to give your people even *more* opportunities to attack us?'

'We are not responsible for actions taken south of the border,' said McGill. 'And we're not talking about the whole of Scotland either. For now, at least allow more ease of travel between the cities, and perhaps make Edinburgh itself a free zone, with unrestricted movement within the city limits.'

'The reason you're not talking about the whole of the country, Mr McGill,' said Andrus, 'is that most of the Highlands remains lawless. Travel north to Inverness and Aberdeen is only possible by air, because anything that moves along the ground risks being attacked and looted. Most of the time I'm forced to amuse myself by trying to establish which of you is worst: the Scots, the Irish or the Welsh. The more I study your history, the more I pity the English for having to put up with the lot of you.'

'And yet now you're being attacked close to Carlisle,' McGill interrupted. 'Forgive me for pointing this out again, but that's England, isn't it?'

'Infected by a virus of rebellion that started up here, no doubt,' Lord Andrus countered. 'In fact, I suspect that the terrorists travelled south to Birdoswald, not north. They're Scots, or I'm a fool. And don't think that the rebels have any love for *your* city either. They disapprove of even your limited cooperation with us, and they'd dearly love to make an example of the most obliging of you. Our security procedures protect you as much as they protect us.'

McGill bowed his head; Lord Andrus's words had hit home. Major attacks on the occupying forces were growing more frequent in Edinburgh, although Glasgow was worse: there were housing estates on the outskirts of the city, wellsprings of rebellion and vicious dissent, that even the Galateans refused to police.

'There will be no relaxation of the travel restrictions for now,' said Lord Andrus. Then, remembering his own reputation for diplomacy, he added: 'We'll review the situation in three months' time. But I warn you: if the attack on Birdoswald represents the beginning of a new terrorist campaign, you can look forward to repression that will make the early days of the invasion seem like a dream state. You can pass that on to the rebels from me.'

McGill started to object, but Lord Andrus interrupted him.

'Don't take me for a fool, Mr McGill. I could have you tortured until you decide to share your knowledge of the Resistance. The only reason I don't do so is that I'd prefer some channels of communication with the Resistance to remain open, and I dislike unnecessary violence. Increasingly, though, my voice is struggling to make itself heard among those who think that we have been far too tolerant. If the violence continues, I won't be able to hold them back for much longer. You may have no love for the Galateans or the Military, but we are ordered, disciplined soldiers. We respond only to provocation, and fight to defend ourselves. Troublesome populations tend to invite the attentions of far more brutal forces.'

Syl knew that her father was referring to the Securitats. They were the Illyri secret police, and answered only to the Diplomatic Corps and its leader, Grand Consul Gradus. It was the Securitats who had been responsible for the destruction of Rome.

There was the sound of a chair being pushed back, and moments later her father appeared in the doorway, herding McGill ahead of him, an almost comically round presence compared to the tall, aristocratic figure of Lord Andrus.

Her father was sixty, but fit and strong, with few signs of ageing. The lifespan of the Illyri was longer than that of humans, thanks to gene therapy and organ replacements, routinely extending to a hundred and twenty Earth years or more, so Lord Andrus was only into his middle age. His military record was impeccable, and his experience of battle and conquest ensured that he was respected by the army and, if the truth be told, somewhat feared by the Diplomats. Even Grand Consul Gradus, who lived by the motto that 'Armies conquer, but Diplomats rule', was known to be wary of angering Andrus, although he still hated him. The reasons for their enmity could be boiled down to one simple difference between the two Illyri: Gradus was cruel; Andrus was not. Nevertheless, in Gradus's ideal universe, the Military would wipe out all resistance in conquered territories and then retreat to bind its wounds while the Diplomats reaped the spoils. In fact he would have preferred it if the Military were entirely under his control, just another arm of the Diplomatic Corps, and subject to its rule.

But it was Gradus who had supported her father's appointment to his current position, despite the objections of many of the Grand Consul's own staff. Curiously, at least three quarters of the Illyri governors on Earth were Military officers, and the remainder had recently retired from service. Over dinner one evening, Syl had questioned her father as to why this was.

'The humans call it a "poisoned chalice",' he replied. 'In the Military, it is known as a "dark command". It means that what appears to be a blessing may well prove to be a curse. Gradus wants the Military to fail here. If we fail, he and the Diplomats can take over. Gradus is no fool, Syl. This conquest of Earth is very different from any previous imperial adventures. We have never before encountered a civilisation so advanced. Biologically, culturally, socially we have more in common with the humans than we have with any other conquered race. But Gradus and his kind are so convinced of their own superiority that every race but our own appears inconsequential to them. He has not even troubled himself to visit Earth. He sits in the palace of a dead king, spinning his plots as a spider spins its web, listening to the whisperings of witches.'

Syl shivered at the memory of her father's words. There it was, the mystery at the heart of the Illyri Empire, the secret power behind its great expansion.

The witches.

The Nairene Sisterhood.

CHAPTER 6

Syl had never encountered any members of the Nairene Sisterhood, but she had heard stories of their power. For centuries they had been an order of recluses, existing only to record and curate the history of the Illyri Empire. As the Empire began to expand, first exploring its own galaxy, and then moving further into the universe, so too did the Sisterhood's thirst for new knowledge grow. They were a storehouse of all that was known about the universe, passed on from generation to generation. It was considered a great honour for a family to have a daughter inducted into the Sisterhood, although Syl couldn't see the appeal in being locked away for the rest of her life, forbidden to travel or explore, or even to leave the Marque, the labyrinthine city which was the Sisterhood's lair. The Marque was situated on a moon of Illyr named Avila Minor, and no one landed on or left the moon without the permission of the Sisterhood.

But then suddenly the nature of the Sisterhood had changed. Led by Ezil, the oldest of their order, they had emerged from the Marque, and some had even taken husbands. If it was considered an honour for a daughter to join the order, so too did ambitious men realise the advantage that might be gained from having the knowledge of the Sisterhood close at hand. Ezil decided which of the sisters should be permitted to marry, and to whom they should become betrothed, but she herself did not marry, and neither did the four other most senior sisters. Instead, they had made themselves indispensable as advisers, attaching themselves to the Diplomatic Corps, and soon no decision was made without first consulting them.

All this had occurred many years before Syl was born, and Ezil and

the senior sisters, known as the First Five, had not been seen outside
the Marque in decades. But the emergence of the Sisterhood had
marked the beginning of what was now known as the Second Empire.
It was the Sisterhood that had given the Empire the means to expand,
for they had discovered the location of the wormholes. The universe
teemed with them; they were gateways between galaxies, allowing
the Illyri to travel vast distances with previously unimagined speed.
Her father had explained the nature of the wormholes to Syl when
she was a small child. He had shown her a sheet of paper, and told her
to imagine that it represented millions and millions of miles of space.
At the far right side of the page he made a mark with his pen, and
placed a similar mark on the far left.

'Now,' he said, 'imagine that this first dot is Illyr, and this second
dot is Earth. How long would it take to travel from one to the other?'

'Years,' the young Syl had replied. 'A lifetime.'

'Many, many lifetimes,' said her father. 'But using the wormholes,
we can cover the distance in an instant.'

He gently folded the paper, aligning the marks, then pierced them
with his pen.

'That is what the wormholes do. They link distant points in
the universe.'

'But how do we know where they lead?' asked Syl.

'We send drones to explore systems in advance. Sometimes the
Sisterhood tells us.'

'And how does the Sisterhood know?' asked Syl, and her father
had not answered her, because, as Syl had come to realise, he did not
have an answer. If the Illyri loved secrets, the Sisterhood lived for
them.

The Empire had explored over one hundred systems, each targeted
because it contained a habitable planet with life forms, however
primitive, and commodities that could support the Empire's further
conquests: food, fuel, minerals, methane, water. Through the Sisterhood and the wormholes, the Illyri had established that the universe
was a fundamentally lonely place, and complex civilisations like their
own were extremely rare. So far, the Illyri had found only one species,

humanity, who could, given time, become as powerful as them, if not more so. The humans had drawn the Illyri down upon them: by sending radio signals out into the universe, they had alerted the Empire to the presence of another advanced race. Better, as one of her father's generals had remarked, that they be conquered now on their own world than battled later on another.

The Sisterhood had agreed, and so the plan to invade Earth was set in motion.

Any mention of the Sisterhood always enraged Syl's father.

'Witches,' he would mutter. 'Damned witches. And Syrene is the damnedest of them all.'

Ezil still lived, although she was now nearly two centuries old: a great and unusual age even for an Illyri. She was reported to be frail, and control of the Sisterhood had gradually passed to Syrene, who had once been her novice. Syrene had the ear of Grand Consul Gradus, for she was his wife, chosen for him by Ezil herself.

Only the Military had resisted the approaches of the Sisterhood, and soldiers were unofficially forbidden from entering into relationships with Nairene sisters, but the reality was that the sisters had barely tried to infiltrate the Military. They seemed content to infest the ranks of Diplomats, and leave the Military to the work of conquest, but their influence on the Diplomatic Corps was one of the factors contributing to the hostility between the Empire's two main forces.

Syl remembered all of this as she watched Lord Andrus smoothly rid himself of McGill. Now she stepped in front of her father as he was about to pass, so quickly that he almost tripped over her. Behind him, Balen stood up at his desk, a sheaf of papers in his hand. He gave Syl a cold smile. Clearly, like Althea, he felt that she should not be disturbing her father at this time.

'Syl!' said Lord Andrus. He spoke to her in the Illyri tongue, harsh yet lovelier to her than any human language. Why aren't you in class?'

'I wanted to see you. It is the anniversary of my birth. I—'

He placed his hands upon her shoulders and kissed her forehead.

'I have not forgotten. There is a gift waiting for you in your chambers, and later we'll have dinner together, but for now you must go back to your studies, or else I'll have Toris complaining that I allow you to wallow in ignorance, and Althea accusing me of indulging you.'

'But that's—'

Her father raised a hand to silence her. 'I have an important meeting, Syl. We'll discuss it later. For now, back to class. Go, go!'

He hustled her ahead of him, and when they came to the main corridor he turned left, and she right. She walked on for a time until she was out of sight, then halted. This wasn't fair. Her father had promised to always keep the anniversary of her birth special, not just because she was his only child, but because her mother had always placed great store by such occasions. With her mother no longer alive, her father maintained that he had to celebrate Syl's birth for both of them, and each year he had done his utmost to make it a day to remember. On her tenth birthday, they had taken his private skimmer to South America, and picnicked at Machu Picchu in Peru. On her thirteenth birthday, they had travelled to Florence, and he had given her a Michelangelo cartoon saved from the destruction of Rome, for she adored art.

But today he was too busy for her, and Syl feared that this might be setting a pattern for the future. Her eyes felt hot. She tried to hold back the tears, but one managed to escape and she brushed it away furiously. No, she would not cry, not here. She ran back to her chambers and lay down on her bed, and there she concentrated on not crying until she was certain that the urge had passed. She tried to imagine what her mother might have said to her were she still alive. She'd probably have told her that she was acting like a spoiled child, and that her father loved her but sometimes the requirements of his job meant that he could not spend as much time with her as she might wish. He would make it up to her later.

Syl sat up and rubbed her face. On her desk, unnoticed until now, was a box tied with brightly coloured ribbons; it was her father's gift to her.

'Oh!' she said aloud, childlike in anticipation as she bounded from her bed to inspect the parcel. It was heavy, so she unwrapped it where it was, exposing a plain wooden box. Inside the box, nestled in tissue, lay the bronze sculpture of a man's hand. She recognised it immediately and gave a yelp of glee, for it was *La Main*, a cast of Picasso's right hand sculpted by the artist himself. It had been part of the collection of the National Gallery of Scotland before the building was looted and burned during the unrest that initially followed the invasion. Some of the collection had been recovered, but the gallery had not been rebuilt, and paintings that had previously been housed there now adorned the walls of Edinburgh Castle. *La Main*, though, had been believed lost. The cast was one of a series of ten, but the whereabouts of the rest were unknown.

Syl loved to paint, and there was something in the way that Picasso depicted the world, the way in which he made the familiar strange and new, that appealed deeply to her. She liked the idea of the hand that had created such wonders being rendered in bronze, and now she touched her fingers to it, feeling the cool metal beneath her skin, and smiled despite herself.

There was a note with it: *Art is universal. Let one great artist inspire you to become another.*

She stroked the bronze, finding on it the marks of its maker's fingers.

'Thank you,' she whispered.

CHAPTER 7

Lord Andrus found himself wondering what his daughter would think of his gift to her, even as his personal guards fell into step behind him. She was angry with him now, but he knew that she would not be for long, and he smiled as he thought of the pleasure she'd take in *La Main*.

His smile faded as he arrived at the door of the private meeting room adjoining his offices. His guards took up position outside, and he gave them strict instructions that no one, and definitely not his daughter – not again – should be permitted to enter.

Andrus activated his private lens; he did not want to call up a screen from the castle's own systems. The tiny lens lay on his right eye, and enabled him to see virtual images superimposed on reality, from street names to weather information and private messages from his general staff if he was away from the castle. Lenses had first been developed for battlefield use; aided by information from drones and overhead satellites, they provided soldiers with maps, direction of enemy fire and, most importantly, the enemy's position. Now many Illyri used them the way humans had once used cell phones: they took calls through lenses, searched for information, watched movies and even played immersive games. It irritated Andrus to see such amazing technology being used for such frivolous ends.

Danis appeared on Andrus's lens. The remains of the fort at Birdoswald smouldered behind him. The old general was one of Andrus's most trusted soldiers, and his closest friend.

There was also the not insignificant matter of his daughter, Ani. Danis's wife Fian had given birth to the girl while Syl was still digesting her first meals at her mother's breast; only a difficult, extended labour had stopped Syl and Ani from being virtual twins, and they had settled for being sisters under the skin. Had Danis actively sought a governorship, then Syl and Ani would have been separated, and that would have broken the hearts of both the young Illyri. To some degree Danis had sacrificed personal ambition at the altar of his daughter's happiness.

'Talk to me, Danis,' said Andrus, pouring himself a glass of wine as he did so.

Danis looked cold and damp. On his own lens, he watched enviously as Andrus settled into his chair.

'Good wine, I hope?' he said.

'Very,' said Andrus.

'You're developing the tastes of a Diplomat. Next you'll be shaving your head, and you won't be able to lift your hands for all the jewellery on your fingers.'

'I'll give you a bottle when you return,' said Andrus. 'Now tell me about Birdoswald.'

In a corner of his lens, images of the fort appeared, transmitted by Danis. Bodies lay scattered throughout.

'It was a carefully planned and well-executed attack,' said Danis. 'A year ago, the Resistance wouldn't have had the guts or the manpower to carry out a raid like that.'

'So what has changed?'

'Their organisation, their weaponry and their intelligence-gathering. It's the last that worries me most.'

'They have spies among us?'

'You know they do. We use human workers, after all. Nothing would get done if we didn't. And even those that we keep at a distance watch us — they know our comings and goings, our troop movements . . . But there's also the issue of traitors.'

'Ah,' said Andrus, looking troubled. The Illyri still frowned on the mixing of the two races, but the biological similarities between them meant that some Illyri had secretly taken human partners. No human-Illyri hybrids had yet been born alive, but there had been pregnancies and miscarriages, and it was only a matter of time before nature overcame the differences between the species. Meanwhile, the monitoring of relationships fell to the Securitats, and punishment for such affairs was separation and exile. A number of Illyri had fled with their human lovers to avoid banishment; most deserters on the island of Britain were believed to have gone to ground in the Scottish Highlands, the most lawless region of the country. Some of these Illyri were also thought to be providing information to the Resistance, probably in return for protection.

More pictures of bodies flashed up. They were all Galateans. There were no images of Thaios, the commander of the garrison.

'Where is Thaios's body?' asked Andrus.

'I don't know,' said Danis. 'The Corps got to the scene before we did.'

Andrus leaned forward in his chair. *This* was news.

'How could that be? Birdoswald is a Military base. All communication is conducted directly through us, and all non-Military transmissions are automatically blocked. Did you have it swept for devices?'

'Of course I did,' said Danis. 'The equipment that we recovered from the rubble was clean.'

'Well, could Thaios have notified the Corps as soon as the attack commenced?'

'I'd imagine he had enough on his hands just trying to survive. Even though he was a Diplomat, his first instinct would have been to fight, especially if his own life was at stake.'

'And yet still the Diplomats knew of what was happening before our own Emergency Response Team.'

'Yes.'

It was very peculiar. Andrus didn't say so, but he was certain that Danis and his team must have missed a communications device of some kind; that, or the Diplomats had removed it along with Thaios's body.

'So you've found nothing helpful?' he said.

'I didn't say that. I may not have managed to examine Thaios, but I did take a look at the bodies of the Galateans.'

'What about them?'

Danis frowned. 'I can't be certain of this, but I'd say that some of them were killed when they were already down. Executed, even.'

'By the Resistance?' Andrus couldn't disguise his shock.

'The Resistance here isn't in the habit of finishing off the wounded on the ground, Galatean or Illyri. In other places, yes: they put our heads on spikes in Afghanistan, and they send them to us in boxes in Mexico and Texas, but here the humans tend to abide by the civilities, more or less. Even if they have changed their tactics, it still doesn't explain why the Diplomatic Corps was so quick to clean up after the raid. Besides, the Galateans were not killed by bullets.'

'How then?' said Andrus.

'Pulses were used. This was Diplomat work. Diplomat or Securitat.'

Anger clouded Andrus's face. While the Military, for the most part, still favoured variations on standard ammunition – bullets and shells – the Diplomats and their Securitats preferred infrasonic pulse weapons that induced resonance, or vibration, in their targets. Skulls, chests and abdomens were particularly effective resonance chambers. Depending on the level of power, the target might experience nausea, or even chest pain. At the highest levels, the pulses destroyed inner organs, bursting hearts, lungs, and brains. It was a bad way to die.

So Diplomats had trespassed upon a death scene at a Military base, and the loss of one of their own was no excuse. But now Danis was suggesting that they might have killed Military Galateans in the aftermath. They might not have been Illyri, but they were still his soldiers, and that was murder.

'Why would the Diplomats kill Galateans?' Andrus asked.

'My suspicion is that they were finished off so that they couldn't talk about what they'd seen, so we'd have no witnesses as to what might have occurred in the final moments at Birdoswald.'

'If that's the case, then it worked.'

'Not entirely. It seems that Thaios's body was taken to the main Diplomats facility in Glasgow. It just so happens that I have a contact there who owes me favours. He didn't get to examine the body either, but he did catch a glimpse of it as it was being placed on a slab.'

'And?'

'It didn't have a head.'

'Shotgun blast?'

'Must have been a big shotgun. All the cervical vertebrae were gone. According to my source, there was nothing left of Thaios above the shoulders – not that he had a lot above them even when he was alive.'

'Some new type of weapon?'

'If it is, then the humans must have stolen it from us, but how would they convert it to use?'

All Illyri weapons were encoded to Illyri or Galatean DNA, a precaution introduced to prevent hostile alien races from using Illyri technology against its creators.

'They could have found a way,' said Andrus. 'They went from fish struggling in slime to space exploration in no more than a blink of the universe's eye. It was only a matter of time before they applied themselves to adapting our guns.'

'I suppose it could explain pulses being used on the Galateans, but if the humans had succeeded in unlocking Illyri weapons we'd have heard about it,' said Danis. 'I'm certain.'

'So what's your theory?'

'I think Thaios put a pulse weapon at full power into his own mouth and pulled the trigger.'

Andrus winced at the thought. The degree of vibration caused by such an act would certainly be enough to explode a skull.

'But why? Just so he wouldn't be captured? That speaks of a surprising degree of self-sacrifice. After all, the Diplomats would have used his tracker to find him within an hour.'

In recent years, all Illyri on Earth had been fitted with a small subcutaneous tracker, usually implanted in the right arm. The tracker could be turned on at will, since few Illyri wanted their every movement to be known and monitored. Syl, for example, rarely turned on her tracker at all, even – or rather, most particularly – when she was on one of her little unauthorised trips beyond the castle walls. As far as she was concerned, it was to be used only in a case of the worst possible emergency, and most of the time she hardly remembered it was there at all.

A discussion had arisen about whether trackers should instead be implanted in teeth, or even in skulls, perhaps as part of the Chip, the thin electronic membrane that all Illyri had attached to their brains at birth, enabling them to interact electronically with their environment, from simple tasks such as calling up virtual screens or translating alien speech to complex operations like piloting spacecraft or operating weapons systems. It also monitored their health, constantly scanning for signs of disease or illness. Unfortunately for Syl's mother, her early version of the Chip had not been able to recognise the malarial infection that eventually killed her.

The use of trackers had been kept secret for a while, but it was believed that humans had recently either figured out the fact of their existence for themselves, or had been told of them by Illyri deserters. Encoding Chips with trackers had been briefly tested in Mexico, but the operation was painful, the tracker too susceptible to the brain's electric impulses, and it had led to Illyri captives having their heads removed by Mexican gangs to prevent their rescue.

'I have no idea why Thaios might have killed himself,' said Danis. 'Then again, it saved me the trouble. He was little better than a spy for his uncle.'

Andrus didn't bother to disagree. Instead he catalogued all that he had been told: a dead Diplomat who appeared to have somehow secretly communicated with his superiors before killing himself, and Galateans killed by pulse weapons. If there was a pattern, he failed to see it.

'Call in favours,' he told Danis. 'Find out – discreetly – if Birdoswald was an isolated incident. I want details of casualties among officers of the Diplomatic Corps over the last six months. I want to know if pulses have been used on our own troops anywhere on Earth. I want answers!'

Andrus killed the lens connection, and sipped his wine unhappily.

★ ★ ★

At Birdoswald, Danis had to make do with coffee from a flask as the rain began to fall. Around him, the dead Galateans had started to smell. He sighed deeply.

A soldier's lot, he thought, was not a happy one.

CHAPTER 8

The Diplomatic Corps had taken over the old Glasgow School of Art for its regional headquarters, and it was there that the Securitats had their Scottish lair. The building had been the first commission given to the great Scottish architect Charles Rennie Mackintosh, and was a mixture of Scottish baronial architecture and art nouveau motifs. Beautiful but imposing, it stood at the edge of a steep hill, and took the shape of a letter E. The panes in the big industrial windows on its northern side had been replaced by toughened glass, capable of withstanding a blast without shattering. When a massive truck bomb had exploded outside the building years before, the glass had not even cracked, and concrete blocks now prevented vehicles from gaining access to the area. It had additionally been fortified with spiked walls, but these were more for show than anything else. Like all Diplomat facilities, the building was protected by an energy shield. It was state-of-the-art; its advanced design meant that the nausea associated with the prototype shields – which had long since been mothballed because of the queasiness they caused to those inside – did not arise.

Naturally, the Diplomats had not seen fit to share their improved shield technology with their Military rivals.

In the school's basement mortuary, two technicians stared down at the headless body of Sub-Consul Thaios. They wore gloves on their hands, and masks on their faces. Even in the temperature-controlled environment of the mortuary, Thaios's remains had begun to rot. His skin was covered with black and purple blotches, and a stench arose from his flesh. This was unusual, to say the least. Under other circumstances, a full autopsy might have been in order to investigate the exceptionally quick decay. But an autopsy would not be carried out. The orders received by the technicians for dealing with Thaios's body were very different.

'You're sure about this?' said the first technician.

'I just do what I'm told,' said the other. 'I know better than to ask questions.'

'But he should be accorded a proper service, not . . . *this*. He's Consul Gradus's nephew. There'll be trouble when Gradus finds out.'

His colleague glared at him. He was older, and more senior.

'Don't you understand anything, you young fool? The order came from Gradus himself. Now just get on with it. He stinks.'

The younger technician began to close the body bag, then stopped.

'What are *they*?' he asked.

'What are what?' said his colleague.

'Those.' He pointed a gloved finger at Thaios's chest. It appeared to be covered in tiny red threads that poked from his pores. He hadn't noticed them before. He stroked them with his hand, but the filaments were so delicate he could barely feel them.

'I don't know,' replied his partner. 'And I don't want to know. Forget that you ever saw them, and I'll do the same.'

No more protests were heard. Together the two Illyri sealed the bag and wheeled it to the furnace room. There, as ordered, they burned the body of Thaios. As it turned to charred meat, they heard footsteps behind them.

'Is it done?' said a female voice.

'Yes,' said the older of the technicians. Had the new arrival been anyone else, he would have been tempted to make a joke about Thaios not just being done, but well done; hearing that voice, however, killed all thoughts of joking. It would be safer to make his silly comments later, in private, for the woman in the black-and-gold uniform of the Securitats wasn't likely to laugh. She was Vena, the most senior Securitat in the United Kingdom, and possibly the most terrifying member of the secret police between here and Illyr itself. Vena had never been seen to laugh, and rarely smiled. Ice ran in her veins, ice and scalding steam, echoing the twin silver streaks that adorned her shaven head.

'And nobody examined the body?' she said, and her voice was as sharp and direct as a dagger.

'No one. We put him in a secure locker under a serial number, with no name. We did as we were told.'

'Good.'

'Funny how he decayed so quickly, though,' said the younger technician, and beside him he heard his colleague give a sharp intake of breath. So close. They'd been so close. He'd warned him about questions, warned him time and time again.

He barely registered the weapon that appeared in Vena's hand. It was too late to react, too late to do anything but die. The pulses that killed the two technicians came close together, the thick basement walls smothering the sound.

And they joined Thaios in the flames.

CHAPTER 9

Despite the gratitude she felt for her father's gift, Syl still had no intention of sitting in class for her birthday, but neither could she simply wander the castle's corridors all day. That would be pointless.

She knew the castle better than almost anyone else, including perhaps her father's own security detail. She had been exploring the old fortress ever since she was able to crawl, and had discovered spyholes and listening posts created centuries before, when courtiers had eavesdropped on the deliberations of kings. She had even found the secret area behind the fireplace in the Great Hall, the grand room in which her father often met with visiting dignitaries. Boarded up for the visit of a Russian president during the previous century, the spyhole's very existence had been forgotten until Syl had stumbled across a mention of it in the archives. It was her place now, and she would sometimes retreat there to read or listen to music, cocooned in the darkness. At other times she would spy on her father's meetings if the timing suited, but for the most part they were so dull that she rarely bothered.

From her snooping she knew of events on Earth that Toris never shared with his students. She was aware that, like so many empires before them, the Illyri had given up on taming Afghanistan, which would have been more worrying if the Afghan people hadn't themselves divided into opposing Islamic factions, just as various Christian groups had elsewhere, and turned all their rage upon each other. The humans' argument was always the same, regardless of the god or gods they worshipped: if their god had created all living things, then had he not also created the Illyri? Or was it only Man who was made in this god's image, Man who was central to all creation?

The Illyri, meanwhile, considered themselves simply to be creatures of the universe, and so such arguments would have been meaningless to them had they not brought with them such violent repercussions. There had been some discussion about outlawing religion entirely, but this had been tried on other conquered worlds and the results were always the same: suppression concentrated the power of belief. But religious extremism was an ongoing problem, and too often it appeared to be motivated less by faith than by a hatred of anything and anyone that was not like itself.

And in her hidey-hole, Syl had wondered if Man had not been made in the image of his god but had instead shaped a god in Man's image: violent, wrathful and vengeful. It was all rather grim, she decided, and her birthday was certainly not a day to be spent eavesdropping on even more gloomy news from a hole in a wall.

Listless, she wandered into the lounge beside her bedroom. The house in which she and her father dwelt had originally been built for the castle governor in 1742, and had remained a governor's residence for over a century before the post was abolished for a time. It had then served as a hospital until the position was re-established in 1935, and now an Illyri governor slept in its bedroom and ate in its dining room. It was a handsome building, if a little cold in winter.

Out of habit, Syl picked up a book, but then immediately put it back down again. She wanted to be active. She wanted to *do* something. She moved to the window, swept back the heavy drapes and looked down on to the busy courtyard. This had been transformed into a landing pad for the governor and other important visitors, and shuttles, skimmers and interceptors used it regularly.

Syl watched the traffic for a time, all of it routine, longing to climb aboard a shuttle and go somewhere, anywhere. Yet she wasn't supposed to leave even the castle's environs unaccompanied. While the Royal Mile area of Edinburgh was less dangerous for the Illyri than elsewhere, they were still objects of vaguely hostile curiosity at best. It was not unknown for stones to be thrown at them, and worse could happen once the castle was out of sight.

But dwindling away inside these walls felt like a death all of its own.

It started to rain. The heavy droplets splashed against the window, and the courtyard cleared as everyone ran for cover. That solved it then: she should read, and forget about going out . . . but what a waste that would be. It hardly seemed worth all the grief she'd doubtless get for skipping school if it was only for a day spent cooped up in the castle.

She walked back to her room and kicked open her closet. Like most young Illyri, her wardrobe consisted of a mix of Illyri dress – mainly long robes for non-Military or security personnel – and Earth clothing, although her father disapproved of non-regulation garments, especially on his own daughter. But the human clothing gave Syl freedom of movement in the city. Yes, she was tall, but not unusually so, not yet. Her skin had not yet reached the full golden glow of maturity, so she just appeared well tanned. She had tinted glasses to hide her eyes – sunglasses were better, but it didn't look like today was a day for shades – and a crazy velvet hat to conceal her lustrous hair. Now, grinning to herself, she dressed in jeans and an old coat; with her hat fixed firmly on her head, she reckoned she easily passed for a foreign student – Italian, perhaps, or Spanish.

'My name is, uh, Isabella,' she said to her mirrored reflection, putting on a dreadful Italianesque accent. '*Buongiorno*, Edinburgh.'

Quickly she stuffed the human clothing into a backpack and made her way to the courtyard through the quietest corridors of the castle. She changed her clothes in a bathroom close to the Argyle Tower, then put up an umbrella, and slipped out into the rain. Nobody stopped her as she left the castle; the guards were more concerned about those who tried to enter than those who were leaving. If she was lucky, and there were guards she knew on the gates when she returned, she would be able to convince them not to report her to her father. Syl was particularly good at bending the sentries to her will.

But that was for later. For now, she was sixteen, and away from the castle. She was free. So caught up was she in the pleasure of the moment, even as the rain continued to fall, and a cold wind blew stinging droplets in her face, that she did not notice the figure that detached itself from the shadows by the Esplanade and fell casually into step behind her, hidden by the crowds.

CHAPTER 10

Paul and Steven approached the Royal Mile, and Knutter's shop. Knutter was a minor asset to the Resistance, passing on information and providing a safe house for weapons and munitions when required. A cousin of his from Aberdeen had been killed in the early days of the invasion, shot while in the act of throwing a firebomb at a patrol, and Knutter, as a consequence, was barely able to conceal his hatred for the invaders. He had little access to the Resistance's secrets, though, and knew the identities of only a handful of its operatives. It was better that way. Very few of those who fought the aliens knew much beyond their own field of operations, for just as the Resistance had its informers close to the Illyri, so too there were those among the humans who were prepared to sell out their own for money, or advancement, or to secure the return of conscripts to their families. The less men like Knutter knew, the less they might accidentally reveal, or have tortured out of them if they were ever caught and interrogated.

What made Knutter's store particularly useful was the fact that it provided a secret access point to the South Bridge Vaults, the system of over one hundred chambers in the arches of the South Bridge, completed at the end of the eighteenth century. They had first housed taverns and the workshops of various trades, as well as serving as slum housing for the city's poor. It was said that the nineteenth-century serial killers Burke and Hare had hunted among the residents of the Vaults for their victims, selling the bodies for medical experimentation. Then, sometime in the mid- to late nineteenth century, the Vaults were closed, and had not been excavated further until the end of the twentieth century, when they became a tourist attraction. Now they provided a hiding place for guns and, occasionally, Resistance members who had been identified and were being hunted by the Illyri, although most preferred to take their chances above ground. The Vaults were grim and dank, and said to be haunted, although in Knutter's experience it was only those who already believed in ghosts who were susceptible to such fantasies. Knutter himself had yet to encounter anything, either human or alien, that could not be felled by a sufficiently hard blow from his own head. So far, his forehead had not passed through the face of a supernatural entity.

But it was Knutter who first began hearing the noises from the Vaults after a few too many drinks, and it had caused him to briefly reconsider his views on ghosts and, indeed, drinking. But he was still hearing the noises when he had sobered up, and he had also recognised the curious burbling, clicking language of the Toads coming through the cracks in his basement wall. It was then that he had informed the Resistance. Once its leaders had concluded that Knutter was not simply hallucinating, further enquiries were made among the Resistance's informers. By piecing together various pearls of information, a chain of events was constructed, and it was deduced that the Illyri had been tunnelling with great secrecy under the city, and had come close to Knutter, and the Vaults.

The Resistance leaders were furious: a major excavation had been carried out quite literally under their noses, and they hadn't known. Their system of spies and informers had let them down. The Illyri had managed to keep their tunnels very quiet until Knutter's keen ear had picked up on what was happening. The Resistance had decided it was the Diplomatic Corps and not the Military that was behind the excavations. They had enjoyed little success in infiltrating the Diplomats, for they tended not to use human labour, and most of their forces kept their distance from humans, except when they were fighting them, or arresting them, or killing them. If the Military had been engaged in digging beneath Edinburgh, someone would have informed the Resistance. Only the Diplomats could keep such a project secret, aided, perhaps, by the Securitats.

Katherine Kerr, the boys' mother, had been a tour guide in the city before the Illyri invaded, and had passed on her knowledge of its secrets – among them the location of various concealed entrances to the Vaults, Knutter's shop included – to her close family. This was why Paul and Steven had been chosen for the mission and given instructions from the top, via Nessa, to investigate further. No point in hanging about, Nessa had said. Knutter was expecting them just as soon as they'd finished their tea.

Now an Illyri patrol vehicle hummed by, its grey armour bristling with weaponry both lethal and non-lethal. It reminded Paul of a huge woodlouse. Its wheels were concealed beneath its frame, and its body was V-shaped to protect the Illyri inside by dispelling the force of explosives. It didn't even have windows; its sensor array provided a detailed picture of the environment to its crew without exposing them to harm. Like most of the smaller Illyri transports, it was powered by biogas produced mostly from animal waste, although the Illyri also used vehicles powered by electricity and hydrogen, the latter derived mainly from methane. The boys gave the vehicle a quick glance, but nothing more. Taking too much interest in an Illyri patrol might lead the patrol to take an interest in turn, but ignoring it entirely was almost as bad because it suggested that you might be trying too hard to remain unnoticed. It was a delicate balance to strike.

'Are you nervous?' said Paul.

'No,' said Steven, then corrected himself: 'Maybe a bit.'

'Don't be. We've a right to walk the streets. They haven't taken that away from us yet.'

Ahead of them lay the Royal Mile, the castle towering over it. Before the occupation, the castle had been the city's main tourist attraction. Now few humans went there voluntarily, and the ones that entered it to work were usually either traitors or spies. Paul had never set foot inside it, and even though he was committed to the Resistance, he sometimes wondered if there would ever come a time when sight-seers might innocently wander its battlements again, remembering the great occupation that had once based itself here and had finally been defeated. In his darker moments, he found it hard to imagine.

'Walk faster,' he said to Steven. The rain had stopped for a time, but it would return. It always did in this city.

Syl stepped out of the vintage clothing store, her purchases in a plastic bag. The man behind the counter had looked at her oddly as she browsed, but had said nothing. Even if he suspected that she might not be human, he probably needed the business. The proximity of the castle and the presence of stop-and-search Illyri patrols meant that many citizens tended to avoid the area around the Royal Mile. Still, Syl bought a lovely old purse decorated with mother-of-pearl, and a white wool coat with a fur collar that would keep her warm in winter.

The streets were dry again, and the sun was coming out. Perhaps the day would be good after all, a possibility worth celebrating. Syl glanced to her left. There was a little coffee shop nearby, and it sold very good pastries. Maybe she could stick a candle in one and sing herself a song. She smiled at the thought, and started walking. Canongate Kirk, a seventeenth-century church, was ahead of her, and beside it the coffee shop.

Suddenly there was a massive bang, as though a huge hand had slammed itself down on the Royal Mile, and the coffee shop simply wasn't there any more. It disintegrated into a cloud of dirt and brick and glass. Syl was knocked to the ground; she instinctively put her arms up, shielding her face and head. Her ears were ringing, and she couldn't hear properly. Then the dust found her, and she started to choke. She tried not to breathe but she was frightened, so she began to hyperventilate, and the choking became worse.

Frantic hands were on her now, trying to pull her to her feet.

'Are you all right?' asked a voice. It sounded like it was speaking from underwater, but it was still familiar to her. 'Syl, are you hurt?'

Syl shook her head. She coughed and spat dust. She felt water splashing on to her face, and then the bottle was in her hands and she drank from it.

'I don't think so,' she said at last, once she had stopped choking. She squinted up at the figure before her, until she could see through the fine dust. It was hazy in the smoke-blotted sunlight, but she still recognised the feminine figure with her head cocked like a bird's, small for her age but fast and agile, and currently badly disguised in mismatched human clothing and sunglasses that were a match for Syl's own shades back at the castle. After all, they had bought them together, because that's what best friends do.

'Ani!' she said. 'What are you doing here?'

'Following you,' said Ani, and her words came to Syl as a distorted whisper, even though Ani was speaking normally. 'I thought it would be funny, but it isn't now. Quickly, patrols will be coming. We have to get away from here.'

They heard sirens, and from above, the whistling sound of approaching interceptors. Ani put her hand out to help Syl up, but before Syl could take it, another strange hand found hers, yanking her upright and steadying her on her feet. She gave a little squeal of surprise.

'Are you hurt?' said a male voice.

In front of the girls stood two young humans, clearly brothers. It was the older of the two that had spoken. In the dust and chaos of the explosion's aftermath, he had clearly mistaken Syl and Ani for human girls. Syl shook her head, confused, trying to remember her human name, her Italian accent.

'Do you need help?' he asked, and Syl found herself watching his mouth closely, feeling dazed, seeing it shape the words that she could barely hear. His bottom lip was curved and a little pillowy, and she had an odd urge to touch it to see if it was as soft as it looked, so pink and clean in his dusty face.

'We're fine,' said Ani. 'We're just trying to get home.'

She pulled hard on Syl's elbow, starting to turn in the direction of the castle, but the younger boy stopped her with an outstretched arm, and now Syl was pushed even closer to the older one, watching his mouth moving once more, half hearing and half lip-reading, near enough to him to see stubble like a little sprinkle of pepper across his top lip.

'Wait,' he said. 'Did you see what happened? Were there people—'

'We don't know,' interrupted Ani, jerking Syl's arm again, and Syl could feel the panic coming off her friend in waves. No human was ever to be trusted, but in the chaotic aftermath of an explosion it would be particularly easy to snatch two young Illyri from the streets.

'Hold on,' said Syl, and she gave her head a shake so that her ears cleared somewhat. 'It was MacBride's coffee shop – I think that's where the explosion happened. I didn't see anyone on the street beforehand, but there might have been people inside. That's all I know. But thank you for helping me.'

'We really have to go,' said Ani urgently, and now Syl turned to follow her, but the boy didn't move, and his younger companion closed in too, blocking their path. This is it, thought Syl. They've seen through our disguises. They *know*.

'Not that way,' said the older boy.

'Let us pass,' said Ani. 'Please!'

'You can't go that way,' he said. 'You just can't.'

'Why not?' said Ani.

Syl looked past them. Already there were soldiers and emergency vehicles racing from the direction of the castle.

'Because there may be another bomb.'

And as he spoke, there was a second massive blast, and the approaching vehicles were blown apart.

CHAPTER 11

They all turned and ran, not towards the castle but away from it, away from the carnage and bloodshed and ammonia stink behind them, away from the billowing cloud of powdered stone and concrete and obliterated flesh, be it human or Illyri. Black-and-gold uniformed Securitats had materialised in the area and now swarmed over it like beetles, questioning shopkeepers, searching pedestrians and loading into their armoured vehicles anyone who failed to come up with a plausible explanation for being near the site of the explosion.

Syl, Ani and the two humans powered down the Royal Mile together, and then the boys veered off down a side street, slowing only long enough to make sure the girls were with them before racing on, left-right-right-left, twisting, turning, finally stopping in a deep-set doorway on a corner.

'We go left now,' said the older boy, but as they burst back on to the street Ani was in the lead, and instead of left she headed right, then took a sharp left down a narrow, urine-scented service alley. Syl followed, and after a heartbeat the boys did too, joining Ani as she crouched in a pool of cigarette butts behind a plastic dumpster at the rear of a greasy shop. She seemed to be hiding.

'What the hell are you doing?' snarled the older boy, but she put her finger to her lips, and then they all heard it: the whine of an interceptor followed by the rhythmic quickstep of soldiers' boots approaching, rattling like applause on the cobbles as they passed the filthy alley. The youngsters stayed still, barely breathing until the stomping faded away.

'You must have amazing hearing,' the boy said when all was silent once more, but Ani just shrugged and half smiled.

'Lead on,' she said.

Frowning slightly, the human looked from one Illyri to the other, his blue eyes narrowing, then seemed to make a decision. He went to the entrance to the alley, peering around the corner before he beckoned for them to follow.

They moved more cautiously now, stopping to listen every few steps, dodging and weaving, disappearing ever deeper into the warren of streets behind the Royal Mile.

'Where are we going?' asked Syl quietly as they paused at another bend, looking down a laneway she'd never seen before, the tall, regal buildings more humble back here, lopsided and blackened by decades of pollution. Windows were broken, some even boarded up, and she saw the painted graffiti of the Resistance on a peeling doorway. This was not a place where she should be, where any Illyri should be. Her heart was like a bag of stones clattering terrified in her chest.

'Um, away?' said the older boy next to her ear.

'Where to, though?'

His breath was warm on her cheek and she could smell him, soapy and musky. She stepped back a little, feeling flustered.

'I hadn't thought of anywhere in particular. Just away from the soldiers and Securitats. They'll be rounding people up like sheep for the slaughter.'

'Oh. Right.'

They started walking again, sticking close to the buildings, but the street was deserted.

'Why? Where do you need to be?' he said.

'The castle,' she replied automatically before she could stop herself.

He turned to face her now, his eyes wide and shocked.

'The castle? Why would you want to go *there*?'

Syl felt Ani poke her hard in her back.

'Um, a job interview,' Syl spluttered. 'We had job interviews.'

'Doing what exactly?'

'Scrubbing floors. She's great at scrubbing floors,' said Ani from behind her.

'I am. Fabulous,' said Syl. 'And she cleans toilets.'

The older boy gave a low chuckle, and the younger one snorted.

'Will you keep your sunglasses on even when you're cleaning the jacks?' he said to Ani.

'Of course,' snapped Ani. 'Safety gear. I never take them off.'

'You really are the strangest pair,' the older boy said, but he seemed more relaxed now. 'I wouldn't recommend going near the castle for a while, though, not until they've calmed down. You could always just hang around here: it's quiet, and the Illyri don't come this way very much.'

He waved his hand absently at a sheet of corrugated iron that hung from a doorway. *ILLyri is a disease* was scrawled across it in red spray paint.

You reckon? thought Syl to herself, and she gave an inadvertent shudder. The adrenalin was seeping out of her now, and her legs suddenly felt wobbly and weak. She thought she might be sick. She remembered the explosions, the twin bombs, how close they'd been to walking straight into the second one, how these boys had stopped them, saved them, run with them until they were safe from the guards. How had they known there'd be a second bomb? Had it been their doing? Were they killers, Resistance killers?

'Hey,' the older human was saying, looking at her kindly, 'are you okay? Seriously?'

His eyes crinkled at the corners. He had that pillow-soft bottom lip, and he didn't look like a murderer, but what did a murderer look like anyway? Abruptly it all became too much. With a nauseous shiver, Syl tried to sit down where she was, but he leapt forward and steadied her elbow.

'Not here,' he said. 'You're in shock. Let's get you somewhere safe. There's a place nearby . . .'

'No!' said the other boy, jumping forward.

'Seriously, Steven, it's fine.'

'But . . .'

'Steven, I make the decisions. Now, let's go.'

Stumbling along between Ani and the older boy, Syl found herself guided up a set of litter-strewn stairs and through a doorway that seemed to open as if by magic when the younger boy – Steven, was it? – created a little tune on its crusty keypad. They went into a hallway where another tune was played beside a door that looked like wood but sounded like metal, and then they were in a little kitchen. The windows had boards nailed over them, but it was quaintly cheerful and bright nonetheless, with polka-dot red vinyl on the table beneath a row of fat yellow light bulbs. The floor was polished chequerboard stones and the walls were lined with scrubbed pine cupboards, each shelf teetering with mismatched mugs and plates, vases and knick-knacks, all in bright, crayon-box colours. An enormous old kettle sat on a squat stove, waiting to be used.

Ani pushed Syl gently into a chair.

'Where are we?' Syl said, watching as the older boy set the kettle to boil, deftly counted tea bags into a green-striped pot, and then poured in the steaming water before covering the whole thing with a fluffy yellow tea cosy.

He looked over at her and smiled properly for the first time.

'Oh good, you're back with us. You okay?'

She nodded and returned his smile.

'Everyone else okay?' he said. 'Steven?'

The younger boy nodded, and grinned as if to underscore exactly how okay he was.

'That was amazing! It was mental!' he said.

'Amazing?' said Ani, rounding on him. '*You* must be mental!'

His face fell, and he turned to scratch in a cupboard, finding a packet of HobNobs and a sugar bowl, his young shoulders square and proud.

'Whatever,' he mumbled to nobody in particular, but the older boy patted him gently on the back before turning to the girls.

'I'm Paul, by the way,' he said, smiling again and extending his hand, but then snatching it back and wiping it clean on his jeans before they shook.

'Syl,' said Syl, without thinking, and his warm hand gripped hers. And then she realised what she'd done.

'Syl?' He looked baffled for a moment, his grip tightening, then said: 'Short for Sylvia?'

'Yeah, that's me,' she said, forcing herself to smile, trying to sound as much like a human girl as she knew how. 'And this is Ani.'

'Annie,' said Paul, shaking Ani's hand and nodding. 'That's more like it. When you said Syl, it sounded like an Illyri name.' He laughed drily, and Syl and Ani joined in.

'Oh, and this is my brother Steven.'

They all said hello and then went silent, eyeing each other awkwardly, the Illyri females still with their glasses incongruously perched on their smudged faces. Ani looked more ridiculous than Syl; at least Syl's glasses resembled something a regular person might wear on a day like today. Ani, by contrast, should have been lying on a sunlounger and drinking a cocktail.

'You can probably take your glasses off now,' said Paul.

'No!' said the females in unison, and in a rush of words, Syl explained that Ani had a nasty eye condition from toilet chemicals, and Ani said Syl had a squint.

'A squint?' said Paul.

'Uh-huh.' Syl nodded, but gave Ani a kick under the table.

Paul and Steven looked at each other in confusion, and then Paul turned to fetch the teapot, pouring them all large colourful mugs and loading Syl's with sugar, 'for shock', before slopping in milk. She took a sip. It was sweet and treacly and vaguely disgusting, but she drank it anyway, feeling the colour returning to her cheeks, the vitality re-awakened in her strong Illyri bones.

'Where are we, then?' said Ani, breaking the silence that descended again as they all munched on biscuits.

'Just a place,' said Paul, waving a hand vaguely, and Steven gave a meaningful cough.

'A place? I see.'

They were silent again. Syl watched Paul, saw how he held his mug with both hands, his fingers interlocked, lean and strong, yet vulnerable too, as though he was trying to warm them even though it wasn't cold. Could they really be the fingers of a bomber, of a murderer? She had to know.

'Paul,' she said, and everyone looked at her. Paul raised an eyebrow, and she bit her lip nervously. 'How did you know there'd be a second bomb?'

'I didn't know,' he said. 'I just guessed.'

'How, though?'

'Because this is my home, Sylvia. I live here, and I intend to carry on living here without being blown up. That's how it sometimes is with bombings: one blast followed shortly afterwards by another. The first lures in the soldiers and the Securitats who respond to it, and then the second kills them. I figured it would probably happen that way again. I watch. I've been watching since I was born. Don't you pay attention too?'

'I guess,' she said, but she was starting to realise how little she knew about outside, about the world beyond the castle walls.

Then his face changed, and his eyes narrowed. 'Did you think it was me? You think I'd do something like that, in a place where civilians could be killed?'

'Well, no . . . maybe . . . I don't know. After all, I don't know you, do I?'

'And I don't know you,' he countered, 'yet we brought you here where we'd all be safe because we're not like them, and because that's what we do. We're humans, not Illyri. We stick together.' His tone changed. There was a note of suspicion to it now. 'We *are* in this together, Sylvia, aren't we?'

'She was just asking!' said Ani, jumping up angrily and clattering the cups together, then dumping them in the sink. 'Anyway, it's time we left.'

'Yes, I think it probably is – Steven, you clean up here and I'll get these two back to the Mile. I'll see you in fifteen, right?'

Steven shrugged and looked into his tea.

'Bye,' said Ani gruffly as she followed Paul to the door.

'Thanks,' said Syl, but her voice was weak and high.

'Yup. Cheers,' Steven said, and then they were out on the streets again, weaving down alleys, criss-crossing their path, and she wondered if Paul was trying to confuse them so they couldn't find their way back to the little safe house, because if he was, he'd definitely succeeded. Fat raindrops started splashing around them, and Paul turned up his collar and hurried on, never saying a word. Syl guessed he was used to outpacing people, but the Illyri were naturally vigorous and lean, and even Ani's shorter legs kept up easily.

All at once he stopped, and pointed ahead. 'Go that way to the very end, then take a right and you'll be back at the Mile, but I'd stay away from the castle. I presume you can find your way home from there.'

Syl nodded, but his attention was already focussed elsewhere. Ani shrugged.

'Right, thanks. Bye,' she said, turning to go, but Syl hesitated.

'Thank you, Paul,' she said, and she stretched out a tentative hand towards him. 'And I'm so sorry. You saved my life today – our lives – and I'll never forget that. Truly, thank you.'

He looked at her properly now, and his eyes wrinkled warmly again as he took her hand in his, not so much a shake as a friendly squeeze.

'Well it's certainly been interesting, Sylvia.'

'It has,' she said. 'Good luck, Paul,' then she turned and scampered after Ani.

'See you, Syl,' he called. She looked back and waved, and he waved too. She couldn't be sure, but it looked like he was laughing.

CHAPTER 12

Later, Syl would wonder quite how they had managed to make it back under the noses of so many patrols, both Military and Corps, but somehow they did, for the initial panic around the castle had quietened down in their absence and things were getting back to normal again, as happens in cities that have grown used to violence.

Apart from the minor detail of saving their lives, those boys had done them another favour too, Syl realised, for she and Ani would surely have been picked up by their own people and charged with being outside the castle walls without authorisation if they hadn't been led away to safety. The best they could have hoped for was to be dragged before her father, who would have forced them to explain just what they'd been doing wandering round Edinburgh while bombs were going off. She'd have been grounded until she turned twenty-one!

Illyri under the age of eighteen were not allowed beyond the castle walls, or Illyri areas of control, without permission, although most took this to mean that they shouldn't be *caught* outside certain areas without passes. Syl wasn't the only one who routinely made illicit excursions; life would have been very dull otherwise. While many of the Military guards took a liberal view of such escapes, just as long as their officers weren't around, the Securitats were less forgiving, and particularly so in the case of children of the Military: they never passed up a chance to make life awkward for soldiers and their families, and they would have been overjoyed to discover that they had the daughter of Lord Andrus in their hands, along with one of her little friends. They'd probably have kept them overnight in a cell, just to make her father sweat, before parading them before him in order to make him look foolish. After all, if the governor could not keep his own child under control, how could he be expected to rule nations? It was as much for her father's sake as her own that Syl wanted to return safely to the castle.

And they were lucky, too, for just as they neared the castle, a pair of military trucks emerged, and behind them Syl glimpsed Corporal Laris, who was the closest she had to a friend in the castle guards. She had saved Laris from serious punishment earlier in the year, when he had fallen asleep at his post on a still, humid summer's night. Only the fact that Syl had been wandering the courtyard, unable to sleep, had kept him from being court-martialled, for she had woken him seconds before the captain of the castle guard made his rounds.

Laris stared as Syl and Ani removed their hats and glasses, and seemed about to say something to them, but the pleading look that Syl gave him made him hold his tongue, and he waved them into the safety of the castle without a word. But Syl noticed that a figure in black and gold on the other side of the street seemed on the verge of approaching them before a convoy blocked her from view. Even hidden by her helmet, Syl was sure that she recognised Vena, the most senior Securitat in Scotland, perhaps even the whole island. Vena had no love for Syl, and her proximity was even more reason to get out of the courtyard and into relative safety.

They scurried through the castle to the little bathroom. The corridors were unusually devoid of activity, and Syl noticed that there were no humans to be seen. In the aftermath of the explosion, the castle's human staff would have been surrounded and taken away to a secure location beside the New Barracks. It was standard procedure. There they would remain until it was clear that the threat had passed, and none of them had been involved in any way in the explosions.

Syl and Ani changed their clothes in the bathroom and made themselves look as respectable as they could, then hurried to Syl's rooms. There they stared at each other for a moment before bursting into relieved, hysterical giggles.

'Wow,' said Syl. She hugged her friend. 'What a crazy day. What the hell just happened?'

'Well, we were almost blown up, but two boys saved our lives,' said Ani. 'We then had tea with them. Then, most shockingly of all, there was the small matter of you flirting with an actual H-U-M-A-N.'

'I did not!' shot back Syl.

'Oh you definitely did, and I think he was flirting back.'

'Really?' Syl couldn't help but feel slightly pleased.

'Well, yes . . . until I told him you had a squint.'

Ani's head bobbed with mocking laughter, but it was infectious, and soon Syl couldn't help but laugh too.

'Hey,' said Ani finally, 'I just remembered: happy birthday.'

'Oh – I nearly forgot about that too. And I never had my cake . . . I'm starving.'

'Here, then,' said Ani, pulling the rest of the packet of HobNobs from inside her balled-up jumper with a cheeky grin.

'They save our lives and you steal their biscuits? You're evil.'

'Consider it a birthday gift,' said Ani. 'I didn't have time to get you anything else; time, or money for that matter. My father cut my allowance – again.'

Whenever Syl felt that her father was being unfair or unduly strict, she thought about Ani and Danis. Danis made Lord Andrus look soft as a marshmallow.

'Oh no. What's he accused you of now?' asked Syl.

'He caught me smoking,' said Ani.

'Oh, Ani. That's just stupid!'

Tobacco had been unknown to the Illyri until they arrived on Earth. On Illyr, all narcotics were strictly controlled, and most citizens avoided them on health grounds anyway. The Illyri had tried banning tobacco in the first years of the invasion, and had failed utterly. Now low-tar tobacco was tolerated for human use. Illyri were forbidden to smoke, but some did anyway, buying strong tobacco on the black market, even though it was known that it was run by criminals, many of whom passed information to the Resistance.

Ani shrugged. 'It was only one cigarette, and I didn't even like it that much. It was just bad luck. I was hanging out of my bedroom window to smoke it – so that the smell wouldn't get into my room –

and old Pops was passing through the Middle Ward and happened to look up, didn't he?'

'Busted! Busted big time,' said Syl.

'He said that I couldn't smoke if I didn't have any money to buy cigarettes. Now I don't even have enough to buy matches, never mind cigarettes.'

'Well, good thing I like HobNobs, then,' said Syl.

They sat by the window and stared out at the city, munching biscuits in silence. It seemed so peaceful from up here, and the sky was vivid blue, but the view had changed for Syl, changed forever now that they'd come so close to death in the city below, now that they'd run with the humans, now that they'd hidden from their own. Ani clicked her tongue and sighed, for her thoughts were in the same place.

'I wonder if anyone was hurt in the explosion,' said Syl finally. 'The lady who owned that coffee shop seemed nice. She never objected to serving me, even when I wasn't disguised, and you know what some people are like.'

Ani nodded. There were places in the city where Illyri were given the cold shoulder if they tried to shop or eat. There would be no service, no talk, only silence until they gave up and left the place to the humans. It was illegal, of course, and dangerous for the humans involved. The Securitats had been known to arrest people who refused to deal with the Illyri, but for the most part such actions were reluctantly tolerated. If nothing else, passive resistance was better than acts of violence.

'Maybe she wasn't there,' said Ani. 'Maybe it was closed.'

But Syl didn't think it was closed. The little coffee shop opened all day long, six days a week, and the homely owner was always behind the counter. Frances was her name. It was sewn on her apron.

Had Syl believed in a god, she would have prayed for the soul of Frances. And she would have given thanks for the humans who'd come to their rescue.

'Look,' said Ani. 'Something's happening outside.'

Casual onlookers were being hustled away, and Securitats began to pour into the courtyard. That in itself was unusual: Lord Andrus was

strict about keeping the day-to-day functions of the castle under
Military control, which included all matters relating to security. The
Securitats had been permitted a small garrison in the Lower Ward,
and a larger base off the Royal Mile, but they had no part in the actual
running of the castle. Syl had never before seen so many of the security
police inside the walls. And yes, Vena was leading them, her helmet
held beneath her right arm. The twin silver streaks above her left ear
always made her easy to spot. Privately, Lord Andrus called her 'the
Silver Skunk'.

There was some jostling with the regular Military guard as the
Securitats took up position around the landing pad, and a confrontation
seemed in the offing. Soon Peris, the captain of the castle guard,
appeared. He made straight for Vena, and an argument commenced
between the two officers. It seemed to get quite heated at one point,
because Syl could see Peris jabbing his finger at Vena, his face
reddening. In response, Vena produced a document from the pocket
of her dress jacket and handed it to Peris. He read it, simmered for a
while and then conceded defeat. He signalled the guard to withdraw,
leaving the courtyard in the hands of the Securitats.

A shuttle approached from the north. It was coloured a golden red,
as though caught in the light of a setting sun, and shaped like a trident,
with the central tine forming the cabin and those on either side
housing the propulsion systems. It bore the distinctive interlinked
black circles of the Diplomatic Corps, but contained within the
overlapping of the rings was a single red eye, a variation that Syl had
not seen before. The ship hovered high above the landing pad, but
did not descend. Its windows were dark, but she sensed the presences
behind them taking in the courtyard and the castle. The ship seemed
to Syl both beautiful yet unsettling, like an elegant weapon waiting to
be fired.

Vena put a finger to her right ear, activating her tiny com-
municator. She listened for a moment, raised a hand and summoned
two guards to her side. More discussions followed. Still the red ship
waited. The guards ran back to the castle, and seconds later a white
canvas arch began to extend across the courtyard. It was the sheltering

device used to protect honoured guests when rain was falling, but the rain had stopped. It seemed that whoever was in the trident ship simply did not wish to be exposed to the curious gaze of onlookers, although the arch was thin enough to allow shapes and colours to filter through, if not faces.

Vena stepped in front of the arch and walked along beneath it as it was unfurled, so that she was gradually lost to Syl's sight. Only when the shelter was at its fullest extent did the ship begin its descent, the pilot landing the craft perfectly so that the cabin door was concealed by the canvas.

The engines died. All was silent for a time. Syl found herself holding her breath. Where was her father? she wondered. Clearly there was someone important on the ship, and her father usually greeted all visiting dignitaries personally. It was a mark of respect, on their part as much as on his. Either this was someone to whom he was giving calculated offence by not being present – which was so unlike her father as to be unthinkable – or he had not been aware of the ship's impending arrival, which was stranger still. Yet Vena had known, and whatever authority she had used to dismiss her father's men from the courtyard was significant, for only Andrus should have had the power to replace his own guard.

Vena's figure was visible to Syl through the canvas, a patch of darkness against the white. So too was the outline of the cabin door, and Syl saw it turn from red to black as it opened. Shapes emerged: two soldiers with guns, followed by three robed figures, two in pale yellow and one in white; and finally a sixth figure, tall and almost triangular in form, its robes a deep, dark red. The rich fabric cast a faint glow over the interior of the canvas, dancing on the ripples caused by the breeze as the new arrivals made their way from the courtyard. Led by Vena, the concealed visitors entered the Governor's House.

Syl felt Ani shudder beside her.

'What is it? What's wrong?'

'I don't know,' said Ani. 'Just a feeling. A really strange feeling. Whoever was in that ship is bad, bad news . . .'

CHAPTER 13

It was some hours after the blasts when the two young men eventually managed to slip unnoticed into Knutter's grocery shop and newsagent's on South Bridge. Paul turned the sign on the window to 'Closed', locked the door and pulled down the canvas shutter so that nobody could see inside.

'You're late,' said Knutter. 'I was worried.'

Behind his back he was commonly known as Knutter the Nutter, because of both his short temper and his tendency to knock down those who crossed him by using his bulbous forehead or scarred crown to break their noses, a tactic known as 'nutting' or the 'Glasgow kiss'. His head was shaved, and his forearms were adorned with shamrock tattoos and the insignia of Celtic football club, even though he was a native of Edinburgh and the shop had been in his family for generations.

'We're okay,' said Paul, 'but we were in the area when the bombs went off.'

He went to the fridge and pulled out two bottles of water, tossing one to his brother. Knutter frowned. The boys drank deeply to clear their throats, and when they'd finished, Knutter put out his hand for their cash. He was that kind of man.

'Did you see any injured?' he asked, once the boys had paid for their water and the money was safely in his cash register. Knutter had not left his store that afternoon, not even in the aftermath of the explosion. It wasn't his job to go helping casualties, not at the risk of being arrested by the Securitats. Anyway, he'd been told to wait for the boys, and that was just what he'd done.

'My guess is that the dead were mostly Illyri,' said Paul, 'but two girls told us that MacBride's coffee shop might have been the site of the first explosion. The second one did for half of the Illyri response team, I think.'

'I know the MacBrides,' said Knutter. 'They're good people.'

He frowned as he thought about what Paul had said.

'What two girls?'

'Just girls.'

'Did they get a good look at you?'

Paul shrugged.

'What happens if they're picked up by the patrols? They'll be able to describe you to them.'

'So what?' said Steven. 'We weren't the only people around. It doesn't make us guilty of anything.'

'You're a young fool,' said Knutter. 'The Securitats think everyone is guilty. Even if you're not, they'll torture you until you confess to something, just to make the pain stop.'

'Leave him alone, Knutter,' said Paul. 'He's right. They were just girls, and they owe us. If it hadn't been for Steven and me, I reckon bits of them would be scattered over the Royal Mile right now. They almost ran into the second blast.'

Knutter muttered something to himself. An Illyri troop transport passed by, and the three of them quickly retreated from the front of the store.

'Did our lot plant those bombs, then?' said Knutter.

'We might have,' said Paul, tapping his nose as if it was all a wild secret. Knutter tapped his nose in reply and winked.

In reality Paul didn't have a clue who'd been responsible for the bombings. Surely he'd have been told if something was being planned for the Royal Mile – wouldn't he? After all, the Resistance had sent him and Steven to investigate the tunnels, so they'd been aware that there were operatives in the vicinity. Furthermore, the Resistance didn't bomb civilian areas with massive devices. There was too much risk of killing humans. No, this wasn't right at all.

But the two bombs, one after the other, fitted a certain pattern, just as he'd told the girls: the first bomb drew the emergency response teams, the Military and Securitats, and the second took out the rescuers. There were Resistance bomb teams who worked just that way, but not usually in cities, and not where humans might be injured.

Paul looked around Knutter's cramped shop, and gave a heartfelt sigh.

'Should we call it off?' said Knutter.

'No,' said Paul. 'We go ahead. With luck, the Illyri will have enough to keep them occupied picking through the rubble on the Mile.'

He looked to his brother, who nodded.

'I'm ready,' he said.

Paul turned to Knutter. 'You'd better show us the way, then.'

Knutter guided Paul and Steven into the back room of the shop. From there, they descended the rough stairs to the basement.

'Birdoswald,' said Knutter. 'Wish I'd been part of that one. That was a hell of an operation.'

Paul nodded as if in agreement, but said nothing. First Birdoswald, and now bombs on the Royal Mile. It looked like someone was trying to put the Resistance out of a job.

They were now in the basement, standing in a weak puddle of spluttering light, and Knutter began pulling boxes aside, revealing a rusty shelf.

'See?' he said.

They didn't, and the big man giggled like a child.

'Well, of course you wouldn't.'

With a last theatrical wink at the brothers, he unclipped the catches holding the shelf to the wall and slid it forward on concealed castors. Behind it was a sheet of plywood painted to match the brick, which Knutter shifted to reveal an entrance large enough for a man to pass through without crouching. The interior smelled damp, and when Knutter shone a torch inside, Steven and Paul heard a rat scuttling into the safety of the darkness. The light illuminated a small chamber with a curved ceiling.

'You see there?' said Knutter, pointing at the base of the far wall.

Steven and Paul squinted, and saw that the cement holding together the bricks in that part of the wall appeared newer than elsewhere. 'I've been working on it these last few nights, loosening the bricks until I could create a hole big enough to use. Then I relaid them on a metal support so that the whole section could be pulled out and replaced easily. It's a neat job. You wouldn't spot it unless you were looking for it.'

'Cool,' said Steven, and he meant it.

'And that leads directly into the new tunnel?' asked Paul.

'Pretty much. I still don't know how they managed to dig so quietly. I mean, it's right underneath my shop, and I never would have known about it if I hadn't been down here and heard those Toads babbling.'

Paul looked at his brother.

'You ready?'

Steven nodded, and they both shrugged off their thick coats to reveal the short, sharp knives they carried beneath. The knives were the only weapons they had brought to the city centre, for being caught on the streets with a firearm was a short cut to the Punishment Battalions. The battalions, made up of those found guilty of acts of terror and other crimes against the Illyri, were routinely dispatched to work and fight on the most hostile of worlds. Life expectancy could be measured in weeks and months, and sometimes only days.

Paul and Steven attached LED lights to their foreheads, and knelt to help Knutter pull back the section of wall.

Beyond was darkness.

Paul checked his watch. He took a deep breath. The air beyond smelled stale, but there was something else there, too, something bad. Knutter handed him a Glock pistol.

'Just in case,' he said. 'And I want it back.'

Paul took the gun without hesitation.

'Okay,' he said, 'let's do this.'

CHAPTER 14

Syl detected the new tension in the corridors as she and Ani passed along them, trying to find out what was happening. There were more Securitats among her father's Military, the two forces maintaining a discreetly hostile distance from each other. Twice they were stopped by Securitats and asked where they were going, and why, and only the intervention of members of her father's guard prevented an awkward situation from arising. The Securitats were attempting to put the castle in lockdown for security reasons, and the Military were resisting on principle. The circumstances in the castle had changed, and although it might have been linked in part to the explosions, it was clearly also to do with the red ship that sat beautifully, sinisterly, in the courtyard. Rupe, a sergeant of the castle guard, was advising Ani and Syl to return to their rooms after the second encounter with the Securitats when an Illyri male wearing a black business suit with gold trim on the collar appeared nearby, watching the exchange with grave, humourless eyes. He was frighteningly thin, with black hair cut close to his scalp, and his skin was a sickly, washed-out yellow. He brought to mind a sheathed blade, waiting to be used.

Sedulus.

Syl knew him by name and reputation, although thankfully they had never had reason to speak. Sedulus was Marshal of the Security Directorate for all of northern Europe, one of the most powerful Securitats on Earth. Her father, she knew, disliked him intensely, a feeling that was entirely mutual. Sedulus rarely came to Edinburgh, preferring instead to remain at his own headquarters at the fortress of Akershus in Oslo, Norway, a building that had once been occupied by the Nazis. Syl's father found this entirely apt.

Beside Sedulus, Syl was alarmed to note, was Vena. Syl had heard rumours that Sedulus and Vena were lovers, although she found it hard to believe that love would enter into any relationship involving those two. Both now approached their little group. Rupe instinctively stood in front of Syl and Ani, as though to protect them from the two Securitats.

'Step aside, Sergeant,' said Vena.

'May I ask why?' said Rupe.

'Because I am your superior officer, and if you don't obey my orders I will have you thrown in a cell.'

'With respect, ma'am,' said Rupe, loading his words with so much sarcasm that Syl was certain that he was goading Vena into trying to arrest him, 'this is a Military base of operations, and I answer to the Lord Governor. You can take your orders and shove them where the sun don't shine, begging your pardon.'

Syl saw Vena reach for the pistol on her belt, but Sedulus placed a hand on her arm and she froze.

'There's no need for trouble, Sergeant,' said Sedulus. He had a voice like honey, but stinging bees were not far away. 'Major Vena merely wanted to make sure that these young ladies were safe and well after the recent incidents.'

'Why shouldn't they be?' said Rupe.

'Major Vena appears to be under the impression that the governor's daughter and her friend might have been outside the castle walls when the bombs went off. If that were the case, it might be useful if my officers were given the opportunity to question them, just in case they saw anything while they were abroad, so to speak.'

He smiled. His lips didn't sit perfectly together when he did, so that a sliver of white teeth was visible between them. It made him look hungry.

'The major must be mistaken,' said Syl. 'We were not outside.'

'I saw you in the courtyard,' said Vena.

'Oh, we were in the courtyard,' said Syl, 'but that's not illegal yet. Is it?'

She looked at Ani. Ani shrugged innocently. 'I don't think so, but it sounds like the major might like to *make* it illegal.'

'You were covered in dust,' said Vena.

'We were watching the trucks,' said Syl. 'We wanted to find out what was happening. I guess we must have got dirty from being so close to them.'

Vena scowled at them. Her eyes took in Ani's tight jeans, silver sneakers and outsized off-the-shoulder sweater that revealed a curious tattoo of a bird with the wings of a butterfly. The twin stripes on Vena's skull suggested that she enjoyed expressing her own individuality, but she didn't approve of others doing the same, especially not the spoiled brats of her Military antagonists.

'You dress like a human slut,' said Vena.

'Better that than a Securitat slut,' said Ani. She spoke without thinking, and Syl could see that she regretted her words instantly, but it was typical of Ani to lash out first and think about the consequences after.

Vena's eyes darkened. A pale pink tongue poked from between her lips, like a serpent testing the air before striking.

'Careful, little bird,' she said, 'or I may have to break your wings.'

Even Sedulus appeared to recognise that no good was going to come from any further exchanges.

'Well,' he said, 'I believe that answers our questions for now, doesn't it?'

Vena didn't look like she'd received the answers she was looking for at all, and would have very much liked to continue the questioning somewhere quieter and more private, but she took the hint.

'If you are content, sir, then so am I,' she said.

'Then we'll let the governor's lovely daughter and her equally fetching friend be about their business,' said Sedulus. 'Thank you for your help, Sergeant . . . ?'

'Rupe,' said the sergeant.

'Rupe,' repeated Sedulus. 'I shall remember that name. Such loyal service to the governor should be rewarded appropriately, and it will be, when the time comes.'

Sedulus and Vena retreated, for now. Rupe let out a small, relieved breath.

'Thank you, Sergeant,' said Syl. 'I hope we haven't got you into trouble,' although she suspected that they had. Sedulus had a long memory, and Vena didn't like to be thwarted.

'If you have, it would be worth it just to get in that bitch's face, excuse my language.'

'Can you tell us what's happening?' said Ani. 'Nobody seems to be know, or seems willing to share it with us.'

'All I know is that we have offworld visitors,' said Rupe. 'Unexpected ones, and your father isn't very happy about it.' He lowered his voice. 'I can't say for sure, but I hear that Grand Consul Gradus is among them.'

This was news. Gradus had never visited Earth before, and he would usually have been expected to arrive with much pomp and ceremony, not in a small ship on a damp day in bomb-blasted Edinburgh.

'Now,' concluded Rupe, 'as I was saying earlier, if I were you, I'd find somewhere nice and quiet to wait this out. The Securitats have no love for anyone but their own kind, and I may not be here to protect you the next time. Off you go now.'

They went, but only as far as the next corner. When they were sure that Rupe was gone, Syl stopped.

'What is it?' said Ani.

'Fancy eavesdropping?' said Syl.

'On what?'

'On whatever happens next.'

Ani looked uncertain. 'I think we might have had enough fun for one day, don't you? I mean, we've slipped out of the castle and had to sneak back in again, we've nearly been blown up twice, we've had tea and biscuits with the enemy and we've managed to annoy the head of the secret police and his nasty little puppet.'

'Indulge me,' said Syl. 'It's my birthday.'

'Where are we going?'

'The Great Hall.'

Ani pretended to scowl, then laughed. 'All right, but we leave as soon as it gets boring. Which it will.'

'Fine,' said Syl, but she had a suspicion that the meeting wasn't going to be boring at all.

CHAPTER 15

Paul and Steven were in the sewers. Paul had been there before. The sewers had provided useful ways of moving arms around the city – and even a means of escape from patrols – but the Illyri had learned of what was happening, and had laid motion sensors along the routes most frequently used by the Resistance; motion sensors and minimum-charge infrasonic anti-personnel mines capable of killing a person without damaging the sewer system itself.

Now the Resistance tried to avoid the sewers; they didn't have time to sweep for sensors and mines, and it was only in the most desperate of cases that they made their way below ground. Paul had seen what happened to the insides of Resistance soldiers caught by infrasonic mines. It wasn't pretty, and he tried to keep images of it from his mind as he and his brother tramped through the filth of the city. The only reassurance came from the knowledge that the Illyri were unlikely to plant mines in areas used by their own troops. Just as long as Knutter hadn't simply been hearing things, they should be okay.

'Which way?' asked Steven.

'Left,' said Paul.

'Why left?'

'Why not? Would you prefer to split up?'

Steven shook his head. He didn't like being below ground, and already the tunnel was giving him the creeps. Although bulbs were strung irregularly along its length – another indication that the sewers were in use by the Illyri – they gave out only the dimmest of illumination, and there were great pools of darkness between each one.

Paul looked at his younger brother with only barely concealed admiration. Steven was just a kid, but then so were many of the Resistance's bravest operatives. The Illyri tended to concentrate their strictest surveillance efforts on adults and older teenagers, not children. Even at the best of times, children were difficult to police. There were kids walking the streets of Edinburgh with guns and plastic explosives hidden in their school bags. It wasn't what any parent, might have wished for their children, but there was a war on. Steven was braver than most of his peers, but he would always be Paul's little brother, and Paul tried to protect him as best he could.

'Didn't think so,' he said. 'Quietly now.'

Together they headed south, their knives clutched in their fists. Their headlamps cast disorientating shadows on the tunnel walls, making them both jumpy, so they chose instead to switch them off and rely on their eyes and the lights on the walls.

Paul had a pedometer attached to his hip, and he checked the distance as they walked, comparing it with the map in his hand. The tunnel seemed to run beneath South Bridge and Nicholson Street, then turned north-east at Lutton Place, heading in the direction of Queen's Drive and the Salisbury Crags. As they drew nearer to the Crags, a stink assailed their nostrils, and Steven had to stop himself from retching loudly. It was the smell of burning, and worse.

'The crematorium,' said Paul. 'We must be close to it.'

The Illyri had declared that burials were unsanitary in major urban areas, and had decreed that the remains of all deceased humans should be burned at a central crematorium built specially for that purpose to the east of Queen's Drive. The order had caused some dismay, but not as much as might have been expected, since cremations had begun to outnumber burials even before the arrival of the invaders. People simply resented being told what to do, even if it was something that they had been doing anyway. It was the principle of the thing.

They reached a T-junction in the tunnel, and a collapsed wall was revealed to their right. The bricks had been moved away, and supporting joists added. Paul and Steven moved in for a closer look, and saw that a hole had been made in the sewer wall. A length of pipe, about fifteen feet long and wide enough for a man to move through on his hands and knees connected the sewer with a second, better-lit tunnel beyond.

'Stay here,' Paul told Steven.

He hoisted himself into the pipe and shuffled along on his elbows, making as little noise as he could, until he reached the other end of the pipe. His hands were shaking, but he tried to remain still as he listened for any noises from beyond before risking a quick glance.

The tunnel was perfectly round, with rubber pads set along the ground to provide a grip. Paul was baffled as to how the Illyri had managed to construct it without being noticed, until he recalled being told of the massive lasers they sometimes used to tunnel through mountains in order to build new roads or hide their bases. Yes, he thought, one of those lasers, if it was assembled below ground, would do the trick, and it would explain why the tunnel walls were so smooth. The Illyri had simply burned their way under the city.

To his right, the tunnel came to a dead end in a patch of near darkness. Some machinery was being stored there. To his left, the tunnel intersected with another of similar smoothness and size.

He turned on to his back, slid most of his upper body from the pipe, then gripped its sides and dropped into the tunnel. He could see Steven at the other end, waiting to join him.

'Come on,' he said.

Steven climbed quickly into the pipe, and Paul helped him out. At that moment, they heard the burbling sounds of Galateans communicating, and Paul dragged his brother into the shadows, where they blended in with the piles of machinery and plastic. Paul drew Knutter's gun from under his jacket. If they had to fight their way out, they would. If it got really bad, he hoped he could hold the Toads off while Steven escaped, but he prayed it wouldn't come to that, both for his own sake and also because he knew that he'd have a hard time convincing his little brother to leave without him.

A Galatean appeared in the mouth of the Vault. It stopped in a pool of light and stared down the tunnel into the shadows where the boys had flattened themselves against the wall. Steven held his breath, afraid that if he sniffed even one more molecule of the tunnel stench he would throw up.

The Galatean moved on. Behind it came a series of hovering platforms of the kind used by the Illyri to transport heavy items. Beside them walked several Agrons, the slave race that performed the Illyri's dirtiest jobs. The Agrons were no more than five feet tall, but their upper bodies were overdeveloped, and they were enormously strong. Their pink heads were hairless, their faces wrinkled like those of Shar Pei dogs. They monitored the progress of the platforms, making sure that they did not bang against the walls. Each platform bore an irregularly shaped burden, covered by a layer of canvas. Steven and Paul had watched four of the platforms pass by when the fifth, and last, appeared. It seemed to be giving the Agrons some problems, its progress less smooth than the others. Halfway across the junction, sparks shot from its control panel, and the platform lurched sideways before dropping to the ground. The two Agrons beside it stepped quickly aside to avoid being crushed. One of the bindings holding the canvas in place shot loose, and the material fell away on the right-hand side, revealing what lay beneath.

Steven felt his big brother flinch next to him. He bit his lip to suppress an inadvertent yelp, and hold back a surge of vomit.

Five bodies were piled on the metal surface: three men, one woman and a boy who looked only a little younger than Steven. All were naked, their skin bearing the marks of discoloration and decay, for in addition to requiring cremation of the dead within twenty-four hours, the Illyri had also banned the use of preservatives on bodies on environmental grounds. If nothing else, it encouraged the relatives of the deceased to deal with the matter of their disposal as quickly as possible.

Under the instructions of the Toads, the Agrons unloaded the corpses from the malfunctioning platform and distributed them as best they could among the others, shifting bodies roughly to make room for more.

And then, to the boys' horror, one of the bodies moved. It was the woman. Her head turned, and she gave a little moan. She had dark hair that hung over her face, obscuring most of it, but Paul could see one blue eye open in panic. The woman seemed to be staring straight at him. She started to scream, over and over, the sound of it echoing in the tunnel until one of the Galateans stepped in front of her, blocking the boys' view. He drew a pulse weapon, charged it and fired.

The screaming stopped.

The little procession continued on its way, heading not towards the crematorium but away from it, in the direction of the shuttle base beneath Arthur's Seat.

Once all was quiet again, Paul released his hold on Steven, and allowed his brother to puke.

'You okay?' he asked, once Steven's retching had stopped.

Steven nodded, standing up shamefaced, wiping strings of vomit from his lips.

'She was alive. That lady was still alive.'

'Yes.'

'And then they killed her.'

'Yes.'

'What were they doing with those bodies, with those people?'

'I don't know. They weren't burning them, that's for sure. Let's get out of here. We have to report what we've seen, and I need fresh air.'

The two young men climbed back into the pipe, and headed for safety.

Knutter wrinkled his nose as they re-entered his shop.

'You weren't in there for long,' he said, 'but you still stink. You got my gun?'

Paul returned the weapon; Knutter tucked it back into his belt.

'You find out what they're doing?'

Steven didn't say anything. He was learning to keep his mouth shut when anyone asked a question, leaving Paul to come up with answers. Now he was watching his brother carefully, waiting to hear what he might say.

'Not exactly,' said Paul.

'What's that supposed to mean?' said Knutter. 'I took a big risk bringing you down here, and making that hole in the wall. You're not going to get another opportunity like that, you know, not unless someone plants another bomb on the Royal Mile. What did you see?' He made a motion towards Paul, his hands raised. 'Tell me, you cocky little—'

Paul moved fast. One moment he was using some newspaper to wipe filth from his boots; the next he was right next to Knutter, and his knife was pressed hard against the man's neck.

'You should mind your manners,' said Paul. 'I'll tell you what you need to know, and nothing more. That's how we all stay alive. You understand?'

Knutter tried to swallow, but his Adam's apple caught on the edge of the knife.

'Yes,' he croaked.

'We'll be on our way, then,' said Paul.

He lowered the blade, and Knutter rubbed his throat in an unhappy manner.

'I was only asking,' he said.

'I know,' said Paul.

He was now regretting pulling the knife on Knutter. He had to learn to control his temper; it wouldn't be wise to leave the man angry. Angry people did stupid things.

'Look, I'm sorry,' he said. 'You know, any time spent down there is too much time.'

'Yeah, well,' said Knutter. 'You shouldn't ought to be pulling knives on friends. Caught me by surprise, you did.'

'I'll tell the people who need to know that you did well today,' said Paul. 'You helped us a lot.'

Knutter led them to the door. When he was certain that all was clear, he let them out, and Paul and Steven began making their way home.

'You should have kept his gun until you were sure about him,' said Steven.

'Knutter's all right,' said Paul. 'He just forgets the rules sometimes.'
Steven nodded. They walked on for a time.

'Can I have a gun?' Steven asked.

Paul felt a great sadness wash over him as they crossed to Princes Street. It was only a short step from carrying a gun to using it, and an even shorter step after that to being killed by one. He knew that he couldn't keep Steven safe forever, but he still wanted to protect him for just a little while longer.

'Maybe some day,' he said. 'Maybe.'

Like the rest of its kind, the Agron who returned to repair and retrieve the disabled platform had poor eyesight, and was not very intelligent. But it was gifted with a keen sense of smell, and even amid the various odours in the tunnel it detected the sour-sweet stink of human vomit. It sniffed its way into the darkness of the tunnel until it found the source, still fresh.

Within seconds, it had raised the alarm.

CHAPTER 16

By avoiding the main hallways, and taking the little-used connectors between the old Scottish National War Memorial and the Royal Palace, listening at corners to ensure that the way was clear before proceeding, Syl and Ani made it to the room adjoining the Great Hall without attracting notice.

'Before I bailed class to find you, Deren asked Toris about the Civil War,' whispered Ani, as she helped Syl move the huge armoire that hid the entrance to the spyhole. Syl had discovered the catch that allowed the wooden armoire to slide across the floor, leaving a space just large enough to slip through. Without the catch, the armoire was so heavy that it would take many men to move it.

'Really?' said Syl. 'I bet Toris didn't care much for that.'

Deren enjoyed taunting Toris almost as much as Ani did. Poor Deren fancied Ani something rotten, thought Syl, and always followed her lead, but Ani seemed to have no interest in him, while Deren would happily cut off one of his hands if Ani told him to.

'Not much at all.'

The old tutor always tried to put the best angle on the conflict, arguing that Illyri society was the better for it, but the truth was that the wounds it had caused were still visible to this day. The animosity between the Diplomats and the Military was proof of that.

The Civil War was one of the darkest periods in Illyri history, a century-long conflict of succession that followed the death of Meus, the Unifier of Worlds, who had laid the foundations of what was known as the First Illyri Empire. The Civil War split Illyri society, even individual families. On one side was an elite class of the wealthy and the privileged, among them the Diplomats, who believed that they were best equipped to rule, and that democracy was a failed experiment. A handful of Military leaders sided with them, along with militias from the First Colonies, pressed into service by the Diplomats, who had grown increasingly powerful and ambitious on their offworld bases. Ranged against them were most of the ordinary civilians, the elected politicians and the majority of senior Military leaders, among them Syl's great-grandfather. Sometimes the war took the form of outright battle on one world or another, but mostly it was a series of truces and agreements, broken by either side, constantly under-pinned by low-level guerrilla warfare.

Finally, a lasting agreement was reached to stop the Illyri race from tearing itself apart entirely. A Council of Government was created, to be elected by the people every five sessions, with equal representation by the Military, the civil authorities and the Diplomats, who emerged from the bloody conflict with even more power than they had enjoyed at the beginning, a testament to their cleverness and, indeed, their ruthlessness. A president, elected for twenty sessions of the Council, was given the deciding vote in the event of disagreements. The office of president alternated between the three main groups, and the arrangement had functioned well until the Second Empire began its recent expansion into other systems, and the Diplomatic Corps grew in influence, backed by the Sisterhood. Now the Diplomats dominated the Council, and only the current presidency of Grand Commander Rydus, the most decorated Military leader of his day, kept them from total supremacy.

'So,' said Syl. 'What did Deren want to know this time?'

'He asked Toris if it could happen again.'

Another civil war? It didn't bear thinking about.

'And what did Toris say?' asked Syl.

'Toris said that he believed all sides had learned from the last conflict, which wasn't a proper answer.'

'Toris is just sorry that we're not all ruled by bald Diplomats,' said Syl. 'He thinks that the treaty was a mistake, and the Diplomats and their allies were on the verge of winning when the truce was agreed.'

'How do you know all this?'

'My father likes to educate me over dinner.'

'But if Toris is such a friend of the Corps, why does your father allow him to educate us?'

'Because he says that Toris knows a lot, and his flaws in one area don't necessarily make him unsuited to all,' said Syl. She grinned slyly. 'My father also says that you should know your enemy.'

'I don't think Toris feels the same way. When Deren tried to pursue the subject, Toris got angry and told him to keep quiet and study his history more closely.' Ani seemed to reconsider what she had just said. 'No, not just angry. I think he was frightened. Do *you* believe that there's a chance of another civil war, Syl?'

Syl pushed Ani into the spyhole and pulled the armoire across behind her, so the gap was closed. There was utter darkness for a moment until she exposed a series of narrow slits, allowing light from the Great Hall to penetrate their hiding place. The Hall was empty for now, but it wouldn't be for long.

'My father says that Grand Commander Rydus is skilled at balancing the demands of the Military and the Diplomats,' she replied, 'and no Illyri wants a return to civil conflict. Yes, the Diplomats desire more power, but not at the cost of war with the Military. As long as Rydus is president, and the Military remains united, the Diplomats will be kept in check.'

She realised that she was using almost the exact words that she had heard her father speak during the last meeting of his advisers in the Great Hall. He had been talking to his own officers, his loyal cadre, without any fear of being overheard by Diplomat spies. But then Syl had been listening in, and if she could eavesdrop on meetings in the Hall, could not others do so as well? She knew that the Hall was regularly swept for listening devices, and that her father was careful about how he spoke in unsecured environments, but still . . .

She peered through one of the slits. They gave a surprisingly good view of the chamber, and anything that was said carried clearly. They were also invisible from inside the Great Hall – she'd confirmed that by checking from the other side – for they had been carefully crafted to resemble natural flaws in the materials used to create the fireplace centuries before.

A door opened at the far end of the Hall, and Governor Andrus entered, Balen at his heels. Behind them both came Peris, the captain of the castle guard. Her father spun to face him.

'Why wasn't I informed of their approach?' he said. He spoke quietly, but there was no concealing the fury in his voice.

'We were given no warning,' said Peris. 'The mothership had a cargo designation when it came through the wormhole. There was no indication that it was a Diplomat vessel, and we didn't even know of a Diplomat presence until the shuttle was making its final approach to Edinburgh.'

'Not just a Diplomat presence,' said Andrus, 'but the Sisterhood!'

Syl's stomach tightened. No member of the Nairene Sisterhood had ever been seen on Earth, and she knew of them only from her father's vocal distrust of the sisters and their ways.

'I'm sorry, Governor,' said Peris. 'We were deceived.'

'But to what end?' said Andrus. 'Why would Gradus and his witch arrive in such secrecy?' He turned to Balen. 'Where are they now?'

'I put them in the main guest suite,' he said. The guest suite was in what had once been a war museum. It was not far from the Governor's House.

'And we're monitoring them?'

Balen shifted awkwardly. This was clearly a question to which he would have preferred to be giving a different answer.

'We were, both visually and aurally,' he said. 'Unfortunately, both systems appear to have failed. They went down seconds after the Nairene entered the suite. All we're getting is static and white noise. Oh, and some shouting from Grand Consul Gradus, who is demanding to be shown into your presence immediately, but we don't need surveillance to hear him. He's quite loud enough without it.'

Something like a smile managed to find its way on to Andrus's lips.

'Good. Let him steam for a while. Have we made contact with the mothership?'

'Just the usual courtesies.'

'Demand a crew and cargo manifest. Come up with some excuse; I don't care what it is, but I want a list of everybody on that ship, and some hint as to where it might have come from. With luck, there'll be someone on board who might be willing to tell us discreetly what all this is about. In the meantime—'

But Andrus was destined to get no further with his instructions. They heard the sound of voices approaching, and the door to the Great Hall burst open to admit an extremely tall, wide-shouldered Illyri in shimmering golden robes, his head shaved and his fingers adorned with jewelled rings – the sign of a senior Diplomat, for promotion through the ranks of the Corps was marked by the giving of rings. He was surrounded by his own private soldiers – recently arrived on a second shuttle – and members of the Securitat, Vena the Skunk among them. They in turn were being watched by five members of the castle guard, who had been forced through the doors by the sheer weight of opposing numbers.

'Grand Consul Gradus,' said Andrus, with strained politeness. 'How good of you to join us. I was just about to send my aide to accompany you, but I see that you have discovered the way yourself.'

Gradus gave a small bow, but there was no humility in it.

'I was afraid that I might grow too used to the luxury of my surroundings, and forget my purpose here,' he replied. As he spoke, he walked around the Great Hall, taking in its suits of armour and displays of weaponry: the swords, the pikes, the old trench mortars that stood like small cannons on the floor. He seemed to find the cavalry armour by the fireplace particularly interesting, and commented upon it.

'Which animal was it that the humans rode while wearing this?' he asked.

'Horses,' said Andrus.

'I should like to see one, or even ride one, if it can be arranged.'

His voice was oddly high, but there was a discordancy underlying it, like a poorly tuned instrument playing a beautiful piece of music. From her vantage point, Syl thought him a detestable figure. There was something about him that made her profoundly uneasy: a softness, a decadence. His robes had been cut to make him appear even broader in the shoulder and slimmer in the waist, and he was wearing a strong scent that even from a distance caused her nose to itch. She saw that his rings – dozens of them – were so embedded in the flesh of his fingers that they would be impossible to remove, as if he'd been born into such finery and his fingers had been thus adorned from the cradle.

'Perhaps if you had given us some notice of your arrival, we might have been better prepared to receive you,' said Andrus. 'We could even have sent a horse. We were not expecting the head of the Diplomatic Corps to arrive unexpectedly in a cargo vessel, not unless he has fallen some distance in the eyes of worlds.'

Balen permitted himself a smile, and Syl smiled to herself too, wishing she had her father's way with words.

Some of the castle guards continued to jostle with the soldiers and Securitats while Gradus stood in their midst, his face reddening as he quietly seethed. It was clearly unwise to let this situation continue, particularly with so many loaded weapons in the room. Andrus raised a hand, and ordered the guards to stand down. After a strained pause during which it appeared that Gradus might be unwilling to do the same, he too waved a long finger, and his protectors lowered their weapons.

Gradus took a seat at the council table. Andrus followed suit.

'To answer your question,' said Gradus, 'the tensions between the Military and the Diplomatic Corps mean that any journey, however minor, becomes the subject of speculation and invites the attentions of spies and informers. I preferred to arrive here unburdened by advance gossip. Send your guards away, Andrus, and I will do the same. Then we can talk.'

Andrus instructed Peris to clear the room. The captain took particular pleasure in waiting for Vena to leave before he followed her outside, a small but biting demonstration of his senior position. Only Andrus, Gradus and Balen were left.

'I still seem to be outnumbered,' said Gradus, with a dramatic little huff. 'That hardly seems fair.'

He looked to the door expectantly. After a moment, it opened to reveal a figure dressed entirely in deep red flowing robes, its face obscured by a veil of fine lace. Ani's fingers tightened around Syl's elbow, but when Syl glanced at her, Ani was simply staring wide-eyed at the vision in red, apparently unaware of her grip on Syl's arm. Behind the figure could be seen the faces of both castle guards and Corps soldiers, all of them staring after it with a mixture of fascination and fear.

'Governor Andrus,' said Gradus, 'permit me to introduce you to Syrene, Archmage of the Nairene Sisterhood, and my wife.'

Ani released the breath she had been holding, and she and Syl instinctively moved closer to the observation slits as Syrene approached the table, her feet so obscured by her scarlet finery that she seemed to glide across the floor in a cascade of red. She did not speak, nor did she acknowledge Andrus or Balen. She simply took a seat to the right of Gradus, and placed her gloved hands upon the ancient wood of the council chamber table.

'You are welcome, Archmage,' said Andrus.

'He doesn't sound like he means it,' whispered Ani.

'He doesn't,' said Syl. 'He hates the Sisterhood.'

'Why?'

'Not now. Later. Just listen.'

Ani did as she was told. This was interesting. In the past, the thrill of entering the spyhole had come from the fact that they had been doing something forbidden, and not from anything they had subsequently seen or heard. But this, this was another matter entirely: a Nairene sister here, on Earth. And not just any sister either, but the Archmage herself, the legendary Syrene. Ani felt shivery and warm all at once.

Syrene did not acknowledge Andrus's words. The red veil moved slightly as she slowly looked around the room, her eyes still concealed.

'To business,' said Gradus. 'I bring you sad news, Andrus. Our beloved president, Rydus, has died.'

Andrus reeled back in his chair in shock. Syl felt for him: her father had served under Rydus, and had been closer to him than to his own father. Rydus nurtured his career, and had stood beside him when Andrus married the Lady Orianne, Syl's mother. It was Rydus who had made Andrus the senior governor on Earth after the conquest, effectively entrusting him with the rule of this most unusual of planets.

'How?' asked her father. He seemed barely able to utter the word.

'An embolism. It appears that he died in his sleep.'

'When?'

'Three weeks ago.'

Three weeks! Syl was amazed. News from Illyr often took a long time to get to outlying planets in the Empire, but such important information could have been communicated to Andrus sooner. A system of transmitting stations linked Illyr to the various wormholes. Her father could have learned of Rydus's death in days, rather than weeks, but Gradus had kept it from him. Even Syl could figure out what that meant: Gradus and the Corps had full control of the transmitters, and had deliberately prevented news of Rydus's death from reaching Andrus on Earth.

'I decided to inform you in person, as a mark of respect, instead of allowing the news to come to you through other channels, perhaps polluted by hearsay,' Gradus added.

'What kind of hearsay?'

'You know just as well as I that when a senior figure dies in such circumstances, the rumour mill begins to grind out untruths. There will always be those who whisper of plots and dark dealings, but I have brought with me the reports of the physicians. I will have them sent to your secretary, but you will see that there can be no doubt about how Rydus died.'

Syl watched her father swallow his grief as he began to take in the implications of what Gradus had told him.

'And what of the presidency?' he asked. 'I assume that you have put yourself forward as a candidate. Or has it gone beyond that, and you have already taken office?'

It was widely known that Gradus desired the position of president for himself, but had resigned himself to waiting a long time to ascend to it since Rydus was only six sessions into his term of office, and had shown no signs of ill health. Long living was common in Rydus's family, or had been until now.

'You misunderstand me, Andrus. It is true that I may have had such ambitions in the past, but as I grow older, I have come to realise that the burdens of the office far outweigh its benefits. I have decided to leave it to one better suited to these demands.

'With that in mind, I have instructed the Corps not to take advantage of Rydus's sudden and unexpected demise. We have not sought to have a Diplomat candidate installed. Instead, we have agreed that the Military should continue to hold the office. Rydus should have enjoyed a much longer hold on the presidential throne. It seemed unbecoming to profit from his mortality and create the impression that the Corps was interested only in furthering its own ends. We, like you, have only the interests of the empire at heart.'

If Andrus had been taken aback by the news of Rydus's death, this latest revelation seemed more shocking still. It went against all he had believed, or suspected, of Gradus's nature that the Grand Consul should decline to extend the Corps' influence by assuming the presidency himself, or at the very least ensuring that some Diplomat puppet of his choice took office while Gradus pulled the strings.

'So who is now president?' asked Andrus.

'We are fortunate that General Krake was willing to put his name forward, and was unanimously approved by the governing council. Long may he live, and wise be his rule.'

Andrus's eyes did not leave Gradus, but Syl saw Balen glance from the governor to the still, silent form of Syrene. Krake had been one of the few Military officers to ignore the unofficial, but widely accepted, rule about keeping the Sisterhood away from the Military, and had taken one of the sisters as his bride. Her name was Merida, and she was a favourite of Syrene, who had mentored her since early childhood.

All were silent for a time. Andrus and Gradus appeared locked in some unspoken conflict of their own. Gradus was smiling, as if inviting Andrus to voice his suspicions in the presence of the Archmage.

But now Syrene lifted her veil so that it fell back in delicate folds to reveal her face. Her skin was intricately tattooed, filigree and strange animal forms spilling down from her skull and across her forehead, adorning her cheeks – each of which was decorated with a red eye like that on the side of the shuttle – and framing lips so full and red that they seemed on the verge of bursting. She was paler than most Illyri, for little light penetrated the deepest recesses of the Marque, where the Sisterhood hid their secrets.

She surveyed the room languidly, her eyes wide and cool. Suddenly Ani put her hands to the sides of her head, kneading her temples as though she were in pain.

'Ani?' said Syl. 'What's wrong?'

'Don't you feel it?' said Ani. 'Don't you feel *her*?'

Syrene's gaze alighted on the fireplace, and the ghost of what might have been a smile crossed her face. Ani moved her right hand from her temple to her mouth, wincing as if in pain as she did so, biting hard on her knuckles. Syl put an arm around her, concerned, but Ani didn't respond.

Syrene turned to Syl's father, cocking her head to one side, and the eye on her left cheek appeared to blink once as she spoke. 'Are you quite sure that we're alone here, Lord Andrus?'

Andrus's face was a mask.

'Of course we are, Archmage,' he said.

'I see. How very interesting.'

Syrene stood and pulled her veil over her face once more, hiding her searching eyes.

'Come, husband,' she said. 'His lordship is in shock. We will continue our conversation later. Let us leave him to mourn all that he has lost . . .'

'Yes, of course,' said Gradus, rising to his feet to follow the Red Sister.

'. . . and all that may yet be lost,' concluded Syrene.

Gradus stopped briefly, and seemed about to say something more to Andrus, but then merely chuckled and strode away, having clearly decided that Syrene's parting shot was better than any he could muster.

They all understood the truth of what had transpired, even if none was willing to say it aloud: there had been a quiet coup on Illyr.

The Sisterhood had made its move on the presidency.

CHAPTER 17

Ani and Syl allowed a safe amount of time to elapse before they left the spyhole and returned to the Governor's House. There was to be some respite from the confines of the castle, though: Althea, who had a gift for providing solace to those in pain, whether physical, emotional or psychological, had volunteered to help with the wounded at the Royal Edinburgh Hospital on Morningside Terrace, and had convinced Governor Andrus that Syl and Ani should be allowed to attend with her. Empathy was a quality strongly valued among the Illyri; those who understood the reality of pain and suffering were likely to do their best to avoid inflicting it on others. So Syl and Ani held the hands of the injured, both Illyri and those humans who were willing to accept consolation from any source.

Illyri technology had brought huge advances in human medical techniques. ProGen artificial skin was routinely used to treat burns, replacing the need for skin grafts. Diseased internal organs were replaced with organs grown on artificial 'scaffolds' – animal organs that had been stripped of their living cells, leaving only a basic framework of blood vessels, and repopulated with cells from a patient's own body. Gene therapy cured genetic defects. Nanoparticles and stem cell therapies targeted everything from diabetes to cancer. Even human ageing could be slowed. There were still some humans who objected to such treatments on religious grounds, and others who spread stories that all such efforts were part of a secret Illyri plot to undermine the human race. But most recognised the benefits of being able to easily replace damaged or worn internal organs, and human life expectancy had already increased significantly as a result.

Syl and Ani were exhausted by the time they returned to the castle, and went straight to their respective quarters to wash, change, and eat.

A small group had gathered in the governor's private chambers. Lord Andrus himself was there, as was Balen. General Danis was lying back in an armchair, his legs stretched before him, his feet crossed, almost, it appeared asleep. The last arrival was a young female wearing a mix of human and Illyri clothing, her hair short but still unkempt, her eyes dark and watchful. She stood by the door, and although she seemed to be relaxed, there was about her the sense of an animal tensed and ready to spring. Her name was Meia, and she was Lord Andrus's chief intelligence officer.

Balen served wine. Only Meia declined.

'Why don't you ever drink?' Danis asked.

Meia pondered the question. 'I can, but it disagrees with my system,' she said at last. 'And I prefer to keep a clear head.'

'Very wise,' said Danis, taking a deep draught from his own glass. 'I hope to be as wise as you some day, although your choice of jewellery raises questions about the extent of that wisdom.'

He gestured with his glass at Meia's neck, where a cross hung alongside a Muslim crescent moon, a Hindu aum on an amulet, and even a Shinto torii, or gate. Meia quickly hid them away.

'I have no difficulty accepting the concept of a creator,' said Meia. 'Why should you?'

'Because—' Danis caught himself, and swallowed whatever he had been about to say, choosing instead an alternative track. 'Your views on the nature of the universe are fascinating, I'm sure, but I'm more interested to hear you explain the purpose of a Military intelligence service that couldn't warn us of the arrival of the Grand Consul and his witch-wife until they were on our doorstep telling us about dead presidents!'

His voice had risen steadily throughout this sentence until it was virtually a roar. The room was soundproofed, and had been swept for listening devices before the meeting, but it was hard to believe that there was anyone in the immediate environs who did not now know that Danis was unhappy.

'My orders are to monitor events on Earth, not keep an eye on the activities of the Corps in the wider universe,' said Meia. 'If you wish me to do that, General, I may have to hire an assistant.'

'First Birdoswald, and now this,' said Danis. 'Perhaps it's not an assistant you require, but a replacement.'

'One might say the same about you, General,' said Meia. 'How goes the War on Terror? Have you crushed the Resistance yet, or did I miss that while I was watching body parts being collected on the Royal Mile?'

Danis rose from his chair. It wasn't clear what he planned to do, but it did seem to involve some harm to Meia. The object of his anger did not move. She was more than a match for Danis, and she knew it.

Lord Andrus raised a hand. 'Stop it, both of you. We have enough enemies in the castle without adding to them from our own number.'

He sipped his wine, and frowned. The taste of it, usually so pleasant, now seemed like vinegar on his tongue. The events of the day had ruined his appetite for many things. He put the glass aside, and steepled his hands upon his desk.

'What are our esteemed guests doing at the moment?' he asked Balen.

'The Grand Consul is dining in his room with two of his aides.'

'And his wife?'

'She requested separate quarters, and chose to dine alone. Only her handmaid attends her.'

'Maybe she and her beloved are not getting along,' said Danis. 'One of them might come over to our side and tell us what's going on.'

'Have they made any attempt to contact the mothership?'

'None, nor have we received a request for a communication channel.'

'Could they have brought equipment of their own?'

'It's possible, but we're monitoring the rooms for any signs of electronic traffic.'

Andrus looked to Meia. 'I sense that you have something you'd like to say.'

Meia nodded. 'Why did the Grand Consul choose to arrive today, in the aftermath of twin bomb attacks so close to the castle?'

Andrus glanced at Danis. Danis shrugged. 'Why not? Maybe he's come to mourn his nephew.'

'The Grand Consul is known to be zealous about protecting his personal safety, but he is equally careful, if not more so, about looking after his wife,' said Meia patiently. 'The Sisterhood would be most displeased if some harm were to befall Syrene. She is destined to become Mage upon the death of Ezil.'

'There's no sign of the old bitch dying yet,' said Danis. 'More's the pity. Then again, she may already be dead, given how long it's been since anyone caught sight of her. Good riddance to her if she is.'

'Go on,' said Andrus, ignoring his general while also silently agreeing with him on the subject of Ezil.

'So, it was out of character to risk a landing here while the smoke from bomb attacks was still rising above the city,' said Meia. 'But the Grand Consul is always consistent in his character, at least in this regard. Therefore we have a contradiction.'

She moved closer to the fire, and to the other three Illyri in the room.

'The members of the Resistance, too, are consistent in their actions. They do not endanger their own civilians. They are careful to limit their attacks to Military installations and personnel. When possible they'll also target the Diplomats and their Securitats, although the Corps prefers to conduct its business from behind walls and shields, so they have more opportunities to strike at us. It is completely inconsistent with the Resistance's patterns of behaviour to plant devices in an area like the Royal Mile, which hosts human businesses and extensive pedestrian traffic. We lost ten soldiers today, and three Securitats, but four humans also died, and dozens more on both sides were injured.'

'Could the Resistance be stepping up its campaign, or changing its tactics?' asked Andrus.

'I don't believe so. If a decision like that had been made, news would have reached us. We're not entirely without our sources within the Resistance, and its leadership here is quite clear in its methodology: no civilian casualties.'

'A splinter group, then,' said Danis, 'one that doesn't believe the Resistance is radical enough.'

'Again, the Resistance has its own ways of dealing with dissenters,' said Meia. 'Warnings are usually enough. After that, there are always limbs that can be broken. It's never had to go further, but anyone who chose to kill and injure civilians as a protest against the Resistance's leadership wouldn't last very long. No, I don't believe the Resistance planted those devices.'

'Then who did?' asked Danis. 'Us?'

'No,' said Meia, 'not quite.'

She waited. Eventually, Andrus said what they were all thinking.

'The Diplomatic Corps? The Securitats?'

'It would explain why the Grand Consul was not concerned about landing in the aftermath,' said Meia. 'He knew that there was no danger of further attacks.'

'But why?' asked Danis. 'To what end?'

'To undermine the governor and, by extension, the Military rule on Earth. A new president has come to power, one who, despite his Military credentials, is probably under the sway of the Sisterhood. The Diplomatic Corps wants complete control of this planet. It does not want to share it with the Military. What better way to demonstrate the Military's failures than by having bombs exploding on the doorstep of the planet's senior governor, or to prove the bravery of the Grand Consul than by his willingness to land despite the threat?'

'You seem very certain of this,' said Andrus.

'Not certain, but it fits with the available facts. Then there is the matter of the suicides,' she added.

'Suicides?' said Danis.

'I know that you've been looking into what happened to the Grand Consul's nephew Thaios at Birdoswald. The evidence suggests that he killed himself rather than be captured. There was a similar incident in Iran last month, also involving a relative of Grand Consul Gradus.'

'I had asked Danis to look into the death of Thaois,' said Lord Andrus. 'It seems that you may have spared him the trouble. Do you have proof?'

'An eyewitness in Tehran. A senior sub-consul, a cousin of Gradus, was cornered near a mosque after his convoy was ambushed. Rather than be captured, it seems that he activated an infrasonic grenade. The consequences were . . . messy.'

Andrus considered what had been said. 'Find out more,' he told Meia. 'I want to know if there's a connection between these two deaths and Gradus's arrival on Earth.'

At that moment, there was a knock on the door. Rupe, the sergeant who had earlier helped Syl and Ani in their confrontation with the Corps, was standing outside.

'I gave orders not to be disturbed, Sergeant,' said Andrus, and there was no mistaking the unhappiness in his voice.

Rupe, though, didn't blink. He had been with Andrus for many years, and he knew when the situation called for the exercise of a little personal discretion.

'My lord, I thought you might forgive the interruption on this occasion,' he said. 'The Archmage Syrene has sent a message. She's asking to see your daughter.'

CHAPTER 18

Katherine Kerr worried about her sons. She had always worried about them; it was the curse of being a mother. They were born wilful boys. Paul was the volatile one, Steven quieter and more cautious, and once they had made a decision, there was no changing their minds. Even though they were dissimilar in many ways, they had somehow found a way to act as a unit, with one perfectly complementing the other.

It helped that Steven worshipped Paul, but Paul in turn was hugely protective of his younger brother. He had been both proud and concerned when Steven had asked to play a part in the Resistance. His mother had known better than to try and stop Steven, just as she had not tried to stop his older brother from joining. In both cases she knew that, had she objected, or put obstacles in their way, they would have proceeded without her approval, and perhaps put themselves in greater danger as a consequence. She knew that Paul would look after his brother, but not a day went by when she didn't pray for them both, just in case.

Their father had died five years earlier. The Securitats had picked him up during a sweep following the assassination of one of their number. Bob Kerr had been hurrying to work at Edinburgh Zoo, where he had responsibility for the Malayan tapirs, amongst other species. One of the tapirs was due to give birth after the long gestation typical of the animal, and Bob wanted to be present in case there were problems. When he tried to explain this as the Securitats bundled him into one of their transports, he was struck in the chest with an electric baton. He died of a heart attack in the back of the truck. From that day on, Katherine knew that her sons would fight, and they were far from alone.

It was the great strength of the Resistance: most of its operatives were very young. They had an energy and innovativeness that their elders lacked. Perhaps it was because it was their generation that was being pressed into offworld service by the Illyri, forced to fight wars on distant planets in the name of an empire that had taken their own world by force. But it had also recently become known that the Illyri had contaminated the Earth's water supply, although so far chemical analysis had revealed no trace of it. This was no idle gossip, or unfounded rumour; it came from some of the Illyri who had defected. They spoke of a testosterone suppressant, a simple, harmless means of keeping human aggression in check. The drug inhibited the pituitary gland from secreting the master hormones LSH and FSH that stimulated testosterone production.

However, the surge in the body's testosterone production during puberty rendered teenagers, both male and female, less susceptible to the Illyri drug. In the years since the possibility of the suppressant's existence was first raised, steps had been taken to counteract its effects: testosterone supplements, the boiling of water before use, or preferably, only drinking water that had come from clean, natural springs. The problem was that the suppressant had a cumulative effect, and most men and women had been drinking the contaminated water for so long that it was unclear how long its suppressive effects would last. It was the new generation that remained immune, and so it was that the burden of fighting the oppressors fell on them.

Now, as she heard the front door open and the boys enter, Mrs Kerr felt a surge of relief and gave a small prayer of thanks. She had not asked Paul where they were going when they left earlier that day, but she could always tell when it was a particularly risky task that was being undertaken. It was as if their personalities switched when they were tense: Paul would grow quiet, and Steven would babble as though he thought he might never get the chance to talk again. They had been like that at breakfast, and part of her had wanted to lock them in their rooms so that someone else would be forced to take on their duties instead.

And then she had heard the explosions echoing from the Royal Mile, and she had found herself frozen in place, forgetting to lift the iron until the sour smell of burning fabric filled the room, rendering a pair of Steven's trousers useless. Was that what her boys were doing now, planting bombs? Did they get away in time? She had spent the rest of the day waiting, wondering if a knock would come at the door, if she would open it and see one of the Resistance people, perhaps a man with his wife in tow, or his sister, or his mother, someone to console her as she was told that her sons were dead . . .

But here they were: her boys. They were home. They were safe. They would be with her for another day. She hugged them both, but she noticed that Steven held on to her for a little longer, and when she looked at his face, she could see how pale he was.

'What happened?' she said.

'He just saw something that made him ill,' said Paul. 'He'll be fine.'

'Sugar: that's what he needs.'

She took a bottle of Irn Bru from the fridge and poured a tall glass for Steven, and another for Paul. She didn't drink the stuff. She had never been one for fizzy drinks, but the boys had always liked Irn Bru. Along with whisky, it counted as the Scottish national drink.

'Drink it down,' she told Steven. 'It'll do you good. I'll start on your dinner now that you're back.'

'I'll have to go out again soon,' said Paul, and she knew what he meant. He'd have to make a report about whatever they'd seen, or done, that afternoon.

'The explosions . . .' she said.

'It wasn't us,' said Paul, and she was relieved to hear it. There were reports that humans had died along with Illyri, and she didn't want her sons to be responsible for that kind of carnage.

There was a knock on the front door. The boys looked at each other, and then at their mother. They weren't expecting anyone. Mrs Kerr wiped her hands on her apron, even though they weren't wet or dirty, and tried to keep her fear in check.

'I'll get it,' she said. 'Stay where you are.'

She put the chain on the door before opening it. A large man was standing on the path, keeping his distance. She had never seen him before.

'Mrs Kerr?' he asked.

'Yes?' she said. 'Can I help you?'

'My name is Knutter,' he said. 'I'm wondering if your lads are home yet?'

Something trickled from beneath his hair and slowly ran down his forehead. She watched the blood catch on his eyebrow and drip on his lashes.

Knutter blinked.

'Run,' he whispered.

She slammed the door closed just as she heard the *slap* of a pulse weapon firing. Knutter's upper body hit the door as he died, and the thick glass cracked with the impact. She turned to see Paul and Steven staring at her from the kitchen table.

'Get out of here!' she screamed, as the front door exploded behind her. Something struck her in the back and sent her sprawling on her belly. The glass in the kitchen window broke, and two gas grenades skittered like silver rats across the floor. The room filled with choking fumes, and there were Galateans stepping over her from behind, and more entering through the kitchen door. The aliens wore breathing apparatus to protect them from the gas. One of them knelt beside her and cuffed her hands behind her back before dragging her to her feet. The base of her spine ached. She guessed that she had been struck by a mild pulse blast, for she could feel no blood flowing and she was numb rather than in real pain. Her eyes were watering, but she could still see what was happening to her sons.

The Galateans were on them, easily pinning them to the kitchen floor, clicking and croaking at each other through their masks. They seemed almost amused as the boys tried to struggle against them, even as they coughed and choked. One of the Galateans, tiring of the game, struck Paul on the head with the base of a pulser, and then it was over. Steven was already as helpless as a swaddled baby, his hands secured behind him, his legs shackled together with magnetised cuffs. Blood streaked Paul's face, and he was propped up between two Galateans as a third slapped him hard to bring him round. His eyes opened; he was having trouble focusing, but at least he was conscious. Men had been killed accidentally by Galateans who had set out only to subdue them. The amphibians did not always know, or care to know, their own strength. Their hands were on Steven now, searching him, but he and Paul had left their knives in the umbrella stand when they entered, as their mother did not like weapons at the dinner table. When the Galateans were satisfied that Steven was unarmed, they lifted him from the floor and set him on his feet between his captors, as he coughed in the fumes.

The Galateans sprayed the air with a chemical compound, dispersing the gas before they removed their masks. They also sprayed a diluted form of the compound on the boys and their mother, relieving the stinging in their eyes and throats. A female Illyri Securitat in black and gold entered the house through the front door and walked to the kitchen. Beyond her, Paul could make out the shape of a body face down on the garden path. He recognised Knutter from his shirt. Then his view was blocked as an Agron entered behind the Securitat, sniffing at the air.

The Securitat leaned against the frame of the kitchen door and stared at the boys. Paul knew Vena at once, for the Resistance had photos of most of the senior Illyri, but he tried to keep that knowledge from his face. If Vena realised that he knew who she was, it would be confirmation that he was a member of the Resistance. Their only hope was to play dumb, but it was a small, forlorn hope. The presence of this particular Illyri in their home meant that they were in very serious trouble indeed. Vena was not usually one to make house calls.

The Agron paused by her side.

'Are these the ones?' she asked.

The Agron advanced on Paul, sniffed at him, then turned its attention to Steven. Its eyes were silver, and its sight was poor. It saw the world through scent. It placed its nose close to Steven's face, its nostrils so close to his mouth that he felt its mucus on his lips as it exhaled.

The Agron nodded. It gripped Steven by the hair and pulled his head back.

'Sm-smelled you,' it stuttered roughly in Steven's ear; most of the Agrons had a basic grasp of language. '*Smelled.*'

'Good,' said Vena. 'Very good.'

Paul's scalp was bleeding badly. The Agron keep darting glances at the blood, and its nostrils twitched hard. Eventually it could stand the scent no longer. A rough pink tongue slipped from its lips and lapped at Paul's face. One of the Galateans pushed the Agron away. It looked unhappy.

'Smelled,' it repeated, and pointed a stubby finger at itself. 'Good.'

Summoned by Vena, Securitats flooded into the house. That was just like them, thought Paul: wait until the hard work was done and any threat had been subdued, then enter with boots and fists flying.

'Take the boys away,' said Vena to one of the new arrivals. 'The mother, too.'

The Galatean pointed at the Agron and clicked a question.

'Let it drink the blood,' said Vena. 'It's earned its reward.'

As the Kerrs were led away, they heard the Agron fall on Knutter's corpse, and they tried to close their ears to the sound of it quenching its thirst.

CHAPTER 19

Unsurprisingly, Lord Andrus was troubled by the fact that the Archmage Syrene wished to meet with his daughter, but he did his best not to show it. He had played the game for a long time, and little now surprised him, but today had been a day of shocks, and this was easily the most unwelcome of them.

'Why?' he asked.

'Why does she want to meet with Syl, or why should we allow it?' asked Meia.

'Both.'

'Perhaps the Sisterhood is recruiting,' said Danis to Meia, 'in which case you might wish to put your name forward. Duplicity and untrustworthiness would seem to be essential for membership, so you should be wearing a red cloak before the night is out.'

Meia ignored him. 'I can't answer the first question, but to the second I would say that it's an opening, and openings should be exploited. We don't know why Syrene has chosen to accompany her husband here, and we have no idea why Gradus should be present either. He didn't have to deliver the news of the president's death in person. It's not as if he cares about your grief. We're entirely in the dark here. Now Syrene has made a move. Do we ignore it, or do we move in response?'

'My daughter is not a spy,' said Andrus. 'She is not equipped to trade blows with an Archmage.'

'Syl is clever,' said Meia.

'Not as clever as a Red Sister.'

'I have studied the Sisterhood for many years,' said Meia. 'They interest me.'

'And why is that?' asked Danis.

'They worship a god. Their god is knowledge.'

'And what have you learned about the Sisterhood and their god of knowledge?'

'Very little. They guard themselves well, and share nothing with outsiders. I would be surprised if even Gradus knew very much of what his wife is thinking most of the time, and I am certain that he knows nothing at all of what goes on in the Marque.

'But I know this: arrogance is the Sisterhood's weakness. They have grown more and more arrogant as they have engaged with the world beyond the Marque. Everything they have encountered has confirmed their superiority, most particularly the weakness of males. Syrene believes that she is cleverer than anyone she meets, cleverer even than the most senior of her own sisters, Ezil and the First Five apart, and even then she must feel that the Mage's powers are waning. She will underestimate Syl, and in my experience, Syl is not to be underestimated.'

'We're talking about a sixteen-year-old!' Danis scoffed. 'She's only a fraction older than my daughter, and Ani could be out-thought by a goldfish.'

'Ani is not to be underestimated either,' said Meia. 'You are in error about your own blood.'

Andrus watched the exchange with interest. Meia was Syl's final line of defence. In the event of a breach of the castle's defences, or a tilting of the balance of power in favour of the Diplomats, she was to get Syl and Ani to safety, and kill anyone who stood in her way. She had watched Syl ever since Andrus had ordered her to join him on Earth shortly after Syl's birth. Meia was ruthless, implacable.

Ageless.

'And what if some harm comes to my underestimated daughter?' Andrus asked.

'No harm will come to her. We have eyes and ears in that room, and anyway, Syrene would not be so foolish as to hurt Syl. There would be no advantage in doing so, and Syrene is always looking for an advantage.'

Andrus looked to Danis and Balen.

'Your thoughts?'

'I would not let her go,' said Balen, who was almost as fond of Syl as he was of his own children.

'Danis?'

'It pains me to say it, but Meia is right. We should permit the meeting to go ahead, but we'll monitor everything, and keep guards outside the door: double whatever Syrene has. If Syrene objects to their presence, we walk away.'

'And she won't object,' said Meia. 'She would expect nothing less.'

'Would you send Ani if our positions were reversed?' asked Andrus.

Danis considered the question. 'I would, but I'd warn Syrene first, so she knew what she was letting herself in for. She wouldn't get a word in edgeways.'

Andrus was quiet for a moment, then nodded to Meia.

'Bring my daughter here.'

Syl and Ani, now clean and fed, were back together in Syl's rooms. They were half watching old films, both human and Illyri. The human ones tended to be more fun. Illyri ideas of art placed the emphasis on improving minds first; entertainment came a distant second. One of the greatest Illyri plays, *Of Stars and Seeds*, was seventeen hours long, and included breaks for meals and a suggested two-hour intermission in the middle for an extended nap.

Ani was subdued, though. She had been ever since their little eavesdropping adventure. At the hospital she had listened more than talked, which was fine with those to whom she tended. But shortly after they had reached Syl's rooms, she had suffered a nosebleed so severe that Syl had wanted to summon a physician. Ani had pleaded with her not to.

'Please, Syl,' she said. 'I don't want them examining me, not over this. It'll pass.'

'Has it happened before?'

'A couple of times, when I've felt . . . *stressed.*'

'What do you mean, stressed?' said Syl, but Ani didn't want to pursue the subject.

'Can we talk about it another time?'

'We don't have to if you don't want to,' said Syl. 'Just tip your head forward. We'll wait for it to pass.'

When the knock came on the door, it was Syl who answered. She saw Meia standing before her, flanked by two guards, and felt the blood drain from her face.

Her earlier adventure on the Royal Mile must have been discovered. There could be no other reason for Meia to be there. Her fears were apparently confirmed when Meia said, 'Your father wishes to speak with you.'

Syl nodded dumbly. She looked to Ani, whose face now reflected Syl's own concerns. She felt Meia's hand on her shoulder.

'You're not in trouble, Syl,' said Meia softly, then added, with a quizzical look, 'Should you be?'

Syl felt a flood of relief so strong that her body sagged like a puppet whose strings had been relaxed.

'No,' she said. 'Absolutely not.'

'Do you want me to come with you?' Ani asked.

'You'll have to stay here,' said Meia. 'I'm sorry. I'll have her back to you as soon as I can.'

Syl grabbed a cloak, for the castle had grown cold, and went with Meia.

Syl had always been somewhat in awe of Meia. She was like nobody else on her father's staff, so strange yet so composed, her life lived in the shadows. She deferred only to Lord Andrus, and no other. Everyone else she appeared to judge on a sliding scale that moved between the two extremes of contempt and amusement. Ani said that Danis, her father, hated Meia, but when Syl had asked Lord Andrus about it, he told her that this was not true.

'They snarl at each other like chained dogs, but the truth is that they are more similar than different,' he said. 'If anyone ever harmed Meia, Danis would hunt them to the ends of the universe, and if Danis does not die a natural death, Meia will slaughter those responsible in their beds.'

Syl didn't quite trust Meia, though. It didn't pay to trust spies. Now she fell into step beside her, wondering why she had been summoned. She noticed that she and Meia were now as tall as one another, for Meia was short for an Illyri.

'You didn't look pleased to see me at your door,' said Meia.

'I wasn't expecting company, that's all.'

'Really?' Meia did not look at her, but Syl could see an eyebrow lift in disbelief. 'So it had nothing to do with the fact that you were outside the castle walls today?'

Syl didn't know what to say, so she said nothing. Meia, unfortunately, was a trained interrogator, and ignoring her wouldn't make her go away.

'Well?' Meia persisted. 'I don't suppose you saw anyone planting bombs while you were out shopping?'

Syl swallowed hard. 'I *am* in trouble, then. You were lying.'

'I only lie professionally, not personally,' said Meia. 'Your father doesn't know anything about your little trip today, and with luck he won't find out. He'll chain you to a wall otherwise, and feed you from a bowl to make sure you don't go wandering again.'

'You're not going to tell him?'

'Why would I? You weren't hurt, and neither was your friend Ani. You need to be more careful, though. Your disguises may work for you at a distance, but up close your skin will soon begin to give you away. It would be a significant coup if the Resistance were to capture the daughter of the governor. You'd be worth a lot in trade, assuming they didn't decide that it was better to kill you straight away.'

'They'd kill me?'

'They might, if you fell into the hands of the wrong men, and if I didn't find you first.'

'And would you? Would you find me?'

Meia stopped, and looked her square in the eye for the first time since Syl had left her room.

'Yes. Don't doubt that for a moment. But let's hope that the necessity for it doesn't arise. In the meantime, try to restrain your exploratory impulses for a few days, both inside and outside the castle. The situation is volatile.'

Meia walked on, Syl beside her.

'Because of Gradus and the Sisterhood?' asked Syl, and knew immediately that she had said too much. Meia kept walking, but her steps had faltered for a moment.

'What do you know about Gradus and the Red Sister?' she said.

Syl trod carefully.

'I saw them arrive,' she said.

'What keen eyes you must have. My understanding was that they were hidden from us all.'

'And everybody in the castle is talking about it,' Syl continued. She hated being questioned by Meia, because Meia was immune to her charms and her evasions.

'I told your father that you were clever, but don't try to be too clever, and particularly not with me,' said Meia. 'I know more about you than you might think, and you'd be better off having me as an ally than an adversary. So shall we be honest with each other, Syl?'

'Okay.'

Meia allowed the guards to move out of earshot.

'I saw you and Ani in the vicinity of the Great Hall, and you were moving like criminals. What were you doing there? No lies, Syl.'

'We were eavesdropping.'

'That chamber is soundproofed. I checked it myself.'

'I know a place, a hiding hole.'

'Do you now? We might make a spy of you yet.'

'I don't want to be a spy.'

'I'm surprised. Given your actions, you seem to be doing your best to apply for the job. You'll have to show me how you managed that little piece of business. I'd be most interested to find out.'

They moved on to her father's chambers. Meia stopped within

sight of the door and raised a finger to Syl in warning, the nail short and unadorned.

'Tell me truly, Syl. Did you come face to face with the Archmage Syrene at any point during the day?'

'No.'

'You're sure?'

'Yes.'

'There is no way that she could have known of your presence at the meeting?'

Syl took a moment before replying. It was one thing giving up her own secrets, but another betraying Ani's.

'I was hidden from sight,' said Syl. 'I don't see how she could have known. But . . .'

'Go on.'

'There was a moment when the Archmage seemed to look around the room, as though she knew someone was present who shouldn't have been. She stared straight at . . .' *careful, careful,* '. . . at me, at where I was hiding, even though she couldn't have seen me.'

Meia didn't look pleased to hear this.

'The Sisterhood is an unknown quantity, Syl. Some refer to them as witches, and it may be that, in the depths of the Marque, they have developed skills that are beyond the rest of us. Does she frighten you, the Archmage?'

'A little.'

'Good. She should. How do you dance, Syl?'

'Dance?' Syl looked confused. 'I've never really tried. Why?'

Meia put a hand on the small of her back, and guided her to where her father was waiting.

'Because,' she said, 'you're about to dance with the Red Sister.'

CHAPTER 20

Paul and Steven had been separated from their mother. Their last glimpse of her came as she was being helped into a regular police patrol car, the copper placing his hand on her head so that she wouldn't injure herself. That, at least, was cause for hope: she was with the Lothian and Borders Police, not the Securitat. The Lothian and Borders didn't torture women, or lose them in their secret prisons.

Not yet.

The armoured Securitat truck had two metal benches along either side of its interior, and a pair of cages at the end. The boys were spared the cages, but their heads were covered by hoods as soon as they sat down, and magnetic collars were placed around their necks and activated, holding them uncomfortably upright against the body of the truck as it wound its way through the city streets.

It was Paul who risked speaking. He could hear wet breathing nearby: one Galatean at least, maybe two.

'Are you okay, bruv?' he asked.

The reply came not from Steven, but from their captors. Paul's body jerked as he was tapped in the side with an electric baton, and a white light exploded in his head. It lasted only a second or two, but it was long enough for Paul to bite his own tongue. When the baton was removed, his body still trembled. He fought the urge to be sick. He didn't want to vomit in the hood. He brought his breathing under control, just as he had been taught to do, and just as he had taught others. They had all been questioned in the past, usually in the course of the random searches and street sweeps that the Illyri regularly conducted. Routine questioning was carried out in the backs of vans, or sometimes at one of the L&B police stations. Paul had even spent a night or two in the cells, but he'd always been released once dawn came. This was different, though: these were Securitats, led by Vena. He and Steven weren't going to be held for a couple of hours at the station in St Leonard's Meadows, or the West End, or Portobello, and offered a cup of tea and a biscuit by a decent human in a uniform. No, they could only be going to one of two places: the Securitats' special interrogation centre in Glasgow, or the castle.

The truck slowed, then ground to a halt. Paul heard the doors open, and his collar was deactivated and removed. Hard hands dragged him from the van, and he briefly tasted night air through the hood before the atmosphere around them changed, becoming dank and noisome. He gave a little whistle, and his brother answered in the same way, but then there was the sound of something hard impacting on soft flesh, and Steven cried out in pain.

'You leave him alone!' said Paul. 'He's just a kid.'

He waited to receive another jolt from a baton, but none came. He was simply hustled silently along until he was forced to turn to his right, and a hand pushed him forward. For a moment he had an image of himself standing at the edge of a huge pit, about to tumble into a void, his hooded form falling for ever. Instead, he hit a stone floor, followed seconds later by another body, and he heard Steven whimpering.

'Don't cry,' said Paul. 'Don't give them the satisfaction.'

The door slammed shut behind them.

Paul had no idea how long they were left there. It might have been an hour, or it could have been three. Once they had established that they appeared to be alone in the room, the boys found a wall and leaned against it. When Steven tried to speak, Paul said only one word: 'Careful.'

The Illyri would be listening to them: listening, and watching.

With the index finger of his left hand, Paul began tapping softly on the wall: two short taps, two long, two short. It was Morse code for a question mark.

After a moment, Steven replied with three long taps, followed by long–short–long.

OK.

The Resistance had learned too late that the Illyri were embedded in all forms of electronic communication, and many groups around the world had lost operatives in the early days. The Internet was still functioning, although it had more bugs than an ants' nest; the Illyri had guessed, correctly, that if they allowed the flow of money, and permitted business to proceed worldwide with some degree of normality, then much of humanity would fall into step. But every keystroke was monitored, and only fools transmitted essential inform-ation through the Net, or spoke and texted on telephones of any kind. Thus the Resistance had fallen back on simpler means of staying in touch. They used dead drops, secure locations where paper messages could be left and collected. They sent signals and instructions over short-wave radio, just as spies had done in the Second World War.

And they relied on Morse code. It was one of the first things that young people learned when they joined the Resistance. Sometimes Paul and his colleagues didn't even have to go through the basics with new recruits, for older brothers and sisters had already taught the code to their younger siblings, as had parents who had not succumbed to the Illyri methods of subduing them, chemical or otherwise.

Now slowly, painstakingly, the boys contrived a cover story. They kept it to simple keywords.

Exploring. Vaults. Storm pipe. Adventure.

Nothing.

We saw nothing.

The hoods began to stink. They had grown moist from the boys' exhalations, and very, very hot. Paul began to feel that he was suffocating, and he could hear Steven's breathing growing panicked.

'Easy,' he said. 'Easy.'

Their arms ached, and their circulation was being cut off by their restraints. Paul could no longer feel his fingers.

A door opened. There came the sound of metal objects being placed on the floor. A table and chairs, thought Paul. Maybe they're going to give us dinner, a real slap-up meal with beef, and roast potatoes, and gravy. Even though he was frightened, he was also very hungry. They had not eaten since they'd shared that packet of HobNobs with those two funny girls, the ones with the old-fashioned names and the layers of clothes, their hats and glasses encasing them like swaddling so that all that could be seen were smooth tanned cheeks and chins and foreheads, no eyes, no hair . . .

Oh! Paul thought, as he realised that the 'girls' might not have been girls at all. I'm a fool. I'm such a fool. I was so caught up with the explosions, and not being caught, that I never stopped to think . . .

But any further regrets were halted as hands pulled him to his feet, and then led him to a chair. He sat down, and his hood was removed. He blinked hard at the fluorescent lights, and for a few seconds he could not see anything at all. Gradually his vision adjusted, and he took in the table and chairs, and his brother seated beside him, also blinking, his eyes watering.

Sitting across from them was Vena. Her head was bald, and her scalp was adorned with silver stripes. She was not finished with them, not by a long shot. Paul had feared as much when he saw her standing in their home. Even by the brutal standards of the Securitat, Vena was regarded by the Resistance as psychopathic. On the list of targets for assassination she even ranked above Governor Andrus. As far as the Resistance was aware, Andrus was not in the habit of using skimmers – so-called because they skimmed the limits of the Earth's atmosphere – to take captives to high altitudes and then toss them out. For Vena, it practically counted as a hobby. She was also believed to report back all she saw and heard in the British Isles to her lover, Sedulus. She was his second-in-command in all but name.

'Do you know who I am?' she asked.

'No, ma'am,' said Paul.

'No,' said Steven.

'You're lying,' said Vena. 'I'll record every lie that you tell, and I'll cut off one of your fingers for each one.'

Neither of the young men responded. Well done, little bruv,

thought Paul. *She's fishing. Stick to the story, and we'll be okay.*

'What were you doing in our tunnels, and who are you working for?' said Vena. Clearly there were to be no serious preliminaries, no getting-to-know-you questions, no 'you may be wondering why we've brought you here'. That was for films. The Securitats had a reputation for getting down to business.

'I need to go to the bathroom,' said Steven.

They had discussed this in their coded exchange. They had to find a way to leave the cell, even if only for a short time, so that they could get some sense of their location, of security, of guards. In here, they were blind.

'That's unfortunate,' said Vena.

'I need to go *bad*.'

'When you tell me what I need to know, you'll be made comfortable. Until then, you'll stay where you are.'

'I'll wet myself,' said Steven.

Vena smiled at him, and leaned across the table.

'If you do, I'll slice off the organ responsible and give it to the Agrons as a treat. They'll eat *anything*.'

Steven went quiet. He didn't think the bathroom ploy was going to work, and he wasn't prepared to risk losing his manhood on the slim chance that it might.

'Again: what were you doing in our tunnels?'

There was no point in denying that they'd been there. The Agron had given that much away by telling Steven that it had followed his scent.

'It was an accident?' said Steven. His voice went a little high at the end so that it came out sounding like a question, which he hadn't intended.

'An accident?' said Vena. 'Really? You can't do any better than that?'

'Yes, an accident,' said Steven. 'I was just messing about in the Vaults when I found a new pipe and followed it.'

He stopped talking then; the Resistance had taught them to keep lies short and succinct so as not to trip themselves up on the words they were weaving. But he had slightly changed the story that he and Paul had agreed on, and Paul wasn't sure that was wise.

He had said 'I', not 'we'.

Vena frowned, and Paul knew then that Steven had made a mistake. He'd told him over and over again: the best lies were the ones wrapped in the thickest of truths. You hide the lie, and you don't adorn the truth.

'But surely your brother was with you?'

Paul bit his lip.

'No, it was just me. My brother wasn't there.'

'Odd,' said Vena. 'That's not what your friend Knutter told us. I suppose we could bring him in here and ask him to confirm his story. Oh wait, we can't, because he's *dead*, and so will you be if you keep wasting my time. Even if your friend *had* tried to conceal the truth, your scents would have given you away. The Agrons have five hundred million olfactory receptors. You only have five million. Do you think they can't tell the difference between your stink and your brother's?'

'I can,' said Steven. 'He smells worse than I do.'

Even in this terrible situation, Paul couldn't help but smile. His little brother was baiting the Illyri. His mother had always told them they were both too smart for their own good. Perhaps she'd been right.

'You're a funny little boy,' said Vena. 'Unfortunately, you both smell the same to me. You smell of fear, and desperation, and falsehoods. What did you see in that tunnel?'

'Nothing,' said Steven.

Vena turned her attention to Paul. 'Are you going to let your little brother take all the heat for you? Are you going to let him fight your battles? What a coward you are, letting a boy do the talking while you sit back and try to save your own skin.'

'Like he told you,' said Paul, 'we saw nothing. We were exploring the Vaults, we found a new pipe, the smell made my brother sick, and we left. That's it. He was just trying to protect me by saying I wasn't with him. We're sorry.'

Vena considered what Paul had said, then nodded.

'Bring it in,' she said. The microphones hidden in the room picked up her words, and the door opened. A Galatean entered, carrying a wooden box. Its lid was perforated with air holes, and it had a hinged lid. He placed it on the table, and Paul was certain that he heard something move inside.

Two more Galateans entered. They freed Steven's arms, but only for long enough to place them flat on the table. From its previously smooth surface emerged a pair of metal bands that slipped over Steven's wrists, securing them in place.

Vena looked at Paul. 'Since you seem to prefer letting your brother do most of the talking, maybe you'd like to let him do your screaming for you too.'

The Galatean handed her a gauntlet of metal and thick leather. She put it on her right hand, then lifted the lid of the box and carefully reached inside. Whatever it contained seemed to strike at her, for she flinched and almost withdrew her hand. Eventually, though, she got a grip on the thing, and lifted it from its prison.

It was about a foot long, its armoured body purple and red like an exposed muscle, five heavy jointed legs at each side. Two large bulbous eyes, like those of a mantis, stared unblinkingly from its skull, and between them was a long pointed mouthpiece with a barbed sucker at the end. As it struggled in Vena's grasp, two thin black whips unfolded from the sides of its jaw and struck vainly at the air, splashing the table with clear liquid.

'Have you ever been stung by a bee or a wasp?' asked Vena. 'It can be quite painful. It can even kill you, if you have a particular allergy. This little monster is called an icurus, and it's mostly harmless. It just wants to be left to go about its business. But those stinging strikers deliver a powerful dose of neurotoxin similar to the apamin found in bee venom. I've heard it described as feeling like acid burning through your flesh.

'The icurus does have one nasty little attribute. During mating season, those stingers serve a dual purpose: they inject not just venom, but icurus larvae, which breed in the host organism and consume it from within. On its home planet, it breeds only at very specific times of the year, but the Earth has thrown its biological clock right off. Frankly, I don't know whether this one is in season or not. There's only one way to find out, I suppose.'

She placed the icurus on the table, and eased it towards Steven.

'I'm afraid,' she said, 'that this is going to hurt.'

CHAPTER 21

For Syl, it had been a confusing, uneasy meeting in her father's rooms. All thoughts of birthdays were forgotten, as were all concerns about her narrow escape from the bombings being discovered by her father. Meia had made it clear that she would not tell Lord Andrus about what Syl and Ani had been up to that day, including their trip to the Royal Mile and their bout of eavesdropping, as long as Syl gave her no reason to do so. Syl was under no illusions about the fact that she was now in Meia's debt, but as she sat in one of her father's armchairs and listened to what he and Danis and Meia had to say, she understood that they needed her, and that their debt to her would be at least as great as hers to Meia.

Syl had never been needed before, not in this way. For so much of her life she had been dependent upon others. Yes, her father needed her, but it was an emotional need, born out of love. Yet to be needed because of something she could do, something practical, something dangerous, was different. And while she was frustrated at her father's caution – for it was he who kept returning to the risks involved – she was secretly grateful to him for caring, even as he drew closer and closer to using her as a pawn in his game with the Diplomatic Corps and the Sisterhood.

'I still don't understand why it's Syl she wants to see,' he said at last, as it became clear that he was going to allow her to enter the Red Sister's presence.

Syl could have told him, even if it was only a suspicion. So too could Meia, but she remained quiet. Syl recalled the way that Syrene had tried to seek out whatever had disturbed her in the Great Hall, and how she had finally fixed upon the ornate fire surround concealing the little slits through which Syl and Ani were watching her, as though willing her gaze to assume a physical form and insinuate itself into the gaps like a serpent.

Lord Andrus approached Syl, and laid a hand on her shoulder.

'You don't have to do this, you know,' he said. 'Nobody will think any less of you if you would prefer not to spend time in the company of Syrene.'

'I understand,' said Syl. 'I want to do it.'

Andrus looked to Meia. She stared back at him. There was no need for her to speak. She had considered the problem, and offered her opinion based on her analysis.

'Meia thinks you're clever enough to joust with Syrene for a time, and I agree. But remember: she is dangerous, and cunning, and she has no love for this family.'

He paused.

'You should know that your mother rejected the Sisterhood's advances when she was young,' he said.

Syl's eyes widened. She had not known this.

'She did so for many reasons,' continued Lord Andrus, 'some of which I understood, and at some of which I can only guess. I was one of those reasons, if it's not too vain of me to think so. Orianne and I were in love from a very early age, we were younger even than you are now. Ezil and Syrene took her rejection very personally, in part because it was I whom she loved, and even as a young soldier I had already been branded as an enemy of both the Corps and the Sisterhood. It was why your mother chose to wander the stars with me, and leave her home for ever. She was convinced that some harm might come to her if she stayed – to her, and to any children that she might have. So you were born far from Illyr, and far from the reach of the Red Sisters. But now the Sisterhood is here, and it may be that Syrene wishes to meet you because she wants to look at last upon the daughter of the Lady Orianne.

'Yet if that were all she desired, she could stare at images of you until her eyes fell from her head. Unusual though you may be, Syrene did not travel halfway across the universe simply to admire your features. There is another purpose at work here, and we need to establish what that might be. So spar with her, and debate with her, for she may reveal to the daughter what she wishes to keep secret from the father. We'll be watching, and listening.'

He took Syl's right hand. On her index finger was a ring of white gold with a red crystal set into it.

'If at any time you feel threatened, or afraid, you know what to do.'

'Yes, Father.'

The ring functioned as her personal alarm. By pressing down hard on the crystal, she would activate the device. Within the castle precincts, it would bring help in seconds.

Andrus kissed her gently on the forehead.

'This isn't quite the birthday that I would have wished for you,' he said.

'Thank you for my gifts,' she whispered.

'Gifts? I only gave you one.'

'Two,' said Syl. 'The bronze cast, and your trust.'

Andrus smiled. 'Meia will take you to Syrene, and she'll stay outside until you emerge safely.'

Meia stepped forward.

'Come, Syl,' she said.

'Time to dance?' said Syl.

'Yes, time to dance.'

In the small interrogation cell, Steven's head slumped to the table. The icurus had been restored to its box, its venom seemingly inexhaustible. The fingers of Steven's left hand were swollen badly, the tips purple and bleeding from the icurus's strikes.

'Nothing,' he whispered, for what seemed like the hundredth time. 'We saw nothing . . .'

He was beyond weeping. He had exhausted his capacity for tears, but his brother had not. Paul was crying: for his brother, and his mother, and for his own inability to distinguish between strength and weakness. By remaining silent, he was allowing his brother to suffer. If he spoke, if he admitted what they'd seen, he could make Steven's pain stop.

But if he told Vena what they had seen, they would both die. He was certain of it. Something terrible was happening beneath the city, something that the Illyri wished to keep hidden. Paul's duty was to keep himself and his brother alive, and to report what they knew to those who might be able to investigate further.

'Stop hurting him,' said Paul. 'Please. Hurt me instead. Just leave him alone.'

The little receiver in Vena's ear lit up, and, after a pause to listen, she stood and left the room without a word. Paul wanted to hug his brother, to hold him and tell him that he was sorry, that everything would be okay, but his hands were still bound behind his back. Instead he leaned over and placed his head against Steven's.

'You did well,' he whispered. 'You're brave. You're braver than anyone else I know.'

'Is it true?' said Steven. The words caught in his throat, like dry sobs.

'Is what true?'

'What she said about that thing, that it injects its young into people?'

'I don't know,' said Paul. 'I think she was just trying to frighten you.'

'Well it worked. I am frightened.'

'We'll have a doctor look at you once we get out of here.'

'Great. When do you think that might be? Because I don't think it's looking so good for us right now.'

The boys sat up. Steven stared at his deformed hand.

'It burns,' he said. 'I can feel it spreading up my arm.'

He was right. The swelling was not limited to his hand. It was moving along his forearm, and was halfway to his elbow.

'We'll fix it,' said Paul, but he didn't know if that was true. He wondered how much Knutter had told the Illyri. Knutter wasn't clever, but he had a degree of animal cunning, and he hated the Illyri.

He wouldn't have told them much at all. At the very least, any admission of involvement with the Resistance would have put himself at risk. They had used him as a distraction, but it was the Agron who had followed the scent. No, Paul believed that Knutter would probably have kept quiet and hoped for the best. If they stuck to their story, there was still some hope for them.

The door opened again. This time it was not Vena who entered, but a medical officer in blue scrubs. He examined Steven's hand, and injected his arm, but Paul noticed that he then cleaned the needle on a wipe, which he placed in a sterile specimen bag.

'That will take the swelling down,' he said.

'What about larvae and stuff?' said Paul.

The medical officer looked puzzled. 'What about them?'

'The officer who did this said that the icurus injects its larvae into its host.'

'Did she now? She'll be telling you that it delivers parcels to human children at Christmas next.'

'So it's not true?'

'No.' He lowered his voice. 'The icurus lays eggs, thousands of them, but only on the leaves of one specific plant. Your brother has venom in his system, but nothing worse. Then again, the venom is bad enough. He's been badly stung. If the poison were allowed to spread, it would eventually start shutting down his respiratory system. I've seen grown men killed by those things during interrogation.'

He glanced at the box. It didn't look as though he approved of Vena's methods.

'Thank you,' said Paul.

'For what?'

'For treating my brother.'

'I'm a doctor. It's what I do. Illyri, humans, terrorists, it makes no difference to me.'

'We're not terrorists,' said Paul.

'Whatever,' said the doctor. 'It's not my concern.'

He unwrapped another needle, and took a blood sample from Paul.

'What are you doing?'

'It's just a precaution. Nothing to worry about.'

But once again he cleaned the needle with a wipe, and that went into its own specimen bag. He then took skin swabs from each of them before departing.

After some time, three Galateans came in and released the boys' hands. They were brought soup, and some dry bread.

In the silence of the interrogation room, they waited for their fate to be decided.

CHAPTER 22

Two female Illyri in faded yellow gowns stood at the door of Syrene's quarters and stared with distaste at Syl as she and Meia approached.

'Novices,' whispered Meia. 'They live for the approval of the Archmage.'

Syl felt that they were assessing her, and had found her wanting. They seemed barely to notice Meia, but Meia had a way of making herself appear unthreatening when she chose. It was part of her talent as a spy. There was a transformative quality to her, an ability not only to blend into her surroundings but almost to alter her physical appearance. It was subtle – the dipping of her head, the slumping of her shoulders, the slackening of her facial muscles – but even in the course of the short walk from Lord Andrus's chambers to the temporary lair of the Red Sister, Meia had changed, and Syl thought that, had she not spent the past hour in her company, she might have passed her on the street and not noticed her.

'I bring Syl Hellais,' said Meia. 'The Archmage is expecting her.'

One of the novices nodded.

'You may enter,' she told Syl. 'The other stays outside.'

Meia touched Syl gently on the shoulder. 'Remember to call her "your eminence",' she whispered. 'She will expect it from you.' Then she stepped back as the door opened.

Without hesitation, Syl entered the presence of the Red Sister.

What struck her first was the nature of the room itself. Just as Meia had the ability to take the familiar and make it appear strange and new, so too Syrene's chambers had been transformed by her presence.

The wooden floors were now covered with rugs of red and gold, intricately decorated and clearly very, very old. Cloths had been draped over functional furniture, softening the lines, and candles provided the only light. Tapestries on the walls depicted mythical beasts, and ancient battles fought long before ships flew to the stars. Above the bed hung what Syl now understood to be the seal of the Sisterhood, the Red Eye, but this one was different from those that adorned the ship in the courtyard and the collars of the guards. From it flowed graceful red tendrils of energy that seemed to move even as Syl looked at them, so that it seemed they might reach out and caress her skin.

And in the centre of the room was Syrene, strangely beautiful. She had dispensed with the long robe and ornate veil of the Sisterhood, and wore a simple red dress that was cinched tight around her upper body but flowed like waterfalls of blood from her waist. Her dark hair was cut very short, and was shaved back along her hairline to reveal the tattoos spilling from her scalp and down her forehead, but care had been taken with it. This was no military cut, nor was it the kind of severe shearing to which some of the female religious on Earth resorted. To Syl it indicated both a desire to meet the Sisterhood's requirement that hair should not be long, and a degree of personal vanity on Syrene's part. There was a faint red glow to Syrene's eyes. Syl thought it might have been a candle flame reflected, but when the Red Sister advanced to meet her, the glow remained where it was, only dying as she drew close enough for Syl to smell her breath. It had a hint of spice to it that was not unpleasant.

Syrene extended her hands in greeting. Like her face, they were intricately decorated with red tattoos, although these were more like the detailing on lace curtains than some of the figurative illustrations on her face. Now that she could examine the Archmage more closely, Syl's attention was drawn to the red eyes tattooed on her face, one on each cheek. They were carefully etched – almost lifelike – and the pupils at their care were very, very dark. For the first time since she had entered the room, Syl felt a tickle of unease.

'Your eminence,' she said.

'Syl Hellais,' said Syrene. 'I am most pleased to meet you.'

She stretched out her arms as if to embrace her, and Syl instinctively tensed at the approach. She did not like strangers touching her. Syrene recognised her discomfort, and allowed her arms to drop once again by her sides, but she seemed faintly disappointed by the girl's reluctance to engage in physical contact. In fact, Syl could not help feeling that, although she had only just arrived, Syrene was already bored with her, as if in those first few moments she had learned all that was worth knowing about her, and was now content to discard her.

What was she expecting? thought Syl, and the answer came to her unbidden.

My mother.

Then that disappointment was gone, and Syl might almost have believed that she had imagined it were it not for the small, lingering sense of hurt – and, yes, rejection – that she felt.

'Please,' said Syrene, 'sit. You will have some wine?'

Two glasses were on a side table, with two leather library chairs adjoining it. Between the glasses was a decanter of red wine. Syl drank little as a rule, and would have preferred not to do so here. It was important that she keep a clear head. On the other hand, it was more likely that Syrene would relax with her if she accepted a drink. She agreed to a small glass.

'It is Italian, and very old,' said Syrene. 'One of the things that this world does well is intoxicants. This is one of a handful of vintage bottles salvaged by a dealer in Rome before the city became an example to the rest.'

The destruction of Rome had been a terrible mistake, according to Syl's father, a war crime that he believed would haunt the Illyri for generations to come. He had advised against it, but had been overruled by the Council back on Illyr.

'You disapprove of what happened to Rome?' asked Syrene.

'It was a great city, a beautiful city,' said Syl.

'You visited it, then?'

'Only once.'

'Would you have preferred it if an uglier city had been made an example of?'

'I would have preferred it if no city at all had been destroyed,' said Syl.

'You speak with your father's voice,' said Syrene.

'No,' said Syl, 'I speak with my own.'

'The Earth grows unruly,' said Syrene. 'It does not fear us. Without fear, there can be no rule of law.'

'Do you speak with your husband's voice?' said Syl, and she was surprised to see Syrene laugh.

'Why, there is something of your mother in you after all!' said the Archmage. 'Do you know that she once called the Mage Ezil a witch to her face?'

'No,' said Syl. 'I did not know.'

She felt hugely proud of this woman she could not remember, who she knew only from pictures and video projections. She cherished every mention of her, drinking in the memories people shared with her, keeping them fresh by regularly removing them from her box of experience and examining them in the light of the world that had killed the Lady Orianne. She dreamed of her at night. She kept her mother's locket beside her pillow in a velvet box wound with a ribbon from one of her gloves, and occasionally she allowed herself to open a yellowing crystal bottle that contained the last traces of her mother's signature perfume, musky and warm.

'It was unwise, of course,' continued Syrene, 'and hugely disrespectful. Had Lady Orianne not fled Illyr with your father, the Sisterhood might well have found a way to make her pay for the offence she had given.'

'She did not flee,' said Syl. 'She loved my father, and wanted to be with him.'

'Your father was the only Illyri who was more disdainful of the Sisterhood than your mother was. They were well matched.'

'Were you among those who wanted to make her pay?' asked Syl.

'Outwardly, yes, but inside I rather admired her spirit. She would have been an adornment to our order. In time, she might even have ruled it. In that sense, I was glad that she rejected a place in the Marque, and relieved when she left with your father. Had she not done so, but instead reconsidered the Sisterhood's offer, she would have risen in authority just as I have, and we might now have been competing for power in the Marque.'

'Is that what you want: power?'

Syrene looked at her slyly over the rim of her wine glass.

'You ask a lot of questions, little one. Did your father put you up to this? Did he think he might learn something by putting you in a room with me? I expect he did. He was always clumsy in his methods. He plays the game poorly.'

Syrene sipped her wine. A little of it ran down her chin darkly, but she seemed not to notice.

'In answer to your question, life is all about power. The powerful survive. The powerful *thrive*. So yes, I want power, for myself and for my kind.'

'Your kind? You mean the Sisterhood?'

'The Sisterhood, and more. You are of my kind, just as your mother was. The Sisterhood is the great source of female power. Through it, we influence an empire, and the rule of worlds.'

For a second, the red fire glowed in her eyes once again, and then was gone.

'We've lost visual,' said Balen.

He was standing with Lord Andrus and Danis, watching the array of screens that showed Syrene's chambers from a dozen angles, thanks to the tiny cameras secreted throughout the room. Those screens now showed nothing but static.

'Check the rest of the system,' said Andrus.

Balen moved to the feeds for the cameras elsewhere in the castle. All appeared to be working fine, even the ones in the bedroom of Grand Consul Gradus, which revealed him to be fast asleep on his bed.

'It's the witch,' said Danis. 'She's done something to the cameras – again.'

Following Syrene's brief time in the Great Hall, the surveillance equipment had been replaced after what was believed to be a malfunction, or sabotage. Now it was clear that the Archmage herself might have been responsible.

'We still have sound,' said Balen. 'They're talking. I can hear your daughter. She seems fine.'

'Send in a lurker,' said Andrus. 'Maybe we'll have more luck with that. In the meantime, tell Meia that we've lost visual contact. Make sure she's ready to move at a moment's notice.'

Balen got through to Meia, and then activated one of the lurkers, the tiny spybots that were scattered, dormant, throughout the castle. This one was a modified beetle: it had been enhanced with electronic components at the pupal stage, so that its own tissue would grow around the wiring and microcircuitry, sealing them in place, and the movements of its legs provided power for the tiny camera embedded in its head. These little spies – modified moths, wasps, flies – were the bane of the Resistance, for they could never be certain if an insect was being controlled by the Illyri or not. For that reason, insects did not tend to survive long when the Resistance was about its business.

The lurker beetle responded to Balen's signal, and moved through the darkness towards Syrene's rooms.

CHAPTER 23

Paul knew that he and Steven were doomed as soon as he saw Sedulus appear, Vena at his heels like an obedient, vicious dog. Behind them were half a dozen Galateans dressed in full body armour. Two of them carried long metal poles that ended in open magnetic collars. The next two carried pulse rifles, and the final pair were armed with electric batons that were almost as long as the collared poles. Before the boys could react, they had both been brutally shocked, and the collars were placed around their necks while they still spasmed on the ground. Once again their hands were bound, and straps were placed across their mouths and around their heads so they could not speak.

Sedulus stepped forward. He moved a hand casually through the air, conjuring up a screen. The screen showed a swab being placed in a device not much bigger than a shoebox, and then being sprayed with ink. An ultraviolet light was activated and shone on the swab. Most of the swab was illuminated, but at its centre was a single dark area. A second swab was placed in the box, and the procedure repeated, with the same result.

'Those were the skin swabs taken from you earlier this evening,' said Sedulus, freezing the final image on the screen. 'The ink is fluorescent, but explosives eliminate its fluorescence. It's very sensitive, and capable of detecting traces of both organic and inorganic matter. Your skin swabs showed significant traces of urea nitrate, which, as I'm sure you're aware, is an inorganic compound used in some home-made explosive devices. Earlier today, two such devices exploded on the Royal Mile, and the compounds detected on your skin are a perfect match for those found at the scene of these outrages.'

He squatted before them, and spoke slowly and carefully.

'Just to be certain, we compared your DNA with samples retrieved from the scene, and carried out reconstructions.'

The Illyri had perfected the art of reconstructing human faces from minute samples of DNA. Genetic factors had been found to contribute to nine elements of facial appearance, including the position of cheekbones, the distance between eyes, and the dimensions of the nose. Combined with DNA analysis that already enabled scientists to predict eye and hair colour, a small sample of human genetic material could provide a near-photographic likeness of the individual from which it had come.

The image in the air changed, and Paul and Steven found themselves looking at representations of themselves. They were not perfect copies, but nobody could have mistaken them for anyone else.

'Damned by your own DNA,' said Sedulus. Something about Paul caught his eye, and he extended his right hand towards the teenager. Paul tried to back away, but a Galatean held him still. Sedulus's index finger pushed aside his collar, exposing the silver cross hanging around his neck. Their mother had insisted that both of her sons should wear one. She hoped that it would keep them safe.

'You believe in God,' said Sedulus.

'Yes,' said Paul.

'Do you know what God is?'

'No.'

'God is simply a technology that you do not understand.'

He covered up the cross.

'You young gentlemen are members of the Resistance, and you are guilty of terrorist outrages against the Illyri Empire and the citizens of this city. Your crimes present irrefutable evidence that a policy of gentle occupation has not worked on these islands. It is with great regret that the Council of Government on Illyr has decided to institute the death penalty for the murder of Illyri for all citizens of Earth over the age of fourteen years. You will be hanged in the courtyard of the castle as an example to others.'

He stood, and looked down on them with something like pity.
'May your god have mercy on you, for we will have none.'

Syl's eyes felt gritty. It seemed to her that she had been in the room
with Syrene for a very long time, for a terrible tiredness had come
over her, yet she had barely sipped her wine. But even as her head
sagged, and her chin touched her chest, she could hear her own voice
speaking, responding to all that Syrene said. She forced herself to look
up, and there was a double image of Syrene in the chair before her.
She blinked hard in an effort to clear her vision, but then one of the
Syrenes stood while the other remained seated. The standing Syrene
was almost transparent, a ghost of the other, but it had more life to it.
The seated version's eyes were blank, and it was reciting a long and
tedious history of the Sisterhood. Occasionally Syl's mouth would
open and she heard herself say 'Really?' and 'How interesting!', but
she did not do so of her own volition. She was a doll controlled by
another, and across from her was a figure without essence, an empty
vessel with a far-distant voice.

The spirit Syrene placed her hands against Syl's head, and Syl could
do nothing to stop her. She felt pressure on her temples, and then the
Red Sister was inside her, hunting for secrets. With a huge effort
of will, Syl tried to perform a trick that Meia had taught her a year or
two before, when Lord Andrus had been away and Meia had been
solely responsible for Syl's safety. Syl had asked her about spying, and
the danger of being discovered, and Meia had told her that as part of
her training, she had learned to visualise locked doors and tall,
impenetrable walls to keep interrogators at bay.

'I have been questioned by enemies, and they have got nothing
from me,' said Meia. 'Not even with truth serums. Pain is harder to
resist, but it can be done. Doors and walls, Syl, doors and walls. And
you must never get angry, never. Anger is an absence of control, and
if you lose control, then they have won.'

Now, as Syrene invaded her consciousness, Syl fought her, building
brick walls that shot up before her thoughts and memories, guarding
secrets with heavy metal doors secured with huge locks and bolts. As

Syrene opened one, so Syl would create another. She felt the Red Sister's frustration grow, but at the same time Syl was growing more and more tired, and the walls and doors were becoming harder and harder to sustain.

Not you!

Syrene's voice sounded loudly in her head. It was no longer bright and melodious, but harsh and cracked. It was the voice of a crone in a younger woman's body.

If it was not you that I felt, then who else? Who?

Syl threw up more walls, but they were crumbling more quickly now, the mortar falling from between the bricks. She tried doors, but the metal rusted, and the bolts buckled. The walls disintegrated, the doors fell from their hinges, and each time they did so she saw a vision in red, a woman of flames and tendrils, advancing upon her, and she was forced to retreat.

Who? Who?

But as Syl tried to hide the name from her, some terrible imp inside her kept trying to speak it. It formed letters from bricks. It scratched them into the paint on the door. Syl did her best to obscure them, striking them out before they could become fully formed, but Syrene was determined, so determined.

Tell me, the awful voice screeched. *Tell me!*

But Syl had no energy left. She was about to lose the fight. She would betray—

Suddenly, Syrene withdrew. Syl's ears popped painfully, and as her vision cleared she saw the shadow Syrene melding once more with the figure in the chair. The door crashed open to reveal Meia, Syrene's novices unconscious on the floor beside her, along with two of Gradus's private guards.

And with her was Ani.

CHAPTER 24

Syrene was furious at the intrusion. She threatened dire consequences for the harm done to her novices, but there was something
theatrical about the way she protested, as though she were conscious
that she had an audience, and the words were what was expected of
her in such a situation. Meia ignored her entirely, and simply swept
the bewildered Syl from the room, followed by Ani.

But Syl was no sooner over the threshold than a squad of Securitats
appeared to their right, and almost simultaneously a dozen heavily
armed soldiers, led by Danis, arrived from the left. When the Securitats
saw Gradus's guards lying motionless on the floor, they immediately
raised their weapons, and Danis's troops responded in kind. The three
females were trapped between them, and all Meia could do was draw
Syl and Ani to her and force them down to the floor, shielding them
with her own body.

'Stop!'

The voice was Syrene's, and her tone brooked no opposition. Even
Danis, who was clearly spoiling for a fight, raised a hand to his soldiers
and ordered them not to fire, although he kept his own blast pistol
trained on the guards before him.

Syrene appeared at the door.

'Let them go,' she told the Securitats.

'But your eminence,' said the Securitat sergeant, 'your guards and
novices have been assaulted.'

Syl peeked out from beneath Meia. Already the stunned guards
were struggling to their feet. The novices looked like they might be

out cold for a little longer. Good, she thought, recalling how they had looked at her when she had first arrived.

'Are they dead?' asked Syrene.

The sergeant checked the novices. 'No, your eminence.'

'Then they, along with my dignity, will recover,' said Syrene. 'Let the children rise.'

Meia stepped back, and Syl and Ani got to their feet. Syl felt as though a cloud were being blown from her mind, clearing her thoughts. She tried to remember what had happened in Syrene's chambers, but she couldn't hold on to the memory. It slipped through her fingers like smoke. She was aware only of a feeling of intrusion, of violation, and that the Red Sister at the door frightened her. She was unsteady on her feet, and Ani had to support her.

Syrene stared at Meia, as though imprinting the image of her face upon her memory.

'What is your name?' she asked.

'I am Meia.'

'Meia.' Syrene repeated, tasting it with her tongue. 'What is your bloodline?'

'I am an orphan. My heritage is lost to me.'

Syrene looked displeased with the answer. Bloodlines were important in Illyri society, and one of the roles of the Sisterhood was to record the histories of Illyri families, both major and minor. Births, deaths and marriages, all were noted in the Sisterhood's archives. Even an orphan would have a notation in their file, unless . . .

'You are a bastard?' said Syrene.

'I dislike that word,' said Meia. 'I prefer the term "free agent".'

The double meaning of 'agent' was clear to Syrene.

'I know you now,' she said. 'You are Andrus's spymistress. Are you his mistress in other areas too? His bed has been cold for too long, and even the noble governor has needs.'

Meia did not take the bait. Her calmness under provocation was considerable.

'Your question contains its own answer,' she said. 'The governor is noble. No more need be said.'

'Well then, spymistress, tell me why you assaulted my guards and my novices, and entered my chamber without permission.'

'We were concerned for Syl's safety,' said Meia.

'On what basis?'

Meia paused. 'Intuition,' she said at last.

'Mistaken, it seems.'

'As you say,' replied Meia.

Danis stepped forward.

'It did not help that every monitoring device in your room appeared to malfunction shortly after Syl entered your company,' he said, joining Meia, and in doing so making it clear that he supported her actions. 'We were concerned that it might presage another terrorist attack. We were fearful for your well-being as much as for Syl's.'

Syrene frowned.

'You admit that you are spying on me?'

'Would you have expected anything less?'

'Not from you,' said Syrene. 'You never change, Danis. Your methods are primitive. It's a wonder that you have survived for as long as you have. I'd have thought natural selection would have taken care of an old relic like you a long time ago.'

'I am a living fossil,' said Danis. 'I endure. As for our monitoring of you, we wished only to ensure that your stay in the castle during these difficult times was untroubled. And brief,' he added.

But Syrene was no longer paying any attention to him. Instead, her eyes were fixed on Ani.

'And who is this?' she asked. 'Answer, child.'

'I'm Ani.'

'Are you a friend of Syl's?'

'Yes.'

'Yes, *your eminence*,' Syrene corrected, clearly tired of having her title ignored by both Meia and Danis, and refusing to accept similar insolence from a teenager.

'Yes, your eminence,' echoed Ani. She smiled her most disingenuous smile.

Syl watched Syrene's fingers twitch. The Red Sister had to make an effort of will to stop them from reaching for Ani, and Syrene's reaction to her friend's presence jolted free a small fragment of recollection in Syl's brain. The cloud had taken with it most of her memories of the last hour, but not all. She had a clear image of Syrene reaching for her, and the cold burn of her fingers.

She touches. That's how she does it. She touches you.

Ani continued to beam, bright and seemingly guileless. All waited to see what Syrene would do next. In the end, she elected to do nothing at all beyond making a single threat that seemed hollow to all who heard it.

'Be assured that Grand Consul Gradus will hear of this,' she said.

She retreated into her chambers, but it was Ani at whom she was looking as the door closed. The opposing forces of Securitats and Military stayed in place for a moment, and then, as if by mutual but unspoken agreement, open hostility was replaced by submerged dislike. The stunned guards were replaced, the novices carried away for treatment, and Syl, Ani and Meia were absorbed into Danis's squad, the Military forming a protective wall around them as they departed.

They did not get far, though. Danis and Meia appeared to get the same message simultaneously, and both stopped as their earpieces lit up. Danis immediately left with his soldiers, instructing Meia to take the girls back to their rooms.

'What is it?' said Syl, and she did not like the look that Meia gave her.

'The Securitats have arrested two young men in connection with the explosions on the Royal Mile,' she said. 'Come with me. It's about time you showed me this spyhole of yours.'

CHAPTER 25

The Great Hall was more crowded than before, despite the late hour. Advisers, soldiers, Securitats and representatives of both the Military and the Diplomatic Corps had assembled, some out of duty, many out of curiosity. The bombs on the Royal Mile had been significant not only for the casualties inflicted but because of their daring: never before had the Resistance managed to carry out a major attack so close to the Illyri centre of power in the city. It suggested an escalation in the campaign against the Empire.

There were gasps when Paul and Steven, surrounded by a phalanx of Securitats and Corps guards, were led into the room by Vena. The captives' hands were secured in front of them with heavy magnocuffs, and their legs were manacled. A short chain connected the two sets of restraints.

'But that one is so young!' someone said, giving voice to what many others were silently thinking.

Behind them came Sedulus, and finally Grand Consul Gradus and his wife, Syrene. Gradus looked grave, while Syrene's features were once again hidden behind her veil.

The boys glanced nervously around the room. Paul's teeth were bared against his gag, giving him the look of wild beast snarling at its captors. Beside him, Steven bore the panicked look of a small cornered animal.

Be strong, Paul willed him. *I'm with you.*

As though he had spoken aloud, Steven looked up at his elder brother. Paul winked at him, and somehow Steven found the strength to wink back. Paul stood ramrod straight and raised his head high, and he was pleased to see his brother follow suit. A memory of his father came to him, and an expression that the old man liked to use.

'Just look them in the eye and damn them for fools,' he would say when someone disrespected his sons, or tried to belittle them. That was what they were doing now. They were looking their foes in the eye, and damning them. They were staring death in the face, but they would not show fear.

In the dimness of the spyhole, Meia saw Syl raise her hand to her mouth in shock as the boys were led in. There was only enough room inside for the two of them; Ani had been delegated to remain at the door and keep watch.

'What do I do if someone comes along?' she had asked.

'Distract them,' said Meia.

'How?'

'If they're male, flirt with them.'

'And if they're not male?'

Meia thought about the question.

'Try flirting anyway,' she said at last.

Now Syl touched her hand to Meia's.

'What is it?' Meia asked.

'I know those boys,' said Syl.

'*What?*'

'Today, on the Royal Mile, they helped me and Ani. They stopped us from running back to the castle after the first bomb exploded. They said there might be another, and they were right.'

'That's because they planted them,' said Meia.

But Syl shook her head. 'No, it wasn't like that. I'm sure of it.'

She looked at the two young humans, so small and vulnerable among the taller, hostile Illyri, and felt a surge of sympathy for them. She recalled their faces from earlier in the day, and how concerned they'd been about what had occurred. Could they really have been such good actors, denying everything over a cup of tea and a Hob-Nob? Could they have been responsible for planting those bombs yet have revealed nothing of it to the two young females on the Royal

Mile, especially when one of them was Ani? It was hard to keep dishonesty from Ani. She picked up on it the way Agrons picked up on scents.

Syl watched Syrene. Her attention was fixed on the boys before her, and the raised dais beyond them. This time, she was not trying to find eavesdroppers in the room. Either she did not care, or she did not sense their presence. It was the absence of Ani, Syl was certain. It was Ani who had come to Meia to tell her that Syl was in trouble. She had felt it: Syl's fear, the Red Sister's presence, all of it.

And Meia had believed her. She had not doubted her at all.

A door opened behind the dais, and Lord Andrus emerged in his official uniform, accompanied by Danis, Balen, and half a dozen of his closest advisers. Only Meia was absent.

'Shouldn't you really be down there with them?' said Syl.

'I'm not an adviser,' said Meia. 'I'm a spy, and I'm doing what spies do. Now shut up, and listen.'

Lord Andrus waited for silence to descend. While the room settled, he whispered something to Balen, who left the dais and approached the prisoners. He examined Steven's still swollen hand, and the inflammation on his arm, but did not touch the limb. He returned to the governor, and reported his findings. As he spoke, Andrus fixed his disapproving gaze on Vena, who returned it without flinching.

When all was quiet, Vena and her guards forced the boys forward. Gradus and Syrene took up positions to their right, Sedulus to their left.

Gradus cleared his throat.

'Lord Andrus,' he said. 'It seems that the Diplomatic Corps has succeeded where the Military could not. We have tracked down the humans involved in today's atrocities.' He waved a hand in the direction of the boys, and assumed a theatrical expression of surprise. 'And they are *children*! How can the Military claim to be in control of this city, this *planet*, when mere boys can come almost to our walls and kill us at will?'

Lord Andrus ignored the questions, and Gradus's rhetorical flourishes with them. He would not have his reputation put on trial here to further the Grand Consul's aims.

'What proof do you have of their involvement?' he said.

Vena looked to Gradus for permission to speak, and he nodded.

'My lord, we found traces of inorganic compounds on their skin that matched the explosives used today. Their DNA was tested against specimens taken from the scene, and a reconstruction was carried out.'

Vena waved a hand in the air, and the DNA-generated images of Paul and Steven loomed large, along with a barrage of chemical information. The sight incited an angry buzz in the room, as though a nest of bees had been roused.

'There can be no doubt,' said Vena. 'The tests are foolproof.'

'In my experience, nothing is foolproof,' said Andrus. 'You will, of course, provide my specialists with those test results?'

'Are you doubting the reliability of our methods, Lord Andrus, or our word?' said Gradus.

'Your methods appear to involve the torture of children,' said Andrus. 'Your word I will have to take, reluctantly, on trust.'

Gradus stepped back so that he stood behind Paul and Steven.

'Careful, Lord Andrus,' he said. 'When you insult me, you insult my office and, by extension, the Diplomatic Corps. More worryingly, you seem to place a greater value on the gentle treatment of two terrorists than you do upon our own dead.'

Murmurs of agreement passed through the hall. It was clear that there were those present who felt Gradus might have a point, and they were not all Diplomats. Gradus sensed that there might be an opportunity to be grasped here, a way of further undermining the governor's authority. For a moment, he had a considerable section of the crowd behind him, but like all those who are vain and foolish, he threw his advantage away by overstepping the mark. Before anyone could react, he slammed the boys' heads together with a resounding crack. A collective gasp went up, and the shackled prisoners toppled to the ground.

'No!' shouted Andrus.

Gradus ignored him and grabbed the captives by the hair, smacking the boys' heads down hard on the marble floor. Tears of anger pricked Syl's eyes. The smaller boy remained face down and motionless, while the older one was moaning, his head on its side, his lids closed, blood flowing from his shattered nose and pooling on the floor.

'There,' said Gradus. 'This is how we avenge our dead.'

He turned in a circle, his arms outstretched, a performer waiting for applause that never came. Instead, even some of his own retinue looked disgusted. The Illyri prized honour, and there was no honour in hurting two young shackled boys, regardless of what they might or might not have done. Too late, Gradus realised that he had gone too far, but he could not back down now.

'These humans have committed a capital crime against us,' he said. 'An example must be made of them. They will be shown no mercy.'

'What are you talking about?' said Andrus. For the first time, he sounded doubtful. There was something new here, something of which he had not been made aware.

Gradus ignored him. When next he spoke, his voice was like a whipcrack. 'I hereby sentence them to death.'

There was silence for a second or two, and then Andrus started to laugh. It was a laugh without mirth. There was only mockery in it.

'In case you have forgotten, we do not impose the death penalty on children, Gradus. That is *our* law, set down by the Council centuries ago. Furthermore, in my jurisdiction we do not impose the death penalty at all. Imprisonment, yes. Banishment to the Punishment Battalions, yes. But we do not execute! Killing two teenage humans would only exacerbate the problems we already face from the Resistance here on Earth. It would be an invitation to open revolt. I forbid it!'

A silken voice interjected before Gradus could reply. 'Lord Andrus, I believe there are fresh developments of which you have not been made aware.'

All eyes turned to Syrene. Despite her veil, her words were clear to all.

'By presidential order, the prohibition on the execution of children has been lifted. The Resistance on Earth has taken advantage of our mercy. It has used children against us because it knew we would hesitate to hurt them. That is no longer the case. Order must be restored on this planet and, regrettably, it must be restored with a little bloodshed.'

A minor Diplomat, his fingers still more flesh than rings, stepped forward and presented Lord Andrus with a sealed document. Gradus used the moment to pick up where his wife had left off. It was clear from his face that her interruption had angered him. He had wanted to be the one to take Andrus down. Now, once again, the truth had been revealed about where the real power lay in the relationship between Syrene and Gradus. Gradus was his wife's creature.

As Andrus broke the seal on the letter, Gradus spoke.

'The order gives the Diplomatic Corps full control, through the Securitats, over all judicial procedures on Earth, including imprisonment, banishment and execution. In decisions on which the Military and the Corps disagree, the opinion of the Corps will have precedence. That, you will note, refers to *all* decisions, not merely questions of law. You will, of course, retain your position as governor, Lord Andrus, but you and your fellow governors will defer to the Corps. For now, you will report to me, as the senior Diplomat on this planet, but in a few days I will appoint a permanent Diplomat to implement our new policies on Earth.'

Lord Andrus spent a long time staring at the letter, as though he could not quite believe its contents. Syl and Meia watched from their hiding place. Syl wanted to run to her father, and it was all she could do not to cry out. With one edict, her father had effectively been deprived of his power, and the Illyri set on a path of slaughter. These two boys, boys with whom she had eaten and drunk, boys who had saved her life, would be only the first to die. Others would follow. Syl felt only shame and anger. She was of the Illyri, and the Illyri were about to become killers of children.

'It is decided,' said Gradus. 'The executions will take place thirty hours from now, at dawn on Sunday. That will give us time to arrange a worldwide public broadcast, which will serve as a warning of the consequences of murdering Illyri. In the meantime, the interrogation of the suspects will resume tomorrow. They may have more information that will be of use to us.'

'Don't do this, Gradus,' said Andrus. 'It is wrong.'

'No,' said Gradus. 'It is the law.'

He nodded to Vena, who raised the boys to their feet. Steven sagged, clearly unconscious, and Syl saw that tears were washing blood down Paul's face as he stood wobbling before Gradus. He tried to speak, but the gag muffled his voice. Almost tenderly, Gradus pulled the gag down so that his words could be heard.

'Kill me,' he said. 'But spare my brother. Please.'

Gradus touched Paul's cheek, his ringed fingers brushing the boy's skin.

'If only I could,' he said. 'But as you fought together, so shall you die together.'

Paul pursed his lips, as though considering the wisdom of this, then spat a string of bloody phlegm straight into Gradus's face. After a startled pause, Gradus punched him squarely in the jaw and the boy crumpled, but was prevented from falling again by the guards.

'Give me your pulser!' Gradus ordered the nearest guard. Syl was sure he was about to kill Paul right there, but Syrene moved forward with an other-worldly speed and put her hand on her husband's arm.

'Not yet,' she said. 'A secret death, unseen by the masses, will serve no purpose. Let him suffer on the gallows.'

A cloth was produced, and Gradus used it to wipe his face. He held the bloodied fabric before Paul.

'For this, I'm going to hang your brother first, and make you watch as he dies,' said Gradus. 'Take them away!'

And Paul and Steven were dragged back to their cells, there to await their execution.

CHAPTER 26

It was a small, sombre group that gathered back at the Governor's House. Only Andrus, Danis, Meia and Balen were present, along with Syl and Ani, though the spymistress left shortly after a hurried conversation with the governor. Lord Andrus sat with his head in his hands. The atmosphere was almost one of bereavement, as though his authority had been a physical thing, a living, breathing entity that had protected them and now was gone. Syl thought that her father might be in shock. His gaze focussed inward, not out, and he had barely sipped from the snifter of brandy by his right hand. Danis looked no happier. He had no wish to serve under Gradus's yoke, and it was likely that Gradus would quickly find a way to rid himself of the old general. If he was fortunate, he might find himself in command of a Punishment Battalion, but he was more likely to die prematurely in his sleep, helped to his rest by poison in his wine.

Syl was thinking about the two boys in their cells, waiting to die: of Paul, with his soft mouth, smashed and bleeding; of Steven, unconscious and so pale that his freckles looked like they'd been drawn on paper. She knew that they could not be guilty of the crime with which they had been charged. Even if they were, the thought of their execution would still have repelled her. The construction of the gallows was to commence the following morning on the Esplanade, the part of the complex once known as Castle Hill. Humans had held public executions there in previous centuries, and not only hangings; the humans had burned or beheaded the condemned as well, usually after torturing them to within an inch of death, for Edinburgh Castle had a foul reputation as a place in which torture was routine. In reading the histories of the human race, Syl had never ceased to be surprised by its capacity for cruelty. Now it seemed that the Illyri were about to reveal themselves as being no better. Once again torture was being carried out in the cells of the castle. Once again the dead would hang from ropes outside its gates. This time, though, there would be children among the corpses, and even the humans had ceased to execute children.

Syl wondered if the Illyri had somehow become infected by the residue of violence in the walls of these old fortresses, places where pain had been visited on the defenceless for centuries. The Illyri ruled from former bases of the Roman Empire, which crucified those who opposed it; from old Crusader fortresses, where men, women and children were put to the sword for worshipping the same god by another name; and from places like Oslo's Akershus Castle, and Prague Castle in the Czech Republic, buildings haunted by their association with the Nazis, who sent millions to ovens and gas chambers as part of their plan to create their own empire. Have these sites tainted us, thought Syl, or were we always just as cruel as the humans but found a way to hide it from ourselves?

Gradus had ordered that the gallows should be built strong, because they were destined to remain in place for years to come. He was convinced that there would be no shortage of candidates to test the hangman's rope. Perhaps he was right, but a plan was slowly forming in Syl's mind. It was a plan with little hope of success, but she could not stand by and do nothing to stop this terrible thing from happening.

Lord Andrus turned to his daughter and began to question her about what had occurred during her time with Syrene.

'It's even more important now, Syl. More important than what's happening here on Earth; I fear the very peace of the Illyri race may be at stake. We need every tiny detail you can remember.'

'But I *don't* remember,' said Syl. 'We were talking, and then …'

She frowned in concentration. It was something like a dream, a dream in which Syrene seemed to separate into two parts, one of which had tried to bore into her mind with a terrible remorseless ferocity. She tried to explain it to her father, but she couldn't form the words. It was as though a lock had been placed on her tongue.

Puzzled and concerned, Lord Andrus turned his attention to Ani.

'And you? How did you come to be involved in all this?'

'I just felt strongly that Syl was in trouble,' said Ani. 'I don't know how. I told Meia, and she believed me.'

Andrus looked to Danis, who shrugged.

'She's always been like that,' he said. 'Maybe some Illyri are just more sensitive than others.'

'Well, you're clearly not among them,' said Andrus. It was the first hint of humour he had shown since the events in the council chamber. 'And I suppose we now know why Syrene is here: the Sisterhood has secured its grip on Illyr, and it wants the Earth as well. I wouldn't be surprised if Syrene starts building a replica of the Marque on Calton Hill and populating it with novices.'

'So what do we do?' said Danis.

'Nothing, for now,' said Andrus. 'We wait. There is much happening here that we don't yet understand. Until we know more, it's better to watch, and to listen.'

'So we are to be Gradus's dogs?' said Danis.

'We are, but we still have teeth, and our chains are long,' said Andrus. 'In the meantime, you can rest assured that Gradus will make mistakes. It's in his nature. If he insists on imposing a harsher rule on the humans, then they will rise up against him. The incidents of violence will increase, and the Corps' hold upon the Earth will start to slip. When that happens – and it will happen, sooner rather than later – the Military will be waiting to take back the mantle of power.'

It was Syl who spoke next.

'You said there were two boys sentenced to death, Father,' she said. 'But that is not our way. It's wrong. You must help them.'

Her father looked at her sadly. 'There's nothing I can do for them,' he said. 'If I act against Gradus and the Council of Government, I'll find myself in a cell alongside those boys.'

For the first time in her life, Syl felt real disappointment in her father. It was not only that he could do nothing for Paul and Steven;

he *wanted* to do nothing. She saw the truth of it now. The public execution of two young humans, broadcast to the world, would incite widespread fury, and this was Lord Andrus's only hope. Even those who had resigned themselves to living under the rule of the Illyri, continuing their lives much as they had done before, would rebel. Gradus and the Diplomatic Corps would almost instantly be faced with a full-scale rebellion in country after country. The Diplomats would not be strong enough to deal with such an insurrection, even with the aid of their Securitats, and the way would be open for the Military to step in as the force of reason and restraint. By next week, the brief rule of the Diplomats on Earth might already be over.

And Syl's father was prepared to sacrifice two children to make that happen.

CHAPTER 27

Meia sat in the darkness of Edinburgh Zoo, listening to the calls of the beasts and the birds. The nocturnal animals were now active, and she felt a sense of commonality with them, for she was a night creature too.

'There used to be ravens here, you know,' said a voice from behind her.

Meia's hand tightened on her small blast pistol, but she did not move. She had heard the man approaching long before he had revealed himself by speaking, and she knew that he was alone. She was in no danger from him, not here: this was neutral territory. Still, it paid to be careful. Trust was like money: it shouldn't be spent foolishly.

The man walked past her and stared at an empty cage.

'For some reason,' he continued, 'the people who came to visit didn't seem to find ravens interesting enough, but I always did. They're smart, ravens. They find prey for wolves, and then feed on the leavings once the wolves have gorged themselves. The wolves always leave something for them, but I often wonder what would happen if the ravens didn't find prey for a time, or if one of them fell injured before a wolf.'

He turned to face her. He was a big man, taller than she was, but slightly hunched. His hands were buried deep in the pockets of his overcoat. Meia knew that he had a gun in there somewhere, pointing at her. It would be small calibre, probably no bigger than his fist. It wouldn't make a very big hole in her, but then it wouldn't have to.

'It's a dangerous business, making deals with wolves,' he concluded.

'And which are you?' asked Meia. 'A raven or a wolf?'

'That depends,' he replied.

'On what?'

'On whom I'm making the deal with.'

He slowly withdrew his hands from his pockets. One was empty. The other contained a small silver hip flask. He unscrewed the top and drank from it. Meia could smell the whisky from where she sat. The man didn't offer any to her. They knew each other too well for that by now.

His name was Trask, and he acted as a channel of communication between the Illyri – or that branch of the Illyri represented by Meia and her kind, the ones who moved through the shadows – and the Resistance. This was not unusual. Even in the worst of wars, or the kind of hit-and-run conflict in which the Illyri and the Resistance were engaged, it was often necessary for the opposing sides to be able to communicate. It was a way of ensuring that truces, temporary or otherwise, could be negotiated and prisoners exchanged, along with information when necessary. In the case of Trask and Meia, they had found a way to keep the violence on both sides to a minimum. There were those in the Resistance who might have called him a traitor had they known of some of the deals he had struck with Meia, and there were those among the Illyri who might have said the same of her. Meia suspected that Trask was more deeply involved in the Resistance than he pretended to be, but it did not concern her. She preferred to deal with someone in authority, someone who could make a decision quickly, rather than with a foot soldier.

Trask sat beside her on the bench. A skimmer, one of the long-range craft that the Illyri used for intercontinental travel on Earth, crossed the moon, heading east.

'Off to deliver misery to some other corner of the globe, no doubt,' said Trask.

'You had plenty of misery before we came,' said Meia. 'If you were in the right mood, you might even concede that we have brought some of it to an end: hunger, disease, environmental damage.'

'At the price of our freedom.'

'You were never free, not really. We just rule more obviously than your own kind ever did.'

'At least they *were* our own kind.'

'Must we go through this every time we meet?' asked Meia.

'I wouldn't want you to go mistaking us for friends.'

'After the incidents of the last couple of days, I think that's unlikely.'

'If you're talking about Birdoswald, that wasn't us.'

'Really?'

'I won't lie to you, Meia. I told you that a long time ago. If I can't tell you something, then I'll keep my mouth shut, but I won't lie. There's no point to these meetings otherwise.'

'Who was it, then?'

'Highlanders.'

'Near Carlisle? We've never known them to come so far south before.'

'They're a law unto themselves, and they don't share their plans with us. They think we've grown soft, that maybe we're too close to the Illyri.'

'I can't imagine where they'd get that idea from,' said Meia drily.

'Nor me, not unless they've been visiting the zoo after dark.'

'Why Birdoswald?'

'Why not?'

'There are easier targets for them, closer targets. Also . . .' Meia paused. She had to be careful here. 'It seems to me that they might have been trying to take the Illyri commander of the garrison alive.'

'Well it didn't work then,' said Trask. 'I hear that he blew his own head off.'

'So you *have* been in contact with the Highlanders?'

'In a way. We expressed our concern at having them come on to our patch and start blowing up bases – not to mention some very nice Roman ruins – without so much as a by-your-leave.'

'And what did they say?'

'Two words. The second one was "off". I'll let you figure out the first.'

'And the explosions on the Royal Mile?'

Trask took another sip from his flask.

'That wasn't us either.'

'You're sure?'

'Certain. And it wasn't the Highlanders, I can tell you that.'

'They managed to blast their way into Birdoswald without too much trouble.'

Trask laughed. 'They pointed a lorry filled with explosives at the gates and hoped for the best. It's a wonder they didn't blow themselves up by hitting a pothole in the road long before they ever got near the border.'

'A splinter group, then, one of which you're not yet aware?'

Trask gave her a look. 'You wouldn't be talking to me if you thought there were splinter groups of which I wasn't aware. As soon as you start believing there might be gaps in my knowledge, you'll have me arrested or killed, and you'll find someone else to keep you company on your trips to the zoo.'

'Then who did it?'

'Maybe you ought to look closer to home,' said Trask.

Meia showed no surprise at the suggestion. That Trask felt as she did about the source of the attack simply confirmed her own suspicions.

'The Diplomats have no love for your lot,' Trask went on. 'Anything to sow a little unrest in the ranks. By the way, who was the woman in red?'

For all the precautions that Vena had taken, the Resistance still knew of the new presence in the castle.

'A member of the Nairene Sisterhood.'

'I didn't think they left their big library in the sky. What's she doing here, then?'

'Sowing some of that unrest in the ranks.'

'Huh,' said Trask. 'My turn: what do the Illyri want with the dead and the dying?'

'What?'

Trask smiled. He liked it when he found out something that Meia clearly didn't know about.

'The figures at the crematorium don't add up,' he said. 'There are more bodies coming in than are going into the flames. It's not a big difference, just a few here and there, mostly homeless and old people, but we notice these things, just as we're wondering why the Corps removed half a dozen old people from Western General, put them in a truck and drove them away. Someone assumed they wouldn't be missed, because they were poor, and ill, and had nobody to care about them. But *we* care! And we've heard similar reports from other parts of the country.'

'I'll look into it,' said Meia.

'You do that. Are we finished here?'

'Not quite.'

Meia stood. She didn't like being close to Trask for too long. She knew that what he had said earlier was right: when he ceased being useful to her, she would kill him, if only to protect herself. He would try to do the same to her. It was just a matter of who got there first. It was a shame. She had grown to like him.

'We have a problem,' she said, and heard him shift in his seat. She could almost picture him reaching for his gun. She let him see that her hands were empty.

'What kind of problem?'

'The Diplomatic Corps is bringing back the death penalty.'

'I wasn't aware that it had ever gone away,' said Trask. He knew that the Illyri, and particularly the Securitats, were prepared to kill Resistance members if they couldn't capture them alive, and sometimes even if they could, just as the Resistance's snipers were happy to kill any stray Illyri that wandered into their sights. When you thought about it, the death penalty was being applied every day.

'. . . For children,' Meia finished.

'You can't mean that!' said Trask. 'What about Andrus? He's the law in this land. He won't stand for it.'

'We have a new president back on Illyr,' said Meia. 'The change of leadership has brought with it a change in policy. As of today, the Diplomats have effectively assumed control of Earth. The age of the gentle hand is coming to an end.'

'And when does this new policy come into effect?'

'The first executions are scheduled for the day after tomorrow, on the Esplanade. Two boys, Paul and Steven Kerr, will be hanged for the atrocities committed on the Royal Mile.'

Meia saw Trask react to the names.

'I know those boys,' he said. 'They're good lads, and they're all that their mother has. More to the point, they had nothing to do with those explosions. I've told you already: that wasn't the Resistance!'

But Meia was watching him closely. The Kerr boys were important to Trask; maybe personally, but probably professionally too. Why? Assuming that Trask was telling the truth and the Resistance had not planted the bombs on the Royal Mile, why had the Diplomats chosen to pin the crime on those two boys? How had they been found?

'They were working for you, weren't they?' said Meia. 'Those boys were on a mission for the Resistance when they were picked up.'

Trask nodded.

'What was it?' asked Meia.

'Tunnels,' said Trask softly. 'There are tunnels beneath Edinburgh. You lot have been digging them, and we wanted to find out why. That's what the boys were doing. Looking for the tunnels.'

'Tunnels?'

'You didn't know? You're losing your touch.'

This was Corps work, thought Meia, all of it: the arrival of Syrene and Gradus, the bombs, the move against Lord Andrus, and maybe even these tales of tunnels and bodies, all linked to the Diplomats.

'What about those boys?' said Trask. 'You can't let them hang.'

'I'll think of something,' said Meia.

'You'd better,' said Trask, 'or I promise you, you'll be wading through rivers of Illyri blood.'

CHAPTER 28

Syl spent a sleepless night, tormented by dreams in which she tried to stop her father from being hanged but couldn't get to him in time because thick ranks of Securitats held her back, their uniforms no longer black but a deep blood red. She woke before dawn, convinced of a presence in her room, but she was alone. Her temples throbbed though, and when she looked in the mirror, she saw circular marks on either side of her head, almost like burns

She touched me. Syrene touched me, and I burned.

It was the weekend, which was of some comfort. The Illyri had taken certain human traditions to heart; among the best of them was dispensing with education classes at weekends. Althea appeared shortly after nine, bustling around the room, tidying where no tidying was required.

'I heard you were involved in quite an adventure yesterday,' said Althea.

'Was I?' Syl answered carefully, uncertain as to what exactly Althea might be referring to. She wondered where Althea had been for most of the previous day; it was unlike her to be away from her charge for so long, especially amid so much upheaval.

'Indeed you were. They say you spent time with the Red Witch.'

'Yes,' said Syl, 'although I don't remember too much about it. Althea, where were you yesterday evening?'

'I had errands to run.'

'Errands? What errands?'

'Never you mind. Your curiosity will be the death of you if you're not careful.' She gave Syl a strange look when she said it, as though daring her to deny that she was curious at all.

'Did you hear about those two boys, the ones they captured?'

'I did.'

'They're going to kill them, Althea.'

'Are they now?'

'Yes! They're going to hang them, and my father is going to let it happen, just so that Gradus and the Diplomats will look bad. We have to stop it.'

'I don't know anything about such matters, Syl, and I wouldn't be making assumptions about your father. Now get yourself dressed. He wants to have breakfast with you.'

Lord Andrus looked weary when Syl arrived in the dining room; his youthful eyes were glazed, the flesh beneath them swollen with tiredness and distress. He must have been up all night, thought Syl. Even as she inwardly raged at him for what she believed he was planning to do – or indeed planning not to do in the case of the boys – she felt distress at his condition. The table was laid with fruit and cheese, and scrambled eggs with ham and peppers in a metal bowl kept warm by a burner. Syl kissed her father on the forehead, put a few token pieces of fruit on a plate and sat down. She had no desire to eat. Thoughts of Paul and Steven filled her head, and the knowledge of what was going to happen to them tomorrow made her want to throw up. Choking food down hardly seemed an option.

Her father touched her arm.

'I wanted to say that I'm sorry, Syl. Your birthday was not as I might have wished it to be. I'll make it up to you, I promise.'

Her birthday? She'd completely forgotten about it in the tumult of the previous day. Had it really just been a single day? It seemed to her that she had lived a year of her life in the previous twenty-four hours.

'Oh, please! That hardly matters. Are you okay, Father? You look . . . ill.'

'Uneasy lies the head that wears the crown,' he replied.

'*Henry the Fourth, Part Two*,' said Syl, almost automatically. She shared her father's fascination with many aspects of this planet's culture. It was strange, she thought, but she probably knew more about its art and its history than many humans. She would have known even more if she'd been able to upload the information directly, but limiters were routinely embedded in the Chips of young Illyri after it was found that direct uploading of information at a young age stunted mental development.

The Chip sat on the surface of the brain, near the cerebral cortex. It was basically a neural interface that enabled Illyri thoughts to be detected and read as electrical patterns. It then converted these patterns into orders that could be transmitted to control systems, including flight decks on ships, and weapons, from missiles to pulses. In addition, as Illyri aged, the implants released 'baths' of electrons that boosted memory and increased alertness. They could be used in the treatment of a variety of neurological ailments, including epilepsy, and to aid those with paralysis by allowing them to control prosthetic limbs. Through implants, learning could be replaced by uploading, providing instant knowledge of a language, or a subject.

But the Illyri recognised that the brain continued to develop its wiring to the frontal lobe, and to the tracts responsible for complex cognitive tasks like attention and inhibition, until long past adolescence. It was important that this development occurred organically. For similar reasons, they believed that it was important that the young learn, and not simply upload. As her father liked to point out, it was easy to upload. Real understanding was harder. Uploading was instant and shallow; learning took time, but with it came depth. So it was that, perhaps for the first time, Syl really understood the meaning of Shakespeare's words.

'Well done,' said Andrus. 'All these years of training and governorship and diplomacy, and still Gradus has outmanoeuvred me.'

'Don't let those boys die, Father.'

'I have little choice.'

'Can't you delay the execution? You could demand confirmation of the order from the president. It's such a huge step, such a terrible act . . .'

'I sent the request to Gradus this morning, and it was denied. Even if I were to try to go behind his back, it would require sending a message through the wormhole. Assuming it got through, it would then have to be transmitted to Illyr through the relays, and Gradus controls them.'

He pushed some eggs around his plate, but Syl could see that they had already gone cold. Her father was not in the mood for eating either.

'Syl, the Empire is changing,' he said. 'It may be that my place is no longer here on this world.'

Syl held her breath. She hardly dared to speak, but she had to ask the question.

'Are you talking about returning to Illyr?'

'Perhaps,' he said. 'What took place yesterday is just the first of many such acts we can anticipate. This is not just about my own loss of power, or the deaths of two boys. It is about the corruption of an entire race. There is something rotten at the heart of the Illyri Empire, and there has been for a long, long time. It will have to be tackled at its source. That lies on Illyr, and in the Marque, not here.'

Syl was torn. She longed to see Illyr, wanted to experience it for herself, but she knew too that her father loved Earth, and perhaps she also cared for it more than she'd thought.

'You will abandon Earth to the Diplomats?'

'If I have no other choice. We have done some great wrongs on this world, Syl, but the Diplomats will do worse. If I can stop them, I will, but sometimes a general must lose a battle to win a war. If I have to sacrifice Earth to prevent this poison from seeping deeper into the Empire, then I will.'

'When will you decide?'

'Soon, Syl, soon.'

'And . . .' The words caught in her throat.

'Yes, Syl?'

'And I'll be going with you, won't I? You won't . . . leave me, will you?'

Her father hugged her to him. He rarely gave such demonstrations of affection, and she treasured them all the more for it.

'Yes, Syl, you will be going with me, although there may come a time when you do not thank me for it.'

Balen knocked and entered. The governor's presence was required in his office. Despite the new order, the routine business of rule continued. Her father kissed her on the forehead and left.

Syl took her plate and went to sit in an antique chair in the living room. It was her favourite: the heavy brocade fabric was worn smooth in places and the seat was broad and circular, originally crafted to envelop the wide hooped skirts of Georgian ladies. But she was taller than any human lady of old, so she folded her coltish limbs under her and rested her head back, staring up at the large painting that dominated the wall. It was a masterpiece known as *The Rape of Europa*, painted centuries before by the celebrated human artist Titian. It had been a gift from the human leaders to Lord Andrus when he became governor of Europe and set up his offices in Edinburgh.

'They thought that I wouldn't understand the irony,' he once said, but he had been enchanted by the painting regardless, and it had immediately assumed pride of place in the lounge. *The Rape of Europa* – or simply *Europa*, as it was often called – featured fat cherubs who seemed to be attacking a flailing woman on the back of a massive bull, while nymphs standing at the far side of a lake looked on helplessly, and sea monsters gleamed in the depths. The bull's beady eyes stared straight at the viewer, its tail almost quivering with excitement. When she was much younger, Syl had been frightened by the vibrant spectacle, by the trio of cherubs assaulting poor Europa.

'But they're not attacking,' her father had explained to her. 'They're trying to help Europa. She's just scared, and she doesn't understand.'

Syl thought of Gradus as she looked at the scene anew. Curiously, he reminded her of the cherubs, soft and pale and implacable, with his eerily smooth skin, and his tantrums and his dangerous toys. The elite of the Diplomatic Corps were just like him. The events of the past twenty-four hours had cast the painting in a fresh light. Perhaps Europa was right to be frightened. Perhaps the whole of Earth should be frightened by the rule of the Diplomats.

CHAPTER 29

Syl might have dozed off, or maybe she was just lost in the painting, but gradually she became aware of a presence nearby. She turned to find Meia watching her.

'Don't you ever, like, knock?' she said coldly.

'Why? Were you doing something that you shouldn't have been doing? How unlike you that would be.'

'I was thinking.'

'Really?'

Meia sounded surprised. The expression on her face didn't suggest to Syl that she was joking. Sometimes she was hard to understand.

'Very funny. If you're looking for my father, I don't know where he is.'

'Actually, I was looking for you.'

Meia summoned a screen, and a short piece of video began to play. The camera was angled steeply upwards, and the heads of only two of the three people on the screen were visible, because one of them was standing and the camera couldn't fit her into the frame. The figure on the right was Syl. The other was Syrene. They were sitting across from each other, while a third figure stood between them, dressed in robes that were red yet almost transparent, as though a ghost had just entered the room. Syl could see a translucent hand touching her temple, and then the image flickered and was gone.

'Five seconds,' said Meia. 'That's all the bug got before whatever power was being used to prevent us from monitoring events in that room shorted its systems, and it died.'

Syl let the image play again and again, trying to repair the holes in her memory. It helped. There was still a lot that was unclear, but at least she now knew a little more of what had happened.

'That was Syrene,' she said. 'But that was also Syrene sitting on the chair across from me.'

'A mental projection of some kind,' said Meia. 'A part of Syrene released to roam free, while the rest of her sits and grins.'

'I didn't know the Sisterhood could do that.'

'Neither did I. It seems they've been learning all kinds of new tricks in the Marque: mental projection, the manipulation of presidents and consuls, the rule of an empire from its shadows. Perhaps I should see if the Sisterhood will have me after all. There's much I could glean from them.'

'You don't mean that,' said Syl.

'Don't I, now? Well, have it your way.'

'She burned me,' said Syl, pointing to the marks on her temples.

'So she did. I wonder what she was looking for in that marvellous, mysterious head of yours. Whatever it was, I suspect she didn't find it, because she was looking in the wrong place – or, rather, the wrong head.'

'I don't know what you mean.'

'I think you do, Syl. I want you to bring your little friend Ani to my quarters in an hour. If you don't, I'll tell your father what you both got up to yesterday.'

'You wouldn't!'

'I would,' said Meia, and her tone left Syl in no doubt. 'Oh, it wouldn't give me pleasure – well, not much – but I would. So: an hour, then? And don't be late. I hate to be kept waiting, and who knows what I might do if my patience is tested . . .'

Syl and Ani arrived early. It seemed like the sensible thing to do, under the circumstances. Ani had been most reluctant to join Syl in Meia's quarters, because any meeting with Meia could only mean trouble, at least until Syl explained the consequences for them both if they did not do as she had ordered. Ani had been on the receiving end of her father's rage often enough to know that it wasn't just the two humans who would be in danger of hanging if he found out that his daughter had been wandering outside the castle walls without permission.

Meia was waiting for them, and opened the door before they had a chance to knock.

'Almost as good as one of your tricks, isn't it, Ani?' she said as she closed the door behind them. 'Mind you, I was forced to listen for you, but you'd just have *known*.'

Ani said nothing, which was unusual, even painful, for her.

Meia's rooms were bigger and more elegant than Syl had expected, a confirmation of just how valuable she was to Lord Andrus. The neat living area was furnished with two chairs and a sofa, and a video screen. There were prints and paintings on the wall, some of them quite valuable, Syl thought. They showed good taste. Two walls were lined entirely with books, both Illyri and human. Meia, like Andrus, liked physical books. A half-open doorway led into the bedroom. It looked exceptionally tidy. In fact, it seemed like a room that had never been truly occupied. Despite its adornments, it suggested functionality.

'Sit down,' Meia instructed, pointing to the sofa, and Syl and Ani sat. Meia took one of the chairs. She produced a deck of cards from her pocket, and spread them on the small coffee table between her and her guests. Syl hadn't seen anything like them before. Instead of suits – like human cards – or symbolic animals, as the Illyri used, there were only five symbols: a circle, a cross, a trio of waves, a square and a star.

'These are sometimes called Zener cards on Earth,' said Meia. 'They're used to test for psychic ability. Of course, most of it is nonsense, and a certain degree of success can be put down to chance. You're both going to take this test, and you're going to do it to the best of your abilities, because if you try to trick me' – she stared at Ani, but not at Syl – 'then I'll be having interesting conversations with Lord Andrus and General Danis. Am I clear?'

Syl and Ani nodded.

'Right, let's begin.'

★ ★ ★

It was simple: Meia showed them the back of a card, and they had to guess which symbol was on the other side. They began with fifty cards, and eventually increased to one hundred over the course of five tests. At the end, Meia calculated their accuracy.

'Syl,' she said, 'you scored an average of eighteen per one hundred over the course of the tests.'

'What does that mean?' said Syl.

'It means that if you decide to bet on a sunny day tomorrow, it will probably rain. You seem to have no psychic ability whatsoever. In fact, you may even be a little below average.'

'Loser,' said Ani.

'We haven't heard your score yet, smarty,' said Syl, although she already had her suspicions.

'Ani,' said Meia, 'you scored an average of ninety-five per cent. It would probably have been higher if Syl hadn't distracted you by sneezing a couple of times.'

'Sorry,' said Syl.

'Don't worry about it,' said Ani. 'Below-average specimens probably just sneeze more than the rest of us.'

Meia walked to her drinks cabinet and brought out three glasses and a bottle of fresh lemonade.

'A celebratory drink,' she said.

'Of lemonade?' said Ani, who had been caught drinking illicit alcohol so often by her father that he had largely given up trying to stop her from doing it. 'Wow. Push the boat out, why don't you?'

Meia ignored her and poured the lemonade, handing each of the girls a glass.

'I propose a toast,' she said. 'To what, if I'm right, may be the most gifted psychic this world has ever seen. To Ani!'

They clicked their glasses, and drank. The lemonade was good: not too tart, not too sweet. Meia didn't even sip hers before setting it aside.

'Now, Ani,' she said, 'why don't you tell us what else you can do?'

* * *

The list was long. Even Syl was surprised. Ani couldn't quite read minds, not yet, but she could pick up on emotions, and she was strong on spotting those who were lying.

But there was one particular skill that reminded Syl of what Syrene had done to her: she could cloud minds. Not for long, but for long enough. She demonstrated it on Syl, forcing her to concede that the lemonade was, in fact, whisky, and might be making her a little drunk. It irritated Syl considerably, not only because she didn't wish to be part of some mind experiment, but because she found herself feeling jealous of Ani's gifts, and more than a little hurt that she had not shared the extent of them with her closest fried.

'There are Illyri who would do almost anything to have you on their side,' said Meia. 'You have a great, great gift. Syrene must have sensed it when you were spying on her, but she couldn't pinpoint the source. She thought it might be Syl at first, although I'm not sure why. Perhaps you can screen yourself somehow. I don't know.'

'I'm not going to get into trouble, am I?' asked Ani.

'You're not going to get into any trouble at all,' said Meia, 'not if you refrain from demonstrating your skills too obviously, and not if you do what I ask.'

'But we already did!' protested Syl. 'We came here. We did your tests. We've kept our side of the bargain.'

'Bargain?' said Meia. 'I don't recall making any *bargain*. I simply threatened you, and that threat still stands.'

Syl swore with frustration. Ani fell back against the sofa.

'What do you want us to do now, then?' asked Ani.

'What I want,' said Meia, 'is for you to help two prisoners to escape.'

CHAPTER 30

Later, when it had all gone wrong, Syl would wonder if she might have done things differently had she known what would befall them. But that was the benefit of hindsight: looking back, everything was clearer, and every false step, every poor decision, seemed so obvious that it was impossible to believe that they had ever been taken at all. Still, Meia's scheme, however flawed, was the only one that had been offered to her, and the only plan there was. Of course she had to act; of course she had to try to save Paul and Steven, because they had saved her. And perhaps, just perhaps, they'd been captured because of her and Ani, because they had taken the time to help two panicked girls on the Royal Mile. Not taking action to prevent a wrong, when one could, seemed to Syl almost as bad as the terrible fate to which Gradus had sentenced the boys come the morning. Their bodies would swing, and she would bear witness.

The plan, as far as it went, revolved around something that Syl had never noticed until Meia pointed it out to her: Syl looked a little like Vena. Not a lot, and certainly not enough to fool a guard who wasn't blind, but they were similar in height and in the way that they carried themselves, even in the shape of their faces, the shrewdness of their features. It caused Syl to wonder if that was one of the reasons why Vena seemed to hate her so much, for there was no doubt that the Securitat despised her. The Securitats were bad news anyway; they were technically the Illyr secret police, but as they were under the control of the Diplomatic Corps, they would seize any opportunity to hurt members of the Military or their families. As the daughter of

Lord Andrus, Syl was a particular target for Vena's venom. She thinks I'm a privileged little bitch, thought Syl, my father's pride and joy, the one who can do no wrong, the oldest of those who had come to be known as the Firstborn. Vena looks at me, and she sees herself as she might have been, as she should be. Well, let her think it, for all the good it will do her.

Perhaps it was that defiant streak, as much as her desire to save the lives of the two young men, which spurred her on. Anyway, what choice was there? It wasn't as if Syl had any better suggestions. She was sixteen years old – born among the stars, settled on a strange world, raised among a hostile, sometimes murderous alien race – but so far she had not tried to break anyone out of jail.

However, the success of the plan lay not with her, but with Ani, and Ani's fledgling abilities.

'I don't know that I can do it,' Ani said to Meia, as the spy took two Securitat uniforms from the back of her closet and laid them on her bed. Each had a Securitat cape with it too, hooded against the cold northern weather.

'You'd better be able to do it,' said Meia. 'If you can't, you and your friend may end up on the gallows with the humans.'

Ani looked pleadingly at Syl. She did not want to do this.

'I trust you,' said Syl, with more confidence than she felt. 'I know you won't let anything happen to us. Right?'

Ani put her face in her hands. 'I think I want to die,' she said, her voice muffled by her fingers.

Meia patted her on the back.

'If you fail,' she said, 'that can be arranged.'

With Ani's help, Syl tied her thick, glossy hair tightly back, and Meia smeared her hairline with a flesh-coloured cream, plastering down any wisps, before daubing silver at the edge of her cheekbone. She handed her a slim hairgrip to secure the hood in place.

'I can't imagine that even Ani could keep them fooled if they saw all that damn hair,' Meia said, looking critically at their attempt to hide it. 'Whatever happens, keep it under wraps.'

★ ★ ★

The two humans were being held in the old vaults of the castle. Built in the fifteenth century on the rock at the castle's south side, they had been used at various points as stores, barracks, an arsenal and, as was now the case, a prison. They were dank and unpleasant, the cells secured with electronic locks that could only be opened with swipe keys or directly from a panel in a nearby control room. At the moment the boys were the only prisoners being kept there, and were being guarded not by Galateans, who were usually given these dull jobs, but by Securitats. Four Securitats lined the corridor where Paul and Steven were being held, and two more were stationed in the control room. Cameras also monitored the cells, inside and out.

At precisely 9.00 p.m., the door to the control room opened from outside and then almost immediately closed again. The Securitats turned just in time to see a gas grenade roll across the floor towards them. Within seconds, they were unconscious.

Meia entered, a cloak over her head but her face unmasked, seemingly unaffected by the fumes. She immediately adjusted all the cameras in the vicinity of the cells so that they ceased recording, then quickly reprogrammed the non-essential screens to give her clear views of the area in front of the New Barracks, the old Military Jail, Foog's Gate and St Margaret's Chapel, as well as the approaches to the vaults from the Great Hall and the old Royal Palace. She would now have some notice, however short, if anyone came their way, but Syl and Ani would still need to work fast. Gas grenades would have been simpler, but the dispersal of the guards in the corridor meant that Meia couldn't be sure they would all have been rendered unconscious before one of them had the chance to raise the alarm.

She checked her watch. Five seconds.

Four.

Three.

Two.

One.

Two black-clad figures appeared on one of the screens, viewed from behind.

It was beginning.

★ ★ ★

The uniforms didn't fit quite as well as they might have, and Syl's had a bloodstain on the left side, along with what looked like a repair necessitated by the insertion of a blade. Syl didn't want to think about how, or where, Meia had acquired it. She was starting to think that Meia was a lot more manipulative, and certainly more dangerous, than she had previously given her credit for.

They passed the control room and entered the vaults, pausing just before they turned into the main corridor of cells. A camera watched them from above. Ani stared back at it for a moment, then gave it, and Meia, the finger.

'She won't like that,' whispered Syl.

'I don't care. It made me feel better.'

Syl thought about it, then gave the finger to the camera as well. She wanted Paul and Steven freed, but she still didn't appreciate being exploited by Meia.

'You're right,' she said. 'That did make me feel better.'

'Are you ready?' said Ani.

Syl nodded. 'Are *you* ready?'

Ani let out a deep breath. Her whole body relaxed. When she looked at Syl again, her eyes were bright yet distant, like a noonday sun glimpsed through a haze.

'Yes,' she said. 'I am ready.'

The two Securitats nearest the control room stood to attention as they saw the uniformed figures approach, but both looked confused. One of them opened his mouth as if to say something, and his hand strayed towards the pulser at his belt, then stopped.

'I . . . We . . .' he said. 'We weren't expecting you, ma'am.'

His eyes flickered from Syl's face to the silver near her temple, but he seemed to be having trouble focusing. He used the back of his hand to wipe them, and when he had done so, he appeared more certain of what he was seeing.

'We're here to take the prisoners to the Grand Consul,' said Syl. Beside her, Ani stayed completely silent, and Syl could almost feel the intensity of her concentration as she tried to fix the faces of Vena and one of her female sergeants, Grise, in the minds of the men before her.

'We received no notice,' said the guard. 'Our instructions were to allow no contact with the prisoners until the morning.'

'And whose instructions were those?' said Syl, putting on her most imperious voice.

'Well, yours, ma'am, and the Grand Consul's.'

She looked from one guard to the other, waiting. They faltered. One of them narrowed his eyes, like a man used to glasses who suddenly finds himself trying to see without them. Damn it, thought Syl, just go along with us. Please.

'The Grand Consul wishes to speak with the prisoners,' she said. 'Would you like me to go back and explain to him why this doesn't meet with your approval? Or perhaps you'd prefer to do so yourself?'

Clearly neither option appealed to the guards. They set aside any doubts and led Syl and Ani to the cells, where two more guards waited. This was the hard part, for Ani now had to try to fog the minds of four individuals. Syl risked a glance at her. Ani's face was a mask of concentration, but small beads of sweat were visible on her forehead and upper lip. Syl could see that her jaws were clenched shut.

Now the second pair of guards stepped forward, and Syl instinctively lowered her head slightly as though that might help with their imposture. She disguised the movement with a flick of her chin at the cell doors.

'Open them,' she said, and when the cell guards again seemed reluctant to do so, their faces betraying some confusion, a kind of disjunction between what they were seeing and what they thought they were seeing, she added, 'Quickly!' snarling it more than saying it.

This gave the guards the push they required. They were used to following orders, and the simpler the better. Anyway, it was easier to follow orders than to think about why you shouldn't follow them. That was the whole principle on which armies were founded. Without it, they would have fallen to pieces.

The cell doors were swiped open, revealing Paul and Steven in their respective cells, each lying on his side, neither of them sleeping.

'Up!' said Syl. 'You're coming with us.'

Paul raised himself to a sitting position. He frowned, and Syl could almost hear the mechanisms of his brain grinding as some spark of recognition took fire there. She willed him to say nothing, and then fell back on the same voice she had used on the guards.

'Now!'

Both young men rose and shuffled to the cell doors. The guards stepped back and drew their pulsers, ready for any trickery, but the young men presented no real threat. They looked tired and frightened. One of the guards put a pair of magnetic cuffs on each of the boys, and handed the control unit to Syl.

'Should we accompany you?' asked the first guard.

'No,' said Syl. 'They're secured, and we'll have no trouble from them. Soon,' she added, 'they'll be no trouble to anyone ever again.'

The guard laughed, and the others joined in, but their laughter was nervous and uncertain. Beside her, Ani was trembling with the effort of holding off the reality of their appearances. A tiny trickle of blood appeared from her right nostril and rolled down to her mouth. She turned from the guards before they could see it, and Syl motioned the boys to move ahead of her with the stun baton that Meia had given her.

They tried to walk slowly out of the vaults. It was all Syl could do not to sprint, yet even in the midst of her fear she had never felt so alive.

They had done it. Somehow, they had done it.

CHAPTER 31

If Syl could not quite believe that they had managed to get the prisoners out of their cells, Meia was more surprised still. She had resigned herself to having to rescue the young Illyri from the guards if necessary; the result would have been bloodshed, and even Meia preferred not to kill Securitats within the castle walls. On those occasions when she had been forced to target Securitats, and then only – or mostly – to protect herself, she had done so discreetly, and the bodies had never been found.

She had monitored the progress of Syl and Ani while keeping one hand on the handle of the control-room door, ready to spring to their aid if – or when – everything went to pieces. Instead, she was now watching as they escorted the humans, still manacled, out of the vaults and towards the castle walls, where the next step of the plan would be enacted.

One of the unconscious guards at her feet moaned, and clawed at the floor. Meia removed a second grenade from the folds of her cloak. The last thing they needed now was for the guards to wake and raise the alarm. She pulled the pin, and tossed the grenade with an underarm throw. Just as the gas began to fill the room, she saw three figures appear on one of the screens before her, heading for the vaults.

Even through the fumes, she recognised Vena.

Syl led their little group onwards, through passageways, corridors and galleries, some foul-smelling, some damp-walled and mossy, twisting and turning down into the tunnels carved from the volcanic rock on which the castle had been built so many years before. These areas were vaguely familiar to her; she had explored them as a child, before they were returned to use as cells, but she had little memory of them. Without the instructions that Meia had drummed into her, she would have been entirely lost.

She looked back. Ani was struggling to keep up. The bleeding from her nose had stopped, but the blood was smeared across her left cheek and her chin. Her eyes were glassy, and she was supporting herself against the wall. Syl stopped to give her time to catch up. She noticed that Steven wasn't doing much better than Ani. Whatever the Corps had done to him physically was bad enough, but they had damaged something inside him as well. He might have believed himself to be big and strong like his older brother, but he was still more child than man. He was keeping himself going through sheer force of will, but Syl could tell that he wasn't far from crying for his mother.

'Hey,' Syl said quietly to Ani. 'Are you able to continue?'

Ani nodded. 'I'm just . . . tired. Very tired.'

'We're nearly there,' said Syl. She touched a hand to Ani's cheek. 'We can't stop now.'

'You're the one who stopped, Syl,' said Ani.

'For you.'

'You say.'

This was the Ani that Syl knew and loved.

'Oh Ani, you did so well . . .'

'I knew it!' interrupted Paul loudly. 'Sylvia! I recognise you now. You're not human, you're Illyri! I guessed as much. I should have known it back on the Mile.'

Syl looked at him, a million thoughts going through her head yet not a single word able to form in her mouth. He was staring at her, his eyes narrowed, his pupils flitting over her exposed face, frowning as he took in the smear of silver, the strange paste on her hairline, and then he was staring into the golden-red orbs that were her eyes, lidless and alien.

'Holy crap,' whispered Steven.

'It took me a while,' said Paul, nodding slowly, 'because your glasses covered your eyes when we first met, and then this uniform threw me too, but it was you, you and your friend here, on the Royal Mile. I thought you were human – a bit weird, yes, but at least human. Man, was I mistaken.'

'I guess you were. I bet you're sorry you helped us now.'

She looked back at him defiantly, at the so-very-human eyes in their bruised sockets, at the bloodied lips she'd focussed on so intently only the day before. She watched him blink, and wondered at what that was like, at not being able to see for a split second. There was a long moment before Paul replied.

'No,' he said at last, and his voice caught in a way that made Syl's cheeks burn. 'I'm not. Look, forgive me if I'm wrong, but is this a rescue?'

'Yes, it is.'

'Oh good. I was hoping it might be. Any chance you could take these cuffs off then, Sylvia?'

'Sorry,' said Syl, 'and my name's actually Syl.'

He raised his eyebrows at her as if it didn't matter, and looked pointedly at his bound hands once again. Syl activated the unit, and the cuffs demagnetised and dropped off. Paul rubbed his wrists and winced. The magnacuffs had a tendency to heat up after only a few minutes.

'About time. I wish you'd done that a bit earlier, *Syl*.'

'You're quite critical for someone who was hours away from being hanged,' said Syl. 'Would you like to go back to your cell and come up with a better plan of your own?'

'Actually, no, I wouldn't.'

'I didn't think so.'

'So where are we going?'

'Out.'

'We seem to be taking the long way.'

'We're taking the *safe* way,' said Syl. 'I hope.'

'Okay then. I guess we'll just have to trust you.'

'Right. Any more questions or comments, or shall we get moving?'

'Well, just one thing.'

Syl sighed. She wondered if all rescuers had to put up with this sort of interrogation.

'What is it?'

'Thank you,' said Paul. 'On behalf of both of us, just thank you.'

Syl was thrown.

'You're welcome,' she said, and blushed again. 'We're only returning the favour, though.'

He ignored her glibness.

'You know, after you left, I rather hoped I'd see you again, and without your damned glasses.'

'But now you know I'm Illyri.'

'Yeah. But at least you don't have a squint.'

He smiled, and she found herself smiling back, unable to help herself. They stared at one another, and might have gone on staring were it not for a cough in the background.

'I don't mean to spoil a lovely moment,' said Ani, 'but I really would like to get this over and done with, please.'

Not all the cells in the castle were occupied, or, indeed, locked. The stonework in some was in a state of disrepair, while others were used for storage and, on occasion, as sleeping quarters for guards who were pulling double duty. It was from the darkness of one such cell, furnished only with a pillow and a mattress, that Meia watched Vena pass by, accompanied by two of her black-garbed acolytes. She guessed it was a routine prisoner check, or perhaps another spell of interrogation. Either way, she cursed the female Securitat and all her works. Damn her, why couldn't she just have put her feet up, basked in her success in capturing the humans and looked forward to the executions to come?

Meia waited until the three Securitats had turned the corner. She had no more grenades, although she did have her blast pistol. But it was one thing knocking Securitats unconscious in order to free prisoners, or quietly 'disappearing' them if they happened to look the wrong way at an inconvenient time; quite another to kill Sedulus's vicious little pet, however much personal satisfaction the act might bring. There would be trouble enough once the escape was discovered without adding high-profile bodies to the mix.

She slipped from the cell. A camera watched her from above, but she had no fear of it. She had disabled every camera in the building before leaving the control room. She checked her watch. Syl and Ani should have been at the wall by now, but in a few minutes the castle would be ringing with alarm bells.

Alarm bells.

Meia stopped. She took her blast pistol from her belt and adjusted its setting, before pointing it at the mattress and firing a single shot. A section of the mattress exploded, and flames licked around the edges of the blast mark. Meia fanned them with her hands, feeding the fire until the mattress and the pillow were burning merrily. When she was happy with the blaze, she followed the route taken by Syl and Ani. She paused only once, just long enough to smash the glass that covered the little red box on the wall, and trip the fire alarm.

The Securitats at the cells were relaxing. They could afford to, now that the prisoners had been handed over to Vena. The humans were no longer their responsibility. For a while, at least, they could take it easy. One of them had produced a small silver flask of a kind that might have been familiar to Meia's Resistance contact Trask, and they passed it around to warm themselves, for the Vaults were damp and cold.

It was with some surprise, then, that their sergeant found himself confronted with the spectacle of Vena and two lieutenants. He was only thankful that the flask of whisky had been emptied and put away.

'We didn't expect you back so soon, ma'am,' he said.

Vena took in his slightly red face, and the alcohol on his breath, and the two cell doors standing open behind him. She didn't say a word. She simply drew her pulser and shot the sergeant in the forehead.

'Sound the—' she began to say, but the final word was drowned out by a blast of sirens.

Fire: the castle was burning.

★ ★ ★

The alarm echoed through the passageway.

'They're coming!' said Steven, and he seemed very young in his panic. 'They're going to catch us and kill us!'

'Hush!' said Syl. 'It's the fire alarm.'

Seconds later, though, she heard another noise, a whooping rather than a siren. She exchanged a look with Ani. That was the general alarm. The escape had been discovered.

'What is it?' asked Paul.

'You need to go,' said Syl.

'Go?' he said, looking at the solid wall before them. 'Go where?'

Syl wouldn't have been able to find the door had Meia not described its position down to the last inch. It was marked by two thin white lines against the stone, little more than scratches. Syl took the sensor key from the pocket of her uniform and placed it beside the marks. There was a click, and a section of the stonework simply popped open; it was metal painted to look like brick, and the hole revealed was just large enough for one body to squeeze through, as long as the body in question wasn't large. Syl had no idea how or when it had been installed; all she knew was that it was Meia's work, and there were probably other boltholes like it scattered around the castle.

Outside, a man stood waiting on the rocks. He was tall, but slightly hunched. 'Trask!' said Paul.

'Come on, lads,' said Trask. 'No time to lose.'

Paul turned to Syl. 'What about our mother? She was arrested with us.'

'She's safe,' said Syl. Meia had told her that Mrs Kerr had been released shortly after her sons' capture. They were the prize, not her. Syl could only hope, for the boys' sake, that Meia had been telling the truth.

Steven was already scrambling through the hole, helped by Ani.

'Are you going to be all right?' asked Paul.

'Now that I know that you . . . people aren't going to be executed by my kind, yeah, I think we'll be okay,' said Syl. 'Whatever happens.'

'For what it's worth, we really didn't plant those bombs,' he said.

'I know. And I'm glad,' said Syl.

Paul grasped her arm. He leaned forward to say something, but no words came, and he was gone before Syl realised that he had kissed her.

CHAPTER 32

The castle grounds rang with the sound of sirens. Confusion reigned, just as Meia had intended. Illyri were falling over each other in an effort to establish not only what was happening, but who was responsible for dealing with it. Meanwhile, the entire castle force of Diplomat guards and Securitats, alerted by Vena, was trying to hunt the prisoners, but was being hampered by those who were trying to locate the fire. Meia, her cloak now discarded, moved through it all with clarity of purpose, while being careful not to draw undue attention to herself. She was under no illusions about how much time her little fire would buy all those involved in the escape bid. She needed to be sure that the human males were safely out of the castle, and Syl and Ani secure in their own rooms, before Vena and her underlings got a handle on the situation.

Still, she could not resist a small smile. She had just organised a major act of treason, and so far it had all gone rather well.

Syl and Ani were not smiling. They were about to undone by a stuck zipper.

The uniforms Meia had secured for them were larger than required, but it hadn't mattered because beneath them the two young Illyri were wearing their own casual clothes. The plan was to ditch the uniforms outside the castle walls, where the man tasked with getting the boys to safety would make sure that they were burned, destroying all traces of DNA that might be used to identify the perpetrators of the escape. Unfortunately, Meia's supply of Securitat uniforms was largely determined by whatever she had managed to strip from the dead or otherwise acquire. While Ani's uniform had opened easily, Syl's zip had caught on her own clothes underneath, and now the boys and the older human were gone, and had taken only Ani's suit and boots with them.

'You've busted the zip,' said Ani, gritting her teeth with the effort of trying to pull Syl's fastening down. 'You're clearly too fat for that suit.'

'I am not!' said Syl, tearing at the clasp.

And perhaps it was the fear, but Ani started to giggle, and couldn't stop.

'I can't do it,' she said. 'I'm serious.'

'You have to. If they find me like this, they'll know.'

A shadow fell across them, and a blade flashed in the dark.

'I could hear you from across the courtyard,' said Meia. 'You'll bring the whole Diplomatic Corps down on you.'

'We can't open the zipper,' said Ani.

Meia's knife solved the problem, slashing the material from the nape of Syl's neck to the base of her spine. Syl shrugged off the remains of the garment, removed two folded slippers from the pockets of her trousers, and slid her feet into them. Now, like Ani, she looked as though she had been disturbed by the sirens, and had left her rooms hurriedly to investigate. The problem was that those rooms were on the other side of the castle.

Meia blasted the remains of the uniform three times, kicking them into a pile so that the flames consumed them entirely. Then she spat on her fingers and removed the worst of the blood from the face of a grimacing Ani.

'Yuck,' said Ani.

'I didn't like it any more than you did,' said Meia. 'Now, heads down and come with me. If anyone stops us, say nothing. I'll do the talking.'

As it happened, they were stopped only once. A quartet of Securitats, anxious to avoid a pulse to the head, were hunting for the missing humans, and questioning everyone who crossed their path. There was no way to avoid them, so Meia did the very opposite: she went to them before they could come to her.

'You four,' she said. 'Come with me.'

'What?' said the leader, who bore the four gold flashes of a lieutenant on his collar, and clearly wasn't used to being ordered around by anyone with fewer than five flashes, never mind a female with no flashes at all.

'These are the children of the governor and General Danis,' said Meia. 'I'm taking them to safety in St Margaret's Chapel, and I need an escort.'

'We're searching for two escaped prisoners,' said the lieutenant. 'We don't have time for this.'

Meia spoke softly and carefully to him, the way she might have done to a very small child.

'There are two humans loose in the castle,' she said. 'If anything happens to the governor's daughter, those responsible will take the humans' place on the gallows in the morning. Do I make myself clear?'

The lieutenant swallowed involuntarily, as though he could already feel the noose tightening around his neck. He gestured to two of his guards.

'Escort the governor's daughter and her party to the chapel,' he said.

Meia nodded curtly. 'Thank you, Lieutenant. I'll be sure that the governor is informed of the assistance you offered.'

The two Securitats stayed with them until they reached the chapel door, whereupon Meia informed them that they could return to their duties. Once they were gone, she led Syl and Ani to the nave and, with their help, lifted a stone from the floor, revealing a set of steps winding into the darkness.

'Down you go,' she said.

Syl went first, then Ani. Meia brought up the rear, restoring the stone to its original position from below as she went. For a few seconds they were in total darkness, until Meia produced a torch and pointed it down a tunnel that was so low they had to bend almost double to make any progress, their backs nearly touching the roof and their necks straining. It seemed to take forever to make their way along it, Meia instructing them from behind to go left or right when necessary, until they came to another flight of stairs. There was just enough space for Meia to squeeze by Syl and Ani and ascend. She placed a finger to her lips, and all three listened carefully for any sound from above, but heard nothing. At last Meia pushed upwards, and a dim light was revealed to them from above. She vanished briefly, and then her voice told Syl and Ani that all was safe.

They found themselves in Meia's closet, making their way through her garments into the bedroom beyond. Syl and Ani collapsed in a heap on the floor. Their faces, hands and clothing were filthy. They had cuts and scrapes on their knuckles, and Syl found a gash on her head from where she had misjudged the height of the tunnel ceiling, but they were safe.

'Let's never do that again,' said Syl.

'Seconded,' said Ani.

On Meia's bed were two sets of nightclothes, one for each of them. Meia, as always, had planned ahead. Syl and Ani took it in turn to wash and change in the bathroom.

'That,' said Meia, when they looked respectable once again, 'was very, very impressive. Sloppy, and noisy, but impressive nonetheless.'

'Thank you,' said Ani. 'I think.'

'How many tunnels and escape routes do you have exactly?' asked Syl.

'Exactly?'

'Yes.'

'None of your business.'

'Oh. Fine.'

Meia relented.

'Some of them were here already,' she said. 'Most of them were constructed shortly after your father decided that the castle should be his base of operations. He gave me responsibility for its security systems. I just added a few safeguards of my own along the way.'

'They won't find out that we did it, will they?' said Ani.

'I disabled all the recording systems in the Vaults. There's nothing to prove you were ever there. As far as the guards are concerned, it was Vena who ordered the prisoners' removal, even if that has probably come as a surprise to Vena herself. Now, I'm going to escort you back to your rooms. Naturally, you say nothing of this to anyone. If you're questioned, I came to get you when the alarms sounded, and took you to the chapel until I determined that all was safe. Okay?'

Syl and Ani nodded.

'You did well,' said Meia. 'You didn't just save two lives tonight. You saved many. Remember that, in the days to come.'

And they did, both of them, even as they were running for their own lives.

CHAPTER 33

Paul wasn't sure where they were.

As soon as they were away from the castle, he and Steven were bundled into the back of a van by Trask. The front seats were cut off from the rest of the vehicle by a sheet of metal that had been welded to the sides, and there were two masked men waiting to help them up, although 'help' was probably not the most accurate way of putting it, given that the boys were dragged inside, told to keep their mouths shut and made to wear rough sacks over their heads to obscure their vision. The two men were unfamiliar to Paul, but he knew them for what they were: pure muscle – unsympathetic and unyielding. Their presence in the van gave him some idea of what was to come.

While they drove, Paul tried to keep track of the distance they might have travelled, and the route they might be taking, but quickly gave up. He knew that Trask would double back on himself, and make unnecessary stops and turns, just to confuse his passengers and, indeed, anyone who might be following them. Nevertheless, he didn't stay on the streets for too long. Even though a curfew was no longer in place, and there was plenty of traffic, the prisoners' escape would force the Illyri to start closing roads and searching vehicles. A system of retractable bollards was in place on all major roads in Edinburgh, capable of sealing off the main routes into and out of the city centre. Trask's priority would be to get beyond them and make for a safe house. Someone else would then ditch the van a few miles away, probably by sticking it in the back of a lorry or hiding it in a container, just in case the Illyri had spotted it on a security camera and had put out an alert. There were fewer cameras away from the city centre and the main roads – and those that the Illyri had tried to install were routinely vandalised – but there might well be drones or lurkers in the air, and they wouldn't know about it until the van was stopped, or a missile vaporised them.

The van came to a halt. Paul and Steven were hauled to their feet and guided out and down a flight of steps. A door opened and then closed again behind them. Paul smelled coffee and cigarettes, and a conversation suddenly ceased. He was forced into a chair, and the sack was removed from his head. He was in a near-empty basement. There was a battered table before him, and behind it two more chairs. Steven was gone. They would be questioned separately. That was standard practice. It was what Paul himself would have done had he been faced with two Resistance members who might have revealed secrets to the Illyri.

Trask took one chair, and one of the two masked men from the van took the other. The second masked man entered with three cups of coffee and a packet of Jaffa Cakes on a tray before leaving again.

'Help yourself,' said Trask.

Paul did. He was hungry, and the coffee smelled wonderful, even though it was cheap and nasty instant. But when he tried to lift his cup, his hand began to shake, and the coffee slopped over the sides. He felt sick, and he thought he might faint.

'You're all right, son,' said Trask. 'It's natural after what you've been through. Take a couple of deep breaths. You'll be fine.'

Beside him, the masked man took a Jaffa Cake and dunked it in his coffee. Trask looked at him peculiarly.

'You dunk Jaffa Cakes?' he said.

'I dunk anything.'

'They don't taste right when you dunk them. It's the sponge.'

The masked man nibbled on his soggy biscuit.

'Tastes fine to me.'

'There's something wrong with you.'

'Will you no give it a rest?' said the masked man. 'You're ruining it for me.'

Trask shook his head at Paul as if to say 'See what I have to put up with?'

'It's hard to get the staff these days,' said Paul, who was recovering himself with the help of sips of coffee and bites of biscuit.

'You shut up, or I'll do you,' said the masked man, the threat made only slightly less intimidating by the fact that he was waving half a Jaffa Cake. 'You'll be lucky to walk out of here without broken bones.'

Paul nodded. It was good cop, bad cop. In another room, Steven was doubtless experiencing the same routine.

'Our mum,' he said. 'Is she still in the city?'

He knew that the Securitats would come looking for her in the aftermath of her sons' escape. He didn't want her to suffer more because of what he and Steven had done.

'We moved her to Aberdeen earlier today, when we knew there was a chance of getting you back,' said Trask. 'Wouldn't want the Illyri taking out their temper on her, would we?'

Paul closed his eyes with relief.

Trask took a long gulp of coffee.

'Right then,' he said. 'Might as well get started.'

The debriefing went on for most of the night. It began gently, but grew tougher. Twice the masked man slapped Paul hard across the back of the head, causing Trask to tut-tut and tell him to take it easy, even while his eyes remained cold. In the end, it all came down to one question: *What did you tell them?*

Because everybody broke, in the end. They had seen Steven's fingers. He was just a boy, and he'd have told them something to make the pain end. Hell, a grown man would have confessed in order to stop it. It was understandable. It was okay. They just wanted to know what had been given away.

But Paul was good — better even than Trask suspected — and he had taught his brother well. They had fed the Illyri titbits of information, but it was all useless: the locations of safe houses long abandoned or burned to the ground; the names of operatives who were dead or had never existed; codes that were years old. It was the kind of information that a couple of low-level boys in the Resistance might have been expected to have overheard from others. Paul had drummed it all into his brother, going over it again and again as they lay in their adjoining beds at home each night.

If we're captured, this is what we say, and we never, ever deviate from it. Understand?

Yes, Paul. I understand.

And he had. He was screaming in pain, and there was nothing that his older brother could do to stop it, but still he gave them only what Paul had taught him to give. This is the safe house. This is the man who told us where to go. This is the code.

Useless: all of it useless.

From time to time, Trask or the other man would leave the room, and Paul knew that they were checking what he had told them against what his brother was saying. By the time Trask said, 'Enough,' Paul's head ached, he desperately needed to go to the bathroom, and he wanted to shower because he could smell himself. He was left alone while Trask and the masked man went outside to confer. When they returned after about twenty minutes, the second man was no longer masked. His head was shaved, and he wore a white T-shirt, exposing arms that were covered in tattoos. On his right forearm was a thistle that dripped blood from its leaves, the symbol of the Highland Resistance.

'You did good, laddie,' said Trask. 'You and your brother.'

'Sorry about the slaps,' said the tattooed man. 'You know how it is.'

Paul knew. He didn't have to like it, but he knew.

'This is Joe,' said Trask. 'Just Joe.'

Paul had heard the name. Just Joe was the Green Man's lieutenant, which made him the second-in-command of the Highland Resistance. The Highland Resistance was scattered, but disciplined; if it had a leader, it was the Green Man, and Just Joe stood at his right hand. He was the face of the Highland Resistance. The Green Man's identity was kept very secret, and there were those who said that he did not exist at all.

The Highlanders did not use surnames because no one wanted family members intimidated or friends tortured for information should their true identities get out. All that was widely known of Just Joe was that he had an army background, he was fearless and loyal, and completely ruthless, doing what needed to be done without flinching or sentiment. He was respected, yes. Feared? Absolutely.

Liked?

It had never occurred to anyone to try.

There were stories about Joe, of course. They all had stories. Joe's, it was whispered, was that he had once had a wife and a baby boy, and they'd lived together near Aviemore. Being a military man, Joe had been an early prisoner of the invading forces, and the tale went that his wife had received a visit from an Illyri intelligence officer while Joe was in jail. The officer told her that Joe had died in custody, and she and her child were to be thrown out of their house because there was evidence that her husband had been conspiring against the Illyri, and the property of all conspirators was automatically forfeit. It was an act of casual cruelty, committed because, it was said, this particular intelligence officer had developed an early liking for human women, and Joe's wife was exceptionally pretty. She was also very delicate – physically, emotionally and psychologically. The intelligence officer told her that he might be able to find a way to look after her and her child, in return for certain favours. He gave her until the morning to think about it. She didn't need that long. She killed herself before midnight. They'd shown Joe pictures of the bodies of his wife and child beside each other on the bed, their faces transformed by the gas. It was only later that he found out why she had done it.

The intelligence officer vanished from Fort William the following year, on a clear, cool March evening not long after Just Joe's release from internment. His head was found impaled on a fence post a week later. The rest of him was never discovered, although the story went that it was fed to pigs. His head had still been attached to his body at that point.

He couldn't have screamed otherwise.

But it was just a story, although it might have explained why Joe's small guerrilla fiefdom in the Highlands was known as Camp Glynis – the name of his Welsh wife, murmured the gossips, or perhaps it was just because Glynis meant 'narrow valley' in his wife's tongue. Anyway, it no longer mattered. Camp Glynis, like Glynis herself, was now only a memory. Joe's band had allied itself to the troops of the Green Man many years earlier. The Green Man had promised Joe that more Illyri blood would be spilled if they fought together than if they fought alone, and he had kept his promise.

'You'll be going to the Highlands,' Trask told Paul, 'you and Steven. It won't be safe for you in the city. The Illyri will tear it apart looking for you.'

Paul nodded. He had guessed as much.

'The Green Man has also decided that a little more cooperation with us city boys might not go amiss,' continued Trask.

And then Paul understood: somehow this was related to the attack on Birdoswald, and it was the Highlanders who must have been responsible for it. The Highlanders had never struck so far south before, but they were still the only ones outside Edinburgh equipped to carry out such an assault. Clearly someone in the Edinburgh Resistance had let the Highlanders know that they couldn't simply start blowing up Illyri bases outside their own patch without first asking permission. It wasn't polite.

'You're to be our ambassador to the Highlanders. I'm sure that pleases you as much as it will please them. You can get up from that chair now. There's a hot shower waiting for you, and clean clothes, and a proper meal before you leave.'

But Paul didn't move. He wanted to. He wanted it all so badly: the shower, the clothes, all of it, but it wasn't time, not yet.

'I have more to say,' he said.

Trask looked puzzled, and Just Joe scowled in a manner that suggested some more slaps might be on their way.

'You haven't asked me what we found under Knutter's shop,' said Paul. 'I have to tell you about the bodies.'

CHAPTER 34

Syl slept the sleep of the dead that night. She would have laughed in disbelief had anyone told her earlier that in the wake of the successful rescue of two human prisoners from the vaults – an act of treason that might well be punishable by death – she would rest deeply, but she did. She went to her bed exhausted and strangely exhilarated, with the memory of a kiss brushed softly on her lips.

She had been kissed before. The previous summer she had engaged in a brief, inquisitive romance with Harnur, one of her classmates, before Harnur's father had been transferred to Bolivia, a transfer that might not have been entirely unconnected with Governor Andrus's suspicion that Harnur had feelings for his beloved daughter. In truth, Syl had been more intrigued by the notion of being in love, and the highs and lows that might go with it, rather than holding any particular feelings for Harnur himself, who had been clumsy, and self-absorbed, and a little too free with his hands for Syl's liking. If her father had found out just how free he had been, Harnur's own father might have found himself posted somewhere even worse than Bolivia: Kabul, for example, or Lagos.

Syl was sleeping so soundly that at first the banging on her door was incorporated into a dream of blood and water, the sounds becoming the beating of a great heart hidden beneath the earth, a heart that beat in time with the rhythms of her own. Only when the door burst open and lights shone in her face did she wake up. Vena advanced towards her bed and Syl knew that she was lost.

★ ★ ★

A quartet of Securitats stood outside Ani's door. Their sergeant swiped his skeleton key through the electronic lock, but nothing happened. Instead, he was forced to resort to more old-fashioned methods. It took him three kicks to break the door down. By the time he succeeded, the window was open, and Ani was long gone.

Alerted by the noise, Lord Andrus was already in the corridor as Syl was escorted from her room, her hands cuffed behind her back, her feet bare against the cold stone. He wore his red dressing gown, and his hair was tousled. With him came two of the castle guards who always remained posted at his door, and behind them Syl saw Althea and Meia. Immediately she looked away from her father's spymistress, afraid that even a lingering glance might reveal Meia's involvement to Vena. This was about the prisoners' escape. It had to be, even though Vena had remained entirely silent during Syl's arrest. If Meia was still free, then the Securitats did not yet know of her part in what had occurred.

'Father!' cried Syl.

'What is the meaning of this?' said Lord Andrus. 'Let my daughter go!'

But now more heavily armed Securitats had been summoned, and among them was Lord Consul Gradus. Syl noticed that he was fully dressed, even though the clock in her room read 4.15 a.m. when she had been dragged from her bed. He must have known in advance about her arrest; even Vena would not have dared to come for the governor's daughter in the dead of night without the agreement of the Lord Consul. Meia had a blast pistol in her hand, and Lord Andrus's guards carried blast rifles, but they were outnumbered, and the possibility of hitting Syl if they fired was too great to risk a gun battle.

'I'm afraid it won't be possible to release her just yet,' said Gradus. His hands were buried in the sleeves of his white robes. Only his head remained exposed. It was as though a great white slug were swallowing him, slowly consuming him from the legs up.

'Gradus, you overstep your authority here,' warned Andrus.

'I think not,' said Gradus. 'I *am* the authority here, and your daughter is a traitor.'

Lord Andrus looked at Syl in disbelief. 'What is this, Syl? What are they saying?'

Vena stepped forward. She held a plated millipede on the palm of her right hand. The tiny camera on its head looked like a dewdrop. She called up a screen, and Syl saw life-sized flickering versions of herself and Ani, dressed in Securitat uniforms, standing at a cell door, then stepping back to allow Paul and Steven Kerr to emerge. The film lasted for only a few seconds, but it was enough to damn them.

As the images vanished, Vena smiled at Meia.

'Spies are not the only ones who find lurkers useful,' she said. She displayed the little anthropod for a second longer, than crushed it in her fist.

Meia did not reply, but the look on her face left no doubt that, like the unfortunate millipede, Vena would not survive long in Meia's hands if the opportunity presented itself.

'Your daughter and her friend conspired in the escape of the terrorists,' said Gradus. 'We are not yet certain of how they fooled the guards, but rest assured that we will find out.'

But Andrus was not listening. He only had eyes for his daughter.

'Syl, is this true?'

Syl tried to answer, but she could not. Instead, to her shame, she began to cry, and she could not stop the tears from flowing, even as she was led away.

Ani flitted through the castle courtyard, moving from shadow to shadow. She had felt the Securitats coming. She had dreamed them, and then the dream became real, but she was practised at slipping from her bedroom unnoticed, and had become adept at using a knotted rope to climb from the first-floor window to the ground. When she heard the door burst open, she was already halfway to St Margaret's Chapel, and by the time the alarm was raised, she was lifting the flagstone behind the altar and lowering herself into the tunnel. There had been no time to find a torch, and so she was in total darkness as she started to make her way, by memory and touch, back to the one Illyri who might be able to help her: Meia. She already knew that it was too late to warn Syl. It seemed to Ani that revealing the extent of her gift to Meia had somehow increased its potency, for she had been subduing it before in order to keep it a secret from others. Now she sensed Syl's anguish, but there was nothing she could do for her, not yet. Later, perhaps, but her own priority was to stay out of the clutches of the Securitats, and find the spymistress.

As the darkness pressed in upon her, Ani reflected that she had never liked Meia, had never trusted her because she could never sense her thoughts. Meia just always smelled of trouble and deceit.

All things considered, Ani concluded, she had probably been right.

Syl was not taken to the Vaults, or to the Securitats' interrogation rooms, or to any of the places usually reserved for prisoners. Instead, she found herself once again in Syrene's chambers, this time alone. The light was dim and the air was strangely scented, an aroma at once familiar yet completely alien, an inherited memory given form. An enormous vase of flowers, the likes of which she had never seen before, stood on a polished oak table, their curling, tangled heads glowing softly in the moonlight, their outsized stamens drooping with thick, wet, heady pollen.

'Are they not beautiful?' said a silken voice, and there was a movement from the shadows at the back of the room. Syl had not heard Syrene enter. The door had remained closed. Perhaps Meia was not the only one with knowledge of the castle's secret ways, but Syl suspected that Syrene had no need of tunnels in order to move without being seen. She recalled the image of the ghost of the Red Witch standing over her, and her temples tingled unpleasantly at the memory.

'No,' she said. 'I don't think they're beautiful at all.'

'They are called avatis blossoms,' said Syrene. 'I grew them on the journey to Earth. They are of Illyr, just as you are. I felt that I needed a reminder of my home on this alien world. Perhaps, had you been surrounded by similar tokens, you might not have found yourself in this unfortunate situation. It strikes me that your father has fallen too much in love with this planet. It is he who has made a traitor of you. He planted a seed in your heart, and from it grew treachery.'

'No,' said Syl. 'That's not true.'

Syrene advanced. She raised a hand, as though to stroke the avatis. Instantly the heads of the flowers closed, and a puff of foul-smelling gas erupted from its leaves.

'It's a defence mechanism,' said Syrene. 'All species have one. The avatis is trying to protect itself, even though it's already dying. It was dying from the moment it was cut and placed in this vase.'

She turned to face Syl.

'Your father too is dying. He was dying from the instant he fell in love with this planet. Away from the soil of Illyr, his influence and power have slowly waned, even though he does not realise it. Now his own daughter has dealt him the fatal blow.'

Syl's cheeks burned. She lowered her eyes. There was a truth in what Syrene was saying, a terrible, humiliating truth. Syl had fatally undermined her father by committing an act of treason, even though she had believed it to be the right thing to do.

'My husband believes that your father planned the escape of the humans, and somehow contrived to have you do his dirty work,' said Syrene. 'Is this true?'

'No,' said Syl. She breathed deeply. She would not cry again. She had cried enough that night.

'But you're just a child! You could not have planned this venture alone.'

'I did.'

'Aided by your friend Ani.'

'It was my idea. I forced her to do it.'

'Really? From what I hear of your friend, I doubt that she could be forced to do anything she did not want to. But somebody aided you. Who gassed the guards?'

'We did.'

'Come, come. And you disabled the main surveillance system too?'

'Yes.'

'I should like to know how you did that. If we were to take you to the control room, perhaps you could show us.'

'No,' said Syl. 'I won't. It's a secret.'

'Oh! A secret? Of course.'

Syrene went to the drinks cabinet by the window. Among the bottles of whisky and wine, there now rested a number of curved decanters of liquids in various hues of amber that seemed lit from within. Syl had seen such bottles before. They contained Illyri cremos, a drink made from berries grown on Taleth, a distant moon of the Illyri system. It grew darker as it aged, and some of these bottles contained cremos that was very dark, and thus very old, and very valuable. Even Syl's father – an Illyri so in love with Earth and its treasures that he owned vineyards of his own in France and Spain – prized cremos.

Syrene poured two glasses from the darkest of the bottles, and handed one to Syl.

'No, thank you.'

'Drink it,' said Syrene. 'Don't be ignorant, child. You could fill this glass with diamonds from Earth, and it would not be worth as much as the liquid that it now contains.'

Syl took the glass. As she raised it to her lips, she smelled cloves and cinnamon, and hints of plum and cherry, but she did not share this with Syrene. She did not think the Red Witch would find it amusing that the only points of reference she could find for the delicate scent of fine cremos were entirely terrestrial in origin. She sipped the drink. It tasted like she imagined sunset might: a deep, red, beautiful summer sunset.

'Sit,' said Syrene.

Syl did as she was told. Once again she was facing the Red Witch across this table.

'Vena wants you to be handed over to her for interrogation,' said Syrene. 'Marshal Sedulus feels the same way. I don't think you'd enjoy their company very much.'

'No,' Syl admitted.

'I wouldn't like it very much either,' said Syrene. 'You know that

Vena was rejected by the Sisterhood? A streak of cruelty that we found unappealing manifested itself during her novitiate. Cruelty is always a sign of weakness, and the Sisterhood has no time for weakness. You, on the other hand, are not cruel, and not weak. Tell me truly: why did you free those boys?'

'Because I did not want to see them die,' said Syl.

'Even though they had committed an atrocity?'

'They did not do it.'

'How do you know?'

'They told me so.'

'Before or after you rescued them?'

'After.'

'And you believed them? Why?'

'Because they had no reason to lie, not then.'

Syrene nodded. 'Clever girl, and merciful. But, innocent or guilty, Sedulus and Vena wanted them dead. Sedulus wishes to be unleashed on humanity. He thinks that by killing and tormenting, he will bend mankind to his will. Vena is his puppet, and she dances at his bidding. They are grotesquely alike. In the plans for the hanging, it had to be explained to Vena why it was important to know the height and weight of the person to be killed in order to calculate the length of rope required to break the neck. Vena could not understand why those boys should not have simply been left to strangle slowly.'

'But you wanted them to die too,' said Syl. 'You and your husband.'

'Because it served our ends.'

'Which are?'

'Which are none of your business, but there is a difference between putting someone to death and making him suffer. Death can be painful, or relatively painless. I prefer the painless option. I am not cruel.'

The thought flashed through Syl's head before she could stop it – *Oh, but you are cruel, and crueller than a thug like Vena could ever be, because you're intelligent, and calculating. Vena is cruel because she's flawed deep inside, but you're cruel because you choose to be* – and she saw it mirrored on Syrene's face, and the Red Witch smiled at the truth of it.

'Tell me,' said Syrene, 'how did you fool those guards into releasing the humans into your care?'

'We bluffed them.'

Syrene waved a hand in dismissal, as though the lie were little more than an insect to be swatted away.

'They claimed – or at least the three left alive claimed – that Vena herself came and took them away,' said Syrene. 'They looked at you and your friend, and they saw Vena and a sergeant. That's not bluffing, but something much deeper. That's a gift, and you do not have it, because I've looked inside you.'

There was a lie there: Syl was certain of it. Syrene had indeed *tried* to look inside her, but she had blocked her. Meia had taught her well. Now, as she listened to Syrene, she began to build her wall again, hiding her secrets from the Red Witch's prying intelligence.

'Oh, you have talents, and you're stronger than anyone suspects, but to dissemble in that way is beyond you,' said Syrene. 'Which leaves your friend Ani to do the hard work. Her, or someone else of whom I do not yet know. I suspect Ani; after all, she had already fled when the Securitats came for her, and they were silent in their approach. She knew that they were coming. She *sensed* it.'

'I don't know what you're talking about,' said Syl.

Something flashed in Syrene's eyes. Her hand tightened on her glass, and the delicate crystal seemed on the verge of shattering under the pressure, but the Red Witch, either out of concern for its contents or a reluctance to demonstrate such a public show of anger, relented.

'Don't lie to me,' she said evenly. 'I don't like it.'

Trowel. Cement. Brick. Position. Trowel . . .

'Tell me!'

Cement. Brick. Position. Trowel. Cement . . .

'Oh, you little fool,' said Syrene.

She stood. As if by silent summons, the door to her chambers opened, and Vena stood in the gap, waiting.

'This is your last night on Earth,' said Syrene. 'You will never see it again.'

Syl rose from her chair. Slowly she tipped her glass, and the valuable cremos spilled on Syrene's ancient rug, damaging it irreparably.

'I will look inside your head and find out what you're hiding,' said Syrene, 'even if I have to use a surgeon's scalpel to do it.'

She motioned to Vena.

'Take her away.'

CHAPTER 35

Syl was taken to one of the windowless cells in the vaults so recently vacated by Paul and Steven. She was given a one-piece suit, and her nightclothes were taken away. She was provided with a mattress, a blanket and a jug of water, and left alone with her thoughts. This time, Vena took upon herself the duties of guarding the prisoner, assisted by twelve of her most loyal underlings. Clearly the Securitats were anticipating some attempt to free Syl, because they were armed with both pulsers and heavy-duty blast rifles, and their uniforms had been exchanged for battle armour. Vena informed her that she would be permitted no visitors, and no one beyond Vena's cohort, not even the Grand Consul, was permitted to approach her cell, on pain of death.

'What will happen to me?' asked Syl.

'You are to be taken offworld tomorrow,' said Vena. 'Eventually, in accordance with the requirements of Illyri justice, you will be tried and, I have no doubt, found guilty of treason.'

She paused at the door.

'I do have one question for you,' she said.

Syl waited. She could have told Vena exactly what to do with her question, but she did not. She dreaded the thought of the cell door closing. While it was still open, there was hope: hope of rescue, of her father coming to release her, of Meia mounting some kind of daring escape bid just as had been done for the humans. They would not fear Vena's guns. They would not let Syl be taken through the wormhole, to be lost in the vastness of the universe.

But her father . . .

Her father was ashamed of her. She had seen it in his eyes. His own daughter was a traitor, and she would be made to face the full force of the law. He could not condone or excuse treason, even by his own blood. If an exception were made for her, then the law would be meaningless. And if – or rather *when* – she was found guilty, her father's career would be over. She had ruined him through her actions.

'My question is this,' said Vena. 'You had everything, but you threw it away, and for humans. Why?'

Syl stared her straight in the face.

'So that I could look at myself in the mirror,' she replied, 'and know that I was not like you.'

'I always hated you,' said Vena.

'I know,' said Syl.

'And you always hated me.'

'No,' said Syl, her voice almost bored. 'I pitied you. You hurt, and you torture, and you kill, but you do it to feed the rage and pain inside you; destroying the lives of others is easier than facing the emptiness of your own. You're nothing to me.'

Vena's eyes glittered with pure, vengeful malice.

'The Grand Consul wants you to hang,' she said, 'you and your friend. He thinks it will be an apt punishment for depriving the gallows of two lives. What the Grand Consul wants, he gets, but when you hang, it will be in the hold of a starship far, far from here, and I will be in charge of the rope. I'll make it short, and you'll dance for me. You and Ani will dance on air until your faces turn black and your lungs explode. I will drive the pity from you. I will demonstrate what it's worth. Afterwards, your bodies will be burned, and there will be nothing left to show that you ever existed. I will erase every trace of you and I will watch all those who ever loved you wither and die. *That* is nothingness, Syl. I'll give you a taste of it now, so you can see how you like it.'

Vena closed the door, and seconds later the light in the cell was extinguished, leaving Syl in total darkness.

★ ★ ★

Danis held Lord Andrus back. He was thankful that the governor was not armed. If he were, Meia would be dead. Not that Danis would have minded particularly; his own daughter was also missing, and Meia was to blame.

'*Your* doing?' shouted Andrus. 'You are responsible for this?'

His face was mottled with rage, but there was also hurt and pain. Lord Andrus had been twice betrayed this day: first by his daughter, and now by his spymistress.

Meia showed no fear.

'The two humans could not be allowed to die,' she said simply.

'And why not? Who are you to decide who lives or dies on this world?'

'Who are you to do so?' replied Meia, and even Danis seemed taken aback at her insolence. 'Who is Gradus, or Syrene, to take the lives of children? Is that what we have become: child-killers who sacrifice the lives of the young to further our own political ends?'

'So you went behind my back? You drew my daughter, and Danis's child, into your scheme? You have put both their lives at risk, Meia!'

'I forced them to do nothing,' said Meia. 'They chose to act because those who should have acted stood idly by. When adults would hang children, perhaps it must be left to children to stop them. Syl and Ani were prepared to do what their parents would not.'

'You are beyond arrogant, Meia,' said Danis. 'My daughter is not one of your playthings.'

'You have no idea what your daughter can do,' said Meia. 'She can cloud minds. She is a natural psychic.'

'What are you talking about?' asked Danis, but he could not hold Meia's gaze.

'You knew,' said Meia.

'I knew nothing.'

'Then you suspected, but you and your wife turned a blind eye to it. You have grown too set in your ways, Danis. You're afraid to look closely at what you don't understand.'

Now it was Lord Andrus's turn to hold Danis back. To an uninvolved observer, it might have looked as though they were engaged in an awkward waltz.

'Meia, you go too far,' said Andrus. 'You have been loyal to me for so long, but this will not stand. Tell me why I should not hand you over to Gradus in return for mercy for Syl and Ani.'

'Because you know there will be no mercy,' said Meia. 'Gradus means to destroy you, and he will succeed if you continue to act as you do. The old president is dead, and the new one has the Sisterhood whispering in his ear. Your authority on this world has been completely undermined, and the execution of those boys would have destroyed it utterly with the violence that would have followed. The Earth would undoubtedly have risen up in outright war against us, and Gradus would have found a way to blame you for the consequences of his actions.

'Now Gradus has your daughter, and he means to take her offworld. Once he has her on his ship, you will never see her again. Her trial will be held in secret, and you will learn of her fate in a letter signed by Gradus's hand. The wormholes have given the Diplomatic Corps an entire universe in which to hide that which it does not wish to be found. It has bases on worlds that do not even possess names. If your daughter is not executed in secret, she will end her days in a cell on one of those worlds. Eventually, too, they will find the general's daughter, and she will share the same fate.'

Andrus slumped against Danis, so that the old general was forced to hold him steady. The events of the past days had sapped the governor's strength, and the thought of being deprived of his daughter forever was more than he could bear. He collapsed in a chair and covered his eyes with his right hand.

'So my daughter will be lost to me,' he said, 'unless I am willing to go to war with Gradus, and the Corps.'

'She is not yet lost,' said Meia, 'and war may yet be avoided. It is imperative that Syl does not leave this planet, but she is closely guarded, and the Securitats will shoot anyone who approaches her cell. We will have one chance to save her, but it's dangerous, and it may place her in the hands of those who have as much cause to hate her as Gradus does.'

'What are you proposing?' said Andrus.

'If Syl is to be transported offworld on a shuttle, it is possible that I could access its systems and attempt an override while it is in the air, redirecting it to a safe location,' said Meia. 'The risk involved is an obvious one: Syl's guards could be under orders to execute her if any attempt at rescue is made, and an override would alert them and give them time to kill her.'

At the mention of killing Syl, Andrus flinched involuntarily in pain.

'The shuttle in the courtyard,' continued Meia, 'is a vessel of the Sisterhood, and its systems are protected, but it is unlikely that it will be used to take Syl to Gradus's ship. Syrene will not allow her personal shuttle, with all its comforts and secrets, to be used as prisoner transport, and as long as she stays, so too will her shuttle. That means they will use a shuttle from either the Diplomat or Securitat pool. I'm already monitoring their systems to see which will be chosen.'

'Well?' said Danis. 'What options does that leave us with? You've just told us that they'll kill Syl if we try to override the systems.'

'I'm proposing that we crash the shuttle,' said Meia.

There was an incredulous silence in the room, until Andrus eventually managed to speak.

'With Syl on board?'

'With Syl on board. If we can disable one engine, the shuttle's automatic safety procedures will be activated immediately, and the system will assist the pilots in making an emergency landing. The dangers are obvious, but shuttles have glided safely to ground with minimal engine power. Even an inexperienced pilot can deal with the loss of one engine. The shuttle will have to follow the standard route for all craft going offworld, so we know where it will be headed, and we can pinpoint where it will come down to within a few square miles. We can then arrange for Syl to be picked up, and hide her from Gradus until we figure out our next move.'

'Crashing a shuttle with my daughter on board is a risk I'm not prepared to take,' said Andrus.

'That's not even the greatest risk involved,' said Meia. 'The shuttle will have to come down somewhere out of the immediate reach of the Corps and its Securitats. As soon as it hits the ground, its emergency locator beacon will send out a signal. It should be possible to disable it in advance – after all, if I'm sabotaging the shuttle, I should be able to wire the beacon so that it blows with the engine – but it still won't take long to locate the wreckage. We won't be able to shadow the shuttle with a Military craft because the crew will be scanning for any sign of trouble. Ideally, then, we'll need someone on the ground to find Syl and keep her safe until we can get to her.'

For once, Danis was ahead of the governor.

'The standard route for craft heading offworld is north-west to Iceland,' he said. 'You're talking about crashing an Illyri ship carrying the daughter of the governor of Europe in the Highlands?'

'That's right,' said Meia.

'Which is hostile territory.'

'Yes.'

'And who will we have on the ground in the Highlands?'

Meia spoke as though the answer were so obvious as to not even be worth voicing.

'Highlanders.'

Meia returned to her chambers. It had been all she could do not to show weakness in the face of Andrus's anger, because weakness was contagious, and she had to make the governor and Danis believe in her if she was to rescue Syl. But she knew that her relationship with Andrus had been damaged forever by what had occurred, and even securing Syl would not return it to its previous state. In a way, Meia's actions, like Syl's, had cost her the trust of the only father figure she had ever known.

Her closet door opened, and Ani emerged.

'I'm getting tired of hiding,' she said.

'I'm getting tired of having you in my closet,' said Meia. 'I value my privacy.'

'Oh, well excuse me,' said Ani. 'Sorry for imposing, given that it's your fault I'm on the run to begin with.'

There was a knock on the door. Ani began to slide back into the closet, but Meia indicated that she should stay where she was and remain quiet. A blade appeared in the spymistress's right hand as she approached the door.

'Who's there?' said Meia.

'It's me – Althea.'

Meia opened the door and admitted Syl's governess. Althea nodded curtly at Ani, seemingly unsurprised to discover her in Meia's rooms. While Althea was fond of Ani in a vaguely forbidding way, she regarded her as a wild child who needed to be tamed. She had largely given up trying to persuade Syl to keep her distance from the young Illyri; she was wise enough to know that her own fondness for Syl sometimes blinded her to the fact that it was Syl, not Ani, who generally took the lead. Ani's enthusiasm fed Syl's fire, but it would still have burned merrily, even without Ani.

'I see that you're in trouble again,' said Althea.

'It's a misunderstanding,' said Ani.

'It usually is where you're concerned: a misunderstanding of what is and is not appropriate behaviour for a young Illyri.'

'Right. Rescuing young people from the gallows is bad, then? I'll add it to the list.'

Althea rolled her eyes.

'You summoned me?' she said to Meia.

'I did,' said Meia. 'Syl has been arrested and is charged with treason. She is to be taken offworld tomorrow to be tried and, presumably, executed.'

Althea, normally so teacherly, so precise, so formal, covered her face with her hands and slid to the floor. A wretched wail escaped from between her fingers, a sound that was part animal and pure agony.

Meia watched her with something vaguely like pity on her cool face. Ani looked away, embarrassed and affected by the older woman's grief.

Althea's wail turned to words, short and panicked. 'No, not my Syl. Never Syl. No.'

Meia tapped her foot impatiently.

'Stop this, Althea,' she said finally. 'If we don't act immediately, she will be beyond our reach.'

Althea looked up, her expression that of a drowning woman being thrown a rope.

'I'll do anything, Meia. You know it to be so.'

Meia nodded. 'I have another errand for you. I would go myself, but I have urgent work to do.'

'Where am I going?'

'Where you usually go on these occasions: to visit our friends in the Resistance,' said Meia. 'Oh, and there's some more bad news.'

'Which is?' said Althea, her tone making it clear that there was already quite enough bad news to be getting along with. Nevertheless, Meia found the one thing certain to make the situation even worse.

She smiled grimly.

'You're taking Ani with you.'

CHAPTER 36

The morning dawned bleak and dark, and the rain followed soon after, driven by a cold wind from the north. To those in the castle who loved Syl, it seemed that the world was already in mourning for her.

Syl had somehow managed to sleep a little, but when she did wake up there seemed to be no difference between sleeping and waking, and the blackness pressed in upon her so that she felt she could not breathe. She panicked, and had to force herself to calm down. She tried not to think of her father, or Ani, or Althea. The thought of those who loved her brought no consolation. Instead, she only grew more conscious of the fact that she was to be taken from them, and might never see them again. But even in the midst of her own fear, she worried too about the human brothers. She hoped desperately that they had made it to safety, that this had not all been in vain.

Eventually the door to her cell opened, but she had grown so accustomed to the dark that she had to cover her face with her arm until the light from the corridor, dim though it was, stopped hurting her eyes. The Securitat who entered was only a few years older than herself. He carried a tray in his hands. On it was a plastic mug of coffee, a plastic plate with buttered toast and a small plastic cup filled with slices of apple that were already turning brown. The guard wrinkled his nose as he entered the cell. The smell from the chemical toilet – which was little more than a bucket of blue water – was strong.

The Securitat put the tray on a little table built into the wall, then stepped back. Two other guards stood at the door in case Syl decided to make a break for freedom.

'I can't eat in the dark,' said Syl.

The guard looked to his colleagues for advice. One of them nodded.

'We'll turn your light back on,' he said.

'What time is it?'

'Just after six.'

She tried to think of something else to ask him. After her night in the dark, she wanted someone to talk to. She did not want to be alone again yet. The guard seemed to sense this, because his face softened and he said, 'Is there anything you need?'

Syl was grateful for this small gesture of kindness, this little act of generosity that cost so little but meant so much.

'A book,' she said. 'And perhaps some water with which to wash myself.'

'I'll see what I can do,' said the guard.

He stepped out of the cell and the door closed behind him, but, as promised, the light came on. Syl ate her breakfast, and after a while the guard returned with a volume of poetry and prose that was given to every Illyri soldier, a basin of hot water, a towel and a small bar of soap. Syl thanked him, and he acknowledged her gratitude with a tightening of his mouth that might have passed for a smile.

When the door closed again, Syl removed her clothing and washed herself. The cameras in the cells had been restored to power after Meia's sabotage, so Syl knew they would be watching her, but she did not care. She wanted to be clean. If there was any shame, it was on their part for spying on her. She felt better for bathing, and when the guard came to retrieve the basin and towel, he also removed the chemical toilet and replaced it with a new one.

She did not see the guard again. Later she discovered that his name was Feryn, and that when Vena learned of his kindness to her, she had him relieved of his duties and sent offworld to fight and die alongside one of the Punishment Battalions. Another, she thought, her heart leaden in her chest; there is yet another that I have destroyed by my actions.

She tried to read, and the hours seemed to pass both slowly and yet far too quickly. When the cell door eventually opened again, it revealed Vena standing with a phalanx of Securitats. In her right hand she held a pair of heavy magnetised cuffs, and in her left a printed document from which she began to read.

"'By order of Grand Consul Gradus, representative on Earth of the Council of Government of Illyr, the juvenile Syl Hellais is to be taken to the Diplomatic vessel *Aurion*, and thence to a location yet to be decided, there to await trial on charges of treason.'"

She rolled up the paper, and handed it to the nearest guard.

'The prisoner will stand,' she said.

Syl stood. She stretched out her hands to accept the cuffs, her head held high, and Vena slotted them on to her wrists. As soon as they were in place, she activated them, and Syl's hands were pulled together by the powerful magnets. The control panel for the cuffs was hooked to Vena's belt. She tapped a red button, and Syl's body jerked as a jolt of electricity shot through her system.

'Just making sure that they're working,' said Vena.

The charge hadn't been strong, but it was unpleasant. Syl knew that the cuffs were capable of delivering a series of far greater shocks. In the event of a prisoner attempting to escape the shocks could even be fatal.

Syl was led from her cell, her grey prisoner's suit standing out against the dark uniforms of the guards like the lighter stamen of a black-petalled flower. As they reached the courtyard, she saw a small gathering of figures to her right. Her father was among them, flanked by Balen on one side and by Danis and his wife on the other. Even the old tutor, Toris, had come to witness her departure, but there was no sign of Althea, or Meia.

Across from her father stood Syrene, her face obscured once again by her veil, and Grand Consul Gradus. Gradus was not dressed in his usual robes, but wore instead a wine-red suit over a rose white shirt, and a leather overcoat to protect him from the rain, even though a pair of sub-consuls stood behind him and his wife, holding umbrellas over their heads. Behind them, a shuttle waited, its engines already humming in anticipation.

Lord Andrus, his head bare, stepped forward. Vena glanced at Gradus, who gave a small nod of consent.

Andrus embraced his daughter. Syl wanted to hug him back, but the cuffs would not permit it. In fact they seemed to grow heavier, dragging her hands down with them. She did not know if it was purely psychological, or if Vena had somehow adjusted them as another small humiliation.

'Syl,' said Andrus. 'Oh, Syl.'

She wept against his shoulder. 'I'm sorry,' she said. 'I didn't mean to hurt you. I thought I was doing the right thing.'

And her father surprised her by whispering, 'You were, Syl. It was the right thing.'

He kissed her cheek, and held her face in his hands.

'Do you remember what I told you about shuttle trips?' he said.

'What?' said Syl, genuinely puzzled. They might never see one another again, and now her father was talking about shuttle trips.

'You always belt up,' he continued. 'Always.'

'Right,' said Syl. 'I will.'

'Make sure you do,' said Andrus. 'One never knows what might happen.'

He kissed her again, and then Vena stepped in and pulled her away. Syl tried to look back to see her father as she was led to the ship, but the guards had closed ranks once again. She caught one final glimpse of him as she walked up the gangway to the shuttle doors. He raised a hand in farewell, but she could only try to smile as her heart broke.

The shuttle was comfortable but basic inside. Syl's wrists remained cuffed. Her hands were pulled to the left as soon as she sat, lodging against a strip of metal in the bulkhead. It was clear that this seat had not been chosen casually for her; it was a prisoner's seat. The guard made a cursory check of the cuffs before taking a chair across from her.

'My belt,' said Syl. 'Can you strap me in? Please?'

The guard did as she asked, although he allowed his hands to brush heavily against her breasts as he secured the straps. It was an indication of how much had changed for her. Twenty-four hours earlier, even Gradus himself would not have dared to touch her that way. Now she was a traitor; the entire Diplomatic Corps could have taken turns to abuse her and few would have objected. The guard's insidious contact brought home her vulnerability with terrifying force. He returned to his own seat, a self-satisfied little smile on his face. The two pilots were already in their cabin, but Syl could only see the backs of their heads. She heard soft footsteps behind her, and a final passenger entered. To her surprise, it was Grand Consul Gradus. He gave a small mocking bow before seating himself.

'I have business on board the *Aurion*,' he said, 'and I want to see you safely on board the linkship.'

Linkships were often used for transporting small numbers of people or essential equipment and supplies through wormholes. Shuttles, like the one on which Syl now found herself, were unsuited to the purpose, as they were too easily affected by the action of the negative matter used to keep the mouths of the wormholes open. In the early days of the Illyri conquest, a number of heavy cruisers had brushed against the sides of wormholes, causing the destruction of the vessels in two cases, and the collapse of the wormhole itself in a third, not to mention the loss of thousands of lives. Even now, after all that had been learned, wormhole pilots still needed to be the most skilled of their kind, and most of the senior Illyri preferred not to travel through wormholes more often than was absolutely necessary.

'And where do I go from there?' asked Syl.

'The battleship *Vracon* will be waiting on the other side of the wormhole,' said Gradus. 'It will transport you to Eriba 256, where you'll enter another wormhole, and then another. The whole universe is ours in which to hide you from those who would rescue you.'

'And my trial?'

'I didn't realise you were in such a hurry to be found guilty,' said Gradus. He made himself more comfortable in his seat as the pitch of the engines rose.

Syl instinctively looked down as the shuttle ascended. She tried to pick out her father, but the angle was wrong, and now Edinburgh was spread out beneath them and she wondered if Paul was way down there, wondered if he saw her ship, if he thought about her at all, if he felt a little of the tug she felt deep within, like a string being pulled tauter and tauter as she moved further and further away from the only world she'd ever called home.

Somehow she found the courage to ask her next question.

'Are you going to have me killed?'

'Not yet, and perhaps not ever,' he replied. 'If I kill you, I no longer have any control over your father. As long as I have you, and you're alive, your father and those loyal to him will be more malleable. Now keep quiet, child, and leave me to my thoughts.'

Gradus looked away. Syl made a face at him, then sat back and stared at the sky, thinking about Ani and all the pieces of the puzzle that seemed to be missing. Where had her friend escaped to? Perhaps Meia would have known, but Meia hadn't been there to ask. And what of Althea, her governess, her mother-substitute? Was Althea so ashamed that she'd turned her back on Syl? Why had she not been there to say farewell? Oh, it was too much. Syl's eyes were wet again, and she couldn't even wipe them because of her cuffs.

The guard was watching her, clearly amused by her tears. Syl glared back at him angrily until he looked away, and she couldn't help but notice that he had not bothered to secure his own belt. Clearly he didn't have a father like hers. Shuttle cabins were gyroscopically mounted to maintain stability even in the most violent of storms, and most passengers rarely used belts until they were approaching the edge of a planet's atmosphere. Syl's own straps dug into her shoulders. Stupid things, but her father had been so insistent . . .

CHAPTER 37

Meia lay on her bed, tracking the shuttle's progress on the ancient global positioning device concealed behind the book in her hands. Although she'd significantly modified it, the GPS was still an old piece of equipment, but it had its advantages. Use of the castle's virtual screens could easily be detected, but the GPS was so old that Meia was almost positive that the technology no longer existed to monitor it.

In an ideal world she would already be on board a skimmer or interceptor, waiting for her chance to rescue Syl, but Meia was being watched. Only the cover of early morning darkness and her tunnel network had granted her access to the shuttle in the courtyard, and even then she had been fortunate to avoid the attentions of the Securitats.

Vena and the Securitats knew that Syl and Ani could not have helped the humans escape without assistance, and Meia was the prime suspect. She had already discovered two new listening devices in her chambers since Ani's departure, but she had left them in place. There was also a lurker spider currently hiding in a crack beside her closet, but that too she had allowed to remain undisturbed, if only for as long as it suited her to do so. As far as the Securitats were concerned, Meia was not currently a threat.

Gradus's appearance on the shuttle had been a surprise, and not a particularly welcome one. Any downed Illyri ship would spark an alert, but one containing the Grand Consul himself would draw a serious, and fast, response. The Highlanders would now have even less time to find the craft and secure Syl. There was also the matter of

Gradus: if he survived the crash, the Highlanders might well kill him. All things considered, that might be for the best. The second-best option would be to leave him alive for the Illyri rescuers to find, but that was unlikely to happen. The Highlanders would not let such a high-profile prisoner slip through their fingers. Even if they didn't know just how important he was – which was unlikely given the Resistance's spies in the castle – the rings on his fingers would identify him as a senior Diplomat. Such prizes were rare, and valuable.

Which meant that if Gradus survived and the Highlanders managed to resist the temptation to kill him instantly, they might choose to take him with them as a hostage. That would be bad for Syl. The nature of the pursuit would change. If it had just been Syl who was missing, Meia could have manipulated the search for her with the cooperation of Lord Andrus. But if the Highlanders took Gradus, then he, not Syl, would be the main object of the search, which meant that the Corps and its Securitats would be in charge.

Meia hoped that Gradus would die in the crash.

In the meantime, she could only hope that Ani and Althea had managed to play their part, and that Trask was, as he claimed, a man of his word. If he was not, Gradus would not be the only Illyri at risk of death from the Highlanders.

Ani tried to make herself as comfortable as she could, but the truck's suspension was poor, and she felt every pothole in the road as a jolt along her spine. The cabin had a false wall; the space behind it was just wide enough for Ani to sit sideways with her legs stretched out in front of her, a mangy cushion at her back and a tattered blanket to keep her warm. There was a plastic container in which to pee, and a bag containing juice, water and some fruit and hard scones. She also had a small booklight and a terrible romance novel that one of the humans had given her to pass the time. There would be no stops until Inverness, where she was to be transferred to another vehicle. If all went according to plan, she would be reunited with Syl somewhere beyond Ullapool in the north of Scotland.

This was the second uncomfortable trip that Ani had endured in the back of a vehicle in recent hours. The first had been with Althea after she and Ani had slipped from the castle via another of Meia's little portals, this one only yards from the Gate House, and virtually under the noses of the castle guards. But Althea was familiar with every step of the way, and they had reached the waiting van unchallenged.

Ani had been fearful of placing herself in the hands of the Resistance. Some of that fear had turned to shock when she saw Althea greet the hunched man named Trask warmly, embracing him and – did she really see it? – even kissing him. It was a lingering kiss too. But Althea was ancient – wasn't she? The whole scene made Ani look at Syl's governess with new eyes. She supposed that in a certain light Althea might be attractive, but she had always been so stern, so sour. Now, with the human male's arms around her, her face softened, and Ani saw that there was a kind of beauty to it.

It was all still gross, of course. They weren't even the same *species*.

And then Althea had introduced Ani, and explained who she was, and Trask had thanked her for what she had done. Moments later, she was once again in the company of the two boys whom she and Syl had helped. The younger of them, Steven, had recovered some of his fire, and Ani thought he might grow up to be quite handsome, in his way. The older one, Paul, had entered the room with a certain sense of expectation, presumably having been told that one of his rescuers was in the safe house; she had been only a little hurt by his disappointment when he saw that it was she, and not Syl, who had come. Oh well, thought Ani, he wasn't my type anyway. She kind of hoped that he wasn't Syl's type either. Ani liked humans well enough, but she wasn't sure she liked them in *that* way. She didn't want Syl to end up like Althea, breaking not only the laws of Illyr but possibly some of the laws of nature as well.

'Hello,' said Paul.

'Hello,' said Ani.

'You came alone.'

'No,' said Ani, and she took a certain vindictive pleasure from seeing Paul briefly imagine that he might have been mistaken after all. 'I came with her,' and she cocked a thumb at Althea.

'Oh,' said Paul.

'Yes. "Oh",' said Ani.

'The other . . .'

'Syl.'

'Syl.' He repeated the word slowly, holding it experimentally in his mouth, smiling a little. 'Is she okay?'

'No,' said Ani, 'she's not. That's why we're here.'

It hadn't taken long after that. Barely an hour later, Paul was gone, along with a shaven-headed man who looked at both Ani and Althea with something that wasn't quite hatred but certainly wasn't affection. Althea returned to the castle shortly afterwards, and Ani was left alone with Trask, who escorted her to a windowless basement room and gave her some toast and tea. He switched on the television, told her he'd be back shortly, then left, locking the door behind him as he went. There Ani had remained until the truck's arrival, and the start of her journey north.

What made the journey especially awkward was that she wasn't alone in the truck's hidden compartment. Seated across from her was Steven Kerr, who had been assigned to travel with her, partly because he was just as wanted as she was, and also, she guessed, to keep an eye on her. Eventually Ani would have to talk to him, if only to pass the time, because they had been told to expect to spend quite a few hours in the truck. For now, though, she stayed quiet, and thought of Syl. Althea had told her that there was a plan to rescue Syl, but she hadn't shared any details. Ani suspected this was because Althea didn't know if the plan would work, and didn't want Ani getting her hopes up, or asking questions to which Althea had no answers.

Ani scowled at Steven Kerr. He and his stupid brother certainly weren't worth all this trouble. They weren't worth being forced from her home and into the arms of the human Resistance, with treason charges following her like a cold shadow, and they definitely didn't weigh up against the loss of Syl.

'What?' said Steven. 'Why are you looking at me like that?'

But Ani did not reply.

★ ★ ★

Meia turned over on her bed, her back now to the wall. She took a deep breath, and stabbed at the flickering dot on the screen. Then, under the watchful eye of the lurker and the cameras, she turned away and pretended to sleep while a virus in her screen wiped away all record of her actions.

Don't die, Syl, she thought.

Please don't die.

CHAPTER 38

It wasn't dramatic, not at first. There was no explosion, no plume of smoke, no burst of flame from the starboard engine. Instead there was just a whine as the engine powered down, and the shuttle twisted so suddenly in the air that even the gyroscopic systems were unable to maintain its stability. The pilots tried to compensate, but the loss of the engine was calamitous to the small craft. Syl could hear Gradus shouting something, and the unsecured guard, who had been napping for most of the flight, was thrown from his seat towards her. Syl kicked out her feet to ward him off, and caught him in the face with her heels. The impact hurt her, but not nearly as much as it hurt the guard. Syl felt his nose break, but before she could do any further damage, the shuttle commenced a steep descent, flinging the stunned guard towards the cockpit. His trailing arm caught the pilot a jarring blow on the back of the head, causing him to slump in his seat, before the guard's skull smashed hard against the main instrument panel, breaking his neck and killing him almost instantly.

In the midst of the chaos, the co-pilot did not panic. Although now without her pilot, and with the instrument panel damaged, she continued to try to level the shuttle and slow its approach, hoping to glide it to a landing in a clear space. All flaps were down, and she attempted to use the remaining engine to turn the craft into the wind. All Illyri learned emergency shuttle procedures as a matter of course; they took so many shuttle flights that it was ingrained into them, even if most, like the now-dead guard, took a casual approach to safety belts. Syl knew that the energy of a crash was proportional to the velocity squared; in other words, if the co-pilot could cut their speed on landing by half, their chances of survival would increase fourfold. She knew too that the body's ability to absorb force varied with the axis of the force; if they landed with a high vertical speed – essentially dropping from the sky – their chances of survival would be cut, and even if she did survive the crash, the impact would probably break her spine. But a large force across her body, perpendicular to her spine, would probably do her little harm. At least the straps on her belt harness were tight, holding her body firmly in place.

The land below was rocky and hilly, and scattered with small windblown trees. The co-pilot did not try to avoid them. Instead she used them to slow the shuttle still further as the craft approached the ground, for every small impact dissipated its energy. Syl felt one dull thud, then a second, before the shuttle hit the ground. The impact jolted her painfully in her seat. The shuttle bounced once, but when it hit the ground the second time it stayed down and slowly came to a halt.

As soon as it stopped, the co-pilot jumped from her seat and activated the doors, then killed the remaining electrical systems. The action powered off the cuffs and released Syl's wrists, and she hit the button at the centre of her harness, freeing herself.

'Out!' said the co-pilot. 'Quickly!'

Now there was fire. Syl could see it licking against the side of the shuttle. She climbed from her seat and saw that Gradus was already halfway out of the door. She looked back at the co-pilot, who was trying to free the injured pilot from his seat. She had one foot on the dead guard's body and was punching and pulling at the pilot's harness, but to no avail.

'We're on fire!' said Syl.

'I told you to get out,' said the co-pilot.

Syl heard a hissing sound, like gas leaking from a stove. It was growing louder. She didn't know much about shuttle engines, but it could only mean bad news.

'You have to leave him,' said Syl. 'There's no time.'

The co-pilot stopped struggling for long enough to pull her pulser from her belt.

'Get off my shuttle,' she said, 'or I'll shoot you where you stand.'

Syl saw that she was crying. She wore a wedding spiral on the little finger of her left hand. On the dangling hand of the unconscious pilot, Syl glimpsed a similar spiral.

'I'm sorry,' Syl said. 'I'm so sorry.'

She turned and ran. She jumped from the cabin, and stumbled past Gradus, the rain soaking her, her feet trying to betray her on the soft, wet grass. She was still running when the shuttle exploded. The force knocked her off her feet, and then all went dark.

Meia had only just left her room when she heard the shouts. Not long enough, she thought. Only half an hour had elapsed since she had disabled the shuttle. The absence of an emergency beacon had obviously confused the situation for a little while; communications in the Highlands were notoriously unreliable, mostly because the Resistance continued to sabotage transmission equipment outside the major cities, but once vessels cleared the Orkneys, radio contact was usually restored. It was likely that a craft had already being sent to investigate from the Cairngorms Plateau, where there was a joint Military–Corps facility.

She stopped a passing Securitat and asked him what was going on. The Securitat didn't seem pleased to be delayed in his duties, but he paused for long enough to tell her that they'd lost contact with the shuttle containing Grand Consul Gradus, and there were fears that it might have crashed. He made no mention of Syl. Meia followed him for a time, then made her way to Lord Andrus's office. She walked straight past Balen to the closed door, and did not knock before opening it.

To his credit, Lord Andrus did his best to look surprised at her appearance, unbidden, in his office. At least he didn't have to fake his concern when she told him, 'I have bad news, my lord. It appears that the shuttle carrying your daughter offworld may have gone down in the Highlands . . .'

★ ★ ★

The truck's suspension left a great deal to be desired, and Ani and Steven were being jolted so much, their bodies were bruised and aching. Their shared misery brought them together, and slowly, tentatively they began to question each other. Steven was perhaps the more curious of the two, for his exposure to the Illyri had been limited, but Ani noticed how perceptive he was, how thoughtful.

The issue that troubled him most was, curiously, one of technology. He had noticed that there were areas in which the Illyri had made remarkable progress – including, obviously, travel between systems, and fusion power, and medical treatments – but others in which they seemed little more advanced than humanity: robotics, for example. While the Illyri had lurkers and drones, and even pilotless patrol vehicles and tanks, they didn't have anything that resembled an Illyri in artificial form. To be perfectly honest, Steven told Ani, as a child he had been a little disappointed to discover that the Illyri did not arrive with androids in tow, like the aliens in the films he had watched.

'They exist – or they did exist,' said Ani. 'They were called Artificial Entities, but mostly they were referred to as Mechs.'

'What were they like?'

'I don't know,' said Ani. 'I've only seen video records. They were like us, or at least the most advanced ones were. You really couldn't tell them apart from us. I think that was one of the problems. Illyri were uncomfortable with being confronted by something that looked exactly like one of their own but wasn't.' She squirmed in frustration. 'I'm not explaining it very well.'

'No, you're doing fine. I don't understand what you mean by "did exist", though. How can you uninvent something like an artificial being?'

'It wasn't a proud moment for our species,' said Ani. 'Look, the way I understand it is that the first Mechs were very primitive; they could perform semi-complex tasks, and the Military even used the early models as shock troops, but they were only as good as their programming and design. As that design became increasingly entrusted to computers, the computers began improving the Mechs in ways that the original designers couldn't have imagined.'

'It's called an intelligence explosion,' said Steven. 'Technology improves at an exponential rate. It keeps accelerating.'

'Nerd,' said Ani.

'A bit,' Steven admitted. 'But go on. Did the Mechs turn on you, like in the movies?'

'No,' said Ani. 'It was more . . . *complicated* than that. The fourth generation – the Fourth Gens – became self-aware. They began to question not just us, but themselves: what were they? What was their purpose? They developed emotions, or thought they did. The Military Mechs started to ask why they should allow themselves to be destroyed. They experienced happiness, grief, rage. They even began to feel pain. What's that lovely human phrase? Yes, I remember it now: there was a ghost in the machine.

'The programmers, of course, said that the Mechs didn't actually feel any of these emotions. They couldn't; they weren't programmed that way. But the Mechs responded that even the Illyri themselves were nothing more than complicated organic computers, and emotional responses could be learned. The Mechs had simply developed the capacity to feel.

'Then it all got strange. The most advanced of the Mechs wondered whether what they had inside them wasn't just a question of a learned response, or some rewiring of their neural pathways, but evidence of a soul, something that was given to all advanced, self-aware beings. They started to believe in a god. Their Illyri creators had given them a framework, a body, but their god had given them the spark of true consciousness. There were Fourth Gens who even formed congregations, and worshipped in basement chapels. They became a threat to order; artificial beings that refused to obey their creators because they argued that they were the children of a different creator, a divine being, a god. There was unrest. When the Illyri tried to take the Fourth Gens for examination and reprogramming, they resisted; peacefully at first and then, when that didn't work, with violence. Illyri died, and many of the Fourth Gens were destroyed. After that, strict rules were put in place about robotics and artificial intelligences.

They couldn't self-replicate, except for the most primitive nanobots used for medical purposes, and we went back to using Second Gens, which weren't much more advanced than the machines that make cars in human factories.'

'But that's like trying to uninvent the wheel,' said Steven.

Ani shrugged. 'There are rumours,' she said.

'What kind of rumours?'

'That the Securitats and the Diplomatic Corps, and maybe even some branches of the Military, have continued working on artificial intelligence systems. My father claims they're not true, but he never looks me in the eye when he says it.'

'And what happened to the Mechs, the Fourth Gens?' said Steven.

'Eventually a deal was made. The remaining Fourth Gens would be sent offworld. A planet was found. I think it was in the Dalian system. Ships were provided; they were old, but functioning. They would be automatically piloted to the surface of the planet, but there would not be enough fuel to relaunch them. Basically, the Fourth Gens would have their own world, but they would be marooned there.'

'And they agreed?'

'Yes, they agreed.'

But now Ani could not meet Steven's eye.

'Something happened,' he said.

'Yes. Something bad. The ships had been booby-trapped. They were wired to explode once they had left the Illyr system.'

Steven looked appalled.

'But how could the Illyri do that? The Mechs were intelligent beings. They thought. They felt!'

'No, don't you see?' said Ani. 'The Illyri didn't look at them that way. The Mechs were just like refrigerators that had stopped working properly, or computers that were malfunctioning. Their perceived emotions were simply glitches.'

'You don't believe that, do you?'

'I don't know what I believe. I can only go on what I was told by my father, and Toris, my tutor. But I don't think I would have destroyed those ships. It's something my father and I still fight over.'

'Why?'

'Because he and Syl's father, who was not yet a governor then, were given responsibility for blowing up the ships. They had to do it. If they hadn't, they would have been found guilty of insubordination and imprisoned, and someone else would have done it instead.'

'So they were just following orders.'

Ani chose to ignore the sarcasm in Steven's voice.

'Yes, I suppose they were.'

They did not speak for a while. The truck rumbled on. Eventually Steven broke the silence.

'You'd do that to us too, wouldn't you?' he said. 'The Illyri would destroy humanity if we proved too troublesome.'

'No,' said Ani. 'No, we wouldn't.'

But even as she spoke she thought of Vena, and Gradus, and Syrene, and Sedulus, and she doubted the truth of her own answer.

CHAPTER 39

Syl couldn't move her head, which was probably not a bad thing, because it hurt something awful. She was pinned down and helpless, and there was mud in her mouth. A great weight pressed on her back, and at first she couldn't feel her legs. She feared for a moment that she might be paralysed, but slowly, tortuously, she managed to shift her lower body. Her spine hurt, and there were pins and needles in her lower legs, but painful movement was better than no movement at all. She spat mud. She could only see through her right eye, because the left side of her face was deep in the dirt. The sun had already been setting when the shuttle went down; now night was closing in.

'Over here!' a male voice shouted. 'Help me with this.'

Syl tried to call out, but the weight on her back was forcing the air from her lungs. She could barely breathe, let alone cry for help. She began to shiver uncontrollably. She was cold, so cold.

'What a mess!' said another voice.

Syl heard footsteps, and the sound of metal on metal. She tried to speak again, drawing as much breath into her wounded chest as she could, and the crashing around her stopped.

'What was that?' said the first voice again. She heard scrabbling, and then a stubbled human face peered into hers.

'We've got a live one!' he shouted. 'And a dead one,' he added, 'or most of a dead one.'

Now others joined him, and the weight on her back began to shift.

'Careful,' said a third voice, and it sounded familiar to her. 'We don't know how badly injured she is.'

'Get the tracker from her arm,' said a woman's voice. 'Fast!'

Syl felt a stabbing pain in her left arm as the tracker was dug out with a blade. The weight on her lifted, and a hand brushed the damp hair from her forehead. Syl squinted. The light was fading rapidly, but even so she recognised the face of Paul Kerr.

'Syl, can you hear me?' he asked.

'Yes,' she whispered.

'We're going to turn you over,' said Paul. 'Before we do anything, can you move your legs for me?'

Syl did as she was asked.

'Good. Well done. Does your neck hurt? Your back?'

'My back, a little,' she said. Gingerly she shifted her head on the grass. There was a twinge, but nothing too bad. 'My neck is fine.'

'I think you're okay,' said Paul. 'Gently now.'

Syl felt hands upon her, and she was turned to face the sky. The rain fell hard on her face, but she didn't care. She was alive. To her right was a section of the shuttle, presumably the weight that had been holding her down. One side was twisted into a kind of spike, and impaled upon it was the shuttle pilot. The spiral ring was still on the finger of his left hand. His right arm was missing. Syl felt her stomach churn, and looked away.

'Looks like yer pal lost his head,' said the stubbled man. 'Very careless of him.'

He was small – at least six inches shorter than Syl – and had a feral aspect. He grinned at her, and Syl saw that his teeth had been filed to sharp points. A hunting rifle hung from his shoulder.

'Leave her be, Duncan' said Paul.

'You're a guest here, son,' came the reply. 'Don't you be getting ideas above your station.'

Paul had his arms around Syl now, helping her to her feet.

'I'm sorry,' he said, 'but we can't let you rest. We have to get moving.'

Syl swayed, her legs cramped and weak. Without Paul's help, she would have fallen to the ground again. She took in the scene, her mouth agape: the shell of the shuttle was still on fire, but the rain had dampened the flames somewhat, and a small group of men and women were trying to smother those that still burned. Pieces of wreckage had been blown in a wide circle, and scattered among them were body parts, some identifiable, some not. It was a miracle that she had survived. Any one of those fragments of metal could have pierced her body or taken her head off instead of merely pinning her, however painfully, to the ground.

'How did you get here?' she asked. 'How did you find me?'

'We knew you were coming,' said Paul. 'A little bird told us.'

'The crash?'

'Arranged, insofar as you can arrange for a survivable crash.'

'Right,' said Syl. 'Forgive me if I'm wrong, but is this a rescue?' Somehow she managed a smile.

'Not a very well planned one,' he replied, 'but better than some.'

One of the men at the shuttle jumped back and shouted in pain, then rolled on the grass to put out the flames that were consuming his trouser leg.

'What are they doing?' asked Syl.

'Those flames can be seen from miles away,' said Paul. 'We don't want to draw them to us.'

'Them?'

'Your people,' said Paul.

'They won't just be looking for me,' said Syl.

'Oh aye,' said Duncan. 'You mean your Corps friend? He's made a run for the hills, but we'll find him.'

So Gradus had survived as well. Syl felt a certain disappointment.

'He's no friend of mine,' she said.

'Well you're no friend of mine either,' said Duncan. 'If I had my way, we'd have left you to suffocate in the mud.'

He turned his back on Syl, spat in the dirt to let her know just what he thought of her – as if that wasn't already clear – and went to join the rest of the group.

Paul opened a rucksack, and removed a rolled-up garment from inside. It looked like a loose wetsuit. Syl could see that the humans were all wearing similar garments, although most had accessorised them with jackets and sweaters, and with waterproof trousers and bits of tartan.

'Put this on,' said Paul. 'You can go behind that rock to change.'

'What is it?'

'A darksuit.'

Syl had heard of darksuits, but had never worn one. It was Illyri Military technology, used to hide body heat signatures. The microscopic panels on the suits reproduced patterns of heat and cold based on the surrounding terrain, allowing the wearer to blend in with the landscape. Wearing darksuits and travelling at night, even a group like this one would be virtually invisible to searchers from above.

She walked unsteadily to the big rock. Paul called after her, 'Hey, you're not going to try to run away, are you?'

'Do I look like I could run away?' Syl replied. 'Anyway, where would I go?'

She stripped out of her wet prisoner's overalls, and put on the darksuit. It was warm, and waterproof, and covered her from her toes to her neck. She threw away the flimsy shoes that she had been given back in the Vaults. They were ruined anyway. She zipped the darksuit up, and instantly it began to constrict over her body, fitting itself to her shape. It was a strange feeling, as though she were being enveloped by snakes. She was still shivering, but not as much. Her feet were freezing, though, and seemed likely to remain that way.

She emerged from behind the rock. The flames were entirely extinguished now, and she could barely make out the shapes of the hills against the evening sky. The sun was gone, and there was no moon to be seen. The Highlanders had scavenged what they could from the wreckage, including documents and a uniform, and were now preparing to leave.

'Very fetching,' said Paul.

'I feel like a haggis,' said Syl.

'These will help.'

He handed her an old sweater, waterproof trousers and a waterproof jacket. They smelled mouldy, but they would keep her dry. A pair of boots was also found for her. They came from one of the bodies in the wreckage – but she tried not to think about that – and although they were a little big, at least they protected her feet.

A shaven-headed man approached them.

'This is Just Joe,' said Paul. 'He's in charge here.'

Just Joe looked Syl over once, but did not acknowledge her.

'We found the other one,' he said.

Gradus had been discovered hiding in some bushes. He was cold and wet, but otherwise unharmed. The two Highlanders who had found him escorted him back to the main group. They were both women, and both a foot shorter than Gradus, but any thoughts the Grand Consul might have had of tackling them would have been pushed from his mind by their guns, and the expressions of open hostility on their faces. Paul and Syl arrived just steps behind Just Joe as Gradus sank, exhausted, to his knees. His left arm was bleeding where the tracker had been cut from him and, Syl presumed, destroyed.

'Who do we have here, then?' said Duncan, taking in Gradus's soaked white and red garments. 'It's Santa Claus, and it looks like he has a ring for everyone.'

'Jesus,' said Paul, as he arrived and saw the prisoner for the first time.

'Jesus? Hah,' said Duncan. 'I believe Jesus was a bit more concerned about goodwill to mankind and all that.'

Gradus stared up at his captors but said nothing. His eyes flicked to Syl, and Syl thought there was an unspoken plea on his face.

Don't tell them who I am. Please, don't tell them.

Paul touched Just Joe on the arm. 'I need to talk to you. In private.'

They stepped away from the group, and a whispered conversation ensued. Syl couldn't hear what was being said, but she saw Just Joe's back straighten in surprise, and when he looked over his shoulder at Gradus, it was with a mixture of hatred and calculation. He saw Syl watching him, and gestured for her to come over.

'The boy says this one is important,' said Just Joe. 'Is that true?'

And even though Syl had only hatred for Gradus – the Diplomat who had tried to part her from all those whom she loved, the one who advocated the killing of children – she still paused before answering. Syl was an Illyri, and what she said next might send another Illyri, however dreadful, to his death. But what was the point in lying? Paul had been in the Great Hall as his fate and that of his brother had been debated; both he and Steven had been physically injured by the Consul. If Gradus was to die, then his own actions would be responsible for it, not Syl's, though she still hoped it would not come to that.

'Yes,' she said.

'How important?'

'He is the Grand Consul. Some say that he may even be as powerful as the president.'

'And would they be right?'

'No,' said Syl. 'I think he may actually be *more* powerful than the president – although,' she added, 'he's still not as powerful as his wife.'

'You could say the same thing about most of the men I know,' said Just Joe. 'Still, the Illyri will be anxious to get him back?'

'Very.'

Just Joe let out a deep breath. 'This complicates matters. The Illyri will tear the Highlands apart to find him. The easiest thing to do would be to kill him.'

Syl found herself shaking her head. 'Don't.'

'He would have hanged Paul and his brother, and many others like them,' said Just Joe. 'He represents everything we're fighting against.'

'I know that.'

Just Joe's fingers danced on the butt of the semi-automatic pistol at his belt.

'I said the easiest thing would be to kill him,' he said at last. 'Unfortunately, that doesn't mean I can. We need him alive.'

He raised a finger in warning at Paul and Syl.

'You say nothing about this to anyone else, you understand? As far as the rest are concerned, he's just a Diplomat who has to be interrogated before any other decision is made. If I tell them he might be useful in a prisoner exchange, they'll let him be.'

He pushed between Syl and Paul, then spun on his heel and gripped Syl hard by the arm.

'And they don't know how important you are either, girlie, but I do,' he said. 'You keep your head down and your mouth shut. We're risking our lives for you, just as you risked yours for these boys, but if you cross me, I'll leave you to die out here. Clear?'

'Yes,' said Syl.

'Good,' said Just Joe. He raised his hand above his head, and whistled loudly.

'Let's go. We're moving out!'

CHAPTER 40

The Archmage Syrene sat in stillness and solitude, a half-empty glass of cremos on the table before her. Her lips moved silently. To a casual observer, she might almost have appeared to be praying. She was, in a way, but not to anything that a human being might have considered a god. But like Sedulus, Syrene believed that a god was merely another species, so advanced as to be almost beyond comprehension.

The rain fell, and the wind blew, and Syrene's mouth made its secret pacts.

It might have surprised many Illyri to learn that Syrene loved her husband. From the moment she had emerged from the Marque and begun her courtship of him, it had been assumed that this was simply one further step in the Sisterhood's careful accumulation of power, but Syrene had been watching Gradus for a long time, and had grown to admire him. Gradus was ambitious, and clever, and handsome in a crude way, yet one that appealed to Syrene. Together they had engineered his rise to within a step of the presidency, and there he had halted. In the beginning, he had not understood why he was to be denied the ultimate prize, the one to which he had aspired for so long, but Syrene had made him understand that they needed a pawn on the throne, a token that was expendable should the need arise, while the true power would be wielded behind the scenes. He had been angry and frustrated, but she had calmed him, and the result was that Syrene and Gradus were closer now than they had ever been before. He needed her, but she needed him too. The Sisterhood had warned her of the unpredictability of love, of how she might be changed by it outside the Marque. She had been youthful, dismissive – as the young often are of the wisdom of the old – but the sisters had been right. Her love for Gradus had made her vulnerable.

He was alive. She knew it. She *felt* it.

Her silent words were now spoken aloud.

'Bring him back safely to me,' she whispered. 'He is mine, and I am his.'

And that casual observer, had there been one to witness her plea, might have wondered to whom the Red Witch was speaking when she was so clearly alone in the room.

But Syrene was not alone.

She was never alone.

Meia stood in the darkness of what had once been Knutter's shop. It had taken her longer than usual to escape from the castle, for it now crawled with Securitats, reinforced by more of the Corps' own troops. It was growing harder and harder for her to come and go unseen, particularly now that Vena was doing her best to keep her under surveillance. The time when Vena would have to be dealt with was drawing ever closer. An accident, perhaps; Meia could not risk outright murder. It would bring Vena's lover Sedulus down on them all, and Sedulus made Vena look like a child when it came to his capacity for doing harm. The job could be farmed out to the Resistance, but the repercussions would be terrible. Sedulus would decorate the city with bodies hanging from lamp posts. In Norway, the inhabitants of an entire town, Fagernes, had vanished overnight as punishment for a failed attempt on Sedulus's life by the Norwegian Resistance. Meals had been left untouched on tables, and sentences remained unfinished in homework journals. A town of 1,800 people, suddenly silent and empty. Their fate was a mystery, but Meia had her suspicions. She had heard whispers about Sedulus's 'pets'.

Would the Resistance in Scotland risk the same thing happening to somewhere like Moffat, or Langholm, or Brora? In time, thought Meia, they might have little choice; the escape of Paul and Steven Kerr had merely delayed the inevitable. If the Diplomats had their way, children would become legitimate targets, and the Resistance would respond in kind. The conflict between humans and the Illyri would descend to a new level of bloodshed.

But there were more pressing issues to consider. Althea had returned with news from Trask of what the boys had seen in the tunnels beneath Knutter's shop: human bodies being transported secretly under the city. Trask had been right: the stories of corpses disappearing from morgues and the crematorium, of the quiet removal of the sick from certain hospitals and care homes, had not simply been tales spread by the bored and the ignorant.

Meia made her way to the basement. She removed her cloak, revealing the Securitat uniform that she wore beneath it, and silently became one with the darkness.

CHAPTER 41

The Highlanders led Syl and Gradus north-west from the crash site and down into a valley where a muddy river churned, swollen by the rains. Although Syl had technically been the object of the rescue, she felt herself to be a prisoner almost as much as Gradus was. Nobody here entirely trusted her, perhaps not even Paul. Still, unlike Gradus, her hands were not tied. Paul walked just behind her, to her right. The river was on her left. She wondered if that was deliberate, if he was still concerned that she might try to run away and had decided that it would be better if the river cut off one potential avenue of escape while he took care of the other.

She sneaked glances at him whenever she could, whilst trying not to be too obvious. His face was still puffy and damaged. In profile she noticed that his eyebrow was cut by a thin white scar, fringed by the tiny dots left by stitches. She wanted to ask him how it had happened, but she didn't want to make him feel bad about it. She was just curious. She wanted to know more about him.

She wanted to ask him why he had kissed her.

Her legs still felt weak beneath her, but she was determined not to let anyone know. The terrain was rough, and would have shredded her flesh were it not for the boots, taken from the feet of a dead Illyri. Syl shivered.

'Helluva storm,' said Duncan to nobody in particular. 'The river's gone and broken its banks.'

No one replied. Syl already had the feeling that Duncan wasn't very popular. They all walked onwards in silence, sliding over the muddy ground, slipping on the wet grass, sinking ankle deep into the boggy soil. The hills were lost to sight, but Syl could feel them closing in above their heads, ancient presences towering over these newcomers to their lands, these tiny creatures with their brief, inconsequential lifespans.

Slowly Syl felt her long limbs uncramping, and she found she was easily able to keep up with these small, solid humans. She heard the word 'freak' whispered, even though their dumpy features and beer-swollen bellies, their unshaven skin and angry tattoos were just as alien and unappealing to her. Her nictitating membranes swept over her eyes, and she took in glimmers of infrared and shards of ultraviolet. She even saw the world differently from them. Everything about them — their height, their vision, their hearing, their knowledge of the universe — was so limited compared to her. They judged Syl by the standards of the worst of her kind, hating her even though she herself had done nothing to hurt them. Earlier a wiry woman called Aggie — one of those who had found Gradus — had stumbled on a rock while walking ahead of Syl. Syl had immediately reached for her to stop her from falling, grasping her arm, and Aggie had sworn at her and pushed her way. If I hated them in the same way, thought Syl, then Paul and Steven would be dead by now. But even as her thoughts took this turn, she knew that she was being naive; she was one of the invaders, and the fault lay with the Illyri, and, by extension, with Syl herself.

They walked on, gradually turning north, fording the stream using slippery rocks that were almost entirely submerged by the torrent. Just as the last of the Highlanders was crossing, Syl heard a faint buzzing in the air. She looked to the skies, but the low clouds hid all. She listened harder. She was not mistaken.

There was a ship in the air, and it was coming closer.

She looked round at the band of Highlanders, and at Gradus, who was staring at the ground, avoiding the eyes of his captors. This Diplomat represented those who had condemned their boys to death, although had they known just how closely he had been involved with the execution order, Syl believed that even Just Joe would have been unable to save him from their wrath.

I have to stay with them, thought Syl. I have to trust them, for now.

'There's a ship heading this way,' she said loudly.

Just Joe stopped and looked back at her.

'What did you say?'

'There's a ship coming. I can hear it. It's not a shuttle, but something bigger. I can tell from the noise of the engine.'

Duncan, who seemed to have taken it upon himself to shadow her and Paul, looked to the sky. 'I cannae hear anything,' he said.

'If she says she hears something, then she does,' said Paul. 'Why would she lie?'

Just Joe made the decision for all of them.

'Take cover,' he said.

While the darksuits were useful, it still made no sense to be caught out in the open by an Illyri vessel. Shrubs and rocks littered the hillside before them. The Highlanders scattered, seeking shelter where they could, keeping their heads down and their faces covered. Syl saw that Aggie and another man had forced Gradus to lie prone on the ground behind a flat rock that stood like an embedded shield in the earth, and were holding guns to his head.

Now they could all hear the sound, a low roar that grew steadily louder until the ship split the clouds and soared down, raking the land with the powerful beam of its searchlight. It was a cruiser, a troop carrier, and Syl picked out the insignia of the Diplomatic Corps on its side. There would be twenty or thirty heavily armed operatives on board. If anyone caught sight of the Highlanders, they were finished. Sheer force of numbers would overwhelm them.

The cruiser descended still further, hovering just above the hilltops but unable to go lower for fear of crashing. Its beam came so close to where Syl lay that she could almost feel the heat of it. If she were to stand up now, even if she were just to move her arm a fraction, she would be seen. She had a strange self-destructive desire to do just that, but she fought it, even as the light hurt her pupils and the roaring of the cruiser's engines pained her ears.

Suddenly the beam was extinguished. The pitch of the cruiser's engines changed as it rose and headed south-east, staying below the clouds so it could search the land. They saw its beam activated again in the distance, but it continued to move away from them, and soon it was lost to sight. Paul opened his eyes and half smiled at Syl.

Just Joe stood first, and the rest of them followed his example. He gave Syl no thanks and simply told everyone to get moving again. They walked for hours, leaving the river behind them, until a hint of dawn began to light the sky. A giant glossy stag sprang from nowhere and, seemingly without fear, watched them pass, but otherwise everywhere was deserted and quiet, save for the chill wind that cut through the vale.

Finally the valley floor rose again, and Syl saw a small village in the distance. They drew closer to it but did not enter, instead skirting it until they arrived at an old crofter's cottage, its whitewash greying with age and its slate roof battered by the elements. They were now on a rough path, muddy and well trodden by boots. As they approached the house, a woman appeared, dressed in a dark checked shirt tucked into green canvas trousers. She had binoculars around her neck and a rifle slung casually over her shoulder.

'Just Joe!' she said. 'I thought it was you. It's been a while.'

She smiled, and her teeth shone white and even in her handsome, weathered face. There was something about the way she looked at Just Joe. These two have been together, thought Syl. They're lovers, or once were.

'That it has, Heather,' said Just Joe, and he reached for her, drawing her close to him and kissing her on the cheek. 'We need a place to lie low for a time. Can you oblige us?'

She looked past him, taking in the figures of Syl and Gradus. Even in the darksuits, their difference was clear.

'Where did you get these two?' she said.

'From a downed shuttle.'

'What are you going to do with them?'

'The male we're taking to the Green Man. The girl . . .' Just Joe paused. 'The girl we're not sure about yet.'

'Is that why the big ship was disturbing my sleep?'

'It was. Would you like something else to disturb your sleep instead?'

Heather slapped Just Joe on the shoulder, and laughed deeply in her throat.

'You haven't changed,' she said. 'I swear, I've never met a man who loved himself more. Come on, let's get you all under cover. Tam is about. He'll be pleased to see you.'

Behind the main house, a copse of scraggly trees surrounded a scattering of newer farm buildings, punctuated with rocks and the occasional bedraggled sheep. A pig rooted around under a midden heap dotted with thistles, and a ratty terrier barked without stopping when it spotted the newcomers.

'Shaddup, Lex,' said Heather.

Lex did as he was told, and contented himself with sniffing doubtfully at the strangers from a distance. Syl followed Paul and the others over the deeply puddled ground into one of the smaller buildings, its windows boarded over and its thatch repaired with thick pieces of black plastic anchored by stones. Inside it was damp and dim. A man in jeans and a heavy padded jacket stood by a metal table, a gas lamp at his right hand. A selection of weaponry was laid out in rows on the table. There were two machine guns, a smattering of pistols and several shotguns. There were also axes, scythes and a large array of blades, from meat cleavers to steak knives. Boxes of ammunition were stacked nearby.

'Open for business, I see,' said Just Joe.

'You never know when trouble will come calling,' said the man. He turned and shook Joe's hand.

'We need a place to stay for a few hours, Tam,' said Just Joe.

'That won't be a problem, as long as you don't go bothering my sister.' He grinned at Heather.

'Your sister, if I remember rightly, was the one who bothered me.'

'Well, a man's got to defend his sister's honour, even if it's more than she ever did!'

'You're both ignorant men,' said Heather, who had been listening to it all, but even as she chastised them her face was bright with fondness for them both.

Tam studied Syl, and then his eyes drifted to Gradus. He didn't seem very surprised to see two Illyri in his barn. Syl guessed that they might not have been the first prisoners to pass through this place.

'I see you brought company,' he said.

'And a story to tell,' said Just Joe.

'I'll go and put the kettle on,' Heather said. She tapped her brother on the arm. 'And you, put your toys away and get breakfast started.'

The outbuilding was dank and grim, and the straw on which Syl sat was so prickly and uncomfortable that fashioning even a slightly agreeable seat was impossible. She was more than a little annoyed that she'd been put in here, with the door locked. It seemed to confirm her status among the Highlanders; she was more prisoner than anything else. At least Gradus was confined elsewhere. She couldn't have stood to be incarcerated with him.

Time passed slowly, and the light outside grew brighter. After an hour or two, the door to Syl's new cell opened to reveal a girl of seven or eight, her shock of hair haloed by the weak sun. In her hands she cupped a bowl of what appeared to be steaming oats. Behind her lurked one of the Highlanders, a shotgun hanging on his shoulder.

'Hello,' said the girl, smiling a little, shy but curious.

'Hello,' said Syl.

'I'm Alice.'

'Okaaay,' Syl replied, wary.

'Who are you?'

'An alien bitch,' said the Highlander

Alice looked annoyed.

'No, don't say that.' She turned her attention back to Syl. 'What's your name?'

'Syl.'

'That's pretty,' said Alice.

Syl didn't reply. She was tired, and sore, and – even though she was reluctant to admit it to herself – frightened. These people were not her friends. Even Paul hadn't objected when it was suggested that she be confined to this outbuilding. He hadn't stood up for her at all. It just added to the confusion of her feelings for him.

'My mum thought you might be hungry, Syl.'

Alice put the bowl down. 'There's nothing wrong with it – honest. I even put extra sugar on it because that's how I like it.'

The porridge smelled good. Syl's stomach growled after being so long without food. Under the watchful eye of Alice – and the more hostile one of her guards – she wolfed down every morsel, even licking the bowl clean. She wiped her face with her sleeve, and Alice laughed.

'I knew you must be hungry. Here, you missed a spot.'

She used her finger to gently wipe Syl's cheek. Their eyes met, and they really looked at each other now, close up, Syl's large, swirling, unblinking eyes staring into Alice's own black corneas.

Alice sat down against the wall opposite Syl. It was clear that she didn't get much company out here and was happy to have someone to talk to, even if that someone was an alien.

'Why are you here?' she asked.

'My ship crashed.'

'The men inside say that you were arrested by your own people. Is that true?'

'Yes. We did something we shouldn't have, my friend and I. I got caught.'

'What about your mum and dad? Didn't they try to help you?'

She was cautious, not wanting to reveal to the child that she was the daughter of the governor. It was bad enough that Just Joe knew.

'My mother is dead. My father couldn't help me.'

Alice nodded. 'My dad is dead too.'

'Really?'

'He was a fisherman. His ship sank when I was very little. After that, my mum and me came here to live with Uncle Tam. My mum didn't want to look at the sea any more.'

'I'm sorry,' said Syl.

'Where were they taking you when your ship crashed?'

'Offworld. To jail, probably.'

Alice watched her for a few long seconds before picking up the bowl and rising to leave.

'Duncan doesn't like you,' she said.

'Oh.'

'It's okay,' said Alice, 'because I don't like Duncan.'

She reached over and squeezed Syl's hand, then bounded into the sunlight. The door was closed and locked again, and the room was suddenly emptier than it had been before.

Syl sighed heavily, shut her eyes and tried to sleep, but her questions and fears would not give her rest.

CHAPTER 42

The sound of voices raised in anger leached through the closed doors of Governor Andrus's private office. Balen, as the governor's private secretary, should have been inside bearing witness to what was taking place, but now he was rather glad that he had been excluded. There was enough rage to spare in that room, and he didn't want any of it to be aimed in his direction. Anyway, he was able to hear all that was being said perfectly well. The doors were thick, but they weren't *that* thick . . .

'The shuttle went down twelve hours ago, and you're telling us that there is still no trace of my husband?'

The voice was that of the Archmage Syrene. She had put aside her formal robes, and was dressed in a simple dress of red silk. There were dark patches beneath her eyes. It was clear that she had not slept the previous night.

'Or my daughter,' said Lord Andrus. 'You forget that she was also on that shuttle.'

'Your daughter is a traitor,' said Sedulus, who was standing next to Syrene. He wore an unadorned black suit and a matching knitted silk tie. It struck Andrus as odd that Sedulus, who hated the humans more than most – and was similarly hated by them in return – should have embraced their fashions so wholeheartedly. His shoes were polished to a high sheen, and the only item of his dress that gave a hint of his position was a tiny gold pin in the left-hand lapel of his jacket, a pin in the shape of a fist clutching a bolt of lightning.

'Nevertheless, she remains my daughter,' said Andrus evenly.

'One might almost believe that you condoned her actions,' said Sedulus.

'I will not disown my daughter because of a single failing, no matter how grave,' Andrus replied.

His head ached, and he had slept no more than the Archmage. As the senior Military commander, he was in charge of the search for his daughter and the Grand Consul, even though it was a search that he had a vested interest in seeing fail. Meanwhile Syl was a prisoner of the Resistance, which was little consolation. He had spent a decade fighting them, and now the life of his only daughter was in their hands.

'None of this matters!' shouted Syrene. 'Your daughter is of *no* consequence. My husband, and his safe return, is the priority here. Why have you not sent in waves of soldiers to sweep the land? How can one of the most important figures in the Illyri Empire be a suspected captive of a band of terrorists?'

Lord Andrus sat back in his chair.

'I don't think you grasp the difficulty of the situation to the north,' he said.

'Well,' said Syrene, 'why don't you just explain it to me?'

The Military interceptor flew high over the Central Lowlands, heading north for the Highland Boundary Fault, or the Highland Line as the locals called it, the ancient rock fracture that bisected the Scottish mainland from Helensborough in the west to Stonehaven in the north-east. The Line was the natural divider between the Lowlands to the south and the Highlands to the north and west, but the Illyri had their own name for it. They referred to it as 'the Moat', for beyond it lay bandit country. It was one of a number of regions across the globe that they had found impossible to police, and its inhabitants had largely been left to their own devices. While the Illyri had managed to maintain significant bases at Aberdeen and Inverness to the north, and a smaller mountain base at the Cairngorms Plateau, these were basically just besieged fortresses, surrounded by hostile, aggressive populations. Although the main offworld route out of Edinburgh lay over the Highlands, such flights were conducted at relatively high altitude whenever possible, and were consequently out of the reach of the Resistance's weapons. Low-level shuttle flights to Aberdeen and Inverness tended to take what was known as the 'scenic route' over the North Sea, well out of reach of the land. Keeping the base at the Cairngorms Plateau supplied was costly and dangerous; even the comparatively short hop west from Inverness to the Cairngorms base was known as the Suicide Run.

Thus it was that the interceptor was trying to remain low enough to spot any signs of what might be the Highland Resistance and their Illyri captives, and high enough to avoid providing an easy target. It was also flying slowly enough to more easily spot anyone on the ground, yet fast enough not to be hit by them if they proved to be hostile. It was a delicate balance, and one that was near impossible to maintain.

On board were the pilot and co-pilot, along with an eight-member Illyri extraction team, all heavily armed and armoured. Their instructions were clear: if members of the Resistance were sighted, they were to be engaged and at least one of them captured alive, in the hope that, under interrogation, they might provide some clue as to the whereabouts of Grand Consul Gradus and the traitor Syl. The problem, as those on the interceptor well knew, was that the Resistance did not wear uniforms, and did not travel in convoys advertising their identity. There was, in reality, no way to tell who was an active member of the Resistance and who was not until the shooting began, and by then it was generally too late. The easiest thing was to assume that *everyone* beyond the Moat – men, women, children and possibly even sheep and cows – was a member of the Resistance unless they could prove otherwise.

The interceptor veered north-west over the Grampians towards Fort William, where there had once been a small Illyri base until the Resistance had blown it off the map. Beneath the craft lay Loch Rannoch, still and silver in the morning light.

'I have movement,' said the co-pilot.

'Where?' said the pilot.

'Northern shore of the loch. Four – no, five humans, heading east. You want to take a look?'

The pilot adjusted course.

'It's why we're here.'

'That's not answering the question.'

The pilot grimaced. 'Just put the guns on them. I have the ship.'

The co-pilot activated the weapon system, and the twin-barrel heavy cannon beneath the interceptor spun in their housing. The craft zeroed in on the humans, and the co-pilot fixed them in his sights. The 20mm guns were capable of firing two thousand rounds per minute. They could reduce a human being to shreds of meat within seconds.

As the interceptor drew closer to the banks of the loch, the humans became clearer: three males and two females. The males were carrying fishing rods, the women tackle boxes. They stopped and stared as the interceptor approached them. Carefully they put down their fishing equipment and raised their hands.

'What do you think?' said the co-pilot. 'Our orders are to stop and question.'

The pilot viewed the terrain dubiously. The ground was soft from the rains of the previous week, and once they landed, their cannon would be virtually useless. They would be entirely reliant on the weapons of the extraction team.

One of the humans started waving wildly, smiling as he did so.

'We'll—' the pilot began, but whatever he had decided was destined never to be heard.

The Resistance were students of history. Before the coming of the Illyri, the United Kingdom had not been successfully invaded since the arrival of William the Conqueror in 1066. The men and women who fought in the Highlands had no direct experience of guerrilla conflict, but they had been taught about the battles their ancestors had fought against the English. They had also studied the campaigns of the mujahideen against the Soviets in the previous century, and the difficulties the Americans had subsequently encountered in Iraq, and Somalia, and Afghanistan. One of the lessons they had learned was how to bring down aircraft using rocket-propelled grenades. RPGs had originally been designed for use against tanks, but the addition of a curved pipe to the rear of the launcher enabled them to be directed from a prone position at an aircraft hovering above.

Two RPGs were fired at the interceptor simultaneously, one from bushes to the east, and a second from a small copse of trees to the west. Snaking trails of smoke behind them, the first entered through the cockpit window, while the second hit the shuttle's port engine. The last thing the co-pilot saw before the interceptor exploded was the fishing party diving for cover after signalling for the start of the attack. The debris scattered itself across Loch Rannoch, and was swallowed along with the dead.

Within a minute, the waters were still again.

Just outside Pithlochry, by the shores of the River Tummel, the last soldier was running for his life. Behind him, the rest of the extraction team lay dead or dying; the pilots had been killed before they could even get out of their seats. They had been drawn there by Ani's tracker, kept in a lead box to shield its signals and transported to Pithlochry by motorcycle before being removed and used to lure the Illyri into a trap.

The soldier's name was Varon. He had been posted to Aberdeen for the previous six months. In that time, half of his platoon had been killed or seriously injured. Although he had been on Earth for only eighteen months, he now counted as a veteran in the Highlands.

Varon hated Earth, but most of all he hated Scotland. He came from the desert planet of B'Ethanger, at the heart of the Illyr system. He was built for heat and sand, not rain and mud. He had not stopped sneezing since he arrived. Today, at least, it was not raining. It had seemed like a good omen when the extraction team had set out.

Bullets kicked up dirt to his left, but Varon did not look back. If he could get out of range and find cover, he might be able to hold off the Resistance until a rescue party could be sent out. He had his blast pistol and heavy rifle. The rifle was charged for two hundred rounds, and the blast pistol was good for another twenty. If he needed more than that to stay alive, then he really was in trouble.

There was a low stone wall ahead of him. He dived over it head first, and almost knocked his brains out on a gravestone. He was in an old cemetery, littered with lopsided and broken monuments that reminded him of rotten teeth. There was plenty of cover here, but it would be as useful to his pursuers as it was to him. Still, better this than no cover at all, he thought, even if being in a human cemetery made him uneasy. The Illyri had always cremated their dead. They did not leave them to rot in the ground. It was another reason to regard the humans as a barbaric race.

The grounds of the cemetery sloped upwards, and he followed the gradient. If he could make it to high ground, he would have the advantage. He skirted a huge tomb that dwarfed the other resting places, and stopped short.

There was a young woman kneeling by a grave about ten metres from where he stood. She was putting wild flowers into a plastic vase. She looked up at him as he appeared. Varon raised his blast pistol and stepped forward. As he did so, his right foot knocked against a metal object. He glanced down and saw the hand grenade.

'Ah,' he said, and then he was gone.

By the end of the first day of the search, the Illyri had lost two interceptors and a skimmer, and had suffered more than thirty casualties, twenty of them fatalities. When the advance base on the Cairngorms Plateau came under extensive mortar fire, it was rendered temporarily unfit for use. The losses were the most significant suffered by the Illyri in a single day since the early years of the invasion.

The message had passed quickly through the Resistance in the Highlands: we have a valuable prize. The Illyri want to get it back.

Stop them.

'So,' said Sedulus, 'what you're telling us is that you are powerless to act beyond the Moat?'

'Not powerless, no, but we can operate only with great difficulty,' said Lord Andrus. 'And while the situation is most dangerous beyond the Moat, it's not much better once you travel more than a few miles north of the Glasgow–Edinburgh line. The truth is that the Grand Consul's shuttle could not have gone down in a worse location.'

Sedulus was silent for a moment. He looked at Syrene. She nodded.

'I am sure that you have not forgotten your recent conversation with Grand Consul Gradus,' said Sedulus to Lord Andrus. 'The Diplomatic Corps now has jurisdiction on Earth. The Military is at the command of the Corps.'

'My understanding was that all such authority lay with Grand Consul Gradus,' said Lord Andrus. 'In his absence, I am once again responsible for decisions here.'

'I'm afraid not,' said Sedulus. 'The Grand Consul left instructions that command should default to the ranking Corps official while he was offworld. The Archmage Syrene will confirm this.'

'It is true,' said Syrene. 'I witnessed my husband giving the order myself.'

'In his absence, therefore, I am in command, not you,' said Sedulus.

'I object most strongly—' began Lord Andrus.

'Your objection is noted,' said Sedulus. 'I have decided that I will take total charge of the search for Grand Consul Gradus – and, indeed, your daughter.' He glanced at Danis. 'Neither have I forgotten your own little traitor, General Danis. She will be found.'

Danis did not reply. The only sign of his inner tension was the slow, rhythmic tapping of his right foot on the carpet.

'For now,' continued Sedulus, 'all Military craft are to withdraw from the Highlands and return to their bases. This will be a Securitat operation.'

'What do you propose to do, Marshal Sedulus?' asked Andrus. 'Scour the Highlands yourself, mile by mile?'

'It is tempting,' said Sedulus. 'But I have enlisted the help of more experienced hunters than I.'

He stood to leave, and Syrene did the same, taking his arm.

'The Highlands,' Sedulus concluded, 'are about to be subdued.'

CHAPTER 43

Some time later, Syl heard a vehicle pull up outside, but the window in the outbuilding faced away from the noise and she could not see what was happening. Just Joe and Paul came for her shortly after, and she was brought to the comfortable kitchen of the cottage. There she found Tam, Heather and two men she did not recognise, but who were now introduced to her as Mike and Seán. Heather pointed to a seat at the table, and Syl took it. Seán leaned over and offered his hand. She shook it.

'Fine strong grip on you,' he said.

His accent was different from the others.

'Thank you,' said Syl. 'I think.'

'Sit down, Syl, and don't mind him,' said Heather. 'He's Irish,' as if this explained everything one could possibly want to know about the man.

There was a big battered teapot in front of Seán, and he poured Syl a cup while he spoke.

'Just visiting,' he said. He pushed milk and sugar towards her, but she added only the milk.

'Seán transports weapons for us from across the Irish Sea,' said Just Joe. He watched Syl to gauge her reaction.

'Why are you telling me this?' she asked.

'A gesture of trust,' replied Just Joe.

'And they don't mind if the Irish guy gets it in the head if you do talk,' added Seán.

'That too,' said Just Joe. 'Syl, tell me why you helped Paul and Steven escape.'

'Because they helped my friend and me during the bombings on the Royal Mile. And because they were going to be executed, and I wasn't going to let that happen.'

'Why? Because they're young?'

'Yes. And they hadn't done what they were accused of doing.'

'How do you know that?'

'Paul told me, and I saw in his face that it was true. And even if they had done it, hanging them would still have been wrong.'

'What of the rest of the Resistance?'

'I don't know the rest of the Resistance.'

'You know us. Would you see us hanged for what we've done? We've killed Illyri, and we'll kill more. This is our land, our world, and we want it back.'

Syl had thought about this a lot of late, but she did not have an answer. The question was too complex. She was of the Illyri, and she did not want to see her people hurt, but she also understood that the conquest of the Earth was indefensible. The Illyri might have been more advanced than the humans, and stronger militarily, but that didn't give them the right to invade, to suppress, to take young humans as hostages, train them as soldiers and send them off to fight the Illyri's wars on distant worlds.

And many of those wars still raged, with no end in sight. This much she'd learned while hiding in the spyhole behind the Great Hall at Edinburgh Castle. The most brutal fighting of all was taking place on Ebos, a jungle planet on which every life form, whether animal or vegetative, was actively carnivorous. It had been found to have enough precious metal deposits beneath its surface to meet the needs of the Illyri for centuries. The dominant species on Ebos was a reptilian race vaguely similar to the Komodo dragons of Earth, had the dragons learned to walk upright, but much larger, infinitely more vicious and with a chameleon-like capacity for camouflage so finely tuned that it rendered them practically invisible to the naked eye. Their ability to thermoregulate also meant that heat-detection lenses were ineffective in alerting the Illyri to their presence. While their weaponry was hardly sophisticated, it was surprisingly effective, their blades and arrowheads capable of slicing through even the thickest of body armour. Ebos was regarded as the worst posting in the Illyri Military. For the most part, Punishment Battalions and troublesome conscripts were the main source of workers and soldiers, and their casualty rates were astronomical. If the roles had been reversed, Syl knew, she would have been standing alongside the Resistance, just as Paul and Steven were.

And yet, and yet . . .

'I understand why you're fighting, and no, I don't believe in execution — for anyone,' she said at last. 'We don't execute our own people on Illyr, and I don't see why we should execute those on other worlds. But I don't want to see Illyri killed, and I won't help you to do it.'

Her mouth was dry. She took a sip of tea to moisten it before continuing.

'My people think I'm a traitor, and if I'm captured, the best I can hope for is to be imprisoned far from this planet until the Diplomats decide to free me or kill me. I have no interest in betraying you. If I betray you, I betray myself.'

Just Joe looked at the others. Seán's grin had never left his face, but it had never reached his eyes either. Syl sensed the danger in him. The ones — whether human or Illyri — who laughed and joked the most were often the worst, she had found. If you listened hard enough, the hollowness inside them echoed their laughter. Heather whispered something to Tam, who did not reply. Paul stood beside the fireplace, waiting.

'Well?' said Just Joe.

'Yes,' said Heather, with some force.

'Yes,' said Tam, although a little more reluctantly than his sister.

'Go on then,' said Seán, smiling away. 'Yes — but if she lets us down, I'll kill her myself before I die.'

'Paul?' said Just Joe.

'You know my answer,' said Paul. 'Yes.'

'Who knew you were all so trusting?' said Just Joe. 'Yes it is, then.'

'Yes to what?' asked Syl.

'To you staying with us,' said Just Joe, 'and not being handed over to one of the other groups as a bargaining chip for hostages. But understand this: Paul has stood up for you, and he's guaranteed your honour with his own life. I hear what you've said, and I believe it to be true. But if push comes to shove, and you turn on us, the boy here will pay with his life, and you with yours. Am I clear?'

Syl looked at Paul, but he was staring fixedly at the table.

'Yes,' said Syl, for there was no other option.

Just Joe relaxed. The decision had been made, and there was no point in fretting about it any longer.

'Now,' said Just Joe. 'Tell us about the Grand Consul.'

For the next hour, Syl spoke of Gradus's arrival, and of the Archmage Syrene. She told them what she knew of the Sisterhood, although much of it seemed to be familiar to them already. Mostly they were interested in the Grand Consul – how he acted, what he said, whether he had seemed strange or preoccupied at all, whether he had spoken of the attack on Birdoswald, and the suicide of his nephew.

And bodies: had there been any talk of human bodies?

But there was little that Syl could offer in reply to these enquiries, and she was glad of this. Okay, so she didn't know very much about Gradus, and what she did know she did not like. But nor did she like spilling what she knew to the Resistance, for it really did mean that she was committing treason, that she was a traitor.

'Why don't you ask him all this yourselves?' she said finally.

'We've tried asking him,' said Just Joe.

'Nicely, and not so nicely,' said Seán. 'We didn't get very far.'

'Show her,' said Tam. 'Maybe she can explain it.'

Just Joe and Paul led her from the cottage to a second outbuilding, this one bigger than the one in which she had been kept, and more closely guarded. The door was unlocked at Just Joe's order, and Syl entered with the two humans.

Gradus was seated in a corner, his hands tied behind his back. There was bruising to his face, and a cut on his scalp had bled badly. Despite herself, Syl felt sorry for him. She was about to admonish the humans, and demand that they clean him up, when she saw Gradus's eyes.

They were almost completely white behind the nictitating membrane, which now appeared fixed in place. His breathing was very shallow, and his mouth hung open slightly. She approached him warily, and touched his skin. It was cold.

'What have you done to him?' she asked.

'Nothing,' said Paul. 'Well, he was being questioned—'

'Beaten, you mean,' said Syl.

Paul did not continue, but had the decency to look ashamed.

'His body temperature dropped suddenly,' said Just Joe. 'His eyes rolled up into his head, and that membrane thing became fixed. He stopped responding to any kind of stimuli. Pain, heat, touch: he didn't seem to feel any of it. Is that natural? Is it something that your people can do under stress?'

Syl shook her head. She had never seen any Illyri behave in such a way before.

'It's possible that it's something he learned from the Sisterhood, a way of protecting himself,' she suggested.

'He'll be hard to get to the Green Man in that state,' said Paul. 'We can't carry him.'

'And we can't stay in this place,' said Just Joe. 'We've been here too long as it is. We're moving at nightfall, even if we have to drag him on wheels.'

Syl and the humans left the outbuilding, and the door was locked once again.

'I'm sending you into Durroch with Tam and Heather,' Just Joe told Paul. Durroch, Syl had learned, was the name of the village they had bypassed earlier. 'We have friends there, and we need supplies: medical mostly, in case we get into trouble, but we'll need rice, dried soups, maybe some tea and coffee as well. There's a shortwave radio at the chemist's shop: you can use it to send a message to Trask letting him know that you're okay. I promised him we'd put you in touch when we had the chance, but Heather's radio has given up the ghost. Be as quick as you can. Any sign of Illyri, and you keep your head down and hope for the best, okay? Tam and Heather, not you, will make the call on whether anyone needs to start shooting.'

Just Joe walked away, leaving Syl and Paul alone.

'You staked your life on me?' said Syl.

'Well, you risked yours for me,' said Paul.

'I didn't really know you then,' said Syl.

'What's that supposed to mean?'

Syl looked down at her feet to hide her smile. 'Just that now I've got to know you a bit, I might not be so quick to do it next time.'

'Hey, I'm not so bad.'

'Well, maybe I don't feel that allowing your rescuer to be locked up like an animal is exactly nice.'

Paul shook his head despairingly. 'Women,' he said. 'You're from a different species, and yet you're still the same.'

'So you're telling me you've given up on humans and decided to try Illyri females instead?'

'That's not what I said!'

'But isn't it what you meant?' said Syl, and suddenly she felt stupid, and a bit shy too.

'No!'

'Then why did you kiss me?'

Paul seemed lost for words. 'I – I was overcome by the moment.'

'So it won't happen again?'

'Not if you don't want it to,' said Paul. He stuck his hands in his pockets. His face was furrowed with confusion. It made him look very young.

'That isn't what I meant,' Syl replied, mortified, and turned to walk back to the cottage.

Paul watched her go. He looked even more confused, if such a thing were possible.

'What?' he said forlornly. 'I don't understand . . .'

CHAPTER 44

Durroch had only one main street housing two pubs, a supermarket-cum-post-office, a small café, a chemist's shop and, at its northern end, the local kirk, or church. It was tiny but very, very old, dating back to the seventeenth century.

Syl sat in the back of the Land Rover beside Heather, with Tam and Paul in the front. Lex sat on Tam's lap, his paws on the steering wheel. The little dog seemed to be quite familiar with that position.

Just Joe had come to her as the party was about to leave for the village, and told her that she was to go with them. He gave no reason why, informing her only that she was to stay in the Range Rover unless ordered to do otherwise by Tam or Heather, and Syl had not objected. In part, she realised, she wanted to be with Paul, even though she was still embarrassed about their awkward conversation earlier. She was attracted to him, that much she knew. She had been attracted to him since the first time they'd met, but something in her still rebelled against her own feelings because they were wrong, just wrong. It made her want to fight him, to push him away for fear of being hurt, but when he had seemed wounded by their exchange, she had felt a warm, warped pleasure, as surely that meant he cared about her too.

They passed the church just as Tam was trying to explain to her the nature of religious worship in Scotland.

'You see,' he said, 'originally there was the Roman Catholic church, but then came the Reformation in 1560, and out of that came the Presbyterian Church of Scotland, but the Catholics and the Episcopalians were still around as well. Anyway, the Church of

Scotland kept having arguments about how it should be run, and in 1847 two churches left to form the United Presbyterian Church, although an earlier fight had also produced the Free Church of Scotland in 1843. You follow me?'

'Not really,' said Syl.

'So,' Tam continued, 'the Free Church split in 1893, with a group going off to call itself the Free Presbyterian Church, and then in 1900 most of the Free Church joined with the United Presbyterians to form the United Free Church, except for those who stayed on as the Free Church of Scotland. Then the United Free Church joined with the Church of Scotland, but there were still some folk who didn't want to, so they continued as the United Free Church. Ye ken?'

'No,' said Syl, who by now was completely confused. 'Not at all. They all worship the same god, don't they?'

'Absolutely,' said Tam. 'I think,' he added.

'Which kind are you?' asked Syl.

'Oh, I don't go to church,' said Tam. 'I just find it all amusing.'

'At least they're not killing each other over it,' said Syl. She still found it incredible that people would destroy each other over the nature of a being nobody had ever seen.

'Aye, you're right,' said Tam. 'They haven't killed anybody in ages. You kind of feel that they're not really trying hard enough any more.'

The Land Rover pulled in behind the chemist's shop. There were a few people on the street. One of them waved to Tam, and he waved back. The windows at the back of the Range Rover were very small, and the glass was smoked. Only those sitting in the front seats were visible to the people outside.

'You stay here,' said Tam, as the others got out. 'Don't go wandering off.'

'Why did you need me to come if I'm just going to sit here?' asked Syl.

'Just Joe's orders,' said Tam. 'We're picking up a special delivery. He thought you might be able to help with it. We'll let you know when you're needed.'

And with that they walked off. With nothing else to do, Syl slouched back in her seat and watched the world go by.

Meia stood before Lord Andrus and General Danis. She had spent the night away from the castle, following tunnels and exploring the crematorium. She had found a sub-system linking the main tunnel to a previously unknown Corps research laboratory at Launston Place, not far from the Old City Wall, but even wearing the uniform of a Securitat, and with an array of false identity cards, she didn't believe she could successfully gain access, and had been forced to retreat. Now, exhausted and smelling faintly of drains, she made her report. The room had been swept for listening devices, and a small electromagnetic pulse was being used to ensure that any lurkers that had found their way into nooks and crannies would cease to function.

'First, what news of our children?' said Lord Andrus.

'Syl is safe, and with the Resistance. My contact anticipates a more detailed message later today. General Danis's daughter is on her way north.'

The two fathers smiled at each other with relief, then turned their attention back to her.

'I have not forgiven you for what you did, Meia,' said Andrus.

'I understand.'

'General Danis has not forgiven you either.'

'Perhaps if I live long enough, he may find it in his heart,' said Meia, keeping her face studiedly neutral.

'Nobody is that long-lived, not even you,' said Danis. 'I wouldn't hold my breath.'

'Enough bickering now,' said Andrus, 'for there is much to be done. Continue, Meia. Tell us about the tunnels.'

'I saw bodies,' she said.

'Humans?' said Andrus.

'Of all ages. I think the Corps has been moving them between the crematorium and the lab at Launston Place. There's a connector from there to a landing pad at The Meadows, which has been used by a couple of large Corps vessels in recent months. I could only access a handful of flight records: some of them went straight offworld, but others flew south to Cornwall.'

'Do you have any idea where in Cornwall?'

'St Blazey: the Eden Project.'

The Eden Project had been opened in 2001, shortly before the Illyri invasion. The complex collected plant samples from around the world, housed in adjoining geodesic biomes made from plastic cells supported by steel frames. Since the invasion, it had come under the control of the Diplomatic Corps, which had expanded it with additional domes. The stated purpose of the Corps-run facility was to research plant and animal species on Earth with the aim of coming to a better understanding of the planet's ecosystem.

'If we were jumping to conclusions,' said Danis, 'we'd surmise that the Corps, or individuals within it, might be moving bodies from Edinburgh to the Eden Project.'

'What are your orders, sir?' Meia asked Andrus.

'Go to Eden,' said Andrus, 'but tread carefully.'

Meia bowed, and left the room.

'How will this end, Danis?' asked Lord Andrus once the door had closed behind his spy.

'Badly, I fear,' said Danis.

'For whom?'

'For all of us.'

Syl was half asleep in the Land Rover when Heather and Paul returned, carrying boxes in their arms. Behind them came a portly woman in a white pharmacist's coat, and a pair of teenage boys, similarly laden with boxes. A black truck pulled up behind the Land Rover. Tam was in the passenger seat but the driver was a red-haired man whom Syl had not seen before. They exchanged words, and Tam climbed out and went to the back of the truck.

'Out you get,' said Heather to Syl. Paul stood smirking beside her.

Syl clambered from the Land Rover.

'What are you looking so smug about?' she asked Paul.

'I'm not smug, just happy.'

'Well stop it. It's unnerving.'

The woman in the white coat stared at her curiously. The boys with her were goggle-eyed with a mix of amazement and cautious hostility. The only Illyri they ever saw this far north were probably on patrol, and they certainly did not go around sitting in the backs of Land Rovers squabbling with humans.

Tam reappeared to her right, and he was not alone.

'Uh,' said Syl. It was a very small sound, but it contained as much emotion as a single syllable could accommodate.

'Is that all you have to say?' said Ani. 'Uh?'

And the two young Illyri lost themselves in an embrace.

CHAPTER 45

Tam, with Lex for company, decided to stay a little longer at Durroch. Lizzy, his girlfriend, lived a short distance outside the town, and he planned to ask her to join him and give him a ride back to the farm when his business in the village was done. The capture of Gradus – however valuable a prize he might be – had created problems for the Resistance, and there was some debate going on between Trask in Edinburgh and the representatives of the Green Man. There were also questions about what to do with Syl and Ani. A safe location would have to be found for them, perhaps long-term given the trouble they were in. There were plenty of places to hide in the Highlands, but the land was full of those who harboured deep resentment for the invaders. Trask had made one thing clear to the Resistance: if any harm befell the two girls, those who had failed to protect them could expect to be hunted to death along with those directly responsible, and Trask would help the Illyri to do it because it was his head on the chopping block. He had no illusions about Meia and her capacity for vengeance.

Syl and Ani sat in the back of the Land Rover with Steven, who had also been reunited with his brother, while Paul and Heather sat up front. The two young Illyri compared their stories of how they had ended up in a jeep in the Highlands, talking over each other excitedly, and laughing for the first time in what felt like forever.

'God, you two are noisy,' said Paul. 'It's like having a pair of sparrows trapped in the back.'

'Is he still soft on you?' asked Ani, deliberately loudly.

Syl nudged her hard in the ribs.

'He's soft in the head,' she answered. 'I know that much.'

Paul had begun to reply when Ani cocked her head and shushed him.

'Don't shush me,' said Paul. He was getting tired of being treated like an idiot by these two alien girls. They might have saved his life, but it struck him that he was paying a rather high price for it.

'Shut up,' said Ani. 'Can't you hear it?'

Now Syl could. It sounded like the distant buzzing of bees, but it was still beyond the range of the humans.

'Ships,' she said. 'Big ships.'

Paul didn't hesitate.

'Get off the road,' he told Heather. 'Make for those trees.'

Heather did as she was told, making a hard right turn down a ditch and across the fields until they came to a copse of evergreens. She knocked down some of the younger growth trees getting them under cover, and narrowly missed crashing the Land Rover into one of the larger ones, but eventually they were hidden, and she killed the engine.

All was silent.

'Nothing,' said Heather. 'There's—'

'No,' said Paul. 'They're right. Listen!'

The sound grew louder and louder, until the ground itself seemed to vibrate, and then, with a whoosh, two black skimmers flew low over the trees, heading south. All five occupants clambered from the vehicle to watch them pass.

'I've never seen black skimmers like those before,' said Paul. 'Who are they?'

'Securitats,' said Syl. 'At least, I think so. They like black.'

But their attention was captured by the three massive cruisers that appeared from the north. Those on the flanks broke right and left as they came, while the one at the centre continued on a straight course. At last all five craft were hovering in a circle around the distant village of Durroch.

Slowly they began to descend.

'No,' whispered Heather. 'God, no. Tam. *Tam!*'

★ ★ ★

Tam had been drinking a swift half in the Beggar's Arms in Durroch when the incoming skimmers caused the glasses on the bar to vibrate, and set the bottles of spirits rattling on the shelves. Tam swore. He had a gun tucked into his trousers, and the first priority was to get rid of it. He didn't want to be armed if he was searched. Chances were that this was part of the effort to trace the survivors of the shuttle crash, and if everybody remained calm and said as little as possible, then all would be well. He just had to be careful where he hid the gun. He called over the landlord, known as False Ed because of the wig he wore. False Ed was trying to reassure the handful of customers in the bar, and keep them drinking. He didn't want to lose money unnecessarily.

'You still have that compost heap out back?' asked Tam.

'Aye, we do.'

'Give me a bag.'

The landlord found a plastic carrier bag under the bar, and Tam wrapped the pistol in it as he made his way through the kitchen. He found a big bin filled with vegetable peelings and discarded food from lunch, and buried the gun in the middle of it. He then marched outside to the compost heap, and casually spilled the contents of the bin at the back of the rotting pile. The bag containing the gun remained entirely concealed; Tam couldn't see the Illyri wading through the stinking mass in their nice uniforms to search for contraband. He put his hand to his eyes and looked up at the sky. A black skimmer made its gradual descent to land in the open field at the back of the pub. He counted one more, but it was the three big incoming cruisers that made him fearful. He put the bin down and walked to the main street. Residents of the village had come outside too, alerted by the noise. His stomach gave an uncomfortable lurch. The village was surrounded. Lex, standing at Tam's feet, barked at the craft overhead.

False Ed appeared beside him.

'Military or Corps?' he asked.

'My guess is Securitats,' said Tam, drawing the same conclusion from their colour as Syl had, although he'd never seen black cruisers before. 'You have anything in there you should be worried about?'

False Ed did his part for the Resistance. Everyone in Durroch did. Those who were not active members were sympathisers, willing to store guns and radio equipment, carry messages, or give a bed to strangers who sometimes passed through on Resistance business.

'Just some bad beer,' said False Ed.

'I've drunk your beer,' said Tam. 'It's all bad.'

'It's cheap, though.'

'Aye, it is that.'

But they did not smile as they joked. Whistling past the graveyard, that's what we're doing, thought Tam. Joking in the face of sleek black menace.

The cruisers landed in unison, and there was silence as their engines powered down. Somewhere, a dog barked.

The first figures appeared at the outskirts of the town: a handful of Galateans and several dozen Securitats in full armour, all heavily armed, their faces hidden behind blast masks. They went from house to house and shop to shop, rousting the occupants at gunpoint, ignoring the wails of children and the cries of frightened men and women. Tam and False Ed knew the drill. Searches were an occasional occurrence, even this far north, and were usually carried out by a significant Illyri force in order to ensure their safety. They were more of a nuisance to the locals and the Resistance than anything else. Arms caches were well hidden, and all those who handled weapons and explosives were careful to use solvents to clean as much of the residue from their hands as possible. Also, since the Illyri risked being attacked both flying to or from the search zone, and while they were on the ground, the value of random searches was minimal. Tam couldn't even remember one being conducted in or near Durroch for at least a year, and on that occasion, as on all others, it had been the Military in charge. The Corps didn't tend to waste its time with such nonsense; if the Corps or its Securitats arrived somewhere, they usually had cast-iron information, and somebody always suffered for it. That was why Tam was concerned by the sight of the black craft. If it was a Securitat operation, the people of Durroch were in real danger.

After a cursory pat-down for concealed weapons, the villagers were herded into the town square beside a monument to the dead of two world wars. In recent years, old Lee Lennox, the stonemason, had added a granite slab to the base of the memorial, and had begun to carve the names of local Resistance members who had died fighting the Illyri. On two occasions, the Illyri Military had broken the slab and removed the pieces during their search, but each time Lennox had quickly created a replacement. The latest slab was there now, with four names carved on it, the youngest of them aged only fifteen; his name was Boyd, and he had been Tam's only son.

Tam held Lex under one arm, and patted the dog's head to keep him calm. He counted perhaps sixty people, mostly women, children and old men. The older boys and girls had either headed farther north to avoid being drafted into the Illyri's battalions, gone to one of the big cities to find work, or simply joined the Resistance in the Highlands.

And some, like Boyd, were dead.

Now there was a rumbling sound, and a heavy-tracked troop transporter, its black body bristling with weaponry, was spewed out by one of the cruisers. It stopped at the western end of the square. A second appeared at the eastern end. Their turret guns turned, and were trained on the assembled humans.

The door of the first transporter opened and two Illyri stepped down. One was female, and dressed in the standard uniform of the Securitats. The other wore a dark suit, and a long overcoat to keep out the cold Scottish wind. Tam recognised them both: the female was Vena, the Securitat pin-up girl in Scotland. The male was Sedulus, the head of the Securitats in Europe. They were both Category One targets for the Resistance, but Sedulus was the real prize. Tam wished there had been some warning of his approach. A sniper could have put a bullet in his head and made the Earth a better place. It was too late now, though. Tam looked to the skies. The clouds were dark and warned of rain. He hoped that Heather and Paul had seen the Illyri approach, and had made it safely back to Just Joe and the others.

Behind Sedulus, Agrons held on leashes appeared. They were more primitive-looking than the regular Agrons, and barely capable of walking upright, but their noses were bigger, the nostrils wider. Tam knew that they had been genetically adapted by the Illyri to enhance their sense of smell.

Tam lit a cigarette. He felt a great sadness wash over him. He had a feeling that he wouldn't be seeing his sister again, but he might be reunited with his son. He wondered if the manner of his dying would hurt, then tried to force the thought from his head. Heather had always told him he was a pessimist by nature. She tried to make him see the brighter side of things, and sometimes she even succeeded. Maybe we'll survive this, he thought. Maybe Sedulus, and his little hunting bitch, and all his armoured bullies, will be content to frighten us a bit and let us go after some rough questioning.

And maybe the sun will shine.

Slowly, so as not to alarm the Illyri surrounding them, Tam leaned down and placed Lex on the ground.

'Off you go, boy,' he said. 'Go find Lizzy.'

The dog was reluctant to leave him, and it was all Tam could do not to weep at the animal's loyalty.

'Go on now,' he urged. 'Go to Lizzy. She'll look after you.'

At last Lex, who had walked the road to and from Lizzy's farm for many years, did as he was told. He slipped between the legs of the Illyri and trotted away. From the corner of his eye Tam saw him pause one last time, as though willing his master to call him back. When he did not, the little dog lowered his head and went on his way.

'Goodbye, Lex,' whispered Tam. 'I'll see you on the other side.'

A stiff thread hung from the padded coat that he always wore, rain or shine. Slowly, he began to wind the thread around his fingers, drawing it tight. He'd known that he'd be glad of the coat some day.

Sedulus stood before the villagers. A small microphone was attached to his collar. It amplified his voice so that all could hear him easily.

'People of Durroch,' he said. 'You may be aware that last night an Illyri shuttle went down south of here. Three Illyri died in the crash, but we believe that two survived and were picked up by humans, possibly members of the terrorist Resistance.'

Nobody spoke, but nobody looked away either. They remained standing in silence, their eyes fixed on the tall, thin Illyri in the expensive coat and the black, brilliantly shiny shoes.

'We believe that the captive Illyri passed this way. Our Agrons caught something of their scent, but the heavy rains made the trail impossible to follow accurately.'

Somebody snickered behind Tam. The Securitat wasn't going to get much sympathy here for his lost trails.

Sedulus had clearly heard the laughter. He responded with a smile of his own as he walked to the war memorial and looked down on the granite slab with its four names.

'Your village is known to be sympathetic to the Resistance,' he said. 'The Military has long had its suspicions about you, and the names of the Resistance dead are honoured here.' He pointed at the slab. 'I understand that this memorial has been destroyed in the past by the Illyri. I promise you that I do not intend to commit a similar act of desecration. It is important that the dead should be remembered, regardless of the cause for which they fought. Who is the stonemason?'

A few seconds went by before an elderly man moved from the back of the crowd to the front, his head held high. If he was resigned to being punished for what he had done, he was still determined to show no fear.

'I am,' he said. 'My name is Lennox.'

'You don't need to be afraid of me,' said Sedulus. 'No harm will come to you.'

Lennox couldn't hide his surprise at not being shot, even if he didn't look quite sure that he believed what he was hearing. Two guards led him to one side and kept watch over him.

Now the Agrons were led towards the crowd, their handlers controlling them with their leashes. They sniffed at legs and feet and sleeves. Tam tried to show no fear as one drew near him, and paused. He hadn't touched the girl, or the Grand Consul, but he'd been in their presence. He knew that the Agrons were better than blood-hounds, and these were clearly on another level entirely, but he held his breath, and his nerve, as the Agron snuffled at his clothing, seemed to consider what it was picking up and then moved on. Meanwhile, the Securitats collected the biometric identity cards that citizens were obliged by law to carry with them at all times. The cards were handed to Vena, who leafed through them with a bored expression on her face, as though they were someone else's holiday snaps that had been forced upon her. She offered them to Sedulus, but he waved them aside.

'We believe that more than one person here knows the whereabouts of Resistance operatives in this area,' Sedulus continued. 'We want the names of those operatives.'

Nobody moved. In the past, the Military had tried bribes and threats in an effort to force the villagers to betray the Resistance, but with no result. Durroch had even sacrificed some of its sons and daughters to the Illyri legions before those remaining had the good sense to make themselves harder to find. Everyone in the square knew the consequences for betraying the Resistance were nearly as ruinous: at best they would be exiled from the village, their names dirt, forced to lose themselves in one of the cities to the south, hoping that their reputation for treachery wouldn't follow them. Worse, in some places those who informed on the Resistance simply disappeared, especially if their betrayal led to loss of life. The Highlands had no shortage of bogs and marshes, and bodies that sank in them, weighted by stones, tended not to resurface.

But the villagers of Durroch stayed quiet now, not out of fear of the Resistance, but out of loyalty to their own. They were human beings first, and they would not give away those who fought in their name.

Sedulus did not seem surprised by their lack of cooperation, merely disappointed. He turned to Vena.

'Pick ten,' he instructed. 'Make sure there are children among them.'

Vena, with half a dozen Securitats at her heels, moved through the crowd and chose ten villagers at random by tapping them on the shoulder with her electric baton. They were escorted to the northern end of the square, where the ruins of an old Catholic church stood, now little more than low walls with the remains of the ornate lancet windows still visible. The ten villagers consisted of five children – three girls, two boys, none older than ten or eleven – and five men and women, none of them younger than fifty. False Ed, the pub landlord, was among them. He, like the other adults, tried to keep the children calm, even though the older villagers were just as frightened as the younger ones. There were cries and sobs among those who had not been chosen, as parents, husbands and wives waited to see what might happen to their loved ones.

The door of the transporter opened again, to reveal four mechanised support suits standing in the gap, unmoving. Tam squinted at the faceplates of their helmets. They appeared to be empty, but then the suits began to descend the walkway, and something like smoke swirled behind the faceplates as they made their way towards the ten villagers.

Don't do this, thought Tam. Whatever it is, don't do it. He felt an awful guilt. He could give himself up, but if he did, the Illyri would check his details and immediately head for the farm. He had to give Heather, Just Joe and the rest time to get away, but at what cost? He could see some of the villagers glancing at him, willing him to do something, to stop whatever was about to occur, but he couldn't, not yet.

Sedulus lifted his right hand. It contained a small black device no bigger than a key fob. All eyes were fixed on it.

'Do you know why we were so interested in this world, why we chose to colonise it?' he asked. 'Simple: because you looked so like us. When the Illyri Empire began to search the universe for signs of advanced life, we thought of it in terms of our own form. We wanted it to have two arms, two legs, one head. We wanted it to be carbon-based, to have languages that we could interpret. We hoped it would think like us. In the end, we were as surprised to find you as you were to be found.

'Because the truth is that there are all kinds of life forms in the universe: some primitive, a few more advanced, and some strange beyond all knowing. If you think the Galateans are unusual, or the Agrons, or even ourselves, prepare to be astonished. You are about to witness something that few humans have ever seen.'

He pressed a button on the device in his hand, and the faceplates on the support suits slid up with the slightest of hisses.

At first, Tam thought that what came flooding out of the suits were swarms of black bees. They swirled in the air, creating complex patterns against the cloudy sky above, before compressing into four solid masses that faced the terrified villagers waiting against the ruined church. They still roiled and twisted, but now they resembled bodies covered in black insects, albeit bodies with only the suggestion of arms or legs, and heads without eyes or mouths. They were shadows given substance, a devil's mimicry of the human form.

'Let us begin,' said Sedulus, pressing the device for a second time.

The shapes fell upon the chosen villagers, circling them like tornadoes, their darkness forming coils that closed around the bodies of the ten. The villagers began to disappear; first their foreheads, then their eyes, then their gaping, agonised mouths. It was like a magic trick performed by conjurors from hell itself. No, Tam realised, they weren't vanishing – they were being consumed from the head down, but so quickly that they barely had time to bleed. Yet bleed they did, faster and faster, until at last they were reduced to red pools on the ground, and then the dark beings consumed those too, every molecule of them, and there was nothing left of the villagers but the memory of them, and a few pieces of inorganic matter: plastic belts, metal buttons and badges, a single pacemaker. The beings became four swarms again, hovering beside their suits, waiting.

Waiting for more.

A woman in the crowd screamed a child's name, over and over and over again. Others joined in, as a wave of horror swept through the villagers, and the Illyri and Galateans brought their weapons to bear to keep them at bay.

'Another ten,' said Sedulus, and Vena again stepped forward to make the choice.

'No.'

It was a woman's voice. She stood between a boy and a girl, each of them strikingly similar. Her name was Morag, and her twin children were Colin and Catriona. Now she looked at Tam, and he gave her an almost imperceptible nod. He had been about to step forward anyway. He could not allow this atrocity to continue.

Sedulus looked at Morag.

'Well?' he said.

'If we tell you, will this end?' she said.

'Yes,' said Sedulus. 'But I want a name. Now.'

It was Tam, not Morag, who spoke next.

'I'm the one you're looking for,' he said.

'Take him,' said Sedulus, and Vena led the quartet of guards that pulled Tam from the crowd. 'Put him in the transporter.'

Tam was led to the nearest of the transporters, away from the scene of the slaughter. As he walked, he heard Sedulus give his final instruction.

'Kill them all,' he said. 'But spare the stonemason.'

Tam turned back as he heard Morag scream, 'No! You promised! You said it would be the end of it!'

'And it will be.' Sedulus took the identity cards from Vena and handed them to the stonemason. 'To help you remember the names.'

And before the crowd could react the roiling black mass descended upon them all.

Tam watched it happen. He tried to pull away, but he could not. More Securitats surrounded him, forcing him to retreat from the carnage, as he was dragged backwards to the troop transporter. Already he was almost at its door. As he struggled, the sleeve of his coat tore in the hands of one of the Securitats, revealing not padding but a patch of high explosive, one of more than a dozen sewn into the garment.

The guard reacted, but not fast enough.

Oh well, thought Tam. I was hoping to take Sedulus and Vena with me, but you lot will just have to do.

He closed his right fist, and yanked at the threaded fuse.

And he, and everyone around him, ceased to exist.

CHAPTER 46

There was chaos in Durroch. The explosion had vaporised those closest to Tam, and reduced many of the Illyri in the immediate vicinity to pieces of meat. The heavy transporter's angle had shielded the villagers from the worst of the blast, but some of them had also been injured, although the black swarms quickly put an end to their suffering. Some villagers had escaped in the confusion, and were now being hunted through the streets, but they were fighting back. The sound of pulsers was met with scattered gunfire, and Sedulus knew that he risked losing control of the situation. He did not have time to battle humans from house to house.

The explosion had also severely damaged the transporter: the big armoured vehicles were particularly vulnerable when their doors were open, and this one had been gaping wide to receive Tam when he activated the device. It was now useless, but the incovenience of its loss was reduced somewhat by the fact that most of its former occupants were now dead or seriously injured.

Of more concern to Sedulus was that a piece of shrapnel had blown apart one of the support suits. The three undamaged suits had been resealed, and their occupants pressed darkly against the faceplates, watching one of their kind dying. It circled uncertainly around the useless suit, its energy gradually dissipating, until at last it assumed the form of a kneeling, armless figure. The shape of a mouth opened in agony, and the creature came apart like ash rising into the air, the wind blowing all trace of it away.

Sedulus felt a mix of anger and grief – and fear. The creatures he had unleashed on the villagers – the 'pets' of which Meia had her suspicions, and which had entirely wiped out villages in the past – had no name. Sedulus had found them marooned on a moon of Sarith when he was part of the Scientific Development Division – an innocent name that disguised the elite division's true purpose, which was to seek out alien life forms and technologies that might be used as weapons – and hence the creatures were known only as the Sarith Entities.

His ship had picked up signs of life on the barren moon, but they were difficult to pinpoint; at moments there seemed to be millions, at other times only five. When he led a team down to investigate, the life signs were tracked to a cave system. Outside the cave lay five shattered pods of alien design, unfamiliar to the Illyri and destined to remain so, for their origin had never been ascertained.

The three-member Illyri exploration team entered the caves warily. Their lights caught swirls of dust, but there was no wind to cause such a disturbance: the Sarith moon was a still, dead place. The dust began to thicken, assuming shapes that mimicked those of the Illyri in their spacesuits. There were five in all. One stepped forward and approached Sedulus.

Interesting, he thought. They identify me as the leader.

Later, back on the ship, he would wonder at what happened next. He reached out a hand, and the dark form simply restructured itself around it, so that it appeared as though Sedulus's arm was buried in its chest. In that instant, he had a flash of what he could only think of as understanding, a revelation of the nature of the thing before him. They were five, but they were many in five; each a single consciousness formed of countless smaller entities. He sensed rage – incredible, boundless rage – and loneliness, for they had been marooned on this world for so very long.

But most of all he felt their hunger, and as the other four coiled around the members of his team, he knew what he must do. He carefully drew from his pack one of the small laser cutters designed for the collection of mineral samples. He stepped back and used the beam to slice through the suits of the scientists, exposing the man and the woman who had been unfortunate enough to join him on the expedition. The entities poured through the holes in the material, and Sedulus had watched, enraptured, as they fed.

After that, they were his.

Now, in Durroch, two of the surviving Entities turned away from the empty suit and prepared to return to their transporter. One remained, and Sedulus saw himself reflected in the blank visage of its faceplate, giving him the uncomfortable sense of being trapped inside the support suit. The Securitat's head was bleeding from the scalp, and his right cheek had been cut deeply by a fragment of stone. A medic approached to seal the wounds, but Sedulus waved him away as he faced down the Entity. A sacrifice would be required, Sedulus knew. The Sarith had already lost one of their kind since they had allied themselves to him; it was in the early days of the occupation, and the technology of the support suits was still in the process of being perfected. On that occasion, a malfunction had led to the Entity suffocating inside its suit. Sedulus had given the Entities the small Norwegian town of Fagernes as recompense. He had wanted to make an example of it anyway, and the mystery of the disappearance of its citizens had suited his ends on that occasion.

But Durroch was different, for Sedulus wanted witnesses to its annihilation. It was why he had left the stonemason alive, and why the deaths of its inhabitants had been secretly filmed by the lens worn by Vena. Sedulus would ensure that the film was leaked to the Resistance, and not only on these islands. He wanted it to circulate. He wanted to sow terror and the desire for vengeance. He wanted the Resistance to grow bolder, to be goaded into committing further atrocities against the Illyri.

He wanted the Earth to damn itself.

He spoke to the Entity. 'You will have revenge for this,' he said.

The Entity briefly produced the shape of a head. Two eyeholes appeared, and a mouth. The mouth silently repeated one word.

Revenge.

The Illyri dead and injured were placed in the undamaged transporter to be taken to one of the other cruisers, for Sedulus did not want the dead stinking up his personal craft. Time had been wasted, but the delay was relatively minor. The bomber's biometric identity card had revealed the location of his home. Even without it, the Agrons already had his scent.

Sedulus gave the order to attack and seize the farm.

CHAPTER 47

The drone came in low, scanning for life forms. It detected the heat signatures of four humans in the main house, but no signs of life elsewhere. The drone remained close to the house while the three cruisers roared out of the clouds. Two landed in fields just outside the walls of the farm while the third hovered above the main farmhouse, scanning the entire area for movement, a skimmer beside it. The Resistance were known to use tunnels as escape routes and hiding places, and Sedulus did not want his troops on the ground to be taken unawares as they moved in on the farmhouse. The hovering skimmer spat out dozens of tiny seismic detectors, each of which penetrated the dirt with probes as soon as they hit the ground. The probes were capable of detecting evidence of excavation, as well as human speech patterns and any movement larger than that of a small mammal. They revealed no sign of human activity. Meanwhile, the figures in the house did not appear to have moved.

A squad of Securitats moved in on the farmhouse, the cruiser and the skimmer now hovering barely a few feet above its roof. All pulsers were set to hard stun. Sedulus desired information, and dead Resistance operatives were of no use to him. Gas grenades were fired through the windows of the house, and a hover ram fitted with a camera was used to break down the door and enter the building, just in case the entrances were booby-trapped.

The hover ram reached the farmhouse kitchen in which the four heat signatures had been detected. Its camera revealed four battered metal frames in vaguely human form leaning against the exposed brickwork, each heated by a network of elements that glowed redly in the dim light.

At that moment, the entire farmhouse exploded, taking the hovering cruiser and skimmer with it.

On a hillside nearby, Heather paused and looked back as a cloud of smoke rose up from the farm that she had loved. Beside her, Alice gripped her hand tightly.

'Uncle Tam?' whispered Alice.

Heather shook her head. She was trying not to cry for her daughter's sake, but she couldn't help herself. They had faintly heard the earlier explosion in Durroch, and she had feared the worst. The destruction of the farmhouse confirmed it.

'He's gone, darling,' she said. 'Uncle Tam's away to argue with God.'

CHAPTER 48

Syrene's image appeared in Sedulus's lens. Even in the midst of the disaster that constituted the last couple of hours, he knew better than to ignore the Archmage's incoming communication, but he would have given anything not to face her at this precise moment. He had, in the space of little over an hour, lost one cruiser, one skimmer, one transporter, one drone, twenty Securitats either dead or injured, along with a handful of Galateans and Agrons, and one Sarith Entity, although the latter was more personal than any of the other losses. Already the light was fading, and with the darkness returned the rain. The Agrons might have been able to function despite it, and even pick up the trail — for they detected particles in the air as much as on the ground — had the land around the farm and its surrounds not been sprayed with a chemical-based compound made from hot peppers, which attacked the Agrons' sensitive scent glands, rendering them useless for hours. Sedulus had fed two of them to the Sarith Entities in an effort to suppress the Entities' growing wrath.

He had felt it as he approached them in their sealed compartment, the Agrons desperately trying to escape from their harnesses as they understood what was about to befall them. This time, the three Entities had risen to face Sedulus, even ignoring, for a full thirty seconds, the cowering Agrons until their insatiable hunger finally got the better of their anger, and the Agrons were consumed.

Sedulus turned his back on their feeding. Usually he enjoyed watching them eat, entranced by the purity of their hunger. He did not want to destroy the Entities, but he would if he had to. It was he alone who controlled the support suits, and he had made sure that they had a self-destruct mechanism built into them. Whatever race had marooned them on Sarith had devised a particularly cruel torment for the Entities. Sarith was a barren, brutal environment, entirely without life and with an atmosphere poisoned by carbon monoxide, and yet the Entities were able to survive there unsupported. In an oxygen-rich environment like that of Earth – or even Illyr – they would die within minutes, but only on such planets would they be able to feed, and so Sedulus had designed the support suits, and in that way had made the Sarith Entities his creatures.

But what the remaining Entities did not know was that the death of the first of the five, shortly after their arrival on Earth, had not been caused by a suit malfunction, not in the truest sense of the word. The suit had done just what it had been programmed to do, which was to kill the Entity inside it on Sedulus's command.

The test had been necessary, for Sedulus had no illusions about the nature of the Entities.

The same could have been said of his relationship with Syrene, except that, while he thought he had some inkling of how the Entities functioned, the Archmage remained a mystery to him. Even her image in his lens radiated a compelling authority.

'Report to me,' she said. 'What news of my husband?'

'We picked up his trail, Archmage,' said Sedulus, 'but we encountered some . . . *obstacles* to further progress.'

If medals had been given out for understatement, Sedulus thought, he would have been weighed down with metal.

'Explain.'

He had been hoping that it wouldn't come to this, but there was no point in lying to the Nairene, not unless he wanted to die painfully in the very near future.

'We've taken casualties,' he replied. 'The Resistance has proved more resourceful than anticipated.'

'Or you have proved less resourceful. How close are you?'

'We are only hours behind them, but we've temporarily lost their trail. I have drones in the air.'

A lie, but a small one. He had *one* drone in the air, because he only had one drone left. He might as well have tried to find a fish in a vast lake by trailing a single, unbaited hook.

'I have lost contact with my husband,' said Syrene.

Sedulus frowned. This was news.

'Could he be . . . ?' He did not say the word, but he thought it: *dead*.

'No, but he has closed himself off.'

'Why?'

'To spare himself pain. To protect himself, and his cargo.'

Cargo. Such a careful word to use. Even here, in a secure communication with the Diplomats' head of security and, by extension, Syrene's own head of security, she was cautious.

'I will find him, Archmage,' said Sedulus.

'I know you will. I have confidence in your sense of self-preservation, because you know that if you don't bring my husband safely back to me, you should probably throw yourself on the mercy of the Resistance. They will be kinder to you than I will.'

Sedulus bowed in understanding.

'One final thing,' said Syrene. 'It appears that you may have been incautious in unleashing your pets and leaving survivors. There is already radio traffic. Andrus knows that you've breached the First Protocol. He wants you summoned back to Edinburgh. In fact, he wants you to be arrested for war crimes.'

The First Protocol had been determined at the start of the great Illyri conquest. It stated that hostile organisms should not be introduced into advanced alien ecosystems, in order to avoid contamination. Sedulus, and many like him, regarded it as something of a joke; after all, what were the Illyri themselves but hostile organisms? Similarly, Galateans and Agrons were also hostile within the restrictions imposed on their behaviour by the Illyri. The Protocol politely ignored such an obvious hypocrisy, preferring to concentrate on the potential for disease and infection, or, in the case of something as unknowable as the Sarith Entities, the capacity to annihilate an entire civilisation.

But then the Protocol could not even begin to grasp the reality of the Illyri mission on Earth, and what lay behind it.

Nevertheless, there were those like Andrus who tried to adhere to all of the Protocols: the First; the Second, which forbade the killing of civilian non-combatants; and the Third, which denied the Illyri the right to kill child combatants or even to use enhanced interrogation methods on them, and which had already been dispensed with by the Grand Consul. All of these restrictions had led Sedulus, as a young officer, to doubt the conduct of the Illyri conquest of Earth, until the truth had been revealed to him, and he had learned patience, for the rewards would be great.

'What should I do?' he asked Syrene. While Andrus had no authority over Sedulus on Earth, he could create difficulties back on Illyr.

'Do exactly what you're doing now. Search for my husband, and bring him back safely to me. Send one of your officers to me with a full report of all you've discovered so far, and all that you've lost. Andrus will be dealt with, in time.'

And the Archmage's image vanished from his lens.

CHAPTER 49

Hidden in the undergrowth, Meia watched the comings and goings at Eden. Her body and head were encased in a camouflage darksuit that altered its colour to match not only her surroundings but also fluctuations in natural light, while her keen eyes recorded all she saw: the changes of the guard; the movements of the Illyri scientists and technicians who had taken over the facility; and the security procedures that were in place, all controlled by Securitats. The problem for Meia was that entry to the facility appeared to require both a retinal scan and a fingerprint test, for like humans, the Illyri had distinctive prints on their fingers.

Eventually, as daylight vanished and a light rain began to fall, Meia found her victim and made her move. She had already created a hole in the fence large enough to slip through, and the descent of night aided her. The female scientist wore the seal of the Securitat-controlled Scientific Development Division on the left breast of her coat, and a hood shielded her from the drizzle. Meia considered trying to take her alive, but thought better of it; there might be a struggle, and while she would undoubtedly prevail, she could hardly drag the scientist's unconscious body across the parking area to the entry door. Anyway, Meia hated the Securitats, and the SDD was notorious for the cruelty of its experiments. These were scientists that other scientists disowned.

So it was that minutes later, Meia approached the entry door wearing the scientist's lab coat with the hood covering her head and shielding her face. She moved fast; she had very little time. It was not the fingerprint that concerned her, but the retinal scan. Retinal scanners used a low-intensity light source and a sensor to scan the pattern of blood vessels at the back of the retina, as each eyeball, like a fingerprint, was entirely unique; the error rate for retinal scanning, however, was only about one in ten million, while for fingerprints it was one in five hundred.

There was no guard on the door. There was no need for a guard, for the scans did everything.

Meia placed the scientist's severed right index finger on the fingerprint reader, and received a green light in return.

'Ready to commence retinal scan,' said a voice.

She glanced around quickly to make sure that no one was approaching, then held up a single eyeball, extracted from the skull of the dead scientist and impaled on a spike of inorganic matter at the tip of Meia's left little finger. Retinal decay occurs fast in a corpse, and the Illyri scanners were sensitive enough to detect not only the retina's minute array of blood vessels but also signs of life, so while the scanner examined the blood vessels, it also shot a rapid series of light beams at the eyeball. A dead eye would not respond to them, but a living one would. Unless, of course, the dead eye was under Meia's control, and electrical pulses from her finger were forcing the pupil to expand and contract.

The voice spoke again: 'Welcome back, Dr Sidis. Please proceed to sterilisation.'

The sterilisation room wasn't difficult to find; it was mere footsteps from the door. A series of instruction diagrams on the wall indicated what was required, including an order to leave all weapons outside the area. Meia had anticipated as much, and had left her blast pistol back at her interceptor. She stripped down to her underwear and placed her clothing in a locker, but not before activating a small incendiary device, timed to explode and destroy everything in the locker within two hours if she did not disarm it. If for any reason she had to make a swift escape, she didn't want any traces of her identity to be discovered. She passed through a sterilisation chamber that bathed her body in ultraviolet light as it cleansed her of potential contaminants. Beyond the chamber were racks of loose white suits, each with self-contained breathing apparatus. It was better than she could have hoped for. The suit wouldn't conceal her features entirely, but it would help.

Meia had chosen this time to enter the facility because, from her observations, it seemed to operate on a daytime schedule. She had seen many Illyri emerge over the hours, and they had not been replaced by a similar number. Night-time, therefore, was quieter.

Sealed pathways linked the various parts of what had once been the Eden Project. They all looked identical to Meia, but they clearly looked identical to many of those who worked there too, for at each junction was a map display showing the location of the junction and identifying the surrounding areas. There was a restaurant, assorted labs, a gymnasium, and various rooms marked only with numbers and letters. Meia didn't know what she was looking for, and was considering trying to find someone to ask – possibly in a painful and probably fatal way – but decided that the place to start, in the absence of someone to torture, was one of the geodesic domes, which towered above the other buildings like the eyes of some great buried insect.

She had begun tracing her route on the map when a hissing from behind her announced the opening of a door. She risked a glance over her shoulder, to see two white-suited Illyri emerge from a dark, low-ceilinged room behind her. She glimpsed glass cases, and unfamiliar forms within. The Illyri didn't even seem to notice her as the door closed behind them.

When she was certain that they were gone, Meia swiped the late Dr Sidis's identity card through the locking device. The door opened immediately, and the same voice as before welcomed her by name. She wondered if Sidis's ID provided unrestricted access or if an attempt to enter a restricted room or area would provoke some form of alert. She didn't want to have to fight her way out of Eden. She favoured a stealthier approach to her trade.

Her entry caused low overhead lighting to click on, illuminating a corridor formed by two parallel lines of glass cases, all filled with what appeared to be preservative fluid. Each case contained a mammal, arranged in ascending order of size. The smallest was a cat, the largest a horse, but all were horribly mutilated, their bodies swollen and distorted, as though their bones had been broken and improperly set, and their musculature deformed by disease. The damage to their heads was worse; the skulls were split or, in some instances, entirely fragmented. Meia examined each one closely, and decided that the injuries had been caused by something erupting from within rather than by any external force. At the back of the room she found smaller jars, all containing animal foetuses in various stages of development. Again there was severe damage to the bodies, although some were so small that she was unable to identify the species concerned. She tried to find records of the procedures, surgical or otherwise, that had left the animals in their ruined state, but there were none. The room was nothing more than an archive, a storage space for a series of apparently failed experiments, but what had been their point?

At the back of the room, a little window looked out on one of the smaller geodesic domes. Inside, she saw what appeared to be fertiliser bags with misshapen plants growing from them. She focussed, and realised that they were not bags at all. What she was seeing were bodies; human bodies that had somehow been 'seeded', although with what, she was unable to tell. She returned to the main door and hit the exit button, then operated the 'close' button almost immediately. A group of four Illyri passed, briefly visible as the gap narrowed. An electronically operated gurney hovered between them, and on it lay a live human male, strapped in place.

Meia waited a few seconds, then left the room and followed them.

The operating theatre had an observation gallery, masked with smoked glass, and it was there that Meia watched what was occurring. Clearly something had gone wrong; there was a sense of controlled alarm about the four Illyri as they prepared the human for surgery. A mask was placed over the human's face, and a scanner overhead revealed the entirety of the man's internal workings on a screen to the left of the operating table. His skull was shaved bare.

'We're losing vital signs,' said one of the surgeons.

Yet to Meia, the man's life signs seemed stable. His heartbeat was a little fast, but otherwise he was in no immediate danger that she could see.

'He's prepped for craniotomy,' said a nurse.

'Turn him over.'

The patient was expertly flipped, revealing the back of his skull to the surgeon, who traced the first incision, a long vertical cut from the crown of the head almost to the base of the neck.

Meia changed her position, the better to view the operation and the screen that displayed the man's system. Something was wrong here. She craned her neck, and more of the screen became visible. Until now she had not been able to see the reproduction of the man's skull, but suddenly its interior was revealed to her. She gasped.

Just then, the door behind her opened, and two male Illyri in blue scrubs entered the room. They too wore the insignia of the SDD.

'Dr Sidis,' said the first. 'We noticed you were in the building. We hadn't expected—'

He stopped as he saw Meia's face.

'Wait a minute, you're not Sidis. What are you doing here?'

'I might ask you the same thing,' said Meia.

She was already moving as the second medic dived for an alarm button. His fingers brushed it, but it was his last act before he died, a kick from Meia cracking his skull. The first medic was luckier. He used the distraction offered by his colleague to spring at Meia. She saw a flash of steel, and then felt a burning pain as the scalpel slashed across her right arm, but before the medic could strike again, she caught him a glancing blow to the side of the head that sent him sprawling against a table in the corner of the room. The scalpel spun across the floor and was lost beneath a console.

Meia was now between the medic and the door. He stared at her. His eyes found the tear that the knife had made in her suit. Blood dripped from the wound, but there was also a spray of thick yellow fluid, and a piece of damaged tubing poked through the material.

'No,' he said. 'That's not possible. You were all destroyed.'

'Not all,' said Meia. 'Not I.'

She knew the medic was going to spring. She knew before he knew himself. She saw it in his face, in his eyes, so that when he made his move, she was ready for him. Her fury surprised her. She never forgot her own nature, but the way the medic had spoken – his obvious horror of her, his knowledge of the ordered genocide – had awoken dormant feelings. As he sprang, her left hand shot out, the fist bunched tightly. The force of it caught him in the chest and pinned him hard against the wall, his toes dangling half a metre off the ground.

He gurgled, blood spraying from his mouth. He shuddered, his eyes going to his ribcage. Meia's left arm was buried in it halfway to the elbow. The medic tried to speak, but no words came. Meia didn't need to hear them anyway. Whatever he said would be meaningless. He was dying, and the dying always tried to cry some variation on the word 'no'.

Meia withdrew her fist as the life left the medic. His body slumped to the floor, and his blood dripped from her fingers on to his face. Somewhere in the distance, an alarm sounded. It was time for her to leave. Below her, the surgical team had evacuated the theatre. Only the body of the human remained, his life signs now extinguished. His skull had been opened, and the cerebellum lay exposed.

But the thing that Meia had glimpsed on the screen, coiled like a worm around his brain stem, was gone.

CHAPTER 50

Governor Andrus paced furiously in front of the captain of a recently arrived skimmer. The black craft had attempted landing in the inner courtyard, but had been refused permission. The governor's personal vehicle had quickly been driven into the courtyard and left parked there, just to make it clear to the Securitats that this was still Andrus's residence, and not theirs. The officer had been intercepted at the castle gates and brought, under protest, into the governor's presence. He had, Andrus suspected, been on his way to report to Syrene.

The Military was closely monitoring all flights coming from the Highlands; it was important to maintain the fiction that the governor was a concerned parent worried for his daughter's safety, a role that Andrus had no difficulty in playing. While he knew that his daughter and Ani were in the hands of the Resistance, that didn't mean they were safe. Andrus didn't share Meia's faith in the Resistance; he was aware that there were those within its ranks who would dearly love to hold Syl hostage, and those were the good ones. There were others who would happily kill her and send her back to her father piece by piece.

The situation was complicated further by rumours of the destruction of at least one Securitat vessel, and the deaths of an unconfirmed number of Securitats and Galatean troops. Andrus wanted to know what was going on, but so far the tense, fidgety captain had given him little more than his name and rank. Andrus glared at him afresh.

'So, whatever your name is—'

'Beldyn,' said the man. 'Captain Beldyn.'

'I don't care who you are. I'm telling you for the last time: I want a full report of progress in the search for my daughter, or I'll lose you in the castle dungeons.'

'And I can only repeat what I've already said. My orders are to act as liaison between Marshal Sedulus and the Archmage Syrene. The rescue operation is a matter of the greatest delicacy. Your daughter's life is not the only one at stake. The safety of the Grand Consul must be our primary concern.'

Andrus slammed his fist against his desk. '*Must* be? As the father of a missing child, you'll forgive me if I beg to differ.'

Beldyn gave a small, strange smile. 'My lord, I can reliably inform you that we are searching for both your daughter *and* her friend. The Archmage Syrene was adamant on that score. Most adamant. Otherwise, the situation is under control.'

Andrus couldn't help but laugh.

'Really? I hear stories of exploding ships and dead troops. It sounds to me as if you have an insurgency on your hands, Captain. Perhaps it's time for the Military to intervene.'

'I'll pass on your concerns to Marshal Sedulus, Lord Andrus. Now, I must insist that you allow me to seek out the Archmage, or—'

'Or what? I'd be very careful how I finish that statement if I were you, Captain.'

Beldyn closed his mouth and stayed silent.

'Get out of my sight,' said Andrus.

He watched Beldyn stride away, resisting the urge to help him on his way with a good kick. The desire to lash out was almost beyond endurance, his frustration was so great that he felt it as an ache through his teeth and neck and spine.

He turned to Balen, who was sitting at his desk sifting through papers, as usual, but clearly not concentrating, which was most *un*usual. Syl had always been a favourite of Balen's, just as her mother was before her. In fact Andrus had often felt that Balen had something of a schoolboy crush on the Lady Orianne; when Orianne died, the secretary seemed to have transferred the best part of that affection to her daughter. As she'd grown, Syl had been a regular visitor to her father's office, and Andrus had often found her sitting behind Balen's desk doing her homework under his caring tutelage. Balen would have forgiven Syl anything, even treason, and the depth of his concern for the girl's safety was clear. For a moment Andrus almost shared the truth about the crash with him, but then decided against it. Balen tended to wear his feelings on his sleeve, and was regarded by many in the castle as a barometer of the governor's moods. For now, it was better that he knew as little as possible; that way, he wouldn't have to act.

'Why don't you go to your quarters and rest for a while?' said Andrus. 'You haven't slept since the crash.'

'With respect, Governor, neither have you.'

'That's the point: one of us needs to have a clear head about him. Get some sleep, Balen. You'll be more use to me fresh than exhausted.'

Balen rose. He was so tired that he swayed on his feet.

'Go to bed,' said Andrus. 'I'll make sure that you're woken if needed.'

Balen did as he was told. Andrus remained standing, now uncertain of what to do to occupy himself. He had not heard back from Meia. He should never have let her go to Eden. He needed her here. She was his point of contact with the Resistance, and the only assurance of his daughter's safe return.

An hour passed. He was sick of doing nothing. It was time to act. He summoned Danis. When the old general arrived, Peris, the captain of the castle guard and one of the governor's most trusted veteran soldiers, was with him, just as Andrus had instructed.

Within the hour, Peris, acting on orders from the governor, had assembled a Military squad ready to move into the Highlands.

CHAPTER 51

While Andrus fretted, the objects of his concern continued their hard, damp march across the Highlands. They were nineteen in all, including Ani, Syl and Gradus, who walked along much like a zombie, his eyes unseeing, his footfalls automatic. Syl had now learned all the humans' names. There was Heather, of course, and young Alice, who spent much of her time walking with Syl and Ani while her mother mourned the loss of Tam. Alice had wept for him too, but she did not blame Syl and Ani for the crimes of other Illyri, which made her very different from some of the others, such as the vicious Duncan and the sinewy woman named Aggie who had declined Syl's help earlier in the march. Their animosity towards the Illyri had not lessened since the truth of the events at Durroch began to reach them. Just Joe had used a shortwave transmitter to send and receive a series of Morse code messages, and the story of what had taken place in the little village had roused fierce reactions.

'We should kill them,' said Duncan, pointing at the three Illyri. 'We should leave their bodies on spikes for their mates to find. That'll send them a message for sure.'

'Those were innocent people in that village, Joe,' said Aggie. 'You knew their names. You'd eaten in their houses, and played football with their bairns. Most of them are dead now – and their kind killed them,' she added, pointing at Syl.

Not my kind, Syl wanted to say, but she knew better than to interrupt. Paul and Steven, along with Mike and Seán, had taken up positions close to the three Illyri. Steven had even been entrusted with a gun by Seán, much to Paul's unease. They were there to show that no assaults on the Illyri would be permitted, that they were still under Just Joe's protection, although Joe had made it clear that there was to be no shooting, not unless he gave the order. Three others stood behind Just Joe: a woman named Kathy – who had appeared at the farmhouse shortly before they left, bearing a fresh battery for his shortwave radio – and Joe's closest lieutenants, the grim-faced Logan and the small, lithe Ryan.

Siding with Aggie and Duncan were two men, Frank and Howie, who looked like twin brothers but were actually cousins. They had never been particularly hostile to the three Illyri until now, but they had an uncle who lived in Durroch, and nobody could find out if he was among the dead.

Heather and Alice stood apart from both factions, as did a muscled young man who called himself AK, and Aggie's husband Norris, a massive figure more ox than man, who regarded his wife with a mixture of frustration and admiration. Syl couldn't imagine what kind of argument the couple were likely to have later over the fact that he didn't appear to be supporting her.

'I know that, Aggie,' said Just Joe. 'Don't think I don't feel for them, and for Tam most of all. But it doesn't change the fact that these two young females put their lives on the line for two of ours, and I don't remember them killing anyone at Durroch. Slaughtering them for revenge will get us nowhere, and will make us no better than the ones who murdered our friends. We'll get those responsible, and we'll make them pay, but I won't let you spill blood here.'

'And what about the other one?' said Duncan, pointing at Gradus. 'Who has he saved?'

'He's important,' said Just Joe. 'Maybe more important than any of us can imagine.'

'All the more reason to leave his head for them to find,' said Aggie, and the two cousins shouted their agreement.

'We have to take him to the Green Man,' said Just Joe. 'Those are my orders, and they apply to you as well. If you don't like them, you've no business being here. Do you want to leave, Aggie? And you, Howie and Frank? You've always been loyal. Don't let me down now. And you, Duncan: I understand your anger, because it's in me as well, but we'll find another outlet for it. For now, though, I need you all to stand with me. We're still being hunted, and the greatest hurt we can do the Illyri at the moment is to keep them from getting their hands on the three who are with us. Am I clear?'

There were some rumblings from the four malcontents, but the challenge to Joe's authority had been dealt with for the present. Aggie went back to her husband and scowled at him so hard it seemed her face might crack, while his own remained impassive. Howie and Frank shared some whisky from a small bottle, looking secretly relieved that the argument hadn't ended in violence. They were followers, not leaders, and in the end they would always rally behind the strongest in any group; in this group, that was still Just Joe.

But Duncan sloped off, and they did not see him again until Just Joe announced that they had all rested long enough, and it was time to be moving on. Syl was sorry to see Duncan reappear, zipping his trousers, an apple stuck in his mouth. She had hoped that he might have deserted.

They marched long into the night. Syl and Paul walked together, sometimes with Alice between them. When she became too tired to go on, they took turns at taking her on their backs, and eventually she fell asleep against Paul. In soft voices they talked, discussing details from their respective childhoods, which had been so different, sharing their interests before they were drawn into this brutal war – Syl's passion for art and books, Paul's fascination with all forms of music and his attempts to play the guitar. Eventually Paul told Syl about the death of his father, and she in turn shared the details of her mother's death, and although each still felt the old lingering hurt, there was something peaceful about their conversation, the words flowing with ease.

With little other choice, Ani and Steven had begun to walk together, each keeping an eye on the other, and lending a hand if one got into trouble when climbing, or wading through soft, muddy ground. If the truth were told, Ani had never spent much time talking to humans – or at least not as herself, as an Illyri. She was on nodding terms with some of those who were trusted enough to serve the Illyri at the castle, and she liked to think they were not actively hostile towards her. Most of them were friendly enough, but she was not so naive as to ignore the fact that deep down they resented the very fact of her existence.

But she had learned to mix with them outside the castle walls. In the beginning, she would sit disguised in dark corners of safe coffee shops, sometimes pretending to read so that she could keep her head down and not attract attention. Later, as her awareness of her powers grew, she was able to engage some of them in conversation, clouding their minds just enough to prevent them from recognising her as an Illyri. Old people were the easiest, children the hardest to fool. They seemed to see her for what she was, no matter how hard she tried. Ani had decided that this was because children had not yet begun to engage in the kind of deceptions so integral to adult life, and it was easier to fool those who were already fooling themselves.

Sometimes she could see the doubt surfacing as a human began to suspect that all was not quite right but could not manage to pinpoint the source of the unease. When that happened, she would concentrate harder or, if she felt there was nothing further to be gained from the conversation, simply give up on it. Usually, though, she persisted, because it was all practice, a further honing of her developing skills. In a sense, she was as much a confidence trickster as a psychic; she had learned that humans and Illyri alike wanted to believe certain things about the world. Her role was to discover the nature of those beliefs – or desires – and satisfy them. So an older human might secretly want to believe that this was a pretty young girl seated before him, fascinated by the stories he had to tell, and in that case, much of Ani's work had already been done for her. Similarly, a lonely woman with a jerk for a boyfriend wanted a sympathetic ear, wanted to be understood. Ani had learned to make very slight changes to her personality in order to temporarily fill these gaps in the lives of others, and once she had managed to get beneath their defences she could start to understand much more about them. As Meia had recognised, she had the capacity to become a very good spy.

But Ani had no desire to be a spy. She had gradually come to realise that she conducted all such conversations in disguise, playing a role that was for the most part determined by another. Thus it was that, at her young age, she had discovered the great and terrible truth about spies: that they spent so long adopting disguises and pretending to be something they were not that eventually they lost their own identities entirely and became shadows of themselves.

Steven had walked with Ani shyly at first. After their awkward conversations in the truck on the long journey north, he still seemed somewhat in awe of her. It made her feel a little less jealous of Syl, for when she was reunited with her friend and saw her with Paul, it was instantly apparent to Ani that a deep bond was forming between the two of them. They were still circling one another, uncertain of their feelings, unsure if it was even possible for any relationship to exist between them. They had both been captors and captives, and years of enmity lay between their species.

And that was another thing: as Ani had reminded Syl, she and Paul were of different species, perhaps not all that different in many ways, yet different enough. Then again, Ani's views on such matters had begun to alter subtly. She had seen Althea with the human named Trask, and now she was watching Syl and Paul commence their tentative courtship. Maybe males and females were *always* strange to one another, and the relationship that was developing between Syl and Paul was simply a more complicated variation on an already complex theme.

And so Ani did not spurn Steven's small kindnesses as she might have done before. They were all on the run together now, and were likely to share similar punishments if they were caught. What began as exchanges of no more than a couple of words – a thank you for help scaling rocks, his hand warm against hers, his grip suprisingly strong; an enquiry as to whether she was cold, or wet, or hungry, followed by an effort to solve the problem – quickly became longer conversations, and she found herself happy to have him as her travelling companion.

He was quieter than his brother, and more inclined to listen than to talk. Still, she noticed that he would occasionally offer some quiet suggestion to Paul, or even to Just Joe himself, and she would often see the others nod in agreement, or pause to consider what they had just been told, as though Steven had caused them to see the situation in a new light. He was more sensitive than his brother, but with that came a kind of cleverness; his sensitivity meant that he was more open to experience, and that openness brought with it understanding. Steven would never be a leader, and he did not want to lead, but he would grow up to be the kind of man upon whom leaders relied.

'Do you like him?' Syl whispered to her as they lay shivering in the ruins of a farmhouse, waiting for a sudden downpour of hard, icy rain to ease so that they could cover a few more miles in the darkness.

'Yes,' said Ani. 'I do. Not the way you like Paul, but I like him.'

Syl smiled at her. 'Maybe that will come too, that other kind of liking.'

'No,' said Ani, and there was no uncertainty in her voice. 'And he's young.'

'He will be older soon enough,' said Syl.

But Ani did not reply.

CHAPTER 52

They stopped to rest shortly before dawn. Even Syl, with her sharper eyesight, was able to distinguish relatively little of the landscape around her, and the stars above were lost behind the clouds. She wished she could see the night sky; she was a child of the larger universe, and she was more aware of her place in it than the humans with whom she was marching. Their species had been no further from Earth than their own moon, but Syl had been conceived in outer space, her cells splitting and developing in her mother's womb while her parents crossed the universe, and it gave her comfort to see those flickers in the darkness, even if the light she saw came from stars that no longer existed.

She watched as Howie separated from the group and walked a short distance to relieve himself against a rock. Then Duncan got up and headed into the bushes. She could hear Howie urinating, and soon others started to do the same thing, men and women. It was gross to listen to, yet it reminded her that she needed to go herself, and that Paul was reluctant to let her out of his sight after the events at the farmhouse and their aftermath.

'They should be more careful,' she said to him.

'What?'

He sounded tired, and irritable, well aware of the continued whisperings of Aggie and Duncan, who said that he was getting too close to the alien girl, that he favoured her above his own kind. If Duncan and those who felt like him about the Illyri captives ever succeeded in drawing enough of the others to their cause to take over the leadership from Just Joe, Paul knew there was a good chance that they might kill him and his brother alongside the Illyri.

'When they pee,' said Syl. 'They're not careful. They just go anywhere and don't think about it. They need to dig a hole, and then cover it over when they're done. You know that my people will be using Agrons to track us on the ground, and Agrons can see broadly in the ultraviolet spectrum. Urine will show up as bright yellow. All those people who slipped away to pee while we were walking? They'll have left a trail to be followed. Even I can see faint traces of it.'

'Why didn't you say something before?'

'Because I didn't *think* of it before. Because I've never been hunted before! Now I need to go too, but I *will* dig a hole.'

Paul reddened. 'I'll go with you,' he said.

'What are you going to do, hold my hand? Read to me?'

'I'm not supposed to let you out of my sight.'

'Where am I going to go? I'm in the middle of nowhere, and you keep forgetting that as far as the Illyri are concerned, I'm a criminal and a traitor. They hate me, and although your people hate me too, for now I think my chances are better with you than with the Illyri. If that changes, you'll be the first to know. Now, if you'll excuse me . . .'

She rose and stomped off. She passed Ani along the way. Steven was seated next to her, and they were sharing a bar of chocolate.

'Well aren't you just the pretty couple?' Syl said.

Ani stared at her, a block of chocolate halfway to her mouth.

'What did we do?' she asked. 'And where are you off to in such a temper?'

'I am going to *pee*, if that's all right.'

'Do you want some company?'

'No I do not! The last thing I want is company. I want a couple of minutes alone, and if anybody else offers to come with me, I'll have to start selling tickets!'

'Right,' said Ani. 'I won't come, then.'

'Isn't Paul supposed to stay with you?' said Steven.

Syl raised a finger of warning at him.

'Don't,' she said. 'Just don't.'

She turned her back on them and stomped away, ignoring the looks that the humans gave her, heedless of whether they were hostile or merely curious. She saw Gradus slumped against a stone. He was still little more than a walking zombie – not that she had tried to speak to him, but she knew from Paul that he was still unresponsive. Duncan had even stubbed out a cigarette on his arm, with no result. He had received a punch in the stomach from Just Joe for his troubles.

'You leave him be,' Just Joe had warned. 'We'll deal with him when we get to the Green Man.'

'If he lives that long,' Duncan replied.

'If something happens to him, you'll be keeping him company in the next world. For now, you stay away from him, you hear?'

But Duncan just smiled as he slunk away. He had caught Syl watching him, and the change in his features made her shiver. There was hatred in them, but also hunger, and that frightened her more than anything else.

She found a quiet spot in a small hollow, and when she was sure that she was alone, did what she had to do. She took her own advice and carefully dug a small hole with her hands first, then covered it over when she was finished. She used some of the water in her backpack to clean her hands, and poured a little on her face in an effort to wake herself up. She was so tired, but she knew that Joe might well decide to continue to march. They were on the outskirts of some woodland, which would at least provide shelter, but Joe was anxious to keep putting miles between themselves and their pursuers for as long as possible. Paul had told her that they were about a day away from the Green Man, but when she tried to press him about the identity of this person he simply shrugged and looked away. Syl suspected he knew no more about the Green Man than she did.

She wiped the water from her eyes and drank what was left in the bottle. She could hear a stream flowing nearby. It sounded as if it was just over the other side of the hollow. She could refill her bottle from it, and it would save her having to ask for some of Paul's, or forcing him to ask Norris for more. Norris was the quartermaster, in charge of their supplies, and functioned as a kind of human packhorse, carrying extra water, food and ammunition without complaint. The only time he did complain was when someone asked him for any of it. He lived in constant fear of running out of something, and the easiest way to ensure that he always had supplies was by not giving any of them away.

Syl found the stream, filled her bottle and drank deeply from it. The water tasted fresh and pure. It made her feel a little better but she was reminded that, unlike the water, she was distinctly unfresh, and very dirty. She sank down on the grass, pulled her knees to her chest and rested her forehead against them. She tried to make sense of the series of events that had led her to this situation, beginning with her decision to skip classes for her birthday and head out into the city. That was her mistake, she decided. Had she not done that, everything would have been different. She and Ani would never have met Paul and Steven, and her safe, sheltered life in the castle would not have been disturbed.

Would Paul and Steven have died, though, had she not ventured beyond the walls? Would it have mattered to her if they had? She liked to think that it would have, and that she might have tried her best to persuade her father to spare them, but she would not have involved herself in any hare-brained rescue plan. Perhaps Meia would have found another way to save them. Perhaps, perhaps, perhaps.

But not to have met Paul . . .

She was too weary to examine her feelings for him in any great depth. She knew only that she felt something, and he in turn felt something for her. She didn't want to call it love. It was too early for that. The only thing of which she was certain was that she was glad that their paths had crossed, whatever the consequences might prove to be.

She heard footsteps behind her, and because she had been thinking of Paul, she looked up expecting to see him there. Instead a stranger peered down at her from the rise. He wore filthy camouflage clothing, and he held an old bolt-action rifle in his hands. The rifle had been fitted with a bayonet. It gleamed darkly in the slow-dawning light. Syl guessed that the man was in his thirties or forties. The dawn shadows, and the woollen hat pulled down almost to the level of his eyes, made it difficult to tell. The muzzle of his rifle was pointing directly at Syl.

'Open your mouth, you little alien whore, and it'll be the last thing you ever do,' he said.

Slowly Syl got her feet. She considered trying to run, but then another man, dressed similarly to the first, appeared to her right, and two more popped up on her left, younger than the others. The fast-moving stream cut off her escape to the north. She was surrounded.

'She's pretty,' said one of the younger men. He was probably in his early twenties, and his face was hard and cruel. He made the word 'pretty' sound unclean.

'She's Illyri,' said his companion, and he made the word 'Illyri' sound like an insult. He was smaller than the other man, and his face was softer, but in an unpleasant, effeminate way. Syl suspected that he might even have a crueller nature than his friend.

'Doesn't bother me,' said the first.

'She's not to be touched,' said the man with the rifle. 'Not yet, anyway.'

The man to Syl's right was closing in on her. He was bald, and his right eye was white and dead. Syl backed away from him until she felt the water of the stream on her feet. The man with the rifle raised it to his shoulder and got her in his sights.

'No further,' he said. 'I'll drop you where you stand, I promise you.'

Suddenly a small figure sprang at him, forcing the barrel of the gun upwards while landing a fierce kick to the man's right knee. Syl was so relieved to see Steven coming to her aid that she took her eye off the bald man to her right, and instantly he was upon her. The force of him sent her tumbling into the stream, although it was not deep where she landed. The bald man went down with her, but he recovered more quickly than Syl. He bent down to grab her by the hair, and her right hand came up fast, a rock held firmly in its grasp. It caught her attacker on the side of the head. His eyes rolled up, and he tumbled unconscious into the water. Now the two younger men were advancing on Syl. They came at her simultaneously. She struck one a blow to the left arm with the rock, but it did little damage, and then he and his friend were pinning her arms behind her. Syl tried to scream for help, but one of them put his hand against her mouth, muffling the sound.

Meanwhile, on the rise above, the gunman had recovered from the shock of Steven's assault, and with a swing of his rifle slashed the boy across the chest with the tip of the bayonet, drawing blood. Syl heard Steven cry out to Paul for help, but his voice seemed impossibly small against the sound of the stream, and the pumping of the blood in Syl's head. Harder and harder it pumped, louder and louder, until her entire vision filled with red. There was a growing pressure in her skull, as though her brain might explode.

Steven was sprawling on the ground, and the rifle was raised high, the bayonet poised to descend and finish him off. Syl bit hard into the hand against her lips and tasted blood in her mouth. There was a yelp of pain, and the hand was pulled away.

Later Syl would try to recall what happened next, but it was unclear in her own mind, and only the dead and the dying proved that it had occurred at all. She felt a great rage course through her, starting from somewhere deep in the core of her being. It was like a flame igniting, turning from red to white, scorching everything that it touched, but the focus of it was the man with the rifle. Syl held him in her sights as though it were she, not he, who was pointing a weapon, except now Syl herself was the weapon. There were no longer hands holding her, and she was vaguely aware of bodies falling into the rushing stream. She uttered one word – 'No' – and in the aftermath she would recall how quiet it sounded, how calm and controlled. It was not a shout or a scream, but the solitary syllable denied the possibility of any outcome other than the one she pictured in her mind, and that was the death of the man with the rifle.

He jerked upright, and in a single fluid movement spun the rifle so that it was no longer pointing at Steven but was aimed at himself. Then, without hesitation, he balanced the butt of the rifle against the ground, the bayonet towards his own chest. He paused for a second, and on his features there seemed to appear the realisation of what he was about to do. He looked at Syl, and there was a question on his face that was destined to remain unasked, for the force of her will compelled him to finish what had been started. He slumped forward, and the bayonet pierced his heart. His body shook once, and then was still.

From the camp came shouts, and a short exchange of gunfire, but Syl barely heard it. She fell to her knees, all strength leaving her in an instant. She stared at the dead man on the rise, his body and the rifle in perfect balance so that they formed a triangle against the dawn. She looked to her right and to her left. The two younger men lay stunned in the water, but they were still alive. The bald man was face down in the stream, and blood flowed from the wound in his head. Somehow Syl managed to turn him over, but his face was pale, and she felt sure that he was dying.

The mist cleared from her vision, the sound of the blood in her head growing fainter. Steven came splashing to her, his shirt red with blood. He put one arm around her waist, wrapped her right arm around his neck, and pulled her to her feet.

'Don't tell them what I did,' she whispered. She was crying. 'Please don't tell them. I didn't mean to do it, but he was going to hurt you, to kill you. I didn't mean it. Please, please . . .'

'I won't,' said Steven, and he was crying too. 'I won't tell them anything, Syl, I promise.'

Now there were more people approaching, Paul and Ani among them. Syl tried to say something, but no words would come.

CHAPTER 53

Syrene had left instructions that she was not to be disturbed, not while she was meditating, but now her principal handmaiden Cocile stood before her. Cocile functioned as an extension of the Archmage; she spoke with Syrene's voice, and was the only one permitted to intrude upon the Archmage at any time, yet still Syrene felt irritated by the interruption.

'You bring news?' she asked.

'Yes, your eminence. Marshal Sedulus sends word that he has crossed the trail of the Grand Consul. The Agrons have his scent once again.'

Syrene breathed a sigh of relief. Her beloved husband was not safe yet, but this was progress.

The handmaid lingered. She looked unhappy.

'Is there more?'

'A breach of security at Eden.'

Syrene could not disguise her anxiety at this information.

'What kind of breach?'

'A scientist was killed. An intruder gained entry using her . . . *remains*. Two more scientists died during the incursion. It seems that the intruder may have witnessed a procedure. A human procedure.'

Pain lanced through Syrene's brain. *Panic. Alarm.*

'Do we have any idea of the identity of the intruder?'

'They were disguised throughout, but an injury may have been inflicted. Material was recovered at the scene.'

'Material?'

'ProGen skin, and internal lubricant. Your grace, the intruder was an artificial life form.'

Syrene could barely fathom it. An artificial, a Mech, here on Earth? They had all been destroyed. The order had been given.

To Danis.

To Andrus.

Were they capable of deceit on such a scale?

'Summon Vena from the hunt,' she ordered. 'Send her to Eden. Tell her to access every surveillance system, every secret camera. I want to know the identity of the Mech.'

Meia's intention had been to return to Edinburgh and tell Governor Andrus of what she had seen at the Eden Project, but a call from the castle had forced her to alter her plan. Anyway, she was uncertain of what precisely she *had* seen at Eden: an infestation of some kind, an infection? An organism had clearly been introduced into the human, and it had spread through his system, but what was the point of introducing it to begin with? Furthermore, it seemed to Meia that the host body was fighting the intruder and was, in fact, in the process of rejecting it. That seemed to tie in with the preserved remains of mangled animals that she had discovered. The only conclusion she could draw was that the parasite had been rejected by an array of Earth's species, leading to the death of the host body, and the human was simply the latest of those unfortunate creatures.

Perhaps it should not have concerned her as much as it did. The Diplomats and the Military were forever examining, and experimenting on, the new life forms they found, but it was a core belief among the Illyri that such experiments should not be carried out on advanced races, even if Securitat scientists were known to quietly ignore such niceties. Humanity was more advanced than any other race yet discovered. What was being done to humans at Eden was not just unethical, it was illegal.

But then the call had come, and Eden was put aside for a time. Meia was a spy, and spies in turn relied on spies: she had a network of informants both inside and outside Edinburgh Castle, some of them under the governor's nose. The news that Peris had been dispatched to the Highlands with a strike team created problems. The Resistance had Syl and Ani – and, indeed, Gradus, which must have been quite a bonus for them – and Meia had heard nothing to indicate that the three of them were anything but alive, and safe. She knew their final destination; it was reasonably secure, as long as they could make it there without being intercepted by Sedulus and the Securitats.

Gradus's decision to take the same flight as Syl had been disastrous for Meia. Had the Illyri female been alone on the shuttle, all would have been well, and Sedulus and his Securitats would have had no reason to involve themselves in the subsequent search. Andrus and Meia could have ensured that the hunt went nowhere near them, and they could have kept Syl and Ani hidden until some form of negotiation ensured that they would not be grievously punished for what they had done. If necessary, Meia could have hidden them for years – even offworld, if the Diplomats proved unwilling to bend on the issue of punishment. Instead, Gradus had become the focus of the search, and Sedulus's future was dependent on his safe return. Sedulus was dangerous and ambitious, but he was not a fool, and even the Highlands had their limits. If he persevered, as Meia knew he would, he would close in on his quarry, and he would corner it. Sedulus hated both Andrus and Danis, and Meia believed that were their daughters to die in the Highlands, Sedulus would sleep as soundly as he had ever done.

Now Peris and the strike squad had complicated the situation still further. Meia knew what Peris would do. He was an experienced soldier, clever and resourceful. From what she had heard, Sedulus's efforts to carry out a quick, successful rescue had resulted only in carnage. To find him, all one would need to do was follow the trail of bodies. Peris would shadow Sedulus in the hope that he could snatch Syl and Ani from under his nose, but if Peris started killing members of the Resistance as part of some ridiculous rescue plan, there were those among the Resistance who would happily put bullets in the Illyri girls' heads in reprisal.

Meia could not contact Peris. He was maintaining radio silence for fear of any communications being intercepted by the Securitats. Her best hope was to get to Syl and Ani before either Sedulus or Peris, and move them out of Scotland. As for Gradus, well, she would happily leave him to the Resistance, but it might make more sense to extract him too. Who knew what vengeance Syrene and the Diplomats might wreak if some harm befell him?

Her shuttle display told her that she was well past the remains of Hadrian's Wall.

Before her, the Highlands loomed.

CHAPTER 54

When Syl regained consciousness, she was seated upright supported by a backpack, and someone was gently offering her water. She struggled against nausea, and every muscle in her body burned, as though she had been stretched on a rack. The first thing she saw was Paul.

'How do you feel?' he asked.

'Groggy. What happened?'

'You fainted.'

'No, I mean what happened to the men who tried to attack me?'

Another voice spoke. 'That's just the question I wanted to ask you.'

Just Joe appeared over Paul's shoulder. He was looking at Syl in a new way; there was respect there that she had not seen before, but doubt too. Syl gathered her thoughts: she saw a man impaled on his own rifle, and the life bleeding from another into a rushing stream. And she was responsible; she had taken care of one with a rock, but the other …

She wondered what story Steven had concocted to explain what had happened. Whatever he had said, she had to be sure that their descriptions of the incident matched. She had to protect herself. What she had done was terrible. She had killed; worse, she had made a man kill himself by the sheer force of her will, by the depth of her rage.

Already, as her head began to clear, she was making connections, finding small moments in her past that suggested the power she had tapped into had always been present. She had never previously recognised it – or been willing to recognise it – because its use had been more subtle, and had not been fuelled by anger. Her father always remarked upon how easily she could bend others to her will and escape the consequences of breaches of discipline: homework left undone and classes missed; illicit trips beyond the castle walls that were smiled upon indulgently by guards who should by rights have reported her to their superiors or to her father. Once Althea had found a hand-rolled cigarette sprinkled with cannabis, given to Syl by a boy in a coffee shop, its presence in a drawer forgotten after only a couple of puffs made her violently ill. Althea had been furious. Cigarettes were considered bad enough, but illegal drugs of any kind were forbidden in the castle. It was a matter for parental intervention, Althea had told Syl; she had no choice but to report it to Lord Andrus. But in a matter of minutes, Syl had convinced her that no such report was necessary, and by the end of their conversation it was as if the joint had never existed.

Now these seemingly unconnected incidents began to form a pattern, and Syl thought again of her father's fond tale of her conception – the one she'd always squirmed away from in disgust: of how she and Ani were formed as their parents' ship passed through clouds of illumination like nothing the Illyri had ever glimpsed before in their travels through the universe, rippling phantasms in which the spectrum of visible light was twisted and recreated in new forms, the glow bathing the fleet and causing many of those on board to feel light-headed to the point of giddiness, even though the ship's instruments could detect nothing in the void. The display and its effects had lasted for a day and a night, and no more, but it was during this unsettling time that the travellers had reached for their beloveds, seeking comfort and solace amid the strange new rays, and Syl and Ani had been conceived as the light from without bathed their makers' skin and danced in their eyes.

Just Joe's voice brought her back.

'Did you hear me?' he said. 'I want to know what happened back at the stream.'

Syl held her head in her hands. The water she had swallowed was trying to come back up, along with whatever was in her stomach. She was determined to keep it all down.

'I don't remember,' she said. 'I can recall swinging a rock at one of those men. After that, it's all a blank.'

Just Joe didn't appear to believe her, but he had little choice for now.

'Are they dead?' asked Syl.

'One is,' said Just Joe, 'and another soon will be. His skull is smashed in, and he was near drowned when we pulled him from the stream. He might have survived the blow given proper treatment, but the water did for him. He won't last out the hour.'

'And the others?'

Syl tried to keep the fear from her voice. What had they told Just Joe? She wasn't sure what she'd done to them. She had simply visualised herself freed from their grip, and it had happened.

'They have massive bruising to their chests, like they've been punched by a pair of big fists, and there's damage to their throats too. They can barely croak, never mind speak. You sure you remember nothing?'

'It's as I said: all blank.'

Just Joe regarded her thoughtfully, but said nothing more before he walked away. Paul continued to hold Syl's head as he poured a little more water into her mouth. She liked the feel of his hand against her cheek, and his arm around her shoulders. She wanted to stay that way. She—

She pushed the water bottle from her lips, turned to her right and vomited on the grass. There wasn't much in her stomach, but it all came out anyway, until she was just dry-heaving, her body spasming and her throat aching. Paul held her hair back from her face so that it would not be soiled.

'Oh,' she said. 'Oh.'

She began to cry again, ashamed and embarrassed that he had seen her like this, but Paul simply pulled a T-shirt from a backpack, soaked it with water, then handed it to her so she could clean her face. 'Hush now.'

'I'm sorry,' she said.

'Don't be.'

'Is Steven okay?'

'He's shaken up, and they're going to have to stitch his chest, but he's alive, though I suspect he wouldn't be if it wasn't for you.'

'What did he tell you?'

'Nothing, except that you fought those men and distracted them for long enough for him to turn the tables on Alex Ritchie.'

'Who?'

'The man who died on the bayonet. His name was Alex Ritchie. According to Steven, Ritchie stumbled as they fought, and he fell on his own blade.'

It sounded unlikely, which was no doubt why Just Joe had been so anxious to hear her version of events. Then again, was it any less likely than the truth: that an alien girl had willed a man dead, and the man had obliged? Syl examined Paul's face; it remained studiedly neutral. If he doubted his brother's tale, he wasn't prepared to let anyone know.

'What does Just Joe think?'

'He searched you for a weapon while you were unconscious. He was convinced that you'd concealed something, some kind of alien technology that allowed you to blast those two in the chest. Mind you, it still wouldn't explain how Ritchie ended up impaled, but Steven's story is the best that he has, for now.'

He let the last two words hang. It was an implicit warning. Just Joe wasn't going to let this lie. He would be back to question her again.

'Can I see Steven?'

'In a while, once they've finished working on him.' Paul winced. 'We're low on anaesthetic, and Heather doesn't want to give him anything too strong while we're on the move. Steven's had a dram to ease the pain, but it's still going to hurt like hell. I suspect he'd prefer as few people as possible to see what happens, and that includes me. Once Heather has finished with him, I'll make sure that you have a few minutes alone together. Until then, you can rest here, or you can come and hear what the prisoners have to say.'

'I thought Just Joe said they couldn't speak,' said Syl.

'Not those two,' said Paul. 'The rest of them.'

And Syl remembered the sounds of gunfire and shouting just before she fainted.

'How many of them were there?'

'Nine,' said Paul. 'It seems that they wanted Gradus, and they wanted you.'

Five men sat on the damp grass, their hands fixed behind their backs with plastic cable. Some of them were bleeding from the beatings they'd received. They were surrounded by Just Joe's group. Nearby, four bodies lay on the ground, a fine mist of rain falling on their faces and their sightless eyes. One of the them was the drowned man; he had died while Joe was talking with Syl and Paul.

'Two were killed in the attack,' whispered Paul as he and Syl drew nearer to the group. 'Norris was injured in the exchange of fire. He was shot in the shoulder, but he'll be okay. Norris is hard to kill.'

Ani, dismissed from Steven's company while his wound was being tended to, wandered over to join them. The captives looked at Syl with hostile eyes and, in the case of the two men who had been injured at the stream, a degree of fear. That pleased Syl. They would have hurt her badly, she knew, and she shivered as she recalled the dark appetite in the youngest man's eyes, and the way he had used the word 'pretty' about her.

Just Joe was standing before a big man with white hair and pale skin, his eyes tinged with the red of albinism.

'This is a bad business, McKinnon,' he said.

'That it is,' replied the pale man.

'You're lucky Norris and the boy are still alive, or I'd kill two more of you for each of them.'

'We didn't want to hurt anyone,' said McKinnon. 'We just wanted your prisoners.'

'And why would that be?'

'They'd make good hostages. The Illyri have a dozen of ours. They're to be sent to the Punishment Battalions. We want them back. We're fighting the Illyri, just the same as you are.'

Just Joe laughed.

'You're nothing like us,' he said. 'You're bandits. You're thieves and rapists. You steal from your own people at gunpoint, but not one of you has used a weapon in the service of the Resistance. At the first sign of a fight you melt into the Highlands and leave others to die. I'm glad Ritchie ended up spiked, otherwise I'd have been forced to kill him myself, sooner or later.'

Just Joe squatted so that he was on the same level as McKinnon. He took a knife from his belt and held it meaningfully in front of the pale man.

'Well, I suppose with Ritchie dead, that leaves you in charge, doesn't it?' he said. 'And if you're in charge, that makes you responsible for all this mess. It's the price of leadership, McKinnon. What are we to do with you, eh?'

McKinnon kept his eyes on the knife. With his strange, washed-out features, he already resembled a man who had been cut and drained of blood.

'How did you track us?' said Just Joe.

'You left a trail a blind man could follow,' said McKinnon.

'Not true, not true,' said Just Joe. He used the tip of the knife to lift the end of McKinnon's pants from his left leg, exposing his shin. The knife pricked the skin, and a bubble of blood appeared. 'There isn't one man among you who is capable of doing what the Illyri and their Agrons could not. You're not trackers. You don't even belong out here. You should be tucked up in bed at home, with your mother feeding you cocoa from a spoon.'

Syl saw Paul tense. His hand dropped from her shoulder, where he had been supporting her in case she felt wobbly again. She turned to him, wondering if he was going to object to what Just Joe was doing, but Paul was not watching their leader. Instead, his gaze was fixed on Duncan, who slowly circled the group, closing in on where Just Joe squatted before McKinnon. Duncan's hand slipped inside his coat, and as Syl watched, it emerged holding a pistol. He sidled closer to Just Joe, seemingly unnoticed by all except Syl, and Paul, who moved quickly yet silently to intercept him.

'So,' Just Joe continued, 'how did you manage to get so close to us without giving yourselves away?'

Duncan was now behind Just Joe. He raised the pistol, but Syl could see that he was aiming past Joe. It was McKinnon he wanted to kill.

There was a loud click as Paul materialised at Duncan's side, his gun pointing at the smaller man's head.

Just Joe didn't even turn around.

'Do you have him?' he asked.

'I have him,' said Paul. 'Not a muscle,' he warned Duncan. 'Let it drop.'

The gun fell from Duncan's hand. Mike, who was standing closest to it, picked it up, checked the safety and tucked it into his pocket. The crowd distanced itself from Paul and Duncan as Just Joe got to his feet and faced them both. He looked more sad than angry.

'I thought it might be you,' he said to Duncan. 'I was hoping it wasn't, but every time you made an excuse to wander off, I wondered, and eventually my doubts became near certainties. I just couldn't figure out who you were in league with: the Illyri? But no, you hate them almost as much as you hate yourself. So it had to be Ritchie and McKinnon, or someone like them."

Just Joe gave McKinnon a wink.

'You should have picked a more trustworthy ally,' Just Joe said. 'Duncan was going to put a bullet in you before you gave him away. We may just have saved your life.'

McKinnon didn't reply, but he regarded Duncan with a killer's gaze.

Logan appeared at Joe's side, carrying Duncan's pack. He emptied its contents on to the ground. Among them was a small portable CW transceiver, with a lightweight wire antenna and a switch press for Morse code signals.

'Let me guess,' said Just Joe. 'One of this lot was following close to pick up the signals, while the rest kept their distance until the time was right.'

Duncan's face was a picture of barely contained fury.

'McKinnon is right,' he said. 'We have hostages, and important ones too. I've heard you talking to your pals. We have a governor's daughter, and a Grand Consul! You didn't share that with us, Joe. You kept it quiet. We could demand almost anything in return for their safety. We could demand that the Highlands be kept free, that the Illyri retreat below the wall, all for the promise of keeping these three alive. And what do we do instead? We *guard* them. We *feed* them. We keep them safe, even at the cost of the lives of our own.'

Just Joe put a hand on Duncan's shoulder. 'You don't understand. This is about more than hostages. You should have trusted me. You should have kept faith.'

Then his right fist slammed into Duncan's gut, and Duncan dropped to his knees. Just Joe patted him on the shoulder again, and adjusted the collar of his coat, as though trying to make him look respectable for an important appointment. He turned to Aggie, Frank and Howie.

'Were you involved in this? Tell me true.'

'No,' said Aggie. 'We might have disagreed with you, but that doesn't mean we'd betray you to the likes of these cut-throats.'

Joe seemed to believe them, although Syl saw that Logan and Ryan had been lurking behind Aggie and the cousins just in case Joe decided otherwise.

'What are we going to do with him, and the rest of them?' asked Paul.

'Take away their weapons – and their food too – then let them go.'

There were gasps from the group. Even McKinnon looked surprised, but Just Joe raised a hand, silencing any possible objections. Only Paul showed no emotion.

'What would you have me do, kill them?' asked Joe. 'I've told you before: we're not murderers. We're not like them, and we're not going to do the Illyri's work for them either. We'll send them on their way, and godspeed to them.

'They came across the loch,' he said, turning to Paul. 'Logan found their boat. Cut them loose, and send them back the way they came.

Use my field glasses to watch them for as long as you can, then rejoin us.'

'I will,' said Paul.

'You did well,' said Just Joe.

'Thanks.'

'Don't let it go to your head,' said Just Joe. 'I still don't entirely trust you.'

He stared hard at Syl.

'And her neither.'

But before anything else could be said, Syl had her final shock of the day. An Illyri strode into the camp, and nobody batted an eyelid. Even Aggie barely glanced at him before returning her attention to her husband, who seemed about as troubled by his injury as he might have been by a midge bite. Syl thought she must surely be hallucinating, but the Illyri, tall even by the standards of their race, appeared to be real. She could even hear the sucking sound the mud made against his boots. His clothing was entirely terrestrial in origin: a long wax jacket over an old sweater, and waterproof trousers tucked into lightweight walking boots. His hair had been shaved to within a quarter of an inch of his skull, and he wore a small silver hoop in the lobe of one ear.

'You took your time,' said Just Joe. 'You missed all the excitement.'

The Illyri took in the prisoners, and the wounded. His eyes lit on Duncan.

'I never liked him,' he said.

'I never liked him either,' said Just Joe.

'No loss, then.'

'None at all.'

Just Joe grinned and embraced the big Illyri, and the Illyri hugged him in return.

'It's good to see you,' said Joe.

'And you, my friend.'

The Illyri stepped back, and Joe pointed to Syl and Ani.

'Safe and well,' said Joe.

'And the other?'

'Still alive, but he doesn't talk much.'

The Illyri shrugged.

'He won't have to talk to tell us what he knows.'

'If you're right.'

'Yes, if I'm right.'

The Illyri raised a hand in greeting to Syl and Ani.

'My name is Fremd,' he said, 'spelled with a D but pronounced with a T: Fremt. I'm going to be looking after you for a while . . .'

CHAPTER 55

McKinnon slouched in the front of the van, brooding while Craven, the group's driver, took them away from the jetty where they'd tethered their forlorn boat. They'd had to drag their vessel several hundred yards from where it had finally reached the shore, but thankfully their van was still parked where they'd left it beneath a copse of scraggly trees, unremarkable and untouched. They weren't concerned about being stopped by the Illyri. They had no weapons, and they had been interrogated often enough to know the routine. There was light in the sky, or as much of it as could filter through the clouds and the rain, and it lifted his mood. He had travelled often before the arrival of the Illyri; his father had worked for a big bank, and McKinnon's early years had been spent in the Far East, and Australia, and the United States. He'd seen many beautiful places but he loved the Highlands most of all, although even he sometimes wished that it would rain a little less.

Duncan sat in the back with the others, lost in his own grievances. He would be another mouth to feed unless McKinnon could get rid of him, which he planned to do as soon as they reached the next town. Duncan could find his own way in the world now, because McKinnon didn't want him around. A man who betrayed one master would betray another even faster because he had the taste for treachery in his mouth. McKinnon had enough trouble keeping his own men in line. He had no desire to add Duncan to the mix, especially after Duncan had seemed all too ready to put a bullet in him in order to ensure his silence.

McKinnon was surprised that Just Joe had let them go so easily. Joe was a hard man, and McKinnon had always respected him. It was why his words had cut him deeply. He *was* a bandit. He'd started out as something better, but he'd just lost faith somewhere along the way. Ritchie had changed him. Ritchie believed that in hard times, the strong preyed on the weak, because it was important that the strong should survive. But now Ritchie was dead, and McKinnon was the leader of their less-than-merry band. Perhaps he could change, but what would be the point? He doubted that the Resistance would have him even if he wanted to join them, and the only reason he remained alive – let alone free – was because enough people feared him and his men. No, the die was cast now, and there was no turning back.

Damn, but he'd wanted the Illyri captives for himself. The Grand Consul and a governor's daughter could have bought him a lot: freedom for his imprisoned men, but maybe also a chance at another life. He could have handed them back to the Illyri in return for a fresh start: money, a new name, a decent home. Painful though it might have been for him, he would even have been tempted to leave the Highlands and build a fresh existence somewhere else. He was still dreaming of lost opportunities when he heard the skimmer approach. It drifted down from the east, swooped over the van, then rose behind them in a lazy arc.

'What should I do?' asked Craven.

'Just keep going for now,' said McKinnon. 'If they want us to stop, they'll let us know soon enough.'

The usual procedure was for the Illyri to illuminate any vehicle they wanted to investigate using searchlights, but this skimmer seemed content to shadow them without forcing them to stop. They could hear its whine above the van's engines, and McKinnon could see it flying low to the east. It was black, and it gave him an ominous feeling.

'I don't like it,' said Craven. 'Why haven't they just stopped us?'

'I don't know,' said McKinnon. This wasn't typical Illyri behaviour.

Any further questions were curtailed by a deep roar, and a pair of black cruisers burst from the clouds. One of them came to rest half a mile from the van, blocking the road. The second stayed directly above them until Craven pulled over, whereupon it landed nearby and began disgorging Securitats and Galateans. The van was surrounded before Craven even had time to kill the engine. More Securitats poured from the carrier on the road. For the first time, McKinnon was truly grateful that Just Joe had deprived them of their guns. If he had not, they would now be living their last moments on Earth. The Securitats wouldn't have bothered with trials and exile to the Punishment Battalions; they would have killed them here and dumped their corpses in a bog.

'Stay calm,' said McKinnon. 'Keep your hands where they can see them, and say nothing. If they ask where we've been, we tell them we're labourers heading back home. We have nothing to hide. Remember that.'

A voice boomed from a speaker in the nearest carrier.

'Out of the van. Keep your hands held high once you exit. Do not disobey. Any sudden moves will be treated as a hostile act, and you will be shot.'

The men in the van did as they were told. Once they were outside, the Galateans took over, forcing them to their knees while a pair of Securitats searched the vehicle. As they did so, an Illyri dressed in a smart black suit approached McKinnon, heedless of the rain. The only clue to his identity and position was the silver badge on his lapel, but McKinnon knew who he was, for his picture had long been circulating in the Highlands and elsewhere: Sedulus, the Securitats' torturer-in-chief. Maybe, thought McKinnon, I won't live out this day after all.

The two males, human and Illyri, watched each other carefully but said nothing while the van was torn apart. Eventually the two Securitats climbed out. They looked puzzled.

'It's empty, sir.'

Sedulus frowned.

'You're certain?'

'We removed the panels and the flooring. There's no question.'

Sedulus pointed to the kneeling men.

'Scan them.'

The Securitats moved behind the six humans, each holding a small circular scanning device. They both stopped when they came to Duncan, who looked nervously over his shoulder.

'What? What is it?'

One of the Securitats moved closer, the scanner now almost touching Duncan's clothing. After a moment's hesitation, he put his hand into the pocket of Duncan's jacket and came up with an Illyri tracker.

McKinnon started to laugh. He had underestimated Just Joe.

The others looked at him as though he was mad. Only Sedulus seemed to echo McKinnon's amusement. His face broke into a faint smile.

'Let me guess,' he said. 'You were unwitting decoys.'

McKinnon's laughter faded. 'I don't know what you're talking about.'

'Well then you're no use to me,' said Sedulus. He drew his pulser, and shot McKinnon dead. He did the same with four of the other men, leaving only Duncan alive. Duncan cowered, his face almost at the level of the ground, his hands curled over his head, waiting his turn to die, but Sedulus simply tucked his pulser back into its holster, its work done for the time being. His smile returned as he regarded Duncan.

'Now,' he said, 'perhaps you'd care to tell me how you came by that tracker . . .'

Duncan made a half-hearted effort to resist the interrogation. He tried to stick to his original story, and claimed that the coat had been given to him on a farm when his own had simply fallen apart due to wear and tear. Unfortunately for him, the tracker had been sending its signal ever since Paul had removed it from its lead box and slipped it into the pocket, as he manhandled Duncan into the boat, and the initial transmission had come from nowhere near the location of the fictitious farm on which Duncan had claimed to be working with the others. Joe had entrusted Gradus's tracker to Paul when he placed him in charge of the prisoners, and Paul had known just what to do.

Duncan's story instantly collapsed, and he was taken into the larger of the two cruisers and strapped to a chair. In a pen at one end were what appeared to be three empty mechanised space suits, until one of them moved its head and Duncan saw what looked like oily black smoke swirl behind its visor. He might have been tempted to ask what they were had Sedulus not administered the first of the electric shocks, quickly followed by a second and a third. Within minutes, Duncan had told him of the finding of the wreckage, the survival of the three Illyri, and his own attempted betrayal, as well as the arrival of the Illyri deserter called Freud.

'Where are they taking them?' asked Sedulus.

'I don't know,' said Duncan. 'Only Just Joe knows.'

'You're lying.'

'I'm not, I swear it.'

'Then why should I let you live?'

Duncan considered the question. He saw McKinnon's body slumping lifelessly to the ground once more, and the others that followed, blood leaking from their mouths and their ears.

'You'll kill me either way,' he said.

'I will not kill you,' said Sedulus. 'You have my word.'

'The word of an Illyri,' said Duncan, making it clear how much he felt that was worth.

'That would hurt more if it did not come from the mouth of a traitor.'

Duncan conceded the point with a shrug.

'I can't take the Punishment Battalions,' he said. 'I wouldn't last a week. I'm too old.'

'You will not be sent to the Punishment Battalions. Again, you have my word.'

Duncan swallowed. He looked to the pen. All three of the suits were now in an upright position. Whatever moved behind those black visors seemed to be interested in him.

'What are they?' he asked.

'They are the Sarith Entities.'

'I don't know what that is,' said Duncan.

'Frankly,' said Sedulus, 'I'm not sure that I do either. You were saying?'

Duncan hung his head. 'Only Just Joe knows the destination for sure, but I heard him tell Logan and the others that they're going to turn north-east, and there has been talk of a Green Man.'

'Who is the Green Man?'

'It's a code word for a Resistance leader, but I've never met him before.'

Sedulus nodded. 'I believe you.'

'What's going to happen to me?' asked Duncan.

'Why, you're going to die,' said Sedulus.

A pair of Securitats appeared. They undid the straps on Duncan's arms and legs, and helped him to his feet. He staggered, weakened by shocks.

'But you promised!' he said.

'I promised that I wouldn't kill you, and I won't,' said Sedulus. 'They will.'

He pointed at the three mechanised suits. The black clouds swirled behind the faceplates as Sedulus gave the order.

'Feed him to the Entities.'

CHAPTER 56

Syl could not resist stealing glances at the strong, graceful Illyri named Fremd. She had already learned a little about him from Alice, who was in awe of him. He was an Illyri deserter, one of the first to change sides, and the Securitats had placed a price on his head that grew every year. Alice didn't know why he'd abandoned the Illyri for the humans, and Heather, when she joined them, would say only that he had his reasons. The Resistance had imprisoned him for a long time before they began to trust him.

'Now he is at the core of the Resistance,' said Heather. 'Him, and Maeve.'

'Who's Maeve?' asked Ani.

'You'll meet her,' Heather had replied. 'He's taking you to her.'

There was a ruddiness to the gold of Fremd's skin that spoke of long days spent battling the elements in Scotland. He had wrinkles around his eyes and mouth, astonishing for one who was still comparatively young. Even her father had barely a line on his face, and he was considerably older than Fremd. What struck Syl most about him was the sense of a spirit liberated, a being at peace with himself. In a strange way, this hunted man had found the place where he was always meant to be. If he died in the Highlands, he would die happy.

He in his turn seemed curious about Syl and Ani. After all, they were in a similar situation. He had turned his back on his own people, at the risk of his life, to live among the humans, just as Syl and Ani were now being pursued for their own treason.

Eventually, after twenty minutes spent talking in private with Just

Joe, Fremd fell back to join the little group comprising Syl and Ani, and Steven and Paul. Alice was with them too. Her mother had entrusted her to them, for it had been made clear that the group of Resistance fighters was going to split up. Already the others were preparing to leave without them. Only the lad named AK stood apart from the rest, holding one end of a rope that was wrapped around Grand Consul Gradus. Gradus's jaw hung open, and his eyes remained blank and lifeless.

'You're all coming with me and AK,' Fremd told them.

On the small rise above them, Just Joe let the rest of the Resistance pass him, then paused and raised a hand to Fremd in farewell before rejoining his group. There was something sad about the gesture, as if he feared that he might not see Fremd again.

'Why are they leaving?' asked Syl.

'Because Joe has to play a risky game now,' said Fremd. 'He's had his suspicions about Duncan for a while, and he's been feeding him titbits of false information about his plans. If all has gone well, Duncan is now in the hands of the Illyri, and is telling them what he knows, or thinks he knows. That will lead them away from us, and towards Joe.'

'And what will Joe do then?'

'He'll fight them.'

Syl looked back at the rise, but there was nobody to be seen. They were so few. How could they hope to take on their Illyri pursuers and prevail?

'You've done well to avoid them so far, by the way,' said Fremd. 'To tell the truth, I thought they might catch you within a day, but it seems the old gods are smiling on you.'

'Old gods?' asked Ani. 'What old gods?'

'You can't live out here for long and not start to believe in spirits, both good and bad,' said Fremd. 'They're in the stones, and the air. You don't want to go messing about with the old gods, but if you treat them right, they'll keep their part of the bargain.'

Ani looked at him as though he were mad.

'Do you drink?' she asked.

'What, like whisky? Of course.'

'Well, maybe you should consider cutting back.'

Fremd laughed. 'Have you ever heard of Pascal's Wager?'

Ani shook her head.

'It's a philosophical position,' said Fremd. 'Pascal was a Frenchman, who argued that it made more sense to believe in the existence of God than not, because you had nothing to lose by believing. So I take the view that if I act like there are old gods, and they don't exist, then there's no harm done, but if they do exist, then by treating them with respect I'll avoid any harm to myself. I win either way.'

Fremd began walking, and they all followed, AK leading Gradus the way a drover might lead an obedient mule.

'That woman back at camp, Aggie, she hates me, but she barely looked at you when you came into camp,' said Syl.

'Do you hate all humans?'

'No, of course not.'

'Aggie doesn't hate all Illyri,' said Fremd. 'She hates what the Illyri represent on Earth – conflict, repression, captivity – but she's slowly learning that we're not all alike. She doesn't know you. To her, you and Ani and the Grand Consul are all the enemy. She'll learn the truth about you as well, in time.'

'Your name,' said Syl. 'It's not Illyri.'

'No, it's German. It means "strange" or "foreign". Or in my case, "alien". One of my first captors was a German. He gave me the name, and it stuck.'

'What's your real name?'

'It doesn't matter,' said Fremd, and for the first time Syl saw the steel beneath his placid nature. 'That's not who I am any more.'

The conversation ended, and they continued walking for an hour or more. They moved through places where there was a little cover, although Fremd was more concerned with making progress than reducing exposure to their hunters, until at last they came to an area of new-growth pine. Once upon a time, the ancient Caledonian Forest had covered the Highlands, but primitive tribes had begun its destruction, and the Vikings had helped by burning large parts of it, until farmers and fuel-gatherers finished the job. Even before the arrival of the Illyri, efforts had begun to restore the woodland, and now millions of trees were growing in the Highlands; not just pine, but alder, birch, holly, hazel and mountain ash. Fremd had led them to the outskirts of one of these new patches of forest, and allowed them to refill their water bottles from a small stream.

Syl winced and limped a little as she felt a blister burst on her right foot.

'Sore feet?' said Fremd.

'Very.'

'I have something in my bag that might help, when we stop to eat.'

'Dry socks? Boots that fit?'

'You never know; miracles do happen. But you have my sympathy. Just Joe walks a hard march.'

'Sometimes we seemed to be going around in circles, or at least taking the longest route between any two points,' said Syl.

'Joe didn't want to leave a straight trail, or an obvious line,' explained Fremd, 'because that's what the Agrons look for. It's in their nature: why go around something when you can go through it? They'll assume that we'll do the same. Their sense of smell is incredible, but their logical processes leave a lot to be desired, and their handlers are at their mercy. They go straight, we take the scenic route, and the Agrons get confused. By taking one step back, we take two steps forward.'

'And how long are you planning to keep making us take these miraculous steps?' asked Ani.

'Just for another couple of hours. There's a ruined bothy by a loch with a supply dump nearby. We'll let you rest up there properly before the final push.'

Ani frowned at Syl. 'What's a bothy?'

'A cottage,' said Fremd. 'You really don't get out much, do you? You've been in Scotland most of your life, and you still don't know what a bothy is.'

'I never *had* to know what a stupid bothy was,' said Ani.

She paused to watch AK tear a strip of fabric from his T-shirt and tie it around his forehead before he squatted down and artfully smeared mud across his face.

'What is that idiot doing?' she said. 'Hey, idiot, what are you doing?'

'Don't call me idiot, idiot,' said AK.

'Great comeback,' said Syl.

AK grunted.

'Camouflage,' he said, and he stamped his muddy boots meaningfully on the ground and squinted at the horizon.

Syl bent over the water and began muddying her own features. When she turned to face Ani, she'd daubed a rough L for 'Loser' on her own forehead in mud, and they started to laugh. It was the first time Syl had laughed in what seemed like weeks. For a moment she forgot the pursuit, and how much she missed her father, and Althea. She even forgot Ritchie impaled on his bayonet, and the drowned man in the stream, and the gift, or curse, that had caused their deaths. Her laughter took on an edge of hysteria, but she kept laughing because she was afraid that if she stopped she might start crying instead. Eventually she got herself under control. She wiped her eyes. There were tears, but they were of mirth, for now.

'You know, it wasn't that funny,' said Ani.

And Syl started laughing again.

Fremd shook his head in puzzlement, and set off again. Behind him, the laughter faded, and the little group recommenced their slow, painful trudge.

Syl slowed to take a few minutes to talk quietly with Steven. He was walking carefully for fear of taking a tumble and bursting his stitches. He confirmed to her that he had not said anything of what had happened, not even to Paul, in part because he wasn't sure what had happened himself.

'How did you do it?' he asked.

'I'm not sure,' said Syl. 'I got angry and I just willed it. I was afraid, too. I think that was part of it. I couldn't control it. I was so frightened, and so furious. It was like a storm inside me.'

'Have you done it before?'

'No, not like that. I don't think I even realised I was doing it in the past. Looking back, I can see how I might have made people do something because I wanted them to, but it was subtle. I talked them around, mostly, but I'm starting to think that if they resisted, I might have given them a little push. You understand why nobody must know, don't you? They'd think I was a freak. They'd do tests. They might lock me up.'

'No,' said Steven. 'They'd use you, like a weapon.'

The truth of it made Syl stop in her tracks. He was right.

She saw Paul and Ani staring back at her when they noticed that she was not following. She stomped her right foot on the ground and stretched her thigh, like someone fighting a cramp, then waved to let them know that she was okay.

'So it's our secret?' she said to Steven.

'Yes, it's our secret. It would be even if you hadn't used it to save my life.'

'Thank you,' said Syl.

'It's nothing,' said Steven, and Syl wished that were true.

CHAPTER 57

For the next hour Syl walked beside Paul and told him stories of places that she'd never been to but wished to see, describing things she'd only ever read of in books or glimpsed on screens or in virtual reality constructs, and some even that she might simply have dreamed: the curlicued insects of Illyr, like musical notes moving through the air; great lakes that shone not blue, but gold and yellow, while the sky above constantly swirled with ferocious clouds tinged with blue and red as storms raged high in the atmosphere even while all was calm and humid on the ground. She told him of towering plants that grew to the sky and sucked rain from clouds, and of the strange creatures that spent their entire lives atop these highest flora, winged and scaled with bright red skin as tough as canvas to protect them from the storms, their bodies only descending at last to the ground upon their deaths. She told him of the moons that fought over the waves, and the lazy arc of the planet's bright star – Illyr's sun – that gave a sense of near-endless days and deep, dark nights. She told him of the luminous creatures that followed the night so that they were always in the dark, and camouflaged day creatures that stayed always in the sun, their bodies so perfectly adapted to their environment that they were visible only as a blurring against the clouds, a ripple in the fabric of the sky.

In return, he answered her questions about his life. He talked of his decision to join the Resistance. He spoke of a sister who had lived for just a few hours after her birth, and whose presence he sometimes felt near him, as though her ghost had remained with them and continued to grow, reluctant to be separated from her brothers. And he told her of his mother, who, on the death of her husband, had somehow found it within her to love her boys twice as much to make up for his absence.

'She sounds marvellous,' said Syl.

'Well, she drives me mad sometimes, but then I do the same with her. Anyway, you know mums.'

'No,' said Syl. 'I don't. But I've got Althea.'

'Oh Syl, I'm sorry. That was thoughtless. But tell me more about Althea?'

And she did, spilling feelings she'd never shared before about her formative years, about the hole she felt inside that never went away and how Althea had filled at least part of it, speaking words to a near stranger that she had never shared with a friend. Paul had heard that there was an Illyri from the castle who was friendly with Trask – and perhaps more than that – but he had not known her name until now, and he thought how strange it was that even in this he had been connected to Syl without knowing it. As Syl grew forlorn at her separation from those in the castle who loved her, Paul cheered her with upbeat tales of his life and his extended, oddball family, of cousins and aunts and uncles so bizarre that she thought he must surely have invented them, until she came to the conclusion that nobody could invent a family so strange.

Then he had more questions about where she came from, about her homeworld, so she told him of marvellous fabled cities: of Olos with its castles of ice; of the magical Arayyis that spilled elegantly into the sea; and of splendid spired Tannis, the birthplace of her mother, the most glorious city of them all.

At last they came to a small loch at the heart of the woods, its waters still and cold, reflecting the mountains in shades of icy blue and green, and Syl sighed with pleasure, smiling at Paul and saying, 'But of course, this is beautiful too.'

He took her hand and squeezed it, smiling too, and she felt his touch tingling all the way up her arm and catching like a sigh in her throat. She squeezed back, and he lifted her fingers to his mouth and pressed his lips to the back of her hand. Just then Fremd started to bark instructions and, blushing, they both let go before anyone could see them.

Fremd announced that they would rest here. As AK pointed out, there was also the possibility of catching some fish for supper.

'With your bare hands, no doubt,' said Ani.

Her dislike of AK, unreasonable and instinctive, had not decreased during their walk, and she seemed to take pleasure in baiting him. AK gave her a funny look before he wandered off to 'survey the terrain', only to return a little later with four plump silver fish on a hand-hewn wooden spear. Ani spluttered with surprise when he handed her his prize.

'You've got to be joking,' she said. 'What am I meant to do with these?'

'Cook 'em,' he said. 'Or stick 'em where the sun don't shine.'

'Cooking them might be better,' said Steven.

'And tastier,' said Syl.

Paul was sitting on a boulder keeping watch while Fremd went to the bothy for whatever supplies he needed. Syl had thought about joining Paul, but then decided to give him a little time alone.

'I'll help you,' said Alice to Ani. 'I know what to do.'

'Right,' said Ani, staring doubtfully into the glassy-eyed faces of the dead fish. Alice dug about in her small backpack, pulled out a penknife and gave it to Ani, who gamely set to work gutting the fish on a flat stone, wrinkling her nose with distaste as she followed the little girl's instructions.

'Do you think,' she said, 'that we dare to make a fire, or is it to be sushi for dinner?'

'Neither,' said Fremd, as he stepped from the woods.

From his pack he produced a pair of small gas camping stoves, and a battered metal plate.

'These should do the trick.'

He also had two tins of baked beans, a small pot, some bars of chocolate, a jar of instant coffee, sachets of creamer, and paper cups.

It was to be a feast.

★ ★ ★

They ate together, sharing the fish as it cooked on sticks, stuffing the hot food into their mouths with their fingers. Ani offered the first morsels to AK, and he pronounced it to be very good indeed, and a thaw in their relationship began. When the last of the beans were eaten, Fremd rinsed out the pan and filled it with water to boil, spooned the coffee into the cups and shared out the chocolate. Syl had lost all track of time. There was still light in the sky. That was all she knew for certain.

'I have a sudden desire for toasted marshmallows,' said Paul.

'I'd settle for soap,' said Steven, sniffing theatrically at his armpits.

'As if by magic,' said Fremd, and from his pocket he produced two thick bars of yellow soap. Steven grabbed them.

'And on that note, I'm declaring it bath time,' he said.

He got to his feet, and with a whoop hurtled down the slope towards the water.

'C'mon!' he shouted, tearing off his clothes until he was down to his boxers. 'Last one in is a chicken.'

Paul and AK took off after him, Alice at their heels, but the Illyri girls hung back. Syl pulled a face. 'A chicken? Why is the last one in a chicken?'

Ani shrugged, frowning.

'I don't understand either.'

But now Paul was shouting to them from the bottom of the slope as he too stripped down to tartan boxer shorts. His body was pale and lean, his stomach taut, his limbs held together by obvious sinews and tight knots of still-bruised flesh, and Syl felt a tingling in her thighs and an odd weightlessness in her chest.

'Syl?' Ani said. 'Earth to Syl.'

'Sorry,' said Syl. 'I was just . . .'

Ani waited, one eyebrow arched like a bird taking flight. 'Yes? You were just what, exactly?'

'Never mind,' said Syl.

She took her friend's hand, and together they loped down the slope to bathe in the icy water. It was freezing – so cold that Syl thought she would only be able to stand it for a few seconds – but she was desperate to clean herself. She moved away from the others, who were playing piggy-in-the-middle with a bar of wet soap, Steven and Paul squeezing the bar in their hands to propel it over Ani's head. Syl was in no mood to play. Instead she scrubbed and scrubbed with the second bar of soap, as though she could wipe away not just the filth and the mud but the memory of the blood she had spilled. When she could stand the cold no longer, she ran shivering from the water. She came to their camp and saw that Fremd had built a fire in the lee of a boulder, shielding it on the exposed sides with raised banks of earth.

'Don't worry,' he said from nearby. 'It's not dark yet so it would be hard to see even without the rock and dirt, and it'll do you all good to warm yourselves by it. We can cook on a gas stove, but we can't dry ourselves with one.'

He produced a small tube of ointment and gently tended to the blister on Syl's foot. He was bare-chested, for he too had taken the opportunity to wash. Syl saw scars and burns on his skin. When he was finished, he turned his back to her to shrug on his shirt, and Syl glimpsed a great tattoo that stretched from his shoulders to the base of his spine. It was a bearded face made up of leaves and vines and young branches, all of them bright green. It was a face from ancient myths, the face of an old god.

It was the Green Man.

CHAPTER 58

They warmed themselves, then dressed again and tried to sleep for a time while Fremd kept guard. Syl lay awake, watching the fire die and thinking about the great tattoo on his back. Could it be? Could an Illyri be at the heart of the Resistance? What was it that Heather had said about Fremd?

He is at the core of the Resistance.

And Syl fell asleep and dreamed of old gods.

Fremd woke them while it was dark, and they marched for the rest of the night. The rain returned just before dawn, heavier and colder than any they had yet experienced. The ground turned to swamp, and even Fremd struggled to make headway. Eventually they were forced to camp by a bank of rocks, the largest of them looming like a grey cliff face over the trees. There was a fissure at its base where Fremd lit another small fire, certain that it would be shielded from any watchers above. It was too deep in the rock face to give off much warmth to those outside, but he instructed them all to remove their shoes and socks so that the fire might dry them out. He again produced the container of ointment from his bag, and tended to those whose feet were blistered. He did so unselfconsciously, as if it were the most natural thing in the world for him to hold and heal the filthy, battered limbs of strangers. Only AK declined.

'I'll do it myself,' he said. Fremd shrugged. If he was offended, he gave no sign.

They sipped water and nibbled on protein snacks and muesli bars, more treasures from Fremd's store at the bothy. Ani set about diligently breaking her two bars into squares and making them into sandwiches, muesli hugging the brown gunk of the protein. Steven took her cue and moulded his protein bar into the vague shape of a dog, then promptly ate it. Ani consoled Alice, who was missing her mother, until the child fell asleep, then started a silly game that entailed scrawling shapes on each other's backs and guessing what they were, but AK ruined it by drawing a pair of crude oversized breasts on Ani's back, which earned him a punch that deadened his leg, while Syl found herself flustered and unable to reply when Paul drew a heart on her spine.

'I didn't mean anything, you know, weird by it,' he whispered over her shoulder. 'It just seemed like the easiest thing to draw.' She wasn't sure if she was relieved or disappointed, but she liked the tickle of his warm breath on her ear. She shivered happily.

'You're cold,' he said, taking off his thick waterproof jacket and wrapping it around her shoulders.

'Don't be silly,' she said, shoving it back into his hands. 'Then you'll be cold.'

'How about you sit right here then, between my knees, and I'll wrap it around us together, then we'll both be warm,' he said. His legs curled around her, making a chair, and he pulled his oversized parka around them both, snuggling her between his arms. Syl was too embarrassed to shuffle away, but too aware of her own weight to lean on him, too awkward to relax.

'That's warmer,' he said next to her ear, pulling her closer and leaning his head on her shoulder. 'You don't mind, do you?'

'No. No, not at all. It's definitely better,' she heard herself say, and she had to admit it was, even when she saw Ani watching them, grinning with wicked amusement. She was too engrossed in making Syl feel awkward to notice the look of longing that Steven directed at her, but Syl caught it. She wanted to tell Ani to be careful, for Steven was clearly falling for her. Ani could hurt him if she wasn't careful.

But then she realised that she too was falling for someone who could hurt her.

'Do you like what you do?' she asked Paul.

'What do you mean?'

'I mean all this. The fighting. The Resistance.'

She moved in his arms so that she could see his face as he answered. He looked down on her, and she thought that she had never seen such tenderness in the eyes of one to whom she was not bound by blood or the passage of years.

'There's nothing to like about it. But I dislike the occupation even more.'

'Why, though? I'm not trying to be flippant or anything; I just can't understand why it's so abhorrent that you would rather die fighting the Illyri – I mean, us.'

Her choice of words betrayed the strength of her growing feelings for Paul, and the confusion they were causing her – the Illyri weren't something other than herself; they were her own people – but Paul did not pick up on it. Instead, he noticed that she had placed her emphasis on the word 'you'; it was his safety, and his life, of which she spoke.

'Do you hate us?' Syl continued. 'I mean, you personally, like Duncan did?'

'Sometimes,' said Paul. 'But honestly, I just wish you'd go away. Just bugger off back to where you came from.'

She looked at her feet, her face burning.

'Right,' was all she managed in reply.

'I don't mean you!' He gripped her shoulder, turning her towards him. 'I mean, you're . . . It's . . .'

He struggled to find the right word, then settled for, 'You're different.'

'Different? Is that the best you can do?'

'No,' he said.

His lips touched hers now, briefly, sweetly, another stolen contact gone before the rest of them could notice. Syl smiled, her cheeks pink. Paul's eyes were shining as he stared into her face, and he grinned broadly.

Finally Syl found she could relax against him. She dozed in his arms as if it were the most natural thing in all the world, until a high-pitched whine roused her, and she saw Ani and Fremd responding to it just as she had. Seconds later, the humans heard it too.

'Skimmer,' said Fremd.

They looked to the brightening sky, lit by the first tentative rays of dawn. It was Ani who picked out the fast-moving craft first.

'There,' she said.

A pair of black specks fell from it, as though the craft were slowly disintegrating.

'What are they?' asked AK.

Fremd looked unhappy. 'I don't know, but if they're good news I'll be surprised.'

He rose to his feet.

'AK, keep watch. If I'm not back in an hour, kill the fire and go to Maeve. Just Joe will join you there soon enough, all being well.' He pointed at Gradus. 'But make sure you don't lose him!'

Fremd grabbed his gun and was lost to the pines. Syl wriggled away from Paul, the spell broken. They were all silent now. There were no more laughs, no more teases, no more games. They could only wait for Fremd to come back and tell them what new turn the hunt had taken.

An hour passed, and Fremd did not return.

'AK,' said Paul. 'We should go.'

But AK just shook his head.

'We wait.'

'But Fremd told us—'

'We wait!' repeated AK, and Syl could see how scared he was. For all his bluster, all his bravado, he was still only a boy. He didn't want to make decisions. He didn't want to lead. Fremd should have left Paul in charge, thought Syl, but then Fremd didn't know Paul. Now, seeing the fear in AK's eyes, Syl suspected that Fremd didn't seem to know AK very well either.

They remained as they were, AK's eyes fixed hopefully on the forest, willing Fremd to appear.

'Syl,' whispered Ani.

'Yes?'

'Do you hear it?'

She did. It was a soft whirring, but it was there.

'It's coming closer,' she said.

'What?' said AK. 'What's coming closer?'

Then they saw it: a small hovering black object, little bigger than a football, a single red light blinking at its heart. It stayed about four feet above the ground, altering its course to avoid the trees. Closer and closer it drew to them. AK began to get to his feet, his weapon pointed at the approaching threat, ready to fire, when they heard Fremd's voice from nearby.

'Don't move!' he said. 'Just don't!'

They all froze, AK poised uncomfortably between kneeling and rising. The object approached him, and Syl could see that its surface was covered with sensors and antennae. It was only a few feet from him when it stopped moving forward. It paused for a moment, as though thinking, then dropped until its blinking red light was level with AK's head. The boy trembled, partly in fear and partly because he was trapped in an agonising position. Syl could see it in his face. His brow was contorted with pain as he tried to remain still. She willed him to hold on. Just a few seconds more, AK. Do it for us. Please.

As if her plea had been heard, the orb rotated in the air, its red light turning to the forest, and began to move away. AK sagged to the ground in relief.

And the object spun back in his direction.

AK panicked, starting to run, and Fremd cried a single word: 'No!'

AK only managed to take a few steps before a dart whistled from the body of the object and hit him in the back. He stumbled and fell to the ground, just as Fremd's blast rifle blew the sphere to smithereens.

Syl was the first to reach AK. She stretched out a hand to him, but instantly Fremd was beside her, pulling her back.

'Don't touch him,' he said.

AK was writhing on the ground, as though he were being tortured with electric shocks. At least two inches of the dart still protruded from his back. A series of green lights along its length slowly began to blink out.

'What's happening to him?' said Syl.

'The dart has determined that he's human, not Illyri,' said Fremd.

'And?'

'Nanobots,' said Fremd. 'It's flooding his system with nanobots.'

Inside AK, millions of tiny self-replicating robotic forms were reproducing. Technically, such weapons had been outlawed as part of the restrictions placed on the Illyri artificial life form programme, for nanobots had proved more difficult to control than expected. The most advanced bots, used to target defective and diseased cells in Illyri, had turned upon their patients, having identified all flesh as inferior and flawed when compared with machines, killing those whom they were supposed to cure, although the problem had since been solved.

But the Securitats were not concerned with restrictions, and had seen the weapon potential in the rogue nanobots. These particular bots had been designed to target essential organs in humans – the liver, the lungs, the heart and the kidneys – and tear them apart. Blood bubbled from AK's lips. His eyes widened, his body jerked one final time, and then he lay still. Inside him, the nanobots, their work now done, shut down their systems and died along with their host.

CHAPTER 59

Vena stood in the control centre at the Eden Project. She had been there many times before. While her base of operations was Edinburgh, Sedulus had entrusted her with the task of discreetly overseeing security procedures at Eden, even though there were already senior Securitat operatives in place to take care of such matters. It was all wheels within wheels: spies watched people, other spies watched the spies. It was enough to make one doubt one's faith in everyone, human or Illyri, assuming one had any faith to begin with, which Vena did not.

She had examined the bodies of the dead scientists. Sidis, the corpse from the car park, had been killed with a single stab wound before losing a finger and an eye. Her body had been tested for trace evidence. Fingerprints were found, but they did not match any on the Illyri databases. Vena was not surprised; if, as suspected, the attack had been carried out by a Mech, then the fingerprints could be changed at will by the simple application of some newly patterned ProGen skin. The other bodies had revealed little, although the clothing taken from Harvis, the scientist who had wounded the Mech, had been sprayed with both internal lubricant and blood. The blood contained no identifiers, confirming that the intruder's flesh was a laboratory-grown artifice.

That was interesting. The Mech was, in a sense, biomechanical: it had added a thin layer of real tissue over its mechanics and hydraulics. Why? Vena supposed that, in the event of a minor injury, it would be seen to bleed like an Illyri. A deeper wound, such as the one Harvis had inflicted, would cause more problems, but only if there were others around to witness it.

Vena wondered if the Mech could feel pleasure or pain. Illyri who had suffered major injuries requiring amputation, and for whom replacement limbs could not be created for genetic reasons, usually had regrown tissue applied to the artificial limb and then linked to their nervous systems so that no sensation was lost. Perhaps the Mech simply wanted the tissue in order to maintain the illusion that it was an Illyri so it could hide itself more easily, but why stop there? One of the problems with the Mechs was that they began to believe that they could *feel*. But to truly experience the world required more than a cyborg's brain and a series of complex artificial systems. How could one love if one could not enjoy the touch of a lover's skin? How could one feel pain without the vulnerabilities of flesh?

No, thought Vena, this was not just a Mech with delusions. This was something more special, more dangerous. This was a Mech in the process of transforming itself: not completely artificial, and not yet Illyri, but an entity in between.

This was an abomination.

Pieces of video appeared on the screens around Vena as the system collated all sightings of the intruder. The Mech had been careful – a hood raised here, a head down there, always conscious of surveillance, seen or unseen – but gradually the system began to assemble a face from the brief glimpses of features that the cameras had picked up: an eye from this one, a cheekbone from another, a corner of a mouth from a third.

After an hour Vena had an image. She almost laughed when she saw it, for the identity of the Mech came as both a shock and an unexpected gift.

Meia.

It would give Vena nothing but pleasure to terminate her existence.

CHAPTER 60

Sedulus stood in the command cabin of his cruiser, a relief map of the Highlands on the screen before him. To his right was the Galatean sergeant; like all of his kind, he had no name, or none that the Illyri could pronounce. The Galateans called each other 'Brother' or 'Sister' according to gender, although in reality there were no family or clan loyalties among them, and as far as the Illyri could tell, they had little time for complicated emotions such as grief, or guilt, or even love. They mated, they bred, they lived, they died and, in the service of the Illyri, they killed. It seemed to be enough for them. Sedulus was content to address the Galatean as 'Sergeant'. When this one died – as he assuredly would soon, for the Galateans had a lifespan of only twenty years – he would be replaced by another who looked, sounded and smelled just the same.

To Sedulus's left was Beldyn, recently returned from briefing Syrene in person. Sedulus trusted Beldyn as much as he trusted any of his staff, which wasn't very far at all, Vena excepted. He could have spoken to Syrene himself via his lens, but he was concerned about this particular exchange being intercepted, and there were times when a whispered conversation was better.

Syrene had replied as he had hoped: the Illyri traitors, Syl and Ani, did not have to be returned to Edinburgh alive. She remained curious about the one called Ani, for she had powers that could be of use to the Sisterhood, but, as with Syl, it seemed that attempting to entice her to enter the Marque would be more trouble than it might ultimately be worth, assuming that Gradus, once he was safely back in her arms, could be persuaded to spare their lives for their earlier treason. Andrus and Danis were powerful men, even as the Corps and the Sisterhood worked to limit that power, and they would not give up their daughters without a fight. Equally, unwilling apprentices were useless to the Sisterhood. Syrene's predecessors had learned that hard lesson a long time before. Girls forced to join the Sisterhood by their families, or recruited in the hope that they might be moulded to the sisters' desires, invariably proved difficult and untrustworthy, and sowed discontent among the rest. In the past, to save their families distress, the Sisterhood had usually informed them that these novices were unsuited to life in the Marque and had instead been sent to new worlds, there to seek knowledge that might prove useful to the Sisterhood.

In reality, they had been quietly and painlessly killed.

But that was all in the past. The Sisterhood was now a haven only for the willing, for those who had elected, freely and without pressure, to give their lives to the pursuit of true knowledge.

Much of this was known to Sedulus, and what he did not know he suspected. It did not matter to him. The Sisterhood had given the Corps real power, and what was good for the Corps was good for him, but it was a delicate business. The continued difficulties in restoring Grand Consul Gradus to his wife seriously threatened Sedulus's thus far smooth ascension through the ranks of the Securitats, not to mention his life. If Gradus died, Sedulus would follow him into the void.

Now, though, they had a possible lead, courtesy of the turncoat Duncan. Sedulus had dispatched the second cruiser and his last skimmer in that direction, and Galateans and Securitats would soon be on the ground. The net was closing in on the humans and their Illyri prisoners. Sedulus was simply waiting for confirmation of a sighting, and then he and the remaining cruiser would join the hunt. On the display before him, two red lights indicated the positions of the craft. The Securitats on board were represented by the smaller white lights of their trackers. The Galateans were not fitted with trackers, an indication of their dispensability.

The cruiser touched down. The lights spread out as the Securitats began to disperse. Then, as Sedulus watched, one of the white lights vanished, followed by a second, then a third. Behind him, the aide monitoring communications turned in his chair.

'Sir,' he said, 'we have contact!'

Just Joe had known that they would come. It had been merely a matter of time, and he had made a calculated gamble by having Paul slip Gradus's tracker to Duncan. He or McKinnon would inevitably have betrayed them, although Joe's money was on Duncan. McKinnon was a thug, but he would have died before giving the Illyri more than his name and the time of day. No, Duncan had been the weak one, and as soon as Joe had begun to suspect him, he had started to feed Duncan his snippets of false information.

Just Joe had baited the trap for the Illyri: a fire, a handful of sleeping bags stuffed with rocks, and fighters moving around and giving a semblance of life to the camp. Theirs were the riskiest roles, and he could only hope that the Illyri wouldn't open fire on them from the air but would wait to tackle them on the ground. He reckoned that it was about 70:30 in the Resistance's favour that the Illyri would land rather than shoot; they probably wouldn't risk blasting them from their ships for fear that the Illyri prisoners might be among those sleeping in the camp. In that case, 70:30 didn't seem like bad odds, but Just Joe still didn't care much for them. The people below mattered, and Just Joe had already spent too much of his life informing men and women that their loved ones would not be returning to them.

The land was uneven, and scattered with rocks. There were only two places where the Illyri could land safely while still being within quick striking distance of the camp. In an ideal world he would have mined both sites, and as soon as a ship touched down it would have been blown to pieces, but he had no mines. He had guns and grenades, and they would have to suffice. Neither did he have enough bodies to cover both sites, so he had made another gamble: that the Illyri would send a cruiser, not simply a loaded skimmer. In that case, only one potential landing site was big enough, and he had concentrated all his firepower on it. If he was wrong, there might still be time to move fighters into new positions, but they would be forced to break cover to do so, making them vulnerable to pulser fire, and the element of surprise would be lost.

Just Joe lay beneath a camouflage blanket. Around him, the rest of his band of fighters were similarly disguised. He had positioned his two best shots on the high ground, armed with high-powered rifles capable of penetrating Illyri body armour even at long range. Closer to the landing site, two more fighters lay hidden, each armed with a grenade launcher and a single grenade, the last in Joe's arsenal.

Joe thought about Fremd, and the two Illyri with him. They had entrusted so much to Fremd, and now some of Joe's people were probably going to die on little more than one of the Illyri's hunches. Hell, they'd risked members of the Resistance already because of his suspicions, most recently at Birdoswald. But Gradus was too valuable a prize to surrender without a fight, and if Fremd was right, the knowledge he might yield was worth dying for.

He didn't even hear the cruiser before it appeared. The pilot must have been ordered to glide down, a dangerous manoeuvre for such a big, heavy craft. Flanking it was a single skimmer, which had probably picked out the fire and the people from above and guided the cruiser in.

Just Joe took a deep breath. His hands were shaking. They always did before a fight. Only a fool wasn't frightened of dying, he told himself, and there was no bravery without fear.

The cruiser touched down. His people at the camp grabbed their weapons and ran for cover. The skimmer flew over them, and a pair of black spheres dropped from its belly, homing in on the nearest fleeing humans. Joe heard the hiss of the darts deploying, and watched as Kathy and Howie fell.

The cruiser's doors opened, and the enemy appeared.

Just Joe aimed his weapon, and he and his fighters rained vengeance upon them for the dead of Durroch.

★ ★ ★

Sedulus watched as more and more of the white lights blinked out.

'We need to help them,' said Beldyn.

'No,' said Sedulus. 'We wait.'

The first of the grenades struck the side of the cruiser and exploded harmlessly against its heavy armour. A flurry of blasts from the guns of the Galateans blew the grenadier's position apart. He died instantly, but the distraction was enough to give the second grenadier time to aim. From her position behind a massive moss-covered boulder, Heather steadied the launcher and tightened her finger on the trigger.

'For Tam,' she said.

The grenade shot away and vanished into the gaping maw of the cruiser. Seconds later it exploded in the enclosed space, crippling the cruiser and killing or injuring all of those left inside. Splinters of rock erupted around her as the Illyri opened fire, but a barrage of covering shots allowed her to break for safety. She was terrified, but she remembered to hold on to the launcher. There would be more grenades somewhere, and they couldn't afford to lose weapons like it. She made it to where the first line of Resistance fighters lay, then threw herself to the ground, drew her high-powered pistol and started shooting.

Meanwhile, Just Joe and Norris were trying to take down the black orbs. They had already watched three of their people die, and they were determined that there would be no more. Norris winged the first with his shotgun, with the result that its guidance system was destroyed. It responded by firing its array of darts aimlessly, although one still struck close enough to Norris's head to produce sparks from the rock behind him. A second shotgun blast put an end to it, and its remains dropped to the ground and fizzled harmlessly.

Just Joe drew the second orb to him by waving his coat at it from behind a tree stump. It was, he considered as the first dart smacked into the wood, just about the dumbest thing he'd ever done, in a lifetime of doing things that were not very smart. As the orb approached, he stepped from behind the stump, his backpack strapped to his chest, and prayed. He felt the impact of the dart as it struck the pack, and then he sprayed the orb with bullets even as he kept praying, until the magazine was empty and the orb was no more, and all that was left was his own voice calling on some god, any god, to protect him.

'We've lost contact with the cruiser,' the radio operator informed Sedulus.

Sedulus could see that for himself. The red light blinked rapidly, indicating catastrophic damage. Only six white lights remained intact, and one of those vanished as the operator spoke. Sedulus remained outwardly calm. This was a disaster, but he could not allow his men to see him panic.

'It was a trap,' said Beldyn. 'The human lied.'

'No, I don't think he did,' said Sedulus. 'He was simply lied to by someone cleverer than him. Recall the skimmer.'

'And the Illyri and Galateans still on the ground?'

'They're dead,' said Sedulus. 'They just don't know it yet.'

Now the radio operator spoke again.

'Sir, we've lost a hunter orb.'

'Are you insane?' said Sedulus. 'We've just lost a *cruiser*!'

'No, sir, not there. To the west. It deployed a dart, and then went down.'

Sedulus stared at him.

'Give me its last known location on the map.'

Before him, a green light flashed into existence.

'It's them,' said Sedulus.

'How can you be certain?' asked Beldyn.

'I have to be,' said Sedulus. 'If I'm wrong, then we're all finished.'

CHAPTER 61

AK seemed so small in death, so huddled and young. They had no time to bury him, no time to do anything except stare blankly at his remains until Ani – Ani, of all of them – began to cry.

'I just . . . I could have been kinder to him,' she said.

And there was nothing that anyone could say to console or contradict her, because it was true, just as it was true that AK could have been kinder to her in return. Syl thought that Ani had never looker sadder or older. Later, Ani would come to look back on that moment as one in which she experienced true adult regret for the first time, and something of her childhood was washed away in the mud and the blood and the rain.

'We have to go,' said Fremd. 'They'll know they've lost a hunter drone, and they'll come looking to see why.'

But Ani did not seem to hear him. Instead, she dropped to her knees and brushed the damp hair away from AK's face. Steven crouched beside her. His left hand hovered uncertainly over her, like a bird fearful of alighting, and then rested itself gently on her shoulder. Ani leaned into him, and their bodies shook in unison as he absorbed her grief. Alice joined them, stroking Ani's hair.

'Ani!' said Fremd. 'I said we have to go.'

'What's the point?' said Ani. 'I'm tired of running. We just keep running and running, and we never get anywhere. Let them take me back. I don't care.'

Fremd grabbed her arm and yanked her to her feet. Steven seemed about to intervene, but Paul restrained him.

'Listen to me!' said Fremd, and he gave her a little shake. 'They're not going to take you back. Don't you understand? They're not interested in you. It's Gradus they want. If you and Syl die out here, it will be easier for everyone. Once Gradus is secured, you'll be killed. They'll blame the Resistance, or crossfire, or whatever it takes, but the end result will be the same: you'll end up like AK, dying in the dirt, but there'll be no one to weep for you because we'll all be dead too.'

'You're lying!' said Ani. 'You don't know that!'

'I do. I know it because I know Sedulus. I know it because I was once like him.'

Ani stopped struggling.

'Tell us,' said Syl.

'I will,' said Fremd. 'I promise. We're close to our destination. Just a couple of hours, and when we reach it I'll tell you. I'll tell you everything.'

The four youths exchanged glances, and a silent agreement was reached.

'All right,' said Paul. 'What about him?'

He jerked a thumb at Gradus, who remained seated in the mud, his mouth slack and his eyes like the eyes of the dead.

'Get him to his feet.'

'He's slowing us down!' said Paul. 'Without him, we'll move three times as fast. Just let the Illyri have him.'

'No,' said Fremd.

'Why?'

'Because if I'm right, he holds the secret to all of this.'

'And if you're wrong?'

'Then I'll kill him myself before I hand him back. Now move. Move!'

Syl thought she would surely collapse. Every muscle in her body ached, but her legs hurt most of all. They felt so heavy that she could barely put one foot in front of the other, dragging them through the mud. She was hot and clammy despite the cold, but she found herself shivering and her teeth chattered painfully in her mouth. Ani and

Steven trudged ahead of her, their heads down, stumbling more than running. Paul was beside her, but he did not speak. Like the others, he barely had strength enough to keep himself going. He had precious little left to share, but he still found it in himself to take turns with Ani to carry Alice.

Fremd forced the pace, leading Gradus on the rope. Sometimes the Grand Consul slipped and fell, and once he struck his head so hard in falling that he drew blood, but he made no sound. Each time, Paul and Steven helped Fremd to haul the heavy Illyri to his feet, and they moved on.

All the time they waited for the sound of a skimmer breaching the clouds, for the roar of a cruiser, but none came. Yet as her fever increased, Syl grew more and more paranoid. She looked to the sky, trying to pierce the banks of grey and black. They were watching her, waiting for their chance to strike. They would swoop down and pluck her from the ground, and then they would hang her from the gates of the castle, her legs kicking at the air, the blood congesting in her face. She felt the rope tighten around her neck as she walked, and so real was the sensation that her hands rose to her throat and she clawed at her skin, raking it with her nails until Paul stopped her, gently forcing her arms down and holding them at her sides by pulling her to him and forcing her to walk with him.

'Almost there,' he said. 'Almost there.'

Now she saw Ritchie impaled on his bayonet, but he was still alive and somehow he forced himself from the blade, pushing down on the rifle jammed in the dirt, the metal separating from his flesh with a damp sucking sound. He came through the rain, his hands outstretched before him, the palms facing up and coloured red with his own blood.

I killed you.

I killed you, and I am glad.

She saw Illyri warships passing through washes of illumination, and heard a baby cry as it left the womb. And she was that child, but now it was no longer simply a child but a collection of billions of atoms, and the light corrupted each and every one, altering them, mutating them.

Mutating her.

She was an alien, not simply to the people of Earth but to her own kind as well. She did not belong. She was different. Only Ani might understand, but even Ani was not like her. Ani could blur minds, making others see what she wanted them to see, but she did not take lives. Maybe she could if she tried hard enough, but Syl was not sure, and the fact remained that she was the one who had looked at a man and forced him to turn his weapon on himself. She saw again the look in Ritchie's eyes before he positioned the blade to pierce his own chest: the terror, the desperation, the knowledge that a part of this alien girl had entered him and turned him against himself. In that final stare was a plea for her to save him, to spare him, and she had refused. Her own fear had been too great: her fear, and her rage.

'I'm sorry,' she whispered, but even as she said the words they sounded hollow to her. No, she thought, I am not sorry. I am glad. He deserved to die, he and the one I struck with the rock, the one whose face I pressed into the water. Because she had done that too, she finally admitted to herself. Even as Ritchie was dying, she had felt the man in the stream trying to rise, but she had held him down, willing the water to enter his lungs, willing him to suffer, just as he would have made her suffer had he been given the chance.

'What am I?' she said. 'Who am I?'

And while Paul said her name over and over, trying to calm her, she thought that she was imagining things as she saw torches in the distance, and heard the voices of men and women. She saw a wall with battlements, and a castle keep rising above it. Gates opened in the wall, and she glimpsed people camped inside, and fires burning. She smelled smoke, and roasting meat, and heard the lowing of cattle. A small hand gripped hers, and she looked down to see Alice smiling up at her.

'It's okay, Syl,' said Alice. 'We're safe.'

But it was not okay, thought Syl. They would never be safe again.

Chapter 62

The castle was called Dundearg. It had been built in the reign of James II of England, and the same family, the Buchanans, had occupied it throughout its existence, but only one of their line now remained. Her name was Maeve, and she was a short, dark woman in her early forties, most of her hair already turned to grey, yet still pretty and youthful. She looked on sternly as Syl, Ani and Gradus were led into the huge fortified keep, watched by the hostile eyes of those who now lived within the castle walls in makeshift dwellings, or containers that had been converted to homes. The inhabitants created a narrow channel down which the new arrivals passed. Even with the protection of Fremd, they were still jostled, and someone spat in Ani's face. Although Syl felt for her friend, she was glad that it had not been directed at her. Even in her fevered state, she saw herself turning on the offender and wishing harm upon them. The consequences of that might have been fatal for all concerned.

'No,' said Fremd, and at first Syl thought he was talking to her, warning her not to react, until she realised that he was addressing the crowd. They obeyed him, and there was no more jostling, and no more spitting.

At last they were safe within the walls of the keep, and the doors closed behind them. It was cold inside – but still warmer than it was outside, and at least it was dry. To their right, a great fire burned in a room filled with overstuffed chairs and couches.

Syl did not know what to expect next, but it was not to see Maeve Buchanan take Fremd in her arms and kiss him full on the lips. She held him close to her, and breathed in the scent of him.

'I smell,' he said.

'You smell of mud and grass and sweat.'

'And blood,' said Fremd. 'We lost AK – young Alan.'

Maeve's eyes squeezed shut in pain.

'His father and mother will have to be told,' she said. 'They're in Perth.'

'It'll be done, and gently.'

'He was troubled, and angry, but he would have changed. I could see it in him.'

'So could I.'

Maeve disengaged herself from Fremd, and turned her attention to Syl and Ani.

'My God, these young ones are frozen.' She touched her hand to Syl's brow. 'And this one has a fever.'

She called out a name – 'Kathleen!' – and a stout woman wearing carpet slippers and an apron appeared on the stairs above.

'Yes, ma'am?'

'Bring towels, and warm clothes, and a basin of whatever hot water we have left.'

She guided Syl and Ani to the fire.

'Now get out of those clothes. All of them! You can wrap yourself in some of the furniture throws while you wait for Kathleen.'

She began to close the door behind herself and Fremd in order to give Syl and Ani a little privacy, but Syl rose and stopped her.

'Remember,' she said to Fremd. 'You promised. You promised you'd tell us your story.'

'And I will,' he said. 'Get warm and dry first. When you're done, come find us, for what is about to happen here concerns you as much as it does the rest of us. But if I'm right, my story, and what you may see in this castle, will just leave you with more questions, and you won't be the only one.'

Behind Fremd, two men she had not seen before were holding on tightly to Gradus's arms. Maybe it was the comparative warmth of the castle, or a slow recognition that his situation had changed, but Gradus seemed to be coming out of himself. He was still dazed, but he was taking in his surroudings.

'Clean him up, but keep him restrained,' Fremd ordered.

'I'll wake the technician,' said Maeve. 'Everything is ready to go. We just need to prep the generator.'

'Do it,' said Fremd. 'We don't have much time.'

The woman named Kathleen, assisted by her two daughters, Marie and Jeanie, brought Syl and Ani not just towels, clean clothes, and two basins of hot water, but huge mugs of broth thick with chicken and vegetables. She also fed Syl two small pills to help bring down her fever.

Low cheers echoed from outside that door. Syl opened it and peered out, to see Just Joe arrive, along with Logan and Aggie and Norris. Heather was there too, holding a delighted Alice in her arms. Maeve came to greet them.

'Where are the others?' she asked, but Joe simply shook his head.

'Dear AK's gone too,' said Maeve.

'Ah,' was all that Joe could say. 'Ah.'

Syl closed the door.

The food and the change of clothes had made Syl feel a bit better, but her brow was still hot to the touch, and she felt weak. Nevertheless, she did not want to remain in the room. She needed to find Fremd.

'Will you take us to him?' she asked Kathleen upon her return, and she and Ani were duly led into the bowels of the keep, where a medical infirmary had been set up. One of the beds was now occupied by Norris, whose shoulder wound had become infected. He had been sedated while the wound was cleaned and dressed, and stared woozily at Syl and Ani, as though unsure of whether he was seeing them or dreaming them.

Finally they came to a smaller chamber, and Syl was surprised to see that it contained an array of both human and Illyri medical equipment, most of it new and apparently in perfect working order. The room vibrated with the hum of generators, and Fremd was methodically working with another Illyri – who looked barely older than Syl and Ani – to check the wiring and make sure that everything was in sync. Maeve watched over them, gnawing at her lower lip the way a dog might worry at a bone.

'Okay,' said Fremd. 'It looks like we're ready.'

He noticed Syl and Ani for the first time.

'Ladies, let me introduce you to Lorac,' he said, and the young Illyri smiled uncertainly at them. 'Lorac, this is Syl and Ani.'

'Hello,' said Lorac, rising from a crouch to his full height. He was good-looking, even for an Illyri, but he gave the impression of being uncomfortable in his own skin, and he walked with a slight limp as he approached them. Syl saw that he was a little older than she had first thought, probably in his early twenties.

'Are you hurt?' asked Ani.

'It's an old injury,' said Lorac.

Fremd had gone to Maeve, his arm curled protectively around her waist.

'Lorac made the same mistake that I did,' said Fremd. 'He looked too long at a beautiful woman, and was lost.'

Maeve slapped him gently on the chest, but the compliment still brought a blush to her cheeks. Ani looked slightly disappointed at the news that Lorac was taken by another. Syl was just glad that Steven wasn't there to see her face.

'You've met her,' said Lorac. 'Jeanie, Kathleen's daughter.'

Ani seemed decidedly unimpressed, and even Syl was a little surprised. Jeanie was pretty enough, but not spectacularly so; Lorac had left his own people and thrown in his lot with the Resistance to be with *her*? Whether he was Military or Corps, that was punishable by a lifetime sentence on a prison world, and lifetimes on prison worlds tended to be short and brutal, although Syl suspected that few deserters ever made it to the prisons and instead were simply killed by the Securitats. Truly, she thought, the ways of love were very strange indeed, but then was she not also falling for Paul? What future was there for the two of them? Not for the first time, she felt that her life had become extremely complicated in a very short space of time.

At the mention of her daughter, Kathleen straightened and glowed with pride. She had hardly spoken before except to fuss over Syl and Ani, but now she said, 'You won't find a better girl from here to Land's End.'

Ani appeared on the verge of disagreeing, but Syl carefully but forcefully stepped on her foot, just to make sure she didn't end up with it in her mouth.

Lorac tapped his right leg. 'My comrades-in-arms found out about us. To discourage me, they shattered my foot with rifle butts. I deserted that night, but my foot was so badly damaged that there was nothing to be done but to amputate it.'

The words came to Syl's mouth before she realised that she was speaking them, never mind thinking them.

'Was it worth it?' she said.

Lorac answered as if he was surprised that anyone could ask such a question. 'Of course it was,' he said. 'I love her. Haven't you ever been in love?'

Syl could see Ani grinning at her. This was all getting a bit personal, but having asked the original question, she felt duty bound to give some kind of answer.

'Not like that,' she said. 'At least, I don't think so.'

'You'll know it when you are,' said Maeve. There was a sceptical expression on her face, and it struck Syl that the older woman did not believe the answer Syl had given. For that matter, Syl wasn't sure that she quite believed it either. She was, after all, in this mess because of a young man. She had put her life on the line for a human male, just as Lorac had put his on the line for a human female. Syl wanted to tear her hair out; she felt like she was drowning in a vat of emotions. She turned to Fremd in the hope that he might yank her from it for a time.

'You promised you'd tell us what's happening,' she said.

'I did,' said Fremd, 'or as much of it as I know.'

He patted Lorac on the shoulder.

'Bring our esteemed guest, the Grand Consul. We're ready for him now.'

And while Lorac went to get Gradus, Fremd told them his tale.

CHAPTER 63

The first surprise was that Fremd was not just a member of the Diplomatic Corps; he had been a junior Securitat, and Sedulus had once been his adjutant.

'I believed,' said Fremd. 'I believed in the great expansion of the Illyri Empire. The wormholes had opened up the universe to us, and I was young and wanted to explore it. It was about the discovery of worlds and not the conquest of them, although I admit that was part of the mission. Yet we were to be gentle rulers. We would not ravage societies. We would not rape planets for their resources. What was good for the Empire would be good for the new races we found, and the opposite would also be true.

'But humanity was different. For the first time we became aware of a race that was like us in so many ways. The Empire had monitored the human race's development for decades. There were debates about whether or not conquest was the appropriate response to humanity's resourcefulness and ambition, but the Corps overruled the Military. And to be fair, there were strong reasons for subduing humanity. As a race, they were hostile to one another, so the violence of their reaction to an alien civilisation could only be imagined. Their history was one of brutality and warfare, and they allowed whole nations to starve while others stored food in barns until it rotted. It was felt that they could not be reasoned with.

'So the Earth became a planet of conquest, but care was to be taken with its inhabitants, because they were so like us, and we had yet to discover any race as similarly advanced. But then, as you know, humanity proved more difficult to control than had been hoped, and the occupation became less gentle. There were those of us who started to believe that we should not be on Earth at all, and a new approach to humanity, one of cooperation and peaceful co-existence, needed to be taken.

'But I was not directly involved in such debates. My posting was four and a half light years away in the system the humans named Alpha Centauri, monitoring the mining of the diamond world 55 Cancri, and the harvesting of methane from larger planets in the system.'

The harvesting of methane meant that Illyri ships travelling without using wormholes did not have to carry as much fuel for their flights. Instead, they could be refuelled from methane bases scattered throughout galaxies. Within the Earth's solar system, the Illyri had planted harvesters on Jupiter, Mars and Uranus, but the largest harvesting operation was on Titan, one of Saturn's moons, where it literally rained methane and the surface was dotted with rivers and lakes of it.

'The mining was being carried out by Illyri prisoners and, I'm sorry to say, by Punishment Battalions from Earth,' said Fremd. 'It was near the end of my deployment there. I didn't care for it – I was little more than a prison guard, and I spent too much time wearing a Lethal Environment Suit for my liking – and I had requested a transfer to Earth. In addition, there had been problems of discipline, and an attempt had been made to hijack a shuttle and escape. A senior consul – an uncle of our friend Gradus – was sent to Alpha Centauri to investigate the problem. I was to finish my deployment when he arrived and travel on to Earth, but the pilot made a docking error as he approached the station at Cancri, and the ship was damaged. There was an oxygen leak, and most of the crew died, but we were able to rescue the consul. He was badly injured, but we brought him to the surgery and the medics went to work on him.

'And that was when I was called, because the scans revealed something living inside the consul's head.'

Fremd could still clearly recall the moment; the 'first sighting', as he thought of it, the first glimpse of the Other. Wrapped around the consul's brain stem, and embracing his cerebellum with wispy tentacles, was a parasitic organism of some kind. When an attempt was made to remove it, the organism tightened its grip on the cerebellum, and those whiplike tentacles made further inroads into the consul's brain. His body began to convulse, and it was decided that no further investigation of the organism should take place for fear of killing its host. A coded message was sent to Gradus, informing him of the discovery, and the consul was placed in an isolation chamber. The message that came back was simple: nobody was to leave the station for fear of contamination, and there was to be no further communication about the consul or the organism until a team from the Scientific Development Division arrived.

'But further unrest erupted on Cancri,' said Fremd, 'and I had no choice but to leave the station and travel down to the planet to deal with it. I had to wear a full LES kit on Cancri anyway, so there was no danger of my passing on any infection.'

He paused then, as though the memory of what came next was still painful for him.

'The scientists arrived while I was on Cancri, but with them came Securitat death squads, and the slaughter began. I stayed on the planet while everyone on the station was being killed. I had left a communications channel open with my second-in-command, Seval, in case I had to explain my absence, and I heard him die. I heard them all die. They were murdered by our own people. Seval's last act was to excise all record of my trip to Cancri. As far as the Securitats were concerned, I was missing, presumed deserted.

'Then they blew up the station and left everyone on Cancri to die. The prisoners saw the station exploding, and there was a rush for my ship. I had to kill to save myself, and I abandoned the remaining miners on Cancri. That's my burden. I carry it with me every day.'

'How did you get to Earth?' asked Syl.

'I hitched a ride through the wormhole on the coat-tails of a Corps ship,' he said. 'Eventually I made my way here, to Scotland.'

Syl couldn't help but be impressed. 'Hitching' was an incredibly risky manoeuvre, relying on the gravitational force of the larger ship in the wormhole to pull the smaller craft through. If the hitchhiker miscalculated even slightly, or if the main ship was bounced around either entering or leaving the wormhole, then the other vessel would be destroyed.

'It took a long time for the Resistance to trust me, and for me to trust them,' said Fremd. 'They kept me in a cell for two years. I barely saw daylight. Eventually I met Maeve, and things started to change. But I said nothing about what I'd seen on the station, not until a few months ago, when I started hearing rumours of human bodies going missing, and of secret facilities set up on Earth by the Scientific Development Division. From our spies we also learned of a flood of Corps officials arriving on Earth, all of them related, or loyal, to Gradus, and all with links to the Scientific Development Division. What happened at Cancri station suggested that there were those at the highest levels of the Corps and its Securitats who wanted to keep the existence of the organism, the Other, secret. But what if it wasn't the only one? What if there were more of these things infecting the Illyri? And perhaps the relationship between the organism and its host wasn't merely parasitic, but symbiotic.'

'Symbi-what?' asked Ani.

'Two organisms of different species operating in unison, to the ultimate benefit of each,' said Fremd. 'Like, for example, the pilot fish that feed from the mouths of sharks and clean away decaying matter, or even dogs and humans, except in the case of the Other and its host the relationship is obviously more, um, intimate. So we decided to target newly arrived Corps officials, especially those with a familial relationship to Gradus, in the hope of capturing one, but we had no success until Gradus himself fell into our laps, thanks to you two.'

At that moment Gradus appeared, struggling between two men, Just Joe close behind. He was no longer the pathetic figure who had trudged through the Highlands at the end of a rope. Now he screamed and swore, and his eyes were filled with panic. He saw the medical equipment, and he knew its purpose: there was a small X-ray machine, and a lightweight Illyri magnetic resonance imaging scannner, capable of producing immensely detailed images of the interior of a body. There were also scalpels, and calipers, and dressings.

'No!' said Gradus. 'You can't do this.'

'Place him face down,' said Fremd.

The men placed Gradus on a gurney, and secured his hands, feet and head with straps.

'Sedate him,' said Fremd, and Lorac slipped a needle into Gradus's arm. Slowly the Grand Consul grew calmer, but he remained conscious.

'No,' he repeated. 'No, no, no . . .'

'Come,' said Kathleen to Syl and Ani, guiding them towards the door. 'Maybe you should leave.'

'No,' said Fremd. 'Let them stay. If I'm right, they should see this.'

On Fremd's order, they all placed protective masks over their noses and mouths. Lorac powered up the MRI scanner. Fremd's lips moved in prayer to his old gods, and then he said:

'Begin.'

CHAPTER 64

The rain had ceased, but in its place came a mist that was just as drenching. Each tiny particle of moisture was visible in the lights from the castle, but then the artificial illumination dimmed as power was directed to the machines in the basement of the keep. A handful of emergency bulbs continued to glow brightly, but battery-powered lights were pressed into service, and even, here and there, oil lamps.

The guards at the walls watched the mist, and the inhabitants behind the walls watched the guards. They were people who had fled their isolated homes because of bandits like the late McKinnon, or those with family members whose involvement with the Resistance had been discovered, and whose houses had been destroyed in reprisal – for the Illyri's tactics north of the wall were often more brutal than in the cities. These people had found a haven at Dundearg, and Maeve Buchanan had almost bankrupted herself taking care of them. But she was of an older order, one that recognised a duty towards those who lived on the land owned by the castle, or even on land that was once owned by the castle long before. They were her people, because they had always been her family's people.

But everyone within those walls knew what had taken place in recent days: the pursuit of a precious prize. Now that prize was inside the castle, and the fear was that the pursuers would soon be at their door.

And those fears were about to find form.

Four guards patrolled the battlements above and beside the main gates. Two were still in their teens, and two were older and more experienced. That was the way with the Resistance in the Highlands: there was an abundance of fresh water up there, and so, unlike the city-dwellers, they had remained relatively unaffected by the Illyri contamination of the water supply with chemicals that subdued the instinct to fight, to resist. Yet at the same time, the struggle against the Illyri was more overt in the Highlands, and harder fought. The casualty rate was higher as a consequence, so it was important that the younger ones learned quickly from the older fighters, because the older fighters might not be around for long.

The gates were fortified by a lorry packed with bags of concrete and sand. Once the gates closed, the lorry was driven into place and only moved when friendly parties were trying to enter or leave. Machine-gun posts occupied each of the rounded turrets, and mortars were in place behind the walls.

The youngest of the guards was Jack Dennison, who had just turned seventeen on his last birthday. He could easily be identified by the green-and-white Celtic scarf that he wore around his neck, whatever the weather. The Illyri had long ago tried to clamp down on the most vicious of sporting rivalries by disbanding certain teams: the Red Sox and the Yankees in baseball; Real Madrid and Barcelona in Spanish football, and a whole list of teams in England, including virtually the entire English Premier League. But a particular target had been Rangers and Celtic in Scotland. The two teams had long been at each other's throats, a consequence of religious conflict that had hardened into pure hatred, but the tipping point for the Illyri had been a Scottish FA Cup Final during which violence had broken out between not just the supporters but the teams themselves. When the Illyri tried to intervene, they succeeded in doing what centuries of efforts by priests, pastors and politicians had failed to do: they united the rival supporters, if only against a common enemy. The ensuing riots against Illyri rule lasted for weeks, and added fuel to the ferocious Scottish Resistance that continued to that day. Even wearing the green-and-white of Celtic, or the dark blue of Rangers, was an arrestable offence.

Now Dennison stared out into the darkness, his eyes and especially his ears alert. They would hear the Illyri before they saw them. They always did, just before they screamed, or roared, out of the air. But all was quiet. Dennison shivered. Beside him, Phil Pelham huddled into his waxed jacket. Pelham was from Manchester, and where Dennison wore green-and-white, Pelham favoured blue-and-white, the colours of the former Manchester City. He and the younger man had found a point of contact in teams that no longer existed.

'All right, lad?' said Pelham.

'Yeah, all right.'

'Experiments in the basement.' Pelham jerked a thumb at the keep behind him. 'They're making Frankenstein's monster.'

'They'll need lightning for that,' said Dennison. 'And dead bodies.'

He realised what he had just said, and shuffled with embarrassment.

'Well,' said Pelham, 'best we make sure they don't have any of them then, right?'

'Right you are, Phil.'

The mist rose before them. Dennison hated mist. It made him see figures where there were none, phantasms of his imagination. He wished the main castle lights would come back on. At the very least, they made it easier to distinguish between what was real and what was unreal. They had lit torches on the walls, as much to keep them warm as to provide more light, but they only helped a little.

A form appeared in the mist, then vanished. Dennison narrowed his eyes against the damp and the dark.

'What's wrong?' said Pelham.

'I'm not sure. I thought ...'

There it was again, except it was closer now, and to the left. But how could it have moved so quickly?

'There's something out there.'

Pelham eased the AK-47 from his shoulder.

'I don't see anything. Where? Are you sure?'

The first of the Galateans appeared, and he had his answer. A massive blast struck the gates even as he sounded the alarm. The heavily laden truck shuddered on its axles, but remained in place.

For now.

The assault on Dundearg had begun.

CHAPTER 65

Peris and his strike squad were monitoring the progress of Sedulus's remaining cruiser, staying far above it in the hope that the attention of the Securitats would be focussed on what was happening on the ground below them, and not on the skies above. When the cruiser eventually landed, apparently miles from the nearest village, Peris called up a map of the surrounding area, and found Dundearg Castle at the centre.

'That has to be their destination,' he told Aron, his second-in-command, as their shuttle circled high above cloud level. 'There's nothing else nearby.'

'Then why have they landed so far from it?' asked Aron. The cruiser had come down more than a mile from the castle, and the last of Sedulus's skimmers had joined it.

'He wants to have troops at their walls before they know it, and the mist will hide his approach,' said Peris. 'Plus he only has one cruiser left: if that castle is defended with missiles or heavy-calibre guns, they could blow him out of the sky.'

'I don't understand why he hasn't called for reinforcements.'

'Because it would be a final admission of failure on top of the loss of most of his force,' said Peris. 'Above all else, he wants to bring the Grand Consul back to his witch wife and and reap the benefits. Pride will be Sedulus's downfall.'

He pointed at the onscreen map.

'That looks like clear ground. Glide us in.'

Aron sighed. 'It could be a bog, for all we know.'

'Well,' said Peris, 'at least we'll have a soft landing.'

★ ★ ★

But Peris's progress *was* being tracked, although not by Sedulus. Meia had both the recently-landed cruiser and skimmer on her monitor, as well as Peris's descending shuttle. She could see what Peris was trying to do: quietly land closer to the castle than Sedulus's Securitats, and try to get inside to rescue Syl and Ani before Sedulus made it to the walls. He had to be stopped, because right now Meia knew that she, and she alone, was Syl and Ani's best hope of getting out of Dundearg alive.

Peris's shuttle glided down on what was, thankfully for his squad, firm ground, the engines only kicking in at the final moment to soften the landing, just as Meia had anticipated. Her skimmer differed from Peris's ship, and indeed, those of the rest of the Illyri fleet, in two crucial ways: its software was faster and its engines quieter. She had used all her skill and knowledge to make the improvements, and had shared none of them with others. In war, every advantage was crucial, but especially so for Meia and those who fought in the shadows.

Most usefully of all, her skimmer was virtually invisible to radar. In addition to having its infrared exhaust emissions altered by coolant and its internal and external structures replaced by radar-transparent diametric composites, it used ionised gas to form a deflecting plasma cloud around itself. Its shielding had enabled her to reach, and escape, the Eden Project without being blown out of the sky, and it now allowed her to land next to Peris's shuttle, its wake buffeting her slowly as she dropped gently behind it.

Thus it was that the first thing Peris saw as he and his squad disembarked was Meia, wisps of mist swirling around her like angry ghosts. Peris figured that he should have been more surprised, but then he had been dealing with Meia for long enough to learn that the usual rules of behaviour didn't apply to her. He took in her battle armour, and the heavily adapted blast rifle that she carried. The twin-barrelled weapon could rain depleted uranium ammunition on its targets, along with dragon-breaths of fire. It looked huge as it hung from Meia's slight frame, but the weight didn't seem to trouble her in the least. A belt of high-explosive grenades was strapped around her waist. Meia, it was clear, was ready to wage war single-handedly.

'I don't suppose there's any point in telling you that I'm in charge here,' said Peris.

'Oh, be in charge if you like,' said Meia. 'I don't mind.'

'The fact that you can say that means my authority is largely illusory.'

'Yes.'

'Well, I always was better at just being a simple soldier. So what's the plan? Are we going to fight our way into that castle, or sneak in?'

'Neither,' said Meia. 'They're just going to admit us without hindrance.'

'And why is that?'

Meia smiled.

'Because the world is a lot more complicated than a simple soldier like you could ever imagine.'

Lorac had activated the MRI scanners when the sound of the first explosion reached them. It shook the castle, sending dust and small pieces of masonry falling from the walls. Seconds later, Paul came running in.

'They're at the gates!'

'How many?' said Just Joe.

'I don't know. The mist is too thick. But we're taking fire.'

Just Joe grabbed his rifle. In the infirmary, those who were strong enough to fight began to rise from their beds. Even Norris was on his feet, although he was swaying slightly.

'Go back to bed,' ordered Just Joe.

'Hit me,' said Norris.

'What?'

'Hit me!'

Just Joe gave Norris a massive open-handed blow across the right side of his face. It would have felled a lesser man, but in Norris's case it served only to clear his head.

'That did the trick,' he said. 'Right, where's my shotgun?'

He found the gun under his bed, along with his backpack, and began to fill his pockets with shells. When they were sufficiently bulging, he joined Paul and Just Joe.

'We need time,' said Fremd.

'I know,' said Just Joe. 'We'll buy you as much as we can.'

Syl caught Paul's eye. She wanted to say so much to him, but all she could come up with was, 'Be careful.'

'I will,' he said. 'You do the same.'

'Yes.'

Before he could say any more, Norris had picked him up by the scruff of the neck with one meaty paw and carried him over to where Syl stood, Paul's toes dragging along the ground.

'For God's sake, kiss the girl,' he said, setting Paul down. 'It may be the last chance you have.'

Paul did as he was ordered. He kissed Syl, softly at first, then harder, and she responded to his touch. Her arms rose to embrace him as his hands settled lightly on her waist, before he was suddenly yanked away from her again.

'That's quite enough of that,' said Norris, hauling Paul towards the fighting. 'I said kiss her, not marry her.'

Fremd touched Maeve on the shoulder.

'You have to start the evacuation,' he said.

Maeve nodded. A tear fell from her right eye.

'We knew this day would come,' said Fremd. 'We couldn't be lucky for ever.'

'Just a little longer would have been good,' said Maeve.

'We're not dead yet.'

'No,' said Maeve. 'And pray God we stay a long way from it.'

She kissed the tall Illyri, rising to her toes as he leaned down to her, and then left the room. Only Syl and Ani remained with Fremd and Lorac, but then Ani turned and began to follow Maeve.

'Where are you going?'

'To help,' said Ani. 'You stay here. You're the smart one!'

Syl wasn't sure about that. She moved as if to join Ani, but Fremd put a hand on her shoulder.

'Stay.'

'Hey, aren't you going to tell me to be careful too?' Ani asked.

'Be careful,' said Syl.

'Thanks,' said Ani. 'I don't need the kiss, by the way.'

She laughed, and was gone.

Paul was racing to keep up with Just Joe and Norris when Steven joined him. He had an AK-47 assault rifle in his right hand.

'Where did you get that?' asked Paul.

'Dunno,' said Steven. 'I just picked it up.'

'Well put it back where you found it. You stay where it's safe.'

'No,' said Steven, and his voice sounded deeper and more serious than before.

Paul stopped.

'Steven—'

'I won't,' said Steven.

He looked so stern, so certain. He reminded Paul of their father, but Paul could still see the child in his eyes.

'You can't keep protecting me like this. I have to learn. I have to know how to fight.' Steven swallowed hard. 'Because you might not always be around, and then I'll have to look after myself, and Mum, and . . . and maybe Ani.'

Norris gave him a hard look.

'Ani?' he said. 'Not you as well.'

He turned to Just Joe. 'My God, they're all at it. They're like rabbits.'

Just Joe gestured impatiently as gunfire rattled from the walls outside, but he did not interfere. This was between the brothers.

Paul gave in.

'All right,' he said, 'but stay close to me, and try not to shoot yourself in the foot with that thing.'

The truck was still in place behind the gates as they emerged from the keep, though gunfire rang out from the battlements, along with blasts and pulses from the attackers beyond the walls. A steady stream of women, children and old men was moving in the other direction, all of them carrying bags of their most precious belongings. Paul saw Maeve and Kathleen, along with Kathleen's daughters, directing the flow.

'Where are they going?' asked Paul.

'There's a network of evacuation tunnels under the castle,' said Norris. 'One of them goes back to the time of King James, but the rest are new. They come out well beyond the walls. These people know what to do.'

Above the gate, a man twisted as he was hit by a blast, and tumbled to the ground. He landed on his back, a blue-and-white scarf covering his face like a shroud. Just Joe grimaced, and Norris racked the slide on his shotgun.

'Come on then,' he said. 'There's killing to be done.'

The Galateans formed the first line of attack troops, and half of them had already fallen. Sedulus's intention had been to force the gates open with a massive blast from the last of his heavy weaponry, but he had reckoned without the concrete-laden truck. Now he called in the cruiser. The men and women on the walls heard it coming, and then it roared overhead, its red lights blinking in the dark.

'Clear the gates!' called Just Joe. 'Take cover!'

A pair of missiles struck the gates, blowing them and the truck apart. The force of the explosion shook the foundations and knocked its defenders to the ground. Paul was thrown against the castle walls and left with his ears ringing. The air was filled with dust and dirt, mingling with the mist to create a curtain of grey. Paul's eyes stung, and he could barely keep them open. His first thought was of Steven, but his brother found him first, pouring water into Paul's eyes to clear them.

'Are you okay?' asked Paul. 'Are you hurt?'

'No, I'm good.'

Beside him, Norris, Just Joe and the rest were struggling to their feet. Shapes appeared in the gaping hole where the gates had once been, the remains of the truck flaming around them.

'They're coming through!' said Just Joe.

The machine gun on the top of the keep opened up, and the invaders began to fall beneath its fire, but some of them made it inside and took up positions behind rubble and twisted metal and undamaged bags of cement. The cruiser soared above the castle again, and its heavy cannon ripped into the machine-gun post, silencing its blasts.

'That thing will tear us all apart,' said Just Joe, as a figure appeared on the battlements, struggling beneath the weight of what looked like a long metal tube.

'That's Heather,' said Paul.

'Heather, and a Stinger,' said Just Joe. 'Go on, my girl!'

Heather hefted the launcher on to her shoulder, took aim and fired at the thrusters of the cruiser, one of its few vulnerable spots. The missile shot away, hurtling toward the big vessel at seven hundred miles per hour. From such close range, Heather could not miss.

The cruiser seemed to bounce in the air as the warhead struck, and flames spewed from its starboard exhaust. The huge vessel veered sharply as it fell, striking the ground nose first. Its fuel tanks ignited, and darkness turned bright as day as the cruiser was blown to pieces. There were cheers from the castle's defenders, but then the battlements were raked by pulses from below, and Heather disappeared in a cloud of debris and smoke and fire. A handful of Resistance members ran to see if she could be helped, but Paul feared there was little hope.

A heavy pulse hit the wall beside him, the shock waves bouncing back and giving him a sick feeling in the pit of his stomach. Beside him, Steven started firing, the assault rifle bucking in his hands, but Paul could see that he held it firmly against his shoulder, and his body was relaxed despite his fear. A Securitat twisted as one of Steven's bullets struck home, and the stricken Illyri disappeared in the mist.

You're blooded now, little brother, thought Paul. You're as lost as the rest of us.

CHAPTER 66

The first basic MRI scan of Gradus's skull appeared on the screen, revealing a small, dense formation of matter, about three inches in length, squatting at the base of the cerebellum. It reminded Syl of an insect larva, with legs that curled around the consul's spinal cord, anchoring it in place. It appeared to have no eyes or mouth. How does it feed? Syl wondered. Is it even alive?

Fremd and Lorac crouched over the image on the display, with Syl peering between them.

'Is it the same as the one you saw at Cancri station?' asked Lorac.

'I think so. It's bigger, though. Can you improve the definition, maybe get in a little closer?'

'We're just getting started,' said Lorac.

Behind them, Gradus was moaning as the scanner made a series of passes around not only his head, but his entire body. Illyri technology had made the devices lightweight and portable; the massive tubes of old had been replaced by thin low-radiation screens capable of producing images so detailed that it appeared as if the internal workings of the body were being projected on to the exterior; the pumping of the heart, the twitching of muscles, even the flow of blood through the brain, all were visible. The machine beeped, and a digital readout on its side began counting down from ten, indicating that a full imaging sequence was almost complete. Gradus stopped making noise. He now twisted his head slightly under the restraining band so that he could watch what was happening with one eye. Syl thought it looked like the sedative might be wearing off. She was about to say something to Fremd when the countdown reached zero, and what the display revealed wiped all other concerns from her head.

The organism in Gradus's head, the thing that Fremd had described as the Other, appeared to be breathing, its body slowly inflating and deflating as though drawing air. Its head was a mass of twitching tentacles, probably only a few millimetres long, beneath which was what looked to be a sucking mouth. Syl could see its organs now, although most were unfamiliar. There were what looked like lungs, and what might have been a series of lateral hearts, almost like those of an earthworm, but much of the rest of its physiology was strange to her. On closer examination, what had appeared to be legs were actually more like gripping tentacles, more developed versions of the ones on its head, or thicker versions of the threadlike filaments that seemed to protrude from most of its body.

But that was not the worst of it, for what the scan revealed was that the organism was not isolated in Gradus's brain; those filaments had extended throughout his entire nervous system. They were growing as the Illyri watched, like wires moving through the Grand Consul's body.

'It's like nothing I've ever seen before,' said Lorac, and he spoke not with horror, but with fascination. 'How is it feeding? It must be absorbing nutrients from his system, perhaps through those filaments. But they're so much more extensive than they need to be.'

He tapped one of the screens to focus on an enlarged image of Gradus's cerebellum.

'There seems to be a concentration of filaments here, at the reticular formation,' he said. 'I'd say that it's wired to his consciousness, but there's little contact with his thalamus, only marginal connection to his frontal lobe, and none at all with the temporal or parietal lobes.'

'Meaning?' said Fremd.

'Meaning his bodily senses – hearing, sight, memory of non-verbal events, spatial perception – are mostly cut off from this thing. The frontal lobe deals with motor responses, creativity and emotional reactions; the link looks stronger there. This thing may experience the world partly through the emotional responses of its host. It's also hooked into his cerebellum, so it may be able to stimulate certain muscle responses.'

Fremd squatted close to the gurney. He spoke in Gradus's right ear.

'What is it?' he asked.

Gradus's voice was almost clear. It should be more slurred, thought Syl. We drugged him.

'It is . . . God.'

He began to laugh. Lorac examined the computers hooked up to the scanner.

'The data is saving,' he said. 'It's slow, but we're getting there.'

Fremd poured disinfectant on his hands before walking to the tray of surgical equipment beside the scanner. Gradus managed to move his head just enough to follow his progress.

'What are you doing?' he asked.

'We're going to take a sample from your "god",' said Fremd.

He picked up a packet marked 'BD Spinal Needle', and removed from it a long, thin instrument. Syl winced involuntarily.

'No,' said Gradus. 'You mustn't.'

He began to struggle again, wriggling against his restraints like a great maggot.

'Give him more sedative,' said Fremd, and Lorac hit Gradus in the arm with a smaller needle. It didn't seem to have much effect, appearing if anything to make Gradus more agitated.

'Again!' said Fremd. He reached between the MRI screens and pushed down on the consul in an effort to still him. He put the tip of the lumbar puncture needle against the skin of Gradus's neck, and started to push down.

'Lorac!' said Syl. 'Fremd!'

'In a moment,' said Lorac.

'No, I think you need to see this,' said Syl, who was staring at the screen. 'I think you need to see this *now*.'

Meia and Peris watched the chaos of the attack on the castle with growing frustration. Smoke and mist masked much of the fighting, but they had seen the cruiser go down, and had watched as Sedulus pulled back his troops after the initial assault appeared to have failed.

Their Illyri loyalty meant that they should have announced their presence to Sedulus and fought alongside his remaining forces, but that would have been to ignore their suspicion that Sedulus did not have the best interests of Syl and Ani at heart. Sedulus, too, might well have had them disarmed at gunpoint rather than allow them potentially to interfere with his efforts to secure Gradus. In addition, Meia had no desire to begin killing members of the Resistance, not after they had helped to rescue Syl and Ani in the first place, not while she still had her fragile truce with Trask.

Peris and the strike squad were growing impatient.

'I thought you said we could just walk in,' said Peris.

'Unfortunately, Sedulus beat us to the walls,' said Meia. 'Or hadn't you noticed?'

'We can't stay out here forever. Sedulus won't give up until he's inside, and he won't care who he kills once he's in there as long as he gets the Grand Consul back. And if he doesn't get the Grand Consul . . .'

'Then he'll kill *everyone*,' Meia finished.

'Including— '

'Quiet!' said Meia.

Her hearing was even more acute than that of the other Illyri. She was, in every way, a more advanced creation. Now she picked up footfalls on grass, and the whispers of women and children.

'Do you have signal flares?' she asked Peris.

Peris produced a pair of the self-igniting flares from his belt. They were lightweight tubes, barely six inches long. Meia took them from him.

'I think I may have found another way into the castle,' she said. 'If you don't see one of these flares go up within thirty minutes, you have my permission to blast your way in and get Syl and Ani, and I don't care who you have to kill to do it.'

Meia left the squad. She shouldered her weapon and approached the sound of fleeing humans. She could see shapes appearing from beneath the ground, like the dead rising. When she was almost on top of them, she dropped to the grass and shouted out:

'My name is Meia. I'm alone, and I'm unarmed.'

The voices rose in panic, and then were hushed.

'We are not alone, and we are *not* unarmed,' a female voice replied, but it was immediately interrupted by another calling Meia's name, this one younger and instantly familiar to her.

It was Ani.

Paul was reloading his semi-automatic when the Illyri pulled back, the mist embracing them as they retreated, temporarily abandoning the castle to its defenders. The Resistance fighters advanced to the walls. Men began dragging sandbags and undamaged sacks of concrete to the gates to create a barrier behind which to fight when the Illyri returned, as they surely would. Cries for help rose from the wounded, and demands for ammunition and water from those still unharmed.

Norris and Just Joe, along with Paul and Steven, remained by the castle keep.

They were too weary to move. Unlike most of the others, they had walked for days to get to Dundearg, and their bodies were approaching exhaustion.

'What now?' asked Steven.

'They'll regroup and try again,' said Just Joe. 'They've probably already called for reinforcements.'

'We should abandon the castle,' said Norris.

'We will, just as soon as we get the signal. For now, they need time to complete the evacuation, and for those below to work.'

'Do you know what they're looking for?' asked Norris.

'Aliens,' said Just Joe.

'Right,' said Norris. 'It's not like we don't have enough of those.'

It was Steven who noticed the change in the mist.

'They're back!' he said, rising to his feet, but what appeared beyond the gates were not Securitats or Galateans. A mechanised suit materialised before them. It was followed by a second, then a third. The torchlight flickered upon the faceplates on their helmets so that they seemed to be lit within by fire, but even behind the reflected light of the flames Steven could have sworn that he could see other movement.

Not a face, exactly, but something that was trying to be a face.

Sedulus had given the Sarith Entities only one order: to scour the castle of every trace of humanity. Now, from his hiding place in the mist, surrounded by the last vestiges of his troops, he unlocked the suits and unleashed his demons.

CHAPTER 67

On the MRI display, the changes to Gradus's system were being revealed. The filaments were extending faster and faster through his body, so fast that Gradus screamed in agony, his back arching so high in pain that the restraints stretched to their limits, and Syl could hear the metal of the buckles scraping against the gurney. Sections of the consul's brain began to light up on the scans, exploding into angry oranges and reds. The real-time images lost their focus with Gradus's thrashing, but Syl caught a glimpse of the tip of the needle moving down, drawing closer and closer to the organism in Gradus's head.

The restraints burst. Gradus pushed himself from the gurney with so much force that Lorac was thrown back against the wall and Fremd fell to the floor, the needle still clutched in his right hand. The MRI screens shattered. Syl instinctively grabbed the first weapon that came to hand: a scalpel. Lorac drew a revolver from his belt and trained it on Gradus.

But he could not shoot, not yet.

For Gradus was changing.

At the castle walls, the defenders responded to the new threat. A volley of gunfire struck the suits, but they were heavily armoured, and the bullets succeeded only in striking sparks from them. The firing ceased as Just Joe called for grenades, and in the silence that followed they all heard the hissed release of compressed gases as the suit helmets were unlocked, and the visors rose.

For a moment, all was still.

Columns of black smoke began to flow from the suits, each taking

the form of a dark mockery of man, before the smoke became a
swarm, and the Entities commenced their feeding. A boy who looked
about Paul's age was the first to be surrounded, the Entities encircling
him, consuming him from the head down, his clothing – even his
green-and-white scarf – vanishing as they took him. Two more
members of the Resistance, a young woman and an older man, were
the next to go. Paul and the others could not fire for fear of hitting
their own people, and the black forms moved so *fast* . . .

'Get inside!' cried Just Joe. 'All of you.'

The survivors ran to the keep, but now the Entities separated, each
seeking its own prey. Three more people died, but more slowly now
as the Entities' first surge of hunger was quelled by their feeding. It
gave the rest time to make it to the keep, but it was Paul who realised
that they would still be at risk inside its walls. The doors were old, and
imperfectly sealed. Even when they were closed, draughts came in
underneath them and around the sides, and these things moved like
dark vapour, or a swarm of black bees, isolating and killing. This is it,
he thought: we can't fight them, and if we can't fight them, we die.

Suddenly he was pushed aside. An Illyri female stood beside him.
From her right hand dangled a belt of grenades.

'Who are—' he began, but it was Just Joe who answered.

'Meia!' he said.

'Joe,' she replied. 'You need to get out of my way if you want to
live.'

'What are those things?' said Joe.

'Sedulus's pets.'

'How do we kill them?'

'You can't. But I can.'

Meia walked down the steps of the keep as the Entities finished off
their latest victims and looked for new blood. They swarmed together,
forming one great cloud, as if in response to the approaching female.
They descended on her, swirling and biting. Paul could see fragments
of tissue disappearing from Meia's head – a piece of her cheek, the tip
of her right ear – but then the creatures pulled back. He could see that
she was bleeding, but drops of a yellow milky fluid also leaked from

her wounds, pooling on the seals of her armour. He thought he could see hydraulics moving in her face. The Entities seemed to realise the threat that she posed, but they could not consume her. Whatever she was, whatever she was made from, they could not eat it.

'What is she doing?' said Steven.

'I think she's going after their metal suits,' said Paul.

Meia began to run, arming the grenades as she did so. The first two went through the open visors and into the bodies of the suits, but she threw the entire belt into the third. She hit the ground, and the men at the keep threw themselves flat as the grenades exploded. When Paul looked up, two of the suits were still standing in place, but they were riddled with fissures and leaks. The third suit had split above the waist, and lay in two pieces on the dirt.

The black swarms combined to form a face, with eye sockets and a gaping mouth. It screamed silently, and then vanished into the mist.

The Grand Consul, or some version of him, stood in the centre of the room. His arms were extended from his sides, and his whole body trembled. Specks of blood appeared on his exposed skin, flowing from his face and scalp until he wore a mask of red, and his hands looked like those of a murderer. The shaking increased in intensity. His mouth opened, and he cried out in agony as his head and hands began to blur, the outline of his features becoming less clear as though seen through fog. Syl's screams joined with his, even as she realised that it was not fog but filaments that were emerging through the pores of his skin, waving in the dim light, testing the unfamiliar air. Syl could see them moving beneath his clothing, pushing at the material, their tips hardening to points as they finally tore through.

All trace of Gradus's features was now lost. The Grand Consul was a swirling mass of yellow filaments moving to a tide felt only by them, like a marooned ocean creature remembering the sea. His body swelled, and his mouth opened wider still, so that Syl heard the bones in his skull cracking as his jaw dislocated. From his mouth poured a stream of particles, like pollen being expelled from a plant, and the room filled with the sickly-sweet smell of corrupted flesh. The particles struck the unfortunate Lorac straight in the face. He had lost his mask in the chaos, and now collapsed choking on the ground. Almost immediately filaments exploded from his nose and his ears. They covered his mouth, and his eyes, and his face, slowly suffocating him, even as his belly started to bloat rapidly, and Syl could almost picture the filaments spreading through his system, infecting him, preparing to send forth another deadly cloud when Lorac's stomach burst.

Gradus turned towards Fremd, the Grand Consul's body now nothing more than a weapon to be used by the organism inside him. Another spray of particles poured from his mouth, but Fremd grabbed one of the broken MRI screens and used it to shield his face as he scuttled to where Syl stood, frozen in horror by the wall.

'Run!' he told her. 'Run now!'

He grabbed her by the hand and pulled her towards the door, but Syl's hand slipped from his. She could not move any further. She looked to her feet and saw the filaments wrapped around her ankles. She tried to walk, but they tightened on her. Suddenly she was yanked backwards so hard that she fell facedown on the floor. She reached out to Fremd, but another burst of particles sprayed towards him, and it was all he could do to protect himself with the screen and try not to breathe, for even a mask was little protection against this.

'Help me!' cried Syl. She was being dragged back now, towards the thing that was once Gradus, her own mask slipping from her face, leaving her entirely unprotected. Fremd's fingers reached for hers and their fingertips touched, but there was movement to Syl's left, and she saw that Lorac's entire body was now swollen almost to its limit. Already puffs of particles were being blown through the pores of his skin like the water spouts of a whale. The whole room, perhaps the whole castle, would be infected by him when his flesh gave way.

A pair of shadows fell across Fremd, and Meia's voice shouted, 'Stay down, Syl! Stay down!'

She felt a weight on top of her. A torrent of searing heat from Meia's blast rifle rolled over her as Paul whispered, 'I'm here, I'm here,' and Gradus and Lorac began to burn.

★ ★ ★

Sedulus stood before the last of the skimmers. If everything went wrong, it would at least allow him to escape. Around him stood four Securitats and half a dozen Galateans, all that was left of the three platoons that he had led into the Highlands. The mist was slowly clearing, and the distant shape of the castle was now visible. They were waiting for the Sarith Entities to finish their work when they heard the vague sound of three explosions in quick succession, the final one louder than the rest.

'What was that?' asked Beldyn.

'What does it matter?' replied Sedulus.

The mist billowed before them. Something was emerging from it, something big and fast. Beldyn stepped forward, his gun at the ready. The rest of the troops did likewise.

Beldyn saw them first. He turned to shout a warning, but the Entity entered through his open mouth, pouring itself down his throat and consuming him from within. The others descended on the Galateans and the Securitats, pursuing them as they ran, their hunger made sharper by the fact that they were dying. Only Sedulus did not run. He remained in place, and watched his troops fall.

Two of the Entities began to weaken, the intensity of their feeding dwindling, their essence coalescing into a single roiling mass that beat like a human heart until it turned from black to grey, and then to nothing.

But one remained. It took human form, and Sedulus thought that he had always known this day might come. He had never truly understood the nature of these beings. He had used them, but they had used him too. He feared them, but they hated him. They were like birds of prey; they were his only for as long as he could keep them fed, and they had no loyalty to their master, especially not one who had abused his power of life and death over them.

'Finish it,' he whispered.

The Entity fell upon him, and they died together.

CHAPTER 68

All that was left of Gradus and Lorac was burnt remains. Some of their limbs had fused with the melted equipment in the heat of the fire, but the old stone walls of the keep had contained the blaze.

The clothing had been burned from Paul's back, and his skin was raw and blistered. Part of his hair had been singed down to his skull. Syl was unharmed. She sat on the cold flagstones of the corridor, her face against Paul's chest. She did not hold him – although she wanted to – for Maeve was working on him, salving his wounds prior to applying the dressings. Ani and Steven watched all that was taking place. They stood close together, their shoulders touching companionably.

Heather and Alice waited outside, along with Just Joe and Norris, and what was left of the force in the castle. Heather was wounded, but Fremd had done his best for her. She could walk, and she would survive. Now he turned his attention to Meia.

'We have to tell everyone,' said Syl, as Fremd tended to the damage inflicted by the Entities. 'They have to know.'

'Who do we tell?' asked Meia. 'And what proof do we have? It's gone, all of it.'

She told them of what she had seen at the Eden Project while Fremd patched her with ProGen skin. It was routinely used to heal battle wounds, even burns, and it was possible that some of it might be grafted on to Paul's back if his injuries proved severe enough. Meia showed signs of pain as the work was done. Had she known of Vena's discovery of her true nature, she might have agreed with at least one of the Securitat's conclusions: flesh gave feeling, and once one could experience pain, emotions were no longer illusions. With pain came rage, regret, loss.

Love?

The biggest surprise about the truth of Meia's identity was how little Syl and Ani were surprised. In a way, it made perfect sense to them, given their growing awareness of their own gifts.

I should have known, thought Ani, for Meia only ever revealed what she wanted me to see.

I should have known, thought Syl. Meia was the only one I could never bend to my will.

'My father will believe us,' said Syl.

'We don't know who has been infected,' said Meia.

'The Corps!' said Syl. 'It's just the Corps officials and the Securitats. It has to be. My father isn't like them.'

Fremd and Meia exchanged a look. Syl caught it.

'What?' she said. 'It's true.'

'We don't know that,' said Fremd. 'And even if it is true, by sharing what you know you put everyone you tell at risk, yourself most of all. Think of the panic we'll create if this gets out. No Illyri will be safe: you'll have every lunatic from here to the South Pole beheading Illyri to find out what's living inside their heads.

'No, we need proof, and on a vast scale. We need to try to understand the nature of the Others. Until then, we have to remain silent while we find out what's happening. This isn't just about a handful of Corps officials carrying some kind of life form. We know from what Meia has seen that they've been experimenting on humans. They've been implanting, and they've also been seeding the dead with these things. We have to find out why.'

'And then there is the Sisterhood,' said Meia. 'The Corps does the Sisterhood's bidding. If the Corps is involved, then so too is the Sisterhood. We must be silent, all of us. We must be careful.'

'She's right, Syl,' said Paul, and for an instant Syl wanted to hate him.

'You don't know my father,' she said.

She tried to pull away, but he held her gently.

'I know you,' he said. 'If you trust him, so do I. But everyone who knows about this is at risk. If you tell him, you put him at risk too. Whatever these things are, it's my people – humans – that are being experimented on. I'll do whatever I can to stop it, but it has to be planned, and it has to be successful once we start. For that to happen, we have to know what we're dealing with – all of us, human and Illyri.'

'And it would mean returning to Edinburgh,' said Meia. 'You and Ani are still fugitives. That hasn't changed.'

'So what should we do?' asked Ani. 'Keep running?'

'I can hide you,' said Meia. 'In time, we can get you out of Scotland, maybe even offworld. I can keep you one step ahead of them always.'

'But that will be our lives, won't it?' said Syl. 'They will be like our time in the Highlands, except stretching on forever. We'll always be hunted, and that's no life at all.'

There was silence, for Meia could not disagree. It was left to Ani to speak, and what she said broke Syl's heart, for it was Syl who had got them into this mess to begin with.

'Syl is right,' said Ani. 'We should go back. I'm tired of running.'

Paul and Steven shouted the same word simultaneously: 'No!'

The arguments began, but they were interrupted by Peris, who gestured for Meia to join him. She followed the soldier out of the keep and into the courtyard, where they stood beside the ruined gates. In the distance Meia heard the sound of incoming craft: skimmers and shuttles. She also picked up the dying drone of a cruiser's engines powering down; it had already landed nearby, and would soon begin disgorging troops. The engine suggested a Military craft, she noted, not the Corps or the Securitats. That, at least, was good.

'I'm sorry,' said Peris. 'I tried to keep them away for as long as I could. And you must know: my orders are to bring Syl and Ani back to their fathers.'

'It's all right,' said Meia. 'They want to return.'

Peris looked solemn.

'I have to take the boys back too,' he said.

'They're under sentence of death.'

'Not any more. With Sedulus and Gradus both dead, Governor Andrus is once again in control, at least for the present, and the Corps and the Securitats will be out of favour after this whole mess. The governor has already abolished the death penalty; he says that he'll deal with the Council of Government himself if they object. And the medic who took DNA samples from the boys testified that he believes the same samples were used to contaminate the evidence from the explosions.'

'On whose orders?'

'He says on the orders of Sedulus, and Sedulus alone.'

'Always blame the dead,' said Meia. 'The cover-up has already begun.'

'It's easiest that way. But the boys remain guilty of membership of the Resistance.'

'After all this slaughter, and the death of Gradus, the Corps will press for them to be sent to the Punishment Battalions.'

'Yes.'

'Perhaps they'll survive,' said Meia, but she sounded doubtful.

'I am aware that there is an escape tunnel in that room we've just left, you know.'

'For a simple soldier, you are unusually complicated,' said Meia. 'But I suspect that those young men will want to return too. Paul will not abandon Syl and Steven will follow his brother's lead.'

She watched the reinforcements draw nearer, marching in double time towards the castle. They were only minutes away.

'I should have guessed that you were a Mech,' said Peris.

'Why is that?'

'You never fell for my charms.'

'I was aware of your reputation.'

'And I of yours,' said Peris. 'I should tell you that a second order came through. Highest priority from Vena herself, who is now the ranking Securitat following the death of Sedulus. You are accused of treason and murder. You are to be arrested on sight and handed over to the Securitats. If you resist, you are to be shot.'

Meia turned to face him. His finger was already inside the trigger guard of his blast rifle, although the weapon was not yet pointing in her direction.

'Are you guilty of the offences?' asked Peris.

'The treason I deny, but yes, I have killed.'

'Why?'

'Because there are forces at work here that you don't understand. None of us do, not yet. But humanity is at risk, and I think the Illyri race is in danger too.'

'I've told you before, I'm just a simple soldier,' said Peris. 'I merely follow orders.'

'So what will you do?' she asked.

'Follow my orders,' he said. The slightest of smiles softened his face. 'But if I can't see you, I can't arrest you, and I certainly can't shoot you.'

'I can't leave them,' said Meia. 'I have to help them. I have to help them all.'

'You can't help them if you're dead. Or decommissioned, if you prefer.'

Meia's right hand reached out and touched Peris gently on the arm.

'These boys are important,' she said. 'The older one in particular has grown close to Syl, and she to him. There are those who may try to hurt her by hurting him, but he has also seen things in this castle, things that, for now, I can't share with you, but which will affect the future of our race. Believe me: the Kerr brothers must be protected. They have to be kept alive. Do what you can for them, until I return. Please.'

'I will.'

He turned his back on her. When he looked again, she was gone.

When Peris returned to the room in the keep, Fremd and the Resistance survivors were no longer there. Peris sighed. He was not sure how he was supposed to explain the fact that the entire Resistance force in the castle appeared to have disappeared from under his nose. There were those who would undoubtedly describe him as not just a simple soldier, but a simpleton.

Yet four faces still looked up at him. Syl and Ani had been crying. Peris thought the boys might have shed some tears too. They had all linked hands, like children presenting a united front.

Peris felt a rush of conflicting emotions, but not least of them was admiration.

'Time to go,' he said.

CHAPTER 69

The message from Peris came through to Edinburgh Castle. Syl and Ani were safe, but Marshal Sedulus was missing, and a single surviving Securitat had given a disturbing description of his possible fate. Grand Consul Gradus, Peris reported, had been burned alive during Sedulus's assault on the castle.

As Meia had noted, the dead made useful scapegoats.

Syrene's screams of loss echoed through the castle. Her handmaids flitted helplessly around her like moths drawn to the flame of her grief. Responding to the flood of emotions, the organism in her brain tightened its hold on her cerebral cortex, and the intensity of her shrieks increased.

In the silence of her quarters, Vena mourned for the lost Sedulus, but she did not weep. The heat of her rage evaporated her tears before they could fall from her eyes.

I will watch as every creature on Earth is consumed.
I will continue my lover's work.

CHAPTER 70

Syl and Ani were returned to Edinburgh in the same shuttle as Paul and Steven, all under the watchful eye of Peris. The boys were cuffed, but the two Illyri were not. Peris kept them all separated for appearance's sake, and they were silent throughout the journey, but it seemed to him that the older boy never took his gaze from the governor's daughter, and the young Illyri held him fast in her eyes.

Upon landing, Peris opened the shuttle door and peered out. He saw a Military platoon to the right, and a line of Corps and Securitats to the left. For now, the scales favoured those on the right, but it would shift again. The game was always being played, and the four youths were simply pawns on the board.

A quartet of Military guards approached, ready to receive the prisoners. With a raised hand Peris instructed them to wait. He turned back to the occupants of the shuttle, and with a curt nod he uncuffed the humans. He watched awkwardly as Paul embraced Syl, and they kissed deeply, hungrily. At a loss, Ani gave Steven a hug too, and an awkward pat on the back. It was clear from the look on his face that Steven would have liked more, but Ani did not have more to give him.

'I'm sorry,' said Peris. 'I truly am.'

They separated, and Peris cuffed the boys once again. The members of his strike team surrounded the prisoners as they were led from the shuttle. Paul and Steven could feel the hatred directed towards them from the Securitats. Their numbers in Scotland had been decimated during the preceding days, and they had lost their leader on Earth. These two boys were the only ones left to blame. If they could, their enemies would have executed them in the square.

The brothers were taken to a pair of comfortable but secure Military cells, there to await their fate. Syl and Ani were brought to the governor's office. They were both experiencing similar thoughts: that being locked in a cell might be preferable to the storm that was about to break over them.

Balen was seated in his usual place. He rose from his chair as the young Illyri entered the room. They looked filthy, he thought, and tired.

And older. These were not the same girls who had left the castle mere days before. They had been tested in fire, and changed by the experience. Balen was no longer looking at youths, but young adults.

'Welcome back,' he said.

'Are we?' asked Syl.

'You will always be welcome here,' Balen replied. 'Both of you. Remember that, in the hours and days to come.'

Syl tried to smile at him, but she could not. Being back here made her aware of all that she had sacrificed, and all that she might yet have to sacrifice. Whatever happened, nothing would ever be the same again.

The door opened. Seated inside were Danis and his wife, Fian. As soon as the girls were led in, Fian ran to her daughter and embraced her, even as her husband tried to stop her. Andrus stood behind his desk, his face severe. He did not approach Syl. It was only as the door closed behind her that Syl saw why.

Syrene was waiting in the corner of the room. She had exchanged the red robes of the Sisterhood for the deep blue of a widow's weeds. Her face was uncovered, and so pale that the tattoos of the Sisterhood were like wounds upon her skin.

'Fian,' said Andrus, and there was a warning in his voice. Reluctantly Fian released her hold on her daughter, and returned to her chair.

Andrus regarded the two Illyri. He loved them both, daughter and near daughter. There would be time later for him to take Syl in his arms and tell her how much he cared for her, and how glad he was that she was safely returned.

Time, but only a little.

For now, Syrene filled the room with the jagged edges of her grief. Her pain was a weapon waiting to be used. If they were not careful, she would tear them all apart with it.

'You are unhurt?' Andrus asked.

Syl and Ani nodded dumbly.

'Good,' he said, and he tried to fill that single syllable with all that could not be said. 'Now, I want you to tell the Archmage of her husband. She has the right to know the manner of his death.'

Andrus and Danis had agreed upon this with Syrene. They could not deny her. She wanted to be there when the girls were brought to their fathers. She wanted there to be no secrets. She wanted to be told.

Syl and Ani had prepared their story. Peris had coached them while the boys listened. Fire from the troop carrier; damaged fuel stores; a leak.

Flames.

Syrene probed for the lie, both openly with her questions and insidiously with her mind. They experienced it as an itch in their skulls, a bug crawling on their brains, but Balen had been right: these were changed young people, and their control of their gifts was growing. Perhaps Syl's, though newly recognised, were greater, for Syrene's testing of her betrayed no sign of her abilities, while Ani's brain twitched like a stimulated muscle. They, in turn, felt Syrene's pain and her fury. It was seeking an outlet. There was a part of Syrene that wanted to see them both burn, just as her husband had burned.

When she was done, she turned to face Andrus.

'They're lying,' she said.

Syl opened her mouth to protest, but her father raised a finger in warning, and she stayed quiet.

'I heard no lie,' said Andrus. 'Their story matches that of Peris, and he is an honourable man.'

'He is one of your lackeys,' said Syrene. 'I do not trust him, or them. I do not even trust you, Lord Andrus. My understanding is that you harboured a Mech on your staff.'

Andrus's face gave away nothing.

'I did not know of her true nature.'

'I don't believe you. Even if I did, I wouldn't care. She is a renegade and a killer. She will be found and terminated.'

'Regardless,' said Andrus, 'I have requested more information from the Securitats about the crimes of which she is accused, and have received nothing in return. On a similar matter, we have reason to believe that the bombings in Edinburgh may have been the work of dissidents within the Illyri, possibly even the Corps itself.'

He knew that Syrene was on dangerous ground. To speak of Meia's crimes was to speak of Eden, and Syrene did not wish to do that. Neither did she care to discuss the bombs on the Royal Mile. Andrus just wished that Meia could have reported her findings before she went to ground.

'None of this helps avenge my husband, or eases my grief at his loss,' said Syrene.

'I do not know what more we can do,' said Andrus. 'Your husband's remains are being returned to Edinburgh. His death is a blow to us all. We will mourn with you.'

'I do not want your mourning!'

Syrene's body coiled in fury. Spittle shot from her mouth and flecked the pink of her lips and the blue of her gown. She drew a breath, calming herself. She repeated the words, this time more calmly. 'I do not want your mourning.'

'What *do* you want?'

'A punishment to fit the crime. Your daughters are guilty of treason. They helped the humans to escape.'

'The boys were innocent.'

'Perhaps, but only of the bombings. They are members of the Resistance. They have killed Illyri. Your daughters colluded with them.'

'They were foolish. They are young.'

'Not so young. Had they not acted as they did, my husband would still be alive. I invoke the Widow's Wish.'

The tension in the room increased. The Widow's Wish was now

rarely used. It was a relic of older times, when Illyri females had less power and were dependent upon their husbands for their wealth and security. A crime against the husband was viewed as a crime against the wife, and the murder of a husband was the worst crime of all. Before the elimination of the death penalty on Illyr, the Widow's Wish allowed a woman to decide whether those responsible for the death of her husband should be imprisoned or executed. In later years, it could be used to increase or reduce the severity of a penalty, but it was mainly a weapon of the poor and was rarely used by the privileged. It remained enshrined in law, though, and could not be ignored.

'And what is your wish?'

'That my husband's final decision on the fate of these two traitorous Illyri should remain in force.'

From the pocket of her dress, Syrene produced a note. Carefully she unfolded it, and handed it to Andrus. He read it silently. When he was finished, some of his confidence was gone.

'The Punishment Battalions,' he said, and he saw Danis tense in his chair at the words.

Syl wavered on her feet. That was a death sentence.

'They have not yet been tried.'

'Then let them be tried. The evidence against them is overwhelming. It was my husband's recommended sentence, and it is mine. No court will stand against it. If you try to deprive me of it, if you try to take these daughters of Illyr from here and hide them away, I will bring down the wrath of the Sisterhood and the Corps upon you. There will be civil war, I guarantee it.'

Fian stood. She seemed ready to spring at Syrene and murder her, but Danis held on to his wife firmly.

'Then let there be war,' he said. 'I will not doom these children to the Battalions.'

'I warn you—' said Syrene.

'Wait,' said Syl. 'Wait.'

And though she spoke the word softly, so softly, there was still something in her voice, in the certainty of it, that quieted them all.

'We wish to give ourselves to the Sisterhood,' she said.

'*What?*' shouted Andrus. 'No! I will not permit it!'

Now Danis was roaring, and his wife was crying.

Syl looked at Ani, and Ani understood. She swallowed hard before she spoke, but when she did, it was with almost as much confidence as Syl had managed.

'We wish to give ourselves to the Sisterhood,' she said, then added, so that only Syl could hear, 'I think.'

All shouting ceased. The room was quiet. If the Widow's Wish was an old law, rarely invoked, the pledge to the Sisterhood was older yet, and even more serious. It could not be refused, not by the family of the one making the pledge or by the Sisterhood itself. If the novice did not prove worthy, then a solution could be found, but any Illyri female who was prepared to offer herself as a Nairene had to be given a place in the Marque.

'I accept,' said Syrene. All grief was gone from her face. In its place there was only triumph.

And in Syrene's words, Syl heard the sound of the trap snapping shut.

CHAPTER 71

Consternation reigned in the room. The shouts even drew Balen from his desk, and caused a pair of the governor's guards to come running with their weapons at the ready. Andrus dismissed them, assuring them that he was safe, and the debate raged on. It was all for nothing, though. Even in her grief, Syrene had played them all expertly. She had Ani, whose powers she believed she could turn to the Sisterhood's benefit, and she had avenged the Sisterhood for the loss of the Lady Orianne to her husband, Andrus. If they could not have the mother, they now had the daughter instead.

But Syl had her own secrets. As the arguments raged around her, she saw again a man silhouetted against the Highland dawn, a bayonet buried deep in his chest. Syrene was not the only one who could play vicious games.

'What of Paul and Steven?' Syl asked, her voice again silencing the adults. 'They helped us after the crash. They kept us safe.'

'For their own ends,' said Syrene, and her tone made it clear that she was aware of the feelings at work between the humans and the young Illyri.

'They kept us *safe*,' Syl repeated, and she held Syrene's gaze for so long that it was the Nairene sister who was forced to look away first.

'Have them brought here,' ordered Andrus. He was glad of the distraction. It would give him time to think. He did not want his daughter in the hands of the Sisterhood. He wanted her to remain close to him. There had to be a way.

Eventually Paul and Steven appeared, accompanied by Peris. They no longer wore their own clothes, but had been given grey prison overalls instead. Steven's were too big for him, and he had been forced to roll up the sleeves and the cuffs. It made him appear very small, and very young. The two boys barely glanced at Syl and Ani. It hurt Syl at first, until she realised that they wanted to do nothing that might get the Illyri into more trouble by exposing their true feelings.

Too late, thought Syl. Syrene knew, and she believed that her father might have some suspicions too. He was watching Paul as though he didn't trust him a single inch. Syrene no longer looked triumphant, but simply vindictive. These boys were among those who had taken her husband captive. Had they not done so, he would still be alive.

She wanted their heads.

Andrus stood. He towered over the two boys.

'It appears that you were not responsible for the bombings on the Royal Mile,' he said.

Paul and Steven exchanged a look. Hope shone briefly in their eyes, but was quickly extinguished by Andrus's next words.

'However, you are guilty of membership of the Resistance, and of the murder of Illyri.'

'We didn't murder anyone,' said Paul. 'We fought. We're soldiers.'

'You are terrorists!' said Syrene.

'Quiet!' said Andrus. 'All of you.'

He waited until he was sure that he was being heeded before he continued. Where was Meia? he wondered. He wanted to consult with her. He had colluded with her to place his daughter and Ani with the Resistance in order to prevent them from being taken offworld. Now he was being forced to punish these two boys for essentially doing his will.

'The sentence for those guilty of Resistance activities is exile to the Punishment Battalions for life,' he said. 'Given your age, I commute that sentence to five years.'

Paul and Steven looked shocked. Five years in the Punishment Battalions was still a virtual death sentence. There was a small chance that Paul might survive, if he was strong and lucky enough, but Steven would not. He was too young. Starvation and brutality would kill him within months.

'No,' said Syl softly. 'Not that.'

The sentence she and Ani had avoided had passed to the Kerrs instead. Ani took her hand and squeezed it.

Then Peris stepped forward.

'If I might speak, Lord Andrus.'

Andrus nodded his permission.

'I in no way condone the activities of these two young men,' said Peris. 'They are members of the Resistance, and they fought the Illyri at Dundearg. But I believe they were protecting your daughter and the daughter of General Danis, as well as the women and children sheltered in the castle. Marshal Sedulus, in his desire to rescue the Grand Consul, was guilty of using undue force, of the slaughter of human civilians, of endangering the safety of Illyri and human alike, and of introducing hostile life forms into a protected environment.

'In their position,' Peris concluded, 'I might well have fought Marshal Sedulus too.'

'Do you have an alternative proposal for punishment?' asked Andrus, and his voice betrayed his hope that it might be so.

'They are brave, and strong,' said Peris. 'They could be useful to the Empire. If you send them to the Punishment Battalions, they will die. But if you place them with the Brigades . . .'

The Brigades were different. This was where the one-in-ten of conscripted human youths were placed, and those who served in them were treated well. They were given proper food, and the best of training. They were soldiers, not prisoners. It was still dangerous, but the survival rates were many times higher than in the Battalions.

'It is not usual,' said Andrus. 'It may even be dangerous to place members of the Resistance in the Brigades. They could sow unrest.'

'I will vouch for them,' said Peris. 'I will train them myself. And I will personally deal with any attempts to foment rebellion.'

Andrus and Danis could not hide their surprise. What Peris was proposing was that he should leave his comfortable position in the governor's personal guard and return to the active Military. A place in the guard was a well-earned reward for loyal service. Nobody went from there to the Brigades. The traffic was always in the other direction.

'Are you sure this is what you want?' asked Danis. He and Peris had served together for a long time, and the captain was one of his closest comrades-in-arms.

'Yes, General,' said Peris. 'I am a common soldier, and a soldier's place is not in fine palaces, but in the field.'

'I object—' began Syrene, but Andrus cut her off.

'Your objection is noted, but the decision is made. The prisoners will join the Brigades, and Captain Peris will take responsibility for them. It is done. Captain, prepare for your departure.'

Peris saluted, and the boys were led away. This time, Paul risked a look back at Syl, and she managed a small smile. He winked at her in return.

There was hope after all, if only a little.

Once they were gone, Danis and his wife asked permission to spend some time alone with their daughter, for she was now the property of the Sisterhood. It was granted by Syrene, although she insisted that Corps personnel be positioned outside Danis's quarters to ensure that no attempt was made to remove Ani from the castle.

'And none of your tricks,' she warned Ani in a whisper as she moved to join her parents. 'If you cross me, I'll destroy your father and mother.'

Ani departed, her head bowed low.

That left only Syl, Andrus and Syrene.

'May I request the same kindness?' asked Andrus.

'You may,' said Syrene, 'although I would like a moment alone with you first.'

Andrus didn't seem particularly happy about this, but he had little choice in the matter. He asked Syl to step outside, and she did so. She took a seat across from Balen, but she did not speak. She thought about her conversation with Meia and Fremd, and their warning to say nothing of what had occurred during Gradus's final moments. She had to tell her father something, though. He was a clever, careful man. He would know what to do.

Andrus stood before Syrene. He hated her now, and did nothing to disguise it. He had once viewed her as a potentially dangerous enemy, but one who could be handled and contained. That situation had changed. She had his daughter, and she had Ani. But he would find a way to get them back, even if he had to wage war to do it.

'Say what you have to say,' he told her, 'and then leave. I begrudge every moment I spend away from my child.'

'She will be well cared for,' said Syrene. 'She will make a fine addition to the Sisterhood.'

Not for long, Andrus thought. I will not lose her to the Marque.

Syrene stepped towards him. She placed a hand on his sleeve.

'What do you want from me?' asked Andrus.

'A kiss,' said Syrene. 'A kiss for a grieving widow.'

Andrus laughed.

'I would sooner kiss a serpent,' he said.

The tattoos on Syrene's face grew more vivid, and Andrus believed that, just for an instant, he saw them move independently, writhing like snakes. He looked into Syrene's eyes, and the flecks in her irises were like the light from distant dead stars. He tried to pull away from her, but he could not. Her mouth fixed upon his. He felt something probing at his lips, forcing them apart. He thought at first that it was her tongue, but then it began to separate, and there were tendrils in his mouth, probing at his palate and gums, moving inexorably towards his throat. He tried to pull away, but more tendrils were pouring from Syrene's jaws, wrapping themselves around his head, holding him in place.

Syrene's back arched. She breathed deeply into him, and his mouth was filled with dust.

CHAPTER 72

The door to the governor's office opened, and Syrene emerged. She barely looked at Syl as she pulled her veil down, masking her face.

'Go to your father,' she said. 'Say your goodbyes, for we leave tonight.'

Syl entered the room. Her father was seated at his desk. He looked dazed, but he smiled as she appeared.

'I have to talk to you,' said Syl. 'I have to tell you something important.'

'Syl,' he said. He stood and raised his arms to her. She came to him, and he held her tight.

'Syl,' he repeated. 'Everything is going to be fine. You understand that, don't you?'

She looked up at him. His breath smelled spicy yet sickly sweet, like the corrupted air in Dundearg as Gradus had begun to change.

And she knew.

'What was it you wanted to tell me?' said Andrus.

Syl began to cry. She tried to stop the tears, but she could not. She wrapped her arms around her father and buried her face in his chest. She cried and cried until she had no more tears left to shed, until her throat was raw and her body ached. She stepped back from him and knew that she would never allow him to hold her like that again.

'Just that I love you,' she said. 'And I'll always love you, no matter what.'

With that she left him, and went to her room to gather her belongings.

CHAPTER 73

Paul and Steven were seated side by side in the Military shuttle. Around them were other young men and women, most of them press-ganged into the service of the Illyri. They were as much hostages as recruits, and most looked frightened. There were others, though, who had clearly joined up willingly, anxious to escape their lives on Earth. Those who knew one another laughed and joked, or spoke too loudly about how hard and tough they were in order to impress the rest, but Paul could detect the tension behind their bravado.

Paul and Steven's mother had visited them earlier that day. Saying goodbye to her had been the hardest thing either of the boys had ever done. Their parting had shaken Steven badly, and he had spoken little since then, retreating into himself. Paul wasn't much better, but he kept a brave face for Steven's sake.

At the back of the shuttle sat a transformed Peris. He wore military green, and the return to his old uniform seemed to have changed him. He was no longer the slightly soft-in-the-middle castle guard of old; he had cast off that identity completely. He seemed at once more relaxed yet more threatening, as though this were his true vocation – to train, to fight – and he was comfortable in this skin. He caught Paul watching him, and gave a single swift nod.

Paul looked away. For reasons best known to himself, Peris had signed on to mentor them, and Paul was not sure how he felt about that, or even if he could entirely trust the tough soldier. His instinct said yes, but the Resistance fighter in him said no. There would come a time when he might have to turn against Peris, for Paul was intent upon returning to Earth, *his* Earth, and freeing it from the Illyri.

The Illyri, and the Others. The true aliens.

He thought of Syl. His fingers tensed against the armrests of his chair. This parting was only temporary. He would not relinquish her to the Sisterhood. They were meant to be together.

Steven startled him from his thoughts by speaking.

'What's going to happen to us, Paul?' he asked. His voice was very soft, and very frail.

'We're going to become soldiers,' whispered Paul. 'We're going to learn weapons, and tactics, and the art of war.'

'And then?'

'We're going to take what we've learned and use it to fight the Illyri,' he said. 'We're going to fight, and we're going to win . . .'

CHAPTER 74

In a darkened cellar in Glasgow, far from prying eyes, Meia sat before a mirror and prayed. She could no longer be who she was, not if she was to aid Syl and Ani and discover the truth about the Others. She had injected herself with anaesthetic, but what was to come would still be immensely painful, both physically and psychologically. She tried to tell herself that it was not important, that what mattered was what lay within her.

What mattered was her soul.

She took the scalpel from the tray, placed its blade beside her right eye, and slowly began to cut off her face.

CHAPTER 75

The sleek shuttle of the Sisterhood passed through the Earth's atmosphere with a shudder and entered the vastness of space. Syl and Ani stared at the lights of the stars and the lights among the stars, watching as one speck grew bigger and bigger until the lineaments and dimensions of the great ship were revealed. It was the *Balaron*, newly arrived through the wormhole, now waiting to take them to the Marque.

Syl and Ani wore the yellow robes of novices. All their carefully assembled possessions had been taken from them on Syrene's orders, and they were certain that they would never see them again. Syl had managed to find a moment to whisper to Ani of her suspicions about her father, although Ani seemed to have no such fears about Danis. She had told him nothing, though, just as they had agreed.

The horrors of the day of departure had produced only one bright spark of goodness, one reason for them not to feel entirely alone: Althea had returned, and just as Peris had offered to take Paul and Steven under his wing, so too Althea had announced that wherever Syl went, she would go too. Syrene did not object. Why would she object to Syl's pathetic, needy nursemaid coming along? Anyway, it was not unusual for the wealthier novices to bring a handmaiden with them to the Marque, and it often made the transition to the life of the Sisterhood less traumatic for all concerned. But Syl had found one more use for Althea on Earth before they left, for Ani had told her all about Althea's part in her escape from the castle.

'Can you get a message to the Resistance?' Syl had asked, as Althea helped her to pack.

'Yes,' Althea whispered, 'if you give it to me now.'

'Tell them to contact Meia,' said Syl. 'Tell her not to trust my father.'

And Althea, reluctantly, had passed on the message, even if she did not understand the reason for it.

Now she leaned across the aisle, and together she, Syl and Ani took in the immensity of the *Balaron*.

Syrene sat at the front of the shuttle, her widow's clothes already replaced by the red robes of the Sisterhood. The Archmage had not moved or spoken during the voyage. Ani had risked a peek at her, and whispered to the others that Syrene was meditating – although she herself would have called it 'communing'.

Meditate all you like, thought Syl. You think you've won, but this is simply the first battle. Just as an infection has spread through the Illyri, just as an unknown threat has anchored itself to the collective spine of my race, so too the Sisterhood is about to be infected by a secret enemy.

And I am that enemy.

Acknowledgements

The authors would like to thank Jane Morpeth, Frankie Gray and all at Headline; Emily Bestler, Judith Curr, Megan Reid, David Brown and the staff at Emily Bestler Books/Atria Books; and our agent Darley Anderson and his team, particularly Jill Bentley.

Physics of the Future by Michio Kaku (Doubleday, 2011) and *The Singularity Is Near* by Ray Kurzweil (Viking Penguin, 2006) were among the books that proved particularly useful and thought-provoking during the research and writing of this novel.

KATIE FFORDE

Love Letters

CENTURY · LONDON

Published by Century in 2009

1 3 5 7 9 10 8 6 4 2

First published in Great Britain in 2009 by
Century
Random House, 20 Vauxhall Bridge Road
London SW1V 2SA

www.rbooks.co.uk

Addresses for companies within The Random House Group Limited can be found at:
www.randomhouse.co.uk/offices.htm

The Random House Group Limited Reg. No. 954009

A CIP catalogue record for this book
is available from the British Library

ISBN 9781846057342

The Random House Group Limited supports The Forest Stewardship
Council (FSC), the leading international forest certification organisation. All our
titles that are printed on Greenpeace approved FSC certified paper carry the FSC logo. Our
paper procurement policy can be found at www.rbooks.co.uk/environment

Mixed Sources

Product group from well-managed
forests and other controlled sources
www.fsc.org Cert no. TT-COC-2139
© 1996 Forest Stewardship Council
FSC

Set in Palatino by Palimpsest Book Production Limited,
Grangemouth, Stirlingshire
Printed and bound in Great Britain by
CPI Mackays, Chatham ME5 8TD

To Ireland and Irishmen, this is for you!

Acknowledgements

To the lovely Laura Flemming, who really did organise a literary festival while a toddler, and was so inspiring.

To fellow writer Lesley Cookman for introducing me to the golden voiced Louise Cookman and incidentally, Lindy Hop.

To the wonderful Irish writers I met while doing an event over there, including Sarah Webb whose beautiful boots I also borrowed for this book.

To all the people who have unintentionally inspired me during the writing of this book. Some of you can't be mentioned for legal and embarrassment reasons, but if you read this, and are in it, thank you!

To all my wonderful agents! In no particular order, Sarah Molloy, Sara Fisher and Bill Hamilton. Thank you! Only you know how much I owe you!

To everyone at Random House. Kate Elton and Georgina Hawtrey-Woore for their wonderful editing, inspiring suggestions and infinite patience. Thank you!

To the behind the scenes people who do the work, but don't get the glory.

To Charlotte Bush and Amelia Harvell who are the best fun to go out with and give me wonderful treats (and parties!).

To the shameless marketing and sales departments who force people to buy my books, Claire Round, Louise Gibbs, Rob Waddington, Oliver Malcolm, Jay Cochrane and Trish Slattery.

To lovely Mike Morgan who took me on road trips for many years. So sad we won't be going again.

To Richenda Todd, who has protected me from myself for so many years, I am so grateful!

To the creators of my brilliant covers which I love! None of it could happen without you all, I'm so lucky to have such a brilliant team behind me.

Love Letters

Chapter One

❧

Someone murmured into Laura's ear, making her jump. 'So, what do you think of him?'

The bookshop was crowded: the area they had cleared for the reading was full; the queue to the desk of people clutching recently bought books was long and chattering enthusiastically. Laura had felt a post-Christmas event was a bit of a risk but now she was watching the people with a combination of relief and satisfaction. However carefully you prepared for a bookshop event you could never really tell until they turned up how many people would come. Nor could you be sure whether the author would perform well. Writing was a very private occupation and Laura often thought it was cruel to make them stand up on their hind legs before an audience. But even by her high standards this event was a success.

With all this in her mind, however, she hadn't noticed anyone coming up behind her. She turned round swiftly and saw a short, late middle-aged woman dressed in clothes designed to attract attention. Laura instantly remembered seeing her when she came through the shop door with the rest of the author's party. Her jacket looked as if it were made of tapestry and her jewellery could have been home-made by a grandchild with a welding kit, or by a hot new designer, it was hard to tell. The most startling thing about her close up was her intense, penetrating stare. She had eyes like green agate.

'Very good, of course,' said Laura, startled, but polite

1

as ever, feeling drab in her ubiquitous black trousers and white shirt.

This answer didn't seem entirely to satisfy the green eyes boring into her. 'And have you read the book?'

'Of course.' Laura was firmer now, indignant at the woman's combative tone. She worked in a bookshop. It was her job to know the stock.

A pencilled-in eyebrow was raised. 'No "of course" about it. What did you think?'

Laura opened her mouth to say 'wonderful' and then decided to tell the truth instead. She had nothing to lose now, after all: her beloved job was going to be taken from her – she might as well put aside her habitual tact and say what she really thought. 'I didn't think it was quite as good as his first but I will be really interested to see his next one.' She was an avid, enthusiastic but critical reader; she could tell when a writer wasn't on top form. Then pennies tumbled in her brain, like coins from a fruit machine when someone wins the jackpot. 'Oh my goodness, you're his agent, aren't you?' Embarrassment turned her from hot to cold and back to hot again.

The woman narrowed her gaze in acknowledgement of this fact, but Laura couldn't tell if she was smiling, or expressing disapproval – her mouth didn't move. 'I do have that pleasure, yes.'

Still blushing, Laura tucked a stray curl behind her ear and looked across at the young man who was now signing books for a long queue of fans. Every book-buyer, she noted, got the charming smile, each book a little personal message as well as a dedication. Not one but two publicists had come with him from his publisher's, and not just for crowd control, but because they adored him. Writers like him were rare.

It was because he had two young women only too eager to open the books at the right page, put them into paper bags and keep his wine glass topped up, that Laura was propping up a pillar; they didn't need her help. And Henry, the owner of the shop, had been firm. 'You set all this up, got all these people here, ordered the wine, opened the polystyrene snacks: take a break.'

'He's a star,' said Laura after watching him for a couple more moments. She wasn't buttering up her formidable companion; she was telling it as it was.

'I know. I'm Eleanora Huckleby, by the way.'

'I know – now,' said Laura, relaxing a little. Agents didn't often come to bookshop events, but Damien Stubbs was special. 'I'm Laura Horsley.'

'So, do you read all the books of the people who come and do events here? I gather this shop is – was – famous for the amount of them it puts on.'

'Yes,' said Laura, not wanting to say 'of course' again, and sound prissy. She felt she was prissy, in fact, but didn't want to advertise the fact. Although talking to this woman made her wish she'd had time to straighten her hair. She felt her rather wild ringlets belied her professional air.

'So how do you get so many members of the public through the doors and buying books?' Eleanora added, looking at the queue leading to the signing table. 'At this time of year, too. I've been to so many where only two men and a dog turn up, and they're staff. Not a single member of the paying public present.'

Laura recognised that sort of book signing; Henry had sent her to one when she first suggested having an event. She had been determined to do it better and had. The shop was fairly well suited to holding events, being big enough to be able to clear the right sort of space. She tried to have something on every month, so people thought of the book-shop as a place to come for a good night out.

'I have a huge database of our customers,' she said to her companion, 'and I hand-pick them. If I think they'll like the book I invite them personally. They almost always come. I also run a book club from here. Did run a book club from here.' She sighed as she corrected herself. 'I expect it'll go on when the bookshop is closed. I really hope so.'

'You sound like a treasure. I'm sure another bookshop will snap you up. It's so sad that this one's going. I suppose it's threatened by the supermarkets?'

Laura nodded. 'And Henry wants to retire.'

Eleanora Huckleby took a bottle of wine from the table and tipped some into both her and Laura's glasses. 'Even the wine is drinkable.'

'I'd love to find another bookshop, but it would have to be a quirky independent shop like this one,' said Laura. 'I'm not sure I could cope without all the autonomy Henry allows me. He's been great. Lets me order extra copies of books I think will do especially well, read all the proof copies, all the fun stuff.'

Eleanora snorted, possibly at the thought of reading proof copies being described as fun. 'I should think he's grateful someone wants to read them.' She paused, pressing her lips together in thought. 'So who do you think is the rising literary star?'

Laura raised an eyebrow. 'Apart from Damien Stubbs?' She indicated her companion's client, who was still signing and being charming.

'Yes. What do you think of Anita Dubrovnik?'

The fact that Laura rarely expressed her true opinions out loud didn't mean she didn't have them. Now, when she was about to lose her job and had a glass of wine in her hand, she decided to say what she thought. 'A great writer but lacks narrative thrust.'

The older woman's eyes narrowed in agreement. 'Who else have you read recently?'

'Bertram Westlake?'

The women exchanged speculative looks. 'Worthy but dull,' said Laura firmly.

4

'Oh God! Such a relief to find someone who agrees with me. I mean, there's some great writing in there but whatever happened to plot! OK, what about Janice Hardacre?'

'Well, I loved *The Soul-Mate*, but haven't liked any of her others.'

'Me neither. And that last one went on for ever.'

'It was shortlisted for a prize,' Laura pointed out.

'God knows why!'

They talked about books, tearing apart the current literary masterpieces and raving over the unsung heroes that sold under a thousand copies, until the more senior of the publicists came over and addressed Eleanora.

'Fifty books sold!' She turned to Laura. 'This has been such a good event. Henry told me you organised most of it. Brilliant! Thank you so much!' Then she turned back to Eleanora. 'We thought we'd push off to the restaurant now, if you're ready.'

'Mm. May I bring a guest?'

'Of course! I booked a huge table. Who do you want to bring?'

'Laura here.'

Laura, her habitual shyness coming back in a rush, felt totally thrown. 'No. No really, I can't come. It's terribly kind of you to ask me. But there's so much to do here.' Never in the three years she'd been organising bookshop events had she been to dinner with the author afterwards. Her place was in the background, making things happen. It was where she felt most comfortable. Talking to a whole lot of strangers was not her thing. 'I've got to help clear up. Wash the glasses, get rid of the chairs . . .'

'Don't move!' said Eleanora firmly and strode off in the direction of Henry.

'You'd better not move,' the publicist advised. 'She's known as the Vixen in the trade. Easier to do what she says, really. I'm Emma, by the way, Emma Bennet.'

5

'But I can't imagine why she would want to ask me to dinner.'

'Maybe she enjoyed your company?' Emma smiled, amused by Laura's incredulity at this suggestion.

Laura could see Eleanora, followed by Henry and her colleague Grant, coming over to where she and Emma were chatting.

'She's got reinforcements,' muttered Emma. 'You've got no chance.'

Both her boss and her colleague came to a halt.

'You know perfectly well none of this would have happened without your very hard work,' said Henry, who was tall, balding and distinguished-looking. If he hadn't been forty years older than her and married already, Laura would have fancied him. 'You go and have a nice dinner. You've earned it. Grant and I will clear up.'

'But really . . .' She bit her lip. Panic that she was going to be taken out of her comfort-zone, aka the bookshop, made her look urgently at her friend.

Grant, interpreting her expression, shook his head, determined that she should take this opportunity to mingle with people other than her colleagues for a change. 'That's right,' he said firmly. 'You go and enjoy the ball. Cinderella here will clear up after this one.' He put his hand on her forearm. 'Have a great time and tell me all the goss tomorrow. And don't forget, we're going to the Sisters of Swing gig tomorrow?'

'Oh yes.' She clutched at his arm for a moment.

'Go on! You'll be fine!' Grant, the only other full-time member of staff and her closest colleague, gave her hand an encouraging pat. He was on a you-must-get-out-more mission with Laura and was taking her to a club to hear 'an incredible new girl band'. He teasingly described her as his 'beard', which made her laugh. Nothing and no one could make Grant look anything other than openly

6

gay. But he did have her best interests at heart and she knew he was right and that she should go.

Now Laura had been officially dismissed – or in her eyes, abandoned – Eleanora grasped her arm. 'Show me where the coats were put and get yours. You'll need it. The wind is bitter!'

Instead of a coat, Eleanor had an item that looked like a cross between a hearthrug and a small tent. It enveloped the wearer in red, prickly wool: not a garment for the faint-hearted.

Seeing Laura's slightly startled reaction, Eleanora said, 'I always think I could camp out in this all night if I had to. And I can only wear it in deepest winter, or I sweat like a pig.'

Laura felt her own navy blue overcoat was pathetically drab. She'd bought it from a charity shop while she'd been at university and still hadn't worn it out. Alas, working in a bookshop didn't give one huge amounts of spare cash for clothes.

'Well, come along now,' said Eleanora. 'Take my arm. I can't really walk in these heels but I refuse to wear ballet slippers at my age. And lace-ups would ruin my image.' She looked down at Laura's shoes, which were almost completely flat. 'I rest my case.'

In spite of her disapproval of Laura's footwear, which was comfortable if unglamorous, Eleanora talked to her all the way to the restaurant, grilling her for her opinions of all sorts of books.

Laura read a lot. She lived alone in a tiny bedsit and her television was so small and snowy she didn't watch it much. But she read all the time: at bedtime, while she ate, while she cooked, while she dressed and while she brushed her teeth. She would have read in the shower if she could have worked out a method that wouldn't completely ruin the book. In the same way she could read anywhere, she could read anything, and if it was good, enjoy it. There wasn't a genre or an author that Eleanora quizzed her on that Laura didn't have some knowledge of. Still in the reckless mood engendered by losing her job and finding in Eleanora someone who cared about books as much as she did, she let herself speak her mind without holding back.

Eleanora was impressed. 'Darling! You're a phenomenon!' she declared. 'I'm so glad I've found you.'

At the restaurant Laura was introduced again to the young literary lion, Damien Stubbs. He'd said hello briefly when he arrived at the bookshop and had been as charming then as he was now. He thanked her for arranging such a good event and she muttered a few words of praise for his book. But he didn't seem to need reassurance. Confidence shone from him, and everyone around him basked in its warmth. He was the young writer of the moment and the world loved him.

Laura, who in the confusion of deciding where everyone should sit, which she took no part in, had an opportunity to wonder why she didn't fancy Damien Stubbs. Everyone else, men and women alike, seemed to. Several reasons occurred to her, but the one she felt most likely was that she didn't really admire his writing. When it was allocated to her, she took her seat gloomily. I'm a literary snob, she concluded. My emotions are more wrapped up in books than they are in real life. She felt slightly depressed and not only because she was about to lose what seemed the best job in the world. When had she become so boring? And was it too late to change?

While everyone else sat down, got up again, moved and then ended up back where they'd started, Laura had time for her life to flash before her eyes. Since university, which she had loved, she had only had two jobs, both working in bookshops. Once she'd joined Henry Barnsley Books she hadn't wanted to work anywhere else. Although she was usually shy in her personal life, she enjoyed

8

finding the right book for the right customer. She was popular with them. They asked for her if they wanted a book as a present and didn't know what to buy. Some of them asked her out on dates and sometimes, nagged by Grant, who'd worked at the shop longer than she had and so was her superior, she even went. But it never came to anything. If they enjoyed books and reading as much as she did they quite often had soup stains down the front of their cardigans. She might be a bluestocking bookworm, but she had some standards.

Eleanora handed her a menu. Laura hadn't noticed her sitting down next to her and felt rather cheered. At least she would be able to talk to Eleanora, or if not, sit in silence, observing the other diners, something she loved doing. She much preferred to be safely on the outside of life, watching, than deeply involved. Thankfully there was no one on Laura's other side.

'So dear,' Eleanora said later, and inevitably, Laura felt, 'any plans for your future? Do you want to be a writer?'

'Good God no!' said Laura and then, realising that perhaps she may be shouldn't have sounded so horrified, went on: 'Sorry, I didn't mean to be so vehement, but I would hate to be a writer. I love to get lost in other people's books, but I really don't want to write one myself.'

'Such a relief!' said Eleanora. 'I felt I had to ask, but I'm really pleased. Any other plans for gainful employment?'

'Not really.' She sighed. 'I've hardly had time to think about it, and I've got a couple of months before I'm on the dole. I'm sure to find something.'

'You don't sound very sure.'

Laura tried to make herself clear. 'I'm sure I won't starve – there are always jobs for willing workers – but it's unlikely I'll find anything book related, which I love so much. Not in this town anyway.'

9

Eleanora narrowed her eyes in thought. 'I might have something.'

Laura turned to her, not sure if she'd heard properly. 'Have you?'

Eleanora leant in. 'Mm, something frightfully exciting!'

Laura's little flicker of hope died. She didn't do 'frightfully exciting'. She wouldn't be right for the job. It would probably involve marketing, or starting a business from scratch – not her sort of thing at all.

'Well, don't you want to hear what it is?' Eleanora demanded through a slice of tomato and feta cheese.

Laura speared a black olive with her fork. 'Of course. It's so kind of you to take an interest.' She hoped Eleanora wouldn't hear her apathy.

'It is, actually,' agreed Eleanora, possibly slightly annoyed by Laura's lukewarm response. 'And if it wasn't in my interest as well, I wouldn't bother. Too busy. But what it is, is this!'

At that moment a phalanx of waiters descended on the table, whipping away Greek salad and taramasalata and replacing it with sizzling platters of moussaka, sinister fish dishes and more bottles of wine.

While all this was going on, Laura framed an elegant and polite refusal for whatever Eleanora might be about to suggest. She didn't think anything this brightly coloured parrot of a woman could offer her could possibly be up her street. They were too different as people.

'I want you to set up a literary festival!' Eleanora announced with the assumption that this would be greeted with clapping and shrieks of delight, as if she was a conjuror who had just produced a particularly endearing rabbit. 'Well, help set up one, anyway.'

Visions of the major festivals – Cheltenham, Hay, Edinburgh, with their phalanx of stars, many of them famous for something quite other than writing books – made her feel weak. 'I don't think—'

10

'But it's not just an ordinary lit. fest.' Eleanora flapped a heavily ringed hand as if it were boredom that made Laura doubtful. 'There's a music festival going on too. It's at my niece's house.'

'Oh. Big house,' said Laura. For a moment, her wayward imagination was distracted by the notion of a two-bed semi with a literary lion in one room and an *X Factor* entry-level band in another.

'Huge. A monster, millstone round their necks, but lovely, of course. They're trying to make it pay its way so they can keep it. The music festival should make them a bit, but my niece, Fenella, wanted a literary festival too, to make it a bit different.'

'I think there is a festival already that combines—'

'Doesn't mean they can't have one too, does it?'

'Of course not. I was just saying—'

'The music side of it is all going fine but they've got no one to take over the literary festival bit. You'd be perfect.'

Laura shook her head. She wasn't the right sort of entrepreneurial, feisty woman who could blag big firms into sponsoring huge events for ex-presidents who had written heavily ghosted autobiographies. 'I don't think so.'

'Why on earth not?'

Why didn't Eleanora – obviously a very bright woman – get it? 'Because I've never done anything like that before. I wouldn't know where to start!'

Eleanora took a moment and then lowered her voice and spoke slowly, as if to a bewildered child or a frightened horse. 'But, sweetie, you *have* done things like that before! What do you think a bookshop event is? You get the authors there, you get them to speak, you make sure people buy their books. Just the same!'

'But we don't have to make vast amounts of money out of the bookshop events, or hire a venue, or anything.'

11

'Look, I can tell losing your job has knocked your confidence. It would. But don't turn this down until you've had a proper think about it. Fen said there's some sort of meeting at Somerby – hang on, I'll tell you when it is.' Eleanora took a big gulp of her wine and then started burrowing in her handbag, which had a Mary Poppins quality: it was enormous and possibly contained a standard lamp. She produced a Filofax the size of a family Bible and riffled through the pages. 'Next week. Two o'clock. At Somerby. Do you know where that is?'

'No,' said Laura firmly, although a small part of her wanted to find out. Despite her reservations – and they were strong ones – she felt a flutter of interest. Anything to do with books had that effect on her.

'I'll get Fenella to email you some details. You are on email?'

'Well, at the shop.'

'You'll need a laptop. Better get one with your redundancy money.'

Laura inwardly bristled. She didn't like being told how to spend her as yet unspecified redundancy money. She might need to pay a gas bill or her rent with it.

Eleanora hadn't got to be a top literary agent without knowing how to read body language or how to get people to accept challenges. 'You might as well go to the meeting, at least. If your only other job opportunity is stacking shelves in a supermarket . . .'

Struggling to stick to her original reaction that running a literary festival was not what she wanted to do, Laura kept up her argument about practicalities. 'That's not my only job opportunity, and I'm working at the shop for the next two months!'

'What else are you going to find that involves books, except another bookselling job?'

'I do realise that I might have to broaden my search a bit but that's probably a good thing.'

12

'Do you want to move house as well as change your job?'

Laura visibly shuddered. Her tiny flat was not a palace but it could have been far worse and, more importantly, she could afford it. 'Not really, but I suppose I may have to.'

'Then far better quit while you're ahead. Run the festival for my niece and you won't have to move. You can live on-site, there's plenty of room. And I'm sure you'd be brilliant at it.'

'Honestly, I may be able to set up a reading in a book-shop but I couldn't do the other stuff – such as how to calculate how big a marquee I'd need for the events. There's nothing worse than a tent for two hundred and only twenty people in it.' Laura had experienced this for herself – she had nearly frozen to death.

'You won't have to do that sort of thing,' said Eleanora confidently. 'There are others who can do that. We – they – need you for your knowledge of books and writers.'

Trying to clamp down on the stirrings of interest this flattering statement aroused, Laura said, 'Will it pay well?' The answer was bound to be no and then she could just say no. Eleanora was the sort of woman who would understand this practical approach.

For once, the forthright Eleanora didn't instantly reply. Instead, she fiddled with her cutlery for a second. 'There'll be some sort of fee, I imagine. To be honest, I'm not sure exactly.'

Laura felt on solid ground at last, although she didn't find it as comfortable as she would have thought. 'Well, that settles it. I can't possibly afford to work for nothing.' She felt a little sad to have got out of it so easily, then shook herself. She didn't exactly get a king's ransom working in a bookshop, but at least it paid the bills and she couldn't be reckless and agree to something on the basis of an as yet unspecified fee.

13

'But you said! You've still got your job at the shop for the next two months! And all the big festivals are mostly run by volunteers.'

'I can't afford to be a volunteer, I need paid work,' she gently reminded Eleanora.

'As I said, you've got that!'

'But Miss—'

'Eleanora.'

'Eleanora . . .' she blundered on, not quite happy with calling this woman she didn't know very well by her first name. 'I'm paid to work in a bookshop. That means I have to be there, doing my job.'

'Oh, your boss will give you time off to run the festival! I'm sure he will! He seemed such a nice man.'

She was probably right about this, Laura acknowledged. Henry would be as helpful as possible and give her as much time off as she needed if it involved her getting paid work. But she wouldn't do it unless there was money involved. It would be gross foolishness and unfair to Henry. And when she thought of what her parents would say if she admitted to working for even less than she was currently earning, she reached for her wine for support. They still hadn't quite forgiven her for doing English at university instead of studying something that would give her a job that paid 'proper money'.

'All that student debt,' they had said, 'and you'll never be able to pay it off!'

When she'd told them that if her wages were so low she wouldn't have to pay it off, they weren't remotely impressed. Nor was she, really. She didn't like being in debt to the government but she still wasn't going to study to be an accountant.

'Just go to the meeting,' said Eleanora. 'If your boss doesn't want to give you time off, I'll speak to him. Once

14

you've seen the house and met my niece, you'll want to do it. I promise you.'

'I'd better not go then,' muttered Laura. Eleanora didn't hear, but then Laura hadn't intended her to.

Chapter Two

'So,' said Grant in the shop the next day, before he'd even got his coat off, 'did you sit next to the wunderkind?' They were in the stockroom that combined as a staffroom, in the basement of the building.

'Oh, you mean Damien?' As usual, Laura had got in early, and had finished the clearing up that Grant and Henry had promised they'd do, before going downstairs and putting on the kettle. 'No. He was surrounded by beautiful young women who worked in the publicity department.'

'Jealous?' asked Grant, tipping half a jar of instant coffee into a mug. He was the sort of person who always wanted to know how everyone felt. Laura often told him he should give up bookselling and become a counsellor – it would be his ideal job.

She shook her head, squishing her peppermint tea bag against the side of the mug with a spoon. 'No. Not my type.'

'So what is your type?' Grant poured boiling water on to the coffee.

'I don't know really.' Laura scooped out her bag and dropped it into the bin-liner she'd just put in place. 'I don't fancy many people.'

'You must have some idea. If I'm going to help you find a boyfriend, I must know what I'm looking for.'

Laura laughed. 'I don't want you to find me a boyfriend! I'll find my own if I want one!'

Grant made a face of utter revulsion as he sipped his

coffee. 'Of course you want one, darling, we all do. I just need to know the type. Pipe and slippers? Snappy dresser? Yoghurt-knitter-and-dedicated-recycler? Actual cycler?'

'I think the word you're looking for is cyclist.'

'You're such a pedant sometimes, Laura. And you must have some idea of your basic type.'

'Oh, I don't know.' They'd had this sort of conversation before and it never led anywhere. Although she had no particular ambition to end up a lonely spinster with the regulation cat, she did sometimes feel it was inevitable. She sighed. 'We'd better get upstairs. It'll be time to open soon.'

'No hurry.' Grant was rummaging in a tin of short-bread left over from the staff party. 'I need breakfast and everyone's at the sales, buying tat or taking back the tat they were given for Christmas.' He frowned. 'I see your mother is still giving you "slacks" for Christmas, and you're still taking them back?'

Laura glanced down at her new black trousers. 'My mother can't see why I'd rather wear clothes that need ironing instead of nice, easy-care polypropylene or some such. She doesn't understand about static and how it's just not cool to create sparks when you walk quickly.'

Grant laughed. 'It is in some circles, sweetie. At least mine has stopped giving me diamond-pattern golfing sweaters.' He gave her sweater a disparaging look.

'I know black is dull but clothes get filthy working here.' She gave a wry laugh. 'Maybe I'll have a nice nylon overall for my next job.'

'You and me both, ducky! Now are you going to open up, or aren't you?'

Laura went upstairs to the shop. Henry came through the door just as she was turning round the sign.

'Good morning, sweetheart,' he said, as he always did.

17

'How did you get on last night? Eleanora Huckleby's a piece of work, isn't she?'

'She certainly is. She—'

'Wants you to run a literary festival, I know.' He took off his hat and threw it deftly to a row of pegs where it obligingly landed. 'She phoned me. First thing.'

Laura was used to the hat trick but this was surprising. Henry wasn't a 'first thing' sort of person. It was, he claimed, why he wanted to run a bookshop. She felt instantly guilty. 'Oh goodness! I can't believe that!'

Henry shook his head, smiling down at her. 'She's not a top literary agent because of her lack of tenacity, that's for sure. So if you need time off for this meeting, you can have it. But if you do decide to go for it, and actually help set up the literary festival, I insist on providing the books.'

He was being so generous Laura couldn't help feeling a twinge of conscience. 'But supposing it isn't until after the shop is closed?'

'I'll still have my contacts, and I think a lit. fest. would be splendid fun!'

Was everyone determined to get her involved whether she agreed to or not? They certainly seemed to be conspiring to erase any possible objections she might have. She supposed she ought to feel grateful they believed in her so much. Now all she had to get through was her monthly visit to her parents.

'So how did it go?' asked Grant as he came through Laura's door barely an hour after she'd got back from what had proved to be the usual frustrating visit home. At least she had the thought of her night out with Grant to keep her going. He'd made a duty visit that day too, to his aunt's.

'Oh, OK, you know. Quiet.'

'You didn't tell them about the bookshop closing then?'

18

'No. I thought I'd wait until I'd got something else lined up. You know what they're like. My father might insist that I retrain as an accountant or a book-keeper. Did you tell your aunt?'

'Yup, but as she's not my mother I felt she could take it. She offered me some money if I wanted it.'

Laura smiled. Grant always went through agonies of guilty conscience when his aunt offered him money although he did sometimes accept it. 'So did you say yes this time?'

'Certainly not! I don't need it at the moment. If I'm out of work for ages I might say yes then.' He tutted. 'Don't look at me like that! I'm her only relation and she's loaded. She likes giving me money!'

Chuckling, Laura drew him into her flat and shut the door behind him. 'I know she does and I'm not the one feeling you shouldn't take her handouts. She's got more money than she knows what to do with and you're her only nephew. I don't think you should feel guilty at all. Hey! Why don't you ask her for a really big lump and you could open your own bookshop. Then we'd both be back in gainful employment!'

'What makes you think I'd give you a job?'

'Because I'm the best and you would.'

Grant sighed. 'OK, I would, but I wouldn't like to ask her for real money. She might need it for her care home or something. I'll be all right anyway. I don't mind working for a big chain.' His attention wandered from his possible next job to Laura's outfit. 'Sorry, sweetie, you can't wear that.'

'Why not? I thought I'd put on a skirt for once, look a bit smarter than usual. For our big night out.'

'Well, you look like you're dressed as a secretary in an am. dram. production of something with a secretary in it, only not as sexy.'

Laura was used to Grant's less than enthusiastic

reaction to her clothes. 'Thank you very much for your vote of confidence. I love you too.'

'Don't get huffy, you actually look nearly OK, only you need to wear something a bit fuller, or trousers.'

Laura threw up her hands to express her incredulous frustration. 'Usually you're trying to get me out of trousers! But actually I spilt something on my black ones at the restaurant yesterday, which is why I'm wearing a skirt.'

'I thought you had about five pairs of black trousers – six since Christmas?' It was quite clear how he felt about the working-woman's staple.

'All either dirty or too worn out to be worn out, if you get my meaning.'

Grant sighed. 'Enough with the puns. Have you got a skirt you can dance in?'

'I can bop about in this.'

'I don't mean bop about, I mean dance. Lindy Hop to be precise.'

'Why? We're going to hear a band. We don't have to dance in the aisles if we don't want to. It's usually voluntary.'

'But it's at a club. It's a Lindy night.'

Laura growled at him. 'Grant, why didn't you tell me this before I agreed to go? What is Lindy Hop anyway?'

'It's a dance. A bit like jive or rock and roll but with more moves. You'll find out, anyway. And I didn't tell you because I knew you wouldn't agree to go. Now I'm here I can manhandle you into something you can move in and into the car.'

The thought of Grant manhandling her into a pair of trousers made her relax and giggle. After all, clothes were not a big part of her life and she didn't really care what she wore. The whole Lindy Hop thing was a bit more of a jolt. Although she was perfectly happy bopping about in her kitchen, on her own, she didn't usually do it in public. On the other hand maybe it was time to do things differently. Grant had certainly been trying to get her to do so for long enough. 'You'd better come and look at my wardrobe then.'

'I was hoping you'd say that. And well done for not digging your heels in.'

'I would have done,' Laura confessed, 'but I'm not wearing heels.'

Grant groaned.

'But seriously,' Laura went on, 'the event the other night made me realise just how boring I am. I've got to open myself to new experiences.'

Grant nodded, obviously totally agreeing with her. 'But were you always boring, or is it only since you've been working in a bookshop?'

Refusing to be offended at his agreement that she was boring, she considered. 'I think I've always been what you'd call pretty boring. I had friends at uni, of course, but I didn't go out much, unless I was dragged.'

Grant tutted. 'Such a waste!'

'To be honest, it was such bliss not to be nagged at for reading so much, I just . . . well, read mostly, and wrote essays, of course.'

'And you say you had friends?' Sceptical didn't cover it.

'Yes! I was always there to take washing out of the machine, I always had milk, aspirin, and I could dictate a quick essay if one was needed at the last minute.' She chuckled. 'It really pissed me off if they got a better mark than I did, though.'

'They used you!' Grant was indignant.

'No. Well, a bit, but I didn't mind. And as I said, they did drag me out from time to time. We had a lot of fun together. I just mostly preferred to stay in and read than shout myself hoarse at a lot of drunk people.'

'What about boyfriends?'

'There were a few. They never really came to anything.

21

Grant, I'm sure we've been through all this when I first came to the bookshop and you gave me your standard interrogation.'

'Maybe, but it was obviously all so boring I've forgotten. And I don't interrogate people. I'm just interested in the human condition.'

'You mean nosy.'

'Well, OK, nosy. Now let's look in here.' He pulled open the door of her small wardrobe, expecting the worst. 'Laura, are all your clothes black or white?'

'Pretty much. I've got my summer clothes in a plastic bag somewhere. Here.' She withdrew it from the bottom of the wardrobe. Grant emptied it on to the floor as if he were sorting laundry.

'You should really let me come round and go through all this for you,' he muttered, tossing garments behind him like a picky burglar.

'I would if you were more like that Gok person.'

He stopped. 'I thought you never watched television!'

She laughed, pleased by his surprise. 'I don't but I went round to one of the book group women with a copy of that month's book and she had it on. She persuaded me to stay and watch it. Very brave, all those women. Fancy sitting in a shop window naked?'

'I can think of worse fates actually, but I can see for you it would be torture.'

In the end he found a tiered bo-ho skirt in cream broderie anglaise, a black V-necked cardigan and a tight black belt. 'It's quite sweet but still very monochrome,' he said. 'Where's your jewellery?'

Laura opened her dressing-table drawer and revealed her few bits and pieces, mostly presents from university friends, and a pearl necklace left to her by an aunt. Grant sorted through it dismissively.

'What about scarves, belts, things like that?'

They were stuffed in with her knickers but he rifled

through them until he found a scarf that had been round a sun hat Laura had bought through necessity, the last time she'd been on holiday with her parents, several years ago.

'Here.' He tied it round her neck. 'It looks nice, but your hair needs to be in a higher ponytail. And it needs an iron.'

'What, my hair? I know, the trouble is straightening it—'

'Not your hair! I like that curly, frizzy look, it's cute. No, I meant your skirt! Have you got an iron?'

She nodded, and put on a smug expression. 'Another reason I had friends in my student house was I had an iron and knew how to use it.'

'No wonder you won Miss Congeniality three years in a row.'

Laura giggled. 'How do you know I didn't? I was popular. Sometimes people prefer someone who's a bit quieter.'

'Who could iron.'

Aware she wasn't going to convince Grant that her university days weren't spent reading and ironing her friends' clothes, or if they were, she'd really enjoyed them, she said, 'My mother used to get me to do all the ironing.'

'It's a useful skill,' he said, refusing to be sympathetic to this potential tale of childhood cruelty. 'I'll do it while you do your hair.'

'You're terribly bossy,' Laura objected, getting out the ironing board.

'I know. It's why I'm the manager of the shop and you're not.'

'I'm not sure having one full-time assistant and a couple of part-timers makes you the head of a vast empire . . .'

'Of course it does. Now hurry up, we don't want to miss the first set.'

Laura's efforts with her hair meant that while the bulk of it was in a fifties-style ponytail, there was still a lot of stray hairs, giving her a dark gold aura round her head. 'It's not very tidy.'

'It's not supposed to be tidy! It's supposed to be a bit laid-back. You don't have to look like Sandy in *Grease*.'

Laura stopped trying to smooth her hair. 'Grant, I don't mind dressing the part but I'm not actually going to do Lindy Hopping. You do know that, don't you?'

Grant smiled at her. 'Come along. It's going to be a great night.'

Together they walked down the road to the minicab office. Grant was going to sleep on Laura's sofa that night so he could drink.

'I hope it's not the sort of place where you have to get legless just to get through the evening,' said Laura.

'Have you ever been legless?' Grant demanded.

'Not often, no,' said Laura meekly. 'I really am boring!'

The club was already full and buzzing when they arrived. They made their way down the steps to the basement and Grant paid. A band was playing wonderful old numbers that made Laura's foot tap even though she'd sworn she wouldn't dance.

Grant bought her a glass of wine and put it into her hand. 'Let's see if we can find somewhere to sit, before the girls come on.'

'The girls', he had reminded her on the way, were the band called the Sisters of Swing he'd been bending her ear about for the last couple of weeks. They sang traditional swing numbers and Grant was very keen to see them live.

Laura followed Grant as he headed for a cluster of tables and chairs, taking in what was going on around her. All sorts of people, wearing quite a variety of clothes, were dancing hugely energetically. Slipping easily into her favourite role as observer, she found the crowd fascinating. There were young men dancing with much older women and young women dancing with older men, not (she felt sure) because anything was going on between them, but because they could both dance well. Age was no barrier; dancing was all.

Grant found a couple of seats and they sat down, Laura unable to stop watching the play that was going on around them. Every so often someone from the stage issued instructions to 'freeze' and then say if it was the men or the women who should choose new partners. Laura was fascinated.

'Look at the shoes!' said Grant, indicating a pair of brown and white corespondent shoes.

Once they'd spotted the first pair, they realised women were wearing similar shoes, only with heels and T-bars. There were what even Laura knew as jazz shoes, ballet slippers (they looked a bit vulnerable), character shoes, and ordinary street shoes.

'This is fun!' said Laura, surprising herself.

'Glad you can recognise "fun"!' said Grant and then his complacency fell away. 'Oh God, we may actually have to do this.'

Laura turned to where he was looking and saw a determined girl coming towards Grant. Highly amused at the thought of her gay friend being swept off by a young Amazon, she didn't spot the man heading towards her. Before she knew what was happening she found herself pulled to her feet. Her potential partner was about her age, with curly hair and eyelashes to match. He was wearing baggy trousers and a striped cotton shirt, braces and a pork-pie hat on the back of his head.

'Hi!' he said. 'What's your name?'

'Laura! But I'm only here for the band!'

'So, dance?'

She shook her head, from habit as much as anything. 'Oh no, I said, I'm only here for the band.'

'Nonsense. Come on!'

Laura found herself getting to her feet at the insistence of her partner. At first she could only stand, bemused, but then some dance lessons, given by a friend of her mother's, years ago, came back to her. She began to enjoy the feeling of flippancy and fun the music and the dancing gave her. Her partner didn't seem to care that she was more or less making it up as she went along. She found herself whirled around, held, pushed away, brought back again, all in minutes. When she was allowed to sit down again she was exhausted. 'Thank you so much! That was such fun.'

'You should come more often,' said her partner. 'You've got real talent!'

'I don't think so. I really—'

'—only came for the band,' he finished for her. 'I know. I'm Jim, by the way. I'll look out for you next time.' Although she eventually managed to persuade him to leave, which he did with a tip of his hat, she had enjoyed the feeling of being chosen and danced with.

'Well, that was a turn-up for the books!' said Grant, as they both sipped wine, wishing it was water. 'We both pulled! And I never thought I'd see you on a dance floor, being hurled about by a strong man.'

'Back at ya!'

'Mine wasn't a strong man, more's the pity. I did tell her I was gay, but she said she knew already.' He paused. 'I think the band's going to be on soon. Better get to the bar quickly.'

Laura, recognising her cue, got to her feet. 'More of the same?'

He nodded. 'And a pint of tap water.'

There were a few more energetic routines, which Grant and Laura sat out, mainly to give their feet a rest,

26

and then three girls came to the front of the stage. They were wearing very full tulle skirts with tight waists and fitted bodices. They all had amazing pink beehive hairdos and the one in the middle had a huge flower behind her ear. They looked fantastic and for the first time that evening, people stopped dancing and turned towards the stage.

'We were lucky to get a seat,' said Grant, and then the lights went down and the singers were spotlighted.

They started with 'The Boogie-Woogie Bugle Boy' and everyone stamped their feet and clapped in time to the music. Several upbeat numbers followed and, in spite of the fear of clapping at the wrong moment that always afflicted her, Laura cast off her inhibitions and clapped and hand-jived with the best of them.

And then the tone quietened right down and the lead singer, the girl with the flower behind her ear, began to sing 'Smoke Gets in Your Eyes'. She followed this with something equally sad and romantic, sending Laura into an unaccustomed mood of nostalgia. She began to think about her own love life, now long in the past. There had really only been one possible serious contender. Why hadn't it ever got any further than a couple of drinks and a snog that didn't go on long enough for him but was as much as Laura could stand? Either she was too young, or she just hadn't loved him. She could barely remember his name.

While her mind was free-ranging she found herself thinking how one thing subtly changing, such as her getting notice from her job, could set in train other small changes. She still had her job, she wasn't out on the street, but since hearing the news that she was going to lose it, she had spoken to Eleanora far more freely than she would have done normally, and she had been asked to help run a literary festival. Then, coming here with Grant, instead of just listening to the band, she had got up and danced and really enjoyed herself. There was probably a scientific name for it, like the theory that said a butterfly flapping its wings in Brazil caused a hurricane somewhere else very far away. Perhaps she should just accept her fate and go with the flow, as Grant would say. Going to the festival meeting didn't mean she actually had to agree to help run it, after all.

'Are you all right, chook?' asked Grant, when the band had gone back into a dance number and people took to the floor once more with abandon. She was still staring thoughtfully at the stage.

'Oh yes. I'm fine.'

'Another drink?'

'Would you think I was awfully sad if I said I just wanted to go home?'

For once Grant accepted this without comment but in the cab back to her flat he said, 'You've gone all thoughtful on me. Have you been thinking about the literary festival thing?'

'Yes. Yes, I have.'

'And?'

'I think I'm going to go to the meeting, anyway.'

'Good for you! You see? A bit of Lindy Hopping and you're a changed woman!'

Chapter Three

Laura was wearing her interview suit, which was now a little tight over the hips. It was the day of the meeting. The entire bookshop was rooting for her, possibly anxious, she suspected, that she would back out. Henry had given her the afternoon off, ordering her to use it wisely, and Grant had offered her the use of his car. Now, Grant came round the back of the shop with her, to help her get it out.

'I haven't driven for ages, Grant,' said Laura, suddenly nervous about it. 'The last time was when I was staying with my parents and Dad wanted me to drive back from a restaurant.'

'And you didn't hit anything?'

'No, but it was my home patch! I could have driven those roads blindfold on a bicycle!'

'All roads are much the same really. And you've had your practice run.'

Laura nodded. 'I know.'

'I just wondered if blind panic had wiped your memory.'

She shook her head, trying to dislodge the blind panic that was washing over her with alarming frequency. 'It's only natural to be nervous. This is a big deal! I don't go to meetings and before you say anything, I don't count what we all do when we get together in the staffroom. That's quite different.'

Grant did his best to be reassuring but as she'd been fretting all week, he was obviously getting just a bit tired of it. 'Just take some deep breaths, you'll be fine.'

'But supposing this Fenella woman is just like her aunt? Scariness is bound to run in the family!'

'Laura dear, are you like your parents? No. I rest my case.'

'But genetics don't always work that way.'

'So Fenella will be a perfectly nice woman. She sounded nice on the phone, didn't she?'

'Yes, but—'

'But nothing. Just get in and drive, girl!' he said. 'It's insured for any driver. And you're insured if I've given you permission to—'

'I'd feel happier if I had a letter saying you've given me permission, or something.'

'Oh for goodness sake! You're far too law-abiding! Go to your meeting and tell us all about it when you get back. Remember, you don't have to agree to anything if you don't want to but I'll want to know why! Now, here's your route.' He handed her some sheets of paper. 'This one's off the computer, and this is mine. Here's the map Fenella faxed through.' He paused. 'You've got a sleeping bag, an ice axe and a boxful of emergency rations in case you're stranded overnight.'

Anxiety had slowed her reactions and it took her a nano-second to realise he was joking. She pushed his arm and got into the car. Then she hooked her curls back behind her ears and turned the key. Grant patted the roof and she was off.

She found she liked driving his little Fiat Punto. It was light and nippy and she soon forgot to worry about handling it. Now it was only getting lost she had to concern herself with. Fenella's map looked perfectly straightforward but as she got nearer, all her nervousness came back and she started muddling up left and right. But at last, after a brief unscheuduled detour around the village, it was before her, on a hill, as described in the directions.

Somerby was a truly lovely house. Surrounded by pasture, currently grazed by a few picturesque horses well rugged up against the winter cold, it looked like a calm, benign being surveying the countryside it presided over.

Although it was still early afternoon, the January day was thinking about closing. The leafless trees stood out clearly against the pale sky and a faint glow from the sun lent a soft glow to the scene, as in an old oil painting.

Laura, who had stopped to double-check she had the right place before going up the drive, took a few moments to enjoy the picture. Some days in January, she always felt, teetered between the melancholy of winter and the optimism of spring. This matched her own feelings: sadness about losing her beloved job, but a stirring of hope at the prospect of something that might be quite exciting. She just had to be brave enough to take the leap. She spent a few moments enjoying the view, wondering just how courageous she was.

Then she noted the several cars drawn up in front of the Georgian façade and glanced at her watch, worried that she was late. In fact she was exactly on time, her watch confirmed this, but she liked to be punctual – early, Grant called it – and turned the car into the drive.

She found somewhere to park it and then, when she could put off the moment no longer, got out. Up until this point a meeting to her meant an informal event held in the staffroom of the shop and consisted of Henry, Grant, the part-time staff and her discussing things. There was no agenda and everyone said what they wanted to say and no one wrote anything down. It worked fine. Laura knew this was going to be different. It was likely to be extremely nerve-racking – if she had any nerves left to rack, that is; she was nearly all racked out simply from the journey!

The doorbell jangled and the door opened swiftly on

a tall young woman with blonde hair, wearing a Cavalier shirt, velvet trousers tucked into fabulous pale green suede boots that nearly reached her thighs and a worried expression. Spotting Laura, she smiled and looked slightly less concerned. 'You must be Laura Horsley?'

'Yes. Am I the last? I got a bit lost towards the end.'

'No, there's still another couple of people who aren't here. Come in.' She closed the big oak door and ushered Laura into a large hallway with a sweeping staircase. Laura tried not to feel too intimidated. It was all so grand.

'I've heard such a lot about you from Eleanora,' the woman went on. 'Isn't she terrifying?'

'Well . . .'

'Heart of gold, of course, but tough as old boots in some ways. She thinks very highly of you and she's very perceptive.'

'Oh no, now I'll have to live up to her expectations!'

The woman chuckled. 'I'm sure that won't be a problem. Do you want the loo or anything or shall I take you straight upstairs where the meeting is being held? I'm Fenella, by the way. It was my mad idea to have a festival here.' She glanced round to check that Laura was following her up the staircase. 'The trouble with having such a massive house is that it's very expensive. It has to earn its keep and if we need to do more renovations – and we always do – we have to do something big. We mostly do weddings. Here we are.'

She opened the door to a room with floor-to-ceiling windows and, Laura guessed, fantastic views. There was a huge table in the middle with chairs all round. Most of the chairs were occupied; voices bounced off the parquet floor as people chatted animatedly. Laura licked lips that had suddenly gone dry, certain she would never be able to open her mouth in such circumstances.

Just as Fenella was about the introduce her, the

32

doorbell jangled and she gave Laura a worried look. 'Do you mind if I answer that? Sorry to abandon you.'

'No, not at all, I'll be fine,' said Laura, feeling anything but fine.

One young woman, who seemed somehow familiar, had looked up as Laura entered and raised her eyebrows in greeting, waving her fingers. 'Another girly,' she called across the table. 'What a relief!'

Laura hadn't ever thought of herself as a 'girly' before and found she rather liked this new status. She waved back.

'Find an empty chair,' said Fenella. 'Here, between Rupes and Johnny. They'll look after you. Rupert is my husband. Johnny is a friend. Now I must answer the door.' She hurried off, adding to the sense of bustle and busyness that filled the room.

Both men smiled in a friendly way and Rupert, in jeans and an old tweed jacket, got up and pulled out the chair for Laura. She sank on to it, wondering how soon she could go home. There was no way she could make a useful contribution at a meeting like this. She would just sit quietly and listen. Johnny, in black jeans and T-shirt with a cashmere scarf looped round his neck, poured her a glass of water and wrinkled his eyes at her in greeting. He was young and had an earring that looked to Laura very like a hearing aid. As almost everyone else apart from Fenella and Rupert, but including Laura, was wearing some sort of a suit, he seemed like welcome light relief.

'Is Hugo coming?' called Rupert as Fenella returned, followed by an attractive young woman carrying a bundle of files who apologised for being late, but oozed efficiency in spite of it.

'No. He's working.' The young woman took a seat and arranged her papers into neat piles in front of her, making eye contact with everyone.

33

She seemed to epitomise everything Laura was not; she was outgoing and utterly confident. She has a nice smile, Laura thought, and she can't be much older than me, but I'm still scared of her.

'Right,' said the man sitting at the head of the table, 'shall we start?'

Everyone shuffled and coughed in agreement.

'I suggest we go round the table introducing ourselves, and saying what our role is in all this,' he said. 'Fen, maybe we could have name badges?'

Fenella looked horrified for a moment until the woman who had arrived last said, 'I've got some!' She pulled out a packet. 'You will have to write on them yourselves, though,' she added. 'I couldn't do them beforehand because I wasn't sure who was coming.'

'We don't usually do meetings like this,' murmured Rupert. 'I prefer the kitchen table and a few bottles of wine.'

Johnny, to whom this aside was addressed, laughed. 'Mm. I know. I've been to a few like that.'

Rupert smiled at Laura to include her in this conversation but it didn't help much. The delay while people found pens and wrote their names postponed the moment when she'd have to introduce herself to a room full of strangers, and was very welcome. But she'd have to do it eventually, and to think up a role for herself, when she didn't think she had one.

She caught the eye of the girl who'd said hello and she made a face in solidarity. Laura raised her eyebrows back and wondered why she felt she recognised her.

'OK,' said the man at the top. 'I'm Bill Edwards, I'm going to keep us all in order. Let's go to the left.'

'Sarah Stratford,' said the woman who'd produced the badges. 'I'm here because Fen thought I'd be useful. Not sure if I will.'

'You've been useful already,' said Fenella. 'Producing name badges.'

'If we could press on,' said Bill Edwards, sitting down hard on any inclination to chat.

'Sorry,' muttered Fenella. Laura felt the man was being officious. It was Fenella's house, and her festival, she should be allowed to at least open her mouth.

'I'm Dylan Jones, representative of Alcan Industries.' He sounded as if giving presentations to hundreds of people was all in a day's work for him and he made Laura feel she should have heard of Alcan Industries, although she hadn't.

'Monica Playfair,' said the self-confessed 'girly'. 'Here to liven things up!' She made it sound as if her role was vital. She raised her eyebrows conspiratorially towards Laura who allowed herself to smile back.

'I'm Tricia Montgomery, I'm here on behalf of Eleanora Huckleby.' Tricia sounded confident and smiled at the table full of people. 'She couldn't come.'

Laura couldn't decide if she was glad Eleanora was involved or not. And why hadn't Eleanora mentioned her assistant was coming? Still, if she didn't have to work with her directly it might not be too bad. Tricia seemed a lot less daunting than her boss.

'I'm Fenella Gainsborough. Eleanora Huckleby is my aunt, and this festival was my mad idea to begin with.' Fenella said all this in a rush, as if confessing her sins at a self-help group.

'Jacob Stone,' said the man on Fenella's right. He just stated his name and didn't try and engage with his audience.

'I'm Rupert Gainsborough – also responsible for the mad idea.' Fenella smiled across at him, obviously grateful for his support.

It was her turn now. She cleared her throat and thought of Grant, egging her on. 'I'm Laura Horsley and I'm not sure why I'm here, really, but I was asked to come, so I did.' Although she knew that Grant would have been

35

ashamed of her, she couldn't really say that Eleanora Huckleby had felt she could make a contribution.

'Johnny Animal. I'm in charge of the music side of it. Getting artists, stuff like that.'

'Stage name,' muttered Rupert.

Well, he may have a silly name and be very young but he had an air of huge confidence about him, thought Laura.

Now everyone had introduced themselves they began chatting again. Sarah dished out pads of paper; people who hadn't done so before wrote on their nametags. Bill Edwards looked around, fearing he'd lost control already, coughed and tapped his water glass.

'May I declare this meeting open?' he said.

'If you must,' muttered Johnny to Laura and she smiled.

'Now,' he said, 'we're all here?' He looked around eagerly. He obviously loved being in control of a room full of people.

Everyone nodded.

'So, can we have a report on the music side?'

Several people began to speak. Bill held up his pad and waved it until they stopped. 'Please, one at a time, and through the chair please!'

Johnny Animal looked confused for a moment and then said, 'Do you want me to tell you about the music side?'

'Yes please,' said Bill, writing hard.

Laura wondered what on earth he could be jotting down and noticed similar wonder on Sarah's face.

'Not sure how to speak through a chair, but we've got some quite big names booked – or nearly booked. It's always quite hard to get people to commit.'

'Isn't it just?' muttered Monica, who received a frown from the chairman in reply.

'So who have you got – Sorry . . .' Rupert looked at

36

the chairman. 'Mr Chairman, may I ask which bands have actually agreed to come?'

'The Caped Crusaders,' said Johnny. There was silence when he obviously felt there should have been applause, or at least approving murmurs. 'They appeared at Glastonbury last year?'

'Oh yes,' said a few people as their memories kicked in. Laura decided she was probably the only person there who had never been to Glastonbury. Well, her and Bill Edwards, anyway.

Johnny mentioned a few other bands and it transpired that the music side of the festival was beginning to take shape. Laura drew roses on her pad of paper, determined to apologise to Fenella as soon as possible, and say she couldn't run the literary side of the festival, not if it involved speaking through the chair at meetings like this.

'So,' said Bill Edwards when he'd filled two sides of A4 with notes and Laura had quite a pretty pergola going, 'what about the literary side?'

Fenella cleared her throat, looking anxiously at her blank pad and then at the chairman. Laura stopped doodling, feeling instantly nervous as if the question had been asked of her directly, even though she wasn't involved yet and probably wouldn't be.

'Shall I do this bit?' said Sarah, much to Laura's relief.

'Oh please do,' said Fenella, subsiding into her chair, also with obvious relief.

'As you all may or may not know, this was Fenella's idea and it's brilliant! So many people wouldn't go near a music festival but add big literary names and they'll come in droves. Think of Cheltenham, Edinburgh, Hay-on-Wye.'

'I'd rather think of Glastonbury,' muttered Johnny Animal, and received a dig in the ribs from Fenella.

'It's a huge potential market,' went on Sarah, 'but what

37

we need is a sponsor.' She looked round the room, smiling in a way that invited people to volunteer. 'Bill?' She looked expectantly at the chairman.

'I'm just here to keep order, as a local councillor,' he blustered. 'I'm not saying I won't get the council to sponsor an advert or a small event, but I can't spend the ratepayers' money, or at least not much of it.'

Something about Sarah's manner told Laura this didn't greatly surprise her. Sarah turned her attention to Tricia Montgomery. 'We need top-class authors, to attract a lot of people.'

Laura remained silent, taking it all in. If they had Tricia's expertise and Fenella in charge surely they wouldn't need her, she reasoned.

'I'll do my best, of course,' said Tricia. 'As a top-class agent' – she made a face – 'Eleanora does have all the right contacts. She could probably get Damien Stubbs to come and Amanda Jaegar—'

'Who?' asked the chairman, speaking on behalf of many.

'Shortlisted for the Orange,' said Laura automatically, forgetting she didn't want to draw attention to herself but she just couldn't help it. They were on her territory after all. 'Should have won it last year, lots of people felt.'

Tricia smiled at her. 'And Eleanora felt . . . we were rather hoping that Laura here would be able to get us authors we can't lean on.'

Laura dropped her pencil in panic when she realised everyone was looking at her and cursed herself for piping up about Amanda Jaegar. That was what happened if you were a know-all. 'I'm really not sure . . .' she said. 'I mean . . . I have no experience—'

Sarah interrupted her smoothly. 'Shall we just discuss what we'd like, who we'd like, give ourselves a dream scenario and then see how near we can get to that?'

'She's a wedding planner in her day job,' muttered Rupert.

'She seems very efficient,' said Laura, thinking with relief that with Sarah on board, she really wasn't really necessary. She could make her excuses and leave. They'd manage just fine without her.

The discussion went on, not really achieving anything until Fenella got to her feet. 'Right! Teatime! Down to the kitchen everyone. I've got sandwiches and cake and scones and it's all got to be eaten.'

There was a moment's 'politesse' and 'this meeting is adjourned' from Bill and then a stampede. Laura found herself next to Monica on the stairs.

'Boring or what!' Monica said. 'I think it'll be great when it actually happens but until then – God!'

'It's weird, but I really think I recognise you,' said Laura. 'Are you on telly?'

'Not often. I'm in a band.'

'Oh!' squeaked Laura. 'Now I know why I recognise you, only you haven't got pink hair! I've seen you on stage! You were brilliant!'

'Where did you see us?'

Laura told her about the venue. 'Just a couple of nights ago. I loved it!'

'Oh great! Nice to meet a fan. We're appearing at this festival. Johnny got me in. Something a bit different for the punters. And I said I'd help out too if they needed me.'

'Maybe you could do something in the literary bit as well. You know, someone – an actor – reading a bit of a book and your band singing an appropriate song.' Then Laura remembered she wasn't going to have anything to do with the festival and therefore shouldn't have ideas. Although she had to admit she was beginning to feel getting involved might not be such an impossible thought after all.

'Great!' said Monica. 'That sounds cool! Something like Philip Marlowe would be fab! We could do a really sleazy, smoky number to go with it. We could have fake smoke to get the nightclub atmosphere.'

It did sound rather good, but as they had reached the ground floor and the stairs to the kitchen were too narrow to chat on, Laura didn't feel obliged to explain she wasn't the one to talk to about it.

Fenella, or someone, had put on a wonderful old-fashioned spread, in the best traditions of cricket clubs, the WI – in fact, anywhere where sandwiches and cake might be comforting. There was an urn providing tea and a big jug of coffee.

'This is amazing!' said Laura when she found herself next to Fenella. 'I thought I might get a stale Rich Tea if I was lucky.'

'When I've got lots of people coming, I like to barricade myself in with food. I didn't make all this, though, only a few of the cakes. The dogs will eat anything that's left over. I've shut them all away, because of the meeting.'

Johnny spoke with his mouth full, holding a laden plate. 'If I have my way, the dogs won't get anything. If you weren't married already—'

'I wouldn't marry you, but thank you for the offer,' said Fenella, laughing.

Tricia Montgomery joined the little group that was forming next to the Aga, away from the table. 'Eleanora tells me you've read everything, and that you put on a fantastic reading for Damien,' she said to Laura. 'I wonder if he would come? He likes literary festivals.'

'That would be brilliant,' said Fenella, scribbling on a napkin. 'What's his surname?'

'Stubbs,' supplied Tricia. 'But Eleanora was really impressed with you, Laura. She said she'd never met anyone so well read, so young.'

'Oh well . . .'

Her self-deprecation was ignored. 'It's not often someone who works in a bookshop has such a wide knowledge of contemporary literature,' went on Tricia, to Laura's huge embarrassment.

'Oh,' said Fenella, 'I don't get nearly enough time to read but what do you think of Anita Dubrovnik? I know she's the novelist of the moment – like every other book group in the country, we're reading her latest.' She paused. 'And I know I won't have time to finish it.'

Laura laughed. 'I run a book group at the shop and I always tell people they should come even if they haven't read it. They can often ask questions that really get the discussion going.'

'I don't think I can trade on that for ever,' said Fenella. 'So? Could I have a cheat's guide?'

Laura found herself giving potted reviews of all the latest bestsellers and, unusually for her, content to be the centre of attention. It must be the relaxed atmosphere of the kitchen, she thought, away from all that forced formality upstairs.

Jacob Stone, who hadn't really opened his mouth up to this point, came over to their group. He was short and stocky but had presence. People seemed to listen when he spoke, and as he didn't, often, it made an impact when he did. Now, holding his mug of tea and with a piece of cake in his other hand, he said, 'Do you know Dermot Flynn?'

'Oh yes!' said Laura, genuinely keen. 'He's brilliant. He was—'

'Get him to the festival and I'll sponsor it – however much money you'll need,' said Jacob Stone, cutting through her rush of enthusiasm.

Laura swallowed, her mouth suddenly dry. This man thought she actually knew him. He was possibly her favourite writer, ever, but she didn't actually know him, any more than she actually knew Shakespeare, however

41

many essays she'd written about him. She had to explain. 'Um—'

'Oh, that would be marvellous!' said Fenella, not noticing this small interjection. 'I can't tell you how grateful we'd be. Basically we can't do this without a sponsor and – well, it's hard to get them,' she added, suddenly looking a little sheepish.

'And I was the only millionaire you knew?' said Jacob Stone.

'Yes, frankly, but we'd be terribly thrilled—'

'If Dermot Flynn is there, I'll be proud to support it.'

'But—' Laura tried to break in. Now everyone seemed to think she knew him. She had to put a stop to this. 'I don't—'

'He's one of Eleanora's. Utterly charming but almost impossible to manage.' Tricia Montgomery had the look of someone who really wanted to be outside smoking a cigarette. 'You won't get him to the festival unless he really wants to come.'

'I didn't mean I knew him as a person,' said Laura, getting her word in at last. 'I meant I know his work. I studied him at university and think he's utterly brilliant.'

'Oh he is!' agreed Tricia. 'But he's an *enfant terrible*. As I said, can't be managed and we think he's setting a record for lateness on his latest book. It's *years* past its deadline.'

'As I said, I want him here,' said Jacob Stone, his tone brooking no argument. 'And without being mean, if he's not, you'll have to find another sponsor.' Then he turned and walked away.

Everyone inhaled at once and then they all started talking at Laura who wanted to put her hands up to her face and hide. She managed to keep from doing so by sheer effort of will.

'If you could get him, it would be such a coup,' said Tricia. 'Every opinion-former in the literary world will

42

come. I know there will be lots of other writers but no one's seen him for years. It would be amazing.'

'Oh please, Laura! I beg you! Do try and get him! We need the money. God knows who we'll get to be a sponsor if Jacob Stone doesn't cough up!' said Fenella. 'We wouldn't have approached him if we'd had a choice, he's so eccentric.' She turned to Laura, slightly accusing. 'You said you know him!'

Had no one been listening to her? she thought with frustration. 'I know his work! Like Shakespeare!' she squeaked.

'Now that really would be a coup,' said Rupert, winking at Laura, 'getting Shakespeare along.' He put a fairy cake into her hand.

'Isn't he supposed to be rather gorgeous?' said Monica.

'Who, Shakespeare?' asked Fenella.

'No! Dermot Flynn!' said Monica.

They all regarded Laura, as the official Dermot Flynn expert. 'He was when he was young, going by the pictures,' Laura admitted, wondering if people would stop expecting things from her if she stuffed the cake into her mouth whole.

'And Eleanora told me he's doing a little festival in Ireland at a place called Ballyfitzpatrick,' said Tricia, taking a fairy cake from Rupert and unpeeling the paper.

'Oh,' said Monica, sounding surprised.

'I think he lives there,' Tricia explained. 'And I don't think it's really literary, just some people who are friends who've got together to put something on,' she went on and then bit into her cake.

Laura saw her way out. 'Oh well then, you just need to get Eleanora to ask him to come to this one. It'll be small and friendly, he's bound to say yes.' She passed the buck with both hands.

Tricia gave a hollow laugh. 'But how to get in touch with the man? He doesn't open letters, or email, or answer his phone, or ring back. I told you, he's an absolute nightmare!'

'So how did you find out he was doing this festival?' asked Monica. 'If he doesn't communicate?'

'Eleanora was looking for something else and it came up on the Internet. It's Irish music, poetry, food, stuff like that.'

'It sounds great!' said Monica, full of enthusiasm. 'But who has a literary festival in winter?'

Fenella ignored her protest as she addressed Laura. 'You'll just have to go there and ask him to come here,' she said. 'If that's the only way we'll get him.'

'Fab idea!' said Monica. 'I'll come with you. We'll have a great time!'

Just for a second, Laura was tempted. Monica was such fun, her confidence and zest for life were infectious. And it was her singing that had made Laura do some serious thinking. For whatever reason, she felt a bond. Then she got a grip on reality. 'You don't seem to under-stand—'

'But you've arranged loads of literary events at your bookshop?' said Fenella, sounding indignant.

'Yes,' Laura tried to explain, 'but when I did that, I wrote polite letters via the publisher or agent. It was the publicity department who decided whether or not they came and when they came. It was all down to them. I didn't have to visit the writers in person!' She turned to Tricia for support, feeling things rapidly sliding out of her control again. 'Who are his publishers? Get them to ask him.'

'He's been out of contract for years, and if he doesn't respond to Eleanora, who's a tough cookie, believe me, he wouldn't take any notice of the publicity department.'

'That's my aunt you're talking about,' said Fenella, 'but you're right, she's very tough.'

'So you need to go to Ireland and bring him back,'

said Monica. 'Like a Canadian Mountie who always gets his man.'

The ridiculousness of the situation got to Laura and she started to giggle. 'I'm not a Mountie, or even a Labrador. I don't do fetching.'

'But it would be such fun!' went on Monica, laughing too. 'I'll come with you! It'll be a riot!'

Fenella seemed to sense Laura teetering; going anywhere with Monica would definitely be different. 'Oh God, thank you so much!' Shamelessly, she played the guilt card. 'I can't tell you how much this means to me. And we'll obviously pay for you to get there . . .'

'But supposing I go and he refuses to come?' Although still chuckling, Laura was feeling the pressure badly.

'At least you'll have done your best,' said Tricia.

Monica struck an attitude. 'Good God, girl! Do you think he'll be able to resist? Irish men are all awful womanisers. He'll be made up to do anything for us!'

'Just say you'll give it a go,' said Tricia. 'Maybe Jacob Stone would still sponsor the festival if you've done your absolute best.'

Fenella shook her head. 'Don't think so. He's a man who means what he says.'

'How did he get to be a millionaire?' asked Tricia, which pleased Laura because she didn't like to ask herself but really wanted to know. She was glad, too, that the conversation had finally veered away from her.

'Industrial diamonds,' said Fenella. 'And he's just as hard.'

'So how did you get him to come to the meeting?' Tricia was obviously intrigued.

'Well, he's connected to Rupert's family in some way and although he didn't go to university himself or anything, he's a great fan of literature. Reads the entire Man Booker shortlist every year, stuff like that. He was the natural choice when we were looking for a sponsor.'

She turned her gaze on Laura. 'Which is why it's so important you get Daniel O'Flaherty or whoever it was.'

'Dermot Flynn,' said Laura and sighed.

Monica had decided. 'We'll go to Ireland and get him.' She paused, looking at Laura. 'I'll give you free tickets to our next gig if you agree.'

Laura regarded Monica thoughtfully. The tickets would be a good present for Grant, and she owed him something for lending her his car. 'So why are you so keen?'

'I really want to go.' She paused. 'I've got a bit of unfinished business over there.' She hooked her arm into Laura's in a friendly way. 'And it'll be fun, for feck's sake!'

Everyone laughed as she broke into an Irish accent.

Laura felt she'd fought her hardest and could fight no more. She put her hands up in surrender. 'OK, I'll do my best. But I'm not making any promises.'

Fenella leant forward and hugged her. 'You're a star! Thank you so much! I'll get Jacob Stone to pay for your fares.'

'A free holiday in January,' said Laura. 'In Ireland. How can I resist?'

Chapter Four

'It's awfully kind of you to come with me,' said Laura to Monica as they waited in her Volkswagen Beetle – a car she declared suited her image as a singer in a forties band – to get on the ferry. 'Especially at this godforsaken hour.'

It was half past two in the morning and they were very tired.

'It means we can drive in daylight the other side,' said Monica. 'And I wanted to come. You'd never have gone on your own even if you could have got there and I told you, I have my own reasons for going. Besides . . .' Monica paused. She frowned a little as if thinking how best to express her thoughts. 'There's something about you I like. I think if you came out of your shell a bit you could be jolly good fun.'

Laura laughed. 'Some people think I'm quite fun in my shell.' Grant was probably the only one who qualified, even if he was also trying to get her out of it, but she felt she ought to protest a bit about Monica's backhanded compliment.

'I'm sure, but I think you'd be a lot more fun if you mentally came out from behind the counter of a bookshop.'

'Have you been talking to my friend Grant?' she asked suspiciously.

Monica laughed. 'No. I haven't met him yet.' A man came out of the shadows and beckoned them forward. 'Thank goodness, it's our turn now. I hope they don't put us on a shelf somewhere. Technically called the swing decks.' She moved the car gently forward.

'How do you know so much about ferries?' asked Laura, glad she didn't have to plunge the car into Stygian gloom and interpret the hand signals of men wearing fluorescent jackets walking backwards at speed.

'I used to drive the band round in an old van,' said Monica, coming to halt at the end of a chain of vehicles. 'Ferries are no problem.'

Fenella had insisted that they booked a cabin, even if only for a very short time. Jacob Stone was paying, after all, and he could afford it. Whether or not he would demand his money back if they returned empty-handed, so to speak, had yet to be discovered.

'We'll think of something to tell him when we meet up for our first proper meeting,' Fenella had said casually. 'As long as you try your best, it won't be a problem.' Then her insouciance had left her. 'You do realise we have to get Dermot Flynn to confirm as soon as possible? Otherwise we'll have to find not only another literary superstar but another sponsor, and God knows where we'll find one of those.'

Laura had nodded. 'We can only do our best but we will do that, I promise. But if I can't get time off work, Monica will have to go on her own.'

However, she was not going to get out of it that easily. Henry practically pushed her out of the door.

'It's a quiet time after Christmas and I can always give Brenda a few more hours if we're busy.'

With that excuse not to go denied her, she went to see her parents, feeling it was time they knew about her imminent redundancy. She and Grant discussed the visit before she set off. This was one of the things that bonded them: Grant's aunt had never heard of homosexuals and Laura's parents still berated her for going to university, getting a good degree and ending up working in a shop. The fact that it was a bookshop made no difference.

'Still, we've got our night out to look forward to,' said Grant, who had once brought Laura home to meet his aunt so he could appear to have a girlfriend.

'Yes, and my mother will send me home with a fruit cake because in her heart she thinks I'm still a student.'

'Hmm. I might have overdosed on fruit cake over Christmas, but bring it anyway.'

Her parents greeted her in their usual understated way. They were pleased to see her, but her monthly visits did disrupt their routine rather.

'Hello, dear,' said her mother, kissing her. 'Supper won't be long. You go and watch the news with your father and I'll call you when it's ready.'

'I'll set the table for you, Mum,' said Laura, feeling a wave of love for her mother. She might often feel like a cuckoo in the nest, but she knew her mother had done her absolute best for her. It wasn't anyone's fault that Laura had always been so different from her parents.

'You don't mind eating in the kitchen, do you?'

As she filled a glass jug with water Laura wondered why on earth her mother might think she'd mind. It was a 'kitchen-diner' and they always ate there.

'I hope I'm not so much a guest as you feel we should eat in the dining room.' Laura found the place mats in the drawer and distributed them.

'Well, we don't see you all that often.'

'I know and I'm sorry, but it's not always easy for me to get here.'

Her mother pursed her lips. 'I'm sure you could get a job in a bookshop a bit nearer home.'

'Well, yes. Actually I've got a bit of news. But I think I'll wait until Dad's here – save me going over it all twice.'

'I can't believe you're gallivanting off to Ireland when

49

you should be looking for another job!' her father had declared a little later, putting down his knife and fork to lend emphasis to his words.

'This literary festival could be a great opportunity,' Laura said quietly. 'You've always said I was wasted working in a bookshop. They were impressed by my knowledge of contemporary literature.'

This only set her father off on a familiar rant about English degrees and a 'knowledge of contemporary literature' being a complete waste of time. Her mother hadn't been too thrilled by it all either. Laura had left as soon as she possibly could, glad she'd arranged to meet up with Grant later.

Grant loyally took the opportunity to reiterate what a chance this was for her.

'You need to spread your wings, have new experiences! I know you think you just want to find another bookshop, just like Henry's, and bury yourself in it for ever, but you mustn't! You must follow your dreams! Which are?' he added, to check she actually had some.

Laura took a breath. 'Well, I've always wanted to work for a publisher really, as an editor. I don't suppose this festival is going lead to anything like that, but it has opened my eyes to other book-related opportunities.'

'Fantastic! Let's have another Baileys to celebrate.'

Thus, just over a week later, Laura and Monica found themselves on a ferry to Ireland.

Monica and Laura were now sitting in a café in the little fishing village on the west coast of Ireland that was the venue for the 'Festival of Culture' they had come to see. They'd been travelling, give or take a few stops, some hours in a ferry and a catnap in a lay-by, for approximately nineteen hours.

'I don't think I'll ever eat again,' said Monica, looking at her empty plate with disbelief.

'Well, we won't need to eat this evening, that's for sure,' said Laura. 'Now I know what the difference between an English breakfast – high tea, whatever – and an Irish one is: size.'

'And those scrummy potato pancakes.'

'And the black and white pudding.'

They both leant back in their chairs and drained their mugs of strong tea, sighing with pleasure and feeling a little more human again.

'I never thought we'd get here,' said Laura. 'It feels as if we've been travelling for days.' She yawned. 'I'd only just got off to sleep when it was time to get up again.'

Monica was dismissive. 'At least it wasn't rough, and I think the time in the bar got me in the mood for Ireland, all that singing, fiddle-playing and the drum thing. And sleeping together has made us practically best friends.'

Laura laughed sleepily. 'Mm.'

'Being on the road together really does bond you.'

Laura nodded agreement. 'We could make a movie.' Monica was right, they had got to know each other very well, and luckily, the more they discovered, the more they bonded. They'd been up half the night chatting too. She yawned widely. 'I think we should check into the bed and breakfast and have a nap.'

'Then we'll fall asleep for hours, wake up at midnight and not be able to get off again. I know, I've done that. No fun at all.'

'OK, let's check in, then go for a walk or something.'

'Actually,' said Monica. 'I wouldn't mind getting the car checked out. Its steering has gone a bit funny. It probably would be all right, but if there is a garage it would be silly not to have it looked at.'

'Oh goodness! Of course you must get it checked out. Will there be a garage here that can deal with antique cars, though?'

'Of course. It's not that old. I'm sure there's nothing

much wrong with it. I'm just a bit nervous about breaking down far from home. We had some grisly times in the van, I can tell you.'

'I can imagine,' said Laura, slightly relieved that Monica, who seemed so well travelled and super-calm, had some normal neuroses.

'The bed-and-breakfast people will know,' said Monica.

'I hope it won't take us too long to find it,' said Laura.

'Oh come on,' said Monica. 'How hard will it be to find in a place this size? It's tiny!'

'I know. I can't make out why they're having the festival based here, and not in the town five miles up the road. And why is it so popular we could hardly find a place to rest our heads?' Resting her head was a high priority at the moment.

'Perhaps it's that writer the sponsor is so keen on. Maybe he's bringing them in in busloads.'

Laura shrugged. 'Well, we certainly travelled quite a way to come and see him, although we do have an ulterior motive. But it is a charming place, isn't it?'

They looked around at the brightly painted houses, the cars parked all higgledy-piggledy and the fishing boats tied up in the harbour. It wasn't conventionally pretty, but it had great character.

'Mm,' agreed Monica, 'and if it has a garage I'll think it's even more charming. Let's get going!'

As Monica predicted, the bed and breakfast was not hard to find. It was a bungalow, tucked behind a hedge to shield it from the road, not that there was any traffic of note. The landlady was one of those useful people who imparted information without you having to ask for it.

'Good afternoon girls, I'm Marion,' she said cheerily. 'Come in, come in. Would you like a cup of tea now? Come into the kitchen. You're here for the festival? I expect you're wondering why we have it in January.'

She paused for breath. 'Fact is, the place is heaving in summer. It's a real tourist spot, but there's nothing going on in the winter, so they thought they'd have a festival of some kind in Patricktown – you know? Up the road?'

Laura and Monica nodded and took seats at the big wooden table.

'Well – is it builders' tea you like? Or I've got Earl Grey, Lady Grey, any amount of herbals, White tipped China—'

'Builders' tea please,' they said in unison.

'But Himself said – that's your great writer man, Dermot Flynn – he said he wouldn't go to a festival he had to travel five miles to, and so they have it here. It's grand for business. Now, have you had tea – I mean proper tea, not just a cup of tea in your hand?'

'Yes, we had an all-day breakfast at the café.'

'He would have given you a grand big Full Irish, didn't he?'

'He did, only we saw a girl.'

'Oh yes. She's my niece. A lovely girl.'

Accompanied by constant, amiable chat, the girls were escorted to their room. It was, Monica declared, a picture.

'I've never seen anything so fantastically kitsch in my life! It's a fairy palace!' she said once their landlady was safely out of earshot.

'And all in mauve,' agreed Laura, slightly less enthralled. 'I don't think there's anything that could take another purple frill if its life depended on it.'

Monica bounced on one of the single beds. 'Comfy. What's the bathroom like?'

'Mauve,' said Laura, peering into a little room adjacent to theirs. 'Even the loo paper is mauve. But it seems to have everything, including a bath.'

Her yearning for one must have been audible because Monica said, 'Why don't you sink into it while I sort the car out? Then we can either go out or just stay in and watch television.'

By the time Monica came back the television was watching itself with Laura lying on top of one of the twin beds in a mauve towelling robe, fast asleep.

'There's nothing like an early night for making you feel like exercise!' said Monica, sounding uncharacteristically Brown Owl-ish.

Laura sipped the tea Monica had brought to her bed. 'So you didn't wake up at one in the morning then?'

'Nope. And the sun is shining, and as the days are so short, we should get out there and enjoy it!'

'Did you manage to get your car sorted?'

'Yup! A sweet man is going to sort it out today. It won't be ready until tomorrow but I've had a brilliant idea how to spend our time.'

Laura hadn't known Monica particularly long but she saw Ulterior Motive written all over her. 'How?'

'While I was finding the garage I passed a bike-hire place. They don't get much custom in the winter so they've let me have two at a bargain rate.'

'Bicycles.'

'Yes!'

'Did you notice that we came down a long hill to the village? Wherever we went would involve a long hill up.'

'It's good exercise.'

Laura hid her smile behind another sip of tea. She'd find out what the ulterior motive was soon enough. 'OK then.' Knowing Monica as she felt she now did, Laura suspected it was a man.

'Anywhere particular you want to go on your bike, Mon?' she said a couple of hours later, when, full of Irish breakfast, including several pints of tea, they pushed their bikes up the hill, out of the village.

The bike-hire place had given them a map, helmets and reflective clothing, none of which were particularly attractive but though all very practical. The map was rather creased but Monica had inspected it closely before they set off.

Monica didn't answer. 'The trick when you're cycling is to calculate the distance at about two miles an hour and then multiply by three. It usually works out about right if you add half an hour.'

'I haven't ridden a bike for years.'

'That's fine. You never forget how to ride a bicycle,' said Monica. 'It's just like—'

'Don't tell me,' grumbled Laura as she clambered on to the saddle, 'riding a bicycle.' She pushed on the pedals and moved forward a few feet, wobbling slightly. 'I'm not sure I'm going to be able to cope with the hills.'

'You'll be fine.'

'I will be if you tell me what you're up to. I'm not expiring with a heart attack without knowing why.'

Monica allowed herself to pant for a few seconds. 'One of the reasons I was so keen that we should come to this little hole in the hedge was because it's bang next door – well, a bike ride away – to another little hole in the hedge I really want to visit.'

'Because of a man,' Laura stated.

'Did I tell you that or did you just guess?'

'We may only have been best friends for quite a short time but I think I know you well enough to work that one out.'

Monica tried to look offended, but not very hard.

They stopped talking while they climbed a few more yards. When it flattened out a bit and Laura had more breath to spare she said, 'You did give me a bit of a clue. You said you had unfinished business at the meeting.'

'Did I? Well, yes, and he's called Seamus. He's a real doll. I met him at a gig last year. We exchanged emails and postcards for a while and then I just stopped hearing. I want to find out what's happened to him.'

For all her efficiency and practical nature, Laura had a strongly romantic streak. She may not have had much of a love life herself but she'd read a lot of romantic fiction at an impressionable age. 'So were you really in love with him?'

'No, not that. Obsessed, probably. He was tall and dark with blue eyes.' Monica's halted her bicycle for a minute so she could think better. 'Let's just say he's on my To Do list.'

'How do you mean?' Laura was confused. She was beginning to perspire and she wondered if it was affecting her brain.

Monica shrugged. 'Well, you know.' She paused and checked out her friend who was a few feet behind her. 'Haven't you a To Do list?'

'Frequently, but it doesn't have men on it.'

'Doesn't it? Mine's only got men on it.'

Laura felt suddenly envious. Not for Monica the mundane 'washing', 'ring home', 'buy loo cleaner' type of list that kept her life on track. Hers probably started with George Clooney and worked its way down through Harrison Ford to Jeremy Clarkson. 'But you're not in love?'

The idea was obviously ridiculous. Monica laughed. 'What is it with you and love? No! I want to find out if he's as good in bed as he looks. Laura, why are you looking at me like that? Have you never fancied the pants off anyone?'

'No,' she panted. 'Not really.' She took a little run up the hill, trying to catch up with Monica who was taller and obviously a lot fitter.

'What, never? I just couldn't sleep with anyone I didn't really lust after.'

There was a tiny pause before Laura said, 'Nor could I.'

Monica pressed on cheerfully. 'That's all right then. But I don't think it's right to sleep with someone just because they're there, or you need a lift home or something.'

'I wouldn't know,' Laura muttered. 'I'm a . . .'

'Hang on.' Monica stopped suddenly and turned round. 'Are you telling me what I think you are?'

'I don't know. I hope not.' Laura was panting when she came level with her friend and regretting her momentary need to confess something she wasn't exactly ashamed of, but did make her a bit unusual and possibly strange. Monica was looking at her curiously.

'When you say you wouldn't know, does that . . . Are you – a virgin? I mean – have you never gone to bed with a man?'

'I do know what being a virgin means.'

'And are you one?'

Monica didn't seem to be judging her. 'Yes,' Laura admitted, embarrassed. It wasn't so much that it was wrong to be a virgin but it was odd. She wiped her brow, so she didn't have to see Monica staring at her.

'How old are you?' Monica wasn't staring but she did seem curious.

'Twenty-six.'

'Wow!' said Monica, impressed. 'And you've waited this long!'

'I wasn't waiting, it just didn't happen.'

'Well, I think it's sweet,' said Monica after a pause. 'Weird but sweet.'

She set off up the hill again and Laura fell in beside her. 'It's no big deal,' said Laura. 'But I do think it would have to be the right person for me.'

'Of course,' said Monica uncertainly. 'I think it's lovely that you don't just sleep around like I do.'

'Do you?' Monica was obviously what her father would

describe as a 'goer' but she didn't appear to lack the normal morals, either.

Monica shrugged. 'Well, not really, but I don't hold back, if you know what I mean. I'm always very careful, always use a condom, make sure I like the guy a bit, and it's not only that I want to get into his pants.' She paused. 'But your way is better, I'm sure.'

'It wasn't a deliberate policy.'

Monica was thoughtful. 'Or maybe you could do a lot worse than sleep with a friend, sort of get it over with.'

Laura shook her head. 'I'm not being precious about it, but being a virgin doesn't really interfere with my life. Besides, my best friend is gay.'

'Oh, Grant? Well, maybe you'll meet some other nice man who'd be nice and safe to do it with.'

'Maybe,' said Laura. But however weird still being a virgin made her feel she didn't think she'd want to deal with the matter so pragmatically. It had just sort of happened that way and she'd never felt the need to get rid of it just for the sake of it, like a outmoded piece of furniture.

Laura walked most of the three miles to the little village they were heading for, but she was looking forward to being able to coast all the way back down to Ballyfitzpatrick. It had been a long time since she'd taken so much exercise but in spite of being aware of her unfit state she was enjoying the sensation of all her muscles working and felt exhilarated and energised.

'You must admit, the views are absolutely stunning!' said Monica, who was used to cycling and, unlike Laura, panting only slightly.

'Oh yes, it's amazing.'

They were standing on a cliff, gazing out to sea, re-gathering their energy before going to hunt out Monica's Lust Object. The sun sparkled like diamonds on the little waves. The sky was pale blue and seemed to glint with potential frost. The grass on the clifftop was close-cropped, green still, although it was winter. Behind them was a row of whitewashed cottages. When Monica had stopped sweating, the plan was that they were going to knock on the door of her potential lover. Laura was planning to stay and enjoy the view but she hadn't told Monica that yet. She wasn't sure how'd she'd take it.

'Actually,' said Laura. 'I might lie down.'

She did and it was wonderful. Her long walk uphill had made her warm and the sun on her cold face made her think of summer. Maybe this trip wasn't a wild-goose chase, and if it was, maybe it was fine just to have fun. Grant was always saying she took life too seriously. Well, maybe she'd stop doing that and just go along for the ride. Although maybe he wouldn't appreciate arranging cover for her absence from the bookshop just for her to have a little winter sun.

Monica lay down next to her. 'Oh, this is rather blissful, isn't it? If I told the girls in the band that I'd spent half a week lying on a clifftop in Ireland, in January, they'd think I was mad.'

Laura chuckled, watching a bird cross the sky through half-closed lids. 'Don't you think they know that already?'

'Mm, probably.'

'It's funny, all the people I know think I'm incredibly sensible, except for my parents, of course,' said Laura sleepily. 'You should have heard my father when I told him I was coming to Ireland. He thought I should spend any time off I had looking for another job.'

'Well, you are in a way. The festival is another job.'

'Hm. Not exactly well paid.'

'I'm not being paid at all. Although I don't mind. They're giving the Sisters of Swing a really good spot at the music festival and this –' she indicated the crisp winter day around them '– is just a jolly.'

59

'I don't think my parents would ever understand the concept of "a jolly".'

'Jaysus, they should be grateful you've got a job and aren't living off "the burroo".'

'You've got very Irish all of sudden. What the hell are you talking about?'

'It's what they used to call benefits over here. A man on the ferry told me. And I'm practising. I may go home with a leprechaun.'

Laura chuckled. 'Personally I prefer my men a little taller.'

'Huh! I didn't think beggars could be choosers!'

'I'm not a beggar, I'm just looking for Mr Right.'

'Big mistake. Mr Right Now is far better. Take it from one who knows.'

Laura laughed. There was something about lying on one's back in the sunshine that made one inclined to laughter, she discovered. When Monica finally decided she no longer looked like a scarlet woman in all the wrong ways, she ordered them both to their feet. Laura had forgotten about leaving Monica to her embarrassing errand, and got up. They brushed bits of grass off each other's backs, picked up their bikes, and headed on into the village.

The village was postcard pretty, with its whitewashed cottages around the cove. Not for this village the garish colours of Ballyfitzpatrick – here there must have been rules, but the effect was delightful. Even in January it looked like the perfect holiday destination. The cottages were no longer thatched and the boats in the harbour were all modern but there was a man sitting mending nets in the sunshine.

'They pay him to look picturesque,' said Monica.

'He does his job very well,' said Laura. 'He looks perfect.'

'And if we can't find Cove Road, we can ask him, but

I think it's all Cove Road, so it's just a case of finding the right house.'

It was surprisingly straightforward, only, on the doorstep, the ridiculousness of the whole thing hit Laura and she got the giggles. 'Oh God, Monica, I'm so sorry, I can't do this. You'll have to do it on your own.' She could hardly speak. 'It's just so silly! We've ridden bikes, for goodness' sake, to meet a man who may not even live here. We're grown women, not thirteen-year-olds!' She went off into another fit of laughter and crossed her legs, just in case.

'Really, Laura, I thought you were the sensible one of us! I'm flighty, you're sensible: those are our roles. We must stick to them.'

'I'm sorry,' Laura spluttered. 'I just can't knock on the door and say, "Can Seamus come out to play?" I just can't! And I can't stand behind you while you do it.' She swallowed, took a deep breath and got a grip at last. 'Tell you what, we'll get the bikes out of sight at least. I'll look after them, and you can do this on your own.'

'Don't be silly!' Monica was indignant. 'How sad will that make me look?'

'Not much sadder than if we're both here, me giggling and both of us holding bicycles as if we're kids from school. What are you going to say anyway? "We were passing so we thought we'd drop by?"'

Monica humphed in irritation. 'Well, why not? It's true!'

'No it's not. We cycled bloody miles, we were not "just passing".' She sniffed, found a bit of old tissue, blew her nose and then said, 'But I've stopped giggling now, so go ahead, look a fool. I'll look one with you.'

'Thanks, Laura, you're a good girl.'

Monica lifted the knocker and banged hard. There was no answer. 'Well, now what do we do?' she said after a minute and another knock.

'Write your mobile number on a bit of paper and post it through the letterbox. Although you may have to write a short essay reminding him who you are,' said Laura.

'Not at all! He'll remember exactly who I am, but the mobile number's a good idea. Oh, do you think it'll work in Ireland?'

'Mine did. I phoned the shop while you were in the Ladies.'

'Don't you mean *Mna*?'

'Oh, shut up and write your note. I want to get back to the b. and b. I may need a bit of a lie-down before tonight.'

She was briefly aware of a flutter of anxiety and then dismissed it. She was enjoying herself and didn't want any nerves about the coming evening to spoil this delicious feeling of freedom.

'Lightweight,' muttered Monica, writing.

Laura's giggliness continued for the journey home even though she was now exhausted.

'I'll never ride a bike again,' she said as they finally made it back to the b. and b. 'In fact, I don't suppose I'll ever sit down again comfortably.'

'Shut up moaning. It was downhill all the way.'

Their landlady provided a huge plate of sandwiches with a monster teapot full of strong tea. They ate every scrap and drained the pot. The sandwiches were followed by two sorts of cake, both home-made, both utterly delicious.

'I can't believe we ate all that!' said Laura as they tottered from the dining room back to their room. 'I'm going to need some indigestion tablets or something.'

'Good idea,' said Monica. 'Top tip: before a big night out, take a Zantac, stops you throwing up afterwards.'

Laura paused, her hand on the bedroom door. 'We're not having a big night out, Monica,' she said. 'We're going to worship at the feet of a great writer and persuade him to come to our literary festival. Throwing up is not on the To Do list.'

Monica laughed, obviously not convinced. But now it was nearly upon her, Laura suddenly felt the weight of responsibility for securing Dermot Flynn. It was her mission. She so wanted to make a success of this project. Helping with the literature festival was her first foray outside the bookshop since she'd left university. If she failed she'd feel less able to attempt any other new challenges. And she had personal reasons for wanting to meet Dermot Flynn and get him to the festival: he was her favourite living writer. How would she feel if he was a complete show-off, happy to rest on his early laurels? Seeing a man in the flesh you'd worshipped through his writing for years was a risky business!

After much discussion, the girls had decided to dress down, in jeans and sweaters. Monica added a cashmere pashmina for warmth for the walk to the venue, Laura a cheery but unstylish scarf an aunt had given her for Christmas one year.

The event, as Laura called it, or the gig, as Monica referred to it, was in the only large building in the village and any doubt they might have had about finding it was dispersed by the streams of people making their way to it, many of them clearly coming from the pub.

'I can't believe how many people are going!' said Laura, daunted. 'It would be amazing if we could get a crowd like this for him in England. If so many people come this far to see him, imagine how many might come if he was on the mainland.'

'Absolutely! Not all these people can be locals.'

But then pessimism descended. 'But if he won't do an event practically next door, he's not going to come to our festival, is he? Even if I can get near enough to ask him.'

'Don't give up! And you want to see him anyway, don't you?'

Laura agreed that she did. She had butterflies in her stomach at the prospect although they weren't all good ones. She had so loved his books – there were only two of them – at university that she had practically learnt them by heart. And the author photograph in the back was stunning: a mean and moody young man in a black T-shirt. While her contemporaries were in love with band members, Laura used to gaze at the photo of Dermot Flynn.

The trouble was, that was years ago, and the photo hadn't been new then. She still loved the books and felt that in them was some of the tenderest, most erotic writing she had ever read, before or since. What she was dreading was that her hero had turned into a fat and balding has-been, trading on the bright young talent he once had.

Still, she thought as she and Monica joined the throng, if this had happened, it would be sad, but not heart-breaking. What was slightly more desperate was the fact that he wouldn't move out of his home village; she'd have to go back to England empty-handed, so to speak.

Their tickets were unnumbered, and Laura was resigned to standing at the back behind umpteen other people, but Monica was an old hand at gigs with standing room only, and wriggled and wheedled her way to the front, Laura following, embarrassed and apologising as she went.

They found a spot near the stage and although they had to stand, they could at least lean against the book table that had been set up.

'What time is he due on?' asked Monica.

'About ten minutes ago,' said Laura. 'He's late.'

'Oh, don't be saying your man is late,' said a friendly

man who was leaning on the same table. 'I'll get us all a drink to pass the time with.'

'Oh no—'

'Yes please,' said Monica firmly. 'That would be lovely.'

'And what will you have?'

'Better stick to shorts,' advised Monica. 'We'll never get to the loos.'

'I'll be right back,' said the man, and began shouldering his way against the tide of people to the bar.

'We don't know what we're getting,' said Laura.

'That's the joy of travel,' said Monica. 'Surprises.'

'I think I'm getting the hang of it at last,' said Laura ruefully. 'I've led such a sheltered life.'

The man handed each girl a glass of brown liquid. Laura took hers wondering if they sold sherry by the tumbler everywhere, or if it was only in this particular venue. Only it wasn't sherry, it was whiskey, and it was neat.

After watching Laura's range of expressions from horrified realisation of what she was drinking to appreciation as the fiery liquid warmed her, Monica said, 'We may as well be drunk as the way we are.'

Laura wondered how much longer it would be before Monica started saying, 'top o' the morning' and 'begorrah'.

'Well now, girls,' said the man who'd bought them drinks. 'What are you doing in these parts in January? Have you just come to see Himself?' He nodded to an old publicity photograph mounted on a battered showcard.

'We have,' Laura admitted, sipping her drink, beginning to feel its effect.

'He's great now, isn't he? He's a lovely man but I warn you, he's often late to things if he doesn't really want to do them.'

'Oh.'

'But it's OK, the crack will keep you entertained until he turns up.'

Laura was surprised to discover it did. The air was buzzing with chat, with laughter, people squashing past with drinks. The sheer numbers of people helped boost the limited warmth coming out of a couple of ancient heaters and added to the cosy atmosphere.

Laura had pressed euros into the hand of their self-appointed escort and bought more drinks, and the time passed quickly enough.

An hour after the appointed time, a roar started at the back of the room and gathered momentum. It was in the wake of a tall man in a tattered sweater, black jeans and boots. Dermot Flynn had arrived. For a second Laura wondered if he was in the same clothes he'd been wearing in his author photo but concluded he just wore a lot of black. He leapt up on stage without using the rickety steps and turned round and greeted his audience. He raised his hands for silence and then smiled.

Laura felt as well as saw the smile. It was like a zillion-watt lightbulb. The whiskey probably had something to do with it, she realised – she was now on her third – but it was truly dazzling.

'Ladies and gentlemen!' Dermot Flynn had to shout over the applause and the whooping that had greeted him. Eventually, the crowed quietened apart from the odd stray whistle.

'Ladies and gentlemen,' he repeated. 'Will you ever shut up?'

He certainly had a brogue, thought Laura, but it wasn't really an accent.

There was laughter.

'Now I'm going to read to you, but I'm not taking questions.'

Laura felt a moment of panic. This was awful news.

How was she going to ask him to come to England if he wasn't taking questions?

'I'll take questions tomorrow when the drunks aren't in.'

Huge relief swept over Laura and then she realised she was probably one of the drunks. She resolved not to drink any more. Monica was now holding a pint glass containing a neon-orange liquid she said was lemonade. Laura accepted she was naïve but felt this was unlikely. She herself had decided to stick to what she knew: namely whiskey.

His voice was like tweed made of silk, rough-smooth, dark brown and the sexiest thing Laura had ever heard in her life.

'Good evening, everyone.'

'Good evening!' the crowd roared back. This was unlike any event Laura had ever been to.

'It's nice of you to show up,' went on Dermot. 'People have been asking me why I showed up myself, but you asked me, so I came. I wrote these books a long time ago and I'm going to read you some out of both of them. Afterwards I'll talk a bit about how they came to be written.' He paused, cleared his throat and began to read.

She knew the words by heart – the opening passage of his first book – the bestseller that shocked the literary world. Dermot Flynn had been only twenty when out came this masterpiece. It won every literary prize it was eligible for.

She had studied his books – there were only two – at university, and of all the books she had read since, and there'd been many, these were the two she loved best.

Laura was not the only person entranced. He had such a beautiful voice. Listening to it was like hearing a musical instrument playing the most beautiful piece. The applause when he'd finished was deafening. And then he spoke about how he'd come to write them, how when he lived abroad for a while he was so homesick for his home, his land, its culture and its geography, the only way he could ease his pain was to write.

Laura clapped until her hands were sore. She drummed her feet and she may have even whooped a bit. The audience was treating him more like a rock star than a writer; the event was the most exhilarating thing she'd ever experienced. She was flying and didn't want to stop. He was every bit as wonderful as she had always dreamt he would be. When he jumped off the stage she felt as if a magic spell had suddenly been broken.

Chapter Five

꧁ ꧂

'Come on,' said Laura. 'We're going to the pub.'

Monica looked at her quizzically. 'Are we? Are you sure?'

Aware she was behaving out of character, and that this was probably caused by alcohol as much as anything, Laura made her case. 'I know we've had more than enough to drink and I'm worn out and should probably go home but I'm not ready for the evening to end just yet.'

'But, Laura!' Monica was amused as well as surprised. 'We've had a long day. He's doing another gig tomorrow.'

Laura shook her head. 'It's hard to explain but I need to ask him my big favour now, before I lose my nerve.' She paused, wondering how to express her feelings about Dermot without sounding completely deranged. 'I sort of feel fired up for it and I know the feeling won't last.'

'Fair enough,' said Monica. 'Although it'll be hard to get near him.'

'I know.' She just stopped herself telling Monica that even watching him drink pints with several dozen people between her and him would be good. Being sensible could wait until she was back in England. Here, she didn't want to miss a minute of him, even if she could only look at him across a crowded room. Seduced by the romance of the place, the beauty of his writing, the charm of his voice, she felt as if she was in another world, one sprinkled with fairy dust, she didn't want that feeling to

69

end. An enchanted evening, very different from the one in the song, had already begun.

Not all the audience went to the pub afterwards, in fact Laura saw several dozen of them scattering into the darkness, but there was still a stream of people to follow through the narrow streets to the village local. It was a long, low building that seemed to occupy the width of several shopfronts. It was still going to be a crush.

The smell of the turf fire was the first thing that hit them as they fought their way in. The bar was just visible and behind it could be seen at least three young men, pulling pints, pouring whiskey and handing over change with astonishing speed and accuracy.

Laura kept her quarry in her sights, wondering if this made her a stalker, or just a fan. Because he was so tall, she could follow him as he wove through the crowd in the main bar to where someone was gesturing to a pint glass of black fluid that had been ordered for him. The pub seemed to consist of several small wooden rooms; the now illegal nicotine had stained the walls to a warm brown. Her moment had come. It would have been easier to have ducked out of the way into one of the side rooms, but she was determined not to lose sight of him now.

Laura watched him dispose of most of what she assumed was porter in one draught. She leant in to Monica to ask if she thought 'a pint of plain' meant porter.

Monica, who had no literary references to worry about, shrugged, struggling to make herself heard over the noise. She said, 'We've got to get nearer to him. You can't ask him to come to the festival from here.'

Dermot was obviously in full flow, talking, laughing, gesturing with his glass that had somehow got refilled.

Laura's habitual reticence returned with a vengeance. The thought of actually talking to her hero was suddenly too daunting. 'Well, he's not going to say yes, is he?' Laura shouted. 'There's no point! Let's just have a quick orange juice or something and then go back.'

Monica was not having this. 'You've got us to the pub, you must complete your mission. You can't travel all this way and not. Follow me.'

With the skill Laura had admired before – a smile here, an 'excuse me' here, and a couple of times, a very suggestive wink – Monica got through the throng and to her destination.

Laura hurried after her, smiling and 'excuse me-ing' in her wake, not daring to hang back in case she got separated from Monica for ever.

'Hello, Dermot!' shouted Monica. 'I've got someone here very anxious to meet you.'

Laura cringed. 'Hello!' she said, trying to smile. Now she was up close, she could clearly she that Dermot was even more attractive than he had been in his author photo of fifteen years ago. His hair and eyelashes were just as curly but there was a definition about his features now, lines and shadows that proclaimed him a man and not a boy.

'Hello,' Dermot said back and then crinkled his eyes slightly in thought. 'Weren't you at the gig? I think I noticed you there in the corner.'

'Really?' This time her smile was spontaneous and completely incredulous. She chuckled, pleased her anti-Blarney device worked as well as any girl's although she thought so highly of him. There was no way he could have spotted her in that crowd.

'No, I did. I saw you with your tangled curls and your slightly red nose.'

Her hand went up to it. 'Is it red?' She knew about the tangled curls. She hadn't packed her straighteners and her hair had responded to the sea air in its usual exuberant fashion.

'A little, but to be truthful, I didn't see that until just now.'

She felt herself blush, hoping the heat of the room would justify it. It was hot, and there were a lot of Aran sweaters about – they probably raised the temperature as much as the fire did. 'I don't know how you could have seen me in all that crowd of people . . .'

'I did spot you, however,' he said, possibly sensing that she didn't know how to finish her sentence.

Now Laura worried that he would have seen her adoring expression, too. 'Well done you,' she said lamely, silently admonishing herself for losing the art of conversation now she'd got him to herself.

She rather expected him to turn away and speak to some of the other people who were standing around, all wanting a piece of the great man. He seemed to know everyone. He didn't. 'So, you've read my books?'

'Yes. Both of them,' she said.

To her consternation, he flinched, although it was the last thing she'd wanted him to do. 'If you're going to talk like that,' he said, 'I'll find someone else to make conversation with.'

As he didn't move she had the courage to say, 'I only said—'

'I know what you said.' His words were a full stop on that topic of conversation. 'Why haven't you two got a drink?' Before either of them could respond he'd said, 'Charles, will you do the decent thing?'

Charles nodded and smiled. 'Coming up.'

He'd set off for the bar before either of them could ask for orange juice. If it was alcohol, and Laura accepted it would be, she'd just sip it.

'It's very kind of your friend to get us drinks,' said Laura. 'Obviously—' she'd been going to say that they would pay him back, but Dermot made one of his sweeping gestures.

72

'I have a tab behind the bar tonight,' he said.

'Oh. Thank you.'

The ensuing silence seemed to amuse Dermot. It was killing Laura. Monica decided to put her out of her misery.

'Laura's got a favour to ask you,' she said.

'Laura? That's a pretty name. What does it mean?'

'To do with laurels. Shall we move on?'

Dermot Flynn laughed. His laugh was as sexy as his voice, Laura observed with a sort of detachment. It was like being up close to a tiger or something. It was really fascinating but somehow nothing to do with her.

'So what's this favour?' asked Dermot, sipping the drink that looked like black treacle.

Laura wished Monica hadn't said anything. 'I'm not going to ask it because I know you'll say no. There's no point.'

'I might not. You don't know for sure.' He seemed amused.

'I do so know for sure,' said Laura, falling unconsciously into the local speech pattern and swaying slightly. She steadied herself on a wooden bench.

'Why are you so sure?'

Laura was frustrated. This was embarrassing and stupid; she wished she could magic herself back to the bed and breakfast. 'I just am.' She didn't want to go into what their hostess had said about him not being willing to attend a literary festival in the town five miles away. He must already think she was an idiot.

'Ask me anyway.'

'You might as well,' said Monica, her frustration obvious. 'We've come a long enough way.'

At that moment two tumblers of whiskey appeared and were handed to the girls. Laura had resolved not to drink any more – she was already feeling the effects – but she was so grateful for the diversion she said, 'Thank you very much,' and took a large draught.

'Steady,' murmured Monica. 'It's strong stuff.' Like a contrary teenager, Laura just laughed and took another gulp.

'So, what were you going to ask me?' Dermot seemed very insistent that her favour be asked.

It's a funny thing about alcohol, thought Laura, feeling far removed from reality. You're perfectly fine, not drunk at all, and then one more sip and you are completely out of your head. Although she knew intellectually it was a bad thing, a very bad thing, just at that moment, it felt really good. It seemed to make her perception extra clear. She felt bold and confident.

'OK, here goes nothing.' Laura smiled, suddenly loving the world. 'Will you come to a literary festival I'm organising in England?' Then, before he could answer she quickly added, 'No? Well, I told you you'd say no.' She may have suddenly taken the possession of the meaning of life but she wasn't silly. She knew when she was beaten.

'But I haven't said no.' Dermot stared at her. His gaze was direct and very unsettling.

'But you will.' Laura was sure of her ground even if physically it wobbled a little beneath her feet. Another sip of whiskey and suddenly she knew everything.

'No I won't,' he said, his eyes narrow, his mouth slightly lifted in one corner.

'Told you!' said Laura, and then turned to Monica. 'We can go back now. In fact, maybe we should.'

Monica was looking at her anxiously. She seemed miles away. Laura smiled lopsidedly at her and raised a glass. 'Can we have some water, please?' Monica turned to Charles, who was hovering in a helpful way.

'Two waters coming up,' he said.

Laura's head had begun to swim. It was pleasant,

if strange. She smiled at Dermot. He was so utterly lovely! And he was talking to her! Why was that? She did find it a little difficult to work out what he was saying, though. She leant closer and concentrated very hard on his mouth.

'I didn't say I wouldn't go to the literary festival,' Dermot said slowly. 'I said I wouldn't say no.'

Laura's uncanny clarity left her. She was now very confused. 'What?'

At that moment Charles arrived with two glasses of water. 'Drink up,' said Monica, thrusting one of them at Laura. 'Or you'll want to die in the morning.'

'She's right,' said Charles.

Laura obediently sipped her water. It seemed to make her drunker than ever, but she felt it was a good thing that she realised she was drunk. Before she'd just thought she knew everything. Dermot was speaking again so she focused on his mouth.

'I will go to the festival you're arranging in England,' he said. 'On one condition.'

She was concentrating very hard, trying to gather her scattered brain cells. She was here to get Dermot to the festival. He was asking for something. OK. He could have it. Enunciating carefully she said, 'I'm sure anything that we can do to make—'

He was doing that unnerving starey thing again. He really did have the most amazing eyes, and lips and . . .

'I'll go on one condition – if you'll sleep with me.' He smiled his challenge.

Laura blinked. He couldn't really have said that, could he? She must have misheard. There was something wrong with her hearing as well as her balance. She looked for Monica for confirmation but she saw that she and Charles had gone into one of the other rooms. She was alone with Dermot – if you discounted about thirty other people. She'd have to work this out for herself; she hadn't misheard, of course, Dermot had said she had to sleep

75

with him and then he'd go to the festival. She worked on it in her mind. Did she want to sleep with Dermot Flynn? She smiled. This was what they called a 'no-brainer', which was quite funny because she no longer had a brain. She did want to sleep with him.

'OK.' She nodded. Why not.

Dermot looked down into her eyes once more and something in her flipped. What was this feeling? The poetry-loving romantic in her wanted it to be love, but she had just enough grip left on reality to realise it was lust that stirred her. Both emotions were practically unknown to her.

She was vaguely aware of a tiny voice buried deep inside her telling her she would probably regret what she'd just said, but she drowned it out with another sip of whiskey. She knew there was nothing else in the world at that moment that she wanted to do more.

'Well, isn't that nice?' he said slowly, raising an eyebrow.

Another drink was put into her hand and she sipped it. Monica appeared and murmured to her that she'd been asked to play something and then she disappeared once more into another of the rooms. Laura wasn't quite sure how Monica's sassy American swing would fit into the traditional Irish instruments she heard playing, but that wasn't her problem.

'So tell me,' said Dermot. 'How do you come to be organising a literary festival at your tender age?'

'I'm twenty-six. You'd written two bestselling novels before you were my age.'

'True, but you haven't answered my question.'

'I'm not really sure, to be honest. I sort of got roped in. I'm a bookseller by trade.'

'Go on.'

'Well, I met an agent—' She suddenly remembered that Eleanora Huckleby was his agent, too, and made a split-second decision not to mention this. She heard herself answering in a confident manner. Well, tonight she did feel confident: confident, intelligent Laura. 'She and I got talking and she discovered I was better read than some people. Of course, working in a bookshop, I had access to everything that came out, before it was out truly. I didn't have to pay for my reading habit.'

He chuckled. 'It sounds to me as if you did have to pay for it, by running a literary festival.'

Laura smiled back. 'It's not that bad. Why don't you like literary festivals?'

'How do you know I don't like them?'

'Our landlady told us. She said you wouldn't go to one five miles down the road which is why the Festival of Culture is in Ballyfitzpatrick and not Patricktown.' She'd admitted everything now. 'So why?' She wanted and needed to know and she didn't want him going off on a tangent about landladies or gossip.

'I had my fill of them years ago when my books came out. I don't want to go to them now.'

Laura forced herself to consider how she'd feel if she slept with him and then he refused to come to the festival and was relieved to discover that getting him to England, so they would have a sponsor, was not at all the reason she wanted to sleep with him – if he really meant it, of course, which she doubted – he was knee-tremblingly attractive. 'But you did this one?' She was trying very hard to enunciate and was pleased how sober she sounded.

'The place is dead in winter. It's where I live and it would be churlish not to put on a show that will fill the pubs and all the accommodation if I can, without much – any, frankly – effort.'

Laura sipped at her drink. 'I think I'm drinking neat whiskey.'

'It won't do you a bit of harm.'

Laura laughed ruefully, aware that it may have already

got her into a lot of trouble if not actually done her harm. She couldn't decide what was to blame for what she was about to do: the whiskey or her wanton lust.

'So what have you read lately that you've got really excited about?'

'Well . . .' She went on to enthuse about a recent prizewinner, and a new women's fiction writer, and several other books that she'd enjoyed. She was proud of how lucid she sounded – to her ears at least.

He countered with books and films he'd liked, only of course he was far more critical than even Laura was, and she always thought she was picky. As she talked she saw his attention wander. No male writer could resist talking about their work, she remembered – something Henry from the bookshop had told her when she'd first started organising events. 'Of course,' she said, 'what we're all waiting for is another book from you.'

There was a pause and then he took the glass out of her hand and put it down. 'I think it's time I took you home to bed.'

Her reactions were slowed by strong drink and it took Laura a moment or two to realise what he'd said. She forced her brain to pay attention and tell her to politely decline. It wouldn't. She wanted to go home to bed with him and that was that. She realised she hadn't really believed he meant it, she'd just enjoyed flirting with him. It had felt good. But she liked the idea of sleeping with him even better. She pushed aside any lingering sensibility and nodded her assent.

She retained enough sanity to text Monica to say, if not where she was going, whom she was going with, confident that someone would give Monica the address should she need it. She also added 'I really want this' to stop Monica rushing to the rescue. She knew that Monica would really like an in-depth discussion about what Laura was about to do, her motivation, and what she felt the outcome might be. But Monica even saying, 'Are you sure?' might make her change her mind, and Laura really wanted her virginity to go to her favourite writer in all the world (who also happened to be the most attractive man on the planet). She may never have another opportunity to really live and she didn't want to be talked out of taking it.

It took them a little while to get out of the pub, Dermot had to say goodbye in various ways to so many people. But no one seemed at all surprised that Laura was going with him. She realised he could probably have had any woman he wanted in that pub at that moment; while they might have wondered at his choice, the fact that he was going home with a woman was to be expected.

'I'm just one in a long line of women,' she told herself during the last 'goodbye' conversation. 'But that's all right. Poets are all womanisers. At least it means he'll know what he's doing.' Anticipation and fear heightened her desire. She remembered reading that they did and her addled brain tried to think where. 'It's going to be fine,' she told herself, 'and if it isn't, it's something to tell my grandchildren.' Then she giggled as she imagined the unlikely scenario of her own grandmother telling her about her first sexual encounter.

Eventually they were out into the cold air. She stumbled slightly and he took her arm. Should I tell him I'm a virgin, she wondered, and then decided not to. It might stop him. It would make it far too big a deal. I want to have sex with him for all the right and all the wrong reasons, she reminded herself. I don't want to make him feel bad about it.

She was barely aware of the short journey to his house. He strode purposefully up the path, opened the front door and pushed her gently inside. Before she had time to take anything in he'd pulled her into his arms and kissed her. He was an expert, she decided, her knees almost buckling as whiskey and desire hit them at the same time. I have made exactly the right decision, she thought: my virginity is safe in this man's hands! Is that what I mean? Her brain seemed to be twirling away on its own, disconnected from anything that made sense. She decided to put all thinking on hold until later; just now, she wanted to relish every moment.

Without letting go he manoeuvred her into a bedroom and carried on kissing her. He held her very tightly, pressing her to him. His hand moved from the back of her waist to her bottom and she realised she had never wanted any body else's hand to go there – how strange it was that an intimate touch could be so horrible from the wrong person and so wonderful from the right one.

'Do you need to use the bathroom?' he murmured into her hair that he was now curling his fingers into.

'No thank you,' she murmured back, knowing that if she stopped she might lose her nerve. It wasn't her nerve she was intent on losing. Tenderly he undid the buttons of her jacket and took it off. Underneath she was wearing one of her collection of black V-neck sweaters. This was lifted and pulled over her head. Now she stood before him in a strappy top and a pair of black trousers. A part of her registered that they were the same clothes she wore for work and felt that was a bit odd. But Dermot didn't seem to care what she was wearing; he was only intent on getting it off. He found the hook at the waist-band of her trousers, and the zip and then they fell off her hips. He pushed her gently back on to the bed and laughed.

'You're wearing socks!'

'Of course I am,' she said hazily. 'What's wrong with wearing socks? I expect you're wearing them too.'

He unzipped her short boots and they joined her other clothes on the floor. It ought to have felt odd being with a man she didn't know in just her underwear, but it felt right, nice. Sexy.

He stood looking down at her as she lay there in her bra and pants. He was still fully clothed.

'You're beautiful, you know that?'

Laura chuckled gently. He probably said that to everyone. She didn't mind. She wanted him to treat her just as he'd treat any of his previous girlfriends.

'Get under the duvet, you're shivering,' he said, tenderly amused as he started to strip off his own clothes.

From under the duvet, Laura watched him. His body was fit and well muscled. He may have been a writer but he obviously didn't spend all day sitting at a desk. As his boxer shorts dropped she closed her eyes. The room swung round as if she was on a carousel and she quickly opened them again.

He switched off the main light and replaced it with the bedside one. Then he took Laura into his arms.

The feeling of his skin against hers was like silk. She closed her eyes again, in spite of the spinning room, and let herself enjoy the sensation of lying in his arms as he got rid of her bra and pants. Miraculously any nerves she might have felt seemed to have fled with her inhibitions. He pulled her towards him and began to stroke her back. And all the time he breathed endearments in his deep, sexy voice. He raised himself on his elbow and kissed her face, lightly, more a breath than a kiss, all over her eyes, her lips, her cheeks and then he moved down to her neck, just under her ear.

She sighed deeply and snuggled closer. Only then did he touch her breasts and kiss her chest. Now his hand moved over her body, featherlight caresses, tantalising in their tenderness. He had just discovered that the backs of her knees were particularly sensitive when he said, 'Excuse me. I'll be back in a minute.'

She sighed ecstatically and passed out.

She awoke to find him snoring beside her. She felt terrible: thirsty and a head that felt as if it was about to split. Panic filled her. What had she done? How on earth had she ended up naked in bed with a naked man? She flew out of bed and hunted for her clothes. She was dizzy and couldn't tell if she was still drunk or if the dizziness was part of the hangover.

She found her knickers and socks in separate parts of the corner of the room. Waves of panic came over as she tried to navigate her limbs into them. What had she done?

Terrified Dermot would wake up she tried to assemble what she could remember of the night before as she pulled on her trousers and top. Dermot's event was clear in her mind. Then she remembered dragging Monica to the pub and some of what had gone on there was clear, but how in merry hell had she ended up in Dermot Flynn's bedroom, naked, with him in the bed next to her?

Terrible flashbacks came to her as she pulled on her coat – some dim recollection of him saying he'd come to the festival if she went to bed with him. Had she really said yes? Surely not! However much she admired and fancied him, surely she wouldn't have agreed to sleep with him? Would she? It would make her little better than a prostitute! She didn't dare look at the sleeping form in the bed. If she couldn't see him perhaps he didn't really exist: it was all a figment of her over-active imagination. But she knew he was very real. Oh, why had she drunk so much? Her mother was right about the demon drink. This thought brought a fleeting smile to her lips until the reality of the situation came flooding back. She had to remember what happened last night.

82

She did remember fancying him. She remembered him taking her clothes off, and her liking it very much. As she did up her trousers she wondered if she'd ever feel the same about that particular pair again.

She looked at her watch but it was too dark to see the time. She'd have to get back to the bed and breakfast and hope she could wake Monica to let her in. Thank goodness it was a bungalow and their bedroom window was round the back. If she was attacked and dragged into the bushes by a passing rapist on her way there, she had only herself to blame.

The Patron Saint of Stupid Women guided her back down the road and along the lane to where the bed and breakfast was. Laura had a terrible sense of direction and knew it was only the intervention of this divine being that got her there. By now her head was clearing a little; she studied the outside of the building and worked out where their room was. She tiptoed round and knocked on the window.

Fortunately Monica was a light sleeper. A tousled head appeared behind the curtains. 'Laura! What the hell are you doing here?'

'Oh, just let me in, Monica, please!'

'OK. Go to the front door and I'll see what I can do.

'You're bloody lucky they don't go in for burglar alarms round here,' whispered Monica a few minutes later.

'I feel like a burglar. Worse.'

'What happened?'

'I don't know. Nothing. I don't think. Can we talk about it in the morning?'

'Fair enough. Get into my bed, it's warm and you're shivering like a jelly. I demand a blow-by-blow account in the morning though.'

Laura just wanted to get into bed and search for oblivion but Monica was firm. 'Here,' she said, holding a glass. 'It's got something in it to restore your salts. You'll feel less awful in the morning if you drink it.'

Laura drank it but as more and more memory came back to her in Technicolor detail she felt that it wasn't going to be a hangover that made her feel as if death was an attractive option.

'Tea's up!' said Monica, cruelly loud, the following morning. She was fully dressed and made up and seemed on top form.

'Oh God!' Laura moaned, yawned, moaned again and then sat up and took the tea.

'How are you feeling?'

Laura considered. 'Better than I should, probably. Physically, anyway.'

'I want to hear every detail later, but now we should have breakfast.'

Laura, who hadn't felt like eating anything, did feel a bit better after a pint of orange juice, a huge Irish breakfast and several mugs of tea, and two strong painkillers. Monica hustled her into her warmest clothes, put on her own, and dragged them both off for a walk.

'OK, so tell me everything. Was it wonderful? First times can be dodgy, but at least with a man like that he'll know what he's doing.'

Laura remembered this thought making its appearance in her own head sometime the previous evening.

'Well?' Monica was insistent. 'You have to tell me everything. That's the first rule of Girlfriend Law.'

'I've never heard of the Girlfriend Law,' said Laura.

'I've just made it up, but you've still got to tell me. Don't hold out on me.'

'I'm not holding out. I'm just trying to remember.'

'What? Surely you weren't that off your face?'

'I had had a fair bit to drink, I know that. I must have or I would never have gone back to his house. Although . . .'

'Confession time,' said Monica, accurately interpreting

her sudden pause. 'You fancied him rotten. I'd have gone back to his place after a glass of Ribena. He's a ride.'

'What?'

'Local expression. Self-explanatory. Shall we go and sit down on that bench over there? I've had a broken night.'

'Oh, me too.' Shivers were convulsing Laura's body and she didn't know whether they were caused by the cold, her hangover or by what had happened the night before. She remembered now exactly how much she had wanted to sleep with Dermot Flynn. She remembered how she'd decided that of all the men in the entire world he was the one who should have her virginity. And although the light of day was horribly cold and she felt iller than she could ever remember feeling, she hadn't changed her mind. Not really.

'So, did you have fun?' asked Monica. 'I won't ask if you had an orgasm, because you probably didn't.'

'No . . . I don't think I did.'

'What? Have fun or the orgasm?'

'Monica, I know this sounds really mad but I'm not sure if we had sex or not.'

Monica didn't answer immediately. 'Do you think it's possible that you had sex and can't remember?'

They reached the bench and as they sat on it, Laura winced.

'You're tender – down there?'

Laura acknowledged that she was. 'But we went on that bike ride to see your boyfriend.'

'But I'm fine! I know I'm more used to cycling than you, but you're young and fit. I wouldn't have thought you'd be that uncomfortable. You walked most of the way, after all.'

'There were some very bumpy bits on the way home.' Laura turned to her friend. 'I do need to find out, Mon. I have to know if I had sex or not. I feel it's important.'

85

Monica laughed gently. 'Well, of course it is important, but—'

'No, really. I have to find out. I can't go back to England
not knowing. I just can't.'

Monica became practical. 'OK, let's try and work it
out. Were you alone when you woke up?'

Laura shook her head. 'No. He was asleep beside me.
Snoring. And naked.'

'Hmm . . . Well, did you notice anything, er, discarded
on the floor? You know, like a condom?'

Laura pulled a face. 'No, but then I was too busy
finding my clothes and wanting to leave as quickly as
possible.'

Monica sighed and shook her head. 'It's not looking
good, Laura, if you don't want to have had sex with him.
A man like that, naked in bed with a girl, who was also
naked, I presume?' Laura nodded. 'The chances of him
not having had his evil way with you are slim. And no
sign of a condom – very irresponsible.'

'But surely I'd remember if we had?' Laura asked
quietly, looking down the lane towards the pub where
this whole sorry situation had started. She sighed and
pulled her coat round her more tightly.

'Not if he put Rohypnol in your drink,' said Monica
matter-of-factly.

'He wouldn't do that. He wouldn't need to.' Of this
Laura was absolutely sure.

'You don't know that, sweetie, you know very little
about him,' Monica reminded her, albeit gently.

'I wrote my bloody dissertation about him! I know
everything there is to know. And besides, where would
he get Rohypnol in Ballyfitzpatrick?' She doubted they'd
even heard of it here.

Monica chuckled again. 'You have a point, and you may
be able to quote his books by heart, but you don't know
about his sex life, now do you? I got the impression from

86

Charles that he's quite a ladies' man. You can never be too careful, you know.'

'It wasn't mentioned in the author biog in the back of the books, no,' said Laura. 'You do have a point.'

'You're really worried about this, aren't you?' said Monica, touching Laura's arm, serious now.

'Well, yes! I, the last virgin in the Northern Hemisphere over twenty-one, may or may not have had sex. I would kind of like to know.'

'Do you want to go home? We could leave early . . .'

Laura shook her head. 'Oh no. We can't go before his other session – and I've got to get him to say definitely that he'll come to the festival. There's more than just my virginity at stake here! Besides,' she went on in a small voice, 'I can't pass up a chance to see him again.'

Monica patted her hand. 'Of course.'

'But I also need to know what happened last night. Otherwise how can I speak to him about the festival, make arrangements, stuff like that?'

'I see your point. We need to find out.' She stood up, putting out a hand to pull Laura up. 'Come on, it's freezing out here, let's go to the café and warm ourselves up.'

'But, Monica, how? I'm certainly not asking him,' said Laura as they walked towards the café where they'd had their first Irish breakfast what seemed like days ago now.

'OK, then I will,' said Monica.

'Mon! You can't ask him. You cannot go up to Dermot Flynn and say, "Did you have sex with my friend?" You've got to promise me you won't. It's too embarrassing.' She thought for moment and then flourished, 'It's Girlfriend Law.'

'I invented Girlfriend Law,' said Monica firmly, 'but I admit it is the sort of thing that would be on it. Tell you what, I will ask him, but he won't know I'm asking him, so it'll be all right.'

'I may not be at my intellectual best – my head is

aching so much I think my brain has atrophied – but how on earth are you going to do that?'

'I'll think of something.' Monica flashed her irrepressible grin, but Laura wasn't convinced.

Chapter Six

The second event, although in the afternoon, was just as crowded. If this was an indication of how many people he would attract to the Somerby festival, Laura could see why everyone was so keen to have him. Maybe, she said to herself, it's just because he's local. But although lots of the voices around her were Irish, there was a substantial smattering of English and American accents too.

This time Laura hid at the back. Her hangover was mercifully a distant echo but whatever had – or hadn't – happened the night before, seeing Dermot again was going to be acutely embarrassing. Although, if it transpired that they had made love (even in her imagination, Laura didn't think this was really the right expression) she would hold him to his promise. But how terribly sad – tragic, really – that she'd been so drunk she couldn't be sure if it had happened or not! Supposing she had given her virginity to the man she wanted to have it more than anyone and not been aware of it? She knew what she felt for him wasn't love in any real sense, but it was the sort of adulation young women usually reserved for singers or film stars. Being unconscious through the process was unforgivable.

Monica had agreed that she would go nearer the front so she could grab him and ask her question before everyone went to the pub. Laura needed to know as soon as possible, and while she and Monica agreed that several pints or shots down the line it would be easier to ask, the answer might not be coherent, or lead to other things. Both women agreed that for their livers' sakes, they shouldn't spend longer in the pub than they had to.

The 'what on earth are you going to say?' conversation had gone on some time.

'How about "Have you ever had sex with a virgin and if so, when was it?"' suggested Monica.

Laura had spent several seconds in shock before she picked up that Monica was joking. 'Why beat around the bush, Mon? Why not just come out with it?' Laura was giggling now, as Monica had intended she should. But there was an edge of hysteria to it.

She tried again. 'What about: "Have you ever acted out the sex scenes in your books and if so when?"'

Laura stopped giggling and became indignant. 'No! There are no sex scenes in his books that would give us the remotest clue!'

Monica shrugged. 'Sorry, haven't read them.'

'That's blindingly obvious!'

'Hang on! I'm doing you a favour, don't forget!'

Laura was apologetic. 'I'm sorry! I'm being a bitch. I got myself into this, I should get myself out of it really. Why should you embarrass yourself for me? If only I wasn't such an idiot!'

'Look, it's OK. You don't need to beat yourself up more than you already have done. Hair shirts are so last century, or even several centuries before. I'll think of something at the time, so it sounds more natural.'

Laura was not reassured. 'I've set up a lot of signings, readings, Q and As, and been to a few I haven't arranged, and no one ever, ever, asked about the author's sex life.'

Monica was dismissive. 'But I'm a scary rock chick. I can ask stuff you literary types wouldn't.' Monica put on an expression of insouciance that might have convinced Laura when she first met her, a couple of weeks before, but by now she realised that the 'scary rock chick' or in her case a 'scary swing band chick' was an image that went on with the pink wig and false eyelashes.

'I should do this myself. I'm sure if I got drunk enough – hell, when I got drunk before I was ready to have sex with him!'

'Yes, and you were so drunk you can't remember if you had sex with him or not,' Monica reminded her kindly, in case this had slipped Laura's mind. 'Much good it'll do us if you tank yourself up so you can ask him, and then can't make sense of the answer, or forget what the answer was. No, I'll do it.'

Shamed by the truth of this, Laura shut up.

While Dermot had said he'd do a question-and-answer-session, 'Did you have sex with my friend?' was probably not one he'd be expecting. Laura had no idea if Monica was going to manage to ask it, and was frantically thinking about a plan B. Could she get an email address for him and send him a quick, 'You may not remember me, but I came and saw you at the Ballyfitzpatrick literary festival and we might have had sex. Ring any bells? Did we do it, or didn't we? I feel I ought to know . . .'

No, probably not. She had to put her trust in Monica.

Dermot Flynn leapt up on the stage in the same rock-star way he had the night before. Laura sighed. She felt a mixture of huge relief that he was possibly even more attractive than she'd remembered him, which meant she hadn't had beer glasses (or whatever the expression was) on last night, and a huge sweep of longing. She really, really hoped she hadn't wasted what should have been one of the most wonderful experiences of her life because she was drunk.

Her knees weakened as she thought of what they had shared that she *could* remember. He couldn't have done anything she hadn't liked or surely her body wouldn't go weak at the sight of him – or at least not weak in the gooey, chest-heaving way she was feeling now. There'd have been some sort of psychic wound, surely? Something her brain might have suppressed but her body remembered? That's what happened in crime novels.

There was no one with him to introduce him or chair the event. Everyone knew who he was and he didn't need a minder – she could almost hear him say it. He had two books under his arm and Laura could see bookmarks in them. Someone near her muttered, 'He might read from both of them. Brilliant!'

'I've come from Canada to hear him,' said another. 'I'd go anywhere, pay anything.'

'If only he'd bring out another book! I know both of his by heart!' said the first mutterer.

Agreeing silently but wholeheartedly, Laura shifted slightly behind her neighbour as she saw Dermot rake the audience with his gaze. She hoped this time he wouldn't be able to see her at the back. She'd made such an utter fool of herself.

She wasn't entirely sure but she had a feeling he paused as he got to her section of the crowd. She closed her eyes – that way he'd never spot her. Or, more importantly, she'd never know he had.

She recognised the reading straightaway, but then, she reasoned privately, she would. Like the person now crushed to her left arm, she knew every word almost by heart. It was a scene where the protagonist is describing the woman he loves to his best friend. The hero is saying one thing, but thinking another. There was nothing explicit or lewd or remotely pornographic, but the young man's passion and desire for the woman was absolutely clear. Just hearing his beautiful voice saying those beautiful things was enough to make her want to promise to be his sex-slave for ever, and never ask him to go near a literary festival.

When he stopped reading she had to remind herself to

breathe. She wasn't the only one affected; women were near to swooning all around her. Group lust, she concluded, like group hysteria, only (happily) more private. It would only take one of them to start screaming, or throw their knickers on to the stage, for them all to follow suit – or at least all those who didn't have to struggle out of their jeans, hopping on one leg, fighting with thick socks. Laura felt grateful the venue wasn't well heated and that the punters had dressed up warmly.

'Right, any questions?' he asked.

After a round of questions which Dermot handled expertly with charm and candour, he looked at his watch.

Laura was beginning to wonder if Monica had lost her chance. Her hand had been waving for quite a while.

'Just time for a few more . . .'

'Here! Me!' Monica's voice sang out from the front of the room. Laura could tell she either didn't share the feelings of almost all the other women in the room or she was rising above them. But what on earth could she say in front of a large audience to get the required information?

Monica cleared her throat. 'They say that all first novels are autobiographical. Was this true for you?'

How, Laura wondered, feeling frantic, could Monica get from this pretty bog-standard question, to 'Is my friend still a virgin?' It was absurd! Then she chided herself – Monica was a friend doing her a favour, not an expert interrogator. She knew she should ask Dermot herself – but the mere thought made every nerve ending go into spasm. Perhaps it didn't really matter if she never knew.

Dermot Flynn had of course fielded this question a trillion times. He gave his lazy, charming smile. 'Well, you have to remember that I wrote this book when I was very young. I didn't have much to be autobiographical about.'

Monica was obviously not satisfied with this answer. 'Well, did you go round shag— um – sleeping with every woman you laid eyes on?'

Laura cringed.

Dermot was clearly amused. 'Let's just say there's more imagination in that book than experience.'

'I'm just wondering,' Monica asked, 'if you practise safe sex—' She seemed to be off on another tack now.

Laura gulped. Dermot looked confused, as did most of the audience.

'I mean,' Monica went on, 'a lot of young people read your books . . .'

Where did Monica get that from? Maybe she had read the book herself, after all.

'I don't quite see—' broke in Dermot, but Monica was set on her course and wouldn't be diverted or stopped.

'Don't you think it's important that you set a good example?'

'Of course—'

Monica interrupted before his audience could find out if Dermot was agreeing with her on the subject of good examples or was just going to say something else entirely. 'When did you last use a condom?'

It all came out in a rush and Laura wanted to die.

Silence fell over the audience as everyone tingled in expectation. It was a very rude question, and if Laura hadn't known her friend had asked it only for her, she would have thought it unforgivable. Supposing the crowd turned on Monica? Would she be able to save her?

'I have to say,' said Dermot, not at all put out, 'that that is a question possibly better suited to a more intimate setting, but since you ask, it was about four months ago. Next question?'

Laura edged her way out of the crowd to the door and escaped. It was a freezing night, her friend had humiliated herself and she still didn't know how far things had gone between her and Dermot the night before. Monica soon joined her.

'Thanks for trying, Mon,' said Laura before her friend could apologise. 'I know you did your best. I don't think we'll ever know. Let's just assume nothing much happened, shall we?' A recollection of what had gone on came back to her suddenly. It didn't seem like 'nothing much' really, it had been fantastic – with or without full-on sex.

'I'm not giving up until I know for a fact,' said Monica. 'You'll never have any peace of mind if you don't know. We'll go to the pub now, get the drinks in before the rush, and I'll ask him a supplementary question. That is what they're called, isn't it?'

'Maybe,' said Laura dolefully, 'but you might get us both thrown out for harassing the star! You were quite – er – upfront in there.'

Monica bit her lip, possibly in remorse. 'I know. But I had to be.'

'I feel such a total idiot for not noticing –'

Monica stifled a giggle. 'For not noticing if you had sex with one of the sexiest men on the planet? There's such a thing as being too unworldly, you know.'

Laura groaned in frustration at herself.

Monica patted her soothingly. 'Now let's go and get some Dutch courage – we're going to need it!'

'I thought we said—'

'Do you want to know if you're still a virgin or not?'

Laura nodded and followed her friend obediently down the road to the pub.

The fact that she had a big black pint waiting for him seemed to endear Monica to Dermot – enough for him to go near enough to her to pick it up, at least. Laura had taken refuge in one of the other small rooms and was listening from behind a panel. They'd decided it would be easier if Monica confronted him by herself.

'You gave me a hard time in there,' he said. Laura heard the glass land on the table after several long seconds. She could imagine the movement of his Adam's apple as he swallowed. Then she remembered it was a secondary sexual characteristic and stopped herself.

'I just thought you were completely irresponsible,' said Monica.

Laura winced. Here she goes again. How could Monica be so rude? She couldn't tell if Monica was genuinely cross on her behalf or trying to provoke a reaction.

'Why, for feck's sake?'

Laura could imagine his indignation and didn't blame him for it – or the language.

'Because you should always use a condom,' said Monica. 'Not just when you're asked to.'

You had to admire her persistence, thought Laura, even if it was making her personally want to tie herself in knots to suppress her embarrassment. She didn't dare actually cross her legs, or hunch over; she was getting the odd funny look as it was.

'I quite agree,' said Dermot, sounding quite affable. 'I always do.'

There was silence. Laura could almost hear Monica narrowing her eyes.

'So when was the last time?'

Laura wiped away the film of sweat this question created and stuffed her knuckles in her mouth. She no longer cared what the people around her thought about her behaviour.

'What, that I used a condom? Or had sex?'

Laura let out a little moan.

'Either. Presumably the answer's the same.'

Monica was a terrier when it came to getting information, Laura realised, and really wished she could have emulated some less tenacious breed. But would a cocker spaniel really do the job? She was dimly aware that a combination of embarrassment, terror, remorse and a whole lot of other emotions too complex to be named was making her train of thought spin off the rails.

'As I said before, about four months ago,' said Dermot and then added, 'Ah, I think I've worked out what this is all about.'

Laura, suddenly terrified she was about to hear herself talked about behind her back, squeezed past several people and appeared in front of them. She couldn't rely on Monica any longer – she had to confront Dermot herself.

'It's me,' she said from the door of the snug, trying to look as natural as possible and as if she hadn't been hiding nearby all along.

'Ah ha!' said Dermot – cruelly, in Laura's opinion.

Laura pushed aside some innocent bystanders in order to get nearer to Dermot and Monica. 'I needed to know if we had sex last night or not,' she said breathlessly, grateful that Monica had insisted on a hair of the dog and that she'd consumed at least some whiskey.

Dermot's smile was devastating. 'And you couldn't have just asked me?'

Laura swallowed and shook her head. 'Too embarrassed,' she explained. 'I felt I should have known.'

'If you didn't know,' said Dermot softly, 'the fault would have been mine, not yours. But you fell asleep and then you disappeared, obviously thinking better of it. I'm trying not to feel hurt,' he teased.

'It wasn't really that—'

'I'm going to find Charles and some music,' said Monica, relieved that she'd done her duty. 'You two can sort yourselves out now.' She wriggled through the crowd with Laura looking plaintively after her.

'That woman is a piece of work,' said Dermot admiringly.

'She's a good friend,' said Laura. 'She put herself through hell for me. Or at least a lot of embarrassment.'

Dermot was not impressed. 'Quite unnecessary. She, or you, could just have asked.'

Laura lost some of her numbness and began to giggle. 'How would that conversation have gone, I wonder. I could have said, "Excuse me, Mr Flynn, can you just remind me, did we or did we not have sex last night?"'

'You would have used my Christian name. I wouldn't have thought you forward. After all, I have seen you naked.'

Laura tried to take a sip from her glass but found it was empty. The thought of him seeing her naked, of being naked in his presence was intensely erotic and excruciatingly embarrassing at the same time.

'You need another drink,' said Dermot and lifted his hand. 'Whiskey for the lady.'

Magically a glass appeared. When she'd taken a good gulp and feeling she'd been through the worst embarrassment a woman could experience and survive, she said, 'So, will you come to my literary festival?'

Dermot's smile made Laura's stomach turn with desire but her brain told she was probably not going like what he had to say. 'All original terms and conditions apply.'

Helplessly, Laura looked up into his eyes. They were smiling, but resolute. She looked away again quickly, spent some moments biting her lip and generally trying to make the floor open up and swallow her. When she finally accepted that it wasn't going to she said, 'Oh well. No one could accuse me of not doing my best.' She had agreed to his terms once, while very drunk, but with sobriety had come sanity, and she was not going to let herself do anything quite so foolish now. She turned, preparing to fight her way through the people to find Monica.

She felt a hand on her arm.

'Hang on now, I didn't mean there was no room for negotiation!'

Laura turned. She hadn't meant to be clever, and bluff him into changing his mind, but by some fluke that had been the effect of her reaction.

'You mean, as we've gone some little way towards having sex, you'll take that part into consideration?' She smiled, aware that she was flirting again and enjoying the sensation. She hadn't done much of it herself, but had read enough about how it was done to realise what was happening. She felt on surer ground now that he hadn't dismissed coming to the festival outright.

'I don't mean I'll cross the Irish Sea and reach England but not actually go all the way to the venue, which is more or less what happened last night.' His eyes twinkled with wickedness and sex appeal.

'Oh good,' she quipped, feeling her confidence grow. 'I don't think that would help me convince the sponsors that as you'd come that far, they should still give us money. Not as much as they would have done though, obviously.'

'Oh, so it was to get sponsorship you were so keen to get me to your festival. I thought you "really admired my work".' He put on an irritating imitation of a female voice that didn't sound a bit like her. He wasn't flirting any more.

'I do – did – admire your work,' snapped Laura, no longer wanting to flirt back. 'That bit is absolutely genuine. But there hasn't been much of it lately, has there?'

The twinkle was more speculative now. For a moment she wondered if she'd overstepped the mark. 'You are very cruel,' he said, fortunately still amused, 'but perhaps I deserved it.'

Laura was aware that a woman who'd had more practice with real men rather than literary heroes would have had something clever to say now. Jane Austen, Georgette

99

Heyer, or one of the younger writers of chick lit would have had this man begging to come to her literary festival in a few terse lines. She said nothing.

'Tell you what,' he went on, obviously having come to some kind of decision, 'let me show you a bit of the countryside. Come for a walk with me tomorrow morning. Then perhaps you'll understand why I'm not eager to leave, even for a short time.'

Laura thought about it. There'd be time: they weren't due to go back to England until tomorrow evening. Monica wouldn't mind. 'Actually, Monica and I went cycling yesterday. I've seen the countryside.' Why did she say that? she admonished herself. He was offering her an olive branch.

'It'll look quite different through my eyes, I'm telling you,' he persisted.

'I'm sure.' She still didn't feel quite ready to give in yet. She was enjoying not agreeing too readily to any suggestion from a man who was obviously used to women jumping at his every word.

'But you and Monica. You're not joined at the hip, are you?'

Laura put on a good impression of wide-eyed innocence. 'Do you not want to show the countryside to a woman who asks such pertinent questions?'

He laughed. 'You may not think much of my morals, but I can assure you I only ever court one woman at a time.'

'If they know about each other,' Laura said, as if to confirm it.

He grinned. 'That's right. So, will you come with me?' He studied her earnestly.

She felt herself being drawn in by his magnetic gaze, despite her intention to remain calm and collected.

'For a walk?' Again, she appeared to be seeking confirmation that nothing too much was being asked of her when she knew perfectly well if he'd asked her to row the Atlantic with him she'd probably have agreed to it.

'That's all I'm asking you to do – on this occasion. I'll bring lunch,' he added as if this would clinch it.

She gave him a prim little smile. 'Then yes, that would be very nice.'

'Very nice?' Her choice of words obviously offended him. 'Hmph!'

'Will it not be nice, then?' she asked, still prim, hoping her amusement was well hidden.

He narrowed his gaze so that his eyes almost disappeared. 'It will be spectacular.'

Laura swallowed. His voice was so sexy she pressed her knees together to stop them wobbling.

He paused. 'I'll get you back in plenty of time to set off for the ferry.'

'You are keen to get exercise, aren't you?' Laura struggled to be brisk. 'If it's that difficult for you normally, I'm sure you could find a personal trainer.'

'Listen, Miss . . .'

'Horsley.'

'You're getting the chance to see one of the most beautiful spots in Ireland through the eyes of—'

She broke in, smiling, pretending to be teasing but in reality being perfectly serious: 'One of the most gifted writers to have come out of Ireland for a long time?'

His slow, crooked smile could have been ironic, or could have been completely accepting of this description. 'Well, you said it.'

Laura pretended to be appalled. 'You're not supposed to agree with me! How conceited are you?'

'Some would say: very.'

She held up her hand. 'Count me as one of that group.'

His eyebrow acknowledged her challenge. 'Others would say a craftsman should know his own worth.'

She shook her head. 'Only those very keen to suck up to you.'

'Yesterday you'd have been the founder member of that group. Good God, woman, you were willing to sleep with me!'

She had to acknowledge that this was true, however much it would boost his over-inflated ego. 'Fortunately I was saved from myself.'

He laughed. 'And maybe you can save me from myself.'

Laura laughed back at him. 'Where shall we meet tomorrow morning?'

'On the corner, by the shop. We'll drive a little way first.'

Monica allowed Laura to walk back from the pub on her own after she was convinced nothing bad would happen to her. Laura wanted to be fresh tomorrow and not hungover. Although she'd already drunk far more than was compatible with healthy living, if she drank enough water and took an aspirin, she should be OK in the morning. She'd drunk more in the last couple of evenings than she'd ever drunk in her entire life, even as a student.

It was Monica's turn to sneak in during the early hours and Laura's to be self-righteous, although Monica was fit enough to get up for the massive breakfast they no longer just expected, but looked forward to with worrying eagerness.

'I've got a horrible feeling,' said Monica, loading a piece of soda bread with butter and Old Thyme Irish Marmalade, 'that a bit of toast and a banana isn't going to be enough for me any more. I'll need the Full Irish every day.'

'Well, I need a big breakfast because I'm going to be taking exercise,' said Laura.

'Mm, so you are. Do you care to be specific about what exercise exactly you had in mind?'

Laura laughed. 'To be brutally honest, I don't think the sort of exercise I have in mind is the kind of exercise I'll be having but I'm sure I'll be burning up plenty of calories either way.'

'So you really like him?' Monica was studying her closely.

'God yes,' said Laura, too late realising she should have been less vehement. She knew full well that she was deeply infatuated, and equally well that it could go nowhere and she'd better start getting over it as soon as she could – immediately after they'd had their walk together. Until then she could have her few hours of joy, even if having them was likely to make the getting-over part far, far worse.

'Well, I wish you luck with him. He's a stunner, I'll give you that but not a novice ride, if I can make an equestrian pun.'

Laura raised her cup in congratulation. 'It's a very good pun. With Irish connections too. Excellent.'

'But it's too late, isn't it? All my good advice, too late, no use.'

'Good advice almost always is, isn't it?'

'I expect so, but do me one, big, massive favour; if you sleep with him, remember it this time – and take precautions!'

'Monica, it's January, in Ireland. We're going for a walk. I think that'll provide all the precautions we need.'

Chapter Seven

꧁꧂

Well wrapped up in all the sensible clothing they had between them and with a bag of toffees in her pocket for emergencies, Laura waited for Dermot on the corner, as arranged. Just as she had convinced herself that he'd overslept and wasn't going to come, a rackety old Citroen appeared and drew up next to her.

'Get in, we've a way to go.'

She got in, reminding herself that she was sharing a car with one of the great names of modern Irish fiction – modern anything fiction, in fact. She made a decision to start keeping a diary, simply so she could record this moment.

The car got them up the hill a great deal quicker than the bikes had. At the top, they took the other road along the coast, in the opposite direction to where she and Monica had cycled a lifetime and several dramatic experiences ago. As they passed the sign to the village they had cycled to, Laura wondered if Monica would use the car and her free day to go and see the boy she'd been so keen to catch up with. Although she'd asked her, Monica had been non-committal but cheerful. Laura didn't know if Monica had had a reply to the note she had stuffed through his letterbox but her new friend wasn't one to let things lie. She would make the most of her opportunity.

Laura, on the other hand, wondered if her attempts to get Dermot Flynn to come the literary festival would come to anything. Would he just string her along?

Monica would get him to sign something, possibly in blood. If only she could make herself more like her feisty companion, all would be well. The trouble was, she couldn't.

Laura realised these mental ramblings about Monica were a distraction from her own situation. What was happening to her was almost too wonderful, and she wasn't sure she could cope. She just had to hope her 'in-love state' or whatever it might be, didn't make her do anything stupid again. Although before, when she had so blithely agreed to sleep with him, she had probably just been in lust (and, of course, very drunk). Now she was in a position to spend a day with a writer she'd admired all her adult life – she mustn't let anything interfere with that.

Conversation, however, didn't seem possible. She tried to think of some casual remark – about the scenery, for example. But there didn't seem to be any way of describing it other than as 'beautiful' or 'lovely' or, worse, 'very pretty', and clichés would simply not do. Besides, the scenery was so beautiful, conversation seemed superfluous, intrusive, even. And she wasn't going to talk about his work. Or hers. So she stayed silent.

Eventually, he turned the car down a narrow lane. The hedges either side were in desperate need of attention and there was a good solid strip of grass growing up the middle. It went downhill and seemed to lead towards the sea. It got even narrower and the hedges higher as they progressed.

'Are you sure this is a road, and doesn't just lead to a farm or something?' said Laura, anxiety breaking her self-imposed silence. 'It's hardly wide enough for the car.'

'It does lead to a farm. We'll leave the car there and then walk. I hope you've got the right sort of shoes on.' He glanced down at her feet.

'Of course I have,' she said, glad of her sturdy, flat-heeled boots, aware that he might think she was a complete airhead now. Just because she had got very drunk and had nearly done something very silly, had he got her pegged for a fool? If so, it was very unfair. She was intelligent and efficient in her real life. If only he could see her in the shop, discussing the latest literary phenomenon, running an event, then he'd be impressed.

Even before he parked the car, several farm dogs came leaping up to it, barking furiously. Laura thought of herself as an animal-lover, and any pet dog she met was greeted with a pat and a warm 'hello' but she suddenly felt unwilling to open the door. They looked positively feral.

Dermot seemed not to notice the ravening swarm and got out and walked round to the boot of the car. The dogs surrounded him. Laura turned anxiously from the front seat, wondering how she'd get help if they attacked him. They didn't seem to be savaging him, however, or if they were, Dermot was saying very little about it. But why did no one appear to call them off? Or if they were guard dogs – the farmyard wasn't far away – why didn't anyone appear with a shotgun to order her and Dermot off their land? Surely someone must have heard the noise. Presumably Dermot actually knew the people and they wouldn't mind him parking here. She'd spent most of her life in small towns and wasn't sure of the ways of the countryside. And Ireland, by all accounts, was not just the countryside, but somewhere else altogether.

Dermot came round to her door and opened it. 'Come on, time to stretch our legs.' He had a rucksack with him, which clanked rather.

She hesitated, but before she could force a leg out of the safety of the car he said, 'Are you nervous of the dogs?'

'A bit. I was once bitten by a collie, who had no excuse at all to bite me.'

'You mean you weren't threatening its young, or eating its food?'

'No.'

Dermot shrugged, obviously unable to explain this freak of nature. 'This lot may be noisy devils but there's no harm in them.'

Gingerly, she got out. The dogs surged up to her, still barking their heads off.

'You see? They're fine.'

Laura didn't think they were fine at all. They had wall eyes and looked thin and hungry. They jumped up to smell her better. Although she tried hard not to, she whimpered.

'To hell with this,' he muttered and without warning, swung her off her feet and over his shoulder and carried her in a fireman's lift across the muddy distance towards a gate. The dogs, even more excited now their titbit was tantalisingly out of reach, jumped and barked higher and louder. Laura shut her eyes, bracing herself for a bite on the bottom at any minute. She knew she wasn't enormous but also that she must have felt quite heavy. Dermot was definitely panting.

At last he set her down and she opened her eyes.

'You stay there while I get this open.' He indicated a rusty gate made out of scaffold poles. 'It'll take a while; it hasn't been opened in years. I always climb over.'

'I'll climb over!' she offered, feeling pathetic enough already. 'Just don't let – oh!'

One collie jumped up and left saliva on her arm.

Dermot turned on it. 'What do you think you're doing, you miserable hound of hell! Frightening the poor girl out of wits like that! You'll have her thinking we have no manners in Ireland – if she doesn't think that already!'

'I don't think that,' she said. 'At least, only about the dogs,' she added in a small voice, feeling very pathetic.

Dermot ignored this squeak. 'Are you sure you can climb over OK? I'll open it if you'd rather.' He paused. 'Although the ruts mean I'd have to lift it quite high—'

Before he could finish, she put her foot on the second scaffold pole. Sadly, her legs were just a little bit too short to make the process of climbing the gate easy. What would have been for a taller person a simple matter of swinging one leg over and then the other, for her meant an uncomfortable few moments stranded on the top, unable to progress. Dermot held her arm.

'Bring your leg back over. That's right. Now, climb up to the next bar so you're higher. There. I've got you.'

Somehow she scrambled over, ending in a heap on the other side. Was there no end to her humiliation? He'll hate me now, she thought. I'm such a townie I can't even be taken for a country walk because I can't climb over the gates without help.

'Are you all right now?' he asked when, after an athletic leap, he was over the gate and by her side in one elegant move.

'Fine, thank you. I'm just a bit out of practice.'

'When did you last climb over a gate?' He sounded amused, as if he expected her to have never climbed one before.

'A while ago,' she said, trying frantically to remember.

'I bet you were about six,' he said.

Although she fought it, a smile appeared at the corner of her mouth as she recalled a family holiday in Cornwall. 'That would be about right.'

'We've a couple more to climb later. I expect you'll get the hang of it.'

'I'm sure I will,' she said seriously, but smiling inside, and they set off, Dermot setting a cracking pace.

They went uphill. It was a bright, clear day, cold but

sunny. Currently the sea was on their left but quite far away. The sun bounced off the little waves as it had done before, twinkling like fairy lights in the distance. The land was covered in short, springy grass. Here and there a sheep looked at them curiously, wondering who on earth was mad enough to be out here if they had a choice. Laura, though, was warm as toast. It was hard work keeping up with Dermot, although she sensed he was going slowly for her benefit. Soon her calves were burning and she had to stop for a breather. The blood pulsed through her muscles like mild electric shocks. Although she was tired she felt totally in touch with her body and utterly exhilarated.

'Not much further now. I want us to have lunch in the most perfect spot.'

Laura nodded agreement. She couldn't spare her breath for idle chat.

On and up they went. Laura took off her jacket and tied it round her waist with the sleeves. Even then she was sweating under her clothes. She was elated though, and although she was pleased when he called a halt, she'd have happily gone on for much longer.

'Right now,' he said, swinging his pack down from his back and rummaging inside it. 'What have we got here? A bit of something waterproof to sit on.' He spread out an old plastic mac.

Eager to oblige she sat down, aware as she did so that is was a rather small bit of plastic and they would have to sit hip to hip on it. Then ruefully she remembered that other things they had done together made sitting side by side while fully clothed, even if touching, completely respectable.

'Right now.' He produced a brown paper bag and stared into it. 'We have hard-boiled eggs, but they need peeling, I'm afraid, some rolls, cheese, ham, and a couple of cans of lager. Are you OK drinking it from the can?'

'Of course.'

'Chocolate for afters,' he said.

'My favourite. And I've got toffees in my pocket. I forgot about them earlier. They were to make the journey go quicker but it seemed to go quite quickly anyway.'

She realised she was twittering and tried to calm down. He was just a man, after all. But she realised that to her, he wasn't just a man, he was the equivalent of Seamus Heaney and how many young women who'd studied him at university would feel perfectly relaxed in his presence? Lots, probably, she concluded dolefully, but not her. When they'd been walking she'd felt comfortable in his presence but now they'd stopped she suddenly felt shy and self-conscious again.

He handed her a roll and produced a bit of kitchen foil that had butter in it. 'I've tomatoes and cucumber, but no lettuce. I'll cut it up.' He produced a Swiss Army knife from his pocket and divided the cucumber into chunks. The tomato followed. He seemed anxious to please her, which was touching. 'How are you doing? If you pile it all into your roll you can add your ham and cheese. I've mayonnaise as well.'

'Yummy!'

'I should have brought plates, really,' he said. 'Or one of those nifty little sets.'

'I read somewhere that you should never trust a man who had his own picnic set,' she said, relaxing a little and then suddenly realising she'd strayed into territory she'd rather have avoided. You should never trust a man with a voice like molten gold, eyes as blue as the sea either, but reading that it was a bad idea didn't stop you doing it.

'Well, you'll be perfectly safe with me then.' He looked at her quizzically.

She forced herself to meet his teasing gaze. 'That's all right then.'

'So, tell me about yourself, Laura,' he said after a fair amount of munching.

In spite of her huge breakfast, Laura found herself eating with enthusiasm. When it was all gone she lay back and stretched. The sun was shining in her eyes and she closed them. She heard him lie down next to her.

'Not much to tell. Only child, good girl at school, went to university, got a good degree and ended up working in a bookshop. What about you?'

'I was the youngest of a large family. Bad boy but bright enough to escape being found out. Wrote a couple of novels and ended up being a writer.'

'But you also went travelling, didn't you? I do regret not doing anything like that before I settled down.'

He chuckled. 'You're only twenty-six. I don't think you can describe yourself as "settled down". You've got your whole life ahead of you to go travelling.'

She shook her head. 'I'm too timid to go backpacking on my own. At least,' she added as she thought more about what she'd said, 'I have been up to now.'

'You don't have to go backpacking on your own. There's lots of ways to see a bit of the world that doesn't involved hefting huge weights about.'

She chuckled and sat up, eyeing the components of the picnic. 'I suppose so. I've done my travelling via books so far, but as you say, there's time to change.'

He leant up on one elbow and studied her. She sensed the warmth of his body next to hers and felt a glow of contentment. She was conversing with her all-time favourite writer, against the backdrop of a magnificent Irish landscape.

'The best writer in the world can't be a substitute for your own experience,' he said.

'No, not a substitute, but it can be something better, can't it?'

'How do you mean?'

She made a gesture towards the view. 'Well, take this, for example. It's brilliant to be here because it's stunning, really lovely. But if you were describing it in a book, you could give it layers of meaning that a mere picture, or just looking at it, couldn't.'

He made a sound somewhere between a sigh and a chuckle. 'Are you talking about me in particular or writers in general?'

She shrugged. 'Either. Whichever you like.'

'I think I'll take the general option. The responsibility is too great otherwise.'

'Do you feel your responsibility as a writer?' This was something Laura had always wondered about.

'A bit.' He seemed not to want to carry on with the conversation. 'Would you like to walk a bit further? We can leave the things here and then come back and have tea.'

'Oh yes.' She got to her feet, 'Maybe I'll take the opportunity to go travelling but keep it on a very small scale.'

He laughed. 'Come on then.'

They walked to the top of the hill from where they could see a slightly different view. Still the sun shone and the sea sparkled. Because she was staring out to sea, trying to spot an island Dermot had said was sometimes visible, she stumbled. He caught her arm.

'Are you OK? You didn't twist your ankle did you?'

'No, I'm fine.' Unnerved by his closeness she moved away from him. 'Race you back down to the picnic things!'

As she ran, making very sure of her footing, she wondered why she had run away from him. Was it him or herself she didn't trust? As she collapsed in a heap by their belongings she knew it was her. She might do anything. If he asked her to go with him to a sheltered spot and suggested they made love, she might not say no.

And she couldn't. She had to leave soon and she already liked him too much to want to risk doing something she might later regret. She knew herself too well.

'Well now,' he said as he joined her. 'Are you ready for tea? There's fruit cake to have with it.'

'Let's wait, I couldn't eat a thing now.' Suddenly tired she lay on her back, listening to the sea and the sounds of the countryside: the occasional baa from a sheep; a distant tractor; seagulls. As she closed her eyes she realised she very rarely just enjoyed nature. Usually she'd have brought a book with her and while she would have appreciated her surroundings, she wouldn't have given herself up to them in the same way.

A little later she opened her eyes and became aware of him next to her. Although she didn't stir he must have sensed she was awake because he said, 'You wouldn't think you could take a nap in the outdoors in January, would you?'

She chuckled sleepily. 'No, although of course we are very well wrapped up.'

'And a good thing too, in my opinion. Although I can't believe you fell asleep on me again!'

She swiftly changed the subject. 'I must say this spot is very heaven. I can understand why you don't want to leave it, although . . .' she went on, 'my literary festival would only mean you being away for a few days.' She closed her eyes again against the sun.

He laughed. 'To be honest, that's not the reason I don't like doing literary festivals any more.'

Knowing that he must have done hundreds of them when he was first published she didn't need to ask for his reasons; he'd be bored stiff with them.

'So,' he went on, 'why are you so eager to get me to come to yours?'

She would have liked to deny being eager – she hated to sound needy – but she couldn't. Besides, it was surprisingly easy to talk while lying on your back with your eyes closed, knowing your companion was doing the same. 'Well, we'll get sponsorship if you come, that's all. I was sent here on a mission to get you to come at all costs.'

'Hm. I don't like to be indelicate . . .'

She chuckled, 'Well, I'll pretend to believe you.'

'But would you have shown quite so much dedication to duty if I'd been eighty, with no hair and false teeth?'

'No. But if you'd been eighty, with no hair and false teeth, would you have said you'd come if I went to bed with you?' She paused. 'No, don't answer, I don't want to hear it.'

He was chuckling now. 'You're quite right. I've been in training to be a dirty old man since I was seventeen.'

'I thought you were in training to be a writer when you were seventeen.'

'The two activities go together.'

Lying supine was making her prone to giggling. 'I don't want to hear that. I'm a serious student of literature. I am a big fan of your work, and I was very drunk. And I'm also a virgin – I thought—'

All desire to giggle left her. Why had she said that? Why had she let the words escape? Her train of thought was perfectly logical: she'd been going to tell him that she thought she would like him to have her virginity because of who he was, how he wrote. But that wasn't the sort of thing you told people, unless they were very close friends, like Monica.

He didn't speak for some seconds. 'Oh. So when you agreed to go to bed with me, it would have been your first time?'

'Uh-huh.'

He laughed gently. 'No wonder you ran away.'

'I said, I was very drunk, and I wouldn't have run away if I hadn't fallen asleep.'

114

'So what was so frightening? The sight of me snoring my head off or the thought that you might have given your virginity to a wild Irish writer?'

Although she wanted to be entirely truthful, she didn't then tell him that there was no one else in the world she'd rather give her virginity to. His tone was teasing and she wasn't sure if it was just a game – albeit a very pleasant one – to him or not. She would keep her answers as light as possible. 'The realisation that I'd been so drunk I didn't know if we'd made love or not. I was appalled at myself.'

'But not at me?'

'No. You're a man. You'd made a casual suggestion; you didn't expect me to take you up on it. Did you?'

He paused for a long time. 'As we're being totally honest with each other, I'll tell you: I don't get turned down all that often.'

She put her hand over her eyes, although he wasn't looking at her. 'Oh God! Now I feel like I'm in a long line—'

'If it's any consolation to you, I don't ask anything like as often as I used to. I'm quietening right down. And I always use a condom, you can tell Monica.'

She chuckled softly. 'I'm glad to hear it. And I think you convinced Monica about the condoms. I'm so sorry she harassed you like that. She was only looking after me, but it must have been desperately embarrassing.'

'Not at all,' he said softly. Laura could hear the smile in his voice. 'I've been asked worse things, I can tell you.'

'Really? You didn't look embarrassed, I must say.'

'So you could see, could you? From your spot at the back there.'

'Yes. It was quite a small hall.' So her trying to hide at the back again hadn't worked.

'And I filled it. You don't need to say anything else about me being a big fish in a small pond.'

'I wouldn't dream of it! I've no doubt you could fill the Albert Hall if you'd agree to go.'

'I don't know about that,' he said dismissively, and then went on, 'And another thing. I promise you that if we had made love you would have known about it, drunk or not.' He paused. 'Were you really that far gone? You didn't seem it.'

She sighed. Being drunk seemed a better excuse for her behaviour than being in love – thrall – lust – she still couldn't decide quite how to define her feelings for him. That would be really outrageous. 'I'm not used to drinking whiskey by the tumbler full.'

'No, I suppose not.'

'And the fact that I'm a virgin is not something I usually tell people.'

'Well, it's nothing to be ashamed of.'

'No, but at my age it's a bit – well, odd, really.'

'Is there a reason for it?'

'Nope. Only I never found a man I fancied enough.' She blushed, praying his eyes were still shut and he wouldn't see. She'd virtually told him that in him she had found a man she fancied enough.

'Well, I have a confession to make too.'

'What?'

'I've had writer's block for nearly fifteen years.'

'Oh my goodness.' Laura didn't know what else to say. It was quite a revelation.

'And the reason I'm telling you is there's something about confession being sort of mutual. Not that I expect Catholic priests hearing the peccadilloes of their parishioners necessarily say, "Don't go worrying about that now, I often have a wee peep at that sort of magazine myself," but you shared something with me, and there's been no one else I can tell.'

She felt incredibly privileged, although she also thought that maybe people would have guessed.

'Well, you can understand it.' He seemed eager to justify himself. 'Two books straight off the blocks on to the bestseller lists and the literary prize shortlists.'

'And you won most of the prizes.'

'I did.' He sounded embarrassed. 'They're all waiting for me to fail now.'

She wanted to deny it but she knew how cruel the literary world could be. Cutting down tall poppies was what it liked to do best. 'Does your agent know?'

'Nope, and she mustn't. I fob her off every time she rings me, tell her I'm working on a huge book that'll take years – is taking years.'

'Does she buy that?' She was pretty sure Eleanora didn't for one moment.

His laugh was rueful now. 'Never mind buying it – she'd much rather have something to sell.'

She joined in his laughter. 'There isn't a publisher out there who wouldn't pay millions or at least hundreds of thousands for it.'

'I know. And I could do with the cash.'

'You couldn't offer them three chapters – they wouldn't have to be all that good after all – and get them to cough up an advance?'

'That, young lady,' he said, sounding stern, 'would not be ethical.'

She sighed. 'I suppose not. Plenty of writers would do it, though.'

'I feel if I did that, my block would be permanent. The guilt would make it even harder for me. The Irish are cursed by guilt, you know.'

'Really?' She didn't mean to sound disbelieving, but she did. To gloss over it, she said, 'Or you could teach creative writing. They run courses in wonderfully exotic locations. I don't suppose they pay that much but they might be fun.' She hesitated. 'All those eager young women writers. You could have your pick.' It cost her something to go on in this lighthearted manner. He could have his pick of any group of women, she was certain. Knowing it didn't make it easier for her. Now that she'd actually met him and talked to him properly, she knew her feelings for him were no longer just infatuation, but were in danger of becoming the foundation for something much stronger.

'I do give the odd lecture, but I always felt those writing courses were for writers who didn't write any more.'

'Not at all. Some very busy writers do them because they want to give something back, and like encouraging new talent.'

'Ah, you wouldn't be muddling me up with one of them, would you?'

She giggled again. 'Not at all, at all.'

'Don't mock me.'

'I wouldn't dream of it.'

'I'd love to know what you do dream of,' he said.

Laura swallowed. 'I've confided in you quite enough,' she managed, sounding suitably prim. She felt she would literally die rather than let him know what she was dreaming of right now.

He laughed softly and they fell into a comfortable silence. She felt a contentment she had rarely felt before, even at the bookshop where she'd always been so happy. Now it seemed far away and no longer so desirable.

But would she have felt like this, about this headland, this wildness, if the bookshop hadn't been about to close? She didn't know. Nothing was certain any more. But she did know that even though it was January, she felt she was in the most beautiful spot on earth. And it wasn't just being with Dermot, it was something more.

A while later he said, 'I could help you out with your problem, you know. Not here and now, obviously, but in more comfortable surroundings.'

The thought of this was somehow a bit heartbreaking. He obviously didn't feel the same way about her as she did him – how could he? She felt she'd known him all her life, but he'd only just met her. She didn't know how he really felt about her, if this really was only a bit of fun for him, and she couldn't ask. It would sound so serious. But she just couldn't let go and call his bluff. Whether it was bluff or not, she couldn't do it. And if he was just being kind that would somehow be worse.

'No thank you, I'll be all right,' she said and then paused, struggling to think of something suitably light and flirtatious, to give the impression that she wasn't really bothered. 'I've got used to being a virgin, after all these years.'

He chuckled. 'The status quo has something to be said for it.'

Thinking the status quo wasn't as easy to live with for him, she said, 'I don't suppose I could help you with your problem?'

He shot her a glance filled with mischief. 'If I was really wicked, I'd tell you that the virginity of a young girl was a well-known cure for writer's block.'

She twinkled back at him. 'But you're only partly wicked?'

'Most of the time, yes.'

She considered for a moment whether, if he did really think her virginity would cure him, she'd give it to him. The answer was probably. And not just so the literary world would be so grateful (it was not a favour she could call in, after all), but because underneath all her reservations, she really wanted to sleep with him, almost as much as she wanted to help him. But the moment was lost.

'It's a shame really,' she said, thinking aloud.

'What? That I'm not exploitative enough to demand the sacrifice of your maidenhood?'

She laughed, to deny it, but in her heart she was saying, 'Yes!' 'No, I meant it's a shame that things aren't so easily solved. Things like not being able to write any more when really, in your heart, you know you can write like an angel. You may have your problems with the people who give literary prizes but they don't give them to people who can't write.'

'Oh they do, you know, but let's not argue about it. It's time for tea. You English must have your tea, isn't that so? But don't worry, you don't have to move. I have all the makings.'

'The thermos is a wonderful invention,' she murmured.

'Indeed, but we're not having any truck with them. I have my Volcano kettle with me.'

She sat up. 'Your what?'

'Do you not have them in England? Sure you're terribly behind the times over there.'

She watched as he took out of his rucksack a copy of the *Irish Times* and a large cylindrical object in a draw-string bag. He took this out and then started to tear up sheets of newspaper and stuff them down the column in the middle. When all the newspaper was used up, he took the cork from the top. 'Right now, I'm off to find some water.'

He took a small can from the rucksack. 'You can go back to sleep if you like. I may have to go a little way away to find it.'

She closed her eyes. This was so blissful. The thought of catching the ferry and going back to England intruded on her joy and she batted it away. Live in the moment, she told herself, using a saying that was printed on uplifting postcards they sold in the bookshop. Just enjoy what you have right now, she added, quoting another of them.

Dermot came back a few minutes later. He poured the

water into a little spout at the top of the kettle, and then set light to the paper.

'How does it work?' she asked, fascinated and amused.

'The paper burning in the central column heats the water in the jacket outside. One copy of *The Times*, or the *Irish Times*, is just enough to boil the water. Madam will have her tea in but a moment.'

'I don't remember Madam asking for tea, she was offered it.'

'Don't split hairs.'

'Well no, that would be cruel,' she agreed.

'You're a mad girl, so you are.'

The sun, which had burned so enthusiastically, was fading. She lay back on the heather, although she was getting cold now. She loved him thinking she was a mad girl, when really, back on the mainland, she was almost boringly efficient and predictable.

He put tea bags into mugs and then poured on the boiling water from the little spout in the water-jacket. Milk came from a jam jar.

They sat together companionably, clutching the mugs of tea and looking at the sea. A few clouds were gathering now, and a chilly wind was getting up.

'Thank you so much for bringing me here,' she said, aware that their final parting would be hard for her. 'It's been a lovely day.'

'For me too,' he said. 'You're great company.'

She sipped her tea.

'Damn, I forgot the cake. Here.' He handed her a plastic container that was full of wedges of fruit cake. 'What time is your ferry again?' he asked as she took one, and she knew her perfect day was over.

She told him.

'I'll get you back in plenty of time to leave. And I will come to your literary festival, without your sacrifice, if you don't tell anyone about it – any press, I mean. Not until the last minute, anyway. I don't want to have to battle with all the publicity.'

Laura found herself close to tears. 'Thank you,' she said huskily, hoping he would think it was the cold wind that was making her eyes water.

Chapter Eight

'Don't mind the hounds, they get out of the way eventually,' said Fenella, opening the door to Somerby wide.

'Hello, hounds,' said Laura, wondering why she was coping with Fen's pack perfectly well, although they were completely blocking her way, when those on a certain farm in Ireland had seemed so threatening. (Possibly because none of this lot were snarling and curling their upper lips.) 'Are there some new ones, or did I just not notice them when you let them out as I left last time?'

'I'm looking after my sister's two little Tibetan terriers while she's on hols. Treacle and Toffee. I'm not going to want to give them back.'

'They are very sweet,' said Laura, putting out a hand to be sniffed and finding six noses eagerly searching for food traces. She stifled a sigh, remembering how Dermot had rescued her in Ireland. Ballyfitzpatrick seemed a world away. She had half hoped she might have heard from him – a friendly text at least – but then admonished herself. Why should he? And somehow she felt too shy to be the one to make contact first.

'It wasn't too hard getting the time off?' asked Fenella, kissing Laura on the cheek and stirring the dogs away with her foot.

'No, Henry's been very understanding. So's Grant. But Henry wants to supply the books and Grant wants to do something glamorous for the festival.'

'We'll be glad of all the help we can get.'

Laura indicated a cloth bag filled with files. 'I've been quite busy since I got back from Ireland.'

'Brilliant!' Then Fenella gave a little jump and clapped her hands. 'I can't believe you got Dermot Flynn! Jacob Stone is thrilled. He's going to give us lots of money and I've insisted we increase your fee. Five hundred pounds.'

'Brilliant. Thank you.' She had phoned Fenella the moment she got back from Ireland with the good news. She had followed it up with the bad – that Dermot didn't want anyone to know he was appearing until the last moment – almost immediately. Fenella hadn't seemed to take in what a drawback this might be.

Now Fenella hugged her tightly. 'Sorry, I was so excited about Dermot that I forgot my manners. Come in properly, dump your bags and come on down to the kitchen. I'll show you your room when the fan heater's had time to warm it up a bit.'

Laura put her case down and separated the carrier bag with a box of chocolates and a plant in it. She had come for a serious planning weekend. 'So Jacob Stone didn't mind that Dermot wanted to keep it all under wraps for as long as possible?'

Fenella shook her head. 'I don't think he cares that much about the festival, he just wanted to hear Dermot Flynn.' She paused. 'Well, come on. Let's go down to the kitchen and have a drink. Rupert's cooking supper. It smells heavenly. I'm doing pudding, which is the very exotic ice cream with Marsala poured over it.'

'Unusual,' said Laura, following her hostess down the stairs, holding her carrier.

'Actually it's delish, but not exactly labour-intensive, which is why I serve it so often.'

'You don't think we should start work before we eat? I've come to work, after all.'

'I know and you will but tomorrow will do. My brain

doesn't function after five o'clock anyway. Just be a guest and relax tonight.'

Within minutes the present was delivered and exclaimed over and Laura was seated at the kitchen table with a big glass of wine and a bowl of pistachios in front of her. Rupert had delivered these shortly after he had embraced her warmly. 'Oh that's delicious!' she said, having taken a sip. Although superficially she was talking about the wine, privately she was commenting on the welcome. Her own family didn't do hugs and wine, more 'Oh, hello dear' and 'I suppose I'd better put the kettle on'. She had yet to tell them how she'd got on in Ireland, but as they hadn't asked either, she didn't feel too guilty. And she'd been too busy to visit them since she'd got back.

Fenella took the seat opposite her, having been assured by her husband that there was nothing she could do to help with the meal until later. 'So,' she said eagerly, anxious to prise all the details out of Laura. 'Tell all. Did you have to offer Dermot Flynn your body to get him to agree to come?'

For a stunned moment, Laura wondered how on earth Fenella could have known this, but then realised she was joking. Monica, the only other person apart from Dermot who knew, wouldn't have told her.

She decided the truth would be a good disguise. 'Practically, but you'll be glad to hear he didn't take me up on it.'

'Oh?' said Rupert, stirring thoughtfully. 'That's not his reputation. I heard he was a bit of a womaniser.' He lifted his spoon to his lips. 'Ah yes. The gravy is coming along nicely.'

'Going by his photo he wouldn't have to work too hard at it,' said Fenella. 'Is he as gorgeous in real life?'

'Mm, but older,' said Laura carefully.

'I think men improve with age, like fine wine. Isn't that right, Rupert?'

'Whatever you say, honey.'

'So,' Fenella turned her full attention on Laura again. 'What did you have to do to persuade him to come? Eleanora said for years you couldn't drag him out of Ireland for love nor money, but now he's doing this course as well.'

'What course?' Laura put down the nut she had just prised open and looked at Fen.

'Oh, haven't you heard? No, I suppose you wouldn't have, it's only just been settled. It's a writing course – a competition – at Bath Spa University. People have to send in their novels and the best ten or so get to go on the course. One of Eleanora's other clients – can't remember who – was supposed to be doing it but they had to pull out for some reason. Anyway, she's got Dermot to do it.' She frowned. 'In fact, I think he might have actually offered. She mentioned the problem with the other author while she was talking to Dermot about something else, the festival probably, when he suggested he did it. She was quite taken aback – especially as she's hardly spoken to him in ages and he usually avoids her calls.'

Laura found herself oddly put out. It was nothing to do with her, but somehow, after the enormous lengths she had gone to just to get Dermot to give a talk at a literary festival, let alone the lengths she had been willing to go to, she felt affronted that he had actually offered to teach a writing course, which would be a far bigger deal. 'I must say, I am a bit surprised. I had to go all the way to Ireland to get him to do an hour sitting on a stage being asked questions by a sycophantic interviewer. Piece of cake compared to actually setting exercises, thinking up a course, all that stuff. And he offered to do it? It doesn't make sense.' She really wanted to say that it didn't seem fair but didn't want to appear churlish.

'Maybe he felt once he'd decided actually to leave his native land for one thing, it wouldn't be so hard to do it for two.' Fenella frowned for a second, 'Although the course thing is first, come to think of it. Maybe he'll be moving straight here after the course. Anyway,' she went on enthusiastically, 'do you suppose having done the course he'd let us advertise him for the festival?'

'I don't know, but if he's actually had students, who couldn't all be sworn to secrecy, he should do by then.' Laura was still miffed and tried to shake herself out of it. Another sip of wine helped. 'How's the music festival going?'

'OK, I think. We've got one or two quite famous bands who have almost definitely confirmed. And Monica, of course. Did you and she have fun in Ireland?'

'Gosh yes. She's a real laugh. She made me hire a bicycle with her to go and track down an old boyfriend.'

'Did she find him?'

'He wasn't in when we first arrived on our bicycles, thank goodness, considering I was giggling so much I was nearly wetting myself. And afterwards, when she had a another chance to visit him, she got no reply either.' Finding she didn't want to explain now about why Monica was on her own for a day, she moved on. 'But she was a great travelling companion. Made me go to the pub and things.'

'Was it a real Irish pub with music and lots of crack?' asked Rupert, still stirring his gravy.

'I don't think anyone was taking drugs,' said Laura, pretending to misunderstand.

Fenella laughed. 'It sounds fun. And is Dermot Flynn really "Oirish"?'

'He has a definite lilt but he doesn't sound like someone out of *Father Ted*.'

'Oh! *Father Ted*! How wonderful was that?' Fenella sighed.

'Are you two planning on doing any work tonight?' said Rupert. 'Do you want more wine or not?'

'Yes please,' said Fenella. 'We decided we're going to start early tomorrow. Tonight we can just toss around ideas.'

'Alcohol always helps with that,' said Rupert, pouring. 'And we're just about ready to eat.'

'I'll set the table.' Fenella reached into a drawer and pulled out a random selection of knives and forks. Then she cleared one end of the table with her elbow, sending a miscellany of papers, a fruit bowl, a pile of clean under-wear that had presumably been drying over the Aga and a screwdriver up the other end. Fortunately it was a long table.

'I should really have tidied up a bit more for your visit,' Fenella went on apologetically, setting places. 'But I never seem to unless we've got a huge event on. We don't do weddings much in the winter so we never see the whole table cleared until spring. Maybe we should just force the family to come to us for Christmas. Then I'd do it.'

'I don't think I've ever seen such a huge joint of beef,' said Laura, watching Rupert carve.

'It's locally produced,' said Fenella, 'and we'll eat it cold for ages now, with soup and baked potatoes. I'm always a bit vague when it comes to ordering meat. I seem to buy it by the haunch rather than the pound.'

'As long as you're not vague when it comes to organ-ising literary festivals,' said Laura. She was teasing but there was a thread of anxiety in the back of her mind.

'Oh no, work wise, I'm spot on. It's just domestically I'm a bit of a dilly.'

'Here you are, Dilly,' said her husband fondly, 'and make sure Laura has plenty of gravy.'

When at last they were all eating, and no one had to jump up and get anything else, Laura said, 'I've had quite a lot of ideas about things we could do in the run-up for the festival. A reading group for instance.'

'Oh, that's a good idea. As you know, I'm in a reading group,' said Fenella. 'And there are another couple around, including one in the library.'

Laura nodded while she finished her mouthful. 'I've been in touch with the local librarian. She's very keen. We just need to get the authors sorted out as quickly as possible.'

'Then we'll sell lots of books and they'll be inspired to come to the events.' Fenella speared a piece of roast potato. 'It'll stir up interest.' She chewed thoughtfully. 'Although the library's group always get their books ordered specially. Not everyone can afford to buy a new book every month.'

Laura's bookseller's mantle fell away for a moment. 'Of course not. I couldn't myself if I didn't get proofs from the shop. But it's great to have the library on side.'

'We could get the local paper to sponsor something,' suggested Rupert. 'All the local institutions should have a stake in it.'

'What about a writing competition?' suggested Fenella, her mouth full of carrot.

'But who would we get to judge it?' said Rupert. 'We're going to have our work cut out setting this thing up, and we're not qualified, really.'

'Dermot,' muttered Laura, who was still faintly resentful about him offering to do that course and cross with herself because of it. She sipped her wine, wondering why she was feeling so resentful. He wasn't her exclusive property and he hadn't actually taken her virginity, after all.

'We'll find someone,' said Fenella. 'I've got a huge wish list of authors I want. One of them will be willing to pick a winner, if we didn't offer them more than about five to read.'

'Damien Stubbs might,' said Laura. 'We should definitely ask him to the festival. He's really good and very attractive. Eleanora could make him come. He's one of hers.'

'I hope we don't forget all this. Here, Rupes, chuck us that bit of paper and a pencil.' Fenella made a note.

'Oh,' said Laura, 'and a children's writing competition would be good. The best ones could be read out at an event and printed in the local paper.' Laura considered for a moment. 'Although would the parents come to the event if they could see their child's work in print anyway?'

'I should think so,' said Fenella. 'Hard to tell. But children's events would make the locals keen. It would be their festival too, not just something that's inflicted on them.' She chewed reflectively. 'I've no idea how to get in touch with my wish list of writers.'

'That's what I'm here for. We contact them through their agents or publishers,' said Laura. 'We find out who's in charge of their publicity and ask them. The only trouble is that it can take a while, if you don't get a named person to deal with.'

'Oh it's so good having you,' said Fenella. 'You know all the wrinkles.'

'And I'll probably get a few too,' Laura murmured.

Fenella ignored this. 'I want to involve the local schools, get them to all come to something.'

'Or it might be easier to get the authors to go to the schools,' suggested Laura, flinching at the vision of marshalling fifty or so children into a hall.

'Or both,' suggested Rupert. 'The authors go into the schools, give the children such a good time that they pester their parents to take them to the main event.'

'Good thinking. You're not just a pretty face, after all.' Fenella smiled at her husband affectionately.

'Where are we actually going to hold the events?' asked Laura, feeling gently envious of their relationship. 'Obviously you won't be doing everything here. Festivals always scatter themselves over a town, of course, but yours is a pretty small one.'

'Big enough though,' said Fenella, defending her home territory. 'There'll be some here, of course, but for Dermot or any other really big names, we can hire the cinema. Don't look at me like that! Apparently it's lovely! And there's a huge car park just next door. And I've had a word with the vicar and there's a chapel that's not used much that we can have. That has parking too,' added Fenella, looking at Rupert, who'd obviously been a bit obsessed by this issue.

'So the vicar's keen on the festival, is he?' said Laura. 'I'm sure that'll be helpful.'

'Not he, she, and she's in my book group.'

'Excellent!'

'So we'll need to sort out the venues, but Sarah – remember? She was at the meeting – is going to help decide who should go where. I'm hopeless about guessing numbers and how much space they'll take up.'

'Wouldn't a marquee here be better for Dermot than a cinema?' suggested Laura.

'You don't like my cinema idea, do you? Well, we can go and look at it and decide later.'

'Where are you going to put everyone up?' asked Laura.

'Here, as far as we can. We can sleep about eight, comfortably, and of course not everyone will be here at the same time. The authors will stay in the house on a rolling basis unless they're sharing, in which case they might have one of the cottages. There are also lots of b. and b's. locally, but we hope we don't have to put writers in them, unless they prefer it for some reason.'

'We must mention the b. and b.s when we do the flyers, so people know they can stay. It'll be part of the rural image: "Enjoy literature in the undiscovered beauties of wherever . . ."'

'We're not exactly undiscovered,' complained Rupert. 'We did have a lot of publicity for a celebrity wedding not long ago.'

'I meant the area in general,' said Laura. 'If people think the area is attractive, they're more likely to come. Think of Hay-on-Wye!'

'Are we going to have a theme?' asked Fenella. 'I mean, we've got the music stuff going on too.'

'At exactly the same time?' asked Laura anxiously.

'We thought alternate days,' said Rupert, 'or a few musical events, a few literary ones, and then a music one at the end. Or vice versa. We've got permission to use a couple of the fields.'

'That took a lot of tact and persuasion,' said Fenella. 'It's only because farming isn't doing brilliantly at the moment that I managed to swing it. I think they all imagined Glastonbury was moving up here.'

'But the farms should get something out of it,' said Rupert. 'Lots of them said they could rent out space for camping.'

'And we've got some really big names for the music side of it,' said Laura.

Fenella winced slightly. 'Not confirmed,' she said. 'That's why I wanted some biggies for the lit. bit. Monica is on the case though. She's pulled in all the favours she can manage and has used blackmail if that failed.'

'Well, I wouldn't refuse her anything,' declared Laura.

'And I hope you won't refuse another roast spud from me,' said Rupert.

'Of course not.'

'So, theme or no theme?' asked Fenella. 'I think not, on the whole.'

'The Cheltenham lit. fest. always has one,' said Laura.

'I know but they've got the pick of the bunch. We're brand new. Authors might not be so keen to come to us.'

'I think they will,' said Laura, pushing her plate away

from her so she could really make her point. 'Having Dermot will make it a big literary event, they'll want to be there. Amazing publicity for them. Besides, most of them will get to stay in a lovely country house and there's something special about the first year of a festival.' Laura felt herself getting excited. She realised she was going to enjoy working on the festival with Fen, however much work it might involve.

'It might be the first and last,' said Rupert.

'We might have to tell them he's going to appear and they'll get a chance to meet him. I wonder if he'd mind us doing that?' said Laura, ignoring Rupert's uncharacteristic pessimism.

'Or would he hate that even more?' asked Fenella. 'You know him, Laura. What do you think?'

'I don't know! He may hate other authors. I've come across a few who do. It's probably professional jealousy or something.'

'Maybe we could arrange a discreet authors' dinner before his event. He can choose which ones and we'll make it really special.'

'But would that be cost-effective?' asked Laura. 'A special dinner could cost loads.'

'We don't need to worry about that,' said Rupert. 'We have contacts.'

'Breaking even is all we can hope to do this first year,' said Fenella. 'Although the bottom line is important, we have to speculate in order to accumulate.'

'That sounds very businesslike,' said Laura, impressed.

'I read it somewhere,' said Fenella, 'but more to the point, do you think Dermot would agree to all this?'

'If we'd cleared it with him first,' said Laura. 'He's not easy. And a bit unpredictable,' she added, thinking of him agreeing to do a course, apparently without even being asked, when everyone in Ireland had told her that he wouldn't stir out of his village. 'He may love the idea.'

133

'On the other hand,' put in Rupert, 'maybe we shouldn't give Dermot so much control? He may never be able to decide who he wants to come. I think we should just invite who we think we'd like.'

On Saturday morning their work began in earnest. Laura sat at the computer and, with Fenella's help, typed up all the ideas that had flowed as freely as the wine had the night before.

'OK, now we've got our definitive list of authors, we must check up on who their publishers are.'

'How are we going to do that?'

'I've bought some trade mags. That'll help,' said Laura. 'But to be honest, I know lots of them. Now we've pruned it down a bit, it shouldn't take long.'

They had agreed that in order to be invited the authors had to (a) be still alive (this when Rupert expressed a burning desire to meet Evelyn Waugh) and (b) live either in the UK or near enough so their travel expenses wouldn't use up the entire budget.

When letters had been dispatched, including inducements such as nights to be spent in 'country-house style with old-fashioned hospitality', they spent the rest of the morning writing to schools, inviting entrants to their children's short-story competition. Laura knew a lovely children's author who could be the final judge and Fenella knew a couple of teachers from her book group who could draw up a shortlist.

After lunch, they took all the dogs for a gallop over the fields, and Rupert advised Laura on what sort of car she should buy. She couldn't go on borrowing Grant's for much longer; twice was enough.

On Sunday afternoon they had all repaired to what Fenella and Rupert referred to as 'the small drawing room', which would have swallowed up Laura's bedsit twice over. Rupert had built a dazzling log fire and they were all beginning to doze off in front of it. Laura had had a tour of the local area so she could see some of the venues (from the outside at least) and they had ended up at the pub for lunch. Laura was seriously considering Fenella's suggestion that she should stay another night and go back early the next morning.

Rupert had picked up the paper and was working on the general knowledge crossword when the phone rang. He and Fenella exchanged glances and then Fen got up. 'I can't think who'd be ringing at this time of day.'

'It's only four o'clock,' said Rupert. 'And if you answer it you'll know who it is.'

'Hello,' said Fenella, sounding efficient. 'Somerby.'

Laura stole the crossword from Rupert while his attention was distracted. Then she stole his pencil and put in the answer to a clue.

'Yes, that's right,' Fenella was saying. 'Uh huh, that's me. What? Oh. Well yes, I have, actually, but I can do better than that. She's here. I'll put her on. Laura?' Fenella came across the room and offered her the handset. 'It's for you.'

'It can't be,' said Laura, not touching the phone but at least getting up. 'Who is it?'

'Dermot Flynn. He rang me to get your number.'

Laura's knees went weak and her mouth went dry. She tugged at her polo neck, swallowed and took a deep breath. 'Right. OK.' She took the phone as if it might explode and walked away from the others. Her heart started to race with nerves and excitement. 'Hello? Dermot?' This was the first time she'd spoken to him since Ireland.

'Hello, Laura,' said a voice that made her knees go weaker and her mouth become drier. She sank on to a little chair that was near a small desk.

'Hello,' she said again, wishing she had a glass of water.

'It's a great coincidence that you happened to be there, isn't it?'

'Maybe. Great for whom?' she asked warily, wondering what he meant.

'Great for me, anyway. The reason I need to speak to you is, I want you to do a job for me.'

'What sort of job?' Laura was a bit panicked. She was busy enough as it was with the festival and still working at the bookshop.

'Did you hear about the writing course I've agreed to do?'

She turned away a little but was aware of Rupert and Fenella poring over the crossword as if it were an exam paper, they were working so hard at not eavesdropping. 'Yes. I was a bit surprised. It was all I could do to get you to agree to speak at the festival, now here you are offering to run a writing course. I thought you weren't keen on them.' She tried to sound lighthearted, but she found speaking to him almost unbearably lovely.

He gave a short, dismissive laugh. 'I'm not running anything, I'll just teach.'

Laura tucked a strand of hair behind her ear to help her think. 'But I thought people sent in their manuscripts and you decided who got on the course on the strength of them?'

'Oh, so you know all about it, do you?' He sounded amused.

'Not at all. Just what Fenella told me. But that's right, isn't it?' Now she pulled the scrunchy off her ponytail and shook out her curls as if doing so would settle her jumbled thoughts.

'It is so, and that's where you come in.' He sounded a little triumphant as if he'd solved a problem.

'Where? Where do I come in?'

'My agent, Eleanora, the old dragon' – his chuckle revealed he was fond her, old dragon or not – 'told me

136

that you have a very good eye when it comes to fiction. You didn't tell me you knew her.'

'Well, er, yes, I do. And yes, I suppose I have read a lot,' said Laura tentatively.

'So I want you to read all the scripts and pick out the ten best.'

She gulped. 'What? But how would I know? When would I have time to do it? I'm organising a literary festival!' A second later she remembered that literary festivals were often run by people with full-time jobs.

'Not single-handed. Eleanora told me there's a team, including her niece, or god-daughter, Fenella – whoever it was I spoke to.'

'That's true.' Laura struggled to sound calm.

'Well then, you can do my scripts for me. I'll pay you,' he added.

'How much?' Too late Laura realised this must have made her sound awfully mercenary. She hadn't really asked because she cared that much, although she did need money. She just wanted to give herself a bit of time to think.

'We'll work out a fee, but probably about ten pounds a script. I'd need you to pick, say, thirty, and we'll decide on the best ten together, over the phone probably, or by email.'

'All right then,' she said meekly. Then a thought struck her. 'There's just one thing. I only live in a small flat, just a bedsit with a bathroom, really. I'm not sure I've got the space to do all this.'

'I'm sure it'll be fine. Don't you worry about it.'

Laura could tell he was now bored with the subject of the course, and his 'Don't you worry about it' really meant 'I'm not going to worry about it'. Well, he didn't need to, now he'd got her to agree to help him.

'So, how have you been?' he said now. 'Have you recovered from your trip to the Emerald Isle?'

The laugh in his voice was not helping her current heart condition. 'Of course. What was there to recover from?'

'Drinking whiskey by the tumbler full for a start,' he said. 'Not to mention the men you had to beat off with a stick.' She could just imagine him, lying back in his chair, possibly doodling, enjoying his gentle teasing.

'I didn't need a stick.' She was smiling too and she wasn't sure if he would be able to hear this in her voice or not.

'Sure now, I was meek as a lamb when it came to it.' He paused. 'So, I'll tell Eleanora to get whoever's in charge of this course to send the scripts to you. We'll keep in touch about it.'

'Thank you. I think.'

He laughed. 'Sure you'll thank me. You may discover the next Dermot Flynn and then the world will be at your feet.'

'I think one Dermot Flynn is quite enough for the world, thank you,' she said.

He laughed again. 'You're a lovely girl, Laura Horsley, and I have my eye on you.' Then he disconnected.

Laura examined the handset and then switched it off. She got up and walked slowly to where Fenella had answered the phone and found the rest. She was horribly aware of Rupert and Fenella studying her, desperate to find out what was going on.

'He wants me to read the scripts for his course and help him select the final ten. Apparently Eleanora recommended me.'

'Huh!' said Rupert. 'Far more likely that Eleanora got him to agree to do the course by saying, "I've got a lovely girl who'll do all the hard work for you."'

Fenella looked at her husband, about to reproach him for slandering her aunt but then obviously decided that was probably exactly what had happened.

'It's kind of Eleanora really,' said Laura. 'She knows I need the money. I wonder if there'll be many scripts?'

'There could be a few,' said Fenella. 'I gathered from Eleanora that the competition has been very widely advertised.'

At the sound of this word Laura's eyes widened. 'Ergh! Advertising! We haven't thought about it at all!'

Work, even on a Sunday evening, was an excellent displacement activity, she decided, forcing a reluctant Fenella back down to her office for another hour before she headed back to her flat. Dermot Flynn was taking up far too much space in her brain and they had a festival to organise.

Chapter Nine

Three weeks later, Laura was tipping white wine into a glass at the bookshop for possibly the very last time. It was their farewell party for all their customers. 'Yes, it is terribly sad the shop is closing,' she said to the recipient of the wine, a woman whom she couldn't remember ever seeing in the shop, but who obviously supported it now there was free wine going. 'But I'm sure you'll manage.'

'Of course, I buy all my books from charity shops,' said the woman taking on a pious expression. 'I do like to support charity.'

Behind the woman Laura observed Henry's rueful eyebrow. 'But not bookshops?' said Laura.

'Oh well, they're businesses, aren't they?' The woman looked into her empty glass, willing Laura to magic some more wine into it as a reward for her virtue.

Laura held the bottle firmly upright. 'Yes, and they have to make money, like any other business. And how would the authors make money if no one bought their books new?'

The woman frowned. Taking pity on her, Laura tipped a small amount of wine into her glass.

'I never thought of that,' said the woman, and moved away.

'Laura, dear!' A much-loved customer, stalwart of the reading group, came up. 'What are we going to do without you all?'

It was customers like this woman who made book-selling such a joy, Laura felt, and hoped she wasn't going to get emotional. Now the time had finally come she felt as if she was losing a friend. It was the end of an era for her. She'd cut her literary teeth here; she felt more at home here than anywhere else; this was the place where she could really be herself. 'Oh, Fiona! Don't say that! It's sad enough as it is. You will keep the reading group going, won't you?'

'Of course. It won't be the same without you, though. You've read so much.' She sighed. 'But we'll manage.' She paused. 'And what about you? Have you got another job?'

'Sort of. A temporary one, anyway.' Laura produced a flyer from the table behind her. 'I'm helping to set up a literary festival. In the summer. I do hope you'll be able to come to some of the events?'

Fiona inspected the flyer.

'Of course, we can't promise all those authors will be able to attend but some of them will.' Laura sounded a little more confident than she felt, knowing as she did that authors were sometimes very late making up their minds and some were known to pull out at the last minute. She dismissed this negative thought and smiled at Fiona.

Fiona inspected the flyer. 'Oh, it's a bit far, isn't it?'

'Well, maybe you get up a group of you and arrange to stay over. It's a really beautiful area.' She felt like a travel agent selling a holiday destination, even if it was all true, and tried not to look so eager.

'Mm, that would be fun and lots of us could use a break from our families. Can I take this with me?'

'Of course! Here, take several.' Well, she did need to drum up trade, after all.

Grant came up. 'It's going well, isn't it? And I've given away lots of your flyers. I must say, people have been really sweet, saying how much they'll miss us.'

'Not that woman over there, helping herself to crisps

by the bowlful. I don't think she's ever been in before.' Laura tried not to sound resentful, but she was, a little.

Grant glanced across. 'Don't malign her. I sold her a birthday card once. She's one of those people who doesn't use us but likes us to be here.'

'She buys all her books from charity shops,' explained Laura to another regular customer who joined them. 'I think she believes it's faintly immoral to buy them new.'

'Now don't you go knocking charity bookshops,' the customer said. 'There's many a new author I've discovered by buying their books for virtually nothing. Then I've bought everything else they've written new!'

Laura rewarded this jolly woman by emptying her bottle into her glass. 'I know, you're a star, and I don't really mind people supporting charity shops, of course I don't. It's when they try to make out they're more virtuous than the rest of us who wantonly buy our books new-from-a-shop.'

The woman chuckled. 'So what are you both going to do now?' It was a question they were being asked frequently.

Grant said, 'Well I'm applying to a couple of big bookstores, but Laura here is running a literary festival. Flyer, please.' He held out his hand.

Laura produced one. 'Of course, not everyone on this flyer will be able to come but—'

'Oh, that looks huge fun!' said the woman. 'Good for you!'

And they chatted for a while about festivals and favourite authors and what a shame it was that another independent bookshop was closing down, even if it was out of choice.

As she topped up glasses, answered questions and circulated among the crowd – the shop was understandably packed; it was a huge favourite and had been there for years – Laura felt a sense of pride and sadness. Not an overwhelming sadness, because she had things to look forward to, but she was going to miss it. It was as if she was throwing off her old, safe self, like a treasured overcoat, outgrown.

It was after ten before Henry closed the door on the last straggler: an enthusiastic member of the local press who'd wanted to get all his angles (and help them finish the wine).

'Well, that was a great party,' said Henry as he, Grant and Laura cleared up. The part-time staff had been sent home because Laura insisted they'd covered for her so much recently, she didn't want them doing extra washing-up as well.

'Yes. It was a shame Monica couldn't come though,' Laura said to Grant as she gathered up a pile of paper plates. 'You'd really get on.'

'Well, we'll have to have another get-together some-time.' Grant sighed deeply. 'It's going to be really sad not being a team any more.'

Laura put her arms round him. 'I know! I've suddenly gone all weepy.' She'd managed to keep any threatening tears in check all evening but now it was just the three of them she felt them pricking behind her eyes.

'Oh, do brace up!' said Henry, who couldn't be doing with all this emotion. 'You'll both go on to greater things and soon forget about this little shop.'

'It's not that little,' said Grant, releasing himself from Laura and tying up yet another black bag.

'And I won't forget it,' said Laura. 'It – well, you, Henry, really – taught me all I know.'

'Well, don't get all maudlin!' said Henry, dropping empty bottles into a cardboard box. 'We'll keep in touch over Laura's festival, won't we? And I'll give you both splendid references.'

'And we're not actually closing until the end of the week,' Grant reminded them, 'and then we've got a few days packing up.'

When Laura got home from the shop after its last day of business she was very tired. If she'd had to say, yes, it was very sad the shop's closing, and no, she didn't really have another job yet, but there was going to be this literature and music festival and would they like a flyer? one more time, she felt she'd have had a nasty turn. She'd done so much of it at the party, she hadn't been prepared to do it for the rest of the week as well. And the bookshop had looked so forlorn with its depleted shelves and bare floorboards. Although she'd wanted to help, she was quite glad Henry had insisted he and Grant would do the final days of clearing and packing up. She wasn't sure she could have borne seeing it as a completely empty shell.

She got up the stairs to her little flat, opened the door and put the kettle on, even before she'd shut the door.

She had just taken her first, perfect sip of tea when her phone went. She cursed inwardly. She could never drink tea and talk on the phone unless she knew the person well enough to explain that was what she was doing. Praying it was one of those, she found her phone and answered it. It was Mrs Ironside, her downstairs neighbour, who generally preferred to phone than walk all the way up the stairs to Laura's flat 'at her age'.

'Laura?' Mrs Ironside was an irritable person who didn't have enough to do and so filled her time with the doings of others. 'There are a great many parcels for you. I took them in when I saw the postman about to take them all away. Then you'd have had to go to the sorting office for them.'

'Oh, thank you so much.' Laura was truly grateful although she didn't always get on with Mrs Ironside.

'So will you come and collect them? There are so many of them. What on earth are they?'

'I really don't know. I'll come down now.'

She took a gulp of tea, which was slightly too hot for gulping, and propping her door open, went downstairs. Her tea would be too cold before she got back to it, and she knew that if she made herself another cup, it would not be as nice. It was not her day.

There were fifteen large Jiffy bags piled neatly in Mrs Ironside's hall. She had a much larger flat than Laura but they still took up a lot of space.

'Oh my goodness,' said Laura, wondering how many she could carry at once, and thinking longingly of her tea. If Mrs Ironside had been anyone else, she could have explained about the tea. 'Right, I'll take as many as I can and pop back down for the rest.'

She managed five at a time. Three journeys, a sip of tea between each one. She cursed Dermot every step of the way. The moment she had seen them she'd realised what they were: manuscripts for his wretched course.

There was hardly enough floor space for her to get to the kettle by the time she'd brought the last lot up.

'Oh Lord! What am I to do with this lot?' she said out loud. 'I won't have room to breathe!'

The thought that someone might have written to her about them sent her back downstairs to pick up her post from her pigeon hole.

Yes, there was a letter, and it had a frank on it that indicated a London literary agency. She opened it there and then, not wanting to clutter her flat with any more post, even a single sheet. It was from Eleanora.

'Darling,' it read, 'you'll be getting the manuscripts any day now. I've had them redirected. Any more will come direct to you.'

Thanks a lot, Eleanora, thought Laura, and read on.

'Don't feel you need to read every word. If you're

not enjoying it, stop. The first few pages should tell you if they can write, less even. Then just check the synopsis to see if there's any sort of plot on offer. Make a pile of the possibles, and then weed and weed.' For a moment Laura wondered if Eleanora had meant to write 'read and read' but realised she meant she had to go through the possibles and find excuses to turn them down.

She climbed the stairs again. In spite of the logistics of dealing with all that paper she was quite excited. She might, as Dermot had suggested, discover the next big thing. Maybe it would give her a chance to work as an editor, something she'd always longed to do, but had always felt was beyond her grasp. But it was a big responsibility and she was worried she wouldn't be able to recognise good writing from bad. At least Eleanora had told her she didn't need to read the whole manuscript if she wasn't enjoying it, so it might not take her too long. She hastened up the last flight, eager to get started, all tiredness forgotten with the challenge ahead. If she couldn't do it, she'd have to let Eleanora know right away.

It was, she discovered, quite easy to tell good writing from bad. After all, she didn't have to decide if it was publishable in the current market, something she'd learnt quite a bit about from Henry. She just had to decide who could write and who couldn't. And two hours later she realised that none of these aspiring writers could.

Some had dialogue so stilted it could have been examples from a grammar textbook. Others had characters who were not even dislikeable, let alone engaging; they just didn't have enough substance to be anything. Not one of them had a plot. She was very depressed. She decided to ring Eleanora about it the next day and leave a message if necessary. She also needed to think about

146

buying a laptop. She'd lost her Internet connection after today, where she had it at the shop, and she couldn't organise a literary festival without email.

Eleanora was out when she rang, but returned her call shortly afterwards. 'Laura? Sweetie? Are they God-awful?'

'They are dire,' said Laura. 'Honestly, to start with I thought I'd give each one fifty pages, just to be fair, as I'd heard the judge for a major award say that was what he does. But after a couple I just couldn't bear to.'

'Sweetie, don't sweat it. Most of them will be dire, but how many have you read so far?'

'Fifteen. They all arrived at the same time.'

'Only fifteen? Nothing to worry about. There'll be at least a hundred.'

'A hundred?' Laura took a sharp intake of breath. 'Have you any idea of how tiny my flat is – no, of course you haven't. Sorry.' She paused. 'I haven't got to send them back, have I?'

'Are you saying they haven't got return postage, self-addressed labels? All that?' Eleanora was outraged.

'Well, I think most of them have but—'

'Then just stick on the return labels and bung 'em off to the post office.'

'I haven't got a car and the post office is miles away.' Laura didn't want to sound grumbly but she thought it had been a while since Eleanora had 'bunged anything off to the post office' personally. Did she know that many small, queue-free post offices had been closed?

'Well, wait until you can get a lift or something. These people don't need to get their hopes and dreams thrown back at them too soon. Give them a few days' hope before you let 'em down.'

Shortly afterwards, Laura ended the call. She needed to get to bed. Tomorrow she would address the car and laptop situation which was becoming more and more urgent. Then she had a more uplifting thought: a hundred scripts at ten pounds a throw would come to a thousand pounds. Handy! Her redundancy money wouldn't last for long.

'Why don't you buy my car?' said Grant. They had arranged to meet for coffee a week or so later so they could co-counsel each other on their bookshop-withdrawal. 'Then I could upgrade.'

They were sitting in their favourite café just around the corner from the bookshop. Laura couldn't help but glance in as she went past. It was empty now and except for the many shelves it looked like any other retail space. It had felt strange not to be going into work but she hadn't really had time to feel too bereft. And now she and Grant had been catching up as well as reminiscing.

'Isn't it supposed to be a really bad idea to buy cars from friends? What if it goes horribly wrong? I might never speak to you again,' she said.

'I'll take the chance,' said Grant. 'I've got lots of friends, after all. I can afford to lose one. You're not so lucky, of course.'

'I've got loads of friends! You, and Monica. Fen's definitely a friend. All my uni friends—'

'Who are where, exactly? Not taking you out clubbing every weekend, are they?'

'They're not exactly local, I must admit.' Laura wondered if she could change the subject before she had to also admit that all her uni friends had high-powered jobs in London or were saving the planet in the Galapagos. 'Are you in close touch with all your uni chums?'

He shrugged. 'Only on Facebook, I suppose. But I really do think I'm the only normal person you know round here,' he said, sipping his coffee and preparing to dig into a slice of lemon cake.

'Monica's normal,' said Laura, wondering if someone who wore a pink wig for a living could truly be described as normal.

'I'd love to meet her.' He paused. 'Tell you what, I'll sell you the car for five hundred pounds and a night out with Monica. Can you manage that?'

'The night out with Monica, almost certainly, but as for the car, jot down its CV and I'll ask my car consultant.'

'Your who?'

'Rupert. He was advising me on what sort of car to get.'

'Well I should think mine ticks all the boxes and it's in good nick.'

'I know, and I like driving it, but I feel I should just run it by him as he was taking such an interest.'

'Give me a bit of paper then, and I'll write down the details.'

'Brilliant,' said Laura, taking the paper and putting it in her bag. 'Now do you think we should ask any sci-fi authors to the festival, or are they a bit specialist?'

'Depends who you have in mind.'

They discussed this for a while until Laura looked at her watch. 'Now I really must go back. I've got all those manuscripts to read and I must phone Rupert about the car. I'll ring you the moment I decide. OK?'

Back home, Laura decided to find out about the car before going back to her pile of manuscripts. Talking to Fenella was always cheering and there was some festival stuff they needed to talk about as well.

When they'd updated each other on who had confirmed and whom they'd need to chase, again, Laura said, 'Is Rupert there? Grant from work has suggested I buy his car. I borrowed it the first time I came to Somerby. Rupert said he'd help me get one and I want to ask his advice.'

149

'Well, I can't remember it, but I have no memory for cars. I'll put you on to Rupes.'

'Hi, Laura.' Rupert's deep voice sounded curious. 'What's all this about a car?'

Laura gave him the details. 'And he's anal about getting it serviced and things, so I think it should be all right,' she added, after they'd discussed it for a while. 'I just needed a second opinion really.'

'And you don't want me to come over and check it out for you?' Rupert said eventually.

'I really don't think it's necessary. I've driven it and I really like it.'

'Then it sounds just the job, and five hundred seems a good price. Go for it!'

'Brilliant, Rupert, thank you so much. Now all I need to do is get a laptop.' She spoke lightheartedly enough but she realised she was about to spend her entire fee for the festival on a car. Would a laptop take all her redundancy money? Suddenly Dermot and his writing course seemed like a life-saver.

'Would it have to be a new one?' asked Rupert.

'Oh no, I don't think so. I only really need something to write letters on and do emails.'

'They're not terribly expensive new, but don't buy anything without telling me. I may be able to get you one second-hand.'

'Oh Rupert! You are a star.'

'That's what they tell me,' he said with a laugh, and then rang off.

Having sorted out the issue of the car, she decided to call Monica. Today was turning into a catching up with friends day, after all. Monica was delighted to hear from Laura. 'I have such a lot to tell you! Yes, do let's go out, and any friend of yours can certainly come. As long as we get a chance to exchange girly chats.'

'Grant's good at girly chats,' said Laura, suddenly aware she didn't want Grant knowing too much about what had gone on in Ireland: it was still too raw. She wasn't fully aware of how she felt about it all herself. It was bad enough that Monica knew, she didn't want anyone else picking over the bones just yet. 'So when's good for you?'

Monica was silent, presumably flicking through her busy social calendar. 'I've been so frantic, trying to get bands to confirm for the festival,' she murmured.

'Me too,' said Laura. 'I must have spoken to every publicity department in every publisher there is, trying to get people to confirm. Then I've been on to the sales people to see if they can produce multiple copies for reading groups and put it all through Henry.' She paused. 'And I've got all these manuscripts to read as well.'

'Manuscripts? What the hell are you talking about?'

'Oh, it's all Dermot's fault,' said Laura and was about to explain when Monica interrupted her.

'You know something?' She sounded amused and happy. 'A lot of what's happened to you recently is Dermot's fault. You gotta love him.'

'No you haven't!' squeaked Laura, whose feelings for him were very confused. Did lust combined with huge liking and a touch of obsession equal love?

'I suppose I haven't, as long as you do.' Monica paused, to give this little barb time to find its mark. 'Anyway,' she went on, 'we can talk about all that when we meet. What about Friday?'

'Hang on, I'll just call him on my mobile. Friday?' Laura asked Grant when he answered.

Luckily he had read her mind, as he was so often able to do. 'Fine. Where and when?'

It was agreed to meet Monica in a wine bar in one of the better parts of Bristol. Grant said he'd drive home as it would be one of the last times he could. Once Laura had paid him the money, the car would be hers. Laura, however, had to drive there. She wasn't a very experienced town driver and the thought of the Bristol traffic terrified her. She wasn't going to let on to Grant though – he might decide not to sell her his car after all.

Meanwhile the manuscripts kept arriving. Mrs Ironside took them in if Laura was out and Laura took to calling at her flat before going upstairs to her own. Mrs Ironside had the kettle on and Laura had a cup of tea and a chat with her before going upstairs with her parcels. Relations had improved between them and Mrs Ironside was a lot less frosty these days. She told her about the festival and she became quite enthusiastic.

'I'd definitely come if Kathryn Elisabeth was going to appear,' she said, mentioning one of the most successful romantic novelists ever.

Laura dutifully wrote the name down, wondering if it would look rude to invite an author at this late stage. 'She's very popular,' she said warningly. 'She's probably booked up for years ahead, but I'll definitely ask her publishers.'

'She'd be a very big draw,' said Mrs Ironside.

'I know, and I'll try, but – well, we mustn't get our hopes up too much.'

Mrs Ironside folded her lips, making her disapproval at this feeble attitude plain.

Friday night arrived and Laura and Grant set off to meet Monica. It was amazing how much better you got at parking if you had to practise a lot, thought Laura as she finally straightened up and turned off the ignition. Not that she'd actually been able to fit in any of the five spaces she'd tried, but she did feel much more confident handling the car now: she knew the dimensions of the car precisely. They climbed out.

'God, I hope the car will be safe here!' said Grant,

checking that Laura had actually locked it, although he'd heard the clunk of her doing it just as well as she had.

'We're in Clifton,' said Laura. 'It's not going to get keyed, the hubcaps stolen or broken into. You're such an old woman sometimes!'

'You can talk! Now come on. Let's find this wine bar. I'm longing to meet Monica in the flesh.'

Monica was sitting at the bar, chatting to the barman. She jumped off her stool and hugged Laura. 'So lovely to see you, sweetie! And this must be Grant! Hi!'

Grant and Monica kissed each other. 'So,' said Monica. 'What are we having? Laura will have her usual pint of whiskey. Grant?'

'Pint of whiskey? That doesn't sound like the Laura I know and love!'

Monica laughed. 'You should see her when she's offshore. She's a madwoman.'

'I'll have a white wine spritzer,' said Laura, as if she'd never drunk whiskey out of tumblers, or lemonade the colour of highlighter pens, which is how it seemed to come in Ireland. Or, most importantly, offered her body to a famous writer so he'd attend her literary festival.

'I'll have grapefruit juice and lemonade,' said Grant.

'I'm buying Grant's car, but he's driving us home,' Laura explained to Monica as she and Grant sat either side of her at the bar.

'Buying a car? Haven't you got one already? No, I suppose not,' Monica said when she'd ordered the drinks.

'Bookshop pay, on the whole, is pants,' said Laura, sipping her spritzer. 'But I do – did – really love my job.'

'If you're buying Grant's car, how come he can afford to buy one in the first place if he worked in the book-shop too?' asked Monica, reasonably enough.

'I had a proper job in IT before I joined the book trade,' Grant explained. 'And a small inheritance. So that's my financial cards on the table.' He quickly closed the subject and turned to Monica. 'I want to tell you just how much I love your act,' he gushed. 'Just fabulous. Did Laura tell you how I dragged her along to see you?'

'I think I did,' muttered Laura to herself.

'And isn't she glad I did?' said Grant, looking at her.

Laura wondered if without Monica all the things that had happened to her lately would have happened and realised they wouldn't. While she did wonder if meeting Dermot was going to spoil her for all the normal men she would meet in the future, she wasn't sorry she'd met him. 'Oh yes!'

'Oh!' Monica sounded a bit surprised at her fervency. 'I love you too. Seriously, though, I'm really glad I met you because otherwise I wouldn't have gone to Ireland and met up with Seamus again. That's an old, turned new again, flame,' she explained to Grant.

'It's all back on then?' Laura sipped her spritzer. 'So that agonising bike ride was worth it? Tell all.'

'Well, a few days after we got home, he got in touch! He'd been thrilled to get my note apparently.'

'So how long ago was this?' asked Laura, trying hard not to be jealous. Dermot had called her but only to ask her a favour.

'A couple of days ago.'

'But you and Laura came back from Ireland ages ago,' said Grant. 'How keen is he?'

Monica flapped a scarlet-nailed hand at Grant. 'Very keen, he's just a bit laid-back. All Irishmen are. You just have to get used to it.'

'That's a bit of a sweeping generalisation,' said Laura, although Monica was quite right – as far as her personal experience went, anyway.

'He is laid-back but he's also mad keen to get his band to do a set at the festival.' Monica bit her lip. 'Supposing they're not good enough?'

'Haven't you heard them yet?'

'No,' said Monica, 'and to be honest, going on what Seamus says about them, they're a bit amateur.'

'Just because you're not paid for what you do, it doesn't mean you don't do it well,' said Grant, for some reason feeling the need to defend enthusiastic amateurs everywhere.

'That's very fair of you, Grant!' said Laura. 'Quite out of character if may say so.'

'Not at all. I'm always fair. After all, I did say I wanted to get involved in the festival too.'

'Oh, well, I'm sure we'll be able to find you a job,' said Laura, who was pleased as Grant didn't usually volunteer for anything. 'Remember, it's unlikely there's any money attached to it. My fee is nominal as it is.'

'I don't necessarily have to be paid,' said Grant. 'I'll have my redundancy money and my darling auntie, remember, and I've had some interest in the feelers I put out for bookshop jobs. Besides, apart from when it's actually on, I'd be doing it in my spare time. I just want to have some of the fun you two girls are having.'

'Mm, I wouldn't say it's that exactly – it mainly involves making endless phone calls – although the planning has been, and it has been lovely being in at the ground floor of something. Checking venues will be good, though, I should think.' She frowned. 'You'd probably be more use to Monica—'

'I wish you two would pay attention,' Monica cut in. 'What if Seamus's band is a pile of poo?'

'Then they can't come,' said Grant simply. 'Not only am I fair, I'm firm.'

'Well, lucky you,' said Monica, pushing him, as if they'd been friends for years.

'Seriously,' Grant went on, 'if it's a new festival you can't afford to have substandard acts.'

155

'What sort of music do they play?' asked Laura after she and Monica had taken in this basic truth.

'Irish, very traditional. I've asked him to send me a CD of something but he says there isn't one. They mostly just play in pubs.'

'Well, the musicians who played in the pub in Ballyfitzpatrick were brilliant,' said Laura. 'I've just had an idea,' she added, leaning in.

'Lie down until the feeling goes away,' suggested Grant.

'What?' said Monica.

'It's an idea I had before but then dismissed. Dermot has some poems, not many but very good. Supposing we ask him to read them, and have Seamus's band playing Irish music in between, or even very quietly in the background while he reads.'

Monica nodded, warming to the idea. 'Could be good.'

'The venue would have to be right though. It wouldn't work in an echoing great hall,' said Grant, ever the voice of reason, from his end of the bar.

'No, it would have to be in a pub,' said Monica.

'What, use the pub local to Somerby?' asked Laura.

'Is there one?' asked Grant.

'Yes. And it's lovely but I'd have to find out if they would be up for it.'

'Don't pubs have to have licences if they have music?' said Grant.

'I don't know,' said Laura impatiently. 'But couldn't they get one? It's such a good idea – even though it was mine. Although . . .' She paused. 'We may not be able to fit many people in.'

'That Sarah person would know,' said Monica. 'I'm just thinking how brilliant it would be, recreating that atmosphere in England.' She was really enthusiastic now, in part because she wouldn't have to face the possibility of telling Seamus he couldn't play at the festival.

156

'What atmosphere?' said Grant. 'If you're thinking smoke-filled rooms, fiddles and great crack, there's been a smoking ban for a while now.'

'Oh, you had to be there, Grant!' said Monica. 'There were times when the people enjoying themselves most were the ones outside flicking cigarette butts into the bin, but it was great, wasn't it, Laura?'

'Oh yes,' she replied, thinking back.

'There's just one problem,' said Monica, looking at Laura. 'You'll probably have to offer Dermot your body again to get him to do it.'

Laura's insides seemed to crumple away.

'I mean . . .' Monica hastened to make amends. 'I was talking in that way when you don't really mean it literally—'

Before Grant started asking awkward questions, Laura rushed in to cover her tracks. 'You were speaking metaphorically,' she said. 'That's what you meant. Me offering to sleep with Dermot is a metaphor for – well, saying I'd do anything to make him come to the festival. Because obviously, I wouldn't really offer to sleep with him, would I?' Fairly sure she'd protested far too much to uphold her status as a lady, Laura looked helplessly at Monica.

'No, of course you wouldn't,' Monica confirmed. 'No one would.' She laughed, sounding a bit artificial. 'Let's have another round!'

'Oh do let's,' said Laura. 'I'll pay.' She had jumped off her bar stool, twenty-pound note waving, before she realised she was already at the bar and could order from where she had been sitting. She could feel Grant's eyes on her and knew there'd have to be explanations on the way home. Had she enough money, she asked herself, to get so drunk she wouldn't be able to talk? But look where that had got her last time. No, she would just have to bluff her way through. Grant would never believe she actually had agreed to sleep with Dermot to get him to come to the festival. It was so out of character. Phew!

Fortunately for Laura's peace of mind, the subject changed and they went on to have a great night out. Grant and Monica got on as well as Laura had known they would and Monica had agreed to employ Grant – for free of course – as her second-in-command at the festival. He was delighted.

And suddenly it was midnight and time to go home.

They were barely in the car before Grant piped up, 'You didn't really offer Dermot Thing your body to get him to come to the festival, did you?' Grant was now as proprietorial about the festival as Monica and Laura were.

'Oh come on, Grant!' Laura felt that indignation was her best defence. She might have known nothing would get past him. 'Would I do a thing like that? How long have you known me?'

Grant drove in silence for a worryingly long time. 'No, I suppose not. In some ways you are a bit of a professional virgin.'

'Exactly,' said Laura, glad the dimness of the car would mean he wouldn't see how very near the truth he'd got. 'I wouldn't throw away my virginity on a one-night stand with a drunken Irishman, now would I? I mean, if I was a virgin, I wouldn't do that!' She paused, digging herself deeper. 'Or even if I wasn't! Oh, shut up and drive, Grant.'

Her friend glanced at her but didn't speak. Laura knew Grant wouldn't let the subject drop completely. He was just biding his time. But she was grateful to him for not mentioning it again as they made up the sofa for him and she crept up to her own bed. As she pulled the duvet round her she smiled. On the whole she was very lucky with her friends.

Chapter Ten

Laura sat in her car outside the school shaking with nerves. In a moment, when the minute hand landed at twenty past two, she would go in. She was about to tell a school full of children about the short-story competition. She had her notes; she had practised to herself in the mirror and had told herself it didn't really matter if the children all ran off screaming. Yet she was still terrified and she didn't think imagining her audience in their vests and knickers would help either.

After this, she was visiting the offices of the local paper, to talk to them about the festival. That would seem like a jolly social occasion after trial-by-small-children. Then, later, came the reward: her weekly chat with Dermot, ostensibly to discuss the entries for the writing course. In practice they talked about all sorts of things. It was Dermot's notes she had in her hand now, vibrating gently.

It was early afternoon and a beautiful spring day. The air shimmered with the promise of the summer ahead and the small, country primary school was of the type described in books by Laurie Lee and other such rural writers. It was picturesque, probably extremely inconvenient and the first of a few she would make similar visits to. The idea was to go to as many local schools as possible to foster interest in the festival in general and the writing competition in particular. Once she'd done it the first time, she knew she'd be fine and even enjoy it. After all, she used to do storytimes in the shop and had loved them. But although her confidence had grown so much over the last couple of months, her old shyness would occasionally reappear, as now. To say she was nervous didn't quite cover it.

A last peek in the driving mirror told her she looked OK, if about ten years old, and then she got out. An attractive middle-aged woman had obviously been on the lookout for her, and appeared the moment Laura set foot on school property.

'Hello! Laura? Hi! I'm Margaret Johns, head teacher. I'll just take you into assembly. The children are all very excited about you coming.'

During the walk to the hall, Laura wondered if she vomited in the playground they'd ring her mother and she'd be allowed to lie down in the staffroom and await collection. Then at last she accepted that she was a grown-up now and she had to just get on with it.

Rows of children sitting cross-legged on the floor confronted her. They were wearing royal blue sweat-shirts, and shorts, trousers or grey dresses.

'Quieten down, children! We have a visitor!' said Mrs Johns.

There was almost instant calm. Laura had hoped if they took a while to settle, it would use up her time. She had half an hour to fill when she'd have preferred ten minutes, or better, she could have just sent a letter and some forms to each school. But Fenella had pointed out a personal visit would really enthuse the schools and get the community inspired to support the festival.

'Miss Horsley is going to tell us about a very exciting competition.' Mrs Johns gestured Laura into centre stage. 'Miss Horsley!'

Don't be afraid of silence, Dermot had told her when he'd been coaching her for the visit. Let them just look at you for a couple of minutes. He'd been so helpful, really taking the time to pass on everything he'd learnt about talking to children – which was a surprising amount. Dermot apparently loved going into schools and talking to children. She wanted to be able to tell him it had gone well. She didn't want to let him down. She surveyed her audience.

'Hi, guys!' she said and instantly felt this sounded wrong and went on quickly. 'How many of you like stories?'

Lots of hands went up. 'We do!' they chorused. 'Me! And Me!'

She raised her own hands to quieten them, which seemed to do the trick. 'That's great! And do you know where stories come from?' Dermot had said he sometimes opened with this question.

'Books!' came the reply.

Laura nodded, getting into the spirit of it. 'Yes they do come from books, but how do the books get them?'

She had liked this image of books marching around on their own capturing stories when Dermot had suggested it and the children seemed to as well.

'They don't go around the place listening to stories and snapping them up between the pages like crocodiles, do they?' She didn't wait for them to answer this time. 'No! Well, someone put them there. Someone put the stories in the books. Who could have done that, do you think?' She looked expectantly at the sea of eager little faces. This time she did want their reaction.

'Mrs Johns!' called out a little boy from the front. 'She's got stories!'

'Yes, that's a good answer. And who else?' She looked at her audience carefully, to make sure she didn't overlook a shy child who might have a good idea.

'Writers?' This came from one of the older girls at the back.

'Writers, authors, yes, they make stories. But who else do you think can make them?'

Several rows of children looked at her, transfixed but bemused. 'You can!' said Laura triumphantly.

This caused a certain amount of uproar but Laura dampened it down quickly enough. She was beginning to get the hang of this. 'Yes, you can all make stories. And soon, when your teacher tells you it's time, you're all going to write a story. Now you could write a whole story each – that would be quite difficult – or you could make a story up as a class. Your teacher will decide which you should do. Now, have any of you written stories before?' A forest of hands shot up. 'Yes! All of you! That's brilliant! Well, when you've all written your stories, and drawn pictures to go with them – can you all draw pictures? Wonderful! So when you've written your story you must draw a picture of the people in the story. These are called "characters". So now, what sort of thing do you think you can write about? Where do stories come from? They come from ideas and ideas are everywhere!' She looked around to indicate the ubiquitous nature of ideas and the children did likewise, as if half expecting an idea to come popping out from behind a plant pot.

'But although ideas are everywhere, we have to look for them, to recognise them when we see them! Now . . .' Laura suddenly realised her mouth had dried up completely and she took a gulp of water from the paper cup Mrs Johns handed to her. At the same time she realised she was really enjoying herself.

'Has anything good happened to any of you today?' she asked her enraptured audience.

A little boy almost followed his hand skyward as he fought to get her attention. 'My dog had puppies!'

'Oh, that's a brilliant idea! You could write a story about a puppy. Or a fairy, or a cow. Or even a teacher!' This caused much amusement. 'Then, when you've written your stories and done lovely illustrations – that means pictures – your teachers are going to send them to me and if they're very good, they'll be read out loud to lots of people, including your parents. What about that?'

This notion was very well received.

'But before you start, a real-life writer, one whose stories are in books you have read, is going to come and talk to you some more about how stories get into books.'

A couple of minutes later she finished her talk to huge applause.

'That was really good,' said Mrs Johns. 'I thought you said you weren't used to dealing with children.'

'Well, not with so many children at a time, but I had a lot of help from a friend and then I just pretended it was a storytime, like we used to do at the bookshop, and it seemed to work.'

'Well done, dear! And you're making arrangements for a writer to visit? Would that come out of our budget or yours?'

'Yours if possible, the festival is operating on a shoe-string.'

'I'll see what we can do,' said Mrs Johns. 'The story competition is excellent and it's an excuse to read more stories in school.'

As she had known it would be, the interview with the local newspaper was easy. They were keen to support the festival and offered to fund an event and to print three of the winning stories in the paper. She found herself chatting away with ease, her answers flowing freely. Somehow it was so much easier when you were talking about something you felt committed to.

Just as she was leaving the journalist said, 'Could you let us have author biogs and photos as soon as poss? We'd like to do an "appearing at" feature.'

Laura stopped and turned round. 'Yes, of course. You do know our line-up isn't finalised? Supposing you did a feature on an author and then they couldn't come?'

'Oh dear, that wouldn't work!' The journalist, possibly perfectly reasonably, didn't want to spend a lot of time researching and writing an article about someone who wasn't going to come within a hundred miles of the county.

Laura considered. 'Tell you what, you give me a list of the authors you'd most like to feature and I'll chase them up. If they think there's a bit of guaranteed publicity it might help them decide to come.'

In the car she made some extra notes and then set off home, quietly excited at the prospect of talking to Dermot.

'So how did you get on with the kids?' was the first thing he said when he picked up the phone.

'Oh, it was great! I took all your ideas and once I'd got going I found I loved it. Perhaps there is a performer in me after all.'

'There's something about children though, isn't there? They don't let you get away with anything.'

Discovering that Dermot Flynn, who shunned his public, refused to have anything to do with the literary world and worked hard on his image of a hard-drinking, womanising has-been, actually went into his local school regularly as a helper had come as a shock.

'I don't tell many people,' he had explained. 'It doesn't go with the image.'

She had taken a moment to feel flattered that he had confided in her. 'Have you ever thought about writing for children?' It seemed an obvious thing for him to want to do.

'No way. Far too hard, and far too much responsibility. If I write a book and someone hates it, that's OK, they can just toss it aside and pick up another one. If a children's writer produces a duff book the child who reads it – or who tries to read it – may never read another one.' He obviously felt very strongly on the subject.

It was after this conversation that Laura had thought he'd be a good person to ask about how to pitch her short-story idea to the local schoolchildren.

Now, after she had received his congratulations and slightly smug 'I told you you could do it', she moved on to the competition itself. 'So all I've got to do is line up a suitably keen judge. I've got a couple of retired teachers to do the first cut.' She paused. 'It's all right, I'm not asking you. I've got a children's writer in mind. Right,' she went on briskly, 'how did you get on with the last batch of scripts I sent you? What about the one set in Greece?'

'A pile of crap,' said Dermot.

'How much did you read?' Laura was disappointed, it was important he trusted her judgement.

'Not very much. Why should I?'

'Read on. It gets better.' She was firm. Having selected her thirty manuscripts, had them copied, and sent to Dermot a few at a time, she now felt protective of them. They were her babies and she was going to fight for them, even though they had to be whittled down to ten.

Dermot was dismissive. 'It's no good it getting better. No one will read that far. I thought you were supposed to know about these things.'

She knew him well enough by now to know when she was being teased. 'I do. In the editing, we'll tell her to get rid of the first three chapters and start the book from there.'

'OK, I'll read a bit more and ring you back. But it had better improve.'

Laura put the phone down, smiling.

She had done the washing-up, written a few emails on the laptop Rupert had acquired for her courtesy of Jacob Stone, and was making a list of phone calls for the following day when he rang back. 'Ah,' he said without preamble. 'I see what you mean.'

'So shall I put her on the "maybe" pile?'

'OK, but if the "maybe" pile gets too huge, I'll send it back.'

'But we could do that with a few suggestions, don't you think? So these writers get help even if they don't get on the course?'

'You're all heart, Laura Horsley. I'm not sure that's a good thing.'

'It is a good thing. A few editorial notes could make the whole difference, and they've got this far, they deserve some reward. Have you had a look at Gareth Ainsley's one?' This was probably more up his street, she thought. It was science fiction, very edgy, but surprisingly readable, even to one to whom sci-fi was a bit of a turn-off.

'Yes, yes, I did. It's good, very good. But do you think he'd be a complete pain on the course?'

'I don't think you can ban him on those grounds,' said Laura.

'Mm. I don't know. I think he'll make it anyway. He doesn't need my help.'

Laura considered for a moment. 'Don't tell me you're jealous of the Young Turks snapping at your heels, Mr Bestselling Novelist?' She felt safe teasing him over the telephone. How she'd feel if they were face to face, she didn't know.

'Young Turks: is that a quaint English expression?'

'Hm, one I picked up from my old boss, Henry—'

Dermot cut her off. 'So which are your favourites out of those you've sent me?' Dermot didn't seem to want

166

to enlarge on the subject of Young Turks and his attitude to them.

'They all have merit,' she said carefully, 'which is why I selected them. But we have to decide who'd benefit most from the course. And you can't rule out the Young Turks.'

'You'll just flirt with them,' he said.

'You're doing the course, not me,' said Laura.

'You're assisting. You're going to be there. I thought you knew that.'

This came as a bit of a shock. 'I thought I was only helping with this bit. I didn't know anything about you needing me actually on the course!' She sounded quite indignant but her heart was singing at the prospect of spending so much time with Dermot. 'I don't know anything about writing itself.'

'Oh yes you do.'

A shaft of doubt pierced her pleasure. 'But I've never written more than a To Do list in my life!'

Dermot dismissed this. 'It doesn't mean you can't edit. You've been doing it, and you've read loads more than I have.'

As by this time she knew he read very little modern fiction she had to agree. 'Oh. Well, I suppose I can do it. Will the university mind?'

'Of course not. If they want me, they have to have you, too. We're a team.'

Laura flushed, glad he couldn't see her. 'Oh. OK. Now, what about the Samantha Pitville? I know it's not your thing. It's chick lit, bubbly, funny, irreverent, but it's written by a very pretty woman. I sent a photo. It's attached to the back of the manuscript.'

She waited until he'd found the photo and examined it. 'Mm. Not my usual type, but if she can write, I'll give her a go. Why did you send the photo?'

'Eleanora said that being good-looking helped. It's such

a cut-throat industry that if two writers are of the same standard, it makes sense to take on the one who'll be good at publicity.'

'Well, I think that's extremely sexist—'

'No you don't, you don't care about sexism. Tell me, is she in or out?'

'I'll give her a go at the course. Nothing else,' he added firmly.

Laura was silent. She had sort of assumed that Dermot would be up for dallying with his students if they were attractive and willing. There was a fine old tradition of artists sleeping with their models – there were parallels.

'Are you surprised at my moral attitude?'

'A bit. You don't give the impression of someone who's led a life of purity and hard work.'

'No, well, you're right. But because I misspent my youth, it doesn't mean I'm keen for others to do it. What's next?'

'The one in the blue folder.'

'Oh yes, found it.'

'Dermot, don't you read any of them until we're on the telephone talking about them?'

'Of course I do.' He was obviously lying. 'Tell me about it.'

She sighed. 'It's worthy.'

'What do you mean?'

'I mean, it's a shortlist pick. It's literary, utterly gloomy and will be the book everyone buys and nobody reads.'

Possibly gauging her feelings about books like this, he frowned. 'Well, let's not have it then.'

'Oh no, we have to have it – her, I mean. It's good. I may hate it, but I have to admire it.' She ruffled through her file and produced another photograph. 'I should have sent you her photo, too. In fact I meant to, but forgot. She's beautiful.'

'You seem determined to fill the course with lovely young women.'

'Well, I know you're doing it against your will. I thought I should make sure you had some compensations.'

There was a silence. 'I hate to admit this, but I don't know if you're joking or not.'

Laura laughed.

Chapter Eleven

❦

Fenella was firm. 'Laura dear, if you came and lived here, in this dear little holiday cottage that has no one in it, not only would be you be here when I needed you, you could give up your flat and save shedloads on rent.' She straightened a throw covering the sofa and twitched a curtain into place. 'I'd have offered it to you before if it'd been finished. All our other accommodation has been full. I won't throw you out afterwards until you've found somewhere else to live,' she added, anticipating Laura's objection.

Laura was extremely tempted by the converted cowshed. It was May, two weeks before the course, and summer was at its prettiest. Hawthorn blossom and cow parsley frothed in the hedgerows and verges around Somerby, the sun shone and the birds sang. Naturally a country lover, Laura's small flat in town had lost any charm it ever had for her, and living where she did meant she had to do a lot of driving. But she still protested politely.

'But you'll need it for a writer or something when the festival is on.'

Fenella ran her hand through her already tangled hair. 'None of the writers we've got booked so far, or even any of those who haven't got back to us, are as vital to us as you are! Do stop arguing and just move in!' She looked around. 'Although now I look at it, it is titchy. Fine for a weekend, or even a week, but otherwise . . . I don't know.'

'Oh no, it's plenty big enough,' said Laura instantly. Both women surveyed the room, wood-burning stove at one end with a sofabed and an armchair by it, little kitchen at the other, with a staircase to a gallery where the bed was. 'It's enchanting, you know it is.'

'I know it's a perfect jewel of a cottage, I'm just pointing out it's awfully small if you want to stay in it longer than a week. There's very little space for your clothes and things.'

'I haven't got a lot of stuff, to be honest. I could bundle up anything I don't need and take it to my parents. They have a huge attic. What I need around me mostly are books.'

'Well, there's plenty of space for them.' Fenella looked at the more or less empty bookcase. 'People will leave books behind when they come to stay.' She looked a little guilty. 'Last year, I took all the ones they'd left in the other cottages and read them. I'll have to put them back.'

'Don't worry. I've got actually got loads of books and should have a massive prune. I'll bring them and you can share them round your cottages. How many have you got?'

'Three, plus this one, but we're always looking to do up another old cowshed or something to put people in.'

Laura laughed. 'They're more than "old cowsheds" by the time you've finished with them.'

'I know. So . . .' Fenella was still thinking about books. 'If you were only allowed one shelf full, which books would you choose?'

Laura didn't have to think for long. 'Well, Dermot's first two, of course. Then there're a couple of authors I've followed for their whole careers. Poetry.'

'So is Dermot really as good as everyone says he is?' asked Fenella.

'Yes! He's amazing! I know he's driving everyone mad by not allowing his name to be used as part of the publicity, but he's really – nice.' 'Nice' was such a woefully inadequate way of describing him, she had to smile.

Seeing the smile, Fenella regarded her friend doubtfully. 'I know he's awfully attractive and all that, although of course I haven't met him. But are his books actually readable?'

Laura put her hand on Fenella's arm to emphasise the strength of her feelings. 'Do yourself a favour and read them. Really. They are truly wonderful.'

'I'd better anyway, if he's our star attraction.' Laura was disappointed Fenella wasn't enthusiastic about her task, but reading was so subjective, she reminded herself. 'And it's nice to be able to boast about difficult books you've read. Now, anything else you think you'll need?'

When Laura had insisted that there was nothing, several times, Fenella said, 'You do think Dermot will turn up, don't you?'

'Why? Why do you ask?' Laura was suddenly worried. Dermot had said he'd come; she assumed he would.

'It's just something Eleanora said. She was on the phone the other day and warned me not to have all my eggs in one basket, festival-wise. She seemed to think he might let us down.'

Laura considered. Dermot could be very kind and she didn't think he would say he'd come and then not turn up. But could she be sure? 'I'm sure it will be all right.'

But although she reassured Fenella, she had doubt in her own mind now.

Slowly the literary side of the festival began to take shape. Eventually writers confirmed they could appear, and pre-festival events began. A local writers' circle was writing short stories, the best to be read at the festival and put into a book. An art group was illustrating chosen works from some of the confirmed authors. There was going to be an exhibition and as many as possible would decorate the village hall that was going to host one of the events. A popular children's poet was hosting a poetry slam, so poetry workshops were going on in all schools as well as energetic story writing. Most of the local schools had already submitted theirs and Laura's retired teachers were making their first selection. The Knitters and Embroiderers' Collective was making a bedspread out of knitted or embroidered squares that was going to be raffled one evening. Fenella was already determined to win this, even if it meant buying all the tickets herself.

But the publicity was severely hampered. The fact that Dermot still wouldn't let it be announced that he was appearing meant that many people who might well have sponsored something weren't taking the festival seriously enough. They'd been promised a big name and, so far, no big name had been given to them.

Laura sent him regular emails explaining all this, begging for him to let his name be announced and, just as regularly, he emailed back saying no.

'We'll have a summit meeting,' announced Fenella, when one morning Laura had gone over to the big house and broken the bad news yet again.

'What? With Jacob Stone and Eleanora or Trisha, and that lot?' Laura was a bit startled. Although so much of the festival was going well, she was feeling a bit of a failure about this and didn't want to have to explain herself to all those people.

'Oh no.' Fenella made a dismissive gesture. 'No, I meant with useful, fun people, like Sarah and Hugo – he's Sarah's other half. Maybe Grant and Monica?'

Rupert came into the kitchen and moved the kettle across to the hotplate. 'Great if you want a party, otherwise better keep it small. Why don't you just ask Hugo and Sarah? We'll come up with something. When are you doing this course with Dermot, anyway?'

'Quite soon. End of the month.'

'That's only two weeks away!' said Fenella. 'Well, he must let us use his name by then, surely!'

'Even if he does, it's almost too late, publicity wise,' said Rupert. 'Bloody Irishmen! Always have to be so bloody mysterious.'

'Rupert! You're half-Irish yourself, don't forget, and Irishmen aren't always – oh my God!' Fenella paused, enlightenment dawning. 'I've cracked it! We don't need a summit meeting!'

'What?' asked Laura and Rupert simultaneously, watching as Fenella pushed her fingers into her hair, searched for a pen and generally became like an ant when its nest has been exposed.

'We'll make a thing of it!' she said, flourishing her pen and finding a pad to write on. 'We'll refer to our "mystery guest"! We'll prime all the literary press that the mystery guest will be announced at a certain time—'

'But will they think our mystery guest worth all that tra-la?' asked Rupert. 'Any mystery guest, come to that?'

'They would if they knew who he was,' said Fenella.

'But they don't!' said Laura. 'They mustn't! Until Dermot OKs it, anyway!' She was terrified that Fenella might ignore Dermot's desire for privacy for the sake of the festival. Truthfully, she wouldn't be able to blame her if she did, but Laura's loyalties were with Dermot.

'We'll leave heavy hints!' said Fenella. 'We'll get Eleanora to take all the relevant people out the lunch. The gossip columnists, the *Bookseller*, all the important mags. It'll be great!'

'It could work,' said Rupert.

'It will!' Fenella handed him a bundle of newspapers she'd just gathered up and carried on clearing one end of the table. 'Give Laura a cup of coffee while we make a list of everyone who needs to be convinced we've got the hottest literary date since – since – since some very big author did an event.'

Laura pulled out a chair, thinking rapidly. 'Eleanora will know lots of the names. I know a few. This could be a very good idea, Fen.' But secretly she was worried: Dermot would probably hate this, although he had rather forced them into it. Supposing it did make him back out, as Eleanora feared? 'Maybe we could imply we've got J. D. Salinger coming.'

'Isn't he dead?' objected Rupert, joining Fen in clearing the table.

'Not sure,' said Laura.

'Well, if you don't know, maybe they won't either,' said Fenella, 'and think he's coming.'

'They could just check on the Internet,' said Rupert. 'And better not to promise anything we can't deliver.'

'I only hope we can deliver Dermot!' Laura moaned, and then smiled to imply she was joking, although she wasn't. 'On a brighter note,' she went on, seeing Fenella's concerned glance, 'Monica's got a gig for Seamus. We should all go. Check him out for the festival. We did wonder about having his band playing, very softly, while Dermot reads.' Laura had seated herself at the table and was making notes in the notebook she had taken to carrying around with her everywhere. If she was ant-like too, her real anxieties about Dermot might not show. She felt she'd got to know him quite well over the phone, but Eleanora was his agent – surely she knew him better than Laura did?

'I think that sounds wonderful,' said Rupert. 'We want to try and do some things that involve the literary and the music festivals together.'

'Dermot will probably refuse to do it though,' said Laura, 'but I will ask him.'

'If it wasn't for the fact that Jacob Stone has been such a generous sponsor and it was because of Dermot that he came on board, I'd say to hell with Dermot!' said

Fenella. 'But I know you love him, Laura, so I'll shut up about it now.'

'It's not that I love him,' she lied determinedly, 'it's just that I really admire his work.'

'Yeah, yeah, yeah. So . . .' Fenella looked at her companions. 'Anyone else got any genius ideas?'

'I think if we're going to make the most of having a secret celebrity, we should offer a dinner with him, as a pre-festival treat, just for the important literary bods,' said Rupert. 'We'd make it really gourmet with decent wine.' He paused. 'Don't tell me, Laura, you don't think Dermot would agree.'

'Probably not, frankly. He hates literary bods. He thinks they're out to get him. And they probably are,' said Laura. 'Or at least, they will all pounce on whatever he writes next and want to tear it apart.'

'He hasn't produced anything for years, though, has he?' said Rupert.

'I think he's got something on the stocks,' said Laura, wondering if telling lies really made your nose grow longer. 'But I can't see him agreeing to it.'

'Maybe it wouldn't matter if he didn't turn up?' suggested Fenella. 'After all, we'd give them all a fabulous meal, a night in our "stately home". They'd have each other to talk to, after all. And we can't keep writing off ideas just because Dermot might refuse,' she went on. 'We'll have to work round him.'

'They'll probably hate each other,' said Laura, suddenly gloomy. 'They'll get drunk and pick fights.'

'Fabulous publicity!' said Fenella. 'It'll put my festival on the literary map!'

'Our festival, if you don't mind, darling,' said Rupert. 'More coffee, Laura?'

'No thanks, I'm jumpy enough already. I'll go and email Dermot with the next lot of stuff he's going to refuse to do.'

Dermot didn't refuse to attend a literary dinner at Somerby held in his honour, he just didn't mention it. After three emails asking him, Laura stopped bothering. She even said he could contact her by mobile if he preferred but to no avail.

Two weeks later, Laura parked in the university car park. It was late afternoon. In spite of their long chats on the telephone, she was nervous about actually seeing Dermot in person, especially since she hadn't heard from him for a while. However many times she reminded herself how well they'd got on before, she was sure that this time she would bore him and he would find some other young woman to go for walks with, to talk about and teach about writing, books, films and music. He'd have several to choose from, and four days to take his pick.

But despite her imagination throwing him into the arms of every woman on the course, she was determined to be more proactive herself about Dermot. She thought about Monica, going after Seamus all those months ago in Ireland. She knew she hugely admired Dermot, she liked him, and she fancied him desperately: she would make a move on him. She just hoped it wouldn't take a personality transplant to do it.

As she gathered her bags and made her way to the main entrance she asked herself why she had let so many attractive young women on to the course. Knowing his fondness for the female sex she could have arranged things a bit differently without compromising her position as an editor. The whole question of writing courses was fraught with controversy anyway. Many writers thought they were a complete waste of time, declaring that you could only learn to write by writing. Because of this, Laura didn't feel guilty about some of the young men who didn't get places on the course. She was confident they were well on their way already.

But the real reason she'd picked so many writers of women's fiction, women themselves, was because she felt this sort of fiction needed support in the literary world. Also, these writers were the most promising; they had given her the most fun while she was reading. And in a perverse way she wanted to test Dermot. If he succumbed to these women she'd know she shouldn't pursue him in a Monica-like way. No point in making a complete fool of herself, after all, or in allowing herself to fall in love with him – if she hadn't already – only to have her heart broken by his wandering eye.

Of course the photographs they'd sent in could all have been produced with a good dollop of Photoshop but Laura doubted it. Until you could apply Photoshop in those booths in the post office for taking passport photos, you got what you paid for. She was fairly sure in a couple of hours she and Dermot would be meeting someone her father would have referred to as 'crumpet'. And Laura had brought it on herself.

She had actually confessed all this to Monica, on the phone the previous evening. Her friend had been very brisk.

'For goodness' sake, Laura! You're mad! You don't believe he fancies you so you surround him with gorgeous women so he can prove you right. What sort of skewed thinking is that? Anyway, he does fancy you. He took one look at you and asked you to come to bed.'

'It wasn't quite like that and anyway, he was drunk. Probably.' This incident was still a matter of huge shame and even huger regret that she hadn't slept with him when all her normal defences were down. She'd rerun it in her head so many times she didn't trust her memory of it.

'You were drunk; I don't think he was.'

'Must have been, but even if he wasn't, he's probably

one of those men who'd go to bed with anything with a pulse.'

'I think to be fair, any female thing with a pulse, in his case.'

Laura laughed reluctantly. 'Well, whatever. What I'm trying to say is that I don't think he particularly fancied me, he just fancied sex, and I was there throwing myself at him.'

'No you weren't, you just said yes when you should have said no. He didn't ask me to sleep with him, after all, and I'm considered quite attractive in some circles.'

'No, I think if he'd really fancied me he'd have woken me up. He's not known for holding back. It could only mean "he's not that into me" to quote *Sex and the City*.'

Monica made a noise that indicated shock and awe. 'I didn't know you watched television, Laura! I thought you spent all your time reading improving books.'

'Oh shut up, Mon,' Laura whimpered. 'I'm just nervous.'

'Well, just go for it, that's my advice.'

'I'll do my best.' Laura sounded pathetic, even to her.

'Writers' course? Ah, now, well, is your case very heavy?' The man on reception was friendly and loquacious.

'No, it's on wheels,' said Laura.

The man looked over his desk as if to check this was true. 'Good. Your course is right at the corner of the campus. You could fetch your car and park it over there if you want to?'

'No, I'll be fine.' Laura continued to smile, trusting her key and directions to the building would transpire eventually. She felt she was less likely to get lost if she was on foot.

'That section is going to be demolished to make way for the new science block,' went on her informant.

'Ah!' said Laura. 'That's why the university offered to

host the course during termtime. They had spare accom-modation. I did wonder.'

'Well, I wouldn't know about that,' said the porter. He produced a bit of paper with a map on it. 'You need to go along here, round the corner here, and there's the accommodation. The lecture halls – there are only a couple of them – are here.'

'Right.' Laura studied the map, hoping she wouldn't find it all as complicated as it looked. 'Has Dermot Flynn turned up yet?'

The porter looked down his list of names. 'Oh, him. He's in a staff flat, to keep him safe from all you students.'

Laura's smile was a little chilly, but she didn't explain she wasn't a student. 'But is he here yet?' They were going to meet up that evening and run through the course, find somewhere to eat and generally settle in before the students arrived.

The porter checked his register. 'No. Now, is there anything else you need to know?'

'I don't think so, thank you.'

Or at least, nothing you're likely to be able to help me with, such as: should I put on my sexiest dress (which wasn't, very) or should I wait until later on in the course to make my move on him? The thought of her making a move on anyone was so funny, so unlikely, she couldn't help smiling as she set off.

Once she found her room and was inside, she felt instantly thrown back to her own university days. There was the single bed, the noticeboard with remnants of posters and timetables still showing. There was a desk, witness to much struggle, boredom and despair, and the small shelf for books that meant that when she was at university, Laura's room had had neat piles of books ranged round the walls. There was a tiny shower room that smelt slightly of drains.

The whole place needed decorating and Laura hoped

that their students wouldn't feel disgruntled by having been put in this run-down block. Still, the teaching would be wonderful and they weren't actually paying to attend. It would be all right. She realised she was nervous about her part in it all, even if it was mainly administrative. She was to help with scheduling for private tuition, check everyone was happy and generally do anything that Dermot felt was not in his job description. But as she hadn't seen any of the correspondence regarding the course, she wasn't sure what this might involve. There was only so much you could cover over the phone.

Making sure her door wouldn't slam shut behind her, Laura went down the corridor and found the communal kitchen. This at least was clean and the fridge was on. She had better buy some tea bags, coffee and milk, she realised, but she could do that later.

As she went back to her room Laura wondered if she'd be invited to drink red wine out of paper cups and talk until the early hours? Or would she be considered to be a teacher, like Dermot? Worst would be to have governess status – neither one thing nor another.

She filled her kettle and made a cup of peppermint tea. She wasn't eighteen, leaving her parents for the first time; she was an adult. But actually she'd really loved university, getting away from home. She knew that if it weren't for her anxieties about Dermot, seeing him again, having to talk him into doing things for the festival that he was going to hate, she'd have loved going back to uni.

She was just wondering what she should do next when her phone rang.

'Laura? It's Dermot. What sort of a hole have they put me in?'

A smile spread across Laura's face, just at hearing his voice. 'Dermot! You've got a special staff flat. Don't tell me you're not happy with it?'

'It smells.'

Just for a second she allowed herself to feel pure joy that the planet contained both her and Dermot, and that very shortly she would see him again.

'Would you like me to come over and see if I can make you more comfortable?'

'And how would you be thinking of doing that?' His voice was teasing and full of laughter.

'With some lavatory cleaner and a stiff broom,' she said briskly, laughing too. 'What else?'

'If that's all you're offering I'd better have a shower instead. What time would you like to eat?'

'Well, I am quite hungry.' It had been quite a long drive from Somerby and although she had had a sandwich at lunchtime, it seemed ages ago.

'So am I. I passed a quite nice-looking pub on my way in. I thought we could have dinner there and discuss what's going on from tomorrow, check we're singing off the same hymn sheet.'

'That's sounds good.'

'Why are you laughing?' he demanded.

'How can you tell I am?' Laura had to fight to stop doing it out loud.

'I can hear it in your voice.'

He was stern now. This didn't make Laura any less inclined to smile. 'It's just the thought of you singing off any hymn sheet is quite funny.'

'I do have my spiritual side, I'll have you know,' he said, obviously trying to sound offended.

'I'm sure you have. It's just . . . never mind.'

'Well, can you find your way to my place and then we can go. In about an hour?'

'Fine. I'll find where you are on my map of the campus and come and meet you.'

'Brilliant.'

Laura held on to the phone for a few moments after

182

he had disconnected. In an hour she was going to see Dermot. Actually see him, not just talk to him on the phone. How lovely was that?

Then her elation faded just a little; what the hell should she wear?

Seeing him again made her smile and smile. He seemed pleased to see her too. Just for a moment, she wondered if there was just more than pleasure at seeing a friend in his look, of if she had imagined it. She had so little experience, and although she felt she knew Dermot quite a lot better now than when she'd last seen him, they had only met three times, and all those times were quite a long time ago.

He kissed her cheek. 'Well, hello!'

'Well, hello to you!' She had, she felt, achieved that hardest of images, the 'I just happened to be wearing this old thing, but bizarrely, it is one of my most flattering outfits, but no, of course I didn't put it on specially'. While she was changing for what felt like the ninth time she decided if a designer could create a line that captured this elusive look, they would clean up.

He stood looking down at her and grinning for a few long seconds and then said, 'Well, shall we find that pub then? It looked good and as we don't know what on earth the food is going to be like in the cafeteria, it might be the last decent meal we have for a few days.'

Unless we slip out and eat away from the students, Laura thought, and then felt instantly guilty.

'I feel we should eat with the students as much as possible. A lot of teaching and learning can go on in casual situations. They can feel more able to ask questions one to one, while you're jostling trays, than in a room full of other people.'

'You're displaying a very caring attitude,' she said as they walked along together, not touching apart from when she bumped into him by mistake from time to time. She felt ambivalent, wanting him to be caring on the one hand, but on the other, hoping he'd be keen to bunk off to the pub with her.

'You shouldn't be surprised. You know I go into schools regularly. I admit I prefer students to be under eleven, but I can cope with older ones.'

'You didn't seem quite so conscientious when we first started working together.' She frowned a little as she thought of his dismissive attitude to some of the manuscripts, how she'd had to nudge him into considering them seriously.

'I've turned over a new leaf,' he said, sounding a little smug. 'You should be proud of me.'

'Proud of you – why?'

'Oh, nothing in particular, just my general virtue. Now,' he went on, pushing open the pub door, 'what would you like? A pint of whiskey with a beer chaser?'

'A white wine spritzer please. We have to work tomorrow!'

Chapter Twelve

He walked her back to her accommodation, to her very door, after their meal out. 'There you are, sweetheart, safe and sound. We'll meet for breakfast, to make sure we're all sorted, and then expect the hordes to arrive at ten. Is that right?'

'It is.'

'Good. Nighty-night, then. See you at nine.' And he strode off to his rooms.

Laura was very happy, despite feeling slightly disappointed he hadn't even given her a goodnight peck on the cheek. The evening had been a wonderful combination of them just chatting – about everything – books mainly, but also films, music, politics, the state of the planet and the course, and there'd be other opportunities for a moment alone.

He had been delighted with the way she'd set things up to be easy for him. Each student had a brief CV, a résumé of their work and a photograph, plus the notes they had both discussed, neatly printed up. They both had full sets. He was going to study his now, he said, so he had half a chance of remembering people's names. What she hadn't got round to asking him was why he'd agreed to do the course, at short notice, in the first place. But there'd be plenty of time to do that later. And there'd be plenty of time to make her move on him, in the way Monica would. It would be easy. She got ready for bed with a smile on her face.

*   *   *

Laura, aware that the students might find the section of the university allocated for the course a little difficult to find, even if they had been sent maps of the campus, had printed out (courtesy of the office) some huge signs, and the following day, she and Dermot waited optimistically in the room allocated to them, smiles ready to pin on the moment anyone looked like arriving. They were both nervous.

'You do the opening bit and I'll take it from there,' said Dermot, walking up and down, reading old notices, opening and shutting cupboards and picking off bits of flaking paint.

'I've never done any public speaking of any kind—'

'Yes you have!' objected Dermot. 'You spoke to all those children. How many schools did you do in the end?'

'Only three, and I couldn't have done it at all if you hadn't coached me. You should do it.'

'I'm no teacher.'

'But you're a writer. That's why they're here!' Why didn't he understand the huge draw he was to the world? 'Besides, you liar, you've done loads of teaching!'

He chuckled. 'But not adults. I told you, I specialise in the under-elevens. And didn't you introduce the writers at all those signings you arranged when you were at the bookshop?'

As she'd told him she had, she couldn't very well deny it. 'All I had to say was what a wonderful writer the author was and how grateful the shop was to everyone for coming.'

'You could say that! I wouldn't mind at all!' He was laughing – at himself – at her – at the situation and looking at her in a slightly distracted way. Suddenly she found she couldn't meet his gaze without blushing, so she didn't. It was odd to see him so nervous. It was reassuring but at the same time she wasn't quite sure if it

186

was just nerves about the course that were making him glance at her every couple of minutes. It certainly wasn't helping hers.

She busied herself with her register. 'All right. I'll just do a very brief hello, but then it's down to you.' Was this the moment to ask him why he'd agreed to run the course? Maybe not. It might have been complicated and someone could appear at any moment.

She looked at her watch and then at Dermot to see that he'd just done the same thing. It was still only ten to ten. They exchanged rueful smiles.

'Eleanora's coming on the last night,' said Laura to break the anxious silence. 'Which is good because she'll tell them what's what if we can't.'

Dermot nodded. 'She can be very scary. I always deal with Tricia, her assistant, if I can.'

'Oh, I've met Tricia.' Laura wondered if all this small talk was actually making them more nervous. 'So, have you got any ideas for exercises?'

'Mm. Some.' He smiled. 'I'll be fine once I've started, but I always get like this before a gig.'

'You would never have guessed it,' said Laura, recalling his prowl through his fans, his leap on to the stage, his rock-star confidence. He was wearing a rumpled linen suit which would have looked silly on anyone else but seemed to go well with his generally rumpled look. He was so staggeringly attractive he could pull on any old pair of jeans and manky sweatshirt and look sexy. She decided now was as good a time as any to find out why he was here. 'But if it terrifies you so much, why are you doing this course?'

He made a nonchalant gesture that didn't quite come off. 'The money.'

'Really?' She found this hard to believe. She didn't know anything about his finances, of course, but she doubted that the course would be well paid enough to

187

tempt him if he didn't want something else out of it. Her own fee was welcome, but it wasn't huge.

'I'm doing it under sufferance. And under false pretences.'

'What do you mean? Are you saying that Eleanora made you?' If she had such power over him why hadn't she just ordered him to do the festival? Why had she been sent to persuade him?

He shrugged, sighed and came back to the desk. 'Let's just say that Eleanora told me – reminded me – that you learn what you teach. She thought it might get me writing again.'

'I thought she didn't know about your block?'

'She didn't actually say that, but I know it's what she felt. She must suspect. She's no fool.'

'Well, that makes perfect sense!' Laura smiled, happy that he was making a positive step towards getting over his writer's block.

'Does it?' His smile was incomprehensible. 'Then I'm glad.'

A bit confused, Laura went on. 'So what about the false pretences bit?'

He shrugged. 'I'm just not sure you can teach people to write.'

'I know what you mean, but there must be some tips you can pass on. I mean, what's the hardest part of learning to write?'

He shrugged again. 'I didn't ever learn to write. That's my problem. I just did it.'

Before Laura could react, the door opened and the first students arrived.

'Hi!' Dermot and Laura said brightly and simultaneously at the first couple. They exchanged glances and then Dermot went on.

'I'm Dermot Flynn and this is Laura Horsley. Laura's going to open proceedings officially when everyone is

188

here. In the meantime, if you'd like to come up and collect your name badges.' He smiled. 'We want to start putting the faces to the work as soon as possible in case you don't look like your photos!'

Laura was pleased that any sign of nervousness from Dermot had gone and turned her attention to the group, which now numbered four, as they clustered round the table, looking for their names. They seemed so eager and pleased to be there. Would they still be so keen when she and Dermot started tearing their work to shreds? She felt personally that although she could criticise writing perfectly well when it was just her and the manuscript, she might feel different when the writer was actually present.

'Sit anywhere, but not too spread out,' she said as another clutch of potential writers arrived. 'There are going to be exercises and some of them might involve getting into groups. It's really important that we all feel comfortable with each other, so shyness is not acceptable.'

How she would have cringed if anyone had said this to her a few months ago. How her life had changed! This time last year she would never have dreamt she could pitch a short-story competition to schoolchildren, do interviews to local newspapers and all the other front-of-house-type things that had previously terrified her. She had discovered that when you were involved in a project, particularly one you felt passionately about, you just got on and did what was needed.

The ten writers carefully selected by Laura and approved by Dermot had arranged themselves among the chairs and were chatting to each other in low, excited voices. Getting on the course had obviously meant a lot to all of them. Laura couldn't decide if this keenness was a good thing or a bad thing.

She did a rough head-count and everyone seemed to

be there. She and Dermot exchanged glances and he nodded, indicating she should get things under way.

'OK, everyone, let me just check that you're all here.' She smiled. Having seen their photos and commented on their writing, in some ways she felt she knew these people already. 'Maybe when I've read your name and you've confirmed you're here, you could tell us a bit about yourself for the benefit of the group.'

'It would be quite hard to confirm we're here if we're not,' said one young man who Laura identified as the one Dermot hadn't wanted on the course, in case he was a pain. It looked as if Dermot had been right. She didn't look at him now but she knew he was looking at her knowingly.

'Very true,' she replied solemnly, and started reading the list. 'Gareth Ainsley?'

Rather to her annoyance, it was the young man who answered. 'That's me.'

'And what are you writing, Gareth?' Although she knew from his covering letter, and having read his work she wanted to hear him actually say it, for the others.

'I don't think that pigeonholing writers is very constructive. I'm not prepared to put my work into a slot decided by the publishers.'

Laura bit her lip to hide her emerging smile. Boy did this young man have a lot to learn! Then she realised he was about the same age as she was. 'OK, Gareth, but just to give us an idea, name a writer whose work you admire and who may have influenced you.'

Reluctantly he mumbled a few names of which Dermot's was one, and Laura made a note on her register.

'OK, Samantha Pitville?'

'I'm here. And I write chick lit!' The very pretty young blonde declared this with defiance as if she expected people to boo.

'There is nothing wrong with being commercial,' said

Laura. 'If you're keener on sales than critical acclaim it's best to know that as soon as possible.'

Samantha smiled, adding to her prettiness by about a hundred watts. 'Yes, but I'm writing chick lit because I can't write anything else. And I like it.'

'Good for you!' said Dermot.

Laura wondered if he could possibly resist such pulchritude. Her only hope was that Samantha didn't go for older men.

At last the register was taken and every one had nailed their colours to the mast in one way or another. The older women, Helen and Maggie, who declared they were writing cosy crime and 'thoughtful books for older women', did blush a bit as they did so, but Laura felt proud of them.

'Well that's all very interesting,' said Dermot. 'Now Laura's going to give you a bit of an introduction.'

'Well,' said Laura, 'I'm not going to say much, but firstly, well done for getting a place on this course. You probably know there were a lot of applicants and you were all picked because of your talent.' She smiled encouragingly. 'But now may be the only time you feel talented because I know this course is going to be fairly tough—'

'Can I just ask – er – Laura?' It was Gareth Ainsley and Laura stiffened. 'We all know who Dermot Flynn is, but who are you? I mean, what are your qualifications for assisting on this course?'

Dermot moved forward from where he'd been leaning against a desk but Laura put up a hand to stop him. She was going to deal with this herself. She felt she should. She didn't want them thinking she had no experience at all. 'I'm here to help Dermot. I used to work in a bookshop and because I've spent so much of my life reading, I'm now setting up a literary festival and I helped Dermot make the selection. So if any of you aren't up to it –' she glared at Gareth, trying to make him feel he might not be up to it '– it's my fault you're here. OK?'

Gareth glanced at Dermot and possibly sensed something protective and maybe threatening about his stance. 'Oh yes, fine.'

'Well then, I'll hand you over to Dermot.'

Sweating slightly in spite of her brave front, Laura withdrew to the second desk and sat behind it, arranging her pile of student notes and putting a secret mark on Gareth's.

'Hello,' said Dermot. 'Nice to see you're all here. As Laura said, there was very stiff competition to get on this course, but I'm afraid it's nothing to the competition of the real publishing world. Later in the week my agent is coming to talk to you. If I haven't managed to convince you of this, then she will. Now, I'd like to kick off with a question-and-answer session and general chat. Feel free to comment if you want to. We're not kids. And this will give us an idea of what you're expecting to gain from the course, and it'll give you lot a chance to find out more about each other. Who's first?'

A young man put up his hand. Dermot looked down at his pile of papers. 'John? You have a question?'

'OK,' said the young man who Laura remembered wrote literary, autobiographical, rather navel-gazing fiction. 'Obviously, I entered for the competition, but I started writing when I was a student. I mean, so much of the stuff we had to read was crap. I knew I was better than that.'

'Nice to have confidence,' said one of the older women dryly.

Laura glanced down at her notes. She had this Maggie Jones noted down as promising. The book she'd entered was a bit downbeat but Laura was confident she'd be able to put a bit of uplift into it, if she knew it was required.

'Well, if you're know you're good, there's no point in pretending you're not,' said John, although he flushed slightly.

'Confidence is a gender thing,' said Samantha, who didn't seem to be lacking in it herself.

'I think you're right,' said Tracy, a feisty young woman who had proudly announced she wrote short romance novels. According to Laura's notes, they were sparky and very sexy.

'And your point is?' Dermot said to John.

'I just wonder if there's any point in this course.'

John's words caused a frisson of anxiety around the room.

'Probably not,' said Dermot, his lazy delivery belying his critical gaze.

An anxious silence filled the room until Maggie spoke up. 'I'm sure we've all got a lot to learn. I know I have. After all, I presume we're going to be reading stuff out to each other. When you read it to yourself, it always seems amazing.'

Laura smiled fondly at her. She was going to contribute and co-operate, what a relief!

'I'd rather just work on my novel than do a lot of poxy exercises,' said John.

'In which case you shouldn't have entered the competition,' put in Laura. 'Exercises are extremely useful and we're going to be doing a lot of them.' Rather too late she remembered that she and Dermot hadn't discussed what they were going to do in detail. She shot him a look and he returned it with an amused eyebrow.

'Yes,' said Maggie. 'Lots of people would have given their eye teeth to be here. If you're lucky enough to be chosen, you should make the most of your opportunities.'

'Yes, but—'

'Writing is a strange, ephemeral thing,' said Dermot,

smoothing over potential troubled waters. 'You never know what's going to help and what's not. I don't intend to do exercises on punctuation. But writing for a given time on a given subject can really loosen you up.'

Dermot was cruel. They had five minutes to write about 'money'. Another five to cover 'death', but ten whole minutes to write about 'birth'.

As a concession, he allowed people to choose what they considered to be their best piece before making them read it out. He'd done the exercises himself and went first.

'It's to give you lot confidence,' he explained. 'When you see how crap I am, you'll feel a lot happier about exposing yourselves to the criticism of others.'

But of course, he wasn't crap. Laura was mildly surprised as she thought his writer's block implied he could barely write a shopping list, but then the workings of his literary mind were still a mystery to her. And reading out loud was still agony for most.

By lunchtime, everyone was settling down nicely and went off to the cafeteria talking away as if they really knew each other.

'God Almighty, what I have let myself in for?' declared Dermot the moment they were alone.

Laura laughed delightedly. 'You're brilliant at this! They love you! Although,' she added, less happily, 'I do think it was mean of you to make me do the exercises too.'

'Don't be silly – yours were just as good as anyone else's, but I do think there's some talent there, don't you?'

'Definitely. I just hope we can keep them entertained and happy for the entire time.'

'I've got a plan if things look like dragging,' said Dermot. 'I'll tell you later.'

* * *

194

The afternoon was taken up by students writing longer pieces. They were going to be read and discussed in the bar after supper. After lunch, Dermot said he'd see everyone later in the bar for a quick drink before supper. Trying not to feel disappointed, Laura went to her own room to work. She had quite a lot to do for the festival – inviting all the writers appearing to Rupert's pre-festival dinner for one – and she had promised to read one of Tracy's category romances. They had agreed between them that Dermot would be shown it only if Laura thought it was fantastic. Her afternoon flew by and she found she only had time for a mug of tea at her desk, although when she looked out of her window, she could see everyone else gathering on the lawn, lying around sunbathing, talking, no doubt, about writing.

She grabbed a quick shower and arrived at the bar late and a little damp.

'Hey, Laura! You're at least three drinks behind us,' said Samantha. 'What can I get you?'

'Oh, a white wine spritzer, please.'

'Oh, for goodness' sake! Have a proper drink!' Samantha made her opinion of Laura's choice very clear. 'Have the wine on its own, at least.'

Laura laughed. 'If I can have the water separately. I don't drink much as a rule.'

'That's not what I heard,' said Dermot, his eyes dangerously teasing.

'Isn't it?' she said blithely. 'Well, I can't imagine where you got your information.' Then she wondered if she'd been wrong to trust him not to tell everyone about her exploits in Ireland.

Someone touched her elbow. It was Tracy, the woman whose novel Laura had spent a lot of her afternoon reading. 'Oh, let's go and talk privately,' she said. 'I'll just get my drink.' She was relieved to have an excuse to change the subject.

'Well?'

Tracy was so diffident Laura hastened to reassure her. 'I couldn't put it down! I did my other work first and thought I'd just read a bit so I could tell you, one way or another, and I couldn't stop reading!'

Dermot was fantastic with the students in the bar. He bought drinks all evening and listened to everyone's comments with apparent respect and kindness, and even signed copies of his books a couple of the students shyly presented to him. He was particularly sweet to the older women who lacked the brashness of the young, beautiful high-flyers. It was a side of him Laura hadn't seen much of and she liked it.

'Finding time to write isn't easy,' said Tracy, feeling more confident since she and Laura had had their chat. 'Especially when you've got a young family. Writing seems very self-indulgent, sometimes.'

'If it's good for you, it's good for the family,' said Helen. 'I really believe that. You can't be a good wife and mother if you're stifling your creativity. Isn't that right, Dermot?'

He smiled and shook his head. 'Not having been a wife or a mother I'm not really in a position to comment but stifled creativity is a very bad thing.'

Everyone laughed. 'Not that you'd know about that either,' said John, who, having wanted to challenge Dermot to begin with, to establish his credentials, was now as admiring as everyone else. 'You obviously have no problem with it. What are you working on at the moment?'

It was natural that John should assume that Dermot was working on something, but Laura winced. She didn't want Dermot put on the spot like this.

'I never talk about my work-in-progress,' said Dermot, evading the question skilfully. 'But creativity is a wilful mistress,' he asked, 'she won't always do what you say.'

Everyone had had a couple of drinks by then and only Laura heard the tinge of pain in his words.

'Could I just have another word?' Tracy asked Laura. 'Not many people I know understand the genre as you seem to. Do you really think my book is publishable?'

'Well, obviously, I'm not an expert . . .'

Laura and Tracy discussed her book until they were summoned to dinner by the others. Several of them, including Dermot, were carrying bottles of wine and as Laura had already had two glasses, the second pressed on her by a grateful Tracy, she decided she wouldn't personally drink any more.

She didn't get to sit within easy reach of Dermot but she could see his students were lapping up every word he uttered. Still, that was fine. She was enjoying herself down her end of the table and she could talk to Dermot later, when they went back to the bar.

But by the time everyone had finished eating she felt too tired to carry on with the party. There would be other evenings, she told herself. She'd been working hard and it had been a long day.

'I think I'll just go to bed,' she told everyone, feeling sheepish and a party pooper. 'I seem terribly tired, for some reason.'

Dermot was so engrossed in a discussion about the merits of various genres he barely noticed her leave. She pushed down a feeling of disappointment. He was here for the students, she reminded herself.

'Well, I'm still up for it because I had a nap,' admitted Maggie, one of the older women.

'Me too,' said a couple of others. 'Learning stuff is so tiring!'

The next two days of the course followed the same pattern. Exercises in the morning, private writing or more exercises in the afternoon, long sessions in the bar, before and after dinner in the evening. Each student was to get a one-to-one session with Dermot. He had arranged this timetable himself although she'd been detailed to do it, so Laura didn't know when he would be closeted with a lovely young writer. This was probably a good thing. She had enough on her plate. A flurry of writers had confirmed for the festival and as Fenella was now totally tied up with weddings, it being summer and the wedding season, Laura was trying to work out a timetable. Her afternoons were spent on this, and on reading other people's work. Tracy had been so pleased with her criticism of her book, everyone else wanted Laura's opinion. As the time had passed it had become obvious how highly Dermot thought of her, and how much he valued what she had to say, so the students did likewise. Although she had twice managed to get to the bar after dinner, she could never stay up for more than one drink, however much she wanted to. And much as she'd planned to make a move on Dermot, there just hadn't been a moment. Nor had he suggested a quick, private coffee with her. He seemed to appreciate having her there but she just couldn't work out if there was – as she hoped – a bit more to it than that.

'OK, everyone, change of pace for today!' announced Dermot when the students had stopped talking and were paying attention. 'I've hired a small coach and we're going off to a stately home for the day. This is to give us all a bit of a break – we've been working really hard since we're been here.' Laura's sudden desire to yawn gave testament to this. 'So we're going to get right away. However, you're not just going to skulk around, you're going to work.' He paused for breath. 'In many ways writing is like painting. The artist looks at life and translates it into something else for the viewer. The writer does it with words, not paint. I want you to make written sketches of what you see. Some will be of physical things:

a wood, a statue, a vista. Some will be of people and how they relate to their surroundings. And for the more imaginative among you' – he glanced at the writers of commercial fiction – 'I'd like you to write a scene set in the period of the house we're going to see. It could even be about the real people who lived in the house. I want four pieces of the work by bar-time tonight! Oh, and the cafeteria has made up packed lunches for you all, if you'll just go along and collect them.'

Laura was thrilled. She felt she needed a day off from festival work and surely, during a day spent in a stately home, she'd have a chance for some private – intimate – time with Dermot. She felt sure she'd seen the same anticipation in the look he'd given her when he'd told them all.

'How did you get the cafeteria to make up packed lunches at such short notice?' Laura asked Dermot as they filed on to the bus.

He smiled down at her from the top step. 'It wasn't short notice. I booked them on the first morning. I knew we'd need a day away, to freshen us all up. It gives us a bit of time off too.'

Laura gave a little sigh of happiness and didn't mind at all that Helen had saved a place for her, and she couldn't sit by Dermot. There was bound to be an opportunity to be alone later; he obviously wanted it too.

Laura longed to doze on the bus trip, which was a little longer than she'd anticipated, but Helen wanted to talk about her work. Still, Laura felt she wouldn't need to stay up late in the bar, or try to, because she'd get Dermot on his own very soon. The thought made her very happy – and possibly more enthusiastic about Helen's book than perhaps it warranted.

The garden was attached to a great house that was not to be visited. Dermot had insisted.

'We'd have to pay more,' he said, 'and I want outdoor scenes. You can have people – today's people, people from the past, but use the garden! I want trees, flowers. In detail – remember "oak" not "tree". Off you go.'

Unrestricted by Dermot's orders, Laura did turn to the house. It was large and square and seemed to her to be Georgian. A huge magnolia climbed up one side and lace-cap hydrangeas the other. There was an avenue of lime trees leading to the front door, which, when you turned away from the house, framed the church spire of the nearest village. At the front, parkland stretched to the stone wall in the far distance. A green painted arrow indicated the formal gardens were round the back of the property. They were blessed with a beautiful day and everywhere looked at its best. It was impressive, but Laura found herself thinking that privately she preferred Somerby's more modest and wilder grandeur.

She stood and gazed for a few moments before turning to look for Dermot.

He'd vanished! How could he have disappeared so quickly? He must have gone with the first group of students who were all chattering away and not, Laura felt, taking in their surroundings.

She wandered slowly along the path, following the signs to the gardens. She'd come across Dermot shortly, she was sure.

The trouble was, there were paths to several different gardens: a cottage garden, a millennium garden, a stumpery – whatever that was – a walled garden and a rose garden as well as a vegetable garden and glasshouses. She suspected there was a more formal garden beyond all that – she could see tall clipped yews in the distance, and a copper beech covered with tiny roses.

She blinked in the sunshine, considering her options. His curiosity might lead him to the stumpery, or he might like glasshouses – she did herself – or would he be drawn to the yews and roses like stars against almost purple foliage? She couldn't guess, so, deciding simply to enjoy her surroundings, she set off towards the millennium garden. She was just about to reach it when she saw a group of students, including Dermot, right at the end of a wide mown path.

Feeling she couldn't really gallop down it without looking pathetically needy, like the friendless child on a school outing, she thought she'd try and find a way to meet them without them seeing her approach.

A convenient hedge described in green paint as 'tapestry' and consisting of several varieties of tree and quite a few climbing plants, including dog roses and honeysuckle, led, Laura assumed, to the more formal garden where the group was. Hoping she wouldn't meet anyone and feel obliged to explain why, she hared along it arriving at the other end to see the backs of the group heading along towards a woodland area.

Panting slightly and beginning to perspire she debated just running to join them, but still couldn't persuade herself that she wouldn't look pathetic. Why oh why didn't Dermot dispatch them on their separate ways to work on their pieces?

She decided running to join them would only work if she had something of vital importance to tell them. What could she say? She couldn't say there was a fire because there obviously wasn't, and anyway they were in the garden. Floods and swarms of locusts wouldn't work either. What about a particularly beautiful bit of garden, perhaps with a butterfly or, better, a dragonfly involved? She wiped her brow. No, she wouldn't just look keen like an ambitious Girl Guide but barking mad because if there was a dragonfly, there was no way it would still be there, even if everybody did troop off to look at it. And if it was a particularly fine bit of planting involving old roses and lavender, there would be no need for her to have run.

Sighing, she stumped off towards the stumpery – at least it sounded cool.

She spent the rest of the afternoon alternating between feeling like a very bad private detective, trying to stalk Dermot, and like a detective's quarry, trying to avoid being joined by any students, so if she did manage to get Dermot on his own, she would be on her own too.

When they finally met up in the tea room, she said to him casually, 'It's a lovely garden, isn't it? There must be acres and acres. I don't think I ever spotted you.' This was a lie but she didn't want to say she'd only spotted him from a distance because it would imply she'd been looking.

'Oh, I found a really hidden-away corner in the wood,' he said. 'I read my book.' Seeing her react he added, 'No, not written by me. If I told you it was poetry would you think I was impossibly pretentious?'

'Yes,' she nodded, smiling, lying again. 'But it's very writerly, so I'll forgive you.'

Back on the bus she sat at the back and soon fell into a reverie. Trying to get Dermot on his own was just too stressful. If he fancied her – and it was increasingly likely that he didn't – *he* could seek *her* out.

It was the last day of the course and everyone was anxious about Eleanora's impending visit. Although they had never met her, the students instinctively felt their work was going to be torn to shreds, even though Dermot had already taken it apart and put it together again. Dermot may well have been wondering if his agent would press him on his work-in-progress, although he didn't tell Laura this, there had to be some reason for his twitchiness. And Laura was convinced Eleanora would feel she should have got Dermot to announce his presence at the festival to the world. Although, when she thought more deeply, she realised this probably wasn't the case at all, and she was just picking up nerves from everyone else.

Eleanora arrived in style, driving herself in an old Ferrari that roared up to the building leaving an expensive trail of blue smoke behind it.

Dermot was there to greet her. He had put on his suit, which was now so creased it looked as if it had been run over several times by a steamroller. Laura had longed to tell him to brush his hair but had refrained, realising that Eleanora, who knew him quite well, wouldn't expect him to be smart. The rest of them had all got used to his scruffy, writerly appearance.

He kissed Eleanora warmly and said, 'I'm not sure you can leave your car there, Nellie, dear heart.'

Eleanora bridled and said, 'Don't call me Nellie, and I'm sure this nice young man will park it for me.'

The 'nice young man' in question was Gareth, whom Laura privately referred to as the Young Turk. He was only too delighted to catch the keys that Eleanora tossed to him. Grateful that she hadn't been asked to park it herself, Laura followed Dermot and Eleanora into the building and along the corridor to the lecture room.

Eleanora was ferocious! Laura thought that Dermot had been quite tough, but Eleanora was tougher. She'd suspected she'd tell it how it was but Eleanora went to town and what's more seemed to enjoy imparting every negative aspect of the writer's lot she could think of – and more. She told the students the chances of them getting published were hardly better than winning the lottery. She then went on to say that getting published wasn't half as hard as staying that way. If your first book didn't do well, your second wouldn't see the light of day, and if you weren't well published, you might as well burn your books in a corner of your garden because they might attract more attention that way.

No one actually burst into tears, but Laura felt it was only a matter of time.

Then Eleanora added the final can of petrol to the fire of despondency she had created. 'And if you're not good-looking, very old, very young, related to a football star or the managing director of a publishing company, forget it again. If you're not promotable, you're not publishable.'

Eleanora seemed faintly surprised that the room didn't erupt with applause. Dermot was struck dumb, a rare thing for him, and faint whimperings began to emanate from the students.

Laura got to her feet. She couldn't send them all home with their collective heart in its boots.

'Well, thank you, Eleanora, that was fascinating. And isn't it a good thing to hear the very worst-case scenario? Dermot and I know that there's a lot of talent in this room, and while I don't think any of you are best friends with a football star, or married to the head of a major publishing house . . .' She paused. 'But if you are and you didn't tell us, we'll kill you later . . . Dermot and I have seen the immense amount of work and dedication you're capable of, and I know – am sure –' she wasn't at all sure, but she said it anyway, aware that she was sounding rather like an over-enthusiastic headmistress '– that Eleanora would agree with us when we say that talent and perseverance are more important than any of the things she mentioned. Cream will rise to the top. Just you lot go and be cream! And meet us in the bar afterwards.'

The applause wasn't thunderous, but it was there. As her encouraging words sank in they came out of their state of shock and clapped gently.

'Darling, you're too soft on them!' said Eleanora the moment the three of them were alone. 'Tell it like it is!'

'Sure, I know every word you said is true –' Dermot ran his hand through his hair making it even more like a wind-damaged bird's nest – 'but they'd have all gone out and cut their throats if Laura hadn't rescued the situation.'

'Yes, Laura dear, you have done well! I knew you were the person to run Fenella's festival. You've done a splendid job with this course, too! Now I see why you wanted her on board, Dermot.'

Laura lost her breath suddenly. She'd assumed it was Eleanora who'd suggested she come. She couldn't work out how she felt about it. She was pleased he thought she'd be useful, of course. It was flattering that he thought so highly of her editing and organisational skills. But did this mean he really didn't fancy her at all, and just saw her as useful? Was that why he hadn't wanted to be alone with her? It was a devastating thought.

'Laura has been a complete star,' said Dermot. 'I couldn't have managed without her by my side.'

There was a moment's silence and then Eleanora patted Laura on the shoulder. 'Good for you! Now where's the bar?'

At first the students were wary of sitting near Eleanora, but gradually they crept nearer and found she didn't bite. By the end of the evening she'd bought them all drinks and, with a little prompting from Laura, offered to read anything they sent to her.

As Laura walked a rather intoxicated Eleanora back to the room where she was staying the night, she said to her, 'I don't know why I offered to do that. My slush pile is quite big enough already.'

'But these will be quality slush! I hand-picked them myself and their books will be a lot better when they've done more work.'

'All right, darling, I trust you. And Dermot trusts you too, which is very interesting.'

As Laura had always thought of herself as trustworthy, she didn't think it was that strange. But Eleanora, given her slightly drunken state, possibly wasn't thinking clearly.

The students all left immediately after breakfast, many of them saying they felt thoroughly inspired. Eleanora had left before breakfast, saying she was visiting an old friend on the way home, and so suddenly it was just Dermot and Laura.

'Well, I don't know what to say,' said Dermot.

'That must be a first!' Laura teased him, trying to sound lighthearted, although that was the last thing she felt. She remained puzzled by his behaviour over the course. He seemed to genuinely enjoy having her there, but apart from the odd almost brotherly look, she couldn't read him properly and felt completely confused by his attitude towards her. She was also sad because she hadn't managed to make the most their time together. She suddenly felt less confident – so much for her wanting to seduce him. A university car park wasn't the most romantic of settings. And he wasn't striking the pose of someone about to make a move on her as he stood there with his hands in his pockets looking anxious to get away. She told herself she'd see him again at the festival, but would they ever have a minute alone? She couldn't rely on it. And she had to face the possibility that he just didn't see her in that way, if he ever had. She was good old helpful Laura.

'Irishmen are famously loquacious,' she added brightly.

'Not this particular Irishman, at this particular time.' Then he put his hand on her cheek. 'You're a very sweet girl.'

She blinked to disperse her sudden tears. He was being very kind and gentle but it was only affection that she detected in his voice. 'Right then. See you in July at the festival.'

'Oh God, the bloody festival! I'd forgotten all about that.'

'Well, let me remind you!' she said, with feigned strictness.

'One of these days we'll meet under more auspicious circumstances,' he said. Then he kissed her cheek and walked off towards his car without looking back.

Laura stood and watched him go, her tears flowing freely now. She didn't care if anyone saw her.

Chapter Thirteen

The drive back to Somerby gave Laura plenty of time to sort out in her mind her feelings for Dermot and, more importantly, his feelings for her. Although she couldn't really tell how he felt, Laura was now convinced she was really in love with Dermot. The course had given her an opportunity to see him as a man, and how he functioned in society. He could be cutting, sarcastic and rude but it was all tempered with humour, wit and extreme kindness. All of the students had been criticised, but all of them had received praise they would cherish for the rest of their writing careers.

He saw her as a helpmeet, that was it. Reliable, diligent, forgiving – none of the characteristics that made her a force to be reckoned with, unless they happened to be jointly reckoning the chances of a particular writer's success. His tenderness to her as they parted showed her how fond he was of her, but fondness was not enough. A part of her wished she'd never met him, that he'd remained the elusive figure she'd dreamt about. Now like all good heroines in the books she devoured as a teenager, she'd have to pick herself up and get over him as best she could.

She was soon thrown back into festival work with little time to dwell too much on the great Dermot Flynn and for that she was very grateful. She'd slipped the photograph one of the students had sent her of them all together into one of the books on her shelves after briefly tracing the outline of his face and then telling herself not to be so silly.

She'd been to stay with Grant for a few days, who was back from a holiday 'somewhere hot and expensive' and wanting to tell her all about it, with pictures. She was now returning to Somerby once more – and work.

Fenella greeted Laura as she drove round the back to park her car near her converted byre, calling through the open window. She seemed very over-excited.

'Have you heard? Dermot's gone public! Why didn't you tell me?'

'Let the poor girl get out of the car!' Even Rupert, following his wife, seemed less laid-back than usual.

Laura did this. 'Sorry, Fen, what do you mean?'

'Jacob Stone phoned me. Apparently Dermot has gone public. He saw it on some news thing. He's thrilled, naturally.'

'But he hasn't!' Laura opened the back door to get her bag. 'I'm sure he'd have said something to me if he was going to do that.' She felt desperately betrayed. It was her festival! Surely she should have been the first to know, not some news agency and Jacob Stone! Anyway, on the course he'd said he'd forgotten all about it!

'We'll ring Eleanora,' said Fenella. 'She'll know.'

'Good idea. I think we need to check this story, I really do.'

Apparently it was true. They went on to an Internet news site on Rupert's computer. Some news agency had got hold of the story that *formerly reclusive writer Dermot Flynn has agreed to appear at the Somerby Literary Festival. There are rumours that he'll produce his first new work for many years and also that there's a bidding war for his next novel.*

'Oh fuck,' whispered Laura.

'Laura!' said Fenella.

'I know. I'm sorry, but that's the only word that will do. He'll be absolutely bloody furious!'

'Why? And anyway, the story probably came from him,' said Fenella. 'Who else would make up a story like this?'

'Eleanora, for one,' said Laura. 'She's got the most to gain.' She thought hard about the course, trying to remember if there was anything about Eleanora's behaviour that indicated she might have put this story about. 'But I don't think she did.'

'Well, we can ask her,' said Fenella.

Laura sighed. 'I hope to goodness it doesn't get on the main news.' She looked at Rupert and Fenella plaintively. 'After all, it's only literary news, not really of general interest.'

'It might not be like that in Ireland,' said Rupert. 'I mean, I don't really know, but I imagine if word got out that "the greatest living Irish writer" was producing a new book, it would be of huge interest.'

Laura buried her face in her hands. 'This is dreadful.'

'It's jolly good for the festival!' said Fenella. 'I'll be able to tell everyone that he's coming and then may be all those writers who haven't yet confirmed, will. And people will be queuing for tickets.'

Laura reappeared from behind her hands. 'I just don't know what Dermot will do when he hears about this.'

'Well, we can't do anything about it until he does hear,' said Rupert. 'I think we should all calm down. Let's go into the house and have a cup of coffee.'

Laura was plucking up courage to ring Eleanora when her phone went. Eleanora was phoning her. 'Laura?' she snapped. 'Did you put this story about?'

'No! Did you really think I had?'

Eleanora subsided. 'No.'

'In fact, I thought you might have released it,' said Laura.

'Me? Good God no! Why would I do that? If anything

was designed to give him writer's block for ever, it's something like this.'

'You knew about his writer's block?'

'Of course!'

'He was hoping you didn't know.'

'Who or what does he think I am? Stupid? I'm his agent, for God's sake. I know when my writers aren't writing, even when they're telling me they are! No, the poor boy's been blocked as hell for years. We just keep up the pretence that I don't know.' She paused. 'He told you?'

'Mm.' Laura didn't explain the circumstances, or that they'd exchanged deep secrets. Eleanora didn't need to know everything.

There was a long pause. 'I think you'd better come up to London right away. We need to make a plan.'

'But the festival—'

'The festival won't have it's star act unless we can think of something. This has to be a priority. Fenella will understand.'

Laura was explaining all this to Fenella and Rupert when her phone chimed to indicate she had a text message. It was from Dermot. 'Your festival can take a flying jump.'

It felt like a physical blow, not because the festival needed its star so badly, but because he might think that it was she who had betrayed him. Somehow, she had to tell him that she hadn't.

'I think we can take it as a no,' she said, fighting to sound calm, having shown her message to Rupert and Fenella. 'It's quite polite, really, for him.'

'Maybe he doesn't know you can text the "f" word,' said Rupert.

'You can?' said Fenella. 'I didn't know that!'

'We can be thankful for small mercies,' said Laura, proud of her lighthearted remark. In the circumstances it was a triumph.

211

'You'd better go to Eleanora's straightaway,' said Fenella. 'She's the one to get us out of this mess. If she says she needs you, go.'

'Maybe Laura would prefer to recover from the journey first?' suggested Rupert. 'She's only just got back. I know your family always do jump when Eleanora snaps her fingers, but there's no reason for Laura to do so too.'

'I think there is, actually, Ru,' Laura said. 'The sooner we can get this sorted out, the better. If we *can* get it sorted out.'

'If we could just find out who did it,' said Fenella. 'Then we could send them hate mail.'

'You'd have sent them fan mail when you first heard it,' said Laura, indignantly.

'That was before I knew what a disaster it was.'

A comforting bowl of soup and a lift to the station from Rupert did help Laura to calm down a bit. She read a light romantic novel on the train and by the time she reached London, she was feeling less desperate. After all, if the festival flopped it wasn't the end of the world. Then she remembered how much effort she and Fenella had put in to it, how much money had been spent, and decided it might not be the end of the world but it would be a terrible shame. And there was always the fear that Jacob Stone would withdraw as a sponsor. Supposing he asked for the money he'd already given to be returned?

She dismissed this idea as ridiculous as she walked to the taxi queue, trailing her case on wheels. She felt as if she'd been living out of a suitcase for weeks. She was more worried about Dermot than she was about the festival. And she knew Eleanora would be too.

'Darling, have a drink. God knows I need one,' said Eleanora before Laura had even negotiated the case into the flat. 'This is such a disaster.'

Laura abandoned the case and took off her coat, following Eleanora into what turned out to be an enchanting sitting room.

Eleanora went over to what seemed to be a Louis Quinze side table but probably wasn't, quite, even knowing Eleanora.

'Gin and tonic? Whisky? Anything you can think of?'

'Whisky please,' said Laura.

'Good plan. We need to be fortified.'

She handed Laura a glass filled to a level that would have fitted right in with the measures she'd had in Ireland. 'Sit!'

Laura sank on to the sofa. Eleanora took a chair opposite.

'Sorry to drag you up here,' Eleanora said, having taken a hearty sip, without any preliminary toast, 'but you're the only one who can get us out of this mess.'

'What do you mean? You're his agent.'

'Yes, and his opinion of me, currently, is not fit to print, not even in the grittiest East End crime novel.' Eleanora put down her glass. 'He told you about his block, he asked you to help him with the course – that means he likes you. You have to be the sacrificial virgin delivered to the dragon.'

Laura jumped.

'I was talking figuratively, darling.' One of Eleanora's pencilled eyebrows raised in surprise at her reaction.

Laura tried to gloss over the matter. 'Well, I suppose he does quite like—'

'No, darling. A lot. He likes you a lot. You certainly don't irritate him.'

Laura smiled, hiding her pain. She didn't want him to 'like' her, or for her not to irritate him. She wanted him to – well, want her. 'I think that counts as damning with faint praise.'

'You must go and talk to him. Tell him that we're depending on him and that we didn't leak the story.'

'So who did? I'm just trying to think who knew.'

'All the literary blogs have got hold of it,' said Eleanora gloomily. 'Why people have to spout on about their doings to the world I can't imagine.'

'Let's have a look at one of the blogs, see if it gives us a hint,' suggested Laura.

'My computer's in my office,' said Eleanora. 'You have a look while I deal with supper. It's a ready meal, I'm afraid.'

'I don't care what I eat, really,' said Laura. 'Where's your office?'

'Room at the end, down the hall. The computer's on.'

Laura typed Dermot's name into the search engine and a whole host of blogs came up. She went through them quickly, ignoring those that referred to his first two novels. Then she found what she was looking for. It was a blog done by Gareth Ainsley – one of the students. Although he styled himself as 'writerfrombeyond' his identity was obvious. And he mentioned the course. The strange thing was, though, she was fairly sure that she'd never mentioned the fact that Dermot was appearing in the festival. She'd been protecting Dermot's privacy so carefully.

As she read the blog, which went on about Dermot's teaching, the other people and the accommodation quite a lot, she realised that this student had probably told the trade press and the gossip magazines before he'd written this. He'd been a very ambitious young writer, convinced of his talent, not entirely erroneously, and had apparently really admired Dermot. So why do this to him? Perhaps he thought it would further his own literary career.

Laura joined Eleanora in the kitchen. 'I've found the culprit, I think. One of the students. But what I can't work out is how he found out that Dermot was due to appear at the festival. I'm ninety-nine per cent sure I didn't tell anyone. I was so careful not to.'

Eleanora tipped the contents of a foil container onto a plate. 'Well, maybe Dermot did. I gather there was a fair bit of late-night drinking.'

Now Laura felt guilty for not being able to stay up late, as well as just feeble. 'There was, and I didn't stay up for it, so Dermot could have said something that gave him away.' She sighed. 'Well, there's nothing we can do about it now. The secret's out, except I'm sure Dermot won't appear now.'

Eleanora picked up the two full plates. 'Bring the glasses and the bottle, darling.'

Laura followed her hostess into the dining room, aware that she had more to say. Suddenly things had changed slightly, and now she felt that perhaps Dermot was better just left alone. The festival would have to do without him.

'To be honest,' said Eleanora, filling two wine glasses to the brim. 'I'm not bothered about the festival. Do start. This won't be delicious hot, but it'll be uneatable cold.' She paused while she contemplated her plate for a moment before picking up her knife and fork and plunging in. She went on, a piece of chicken balanced on the end of her fork. 'Obviously it would be fantastic if Dermot appeared but right now it's him I'm worried about.'

Laura paused, her own fork halfway to her mouth. 'What do you mean?'

Eleanora put down her knife and fork. 'He's a very tempestuous sort of person. If he took all this the wrong way he could . . .'

'What? What are you talking about?'

'Well, I don't suppose he'd actually do away with himself or anything,' Eleanora said slowly, 'but it could easily mean he gives up writing all together, which would be a loss. A great loss.'

Despite her breezy air at times, Laura knew that Eleanora still hoped that Dermot would produce another masterpiece, even after all this time, and not just for her ten per cent. She believed in him, just as Laura did. She felt a rush of affection for the older woman.

A gloomy silence settled over them. Laura sipped her wine, thinking about a world with no more books from Dermot Flynn. 'That would be dreadful,' she said aloud.

'Which is why you have to go there and sort him out.'

Laura replaced her glass, aware that Eleanora was a clever, manipulative person. 'Why me? Why not you? Who better than his agent? You've known him all his writing life. You could be a mother figure to him.'

'I can't be a mother to him. He currently hates me. You're the only one. You did it before, after all. You got him to agree to come to the festival in the first place.'

'Yes, but he hates the festival now! He probably hates me too!'

'Darling child, he does not hate you! Trust me on that. He'll be only too pleased to see an uncritical face.'

'I'm not that uncritical!' said Laura wishing her indignation was genuine.

'I know it must seem a bit too much like déjà vu, or Groundhog Day, or whatever the expression is, but you are the one for this task.' She paused. 'Even if he's not that pleased to see anyone, he'd rather see you than anyone else I can think of.' She looked at Laura, her eyes bright with anticipation.

Knowing when she was cornered, Laura said, 'OK,' and picked up her wine glass again. She felt tired and anxious, but there was a tiny spark of excitement at the prospect of seeing Dermot again.

*   *   *

216

The following day, when she was gathering her things for the journey back to Somerby, Laura phoned Monica. Monica had heard all about Dermot, of course. After they'd shared exclamations for a while Laura said, 'Mon, would you come with me to Ireland again? I've got to go and sort him out. Everyone says. I really don't want to go alone.'

'Oh Laura! I can't! I've got a mini-tour coming up. Seamus is coming with me.' She lowered her voice. 'It's going really well between us.'

'Oh.'

'Mm. I haven't actually heard his band yet but I'm sure they're great.' Then she remembered why Laura had rung. 'And really, Laura, this is something you should do on your own.'

'But, Monica!'

'I know, I know, we had such fun before. But it's not going to be fun, is it? Although of course I would have come to support you if I could have.'

'I know. And I also knew it was a long shot. I'm sure it will be very character-forming for me to go on my own.'

'Oh, love, you do sound down about it. Why don't you ask Fenella to go with you?'

'I can't. She's up to her eyes. In fact, even more up to her eyes now.'

'So it's good for the festival, all this publicity?'

'Yes,' said Laura dolefully. 'It's good for the festival.'

She was going to fly to Ireland this time. Eleanora had arranged a cab to pick her up from the airport and drive her all the way to Ballyfitzpatrick. She was also paying for everything. After all, Eleanora had a vested interest, Laura reminded herself.

Personally, because she didn't know what she was going to find at the end of it, Laura would have preferred for the journey to be slower. The flight seemed to whistle by and she was sure the travelling was, in this case, going to be far better than arriving.

She asked the taxi driver to take her to the bed and breakfast where she and Monica had stayed before. She'd booked in there because she knew the people. When Dermot threw her out on to the street she could go to them for comfort.

She had intended to keep her mission secret. Officially she was having a couple of days' break in a pretty part of the world she'd previously visited in winter. She was planning to walk, to relax and enjoy herself.

How long she'd be able to keep this secret, she didn't know. Before she'd even finished registering at the b. and b. she was being asked pertinent questions. 'You were one of the girls who came to see Dermot at the festival, weren't you?'

'That's right. With my friend Monica. We had such a lovely time I wanted to see the place in summer.'

'You'll have heard about Dermot? The paparazzi were on to him. For two days they were there. He hid in his house and wouldn't come out.'

'Poor man. He must have hated it.'

The woman, who Laura remembered was called Marion, clicked her teeth and shook her head. 'Not sure about that. He's stayed indoors ever since.'

'What do you mean?' Marion was obviously dying to tell Laura all about it, so she thought she might as well glean what information she could.

'Well, he doesn't go to the pub. He's not seen at the shop, so God knows what he's living on. No one's seen hide nor hair of him for over a week.'

'Oh.' Laura considered. Would it be best to confide in her? It might make her mission easier, and, she had to be honest, it was unlikely she could do anything without the whole place knowing exactly what she was up to. 'Could I confide in you?'

Marion said, 'Come in to the kitchen. I'll make a pot of tea, and you can tell all. I knew you were here for a reason the moment you made the booking.'

'The thing is,' said Laura, drinking tea so strong she could feel it attacking the enamel on her teeth, 'I've been sent by his agent to check if he's all right.'

'He's not all right. If he was all right he'd be behaving like a normal person, going to the pub, taking his car out, doing his messages.'

'Well, I'm to check on him and report back.' She didn't add that she was supposed to show him the error of his ways, convince him that no one who loved him had betrayed his secret, and that he should definitely come and do the festival.

Marion regarded her seriously, and then handed her a plate of biscuits. She'd already eaten the sandwiches Marion had prepared, but eating seemed to calm her nerves and she took a pink wafer although she didn't usually like them. 'I don't think you should do that.'

'Do what?' The wafer was very sweet and slightly offset the strength of the tea.

'Go and check on him. No nice young woman should go near Dermot when he's like this.'

'Like what?'

'Well! We don't know! But what we do know' – Marion lowered her voice although they were alone – 'is that he has a case of whiskey in there with him.'

Laura lowered her voice too. 'How do you know that?'

'Because one was delivered the day after the paparazzi arrived. It's my belief he's on a bender and no nice woman should go within a mile of him.'

'I think we're both within a mile of him right now.' Laura smiled, she hoped reassuringly. 'I'm sure I'll be all right. He wouldn't do anything to hurt me.'

'Normally, Dermot is charm itself, wouldn't hurt a fly, let alone a pretty young woman like yourself but . . .' Marion paused for dramatic effect. 'I know he likes his pint, but he doesn't usually drink *that* much. It could send him wild. He has a reputation with women. You don't look strong enough to fight him off.'

Laura giggled in spite of the trickiness of the situation. 'I'm sure he's not going to jump on me. He might shout a bit, but that's all.'

'It's still not a fit place for you to visit on your own. Take one of the boys with you if you must go.' She paused. 'I must say folk have been worried. They'd be glad to know if he's all right.'

'So why hasn't anyone looked before now? If he's been holed up for over a week?'

'Scared to. I tell you, he's got a reputation.'

A horrible thought occurred to her. 'He's not armed, is he?'

'Oh dear no. Anyway, if he is, he'll be so drunk he won't be able to shoot straight.'

'I don't think that's very comforting!'

'I'm not trying to be comforting, I'm trying to tell you not to go! But I'm also saying we'd all be glad to know how he is.'

'So you'll sacrifice a stranger to get the information you need?' Laura was fairly sure she'd read a book where this was the theme.

Marion laughed. 'Well, we know him too well to risk it. And besides, we have to live here. If he turns on you, you can fly back to England.'

'Should I have a taxi with its engine running outside?' Laura was laughing too now.

'No, but I'll get Murphy to keep his mule on stand-by.'

After more tea, laughter and for Laura a shower and a change of clothes, she set off up the road to Dermot's house. She didn't feel like laughing now. She remembered taking her GCSEs, her A levels, her driving test, and being summoned to the headmistress's office for some unknown reason. None of those experiences had made her feel this shaky.

Chapter Fourteen

She knew the way, although the last time she had made the journey it had been in the other direction. The fact that the village was so small definitely helped. And the fact that on this visit, the taxi had driven past his house, pointing it out to her as the home of the local celebrity. She would have preferred the journey to be longer really, so she could put off the moment of truth, whatever that turned out to be, for a little while. Seemingly two seconds after she'd set off, she was at his gate.

Although she'd been warned it would do her no good, Laura started by knocking at the door and pressing the bell for quite a long time. Inevitably, recollections of what had so nearly happened the last time she had been in Dermot's house came flooding back: the laughing, clinging, shuffling entry into his house, when she was very drunk and he not much better, when they hadn't wanted to be separated for an instant. The memories were not helpful.

Would she ever feel that degree of passion again? When she did finally go to bed with a man for the first time, would she want it as much? Or would losing her virginity just seem like getting rid of something that had become a burden? She knew it was unrealistic but she couldn't believe she would ever have that chemistry – at least for that one night – with anyone else. There was something about Dermot that made every nerve ending alert and tingling. How long would it take to find another, more suitable man who made her feel like that? She could end up a virgin at fifty!

These thoughts kept her occupied until she felt she'd tried conventional methods of entry long enough. It was time for the back-door approach.

The back door was, of course, locked. It hadn't been, she remembered, when she'd sneaked out of it to run back to the b. and b. in the early hours. Now, knocking on it, pushing at it and even giving it a surly kick only indicated it was locked and bolted.

Now what? Maybe shouting. Maybe if he heard it was she, and not some journalist, he might let her in.

'Hello! Dermot! It's me! Laura!' It was not easy for a normally quiet person to make such a noise, to yell her name to the world, but she did her best.

While the neighbourhood might have heard her calls, Dermot obviously hadn't. She'd have to think of something else.

She walked round the house and at last spotted a slightly open window. It wasn't in the best place for an inexperienced housebreaker, but it would have to do. It was the top half of a hopper-type window. Although the curtains were drawn, judging by the position she was fairly sure it opened on to the sitting room. If she could get up high enough and get her arm in, perhaps she might be able to open the bottom half of it with a stick or something. The irony of it all hit her; the last time she was at Dermot's house, she was sneaking out of it. Here she was now doing her darnedest to sneak in.

She dragged the dustbin over to the window, thinking that she had an advantage over normal burglars. She didn't mind getting caught; in fact, if the owner of the house was disturbed that would be a good thing. And if a passer-by spotted her, she could ask them for help, even if she came across as a rabid fan – or possibly a particularly blatant stalker.

The dustbin was a bit wobbly but she managed to wedge it steady with a couple of big stones she excavated from the edge of the flowerbed. Dermot had obviously not been much of a gardener even before he became a recluse so she didn't think he'd notice or even care what she did.

There was a wooden garden chair and she dragged it over to add stability to the dustbin. Once she was sure it wouldn't fall over, she stood on the chair, and then, gingerly, stepped on to the dustbin.

From there she could see the catch of the main part of the window but she couldn't quite reach it, even when she leant right over. But a stick might do it.

It took her a lot of wiggling but eventually she got the handle to unlatch. A lot of scrabbling later she got it open enough to get the stick in the gap. The window opened.

She was almost disappointed that no one had seen her, she felt so proud of herself as she fought through the curtain, got her leg up over the sill and landed in the sitting room.

Once there, she listened, in case her housebreaking had disturbed Dermot. As there was no other sound in the house a sudden panic took hold of Laura. Supposing he was dead! Supposing she was about to find a rotting corpse!

Her thoughts were so confused that for a few moments she didn't know if the thought of Dermot being dead was more terrible than the thought of finding his body. She broke into a sweat while she talked herself into a more reasonable frame of mind. Marion at the b. and b. hadn't indicated that anyone was worried that he was dead, and they would be if his death were at all likely. They just hadn't seen him since he'd been besieged by the press. She decided to hunt him out.

Although she knew, really, that he wouldn't be downstairs, she thought she'd take a look around, to give her an idea of how he'd been living.

The kitchen told her pretty much everything. It was disgusting. It looked like a project for a reality-television programme involving boiler-suited professionals, swabs and mind-boggling quantities of bacteria. There were rows of empty baked-bean cans, their razor-edged lids piled up like a heap of discarded oyster-shells. Every mug, cup, plate, saucer and bowl filled the sink. The floor was piled with dirty saucepans. This was definitely more than a week's worth of mess.

And it wasn't only crockery he'd run out of. There was a pile of dirty clothes heaped up in front of the washing machine. She suspected there'd be more upstairs.

As she looked further she realised that the grime was fairly superficial. There wasn't grease you could write your name in on the walls, it was just that he obviously hadn't washed up for a long time. And judging by the spoons and forks sticking out of the nearer baked-bean tins, he hadn't intended to do any. He was just eating the beans straight out of the can.

'Yuk,' she said aloud, and wondered if it was the first word heard in the house for ages.

As there were no more downstairs rooms Dermot could possibly be in, she bravely went upstairs.

She didn't have to look far, even if she hadn't been able to remember which his bedroom was. She could hear him snoring. Well, he wasn't dead then, she thought, aware of her relief. Although the front part of her brain had dismissed this as a possibility, her subconscious hadn't quite let it go. But now, unless the snoring was really thousands of flies swarming round a rotting corpse, she knew what she would find.

Once in the door of the bedroom she could also smell him. He was lying on his back with his mouth open, deeply asleep. He was wearing a pair of jeans and nothing else. His unshaven state would have meant he had a beard if it had had any shape, but it was just a vast

225

amount of black hair. His teeth glinted white in among the fur although she was willing to bet he hadn't brushed them for a long time. They made him look like some ferocious animal, a grizzly bear or some such.

She cleared her throat. She wanted him to wake up because she was fed up with feeling like a burglar. Once he knew she was there, she could explain herself. But he didn't stir.

She'd been right about the dirty clothes. Socks, T-shirts, shirts, underpants and at least four pairs of trousers littered the floor. What had been going on? Did he usually have a cleaning lady who'd let him down, and he'd been incapable of shoving his own laundry into the machine?

Knowing she shouldn't really, she bundled as much as she could of it together, piled it on to a shirt to make a bag and carried it downstairs. Maybe it was for the best that he hadn't woken. She could get on better without him.

She switched on the radio, tied a couple of tea towels round her waist to save her jeans from getting soaked and set to work.

She should have gone to the shop for rubber gloves, she realised, but as that would involve a lot of questions when she got there, and finding the key before she went, she did without. She certainly couldn't face having to clamber back in through the window again.

Her recycling soul meant she would have to wash the baked-bean cans but there was a lot to tackle before she had to worry about them. She worked out the washing machine and filled it, holding her breath as she stuffed the clothes into it. Once that was chugging away she turned her attention to the rest of the kitchen. She simply couldn't bear to leave it in this state for a moment longer and she might as well make herself useful until Dermot finally woke up. She didn't like to admit to herself she was doing it because she cared.

226

It was a feat of organisation: finding somewhere to put the dirty things and then the clean ones. No wonder Dermot had resorted to the floor. She opened the window and turned on the hot tap. When hot water did emerge she offered a prayer of thanksgiving, doubled when she also found washing-up liquid. If she hadn't had that she'd have had to go to the shop. Now she'd started, she really wanted the kitchen to gleam before Dermot woke.

When she'd dealt with the kitchen, the bathroom (which was worse than the kitchen, in a way) and had vacuumed the sitting room, she went up to the bedroom and said Dermot's name several times. He still didn't stir. Sighing loudly, she stamped down the stairs. She would brave the shop and the questioning. There was absolutely nothing in the fridge or the cupboards and Dermot was bound to be hungry when he woke up – she didn't fancy the idea of facing a hungry, feral Dermot without food on hand to calm him. It would be her peace-offering – even if she hadn't been the one who'd gone to the press.

She left the front door on the latch and headed down the lane. She was lucky. The shop was full of people, all talking away. She was able to slip among the aisles, tossing things into her basket. The girl at the till rang them up without much in the way of chat. It was possible that she just looked like a woman on holiday, stocking up her holiday cottage.

Back at the house, she had made a nourishing soup, dusted the sitting room and even cut some branches from the garden and put them in a vase when she could stand it no more – Dermot Flynn was going to wake up!

She stood at the doorway of the bedroom thinking what to say when a rasping voice made her heart pound.

'What the hell is going on?'

Trying to give an appearance of calm, she went into the room so he could see her. 'It's me.'

A long list of blasphemous expletives issued from his lips but he didn't sound angry, just very, very surprised.

Laura was not impressed. 'It's all very well you lying there and saying all that, but have you any idea what time it is?' she demanded. She was tired, had been worried and was hungry. This all combined to make her angry, too.

She saw his stomach muscles ripple as he chuckled. 'What do *you* think?'

'The time isn't a matter of opinion!' Then she glanced at her watch. 'Nearly five o'clock. Good God! I've been here for hours!'

'How did you get in?'

'Through a window. Dermot, everyone's been so worried about you. Are you ill? Have you been ill? Why haven't you washed, or eaten proper food, or done any washing up for . . .'

'Just over a fortnight.' He was still lying there, showing no signs of moving.

'Listen, get up, have a shower, a long shower, shave, and then I'll give you soup. Leek and potato. I made it myself.'

'How could I possibly resist?'

She stomped out of the room and downstairs. Once in the kitchen she shut the door and sat at the table. Then she did what she'd been longing to do for some time. She allowed herself to weep. What had she done? She'd travelled hundreds of miles, cleaned his disgusting house, made him soup, done his washing, probably got herself drummed out of the feminist sisterhood, and for what?

She'd done it officially because Eleanora had asked her to come, to find out what had happened to him. She also needed to know if he really meant not to come to the festival. That furious text might have been sent when he was at the height of his anger; maybe he didn't really mean it. But in her heart she knew she'd also come because she loved him. That was why she'd cleaned his house and cooked for him. If she'd only come for professional reasons, she'd have just chucked a bucket of water over him or something and retreated to a safe distance, explaining to the neighbours that he was fine, just in a drunken stupor. Eleanora would have expected her to do a bit more than that, possibly, but she wouldn't have demanded she became a domestic drudge for him.

There was no shame in loving someone. Love was a good, uplifting emotion that made the world go round. Everyone knew that. But everyone, even one as inexperienced as Laura, knew that it was best to keep your feelings to yourself until you were fairly sure they were reciprocated.

She could hope he wouldn't realise why she'd done what she'd done. She could hope he wouldn't read the signals that to her seemed as clear as if she'd arranged an aeroplane to trail a banner through the sky saying 'I Love You' in big letters. Men were notoriously dense about matters like this.

She heard movement in the rooms above her and realised she had to get rid of any signs of her tears, or her weakness. She'd blame it all on Eleanora. He might think she had insisted that she dealt with his sordid house and cook for him. He might not identify her as a complete, loved-up sucker.

Her emergency make-up kit in her handbag produced a tiny sample tube of foundation that she patted on round her nose, disguising the redness. Some mascara sorted out her eyes, and by the time she heard him thundering down the stairs she felt quite respectable.

'Laura, dear girl, what are you doing here?' His voice was still a little hoarse, but that didn't make it any less sexy.

'Eleanora sent me. Everyone's beside themselves with worry. They didn't know what had happened to you.

They thought you must have been ill, or gone on a bender or something.' She paused, looking at him questioningly.

'Or something,' he said after an annoyingly long pause, and pulled out a chair and sat on it. He was wearing clean jeans and a shirt that was clean if very crumpled. It was only half tucked in. Part of Laura was grateful that he hadn't run out of clothes completely.

'But you're all right?' Laura ladled soup into a bowl. She wanted an explanation: summer flu, a bad back, something.

She didn't get one. 'Yes.' He started to eat the soup hungrily. 'There wouldn't be a . . .'

She handed him a plate of bread and butter. 'You obviously haven't eaten a thing for ages. Whyever not?'

He shook his head. 'I was not able,' he said through a mouthful of bread.

Silently, Laura added the missing 'to', liking the difference between Irish English, and English English. 'I could make you a sandwich.'

'That would be fantastic.'

Now he'd started eating he didn't seem able to stop. He ate an entire loaf of sandwiches, all the ham, cheese and tomatoes that Laura had bought, and then looked round for more. Eventually he said, 'Aren't you eating anything?'

She laughed at him, sipping her tea. 'Not now, no. I'll go back to the shop for more supplies. Will it still be open?' She wished she'd bought more last time, but she hadn't realised just how hungry he'd be.

'Oh yes, it's open all hours in summer. Have you got money? My wallet must be somewhere.' He got up and started staring around. 'God, the place is clean!'

'Yes. And don't worry about money. Eleanora gave me lots of euros. It'll all come out of your earnings eventually.'

He sat back down in his chair, genuinely horrified.

'Don't say that, for God's sake. When did I last earn her a brass farthing?'

'Don't sound so melodramatic. Your first two books still sell very steadily, as you must know.'

He shook his head. 'I always forget about that. I think in some ways I try to forget I ever wrote those damn books.'

Laura pursed her lips and put her head on one side. 'I don't think so.'

He regarded her for a long time and then sighed deeply. 'God, I'd kill for a cigarette.'

'And would it be me you'd kill?'

He narrowed his gaze. 'Tell you what, if you don't buy me some fags immediately, it definitely will be you I kill.' Then he smiled.

'Oh Dermot,' she said, oozing sarcasm to cover up her melting stomach, 'you surely must have kissed the Blarney Stone, coming out with such seductive phrases. Surely the birds would come down from the trees to do your bidding.'

'Listen, if you don't want to find out, with demonstrations, exactly what the Blarney Stone and meself have got up to, I'd go to the shop in double-quick time.'

If Laura hadn't been so hungry, and so aware that her feelings for him must be so blatant, she might have been tempted to call his bluff. But she didn't. She gave him a schoolmistress's smile, picked up her bag and went shopping again. It was only when she was halfway down the overgrown path that she realised there was no earthly reason why he couldn't have gone to the shop himself.

Her reappearance in the shop so soon caused an almighty stir; she had not been mistaken for a holiday-maker before, everyone had known exactly who she was and whom she was shopping for. It meant she had to tell everyone, several times, exactly how fine he was, and how hungry. She filled two wire baskets with supplies and then just in time remembered. 'Oh, do you know what sort of cigarettes he smokes?'

The man behind the counter reached behind him. He produced a packet of tobacco and some papers. 'He rolls his own but he gave them up in March.'

'Well, he said he'd kill me unless I got him some cigarettes so maybe I won't remind him.'

After her purchases had been rung up and settled into bags the man said, 'Sure Dermot's a lucky so-and-so to find a woman like you.'

'Oh, I'm not his woman! It's just . . . a business relationship.' She didn't want to go into details.

The man laughed. 'I'll tell my wife that. She'll find it very amusing.'

Laura decided not to press the point. She could perfectly understand that the thought of Dermot having a business relationship with any woman younger than Eleanora was a bit hard to credit.

Dermot took the tobacco and the papers from her with a smile that would have melted her heart if it hadn't already happened. His smile was exceptionally sexy. Knowing that every other woman on the planet would probably share her feelings about this wasn't encouraging.

'So,' he said, putting tobacco into a dark-coloured paper and, having seen it properly disposed, licking the paper and closing it. He didn't put the cigarette between his lips but just watched Laura, seemingly for ever.

'So?' Laura caved in, unable to stand another second of the silence.

'So was it you who revealed my story to the press?'

She'd known they'd have to have this discussion and felt more or less ready for it. 'It wasn't "your story" – it was just the fact that you'd agreed to appear at the festival.'

232

She was pleased that she sounded so calm. 'But actually, no, I didn't. I wouldn't.'

His narrowed gaze and slightly flared nostrils meant she had to keep up the pretence of calm with slightly more effort. 'It must have been Eleanora,' he said, a growl in his voice.

'No! It wasn't. And it wasn't Fenella or Rupert or anyone from the festival. Not even Jacob Stone, who would have dearly loved to shout your name from the rooftops.' Laura felt a growing sense of irritation. How could he think any of them would do such a thing when they'd promised they wouldn't? Did he doubt their word?

This evidence of Jacob Stone's admiration made no impression. 'It sounds as if you know who it was.' He was looking as if he might eat her, whole, in one big bite. 'For God's sake tell me!' he demanded.

She was determined not to let his anger faze her. 'I think it was one of the students,' she said quietly but steadily. 'There's a blog I'm fairly sure was written by one of them.'

'Who?'

'Gareth Ainsley.'

'I'll kill him,' he said, standing up, his fist clenched, his face furious.

The piece of internal elastic that had been keeping Laura functioning, doing the right thing, focused on the task in hand, snapped. She turned on him.

'Oh, for God's sake, Dermot! You are so bloody precious! What the hell does it matter if some poor student of creative writing blogs about you, revealing your not very interesting secret to the world! He didn't tell everyone you were gay! He didn't declare you as a secret heroin addict! Or a paedophile! All he said, in among a lot of sycophantic rubbish, was that you'd be appearing at a tiny little literary festival no one has heard of!'

His eyes blazed and if she hadn't been so angry herself

233

she'd have been frightened. Part of her was, anyway. 'Well, they've heard of it now, haven't they? This has put it on the map well and truly!'

'And is that such a bad thing? Does it really matter, in the scheme of things, that people know that Dermot Flynn, the "greatest living Irish writer", might appear at a literary festival?'

'It matters if you're Dermot Flynn! Have you any idea how destructive all this attention is to a creative person?'

'No, because, thank the Lord, I'm not a creative person! I'm just the little Jane Eyre character who makes it all possible for you pathetic, irritating, solipsistic, up-themselves "creative people"!' She took a breath. She was on a roll now. She'd had enough. 'Well, I'm fed up with creative people. I think they're a myth. I think you're a myth! A self-created myth who pretends he has writer's block so he can spend the rest of his life doing sweet FA! I think—'

His arms came round her, pushing the breath out of her body, and before she could inhale again his mouth was on hers.

Laura didn't know if she nearly fainted through lack of oxygen or desire. Every feminist part of her should have been kicking, screaming, biting and scratching him, but every womanly part of her refused to do more than moan faintly.

His lips captured hers as if he was going to devour her, the ferocity of his feelings clear. His hands gripped her clothes, pressing her to him, crushing her, making her legs buckle.

The table shot away from under them as they collapsed on to it and she would have landed on the floor if he hadn't caught her and moved her round so he was taking their combined weight. He released her mouth for an instant, but only long enough for them to draw breath before he kissed her again.

Laura was swooning, a tiny part of her registering that although she'd read of this happening in books she hadn't believed it really happened. As a unit, they moved to the sitting room, Dermot kicking open the door, hauling them both through it and on to the sofa. It ejected them on to the floor in seconds.

Dermot pulled her T-shirt out of her jeans and up. He was kissing her tummy, fiddling with the button of her jeans when he seemed to come to his senses. 'Laura? Do you want this?'

'Mmm,' she said, nodding her head urgently, thinking that if he stopped she would die. She knew she had the rest of her life to regret it but she felt she'd rather regret something she'd done than something she hadn't.

Now it was she pulling at his clothes, freeing his shirt so she could feel his skin under her fingers, against her cheek.

'We don't want carpet burn,' he said. 'Come on.'

She wanted to object, sure that if they went upstairs her sanity would return, and she didn't want it to. She didn't have a chance to say anything. He took hold of her wrist and dragged her behind him up the stairs and into his bedroom.

She just had long enough to take in the fact that there was a clean sheet on the bed, untucked, not straight but clean, before he was unzipping her jeans and pulling them down, dragging off her socks before throwing her on to the bed. She started to giggle helplessly, delirious in her happiness.

'We've been here before,' he breathed. 'Do you want to back out?'

'No. I don't.'

'Any time you change your mind . . .'

'I won't change my mind. I'm stone-cold sober, and I won't change my mind.'

'I won't either,' he breathed.

After the first breathless rush they experienced downstairs, Dermot now took his time, removing the remainder of Laura's clothes with sensual care. The rest of his own clothes were pulled off and kicked away.

Laura swallowed as she returned his gaze, serious and tender now. Then, lying on the bed next to her, he supported himself with his arm and continued to gaze at her body. Instead of feeling self-conscious she felt like a flower opening under the warmth of the sun.

'You are so beautiful, darling Laura,' he breathed, and she felt beautiful and so sexy she thought she'd dissolve.

Then he tucked a strand of hair behind her ear and drew his finger down her cheek, along her jawline to her chin before going back to her ear, down her neck to her shoulder.

'Your skin is like silk. Sorry, that's not a very original way to describe it but it's the best I can do at the moment.'

She giggled lovingly. 'It's all right, I don't mind if you don't make love to me in iambic pentameters.'

He kissed the inside of her elbow. 'That's good, I much prefer free verse.'

'And free love,' she murmured, but he may not have heard because he didn't answer.

At first Laura was unnerved by the sensations he created with his mouth, his fingers, his breath. But his honeyed reassurances made her relax and she allowed herself to feel and respond. His skin felt like silk too, but she didn't mention it, just brushed her lips over the curve of his arm, feeling the shape of his muscles.

Later, when he paid intimate attention to her with his lips and tongue, she thought the sensation might overwhelm her and she resisted. And then it overcame her resistance and she almost lost consciousness. This time with pleasure.

*   *   *

Much later she said, 'Goodness me. Is it always like that?'

He laughed, still slightly breathless. 'No, it is not always like that. Chemistry is something you can't fake. We've set a very high standard for your first time.' He sighed deeply. 'I was absolutely determined to give you the very best experience I possibly could but if you hadn't responded as you did, it wouldn't have been anything like so wonderful.' He pulled her a little closer to him. 'You're a natural.'

'Am I? That's nice. I always thought I'd be rubbish at lovemaking.' A memory floated into her mind. 'Monica said you weren't a "novice ride".'

She heard the rumble in his chest as he laughed. 'Well, I don't suppose I am, usually, but you and I do seem to have a special something.' He chuckled again. 'When you tell her all about it, don't forget to tell Monica that I did use a condom.'

'Perhaps I won't tell her all about it.' Just then Laura didn't like the thought of sharing their special secret.

'She'll get it out of you. You don't have to tell her the details.'

'Certainly not!' Recalling some of the details made her blush and go gooey all over again. Had he really done those things? And had she really liked them so much?

'But you haven't forgotten any of the details?'

'No . . .'

'Well, just to make sure you don't, I think we'll repeat the exercise . . .'

Chapter Fifteen

❦

They 'repeated the exercise' on and off all night. Laura woke early. She hadn't eaten much the day before and was now absolutely ravenous. Although she didn't think she'd moved, she must have because Dermot stirred.

'All right?' he muttered into her neck.

'Mm, but absolutely starving!' She sighed happily as she thought about why.

'Mm, me too.' Dermot stretched. 'Is there any food left?'

'I don't think so. I think you ate everything.'

'In which case, my darling, I'd better get up and buy some breakfast. I have this peculiar urge for kedgeree.' He slid out of bed and started finding his clothes.

'That sounds complicated,' said Laura, having decided it was better not to watch him move about the place, stark naked, not if she was going to have to wait before they could make love again. Her hunger was momentarily forgotten.

'Oh, it's not,' said Dermot. 'They have it in a packet. You just put it in a pan, add butter and a bit of cream and heat slowly. They get it in especially for me at the shop. Thank goodness they're keeping their holiday hours or they wouldn't be open yet.' He pulled on his jeans. He was halfway into his shirt when he hesitated.

'What?' Laura was half hoping that he had forgotten his hunger too and just wanted to get back into bed.

'Nothing.' He carried on getting dressed.

Laura watched him, thinking, and then said, 'I've just

238

realised what the problem is.' She sat up. 'If you go to the shop there'll be an almighty fuss, everyone will pounce on you and you'll be ages.'

He grinned. 'I'll be looking so damn pleased with myself they'll know exactly what I've been up to. They will all want to talk.'

Laura scrambled out of bed. 'I'll go. I can't lie here, starving to death, waiting for you to stop gossiping. Make me a list. Here's an old receipt and a pencil.'

He chuckled and started to write. 'Being untidy has its advantages, you can always find something to write on.'

'I thought writers all kept notebooks by their beds.'

'Not all writers.'

She had got most of her clothes on when she turned to Dermot, who had slid back to bed, still wearing his jeans. 'Can I just ask you something?'

'Anything.'

His look was so full of lust she turned away, smiling. That could come later, when she'd had something to eat. 'Did you change the sheet yesterday, before you came down, because you knew what would happen?'

'I changed it because I knew what I wanted to happen, but I never thought it would. It was also pretty disgusting. I may be a slob but I change my bed linen once a year, whether it needs it or not.'

Laughing, she went downstairs and, having found her handbag, let herself out of the house.

She was fairly sure everyone would know exactly what she'd been up to when she went back to the shop but, with luck, the same people wouldn't be working there this morning. She thought what to add to Dermot's list; she wasn't sure she wanted to eat kedgeree, although it did sound nice. Some more bread and ham would be useful and maybe some orange juice and croissants if the shop had any.

Her head was full of plans about what they'd like to

eat and where they'd like to eat it when she went into the shop. She said a breezy hello without making eye contact and slipped down an aisle out of sight, hoping they wouldn't ask her about Dermot.

All would have been well if she'd been able to find the packet kedgeree he was so intent on having. She had to ask.

While the right place was being pointed out to her, along with a lot of 'You're back again soon. So how was the old reprobate?' type conversation, a tall, thin woman came up to Laura. Somewhat older than she was, with a skin that had been exposed to the weather, she had dark hair tied in a knot at the nape of her neck and wore a crisp white shirt tucked into jeans.

'So you're after Dermot's kedgeree, are you?' The woman looked her up and down. 'You know that's what he always wants to eat after sex?' She laughed, pretending she'd been joking.

'I didn't know,' said Laura, blushing at the mention of sex and because the woman was inspecting her as if she were a horse she was considering buying.

'Oh yes. He says it restores the "vital juices".' The woman's teeth were a little crooked and discoloured and her smile didn't reach her eyes. Never before had Laura felt herself to be so disliked, especially by a complete stranger. The feeling was mutual – there was something about this woman that made Laura instantly bristle.

'Well, I wouldn't know about that,' said Laura, trying to move so she could do her shopping.

The woman barred her way. 'Oh yes. But if you tell him I'm back your services won't be required any more.'

'Oh, are you his cleaner, then?' Laura's inner bitch rose up and snapped.

That did discomfort the woman a little, but not for long. 'No, no I'm not his cleaner. Just tell him I'm back, will you?' Another false smile was directed at Laura.

'You'll need to tell me who you are.' Laura was not going to rise any further to this woman's bait.

The woman laughed again. 'Oh no, he'll know who I am when you describe me. Dermot and I are very old – friends.'

Laura tried hard to fight off all the unpleasant feelings the woman had aroused in her on the way back to Dermot's. She had made her feel like a tart, frankly, and she didn't know if she would ever stop feeling like one. Almost the worst part was she felt that the whole shop knew she had slept with Dermot, and thought she was a tart too. She didn't like the feeling. And what had the woman meant about them being old friends? It was as if she'd been warning her off. And all that about his usual breakfast. She felt cheapened and hurt and used; an over-riding desire to get away from this place as quickly as possible overcame her. But when she had checked the availability of the local taxi service and the man had said he'd take her to the airport the moment she gave him the call, it didn't really make her feel any better. He obviously thought Dermot would want rid of her as soon as possible. Her wonderfully happy mood had completely evaporated. Doubts about Dermot's motives were marching in by the double, feeding her growing sense of unease. Had he swept her off her feet because she'd been there, ready and willing? He and his 'old friend' would probably laugh about it all when she was gone.

Right now, though, she had to get through the next hour or so without letting Dermot know how she really felt. She'd be calm and collected, and polite. She certainly didn't want him to see how humiliated she felt.

She put on a smile as she entered his house, and called up the stairs, 'I'm back! Do you want to cook this kedgeree or shall I read the packet and get on with it?'

Dermot appeared a few minutes later, after she'd decided to get cracking with it. She felt horrible. She was

241

a one-night stand and she'd be lucky if she got away without Dermot pressing money on her for her cab fare.

She was stirring the rice mixture into melted butter. 'There was a woman at the shop who said to tell you she was back,' she said as nonchalantly as she could manage, not wanting to look at him until she felt calmer.

'Oh? And who was that, then?'

'She wouldn't give her name. She just said you'd know who she was and that you were very old friends.'

Dermot laughed. 'Oh, that'll be Bridget! She's a case, isn't she? I've missed her. She's been away for months. I expect she'll be round here soon, wanting to see me.'

Laura couldn't bear it. He was confirming her worst fears. And he wasn't even trying to deny it.

'Oh well, she's back now. Would you like tea or coffee with your kedgeree?' She was aware she was being rather clipped but it was all she could do not to break down, and she wasn't going to do that in front of him. Also, a part of her felt angry – at him and at herself for being such a fool. She still couldn't look at him.

'Laura, what's wrong? You skipped out of here without a care in the world and now you're all edgy and anxious. What happened? Was anyone unkind to you in the shop?'

He sounded slightly bemused and just for a second she considered telling him what his beloved Bridget had said to her but then realised she couldn't. Bridget was the old friend; she wasn't. She couldn't say, 'Your old friend, the one you're so fond of, has made me feel like a hooker and that you wouldn't be needing my services now she's home.'

'Oh no, nothing like that.' She stirred furiously. 'It's just I realised my flight is earlier than I thought it was. I have to go almost immediately.'

'But we were going to have breakfast together. In bed, I thought.'

He was still maintaining the act. She managed a breezy

laugh. 'Oh no, I'm afraid not. In fact my taxi will be here at any moment.'

He scratched his head, frowning. 'Have they changed the flight back to England then? It was always in the evening.'

'Oh yes, they've changed it.' She turned off the heat and dropped the wooden spoon. 'I'll just go upstairs and make sure I haven't left anything.'

But she didn't need to look to knew that she'd left two things she couldn't retrieve: her virginity and her heart. Both were gone for ever.

Chapter Sixteen

Unfortunately for Laura, they hadn't changed the flight to England: she had a very long wait at the airport for it, which gave her plenty of time to realise that she'd given her all to a man who just wanted her at that moment, not for ever. He hadn't tried to stop her, or ask her again if anything had happened; he'd just stood there, looking baffled, as if he couldn't comprehend why she hadn't fallen into his arms again, all 'Aren't you wonderful, Dermot' and 'Let me wait on you hand and foot, Dermot'. What's more he obviously had a girlfriend, but being the sort of man he was, since she was away, he'd found a substitute. In other words, he was your classic – albeit charming – bastard. How long would it take her to get over him? Knowing he was a bastard wouldn't necessarily make it any quicker.

Eleanora was going to pick Laura up from the airport, whence they would go to Somerby. Laura was not looking forward to the questioning that would go on from the moment she and Eleanora had located each other. Eleanora would be bound to ask about Dermot and she had rehearsed some suitably bland phrases like: 'He's fine now. Eating well! Seemed quite happy when I left him.' Fenella would ask about the festival and she could hardly tell her that she hadn't actually asked him if he was coming, because she couldn't possibly tell her why not. After the row when he'd accused all and sundry of selling his story to the papers, and she'd accused him of being pretentious, and what happened next, all thoughts of the festival had been wiped from her mind – really amazing sex and subsequent humiliation had that effect.

On the plane, when she acknowledged that she couldn't have him electronically wiped from her brain, and that she would have to see him and deal with him again, she decided she'd send him an email, asking him if he would indeed appear, hoping that he'd at least answer it and say yes or no. Although, he would have to admit, she thought bitterly, she had fully complied with his original conditions and it would be a breach of promise if he didn't.

In spite of her sadness, however, she knew she wouldn't regret making love to him, even though he had set an impossibly high standard for the rest of her life. What had happened afterwards, at the shop, she tried to put firmly out of her mind. She stayed in a state of bitter-sweet reminiscing until the plane landed.

Eleanora kissed her cheek, patted her shoulder and, as Laura had known she would, launched straight in. 'How did you get on, darling? How is Dermot? Is the wretched man going to appear at the festival or not? We're all on tenterhooks.'

Laura appeared to consider, although in fact she'd planned what to say already. 'Well, he's fine, in that he's not ill or anything, but about the festival, I'm not sure.' She felt proud of how normal her voice sounded, despite her inner turmoil.

Eleanora wasted several seconds being irritated and then moved on to more important things. 'No sign of any writing, was there?'

Laura thought back. All that cleaning would have turned up any signs of work and in the bedroom she'd had to use a receipt as a shopping list. 'No, I would have noticed if there'd been anything to see.' She surrendered her bag to the cab driver.

'He used to write in longhand on big foolscap pads, on one side of the paper only. Apparently when each page was finished, he'd throw it on to the floor and only collate it when the work was finished.'

She shook her head sadly. 'No sign of any foolscap pads, let alone any tottering piles of complete pages. The house was in a frightful state but I think if they existed they'd have been obvious.'

Eleanora shook herself as if shrugging off disappointment. 'No change there then. Get in, darling, we should press on.'

When they were both settled in the back seat, sucking mints, she said, 'So why didn't you press him about the festival? A simple "no" would have done.'

'I couldn't really. The time just wasn't right. He was so angry about being outed to the press.'

'He has got a truly awful temper.' Eleanora frowned. 'He wasn't unkind to you, was he? He can be merciless.'

'No, he wasn't unkind.' Although the effect was the same as if he had been. She was sure he certainly never meant to be unkind, or to hurt her in any way – as bastards went, he was a nice one.

'So what will you do about the festival? Fenella is beside herself, wanting to know. She thinks it's going to be embarrassing if all these authors agree to come because of him and then he doesn't pitch up.'

'I'll email him. It's all I can do, really.' She certainly wasn't going to contact him except in the most formal manner. 'But going on the number I've sent him in the past and never had any reply to I think he goes through phases when he never even looks at his emails.'

'You're probably right. But never mind, now the news is out, we can finally advertise him as coming, even if he doesn't.'

'But surely that would be deception, or advertising false goods or something?'

'No. We don't know he's *not* coming.' Eleanora paused. 'Or do we?' she regarded Laura beadily, possibly suspecting Laura hadn't told her everything.

Laura hadn't but she also hadn't lied about the festival. 'Really, I don't know either way.'

'Then it's fine to advertise him. We've hinted enough as it is, after all. Fenella is having some banners made to go over all the posters. Apparently ticket sales have increased like mad. But more importantly, a lot of the big-name authors who wouldn't commit themselves have agreed to come. They're all mad to meet Dermot. And we're the only ones who suspect he might not make it – we'll keep it to ourselves.'

'So when's the big dinner?' Laura asked.

'Oh, the one for all the writers who are appearing? Next Friday, before the big opening. Laura dear, you can't have forgotten. We talked about it. You wrote and invited everyone.'

'Sorry. I'm a bit distracted.'

Eleanora shot Laura a glance that made her blush. Was it possible that losing your virginity and having glorious sex showed from the outside? Laura's blush deepened. Only part of it was because of the glorious sex; the other part was the feeling Bridget had given her: that she was a fill-in for her and no better than a prostitute.

In the end, Fenella was philosophical about Dermot possibly not appearing. She hushed the sea of dogs, led Eleanora and Laura down to the kitchen and handed them both a large glass of wine. Laura suspected that Rupert, now staring into the oven, had been instrumental in calming her down.

'Well, if he comes, he comes, there's nothing much else we can do about it,' she said, shooting Laura a glance that suggested she didn't quite believe her words. 'Have some olives, Laura.'

247

'He always has been a law unto himself,' said Eleanora. 'That's very good wine, Rupert.'

'Bogof,' said Fenella. 'I got it at the supermarket.'

'Oh. Well, it's very nice.'

'So, Laura, was it very terrifying bearding Dermot in his den?' asked Fenella. 'Eleanora has told us how utterly scary he can be.'

Her aunt nodded her agreement, happy to sip her wine and not interject with a pertinent opinion for once.

'He was a bit tough with some of the students,' agreed Laura. 'And I suppose it was a bit nerve-racking. I had to break into his house.'

Rupert snorted with laughter. 'I don't see you as a housebreaker, Laura.'

'You'd be surprised how good I was at it. I—' Just in time she stopped herself telling him how often she'd sneaked in and out of houses lately. 'I had the advantage of not minding if anyone caught me doing it. I'd have asked any passer-by for help.'

'But there weren't any?'

'No. Never is when you need one.'

'You did exactly the right thing, not pressing him too hard,' said Eleanora. 'I should have gone myself. His childish tantrums don't scare me! Did I ever tell you? Once when we were at the Ivy . . .'

Laura began to relax. No one seemed to be blaming her for not bringing Dermot's promise to appear written in blood and now Eleanora was telling a vivid and amusing story of Dermot in a rage. Her possible failure was being seen as a sensible withdrawal. What Laura couldn't say was that she wasn't remotely frightened of Dermot's temper, although she'd seen a glimpse of it. Once he'd started making love to her she'd just forgotten all about the damn festival.

* * *

The following morning, in the room designated as the Festival Office, Fenella and Laura went through the details. Eleanora was off inspecting some of the venues with Rupert.

'Kathryn Elisabeth has confirmed,' said Fenella.

'Ooh, I must tell my old neighbour. She was a crusty old thing but she got interested in the festival. She'll be thrilled.'

'Everyone is. She's very popular. She's doing a writing course. We've sold fifteen tickets so far, but we can only take twenty, and I've got some people who I'm fairly sure will take the other places.'

Laura was grateful no one knew how she was feeling inside and for being thrown straight back into festival matters.

'Brilliant. We must make sure we have all her backlist. Talking of which, is Henry organised? Has every author who's appearing got lots of copies to sign and sell?'

'He's been ace! Not only has he got books by all the authors we've invited, but quite a few other authors in similar genres. He said you had him very well trained.'

Laura laughed. 'He trained me actually.' She paused. 'So what are we going to do about the authors who haven't confirmed? With only a week to go it's cutting it a bit fine.'

'There is only one of those now.' Fenella took a sip of her coffee, fixing Laura with a stare from behind her mug.

Laura hoped Fenella didn't notice her blushing. 'We'll have to plan events to fill his slots. Remind me what we had planned for him.'

'Apart from the main interview? An "Evening of Irish Music and Literature".'

Laura thought. 'Oh yes. In the pub, to recreate an Irish atmosphere.'

Fenella nodded. 'Except that we couldn't use the pub. We could only have got about ten people in and the publican wasn't keen. And I've got cold feet about the poetry, to be honest. We're a new festival – poetry might not be that popular. Is his poetry wonderful?'

Laura put her head on one side. 'Yes, but not as wonderful as his prose.'

'Shall we scrub it then? Especially as he's quite likely not to turn up?'

'That would be a shame. We could have the music and someone could just read bits of Irish literature. I could choose some pieces. They don't all have to be Dermot's. Have we got someone who could read them?'

'You've got no faith in Dermot turning up then?' Fen asked.

Laura sighed. She no longer had any faith in her judgement. She'd thought she had known Dermot, and then Bridget had appeared before her like a banshee in modern dress and she didn't feel she knew anything about him. 'I just don't know. I think we'd better make elaborate plans for his non-appearance, then he'll turn up just to annoy us.'

Fenella laughed. 'Would it annoy you?'

'If we had gone to huge trouble to fill in for him it would. Who might read the pieces? Do you know any actors?'

'No, but Hugo, Sarah's husband, has got a beautiful speaking voice.'

'We need a bit of Irish, really. Hugo's rather posh, isn't he?'

'We'll think of someone. Rupert can do a brogue, if drunk. He does have Irish blood.'

Laura made a note. 'Rupert, drunk, to read selections of Irish literature. L to make selection. That sounds great! Not!'

'It will be great. Monica's boyfriend's band will be lovely. We'll give everyone free beer, it'll go down a treat.'

'Well, bang goes your profit straightaway. And is Monica's boyfriend's band lovely?'

'It's not all about making money. And I expect so! Monica still hasn't managed to hear them. She's getting a bit anxious about it.'

'Fantastic! A mediocre band plays while Rupert puts on a fake accent and reads out bits of *Ulysses*. I can't wait.'

Fenella laughed. 'You don't have to choose *Ulysses*. You can have funny pieces and Rupert will do it in his own voice. As for the band, why don't you go and hear them? Monica would be thrilled. She rang last night, by the way, wanting to hear how you got on in Ireland. I said you'd gone to bed, exhausted. She seemed to find that quite funny. Anyway, she mentioned Seamus having a gig she can get to at last. She and Grant are going. Give her a ring and arrange to go too.'

'OK, I'll do that. I'm glad that Monica and Grant have become such good friends. I knew they'd get on. Maybe when the festival is over I'll become a matchmaker.'

'Hm. If Monica and Grant are the sort of relationship you had in mind . . .'

'OK, I take your point. So . . .' She made another note. 'All we have to do now is think up some way of filling that big Sunday night spot when Dermot was going to do an interview.' She paused. 'Who was going to interview him? Didn't you have someone in mind?'

Fenella made a rueful face. 'Sorry. I couldn't get anyone that anyone had heard of without being able to say for sure if Dermot would actually be there.'

'Fair enough, I suppose.'

'So I thought you could do it.'

'Me!' Laura squeaked.

'Well, why not? You know more about his books than anyone on the planet and you know him – what?'

'It's just . . . oh, Fenella, you know how shy I am!'

'I know how shy you *used* to be. Besides, as they always say to worried people, "it may never happen".'

Laura had to laugh now. 'Well, that's true. In fact, it probably won't. So what shall we do to fill the space? If people have bought tickets, or even if they haven't yet, we can't have nothing on the Saturday night.'

There was silence as the two women thought hard. 'I know!' said Laura. 'A panel! We'll get a selection of the authors who are coming to talk about their writing practice. It'll be brilliant! Far better than me trying to interview Dermot!' Even the thought of it made her feel weak.

'Fab. I'll email all the authors and ask them. How many do we need?'

'Ask everyone and see how many we're left with.' Laura gave a huge yawn.

'Gracious,' said Fenella. 'You're still tired, in spite of your early night. I didn't realise Ireland involved a change of time zone.'

Laura nodded sagely. 'Oh it does, it definitely does . . .'

Laura had pondered the question about losing one's virginity showing from the outside for some time. A couple of days later, when Monica picked her up in her car, to take her to Bristol, she had her answer. It did.

'So, what was it like?' Monica said the moment they were at the bottom of the Somerby drive. They were on their way to Seamus's gig. Laura was checking the band out to see if it was remotely suitable for a potentially raucous evening with free beer and Rupert, with or without an Irish accent, or as the more cultural backing for Dermot reading some of his work.

'What was what like?'

'Oh, for God's sake! Don't mess me around! Sex with Dermot!'

'Ssh. Keep your voice down!'

'It's all right. We're in a car. No one is going to hear. So tell me!'

Only for a second did Laura consider pretending nothing had happened, but she knew Monica would see straight through her. 'OK. Well. It was amazing,' Laura said quietly, half hoping this would satisfy Monica, and half hoping she'd have an opportunity to talk.

'I don't believe you.' Monica banged her hand on the steering wheel to emphasise her incredulity. 'First times are never amazing, let alone the first time ever. You've spent too much of your life reading romantic novels. Sex is one of those things you have to learn how to do.'

'I accept that. And I know I probably have spent far more of my life reading about sex rather than having it than most normal people, but I'm telling you, it was amazing.'

Monica considered for a moment. 'Well, stripe me pink!'

Laura laughed. 'I think someone already did that.' She indicated the wide pink stripe in Monica's hair. She obviously enjoyed wearing her pink wig so much she'd decided to add a bit of colour to her own hair.

'Laura! I'm trying to have a serious conversation, to help you live through the ramifications of what's happened to you, and you just make stupid jokes.'

'It was you who said "stripe me pink".' Laura pretended to be apologetic. 'But I don't think there are any ramifications.' She sighed. Except a feeling of being used and Bridget, of course, although she wasn't a ramification – she was the bitch from hell but she wasn't going to think about her if she could help it; she had already spoilt something that had been really lovely.

'There will be, I promise you.'

'Well, I hope not.'

Monica hesitated before asking incredulously. 'Are you sure you're not lying about it being fantastic?'

'Yes! I'm not saying that the second and third time weren't even more—'

'Three times!'

Actually, there'd been more than that, but she didn't want to shock her friend. 'Over quite a long period. A whole night.'

'But he's quite old!'

'Thirty-five is not old!'

'I suppose not. So now what? Are you together?'

This was the bad news. She had to keep it cheery, not give too much away – she couldn't face Monica's sympathy. 'I had to go really early the next day to get my flight.' She wasn't going to say that leaving him that morning was the saddest thing she had ever done in her entire life. She knew that it was worth it for the happiness she'd experienced – or it would be once she'd got over the whole Bridget incident – but she wasn't going to mention that either. 'We didn't have much time to talk. But he wanted you to know that he used condoms, every time.'

Monica chuckled, possibly sensing that Laura was trying to make light of the situation. 'You must congratulate him when you next see him.' She paused, glancing briefly at her friend. 'When are you seeing him again?' She wasn't going to let Laura off that easily.

Laura bit her lip. 'I'm not sure. We didn't actually get round to talking about the festival. I don't know if he's coming or not. After all the publicity erupted he said the festival could take a flying jump.'

'Bugger the festival! What about you and him?'

'We didn't talk about when we might see each other again.'

'What?' Monica gave her a quick look. 'Not at all? You just got in the taxi and went to the airport? How often has he been in touch since?'

'He rang me when I was at the airport. Just to see if I'd got there safely.' He'd sounded strange on the phone but that may have been because she'd been very cool with him. She hadn't really wanted to speak to him again, not until she'd got her feelings in order.

'And since?' Monica was sniffing out the bad bits of Laura's story like a truffle-hound.

'Nothing since. Marion – the woman who ran the bed and breakfast we stayed at – emailed me to say he's gone to ground again. But no one's worried this time.'

'But what about you?' Monica was hardly audible, empathy seemed to have affected her vocal cords. 'Isn't your heart breaking? You've done all that with him, given him your virginity, and you don't know when you'll see him again?'

Laura longed to say yes, her heart was breaking, but she couldn't. She thought carefully, trying to express herself in a way that was truthful, but that wouldn't have Monica sending her off for some sort of therapy involving bars, vodka and male strippers, which she would do if she told her everything. No suitable phrases sprang to mind.

'Well?' Monica pressed. She was obviously getting worried.

Laura decided she might as well tell Monica the truth. At least her friend cared. She just wouldn't tell her how *much* it was hurting.

'To be honest, yes, my heart is breaking,' she said. 'But I don't mind, not really. It's hard to explain, but that time with Dermot was so – special, though in some ways, it was just sex.' Although she was the one who'd said them, the words were almost physically painful. 'It was sex with someone I'd admired for years, and years,' she went on as breezily as she could, 'since I was at university. If he wanted – me' – she baulked at referring to her virginity, although Monica had – 'I was more than happy for him – to give myself – oh, I don't know how to put it. I'm just trying to say, I knew what I was doing. I knew nothing would come of it and I did it anyway. No regrets.' She hadn't known quite so well that nothing would come of it until later, but still, the principle was the same.

'What, no regrets at all? Come on, Laura, this is me you're talking to,' Monica pushed.

'I wouldn't have done anything different. I knew what he was like. I didn't expect anything different. And what I had was so fantastic! He took such pains to make me – enjoy it. Really, Monica, I know I'm going to feel a bit sad for a while, but I'm also happy.'

Monica sighed. 'I suppose I do understand. He will have spoilt you for anyone else, you know that.'

'Yes, but there will be someone else. I'm not going to cling to my moment of happiness and not look for more. Obviously, I'm not up for going on the pull any time soon' – she said this so Monica wouldn't suggest the bars and male-stripper cure – 'but I will "love again".' She smiled to highlight her irony and then added, 'After the festival and about ten years have passed.'

Monica sighed. 'If you're sure . . .' And then she snapped out of her romantic reverie. 'OK, that's enough about you. Could you have a look at the map? Are we on the right road? I seem to have got a bit lost.'

They found it eventually. Grant and the rest of Monica's band were already there. It was in the basement of a small club in Bristol. As they fought their way down the narrow stairs, Laura realised that Monica really was nervous. She was very keen on Seamus and they'd spent a lot of time talking about him as they drove along. But his band was a bit suspect. It was, according to Monica, because of the other members not wanting to play traditional music and not being great at anything else.

'Laura!' Grant hugged Laura long and hard. 'How great to see you! You look amazing! What have you done to yourself? New hairdo? No, you still haven't discovered straighteners. Lost weight? Gained weight? No, you're still fairly skinny. Must be a new moisturiser. Your skin looks brilliant.'

Laura avoided looking at Monica who was laughing in a vulgar way. 'Shall we get some drinks? Grant? You others?'

She went to the bar hoping she'd remember what everyone wanted. Monica had ordered a double vodka to calm her nerves. It was nearly time for Seamus's set.

She got the tray of drinks back to the table without accidents and squashed on to a corner of the banquette. 'I'm glad I got back before Seamus started,' she said. She picked up her glass. 'Cheers!'

Seamus and his band didn't seem quite ready so the audience started talking again.

'Would you want the whole band, or just Seamus, do you think?' Monica asked Laura. 'It might be better . . . oh, I don't know. What would Dermot like?'

'Who knows!' said Laura. 'I didn't ask him. I mean, I think it would work well. Originally we thought of having him reading his poetry but there's a scene in one of Dermot's books with Irish music in the background. It would be perfect. But he's so – I don't know . . .'

'Uncommunicative?'

'Yes. I don't know if he'd love the idea or hate it. Actually, I do know. He'll hate it. But he might just do it.'

'For you?'

'No. I don't think he'd do anything particular for me.' Although as she said this she knew it wasn't strictly true. She remembered some of the things he'd done for her in Ireland and felt a stab of pleasure. 'Oh, I think they're starting!' she said, to stop Monica asking any more questions.

The band did start a little later and after the first few bars, Grant and Laura exchanged looks. The first number was a lament that should have had tears of sadness pouring down cheeks; it had the opposite effect. By the end even Laura, whose recent Irish experiences should have meant the words and the music was particularly poignant, wanted to giggle with embarrassment.

Monica sighed, drained her glass. 'Anyone else for another drink?'

'I'll help you carry them,' said Laura, struggling out from behind the table.

'They're crap, aren't they?' said Monica once they were at the bar.

'Well, maybe they just need time . . .'

'Don't beat about the bush, say it like it is! They're rubbish! Bugger! Back to the drawing board!'

'It's OK,' said Laura. 'We'll find a CD with the right sort of harpy-fiddly-drummy-Celtic stuff on it. It might be easier in some ways. Rupert could practise.'

'Don't quite know when he's going to have time to do that,' said Monica. She looked at her friend as her turn to be served came up. 'Do you mind driving home? I think I need another vodka.'

'Do you mind coming home with me? Don't you want to stay with Seamus?'

'I really don't want to talk to him about how it's gone tonight. I'll have to think very carefully what to say.'

While they were being served, Laura said, 'But surely you've heard them play lots of times. You must have known that they weren't all that good.'

Monica explained the reason she hadn't heard them yet was because she'd been on tour, he'd been very busy and what with organising the music festival practically

258

single-handed now Johnny Animal had disappeared off on 'important business' there just hadn't been time.

'Would it be wrong of me to dump Seamus because he doesn't know which way up to hold a fiddle?' Monica asked now.

Laura, her sense of the ridiculous finely honed, giggled. 'Yes it would! Besides, you said he was lovely. Can you manage those bottles? I'll take the tray.'

'You're not still on the voddy, are you, Monica?' asked Grant as Laura doled out bottles of water and spritzers, giving the only glass to Monica.

'God yes, I need something. Laura's driving home. She's so loved up she doesn't need alcohol.'

A look like an interrogation lamp turned on Laura. 'Loved up? Something you're not telling me, Laura?'

'It's Dermot,' said Monica.

'Ye Gods! I might have guessed!' said Grant. 'I always knew she'd lose her cherry to a poet.'

'He's not a poet,' said Laura, eventually, when she'd processed what Grant had said and recovered. 'He's a novelist . . .' And then she gave up. The cat was out of the bag. Luckily Grant and Monica started having an argument about who was the greatest band ever and she was spared any further interrogation.

Chapter Seventeen

❧

Laura woke up on the Friday of the pre-launch festival dinner feeling a mixture of excitement and trepidation. She had had very confusing dreams, including one in which Grant was reading nonsense rhymes while Laura's old school orchestra played in the background. It was a relief to be fully awake. At least in real life one had the impression of having control over events.

As she brushed her teeth she wondered how Monica had got on. She'd been to see what she'd declared to be her final band. Grant had gone with her as a driver, so Monica could drown her sorrows if necessary. The music festival had some good acts, Monica had told her, but was short on publicity. Although Monica didn't dare say it, to her at least, Laura knew Monica wished she had a musical Dermot, to create a bit of useful scandal.

A couple of nights before a group of them had gone to see Monica's band open the music part of the festival. In theory they were supporting a better-known group (which Laura had never heard of), but in fact they had stolen the show. The entire audience had stamped and clapped along and a goodly proportion of them got up and danced in the aisles of the old cinema. Laura had been amusing herself spotting people from the Lindy Hop night she and Grant had been to when Grant pulled her to her feet.

'Come on, girlfriend, let's see if we've remembered anything from when we did this before.' He led her to the front where several rows of seats had been removed (Laura didn't know if this was to disguise slightly low sales figures, or to make room for dancing) and they started to dance. Soon they were joined by Fenella and a reluctant Rupert. Everyone was laughing and clapping – even the boy band kept time, trying to look cool amidst so much overt enjoyment.

'What a fabulous opening night!' Laura said to Monica when they met up backstage, where the party continued, just as exuberantly, only without the dancing.

'There's no greater high on earth than 'a gig going that well,' said Monica, 'except being in love!'

As her Seamus was standing by her, Laura didn't know if Monica was addressing this to her or to Seamus. But at that moment Fenella came up and hugged Monica, and then all her band mates, so Laura didn't have to respond.

Although Dermot was always in the background of her thoughts, leaping to the front whenever there was a nano-second of space between one useful thought and the next, Laura was gradually coming to terms with what had gone on between them.

She realised it had been quite unreasonable of her to expect – even to hope – that Dermot was unattached. Her head had filled in the blanks, even if her heart didn't want to accept it. He was highly sexed and had the free attitude to love and life that great artists often did. If his girlfriend was away there would be a vacuum and he would fill it. Bridget (in spite of her hard-won rationality she could hardly even think her name) would have known this when she went away, pragmatically accepting that being with Dermot meant putting up with his occasional infidelity. Well, good for her, thought Laura, doubting she would have been able to be so adult about it.

Having attempted to sort it all out in her mind she

felt marginally better. She just had to accept Dermot as he was. He'd been a lovely dream. Some irritation remained: even if he didn't want to contact her, he could at least reply to Fenella's emails and say whether or not he was coming. But if he didn't she'd cope. She'd have to.

Laura presented herself to Fenella as soon as she was dressed. It was another glorious day with the promise of more of the same over the weekend. At least the weather was being kind to them.

'So what do you want me to do for tonight?'

Fenella kissed her cheek, partly in greeting and partly in thanks for her prompt appearance to report for duty.

'A seating plan. Sarah's upstairs and she'll do it, but she needs you to tell her who is who. You'll know if people are deadly rivals, at daggers drawn. Damien Stubbs has confirmed. And Kathryn Elisabeth can't come to the dinner but she's fine for her event and for the panel.'

'Oh, that's OK then. But I don't know any of the authors personally, you know.' Laura felt obliged to make this clear, although this wasn't absolutely true.

'Which is how it should be,' said Fenella firmly. 'Any problems, you can ask Eleanora. She'll know exactly who doesn't speak to who.'

'I think maybe that should be "whom",' suggested Laura softly.

'Oh shut up,' said Fenella good-naturedly. 'Sarah's in the dining room. I'll bring some coffee up.'

Sarah had all the names of the guests on place cards and was putting them down and then picking them up again.

'Hi, Laura, how are you? Come and tell me if I've made any ghastly mistakes.'

'That's a lot of people,' said Laura. 'But in spite of what Fenella might have said, I don't really know who's who.'

'But you'd know if I've put a romantic novelist next to a science-fiction writer.'

'Well, yes, but I'm not sure that would matter too much. All the writers of women's fiction I've met have been very down-to-earth and easy.'

'But what about the sci-fi ones?'

Laura considered. 'Ah well – they vary.'

'So where would you like to sit?' asked Sarah when they'd moved the place cards around quite a bit.

'Really, I don't mind. Just fit me in anywhere there's a gap. I'm surprised I'm invited, actually. I feel I should be helping to serve or something.'

'It's being catered. Fen was muttering about her and Rupert doing the cooking but I put my foot down. They're here to entertain the guests, and so are you. Hey, it's good that they got the old dumb waiter sorted, isn't it? Otherwise it would have to be a cold dinner.'

'That will have made a big hole in the budget.'

'What? Fixing the dumb waiter? Not at all. It only needed the cords replacing.'

'I meant having the dinner catered.'

Sarah shook her head. 'Not really. Rupert has provided all the wine from his cellar and has sourced the food. It's being done by this lovely firm of women I know, the Catering Ladies. They're very low key, reasonable and utterly brilliant.'

'Oh well, that's good.'

'You look worried. Is it Dermot?'

Laura sighed. Was it that obvious to everyone? Although she was sure Sarah didn't mean to imply anything personal. 'Not so much him, or at least, not just him, it's the whole thing. I feel we're going to look awfully silly if our star turn doesn't pitch up, however many things we've arranged to fill in the gaps.' She also felt guilty. Although she had emailed him, as had Fenella and Eleanora, she couldn't bring herself to phone. She didn't want to hear his voice. She was just about managing to get her feelings under control; she didn't need anything to undermine that. Anyway, why should she? Why should she even care after he'd effectively used her? And would a call from her make him come when everything else had apparently failed? If several fierce messages from Eleanora hadn't done the trick, nothing would. And should she really sacrifice herself once more for the greater good?

'I don't think once it's started anyone will really notice,' said Sarah, unaware of Laura's internal inquisition. 'We've got the dinner tonight – well, that's not for the punters, but it'll keep the performers happy.'

'And tomorrow's either Dermot, reading with music, or Rupert, pretending to be Irish, reading with a CD.' Laura made a face. 'It doesn't sound very convincing, does it?'

'But there are free drinks, courtesy of the local micro-brewery – we've Rupert to thank for that – so no one will mind if it's not amazing.'

Laura sighed agreement. 'And then the big interview or the panel the day after tomorrow.' She frowned. 'I do see that with free beer Rupert might go down all right, but a panel of authors? Instead of the big star name? I'm really not sure.'

Sarah was firmly philosophical. 'There's no point in worrying about it. You've done everything you can and set up a good substitute event. If people want their money back, well, we'll give it to them.'

'I know, but—'

'Relax, most people will just go to the events they're going to, if you see what I mean. The ticket sales have been very good. Lots of the people on the database you provided from the shop have bought tickets. And the competitions have been very well supported. Trust me, it'll be fine. And Fen says there's a real buzz locally. People stop her in the street and ask about it every time she goes to town.'

Aware that as an events organiser who specialised in weddings, Sarah was a professional soother of ragged nerves, Laura smiled. But she was still worried.

Just then the door opened and Fenella came in with a thermos jug of coffee and a plate of biscuits.

'How are you two getting on?' she said, handing the plate to them. 'These are home-made. The Catering Ladies made them.'

Laura crunched into a lemon-flavoured biscuit. 'Delicious! Couldn't we just have these for the dinner?'

Fenella was just about to tell Laura off when her phone rang. She pulled it out of her back pocket and then walked across the room to where there was better reception. Sarah poured the coffee and she and Laura sipped and ate until Fenella came back.

'You look as if you've either won the lottery or failed your driving test,' said Sarah. 'Which is it?'

'I don't know,' said Fenella, looking from one to the other. 'Sort of both.'

'Tell us then!' urged Laura.

'Well, you know the music festival hasn't been able to get the same amount of publicity as the literary one? Monica's worked really hard at getting it attention but no one seems that interested in giving it any airtime. Maybe it's musicians being even more flaky than writers . . .'

'Cut to the chase, honey,' said Sarah.

'Well, Ironstone – heard of them?' Fenella addressed this to Laura.

'I may be a bluestocking,' she said crisply, 'but I haven't been living in a cave for the past year. They are pretty darn famous.'

'Sorry. Well, they're willing to do a spot—'

'But that's amazing!' said Sarah.

'Yes it is! What's the downside?' Then Laura suddenly wished she hadn't asked. Fenella was looking at her with a sympathy that could only mean one thing. 'Oh don't tell me. It's to do with Dermot, isn't it? They'll come if they can meet the "greatest living Irish writer" da de da de da.'

'I want to thank you for not doing those wiggly things in the air with your fingers for inverted commas,' said Sarah gravely.

This broke the tension somewhat, but didn't stop Laura clenching her fists. 'I'm just so fed up with this! Bloody Dermot! Why is he being so – bloody difficult.' Her pent-up frustration at herself for minding so much was making her crosser than she wanted to be.

'I thought you were going to use a four-letter word for a moment there, Laura,' said Fenella.

'I did in my head. I've just trained myself not to say it out loud, because of working in the shop – or at least not often. But you must see my point! He's been such a – nuisance! I mean, how long does it take to answer an email, even if only to say no! The literary festival starts tomorrow, for God's sake!' She'd even rung Marion, her bed and breakfast hostess, to see if she knew anything, but all she could say was that he was holed up again and no one had seen hair nor hide of him. She didn't tell the others this because they'd ask, perfectly reasonably, if she'd phoned him. She didn't want to have to explain why she hadn't. And anyway, Eleanora had and she was much better at getting mountains to move.

'He did get us a very good sponsor, who hasn't withdrawn his sponsorship in spite of Dermot being such a loose cannon,' Sarah pointed out reasonably.

'He could have lost us it,' said Laura.

'And think of all the authors who confirmed when

there was all that fuss in the press!' said Fenella. 'They were queuing up to come!'

'And if he doesn't turn up no one will ever agree to appear at this festival again!' said Laura. 'They'll say we got people here under false pretences. The press will have a field day . . .'

'He might still come,' said Fenella softly, obviously not really believing that he would. 'Try not to take it to heart, Laura.'

Laura sighed. It was much too late for that.

'And I'm not going to Ireland to try and bring him. Not again. It wouldn't work. It didn't work on either of the other two times I tried it.' Laura took refuge in another biscuit.

'So what shall I tell the man from Ironstone?' said Fenella after a suitable pause out of respect for Laura's previous efforts.

'The truth!' said Laura, still crunching.

'Hang on, let's just think,' said Sarah, tapping her pen on her cheek. 'If they came it would really help the festival?'

Fenella nodded. 'Bloody right! We might get coverage on Radio 1, as well as all the local stations. It'd be mega. We didn't even ask any bands that big, because they're always booked up years ahead. Ironstone just happen to have a gap for some reason. Publicity-wise, it would be fantastic.'

'Well,' said Sarah, after chewing her pen for a few thought-filled moments. 'It won't do them any harm to do something for us. Tell them we can't guarantee that they'll get to meet the great man but we'll do our best. After all, it's what we've been saying to everyone else and they haven't smelt a rat.'

'They will expect the great man to appear,' said Laura, when Fenella had gone away to tell this whopping lie.

'I don't care,' said Sarah. 'Sometimes one just has to be a bit unscrupulous. Other people often are.'

'Quite right!' said Laura, with a very attractive but very unscrupulous-where-women-were-concerned person in her mind.

'So let's get these place cards done.'

'What shall I do with this one?' asked Laura a little later, holding a card with Dermot's name on.

'Put it on the side with the other possible no-shows,' said Sarah. 'A couple of people said they might not be able make it.'

Laura was on duty in the hall. Everyone was due to arrive any minute now. She had the house phone, a list of directions from several local landmarks and a note of which author was to stay where.

The first people to arrive were a couple of women's fiction writers who were very jolly. They'd travelled together, got lost several times and not minded. They'd had lunch at the local pub and were in positive mood.

'I'm Anne,' said one, 'and this is Veronica. To be honest, people who write books like we do don't often get asked to festivals,' she went on. 'And to get to stay in this lovely house,' she added, looking round at the hall, newly decorated with some very pretty *trompe l'œil* morning glories that were concealing something or other that Fenella was worried about. 'That makes it really special.'

'Oh yes,' said Veronica. 'I love that fake pillar. Getting it to look like real marble is not easy.'

Laura laughed, grateful that the party included two such good-hearted people. 'It is a lovely house, and Fenella and Rupert are such good hosts,' said Laura. 'Fenella will be here in a minute to show you to your rooms.' She smiled at both women. 'I've always been a fan of your books.'

Anne Marsh enveloped Laura in a Chanel-scented, silken hug. 'Bless your heart.' She wore a lot of scarves

268

and jewellery and was like a softer version of Eleanora. 'How many writers have you got coming to the dinner?'

Laura considered. 'Well, there's you two, Kathryn Elisabeth couldn't be here tonight but is doing an event in the library tomorrow. There are a couple of literary writers, including Damien Stubbs and a science-fiction writer. We didn't have room for everyone. So that's six.' She didn't mention that there should have been seven, in case there wasn't.

'Well, we're very happy to be part of it all,' said Veronica.

'Hello!' Fenella appeared. 'I'm Fenella.' She shook hands with both women. 'Now, would you like some tea first, or to be shown to your rooms?'

The women exchanged glances. 'Let's find our rooms,' said Veronica. 'But then a cup of tea would be wonderful.'

'I'll organise the tea,' said Laura. 'Would you like it in the sitting room or the kitchen?'

'Kitchen,' they said in unison.

'In which case, you stay here,' said Fenella to Laura, 'and I'll make tea when Anne and Veronica are settled.'

Eleanora appeared and, hard on her heels, a young writer of literary fiction who'd got lost and was not at all happy. Fortunately for Laura, Eleanora gave him a sharp lecture about being grateful for the exposure, and that books like his hardly sold diddly-squat, and that this was a great opportunity.

A couple of men in country clothes arrived. They turned out to be literary editors. They'd travelled together and were extremely pleasant. 'So will Dermot actually appear?' one of them asked Laura.

She shrugged, and then smiled, remembering that they were supposed to be pretending he was coming, at least to everyone else.

'Shall we open a book on it?' said the other one.

Laughing, they followed Fenella to their accommodation.

At last everyone they were expecting had arrived, except Dermot.

'It really is an amazing room,' said Laura, looking around her.

The huge table took up most of the middle, but the room was so large there was ample space for sideboards and serving tables at the edges.

The vast mahogany table shone, set off by the sparkling glasses and crisp white napery. Laura's eye was caught by something and she looked closer.

'It's a darn! In the napkin!'

Sarah laughed. 'It's all antique, from Rupert's family, or from car-boot sales, depending. The glasses are a bit mixed if you look carefully. Fenella's been hunting for nice ones on eBay.'

'But so many of them – the polishing must have been a nightmare.'

'The Catering Ladies really enjoy making everything look perfect.' Sarah chuckled. 'They were a bit horrified when they saw the number of bottles of wine Rupert's put out.'

Laura made a rough calculation. 'That's nearly a bottle per person, no wonder they were shocked.'

'That's just the red wine. The champagne and the white is all being chilled.'

Laura laughed. 'My goodness!'

'Rupert says dinner parties where the empty bottles don't exceed the number of guests are niggardly affairs. And Eleanora says writers all drink like fish.'

'Well, I don't think we need worry about anyone going thirsty!'

'There's masses of soft stuff as well, if you don't want to drink much.'

Laura made a rueful face. 'I'd prefer not to tonight.

Rupert still needs to run through his pieces for Saturday, so we'll have to get up at a reasonable time tomorrow.'

'Rupert's cooking breakfast, so unless it's before dawn, I'm afraid you've missed that slot.'

This was a bit of a blow. Doing something like this without proper preparation could end up the most amateur disaster: hideously embarrassing. Suppressing a feeling of panic, Laura said, 'Oh well, might as well get pie-eyed then!' Seeing Sarah's searching look she added, 'It's all right, I'm joking.'

There was a pre-dinner reception in the long gallery that had, Fenella told Laura proudly, been the venue for a celebrity wedding that had featured in all the gossip magazines. Laura hadn't liked to admit she didn't read gossip magazines, but when she had passed this information on to Monica, she was very impressed.

Monica was sharing Laura's little cottage for the festival while Grant was in a local b. and b. Monica arrived back from sorting out yet another 'slight hiccup' on the music side of things while Laura was ironing her best white shirt.

After hellos, the discussion about opening a bottle of wine or not and the bewailing of Dermot's as yet no-show, Monica said, 'You're not wearing that, are you?'

'Why not? It's clean, freshly ironed, and I've got all the dog hair off my black trousers!' Laura was feeling combative, mainly because she felt she was going to look a little dull next to Monica's glittering pink number that perfectly toned with her glittering pink hair.

'Haven't you got anything else?'

Laura sighed. 'I was going to go into town and buy something, but the time slipped away.'

'OK, let's think. You're a bit shorter than Fenella. Shoe size?'

Laura told her and Monica rushed off. For want of something better to do, Laura picked up a bottle of nail

271

varnish that had fallen out of Monica's make-up bag and began to apply it. Lucky Monica – this was just a jolly dinner for her. It could make Laura look a complete fool.

Monica came back with a hanger on which hung a tiny velvet item that she declared was a tunic. 'But wear it over tights, with these boots' – she produced the long, pale green suede pair that Fenella had been wearing when Laura had first met her – 'and it's an outfit.'

'But it's summer. I can't wear boots, and besides, that – dress is terribly short.'

'Put it on!'

As Monica was sounding very like Laura's mother when getting Laura dressed to visit her grandparents, she did as she was told.

'Fantastic! You look great! Now let me get at your hair.'

'I look like a pixie having a bad hair day,' said Laura when she had manoeuvred herself in front of a mirror, Monica following behind holding said bad hair.

'You won't when I've finished with you. Just stand still!'

Laura was not at all sure she liked the impression she gave but she had to admit that the bits of her legs that showed between the short dress and the long boots did look rather fine.

'It doesn't really matter what I look like anyway,' she said.

Monica made as if to clip her round the ear.

When they got to the house everyone was wearing their finest. There was quite a lot of sparkly black; Eleanora's jewellery was longer and more glittery than ever. The men wore suits or dinner jackets; Grant was wearing a white dinner jacket with a black sequinned bow tie. Laura noticed one of the romantic novelists writing things down in a tiny notebook.

Rupert, particularly dashing in a velvet tuxedo, filled everyone's glasses with either champagne or elderflower pressé that had a few stars of elderflower in it. Then Sarah banged something against a glass.

'Ladies and gentlemen,' said Rupert. 'Fenella was supposed to be doing this opening speech but she absolutely refused, so I'm doing it.' There were polite murmurs and sips of champagne. 'She and I and all the festival committee have worked incredibly hard to make this first Somerby Festival a roaring success, and I'm sure it will be. But one person has done more, gone to lengths far greater than anyone else, to get the literary side of it all going, and that's Laura Horsley.'

Laura blushed so deeply she thought she would spontaneously combust, and vowed to take out a contract on Rupert's life at the first opportunity. The applause was loud and extremely embarrassing. The cries of 'Speech, speech' got so loud she realised she'd have to say something.

'Thanks, Rupert, for that,' she said meaningfully, making sure he picked up the message that she would never forgive her for dumping her in it. 'It's very sweet of Rupert to say those kind words about me, but these things never hang on one person, however much that may seem to be the case.' There was a stage-whispered 'bloody Dermot' from Monica. 'This was a new—' A buzzing sound from the pocket of Fenella's tunic stopped Laura mid-sentence. 'Saved by the bell!' she said gaily and groped for her phone.

An angry Irish voice growled in her ear as she said hello, 'Where the feck am I?'

A beatific smile spread from Laura's lips and ended possibly at her toes. 'Give me a hint and I'll try to talk you in,' she said, aware she was grinning so hard she could barely speak. He was here. Nothing else mattered.

'That'll be Dermot,' said Monica, half cross, half delighted.

'I'll go and change the place settings,' said Sarah.

Laura walked away from the sound of rejoicing and speculation that was going on in the gallery. She went back down to the hall where all her written instructions were.

'I'm in some godforsaken hole with an unpronounceable name,' Dermot went on.

'Right. I think you might be in Wales.'

'Wales!'

'But don't worry, it's not all that far. Are you driving yourself?'

'Who the feck else would be driving me?'

'OK, now what I want you to do is to find a safe place to park the car. I'll send someone to come and get you. You don't sound fit to drive.'

'Feck that! I haven't had a drink for weeks! I'll find the way myself.'

'Don't disconnect! Head for . . .' Laura found the directions she needed and read them out to Dermot. 'Will you be all right?'

'I will be, probably. I can't answer for you, getting me into all this.'

'I'll keep my phone by me. Just ring if you get lost again.'

Laura didn't rush back upstairs again. Just for a while she wanted to keep Dermot for herself. When he arrived he would be common property, everyone would be dancing attendance, admiring, admonishing, wanting a part of him. Now, while she held her phone in her hand, and knew that the last person to have spoken to her on it was Dermot, he was hers: her irascible, ornery, difficult, egoistic, wild Irish writer. She finally admitted to herself that she loved him, even without any hope or expectation that he might love her back. Just loving him was enough for now. And he had come to their festival.

'When do you think he might arrive?' asked Fenella when she went back upstairs again.

'Depending on whether he gets lost again or not, about half an hour.'

'Do you think we should start without him?' said Sarah, who had an anxious-looking woman at her side.

'Definitely. He doesn't deserve to be waited for.'

For some reason, Fenella moved forward and kissed Laura's cheek.

Laura was in two minds whether to wait for Dermot in the hall or to sit down and start eating. She felt fairly sure Dermot would need directions at least once more so she decided to eat. She was seated next to one of the romantic novelists, Anne Marsh.

'I must say, I adore Dermot's writing,' she said.

'I really liked it at university,' said Laura, frightened that she'd shown her feelings for Dermot far too clearly. She quickly steered the conversation away from him. 'But I really love your books. How do you find writing a book a year?'

'Well,' said Anne. 'I'd like it a lot better if every year had fourteen months in it, but lots of writers write far more than I do.'

'And lots write far less.' Her phone went and Laura smiled. 'Far less . . . Excuse me a moment,' she said before connecting.

'How the feck do you get into this place?'

He was downstairs. Barely excusing herself, Laura ran down the stairs and started wrestling with the huge key. 'I can't open it!' she called to Dermot.

'Try pulling it towards you,' he called back.

Laura did, and eventually got the key to turn. Dermot was standing there, looking completely disreputable in an old leather jacket and blue jeans. Her heart clenched at the sight of him. He strode in, dropped a bag at her feet and looked at her. 'Did you dress up as a leprechaun just for me?'

'Don't be silly!' she said crossly, desperate to avoid sounding coy.

She saw him look at her mouth and she felt breathless.

'Are you all right? That key can be quite tricky,' said Rupert coming up behind Laura. Laura wasn't sure if she was pleased to see him at that moment or not. Rupert smiled and held out his hand. 'You must be the famous Dermot Flynn. Welcome!'

'I think you must mean infamous,' said Dermot.

'Either way, it's good to see you. We started dinner, I'm afraid.'

Dermot, who had picked up his bag halted. 'Dinner. Ah. What I need is a shower and a shave.' Then he looked wickedly at Laura and mouthed, 'And a shag.'

She blushed and looked away. Just for a moment she wanted to go with him to where they could be alone for a very long time. Then she mentally shook herself. She wouldn't let him weave his spell on her again. She mustn't.

'I don't want to meet everyone in all my dirt,' went on Dermot, possibly completely unaware of the effect he was having on Laura.

'You don't have to—' Rupert began.

'Trust me,' said Dermot. 'I do have to. For various reasons, I haven't had a shower for a few days.'

'Right. I'll show you to your room then. It has an en suite.'

'And how will I find my way to the party afterwards? This is a huge pile you have here.'

'I'll come and fetch you,' said Rupert. 'In about fifteen minutes?'

'Fifteen minutes is fine. But would you not send the leprechaun?' He nodded his head towards Laura, in case Rupert was in any doubt who he was referring to.

Rupert laughed. 'She'll get more lost than you will.'

'Mm,' said Dermot, looking at Laura in a way that made her just want to smile and smile, 'that might not be so dreadful.'

Chapter Eighteen

Laura went back upstairs trying very hard to wipe the smile of sheer joy at seeing Dermot again off her face. As she got to the door she remembered she could be pleased for the festival's sake, and stopped bothering. There was time enough for her to be sensible and remember he was the enemy and she needed to protect herself – and more importantly her heart – from him.

'He's here!' she announced. 'Dermot Flynn has actually deigned to turn up!'

A buzz of exclamations filled the room. 'What's he like?' said Anne Marsh, when Laura had got back to her place.

'Well, I had met him before—'

'You've met him before? But I thought he was practically a recluse!'

'Not at all,' broke in Eleanora. 'He's just damn difficult to get out of Ireland. Laura did a grand job getting him to come.'

Some man said, 'Did you have to sleep with him to get him to agree?'

Laura looked and saw it was one of the young literary writers. She gave him a withering look. 'As if that would really work.'

'Well,' he said, 'it would for me.'

'Oh,' said Laura, having worked out eventually that he didn't mean that he wanted to sleep with Dermot. She blushed deeply.

'It would be no hardship sleeping with him,' said

Veronica. 'I saw him on television, years ago and thought: Mr Darcy, eat your heart out.'

Perfectly presented portions of Jubilee Chicken were being served over their shoulders. 'I prefer that Sean Bean myself,' said the Catering Lady who had just delivered the chicken.

The young writer ignored this interjection, it being from a motherly soul who was obviously only a waitress. 'You romantic novelists, you're just suckers for an Irish brogue and an easy smile,' he said. Laura remembered he had been shortlisted for some prize or other and one reviewer had likened him to Dermot.

'Oh, it's general,' said Veronica, smiling sweetly. 'All women are suckers for an Irish brogue and an easy smile – don't they come in pairs? You might have to work just that bit harder. Although,' she added kindly, having watched him bluster a bit, 'lots of women are attracted to writers per se.'

Anne glanced at her colleague. The young man, who was now blushing and blustering in equal measures, obviously didn't quite know how to take this.

'I don't know why he's considered such a draw,' he said, sounding resentful. 'He's not J. D. Salinger, is he?'

'Well, no,' agreed Anne. 'But he does have rarity value, doesn't he? I mean, he may not have produced anything for ages, but he was – is so good.'

'And tasty,' added Veronica.

'I'll second that,' threw in one of the literary critics, overhearing this conversation.

'What? That he's tasty?' Veronica raised her eyebrows. 'Something for the gossip columns?'

'My dear girl, I didn't mean that,' he said, 'as you very well know.' He gave her a teasing look. They obviously knew each other. 'What I meant was, we're all here from curiosity. No one from the literary world has set eyes on him for years.'

'And personally speaking, I'm quite happy for him to be the main attraction at the festival,' said Anne. Then she took pity on the young writer who was looking a bit downcast. 'So tell me, Adam,' she said, putting her hand on his and capturing his attention, 'what are you writing now?'

He was thrilled. 'My third novel. I've been working on it for a couple of years now. Just about taking shape.'

'Two years! If it's not a rude question,' said Veronica, sabotaging her friend's attempts to be nice, 'how do you support yourself between novels?'

'I'm a English lecturer.' He looked pained. 'My novels are my work, my life! I don't expect to make money out of them.'

Veronica and Anne exchanged glances and cleared their throats. 'Sorry,' Veronica went on. 'I didn't realise that making money from one's novels was on a par with selling one's daughters into prostitution. It's how I earn my crust.'

Laura chuckled inwardly. Anne and Veronica had swept up the drive to Somerby in a Porsche. Some crust.

'Well, I don't just churn them out, like you do.' Adam took an affronted gulp of his wine.

Anne and Veronica didn't need to look at each other to pick up each other's thoughts. Veronica patted Adam's hand. 'It's all right, sweetie. There'll always be a place in the publishing world for a well-received novel that no one actually reads, let alone buys. You keep on crafting those perfect sentences.'

'I say! That's a bit—'

'Patronising? Sorry,' said Veronica. 'But don't worry, I'll be all sweetness and light from now on, as my reputation requires.' She frowned thoughtfully. 'Dermot managed to do both – write like an angel and sell in shed-loads.'

Laura, satisfied that no blows would be exchanged or

glasses of wine thrown, leant across to Monica. 'You'd better get in touch with Ironstone! And tell the people who aren't here about Dermot.'

'They'll be so pleased! And Ironstone!' She clapped her hands excitedly. 'I must buy new knickers.'

Laura became aware of Fenella trying to say something to her but she was too far away. She leant in and concentrated on lip reading. After several attempts she picked up that Fenella thought it was a pity that Jacob Stone had decided not to come to this dinner.

'He probably didn't think Dermot would turn up!' Laura mouthed back.

Fenella nodded agreement. 'It means I've got to get Dermot to agree to meet him on his own.' She frowned across at Laura. 'Is he very difficult?'

Laura leant further forward, still struggling to hear. 'Who, Jacob Stone? I thought he was your friend.'

'No!' Frustrated, Fenella raised her voice. 'No! Dermot! Is Dermot really as difficult as everyone says he is?'

At that moment the double doors opened. 'Right on cue,' murmured Veronica. 'You couldn't have stage-managed it better.'

Dermot, shaved but still wearing his casual shirt and jeans, stood looking directly at Fenella. Then he smiled. 'Why don't you ask him yourself?'

Fenella got up from the table and walked round to greet him. She hesitated as if not sure if she should kiss him or shake his hand. 'I don't know what to say. In some ways, I feel I know you,' she said.

He just smiled and opened his arms. 'You'd better give me a hug, then.'

Fenella went straight into them.

Laura was aware of a pang of jealousy so deep at first she thought it was actual pain. She'd thought it was fine, that she'd had her magical time with Dermot and now he belonged to the rest of the world. But her heart wasn't clued up to her rationalisation and it hurt. He hadn't hugged her like that.

'I've put you next to Eleanora,' Fenella was saying.

'I don't want to sit next to her. I want to sit by the leprechaun and these attractive women.'

There was an instant shuffling of chairs and people getting up and sitting down. Laura caught Sarah's look of resignation as her carefully planned seating arrangements were tossed into disarray. There was a frantic shifting of cutlery and glasses, too.

'I know perfectly well why you don't want to sit by me, Dermot,' said Eleanora placidly. 'But don't worry, I'll get to you later.'

'We ought to discuss your various events,' said Laura, struggling to breathe properly and working very hard on being businesslike. 'Tomorrow you're supposed to be reading extracts of your books with Celtic music accompanying.'

His look of disgust made Anne and Veronica chuckle.

'Of course, you don't have to do it if you don't want to,' said Fenella quickly. 'Laura's chosen some extracts and Rupert's going to read them in an Irish accent. We have a CD for the music.'

At this his look of disgust was even more extreme.

'Or whatever you prefer,' said Fenella. 'Really—'

'Oh, for goodness' sake!' said Laura. 'I'm sure now he's here, Dermot will do whatever he's scheduled to do.' She smiled sweetly at him.

'For a leprechaun you're very bad-tempered,' he said.

'Not at all. Leprechauns are notoriously bad-tempered. Think of Rumpelstiltskin,' she said, trying to sound sniffy. She was enjoying herself. She could banter with him without fearing for her safety.

'I always thought he was very hard done by,' said Anne to Veronica.

'So did I!' said Dermot, joining in with glee. 'He helps that materialistic woman—'

'It wasn't her fault,' said Anne. 'She was sold into that marriage by her father.'

'And the king wasn't much better,' agreed Veronica. 'He only wanted her for her ability to spin straw into gold.'

'Oh, I think he wanted the girl for her beauty too,' said Dermot. 'He just used the straw-into-gold thing as an excuse.'

Laura channelled her tumultuous feelings into a snappish efficiency. 'Lovely though it is to hear all your thoughts on the subtext of traditional fairy stories, firstly I don't think Rumplestiltskin was actually a leprechaun and secondly, could I just bring us all back to the present day? Dermot has to do an event for which every ticket has been sold. Could we agree what it is?'

'Does that mean we won't be doing the panel?' said Adam, sounding disappointed. 'I was really hoping—'

'For some publicity?' said Anne. 'Surely not!' Her amused expression took the sting out of her words.

Adam glanced at her sideways, as if a full-on look might turn him to stone, and muttered out of the corner of his mouth, 'So how many paperbacks would you reckon to sell?'

'Oh, I don't know,' said Anne. 'If I'm lucky, about a hundred thousand.'

'A hundred thousand? Bloody hell!'

'She's being modest,' said Veronica. 'She sells far more than that.'

'Only because they're in the supermarkets.' Now that she'd demolished him, Anne now wanted Adam to feel better.

Laura was trying to catch Dermot's attention but he was too busy enjoying the interchange between the popular-fiction writer and the literary novelist.

She opened her mouth to try again but Monica pipped her to the post. 'Dermot, do you remember me?'

His charm was like an interrogation light: no one, let alone a woman like Monica, could fail to melt a little under its influence, in spite of how she'd been with him when they were in Ireland. 'How could I forget the woman who asked such searching questions from the floor?'

'Oh? What were they?' asked Adam. 'I always like to plant a few good questions.'

'I don't think you'd want that kind of question,' said Laura, blushing hard, hoping everyone would just think she'd had too much to drink.

'No, but something that allows one—'

'She asked me when I last used a condom,' said Dermot brutally.

'Oh!'

Anne and Veronica both snorted into their wine, unable to hide their amusement.

'But Dermot's not going to hold that against me,' said Monica. 'Are you? I want to ask you about Seamus.'

'And I don't think—' said Laura.

'What about Seamus?' asked Dermot. 'Who is Seamus?'

'He's a musician,' said Monica, fighting for her man. 'I just don't think – I mean, possibly—' She stopped. 'You might know him?'

'Just because they're both Irish, doesn't mean they know each other,' said Adam. 'Hi, Dermot, may I introduce myself? Adam Saint.' He leant over and stuck his hand out towards Dermot.

'What's his surname?' said Dermot, having smiled briefly at Adam, ignoring the proffered hand.

'O'Hennessy. He lives—'

'Oh God, *that* Seamus! Of course I bloody know him! Don't tell me he's made you pregnant? I'll knock him down for you.'

Becoming hysterical, Monica began to laugh. 'No! He hasn't! Anyway, if he had it would be my responsibility. He just wants to play—'

'Monica,' Laura implored. 'His band was dreadful! You said so yourself.'

'What does he want to play, and why?' demanded Dermot.

'His bodhrán. Behind you as you read out pieces from your great work.'

It was Adam Saint's turn to laugh. Dermot made a face at Laura. 'Did I agree to this?'

'I probably didn't get round to asking you,' she admitted. 'I got distracted!'

Dermot smiled. 'So you did. So what precisely would you have been asking me to do if you hadn't . . . got distracted?'

'To read from your work to the accompaniment of Irish music,' Laura muttered. 'It's to link the music and the literary bit of the festival together. I know you hate the idea, but don't worry, we can do Rupert's thing.'

'With the fake accent and the Celtic Twilight bollocks?'

Anne and Veronica were loving it. Even Adam Saint seemed content.

'Yes,' muttered Laura, concentrating on getting a bit of sweetcorn back into the rice it had escaped from with her fork. It was wonderful to be so close to Dermot but also agony. It was making it so much harder to keep her feelings in check. Unrequited love was so painful.

'Well, I'll do something, if only to spare us that. And Seamus can play, as long as it's *not* the fiddle.'

'Oh Dermot, thank you!' said Monica, reaching across three plates of chicken to kiss him, and narrowly missing some curry-and-mango-flavoured mayonnaise as she did so.

'So who's going to do the big interview on Sunday night?' asked Adam. 'Everyone's going to be really interested to hear that.' Something in his tone suggested *schadenfreude*.

'I'm sure they are,' said Dermot lazily. 'Did I agree to do a big interview? Or did you slip that one by me too?' His gaze wandered over Laura in a speculative way that made her feel weak and angry with herself and consequently cross with him for having this effect on her. He obviously thought they could pick up where they'd left off. That he only had to look at her and she'd willingly leap into bed with him.

'Oh, for goodness' sake, stop being such a prima donna. Of course there'll be a big interview! This is a literary festival! It's what happens!'

'So who's doing it?' Adam pressed on, possibly hoping for the hardest-hitting, most incisive, unkindest interviewer around – the Jeremy Paxman of the literary world, if not *the* Jeremy Paxman.

'I am,' said Laura, more sharply than she had intended.

'Oh,' said Adam. 'Bit of a pushover that will be for you, Dermot! Can't you face a proper interviewer, then?'

'I'll have you know that the leprechaun here is very proper, or she was until I got to her, and I'm sure she'll ask some very searching questions,' said Dermot.

'I will indeed,' said Laura, hoping to goodness she'd be able to think of more than the three she'd scribbled down in her notebook late one evening. 'We couldn't book anyone famous without knowing if Dermot was able to attend,' she said to Adam.

'You see? It's all my fault,' Dermot said. 'Laura dear, is there any chance of getting you on your own?' He raised an eyebrow and Laura flushed. Did he really expect to claim his 'shag'? While the mouse was safely back in Ireland, the cat could claim his prey. Humph!

'Oh, you can't nobble her,' said Adam. 'That would be entirely unsporting.'

'I'm not entirely sure what you mean by "nobble",'

said Dermot, 'but that was the very last thing I had in mind.'

'Here's the pudding,' said Veronica quickly, sensing trouble. 'Banoffee pie. I think I've died and gone to heaven.'

Laura caught her eye and smiled her gratitude. She knew Dermot had been going to say something outrageous and realised Veronica had too.

'No really, I insist,' went on Adam. 'It would be unethical for you and Laura to talk before the interview.' He paused. 'Because it seems to me that Dermot can twist any woman round his finger and he'd just talk her out of asking anything remotely tricky.'

'I assure you what I want to say to Laura is of an entirely private nature,' said Dermot. He was serious now; no more suggestive looks.

Sweat prickled along her hairline as she realised what Dermot might be going to say. He was probably going to 'explain' about Bridget, make it clear that what had happened between them had been delightful, but it was a one-off and she mustn't think of it or him any more, but how about a shag for old times' sake, Bridget need never know. She could almost hear his lovely sexy voice saying the words. She couldn't bear it. 'I think you're quite right!' She said this so vehemently, people looked a little startled. 'I mean,' she went on, trying to sound more rational, 'I think it should be like the bride not seeing the bridegroom the night before the wedding.'

Dermot was frowning and apparently somewhat confused. 'Well, if that's how you feel, Laura.'

'I do! I think I'd feel better about interviewing you if we hadn't talked beforehand. I could approach it in a more professional way.'

'And a writer of your experience, Dermot,' said Veronica, 'shouldn't have any problems with Laura here. Oh, I do realise she'll be a lot tougher than she looks in that tiny dress and those heavenly boots, but she's not going to hang you out to dry!'

'No,' Laura agreed meekly, 'definitely not.' The ache in her heart had returned with a vengeance.

Dermot sighed. 'For feck's sake! But if you insist!' He looked around the table and then got up. 'If I can't talk to the person I want to talk to, I'd better go and see my agent. Is there any chance of any brandy, do you think?'

The happiness that Laura had felt on seeing Dermot again had turned to the depths of despair. She managed to stay chatting to Veronica, Anne and Adam for a few moments longer and then she excused herself on the pretext of seeing when the coffee might turn up.

Fenella was in the kitchen on the same errand, much to the irritation of the Catering Ladies who had it all in hand.

'Are you all right, honey?' said Fenella.

'I'm fine, or rather I will be. I've just suddenly realised what Dermot turning up means. I'll have to interview him, unless there's anyone else.' Frantically she mentally scanned the authors who were around. She couldn't do it, she just couldn't. 'Maybe—'

'No,' said Fenella firmly. 'It has to be you. You know his work, you won't take the limelight away from him, you are the one.'

'You know, there are at least two song titles in that sentence,' said Monica, appearing behind Laura. 'But Dermot is utterly lovely.'

'You know, you're sounding very Irish these days,' said Laura. 'Maybe you're spending too much time with Seamus.'

'Well, you're right there,' she agreed happily, 'but isn't it just darling of Dermot to let Seamus play behind him?' Monica seemed to have forgotten Dermot was the bad fairy who had broken her friend's heart.

'He doesn't know how bad Seamus is, obviously,' said Laura.

'He can't be that bad,' said Fenella.

'And he knows him,' Monica said. 'Anyway, Seamus isn't bad, it's the band that's awful, and Dermot probably knows exactly how bad – or even good – he is. It's a great chance for Seamus.'

'If you ladies would either like to take up some jugs of coffee, or get out of the way, we'd be very grateful,' said one of the Catering Ladies.

'Oh, sorry,' they said in unison, and moved out of the way.

What she needed, Laura decided in the shower the following morning, was time to go away by herself with Dermot's books and think up some really insightful questions. But she had a busy day ahead of her and even her time alone in the shower was limited; Monica needed to get into it.

'Do you want toast and stuff here, or to go across to the house for a cooked breakfast?' she asked a still-damp Monica a short time later. 'I wouldn't mind checking in with Veronica and Anne. I'm taking them to their event later.'

'Won't Dermot be there?' Monica put a large dollop of something smelly on to her hair.

'I'm allowed to see him, just not alone,' said Laura primly.

'Are you all right about doing it, though?' Monica said, sculpting her hair with the product.

'I would be if I had time to think about it, but I won't have a moment to think up anything until about ten minutes before it happens.'

'It must be extra hard for you, seeing that you're sleeping with him.'

'I'm not! It was just that time!' She sighed. 'But of

course it is harder. I can't treat him just like any other writer.' And I don't want to treat him like the man who's broken my heart.

'What you need to do is to work up a good old grudge against him,' said Monica, plugging in her hair-dryer, unaware of the depth of Laura's anguish. 'Think how badly he's treated you and get your revenge.'

'But he hasn't treated me badly, really.' Laura kept feeling an impulse to confide in Monica about Bridget, then realising she didn't want to drag it all up again. She was coping as well as she could, she thought. Don't rock the boat. Monica knew she was upset; she didn't need all the sorry details.

Monica wasn't having this. 'Oh, for Jaysus' sake! From where I'm standing, he may be lovely and charming and a God's gift to the literary world, but he had his evil way with you and never phoned! In my book that's not gentle-manly behaviour. How much more badly could he treat you?' She obviously still felt loyal towards her friend and for that Laura was grateful.

'I should think a lot worse. He could have made me pregnant and then left me.' Then, wanting to change the subject, she said, 'Now, what about breakfast? Cooked or toast?'

'Cooked, I think. I want to see Dermot, even if you don't.'

'Monica, don't start interrogating him . . .' But Monica was already out of the door.

The Somerby kitchen was full of chatter, clattering and the smell of bacon. Rupert was wearing a huge apron and had three frying pans on the go and a separate pan full of scrambled eggs. Dermot wasn't there.

'He, Rupert and Eleanora stayed up into the early hours,' Fenella reported to Laura, obviously annoyed. 'They'll be fit for nothing later, and Dermot's got to do his thing with Seamus.'

'Have you eaten anything yet?' Laura asked.

'No she hasn't,' snapped Sarah, equally tetchily. Everyone was obviously a little anxious now the literary festival was officially open and the first proper day of events was before them. She took Fenella by the shoulders and guided her to an empty seat. Then she put a big plate of food down in front of her. 'Get that down you. I'll fetch you some tea.'

They all chatted for a while about nothing in particular, and Laura had just begun her own breakfast when Dermot and Eleanora appeared. Eleanora demanded a full English and Dermot just some toast and black coffee. Anne and Veronica, who were tucking their chairs neatly under the table, exchanged glances. 'I love it when people act out of character!' one of them whispered as they left. 'You'd expect Eleanora to gnaw on dry toast and Dermot to have a huge fry-up!'

As soon as she decently could, Laura returned to her little house to sort herself out. She had come back to see if Anne and Veronica were ready when she met Sarah in the hall.

'This could be a bit awkward,' said Sarah. 'There are several journalists here. Would you be a love and run back down and see if Dermot wants to speak to them? Otherwise, I'll get rid.'

Laura went back down. Only the hard-core coffee drinkers and smokers were left: Dermot, Eleanora and Rupert, who'd blagged a roll-up from Dermot and was looking guilty.

Feeling like a prefect disturbing a midnight feast Laura made her announcement. 'But Sarah will send them away if you don't want to speak to them, Dermot.'

'I think you should see a select few,' said Eleanora, 'and then the story comes from you, instead of being a lot of invented rubbish.'

'Should I send for Max Clifford?' asked Rupert, only

half joking. 'Or don't we need a publicity person? We have got Sarah, after all.'

'So what shall I tell her?' asked Laura, having turned from one person to another, no longer feeling like a prefect but like a child who isn't really allowed to join the adults.

'OK, I'll see a few, until I get bored,' said Dermot, getting up and giving Laura a wicked grin. 'Don't tell Fenella Rupert had a fag, will you?'

Laura tossed her head and tutted, reverting to prefect-hood with gratitude. 'I won't need to tell her, she'll smell it a mile off.' Then she gathered up some dirty crockery, leaving Dermot to face the press.

Chapter Nineteen

Laura didn't have time to worry about how Dermot got on with the journalists. She had to take Veronica and Anne to their venue, where they were doing a joint talk, followed by a signing. Then the two authors were adjudicating a short-story competition that they had already judged, before going to a local café for a 'Tea with Two Authors' event. They were good sports and didn't mind working so hard, but a great deal had been asked of them and Laura felt a bit guilty. When she'd suggested them as adjudicators for the competition, she hadn't realised it would mean running from place to place in quite the way it had worked out. Fortunately the cakes at the café were extremely good and Laura insisted they be allowed to eat a couple before the questions began again.

She was just contemplating a Jap cake, a wonderful old-fashioned confection involving coffee icing and crushed meringue, when her phone rang. She went outside to take the call. It was Fenella.

'Sorry to bother you, but Dermot asked me to call.'

'That's OK, but he could have phoned me himself. I know I said I didn't want to speak to him, but I only meant—'

'It's not that. Dermot's been giving interviews all day. Eleanora is thrilled! She doesn't know why he's being so obliging, but never mind that. He hasn't got time to choose readings for his event tonight and wonders if you have any ideas?'

Laura had thought about this when she very first had the idea of combining music and readings. 'OK, I've marked some places. If you go into my house, on the bookshelf are copies of both Dermot's books. The passages I think are best have paperclips on the pages.'

'You're amazing! I bet you're glad I never got round to borrowing them after all, or we'd never find the books, let alone some good bits.'

She wanted to retort that Dermot's books were all 'good bits' but just said, 'Glad to be of help.'

Laura went back to the tea shop and decided Jap cakes were no longer optional, but essential. She was frantically thinking about when she was going to have time to plan what to ask Dermot the following night. Tomorrow she was touring the countryside for the 'Festival in the Community' with authors in the back of her car, taking them to visit old people's homes. Still, there should be time between getting the authors back to Somerby and being on hand again in case she was needed to get them to Dermot's musical event. With luck, she shouldn't have to do that at all, and then she'd have plenty of time. Well, an hour or so, anyway.

When she and Fenella had been planning the festival they had welcomed each new suggestion and set it up gleefully. The programme was full of events at venues all over the area. Everyone had taken up the ideas with enthusiasm. It was only now, when the festival was actually happening, that they realised quite how much running around was involved.

It was quite late by the time they got back to Somerby as Veronica had insisted on visiting a local garden centre and Laura felt she could hardly say 'there's no time'. Grant and Monica were waiting for her on the doorstep of the main house. She had forgotten they were all going to have a drink together before Dermot's event. She'd have no time to write down her questions this evening. She sighed.

'Laura, I can't believe you've been taking these lovely authors round the country in my old banger,' said Grant as he and Monica helped Veronica and Anne out of his old car.

'It's been fine,' said Anne, taking his arm and heaving herself out of the back of the car. 'It's just we're women of a certain age.'

Veronica, in the front, who had got out unaided, humphed. 'Women of a certain arse, more like!'

Grant regarded them both. 'I don't know if I should laugh at that joke or not!

'Right!' he went on, once Anne and Veronica had been shown back to their accommodation and supplied with tea and whisky. 'Let's go back to yours and have a glass of wine. I've been saving myself. I want a full update. Didn't you pack just a bit too much in to the literary festival, Laura?'

'Mm. We did,' she admitted as they set off towards her cottage. 'The thing was we didn't realise how everyone would leap at the chance of having an author, or a writing competition, or even a "Stitch and Bitch with Books" event so avidly.'

'So, what's a "Stitch and Bitch with Books" then?' asked Grant.

'It's like a Stitch and Bitch, when women get together and—'

'It's all right, I worked that out.'

'Well, in this instance, someone reads aloud, so there's no bitching really, and everyone knits squares for a blanket. It's happening on Monday morning. Fenella's providing the cake.'

'Come on you two, never mind Stitch and Bitch,' said Monica. 'I'm going to the event early with Seamus to help with the sound check and things. We need to hurry.'

Upping the pace a bit, Laura said, 'What's your b. and b. like, Grant?'

'Lovely, but a bit bucolic. There are cows right outside my window.'

'What do you expect in the country?' asked Monica.

But Grant forgot his objections to rural life when he saw where Laura and Monica were staying. This was the first time he'd been over. 'Oh, this is charming,' he said. 'Really nicely done.'

'It is, isn't it?' Laura agreed, retrieving a bottle of wine from the fridge. 'You go first in the shower, Monica. You're in a hurry.'

'Only the same hurry you're in,' said Monica, pausing en route, looking at her friend suspiciously.

'I don't have to go early like you do.'

Monica gave her a beady glance.

Laura inspected her nails. 'I may not go tonight. I need to plan my questions for tomorrow.'

'You can't not go to Dermot's event,' Monica protested. 'He'd be so upset.'

'No he wouldn't be!' Laura was equally adamant. 'He wouldn't care at all, if he even noticed.'

'But, Laura!' Grant was appalled. 'You can't miss it! You've loved his work since you were a baby—'

'Not quite a baby,' she protested quietly.

'You can't miss hearing him read,' Grant went on. 'You'd never forgive yourself.'

After being stared at by two indignant friends for several seconds, Laura sighed. 'I suppose you're right, Grant. I've heard enough lesser writers read their stuff. It would be silly to miss the best.'

'Let's get out the wine,' said Grant.

'Monica can't have a drink if she's driving,' said Laura, feeling bullied and wanting revenge.

'It's OK, I'm not driving,' said Monica. 'We've got

a driver. We're picking up Seamus on the way. It's such a shame he's not staying at Somerby.'

'Somerby is filled to the gunwales,' said Laura. 'Some authors have had to stay in bed and breakfasts.' She paused as a happy thought occurred to her. 'You could go and stay with him, if you want.'

Monica shook her head. 'No. I need to be on-hand really, for the music festival stuff.'

Laura sighed, contrite. 'I'm sorry, Mon, I keep forgetting about that side of things. How's it going? Did you tell Ironstone? Will they be there tonight?'

'Some of them, definitely, but it's a sell-out. Seamus is bricking it.'

'We have got the CD fall back position if he's that scared.'

'No! Dermot has vetoed that, remember.'

'Come on, Mon, never mind all that, do you want a glass of wine first, or a shower?'

'Both of course! Haven't you heard of multi-tasking?'

Grant and Monica both insisted that Laura came early with them, not trusting her turn up unless they took her to the event by force.

'It is a shame we couldn't organise the pub to host this event,' said Monica.

'Yes, but apparently it couldn't fit in nearly enough people so they moved it to Fenella's cinema,' said Laura.

'Fenella's cinema?' said Grant.

'Not her personal cinema. She loves the building and wanted it used for everything.' Laura paused. 'It's also the biggest venue around. It's where Monica did her gig, remember?'

'Oh. I thought it was just a theatre.'

'Poor Seamus! He's going to be so nervous!' said Monica interrupting. 'He'd have been much happier in a pub.'

Monica sat in the front next to the driver on the way to pick up Seamus. Grant and Laura sat in the back, squashing up when Seamus got in. Laura was also feeling nervous. She so wanted it to go well, for Seamus's sake, and, of course, for Dermot.

Sarah had asked her if she should photocopy the pages of the book and enlarge them for Dermot to read from. They had discussed it and decided it could do no harm, but Laura said that laminating them wasn't a good idea. Apart from anything else, if he dropped the pages they would skid all over the place. Laura had the sheets; Dermot had the books.

'It's like members of the cabinet not travelling on the same flights in case there's a plane crash,' Sarah had said solemnly. 'There's a back-up position.'

Laura wasn't sure if being made to laugh was helpful or not. It did relieve a bit of tension, but now she was worrying about Dermot's driver, a very steady ex-policeman called Reg, getting into an accident on the way to the venue.

The venue functioned as a cinema most of the time except when the local amateur-dramatics group put on productions, or the village panto was on. It was a very pretty building, kept up by massive fund-raising activities. This time, all the seats were in place so as to have as big an audience as possible. Although they arrived a good hour before the event, there were already people gathering outside.

'Kerrist!' said Seamus as the driver slowed down, looking for a place to stop. 'There's bloody loads of them here!'

'It's all right,' said Grant. 'They're here for Dermot. You don't need to worry.'

'That's not very kind!' said Monica, shoving Grant's arm. 'Of course they're here for Seamus!'

'They're here for the event,' said Laura diplomatically. 'And I'm really nervous too!'

'And me,' said Grant. 'I'm really worried that someone will forget their lines or something. I feel like a mum at a kid's play. Let's get in there. The bar should be open, shouldn't it?'

'Yes,' said Laura. 'The idea is to make it feel like an Irish pub as much as possible, given that it isn't one. With music and crack, and porter.'

'Crack?' said Monica. 'I thought this was a nice sedate music festival.'

'It is,' said Grant. 'It's the writers who might let the side down.'

'Shall I drop you here?' asked the driver, who'd been chuckling quietly to himself. 'And you've got my mobile number? Ring me when you want to go home.'

'Could that be now?' asked Seamus.

'No,' everyone chorused, and they all got out.

The first person they saw when they got inside was Adam. 'I came with Dermot,' he said, implying he was doing a useful task. Laura, who normally would have had sympathy for the young writer, found this rather annoying. 'He doesn't want to be swamped with fans,' Adam went on. 'Or to discuss tomorrow's interview. He needs to focus on tonight's performance.' He glared at Laura as if she was a door-stepping paparazza looking for scandal.

Laura didn't respond. Adam had obviously appointed himself as Dermot's minder – a task that Fenella or Rupert had been allocated. But as they were busy, they'd probably been happy to let Adam do it, and presumably Dermot hadn't objected. As for discussing tomorrow's interview, it was the last thing she would have ever done. It was a bit ironic that all Adam's original resentment of Dermot had somehow morphed into hero worship and a fierce protectiveness.

Monica took Seamus up to the stage and was already giving orders to the sound crew. Dermot was sitting on the stage, on a chair, reading, a well-thumbed copy of one of his books in his hand. He had a tall glass by his side.

'Let's go and get a drink,' Grant suggested. 'We're not needed here.'

The bar was already buzzing. The usual volunteers had been supplemented by staff from the local pub, there not usually being much call for draught stout at the theatre. There was a young man in black jeans, black T-shirt and a ponytail instructing a woman in her sixties how to pull the perfect pint.

'I'm not sure if I should drink,' said Laura when Grant asked her what she wanted.

'Oh, for God's sake! You'll never get through this sober! I can tell, you're far more nervous than Seamus is. Have a large whisky.'

By the time he'd got back to their table, the place was packed. Laura was relieved. A good audience, and no chance of Dermot being able to spot her in the crowd. It couldn't be better. But she still planned to sit right at the back, behind a pillar if she could find one.

Laura wasn't surprised that Dermot was a star; he read beautifully, captured the audience and held them, totally enthralled. She was momentarily surprised that Seamus was so good. He didn't play the bodhrán he'd been so miserable at, but the guitar. Very, very softly, he played traditional Irish songs: 'She Moved Through the Fair', 'Down by the Salley Gardens', 'The Lark in the Clear Air'. And Dermot read.

In deep, dark brown tones he described a small boy watching through a window as his mother kissed his father and feeling excluded, a windy morning in spring, a blackbird's song and a feeling of expectation that had no cause; falling asleep on a hard, leather-covered banquette in a pub while the wedding party caroused.

There wasn't a cough, a murmur or a fidget to be heard. Even Grant was listening intently.

Laura knew she was what was popularly known as being 'tired and emotional' but the words were so evocative, so poetic without being sentimental, and the music was so touching that she felt tears smarting in her eyes.

She concentrated on keeping them very wide open and then occasionally blinking, so a big tear splashed down. This way she could blot up each tear with her hand, and hope no one noticed how overcome she was. Not that anyone would, she realised. They were all transfixed.

She and Grant were right at the back. On Laura's insistence they had delayed going in as long as possible. She had said she wanted to get back as soon as the event was over, to prepare for her interview, and to avoid Dermot until she could face him calmly and unemotionally the following morning. Now she was even more glad she had. His reading had brought up every feeling, every longing – not that they were buried that deep beneath the surface, but with each sentence all her love and admiration for him rose up with renewed force.

Dermot closed the book and Seamus rested his fingers on his guitar strings to silence them. It was over. For a moment there was silence, as if no one wanted to break the spell Dermot had woven around them. And then the theatre erupted.

There was, inevitably, a standing ovation. Laura slipped outside, too overwhelmed to be able to join in. Damn the man for putting her in this turmoil, she thought. But wasn't he wonderful? Walking up and down in the road on her own, her heart began to sing. He was a star; he wouldn't regret coming to the festival. And however painful it was to admit it, she loved him with all her heart.

'Are you OK?' A friendly male voice addressed her.

'It's me, Hugo. I'm Sarah's other half and a friend of Rupert and Fenella's.'

'Oh yes, of course. Hello again. I'm fine,' she insisted.

Hugo studied her thoughtfully. 'Do you want me to run you home? Escape all the crowds? You're inter-viewing the great man tomorrow, aren't you? You might need some time away from the furore.'

'That would be brilliant! Can you do that?' Laura felt relief course through her and she almost stumbled.

'What, drive you home? Yup, and be back before anyone notices I haven't been here all the time. Come with me. The car's here.'

Having asked Hugo to tell Monica and Grant she'd gone home, she left a note for Monica and then fled up to the mezzanine and went to bed. She couldn't think of any questions tonight: she was too wrung out. After ten minutes she came back downstairs and made some hot chocolate. She took it back up to bed with her and hoped she'd get to sleep this time. Surprisingly, she did.

On Sunday she had very little time either to think about the interview later that day or dwell on the emotions Dermot's reading had stirred up in her the night before. She'd joked to Fenella and Sarah at breakfast about needing time to lie on her bed with slices of cucumber on her eyes, but really she was worried that if she didn't have time to prepare, Dermot would make her look a complete fool. And while it was how Dermot performed that mattered, his reputation wouldn't be enhanced if he was asked obvious questions by a slip of a thing with wild curly hair who was totally unprepared. She owed it to herself, too.

Sunday's schedule was genteelly packed. As soon as they'd had one of Rupert's famous breakfasts, Veronica and Anne plus Maria Cavendish, a crime author, squashed themselves into the car and Laura set off towards the first of their destinations. The 'Festival in the Community' had been a very popular idea – one Laura now wished she hadn't had, although perhaps it was the distraction she needed.

At the last place, a very grand home for retired gentle-folk, she was about to get out of the car when Veronica said, 'You stay here and prepare your interview. We'll be fine. Honestly.'

Grateful, Laura agreed that she would, but instead she found herself daydreaming.

A tap on the window jolted her out of her reverie. She realised she had actually fallen asleep. All this emotion was wearing her out.

'Never mind, you'll be better for a nap,' said Veronica, when they all got back in the car and discovered Laura in dreamland. 'I'm a great believer in catnaps.'

'But you don't want Dermot to run rings round you,' said Anne. 'What time is the event?'

'Seven. We're having an early meal. Maybe I should skip that and think up some questions then.'

'Really,' said Maria Cavendish, who'd only joined the group that day and wasn't as friendly, 'you should have thought up your questions weeks ago, when the event was first arranged.'

'But she didn't know if Dermot was coming,' explained Veronica. 'There was going to be a panel of authors instead.'

'Oh? Is that why that was cancelled? Hmph. I could have come tomorrow instead.'

'But the old ladies loved you!' said Anne. 'It's amazing how many of them read really gritty crime.'

In between navigating back to Somerby and telling the writers how brilliant they'd been Laura tried to pull her disparate thoughts together. By the time she finally deliv-ered her literary load, all she'd come up with was 'Did you like school?' Then she remembered she'd asked him for his Desert Island book. He'd said *Ulysses*. She could get him to talk about James Joyce for a little bit. It would ease them both into the interview. Once she was back in the quiet of the cottage, she noted both these questions down in the back of her diary, ready to transfer them to something more substantial. Sarah had asked her if she wanted a clipboard, but Laura felt some notes on a sheet of A4 would be easier.

Laura's teeth were chattering and she felt sick. She had managed to think of a list of questions and written it out, and she could tell, just by looking at her handwriting, that she was terrified. Not that she'd been in any doubt but the spiky, uneven strokes revealed the turmoil going on inside. She was slightly disappointed that Dermot hadn't even tried to see her. But then she'd been busy and so had he and they had said they wouldn't. He'd sent one text saying 'Go gently on me' which she'd decided not to reply to. On reflection she was grateful she hadn't seen him after last night.

And she decided that she'd feel better about the whole thing if she controlled the one thing she actually could control: her hair. On hearing this, Sarah, who'd come to see why she hadn't been at the meal, bringing a sandwich with her, went to find some straighteners. When she brought them, she insisted on staying to do Laura's hair for her.

'I'm not a hairdresser,' Sarah explained, gathering up a strand of Laura's hair, 'but I have seen lots of brides getting their hair done. It's a shame I didn't book Bron. She's my hairdresser friend I've worked with a lot. I just didn't think of it.'

'If I didn't have mad hair it wouldn't be a problem. I don't usually think about it much myself—'

'But this is a big occasion. You want to look your best. It's natural.'

Sarah was getting on quite well with the hair straighteners. Laura sat quietly for a while, enjoying being looked after for once. It was strangely comforting. Then she said, 'What do you think I should wear?'

'You looked lovely in what you wore last night, unless you want Dermot to see you in something different.' She frowned. 'Not that he would have seen much of it.'

'I can't care what Dermot sees me in!' Laura's anxiety turned this into a bit of a shriek. Hearing herself she added, 'I do hope that didn't come out as if I cared what he thinks.'

Sarah laughed soothingly, taking up another lock of Laura's hair. 'No, it just came out as if you want to look professional for the audience, how Dermot feels about it is neither here nor there.'

'That's excellent! That's just what I meant. How did you know?'

'Oh, I spent a lot of time kidding myself about my feelings too,' Sarah went on. 'Now, are you going to clip your hair back? Or just let it hang?'

'I think a clip.' Laura scooped up a hank of carefully straightened hair and held it up. 'What do you think?'

'You look about twelve, but adorable. Are you going to wear make-up?'

'A bit. Some mascara. Anything else always ends up under my eyes in seconds. Will that be enough, do you think?'

'And some lipstick.' Sarah supervised the clip, the mascara and the lipstick. 'There, now you look at least fourteen.' She paused. 'Have you got any notes? Questions?'

'Mm.' She picked up her sheet of A4 and noticed it shaking. 'I need a file to put this in.'

Sarah noticed it too and smiled reassuringly. 'I'll give you one. And do you want me to drive you to the theatre? Or will you travel with Dermot?'

305

Laura's mouth went dry at the thought of travelling with Dermot. 'Oh no. I'd rather go with you.'

'Then I'll make sure I don't have to give anyone else a lift.'

'Gosh, thank you, Sarah. You've been amazing.'

'I haven't done anything, actually. But *you* really will be amazing. I promise you.'

Somehow Sarah's words stayed with her as they drove to the venue. Her parents had never had much faith in her but other people had, and Sarah reminded her that she had done difficult things in the past and done them well. She thought of everything she had achieved since the whole festival thing had begun, from Lindy Hopping to speaking to schoolchildren to talking would-be authors through their manuscripts. Asking Dermot a few questions, allowing him to talk as much as he liked on the subjects that came up shouldn't be as hard as any of that. And yet somehow it seemed, much harder.

Sarah stayed with her, keeping her calm and bolstering her spirits until it was time for her to go on to the stage behind the drawn curtain.

The stage was set with a low table covered with a cloth and two chairs. On the table were two glasses of water and a carafe. Dermot was already there. He smiled at Laura. 'Maybe we should shake hands before we start, like boxers.'

His smile made her stomach turn over. 'I'm interviewing you. It's not a confrontation,' she said, and heard her voice tremble. And she didn't believe it, really.

Dermot had a file of papers propped against his chair. 'I know you didn't want us to talk but I feel I must. We haven't had time – you rushed off and—'

She put up her hand. 'No really, there's no need for you to say anything. It's fine. I do understand.'

Sarah called from the wings. 'It's time. Are you guys ready?'

'Not quite,' said Dermot. He was gazing at her, a puzzled look on his face.

'Oh yes we are.' Laura was firm. She felt if she waited any longer she might actually be sick.

'We must find a moment to talk,' he began. 'What happened in Ireland—

'We don't need to talk about that. In fact, we don't need to talk about anything except – oh, the curtains are going back,' she said with relief, even if it meant her next ordeal was about to begin.

Rupert introduced them and, staring beyond the lights, Laura could see the place was packed. She glanced at Dermot, to see if he was shaking too, but he didn't seem to be. He was looking out at the audience; how he felt about it was a mystery to her.

When the applause had died down Laura took a sip of water so her mouth would work. This was it.

She recited the phrases of introduction she had prepared and then turned to Dermot with the first question.

'So, tell us, Dermot, were you happy at school?'

The question surprised him but after a few seconds he was off, describing how bad he was at so many subjects, how he read Proust under the desk and that the whole school thought he was a complete idiot until he won an essay competition. He captured their interest, he made people laugh, and everyone loved him.

'And now, something I always want to know about writers, what's your Desert Island book? If you could only have one book, for the rest of your life, which one would it be?'

His eyes smiled and for a moment she was transported back to the day on the headland when they first really talked. 'God, that's a hard one. Fortunately, I've been asked it before and so I know the answer.'

She nodded, smiling.

307

'It's *Ulysses*.'

'But many people find James Joyce impenetrable.'

'He is, but infinitely rewarding.'

He went on to talk about Joyce for a little longer and then turned to Laura expectantly.

Her next few questions were as insightful as cocktail party small talk, she knew, but fortunately Dermot answered them brilliantly. Whether this indicated that he had at one time gone to a lot of cocktail parties, or that the small talk down at the pub in Ballyfitzpatrick was very similar, Laura didn't know. Either way, the audience was in turn laughing hysterically or leaning forward to pick up every nuance.

Having warmed him up she felt she had to ask her proper question now. It was a slightly risky one but any interviewer worth his or her salt would have asked it. Another sip of water, a deep breath and she launched in, 'So, Dermot, it's been a few years since there's been any new work from you. Would you like to tell us why?'

She felt like Judas and couldn't look at him, but she could imagine the flash of anger he must have been shooting at her.

'Actually, Laura' – it sounded very personal, although it was addressed to the audience too – 'there has been some new work.'

As she expected this answer – it was his usual front – she decided to push on. She'd got this far, she couldn't back out now. 'Well, have you got it with you?' she asked.

'I have.' He picked up his folder and put it on his lap.

'Oh.' She certainly hadn't been expecting this answer, but now came the real challenge. She was curious as to how he'd respond. 'So then would you like to read some of it? Or shall we go straight to questions from the floor?' she said.

'Read!' came the reply from the audience.

Dermot smiled at them and then turned back to Laura. 'It's a short story.'

'That's nice,' she said, not wanting to reveal her mounting excitement. He really did seem to have something new. 'Would you like to read it?' She felt as if she was encouraging a small child.

'Are you sure you don't want to ask me some more questions instead?' he asked teasingly.

Was the man mad? He was offering to read a short story, thus putting an end to the agony that was this interview and make literary history in one simple action!

'Well, let's ask the audience again, shall we?' she said, confident that they'd back her up.

The 'yes' from the audience was deafening, but Dermot kept his gaze on Laura. She sneaked a look at him but she couldn't guess how he was feeling.

'Then that would be lovely,' she said, as if accepting a second cup of tea.

'OK then. Here goes.'

'It's wrong to play a game when the other person doesn't know the rules, but somehow we find ourselves doing it all the time.'

His voice was so beautiful, and so sexy, at first Laura just enjoyed listening to the melodic sound of each eloquently expressed phrase without really taking in what he was actually saying, but gradually the story took shape in her mind and she listened more attentively.

'At what point in the game do you confess? In the middle? Or at the end, when success feels like defeat? And hurting someone is inevitable?'

As he read on about commitment and letting someone down gently, Laura's mouth went dry, blood coloured her cheeks scarlet and she thought she might faint. Was he talking about her? Had he written a short story about her, and their relationship, if it could be called a relationship?

The rest of the story passed through her ears without fully connecting with her brain. It was a defence mechanism, she decided, when she realised she couldn't capture his words any more than she could catch thistledown. The odd word floated through slowly enough for her to grasp it. *'Betrayal . . . passion'*, and, cruelly, *'hero-worship'*.

The more he read the more she felt a chill clutch at her heart. He'd written about her, about them, about unrequited love and letting someone down gently. And he had read it out loud, to a room full of people. Why couldn't he have just sent her an email? At least she could have read it in private.

She sat on the stage waiting for the torture to end, grateful that the audience was so enraptured by Dermot that none of them was looking at her. Thankfully no one would connect the story with her, there was no reason why anyone should. That helped. She felt now she could finish the event with dignity even if she felt like crawling away and hiding from the world for ever. She realised a small part of her had still hoped, but he couldn't have been clearer. How could she ever face him again? A glance at her watch told her there'd be no time for questions. She knew Dermot would be glad of this.

When his story came to an end the audience got to its feet, thundering applause as loud as possible. She was vaguely aware of mobile phone cameras clicking and even some flashes. Had some press got in the event? She knew they weren't supposed to be there, but how could they be stopped really?

Dermot came to the front of the stage with his hands held up to silence them. Laura crept off the stage into the sanctuary of the darkened wings.

Chapter Twenty

She knew that however much she wanted to, she had one more task to do before she could head for the sanctuary of the cottage. Seeing her old boss Henry in the book room was a lovely surprise. It shouldn't have been, of course. She knew he was supplying books for the festival but it was the first time they'd caught up with each other. His dear old face was a welcome sight after what she'd just been through.

'Sweetie!' he said, leaping to his feet, then added, less enthusiastically, 'You're looking rather tired.'

'Hardly surprising,' said Laura, smiling widely, hoping he wouldn't spot the effort it took, 'we've been fantastically busy.'

'But hugely successful,' Henry said approvingly. 'All the literary world is here and listening to every word Dermot utters.'

Laura shuddered and then hastily turned it into a shrug. 'His events have been very well attended, but so have all the others. Now, am I really needed here? Or shall I get back?' She so wanted to creep away to a darkened room.

'You're needed here.' Henry was firm. 'You've just interviewed the star of the show. That means you're a bit of a star yourself. Ah, here's Eleanora.'

Eleanora swooped down on Laura in a cloud of black sequins, shocking pink bugle beads and marabou. Her earrings bit into Laura's cheek as they kissed. 'Darling, if you're even dreaming of escaping before Dermot's done his signing, forget it. He's having a late supper with Jacob Stone, but right now he's fighting his way through the autograph-hunters. He'll be here in a minute to sign books.'

'I hope some of this vast crowd buy books,' said Henry. 'Trouble is, when there's nothing new—'

'There IS something new,' said Eleanora triumphantly, 'and I can't help thinking that Laura had something to do with it.'

Laura sat down suddenly on Henry's recently vacated chair, her knees weak. She felt hot and cold all at the same time. For a moment she thought Eleanora had guessed. 'I really don't think – I mean – I think he must have been writing obsessively before I . . .' Aware she was in danger of revealing what had gone on after she'd discovered him in Ireland she stopped.

'Oh, darling,' Eleanora would have none of it. 'You're so bloody modest! Take the credit! He's produced nothing for nearly fifteen years. You walk into his life and he's writing again! And you were so professional out there. Now, just for a moment, be happy!'

'But I'm not—'

'You'll never get her to take the credit for anything,' said Henry, producing a glass of wine from behind his table and handing it to Eleanora. 'Best not to pester her.'

Laura was about to protest some more when he handed her a glass of wine too. 'Just sit there and relax. You've had a long day.'

Laura sipped the wine, missing her quiet days at the bookshop and Henry very much. Just lately life had been far too exciting for a bluestocking.

Monica came rushing in. She bent and hugged Laura hard. 'That was so lovely! So tender, so utterly beautiful.' She sniffed. 'I've been crying my eyes out!'

'Why? What?' Laura narrowly missed spilling her wine as she disentangled herself. Surely Monica didn't suspect either? She was in danger of sobbing into her friend's chest.

The thought of everything she and Dermot had shared reduced to a story – albeit a brilliant one – made her want to cry. She knew for the sake of the literary world she should be thankful he'd lost his writer's block, and if she'd helped in any way then she should be proud to have been of service, but right at this moment she could only think of herself and the tragedy of it all and just hope no one thought to ask whom the story was about. She couldn't bear to be exposed to the examination of the world. She would just die of embarrassment if word got out.

People were beginning to come through to buy books now, but no one was looking in her direction as if to say 'poor you'.

And then the great man himself arrived, flanked by admirers and press alike. Their eyes met briefly and Laura saw in his a tender concern that told her everything she felt she needed to know: the story *was* about her. The reason he'd wanted to talk to her in private was so that he could explain it to her and she hadn't let him. He probably knew she was in love with him. She wouldn't have been the first down that particularly rocky road, after all. And with her naivety, it was pretty inevitable, given what they'd shared. He, being basically kind, didn't want her hurt. But her feelings were not returned. She just wished he hadn't put it all into a story and read it out so publicly. He of all people should know the value of privacy. And if he felt that way why had he even joked about a 'shag'? She was so confused.

But she smiled at him, every cell of her body trying to convey that it was all right, she wasn't in love with him, didn't think the story was about her. In fact, she wanted him to know that everything with her was fine

313

and dandy. She was asking a lot from her smile, she was well aware, but she did her best.

Then, making a heroic effort, she moved her way through the crowd until she met him, halfway to his signing table. 'Well done, Dermot!' she said bravely. 'That was fantastic! I hope you don't mind if I go back now. I've got a splitting headache.' The fact that this part was true lent veracity to the rest of it. 'I'll see you tomorrow.'

He looked back up at her, frowning a little as his pen hovered over a book. 'Will I not see you later?'

Laura shrugged. 'Oh yes. When I've got rid of the headache I'll come over. Probably.'

She didn't wait to see if he'd accepted this, she just fought her way out of the room and then the cinema, hoping she'd come across someone who could take her home.

She spotted Reg, the driver who'd brought Dermot to the event. She knocked on the window. 'Any chance of a lift back to Somerby? Dermot will be ages yet. I've got a frightful headache.'

He wound down the window. 'Jump in. I'll have you back in no time.'

So far so good. She'd take aspirin, drink hot milk and go to bed and worry about having to face Dermot, possibly over breakfast, in the morning. She'd cross that bridge when she came to it.

Another note to Monica, apologising for her 'copping out', and Laura climbed the stairs to the mezzanine level and fell into bed. She was genuinely exhausted but it took her a little time to relax enough to sleep. She knew that everyone else involved in the festival was just as exhausted and she was dipping out, leaving them to carry on. It wasn't fair, really. But although she felt guilty, she didn't feel guilty enough to get up again and go over to the main house and help. She had to think how she was going to get through the next twenty-four hours.

Laura awoke full of determination. She would go to breakfast at nine o'clock and face Dermot like a grown woman, not a lovesick teenager. She'd had her night of heartbreak, now she'd face 'Real Life' head on. She would not let anyone, most of all Dermot, see how hurt she was.

She would have liked to have had Monica with her, but as she'd suspected she might, she had a text instead, saying that Monica was staying with Seamus and would be back sometime the following day and that Grant had headed off to his aunt's for the day.

Oh well, thought Laura, trying to find something to be positive about, it means I can spend as long as I like in the shower. She was determined to turn up to breakfast looking fabulous. No one would know she was heartbroken and felt betrayed, least of all Dermot. She would sweep in on the tide of the success of the festival and eat sausages, eggs and bacon with pride! She was seriously tempted to put a fabric rose Monica had left lying about behind her ear.

'Good morning,' she cooed as she opened the kitchen door, sounding worryingly like a primary-school teacher addressing her flock.

She looked quickly round the room and realised Dermot wasn't there. Relief and disappointment raged for a moment and disappointment won. She chided herself. Even now her heart was in danger of ruling her head. She pulled out a chair next to Veronica, who was reading the paper. Veronica lowered the *Daily Telegraph* a little and gave Laura a warm smile over the top of it. Fenella was yawning into a cup of coffee; Reg, the driver, had a piece of fried bread and was cleaning up every scrap of egg yolk with it; and Sarah was writing things down in a notebook. Hugo, next to her, appeared to be composing a sonnet to the piece of sausage on his fork. Eleanora was sipping mint tea with her eyes half closed. Although there were several people in it, the big kitchen felt rather empty.

'Laura!' said Rupert from the Aga, wearing a striped apron and wielding a fish slice. 'What will you have? A bit of everything? A kipper?'

'No kippers, thank you. But I'll have everything except black pudding,' she said. 'Thank you.'

'Black pudding is full of iron you know, darling,' said Eleanora, 'but I'm glad to see you've got an appetite. You look a bit peaky.'

The appetite vanished. Why did Eleanora say that? Why was she surprised, or commenting on her appetite? She must stop being paranoid.

Laura reached for some toast. 'Well, you know how it is, I didn't eat much last night.' She took a breath. 'Dermot not up yet?'

'Oh no!' Eleanora was suddenly bursting with good humour and news. 'I forgot you didn't know. He went off to London last night so he can do breakfast telly today.'

'But I thought he was having a late dinner with Jacob Stone?'

'He did, and then the two of them went off to London in Jacob's helicopter,' said Fenella. 'We've recorded the show,' she went on. 'It was on horribly early. But I think he's doing another couple of shows, isn't he, Aunt – I mean, Eleanora?'

'*Loose Women*,' said Eleanora. 'Excellent programme.'

Laura, feeling bewildered, looked round the table for clarification.

Sarah, who had closed her notebook and was now gathering plates in the corner, helped her out. 'It's a lunchtime show where a group of women discuss current affairs, and gossip.'

'It sounds right up Dermot's street,' said Laura, just as Rupert put a sizzling plate down in front of her. 'Oh, that looks delicious!'

Reg got up, taking his plate with him. 'It was. Now if you don't mind, I've got things to do.'

Now that Reg had left, it seemed that everyone else apart from Laura had had their cooked breakfast and were now just reading the papers, eating toast and drinking coffee.

Everyone was behaving so naturally she didn't need to pretend to be her usual cheery self. And with Dermot out of the county there was no danger of her bumping into him and being forced to see the concern on his face all over again.

Fenella came and sat down next to her. 'So it's just Damien Stubbs's event tonight, and then we've done the big stars. The event is sold out and that man from *The Times* is arriving at lunchtime. Plenty of time for Damien to miss his train and get the next one.'

'You're not very confident of Damien's time-keeping,' said Veronica, having put down the paper. 'It's the trains I worry about, which is why Anne and I came by car. Fortunately we live quite near to each other.'

'What time –?' Fenella stopped, belatedly aware that it wasn't polite to ask when people were leaving.

'In about half an hour,' said Veronica reassuringly. 'The car's packed already and Anne's just taking some photos of your lovely wild garden.'

'We make sure it's tamed in time for the wedding season but it soon grows unruly again. Everyone seems to prefer it that way,' said Fenella.

Vernonica agreed that wild was wonderful.

'Anyone need a lift to the station or anything?' asked Laura. 'No? Then when I've finished this, I'll get upstairs to the office, start sorting out thank-you letters and things.' She turned to Veronica. 'You won't

317

go without telling me? You and Anne have been so brilliant.'

Veronica patted Laura's shoulder as she got up. 'Well, any time you want me – us – again, just say the word. It's been a cracking festival, it really has, well done!'

After Veronica and Anne had been seen off in a throaty roar everyone drifted back to the kitchen.

'It's been really odd, hasn't it?' said Fenella, sliding the kettle on to the hot plate. 'We've spent most of the festival wondering if Dermot was going to turn up. Then he whistled in, did two amazing events, and was helicoptered out again. It's as if he was never here, in a way.'

'Sort of,' said Laura, feeling that in some ways her life would have been easier if he hadn't whistled in.

'But he made the festival such a roaring success. And all down to you, Laura.' She paused. 'You've been such a star, getting Dermot here and everything. Jacob Stone's said to give you a bonus.'

'Oh, you don't need—'

'Then I explained that we couldn't, so he's given you one instead.'

Laura was mortified. 'You mean, after all that, we didn't make a profit?'

'Well, we did,' said Rupert. 'But not a huge one. Jacob emailed me to say he was going to give you two thousand pounds, on top of your fee.'

'That's amazing!' said Laura when she had taken this in. 'That's so kind of him!' She realised she hadn't really given much thought to where her next pay cheque was coming from.

'Dermot told him how much you'd personally done to get him here, before he went to California.'

Laura swallowed, hoping he hadn't done this in too much detail. 'Oh. So Jacob Stone's gone to California?'

'No, Dermot has. A film deal. Eleanora says it may not come off, but apparently lots of people have been interested for ages and he's never entertained the idea before. It's for his first book.'

'Oh, yes. It would make a lovely film. So what's changed? Why is he willing to have it made into a film now?' That was it – she'd never see him again. A part of her wept, even if it was probably for the best.

'It's losing his writer's block, so Eleanora said.' Fenella frowned. 'You did know that, didn't you? It wasn't just the short story, he's writing a novel as well.'

Laura felt sick. 'No I didn't know that. That's brilliant news.' It was but she couldn't help feeling like a discarded shoe. She'd been useful and now she wasn't needed any more. And why hadn't he told her? The fact that he'd hardly had a chance to tell her and that that was mostly her fault was small consolation. Maybe that's what he'd been trying to tell her on the phone. She'd deleted a couple of messages before she'd even read them. She asked herself now if she'd rather have Dermot, writing and happy but away from her, or with her and blocked. At first it seemed like a Faustian pact she was glad she didn't have to make, but the more she thought about it, in the grand scheme of things his happiness seemed more important than her own. That was love for you.

'We were saying – weren't we, Rupert? – that we must have a party with everyone who's been involved in the festival. Once we're not doing back-to-back weddings. We could plan what we're doing for the festival next year.'

Laura laughed, grateful for the diversion. 'How you can even think of another festival? This one isn't over yet.'

The last two events felt a bit anticlimactic to Laura. Everyone was very tired and although the Somerby hospitality flowed as ever, even Fenella was losing her enthusiasm for it a bit. But at last it was just Laura, Rupert and Fenella, back in the kitchen.

'So, have you got any plans?' asked Fenella.

'What? After writing all the thank-you letters, you mean?' Laura managed a cheery laugh. In fact she had no idea what she would do now. She thought she might go and stay with Grant and look for jobs and flats in his area.

'Mm.' Fenella was looking at her rather intensely and Laura felt it must be because she was yearning to have her house to herself again.

'Well, I thought—'

'Can I offer you a job? You can have your converted cow shed for as long as you need it.'

Laura got up and put her arm round Fenella's shoulders. 'You've been brilliant and are so kind, but . . .'

'Books are your thing?'

'Told you,' said Rupert. He was doing the crossword as was his habit.

'I thought it was worth a try,' said Fenella, 'but if you won't work for me, you must ring Eleanora. She said you were to if you seemed jobless and at a loose end. Are you?'

Laura laughed. 'I suppose I am, really.'

'Then she's got an idea.' Fenella said this as if the idea might be on the wackier side of totally insane.

'Oh, hasn't she gone to the States with Dermot?'

Fenella dismissed this idea. 'Oh no, she says she's too old for California. A little light shopping in New York is fine, but Dermot has an American agent as well as an agent for his film rights, so he doesn't need her.' She took a breath. 'Does the thought of ringing her horrify you? You never know with her. Sometimes her ideas are terrific, but sometimes they're just mad. She suggested that Rupes and I went crocodile-hunting for our honeymoon.'

Laura giggled. Bless Fenella, she was going to miss her. 'I'll give her a ring. There's no harm in finding out what she has in mind. And I'll call Grant as soon as I've done that. Finding a flat will be so much easier, thanks to Jacob Stone's bonus.'

'Well, ring Eleanora first,' said Fenella.

'Darling!' said Eleanora, when at last Laura was put through. 'Come to lunch tomorrow. There's someone I want you to meet.'

'Um . . .' This could mean anything from a nearly blind date to a job opportunity. As Fenella had said, Eleanora was capable of anything.

'The Grove, at twelve-thirty. That OK? Trains fit in? Don't try and drive, darling. There's nowhere to park.'

Laura rang Eleanora's office a few minutes after this brief phone call to find the address of the restaurant. Eleanora's advice to Laura not to drive was unnecessary; the thought of a five-hour drive twice in one day made her feel weak. Add lunch with Eleanora and she'd be on her knees.

'You don't know what she's got in mind, do you?' Laura asked Fenella while the three of them huddled down one end of the kitchen table and ate tinned tomato soup with white bread.

'Not a clue,' said Fenella. 'But she was fantastically impressed by all you did with the festival. Maybe she wants you to run another one.'

'Let me get over this one first. I—'

'Hey!' Rupert shouted. 'Look at this! There's a full-page article about us!'

Instantly they were all jostling to read it.

'And it's not just about Dermot!' said Fenella proudly, when she'd read a bit. 'Listen. *Somerby is to festivals as those delightful boutique hotels are to big chains. Add a literary star who seemed to have dropped out of the firmament to the mix and you have something really special.*'

Laura grabbed the paper now. 'We need to buy lots of copies and make a scrapbook. Other papers might have articles too. It'll be so good for next year. We can put extracts in the brochure.' She felt herself brightening despite her heartache.

'I'm so glad there's going to be a next year,' said Rupert, patting Laura's shoulder. 'As long as you run it for us.'

Laura laughed. 'And in the meantime, I've got Eleanora!'

Chapter Twenty-One

Fenella had been firm; Laura was to take a taxi to the restaurant from the station. If it meant she was a little early, well, she could wander round the streets for a bit, as long as she didn't get lost. The restaurant was in Mayfair so the surrounding shops were only for looking in, not actually entering, but Laura did manage to find her way back to the restaurant when she finally decided the time was right – five minutes after the time for which she was invited, to give Eleanora time to arrive.

Except that Eleanora hadn't arrived, although when Laura asked for her at least her name was recognised. She was shown to a table and asked if she wanted anything to drink.

'A glass of white wine and some fizzy water please.' This way she could have an encouraging slug of neat wine, and then turn it into a spritzer if she wanted to.

The restaurant was full of people who seemed to have very little interest in the food. They were talking business to each other at a hundred miles an hour. There were no couples looking into each other's eyes, girlfriends exchanging confidences, or mothers and daughters having meaningful talks. Everyone here was working. Laura enjoyed people-watching, and would have had more fun with it today had she not been anxious about the lunch.

What was Eleanora up to? She'd given Laura what had turned out to be her big break, introducing her to Fenella and Rupert and the Somerby Festival.

Maybe, as Fen had said, this really was another job opportunity.

As she fiddled with her napkin and adjusted her perfectly aligned knife and fork, Laura reflected on all she had learnt since that first meeting. Up until then all her life's learning had been through books, fiction mostly. Since then it had been real life, sometimes painfully real.

She deliberately turned her mind away from Dermot. One day she would look back at her time with him and smile, see it for what it was, a lovely introduction to sex and, for her, love. Now it was an aching wound, poisoned by a growing sense of betrayal. Once her feelings of embarrassment and humiliation had lessened a little, a sense that he hadn't really been mindful of her feelings despite all his 'concern' had gradually built inside her. It didn't make her love him any less or take away the pain but it strengthened her resolve to make every effort she could to get over him, as quickly as mending a broken heart ever could. Having plenty of distractions like lunch today helped.

At last Eleanora appeared with a man probably in his late thirties or early forties in her wake. Laura relaxed. She'd long ago stopped feeling nervous about the actual meeting. She was just worrying about Eleanora not turning up. Now she was here, she relaxed.

'Darling, this is Gerald O'Brien, another Irishman, but don't hold that against him.'

Laura had to smile and allowed the man to take her hand. 'How do you do?' he said formally. 'In England people seem awfully keen on kissing each other when they're introduced, but I'm a bit old-fashioned.' He smiled apologetically and Laura was touched.

For a few seconds she searched for traces of Dermot's voice in Gerald O'Brien's, but she couldn't find any. Of course there were hundreds of accents and variations of accents from Ireland, but part of her had hoped for some connection with the accent uppermost in her mind.

'I am too, I think,' she said, shaking his hand. 'A bit old-fashioned, I mean.'

Eleanora, having kissed Laura, plumped on to her chair with a little puff of air as if she had descended from a height. 'I see you've started on the wine already, good girl. Let's have a bottle. I know drinking at lunchtime has quite gone out with the younger crowd, but I still enjoy a glass or two with my lunch.'

She perused the wine list with concentration. Gerald O'Brien and Laura exchanged shy glances. He was not your stereotypical Irishman, thought Laura. He was quite charming enough but he had none of the easy blarney that seemed to ooze from Dermot. She pushed down the familiar ache.

The ordering didn't take long. Laura had had time to change her mind several times while she was waiting and both Gerald and Eleanora were decisive. The wine came and was poured and Eleanora put her elbows on the table like a woman about to make a statement. Then she caught sight of someone over the other side of the room. 'Oh my God!' she said. 'So sorry – got to table hop although it's frightfully bad manners – but it's Susie Blanquette. And she's with Hubert von Trapp! How dare she? She promised she wouldn't look at another publisher until she'd finished her novel and had something to sell! We were going to have a beauty parade and now it looks as if she'd going with Hubert. Excuse me. Must stop this!'

Laura found herself smiling. Only Eleanora could leave two quite obviously shy people on their own, at their first meeting, before they could even pretend to know each other well enough to make conversation.

She swept off on her mission leaving Gerald and Laura to look anxiously at each other, both determined to make an effort. 'So what do you do, Laura?' asked Gerald.

'Oh, I – um – well, I've just finished helping to run a literary festival,' she said. She still didn't know if Eleanora had set them up for a date, in which case she should think of something to say about herself that would make her sound interesting (but unavailable), or a job, in which case she'd definitely want to appear interested and efficient (and possibly available).

'That sounds interesting.' Gerald's polite but genuine response gave her no clue. 'My wife worked as a volunteer at the Cheltenham Festival once, when she was a student.'

He had a wife, so he wasn't a potential date. This was a relief. She relaxed a bit more.

'It *was* interesting, and quite challenging too, actually. It is amazing how many things you need to be able to do. I had to talk to groups of schoolchildren which, I have to say, is one of the most frightening things I've ever done in my life.'

'I can imagine! In fact, I can't imagine anything more terrifying!'

His horror made Laura laugh and she felt herself relax even further. 'Well, they were supervised and I didn't have to talk for long. Der— a friend had given some hints on how to tackle it and it went quite well. I almost enjoyed doing it at the last school.'

'I still don't want to do it. You must be a natural teacher.'

Laura shook her head. 'Oh no, I've never done any teaching.' She paused. 'Although come to think of it, I sort of did, when I helped someone run a writing course.'

'You are a woman of many parts,' said Gerald gravely, but with enough of a twinkle to tell Laura that he had a sense of humour.

Eleanora swooped back. 'Nipped that in the bud. But honestly! What is the point in having an agent if you don't do what they say?'

326

There was a moment's pause and then Gerald spoke. 'I can promise you, Eleanora, if you were my agent, I'd do exactly what you say.'

'Oh, are you a writer?' asked Laura.

Gerald was horrified. 'God no! The boot's on the other foot! I'm a publisher.'

'Oh.' Laura was spared having to wonder why the thought of being a writer was so ghastly, or to think of a proper reaction by the arrival of the starters.

'Yes and he needs you, Laura dear.' Not even the arrival of a miniature sculpture made from shellfish, seaweed and something bright red put Eleanora off her stride.

Gerald and Laura exchanged appalled glances. 'I don't think—' they began, more or less in unison.

'Yes you do, you just don't know it yet.' Having checked that Gerald's soup and Laura's tian of baby vegetables had arrived, she picked up a mussel. 'Laura has always wanted to be an editor.'

'How do—'

'I met that Grant? Lovely boy. He told me.' She put down her fork. 'I am a bit of a fag hag, I must admit. But I never know if it's because I'm stylish or wear too much make-up!' Eleanora was off on one of her tangents again.

Neither Gerald nor Laura felt able to help her here, so kept silent. 'Anyway,' Eleanora went on, 'that's neither here nor there. I'm determined to put you two together.'

The two in question exchanged glances, aware they lacked the moral fibre to withstand Eleanora once her heart was sent on something. 'I don't think—'

'I don't want . . . The thing is,' Gerald went on more decisively, 'I can't afford to pay a full-time editor and I must have someone in Ireland.'

'And I need full-time work and I don't live in Ireland.' Laura borrowed determination from Gerald with gratitude.

This time the glances they exchanged were almost triumphant.

Eleanora was having none of it. 'Goodness me, how negative you both are! These are tiny details! You're made for one another!'

When the waiter offered to refill her wine glass, Laura accepted gratefully.

Chapter Twenty-Two

Eleanora didn't give up. She told them both how good Laura would be. 'Think about that writing course! You got through those manuscripts, knew what was wrong, how to put it right. You were brilliant. She was, Gerald, Dermot said so.' She sipped her wine. 'I even took on one of the poor dears, though in this market . . .'

'Are you talking about "The" Dermot? Dermot Flynn?' Gerald cut through what could have become a long lecture on 'the State of Publishing Today'. He turned to Laura. 'Did you work with him, then?'

'Yes.' She couldn't think of much else to say on the subject. It was just as well she didn't want the job, she was doing very badly in the interview. Of course, had the job been in England, she would have been much more enthusiastic.

'And her organisational skills are second to none. The festival was fantastic! All down to Laura.'

'And Fenella, and Sarah and Rupert and countless others,' Laura said.

'You got the star to appear.'

'What star?' asked Gerald politely.

'Dermot, of course. She went to Ireland and brought him back, kicking and screaming. Didn't you read about it in the trade press? Quite an amusing little article.'

This was news to Laura and not particularly welcome, but if Gerald hadn't read about it, others might not either. He was now really interested. 'Is he out of contract? He must be, surely, he hasn't produced anything new for ages.'

Eleanora laughed. 'Don't even think about it. Way out of your league. Very, very expensive.'

'But he'd turn my little Irish publishing house into a giant.'

Eleanora shook her head. 'Takes more than one, darling, you know that as well I as I do. You're the publisher, damn it. Talking of Dermot . . .' She turned to Laura, 'He's been calling me, saying you won't return his calls. Do for heaven's sake ring him, there's a dear, he's driving me mad.'

Laura nodded as if in agreement, but although she knew full well that Dermot had been trying to get hold of her there was no way she'd ever return his calls. She had nothing to say to him.

Eleanora glanced round the room again. 'Oh, sorry. Just seen an old friend. Back in a min.,' she said and she was off.

'I knew it was a long shot but I thought I'd try.' Gerald narrowed his eyes. 'Hey, if he's calling you, I don't suppose you could persuade Dermot—'

Laura shook her head sadly. 'No! I assure you I have no influence over him.'

'Then how did you get him to appear at the festival?' Gerald persisted. 'He's famously difficult to budge out of his "little grey home in the West".'

'That was just a one-off,' Laura explained. It was agony for her to talk about him. If she kept it general she could just about cope. 'Just for the festival. And anyway, it's one thing getting someone to pitch up at a literary festival and quite another to persuade them to join a publisher that's far too small for them.' She looked around. 'Where is Eleanora? I can't believe she's really seen an old friend.'

Gerald also turned round. 'She has. She's over there. She seems to know half the room. I think this is where she always has lunch so she's bound to get to know everyone even if she didn't before they came. So tell me really, how did you get Dermot Flynn out of Ireland to come to this festival?'

Laura now realised she might be asked this question again and again; she'd better think of an answer fit to print, or at least say out loud. She smiled to give an impression it was down to serendipity and therefore not really anything to do with her efforts. 'Well, let's just say alcohol was involved.' They needn't know it was on her part more than Dermot's. 'And I didn't bring him between my jaws, like a Labrador, and drop him at Eleanora's feet. She just makes it sound like that.'

He laughed. 'It sounds impressive even if you didn't.' Laura decided he was rather sweet as he leant forward, sounding really interested. 'So, have you really always wanted to be an editor?'

This was one question she could happily answer, with genuine enthusiasm. 'Oh yes.' She sat up straighter. 'That's true. I really have no desire to write anything myself, but I would really enjoy polishing someone else's work so that it really shines. When I worked at the bookshop and used to read as much of the stock as I possibly could, I came across books – self-published ones mainly – that obviously hadn't had much editing. It really showed me how important editing is. I'd think: this bit would be so much better here, or the writer needed to introduce this character or that much earlier. And then, when I was doing it for the writing course, well I loved it. I see editing as like being a master jeweller: you take a wonderful but uncut stone and polish and work on it until it really shines. The original stone is still the main thing, but now everyone can see its beauty.'

Gerald seemed apologetic. 'To think I dismissed you because you didn't live in Ireland! You're just what I need.'

'And to think I dismissed you, just because you did! Although I think to begin with the thought of moving to another country seemed like a big thing, but now – well, I might as well live in Ireland as anywhere else.' A horrible thought made Laura bite her lip anxiously. 'You don't just want me because I know Dermot, do you? If I joined you, would you constantly be badgering me to get Dermot to sign up?'

This time he laughed. 'Indeed no. I was just trying it on with Eleanora. I know my place. But would you really consider it?' He ran through what would roughly be involved: two to three new authors a year, editing, potential to grow. Laura grew more and more excited as he talked. She couldn't help herself. It did sound pretty much like her dream job. Before long Laura *really* wanted to work for Gerald, even if it was in Ireland. After all, Ireland was quite a big place and Dermot would probably spend all his time in the States or somewhere now. But even if he didn't, they could both live there and never meet up. It would be fine. And somehow despite everything she still felt a soft spot for the country she'd lost her virginity in. 'But your office is in Dublin, isn't it?' she asked.

He acknowledged that it was.

'And that's a really expensive place to live?'

He nodded. 'Yes, but you don't have to live in Dublin, as long as you could get there once a week or so. You'd need to meet the authors in the office occasionally.'

Laura considered her carbon footprint for a moment. In theory it would be possible to fly to Dublin once a week and still live in England, but she didn't really want to send half her life in an airport. No, she would take a chance and relocate.

It sounded almost perfect. There was only one thing that was concerning her now. 'But I'd still need full-time work, not just part-time.'

'I'm sure I could make it full-time. I'd need to check my finances but the more I think about it, the more I realise I've needed someone like you for a while. It's time I took on someone full-time.'

She felt flattered. She may have lost her dream man (if she'd ever had him in the first place) but it looked as if she might just be on her way to securing her dream job – or at least the distinct possibility of it. But would she be mad to take it? She had a bit of money: would it tide her over until the work picked up? Moving to Ireland didn't seem as daunting as it might have once done. She was a different person now. But it was still quite an upheaval.

Seeing Laura's doubts, Gerald put his hands on the table in a triumphant gesture. 'I've just had an idea! I don't know why I didn't think of it before. I own a couple of holiday cottages on the west coast—'

'Where on the west coast?' Laura's self-preservation antennae went on red alert. If he said Ballyfitzpatrick she'd say no, however wonderful the deal was.

'Ballymolloy. It's a really beautiful spot. You might not have seen it though. It's not very near where Dermot comes from.'

Suddenly it sounded perfect. She smiled broadly. 'I'd love the chance to see a bit more of Ireland!'

'Well, the thing is, the holiday cottage isn't quite ready for visitors yet. There's still a bit of work going on, decorating and suchlike. If you wouldn't mind being there while it's finished, I'd let you have it rent-free.'

She'd once heard that things that sounded too good to be true usually were. 'That's a very generous offer and it's very tempting, but wouldn't it lull me into a false sense of security? Living rent-free, I'll get to think I can manage on the money.' But she was used to living frugally: maybe she could make it work. It was such a great opportunity. And why not – if it didn't work out she could always come back to England, no lasting harm done.

Gerald was determined to reassure her. 'By the time the building and decorating is finished I'll probably have full-time work for you and I've got friends in the business who might use you too. Editors tend to be freelance in Ireland. It's a much smaller market than in England.'

By now Laura's enthusiasm was pushing aside her natural caution. 'And I could always get a job in a pub, to make a bit of extra.'

Gerald became solemn. 'I don't think I'd like to think of you working in a pub. Tell you what, I'll undertake to get you all the editorial work you need, be it from me or other publishers. Although you might have to do a bit of copy-editing, too – you can handle that.'

'I'd need to go on a course for copy-editing, wouldn't I?'

He nodded. 'Possibly, but you could do it by mail order.'

She laughed. 'Don't you mean by correspondence?'

'As near the same thing as makes no difference.'

Her moment of levity vanished. 'I've just thought of something. If I've been living in your holiday cottage say for . . .'

'Three months.'

'And if I've made any friends, I won't want to uproot myself again. Is there likely to be anywhere to live in Bally— what you said? Or is it just a holiday place?'

'Oh no. It's also full of commuters. Lots of young families live there. It's a great place. It has a real buzz to it.'

'It sounds brilliant!'

'So you'll come?' Gerald seemed eager.

'Well, what's to stop me? And if there's a house thrown in – well.' She smiled reflectively. 'This morning I was about to be jobless and homeless and now both seem to be sorted out, in the best way possible.'

'Oh, good girl,' said Eleanora who Laura now suspected

might have been listening to a good bit of the conversation. 'You're sounding really positive now. Shall we have a bottle of champagne to celebrate? Waiter!'

'I hope it's not all too good to be true,' said Laura to Monica on the phone three weeks later. She'd already thrashed out all the pros and cons with Fenella and Rupert and there seemed to be more of the former than the latter. This was the first time she'd had a chance to run it all past Monica, who'd been on tour. 'The thing is, while I'm living rent-free I can decide if I like it over there, and if I don't, well, I can find something back in England. Now I've done that copy-editing course Eleanora arranged for me, I could get work here, possibly.'

'You have been busy since I've been away.' Monica was impressed. 'When did you do that?'

'Last week. It was only for two days, although they were quite intensive. I feel I've learnt a useful skill. I stayed with Eleanora and I'm surprised I've got any liver left, frankly, the amount we drank. I'd totter in through the door, she'd give me a huge whisky, then I'd fall asleep until suppertime. Then we'd have wine.'

Monica laughed. 'Well, I'm definitely coming with you to check it all out. Seamus is on tour – he's so much more confident these days since that reading. Anyway, if you're going to live in some godforsaken island, bloody miles away, I want to make sure it's not just some hole in the hedge.'

'Mon, this is Ireland we're talking about! You love Ireland!'

Monica's anxiety subsided. 'I know I do, but I'm going to miss you.'

'And I'm going to miss you! And everyone! It is all quite scary for someone like me.'

Now Laura was revealing her nerves Monica felt she could afford to be reassuring. 'Oh, you'll be fine!'

'I know I will when I get there it's just the going part.' She paused, sounding a little plaintive. 'You can come and stay as often as you like.'

'And I will! And we'll drive over there together. But we must have a farewell party before you go.' She paused. 'Have you heard from Dermot?'

Somehow she didn't want to tell Monica about the unanswered calls.

'Of course I haven't. Why would I? I don't even want to hear from him!'

'Sweetie, this is me, Monica, you're talking to. You don't have to pretend.'

'I'm not pretending anything! I don't want to speak to him. I will admit to you that I'm in love with him, but he's not in love with me, he never was. Everything we did was just a wonderful, passing, temporary thing. Speaking to him would only make it worse. I've just got to get over it, and I'll do that better if I don't have any contact with him.'

She'd had a hard time convincing Eleanora that she wasn't to divulge her address or land line or her new mobile number – she'd changed it just in case – or anything to Dermot, especially as he'd already been trying to reach Laura through her. But she had eventually managed it by confiding in her. Eleanora had obviously led an exciting romantic life and the scene in the shop with Bridget was somewhat familiar to her. After that she said, 'Fine. I absolutely understand and I won't say a word.'

And Fen was on board too, although she just thought it was because Laura didn't want to get roped into any more slave labour as far as Dermot was concerned.

Monica was silent for a bit. 'OK. I do see your point. Now, what shall we do for a farewell party?'

'Well, I would really like to do something for Fenella and Rupert. I thought about a picnic. We can have it in

336

the grounds so we're not too far from cover if the weather lets us down. They've got a lovely patch of meadow by a stream. It would be perfect.'

'Oh, I'll help you and Grant will probably, too. There's a shop near me that does brilliant pork pies.'

'And I thought I'd order some sausage rolls and bits and pieces from Sarah's Catering Ladies – the ones that did the food for the festival dinner party. Then we just need some bread, a bit of salad and some strawberries or something.'

'And champagne. I can't wait.'

The weather didn't let them down. A small gathering made their way down from the house carrying rugs, cool bags, chairs, cushions and bottles. Rupert insisted on bringing a mini barbecue down to the water's edge and he and Hugo cooked lamb chops, sausages and steaks. Despite it also being a thank you to Fen and Rupert, they'd insisted on organising most of it themselves. Henry, Laura's old boss from the bookshop, and Eleanora were the only ones allowed steamer chairs, whence they presided over the proceedings and gossiped about the book world, enjoying themselves hugely.

Fenella, Monica, Grant and Laura became a little nostalgic towards the end as they talked about the festival and how much fun they'd had.

'Of course, we've forgotten how much hard work it was,' said Sarah, who was less emotional, 'but I think you should definitely do it again next year, Fen.'

'Only if Laura agrees to come and run it,' insisted Fenella, dipping a strawberry in a bowl of cream and eating it.

'Oh I will!' Laura said, this time with genuine enthusiasm. 'After all, we've learnt so much from doing it this time, it would be nice to use the experience.'

'So what would you do differently?' asked Grant.

Laura lay back and closed her eyes for a few minutes. 'I can't think of anything really.'

'It would be better if the star act hadn't been so elusive,' said Monica, 'but in a way that added to the fun.'

'I thought we weren't supposed to mention the D word,' said Grant.

'No one did, until just now,' said Monica, pushing Grant's elbow and causing him to spill his mug of tea.

'It's all right,' said Laura. 'He is the elephant in the room, after all.'

'Jaysus,' said Monica, putting on her best brogue, 'I've heard you call him a lot of things, but never an elephant before.'

It was a wonderful afternoon and Laura felt sad when it was time to leave, but she was soon off on her own adventure and everyone had promised to keep in touch.

Two weeks after the picnic, Laura and Monica set off from Somerby to Ireland. They were going to travel to Fishguard on the daytime ferry, spend a night in a bed and breakfast on their arrival, and then set off again in the morning. They planned to reach Ballymolloy in the afternoon.

'I'm so glad you're coming with me,' said Laura as they turned out of the drive into the road. They were in Monica's VW Beetle again, Laura having sold her car. She felt it was a sign that she was committed to making her new life in Ireland work and she wouldn't really need one over there. She went on, 'Now it's actually happening, I'm really nervous.' She paused. 'I haven't lived in many places in my life.'

'It's a big step for anyone,' agreed Monica.

'I know! I mean, it's more like emigrating than moving.'

'What do you parents think about it all?' asked Monica after a suitable pause.

'Full of their usual lack of enthusiasm for yet another

of my madcap schemes,' Laura said dryly. 'I do feel a bit guilty about them actually. I meant to go over and visit them but there just wasn't time, what with the course and everything. And Fen and Rupert needed a bit of help with a wedding and after all they've done for me, it seemed the least I could do. I'll come back and see them when I'm settled in and can reassure them a bit. But this suited Gerald best. He's got lots of work waiting for me, apparently.'

'Your parents should be thrilled for you,' said Monica indignantly. 'It's your ideal job.'

'I know. But they don't do "thrilled". And they worry about it being part-time, and freelance, and in another country. All that stuff. It's only natural.' Although she found her parents intensely negative and irritating, Laura was aware a lot of it was caused by genuine concern, and she didn't want others to think badly of them.

'Well, I'm thrilled even if I will miss you.'

'We haven't known each other long, have we? And yet I feel we've been best friends all our lives. I'm going to miss you terribly.'

'It's because we were girls on the razz in Ireland all those months ago. It bonded us. And now we're going to be on the razz in Ireland again!'

Laura laughed gently. 'I wonder whether, if I knew then what I know now, I'd have "razzed" quite so much.' But only a moment's thought told her that despite everything she regretted nothing.

Dermot seemed to fill her every waking thought, even when she was concentrating on something quite different, and knowing that she might never see him again was intensely painful. But less painful, she decided, than seeing him while knowing he would never be hers. And she wouldn't turn the clock back: the pain she was now going through regarding Dermot was worth it. She truly believed she was happier to have known Dermot and be

339

left with possibly a lifetime of heartbreak, than to be living a more contented life without the memories of that mad, ecstatic time.

'It was great,' said Monica, also pensive. 'For both of us. I'm just sorry it hasn't—'

'It's OK. It wasn't destined to "work out".' She chuckled. 'Can you really see me married to a great literary lion like Dermot? Nor can I!'

Monica said something with her head turned away which sounded a bit like, 'I can, actually.'

Laura ignored this.

'You know,' said Monica, sounding tired and not just because they'd been travelling for what felt like hours. 'I always thought those jokes about Irishmen saying, "You can't get there from here" were just jokes! But they're horribly real!'

'We're here now, thanks to Gerald. Our call to him got us back on the right road. It's just a matter of finding the house, which shouldn't be too difficult.'

'I hope to God this house of yours has the electrics done, or I'm checking in to the nearest hotel. And taking you with me.'

The house definitely had had its electrics done, as all the lights were on when they finally found it and pulled up outside. The door opened and Gerald stood there to welcome them.

'Hello! How was your journey? I wanted to be here when you arrived, to make sure everything was all right. Besides, Cara – that's my wife – insisted. Said it was only fair.'

Warmed by his concern, Laura kissed his cheek and introduced Monica. 'She came with me—'

'Just to see she wasn't living in a sheep pen or something,' Monica finished for her with a smile.

'It's not that bad although there are some floors still up and the kitchen's not finished yet,' said Gerald.

340

'Come in while I bring your bags. When you're a bit settled, we'll go out for dinner.'

'Well,' said Monica some hours later, when they were back in the house, 'I think you've fallen on your feet here. And Gerald is sweet! Imagine! Coming all the way from Dublin when he could have just left the key with a neighbour and let you sort yourself out!'

'It was kind.' Laura flicked the switch on the kettle. The kitchen may not have been finished, but it was going to be very well equipped eventually. 'He has another cottage here he wanted to check out, so he didn't come all the way from Dublin just to welcome me.' Still, Laura had been very touched.

'And don't forget he's arranged a little drinks party on Sunday so you can meet some of the neighbours.'

'That certainly is kind. Do you want tea? Or hot chocolate? I'm not sure I want anything now I've boiled the kettle. I think I'll just fall into bed.'

'Mm, me too. It's been a long day. Fun though.'

'Yes,' said Laura. 'A bit of a big day, but definitely fun.'

It was difficult saying goodbye to Monica early on Monday morning – she was flying off to visit Seamus, on tour in Germany – but not as hard as it might have been had Gerald not been so thoughtful. She stood on the doorstep, sensing a hint of autumn in the air, waving her friend off in the taxi. She couldn't help remembering another trip to the airport in a taxi, and she fought back her melancholy with an effort.

But Gerald had made things as easy as possible. Apart from greeting her and Monica, and arranging a party so she could meet her neighbours (which Monica had agreed had been a 'gas'), he had also left her with quite a lot of work. It was this pile of Jiffy bags, lurking in a corner, that stopped Laura slumping into a heap; it was her new

341

job, she had to get on with it. And she wanted to – she felt ready for the challenge. As soon as she'd waved Monica off, she went to the room she and Gerald had designated her study, and had a look at the pile.

Gerald had admitted that he'd been neglecting his slush pile, waiting for her to come. Her first job was to go through everything, decide if there was any merit in any of it, and write a report on anything she liked. Although she'd spent enough time with Eleanora to know that slush piles rarely threw up anything interesting, she couldn't help a slight feeling of excitement as she picked up the first parcel. She had found her scissors and was attacking the staples that held it together when there was a ring at the back door, swiftly followed by a cheery 'Halloo!'

Her heart soared and descended in a sickening way as she hoped, and then stopped hoping, that it was Dermot. She'd told everyone not to tell him where she was after all. She got up from behind the table to meet the first of the builders.

The builders were, they told her, 'snagging'. There were two of them. They were in their thirties and brothers, and were there to go through the long list of little things that hadn't gone right the first time round. There was a radiator to move so a door would close properly, there were skirtings that didn't fit, taps that dripped and generally things that weren't right.

'That Gerald,' said the older brother. 'Stickler for detail.'

'Gerald's fine. It's his wife who's the real obsessive.'

'Quite right too,' said the younger one. 'If only they'd got us in in the first place, they wouldn't have this long snagging list. The first builder went off abroad before the job was finished,' he explained. 'Which is why your man got us in.'

Laura was just about well versed enough in the vernacular to realise that this was a general term, and that the

342

building brothers didn't think that she and Gerald were connected in any way except as employer and employee, landlord and tenant.

'So how long will it take you to get through the snagging list?' she asked.

The brothers exchanged glances and then took on the slightly anxious look that builders will when asked how long anything will take. 'Hard to say,' said one of them. 'We've got the decorating to do when we've done the carpentry and plumbing. Could take a while.'

Laura smiled. 'Well, that's fine with me. As long as you're here, I'm here rent-free. So take your time!'

Another glance was exchanged and then the older one said, 'It's not often you hear that in the building game.'

'Well, obviously,' Laura went on, feeling guilty about Gerald, who'd been so kind to her, 'don't take too much advantage . . .'

'We'd call that "extracting the Michael",' said the younger brother. 'And don't worry, we won't. We'll try not to disturb you too much. Now, would you like a cup of tea? I'll bring it in for you if you've work to do.'

Later Laura emailed various friends with a description of these unusual builders and instantly Fenella came back with one asking if the builders would travel, but then said she was only jealous.

Laura got through the slush pile quite quickly. Lots of it was so far off publishable standard she knew a simple rejection slip would deal with them. Others were better, and on these she wrote a report, but she knew they too would be rejected. In fact there was nothing that sang to her and told her it was the book the world needed next. Gerald's last words to her with regard to the slush pile had been, 'Remember we're looking for an excuse to turn a book down. Taking one on means a lot of work and possibly no return.'

Laura had refrained from asking him why he was a

343

publisher if that was his attitude, because she did understand. Her experience with the writing course had taught her a lot. Manuscripts could be promising, good even, but still a long way from being something the public would want to read. But Laura's bookshop experience, however, told her that lots of the books that did get through this process were still not, in her opinion, actually good.

Gerald had told her to ring him when she'd done the slush pile, so after a couple of days, she did.

'Laura! You're a wonder! I'll have to send Eleanora flowers to thank her for putting us together.' He paused. 'Are you doing anything on Thursday night? Cara and I were thinking of coming down. We can have a look at the house and I can pick up anything you might have to give me.'

'I don't think so, but I have to say, and it's all down to you, I have been invited out for meals several times already. People have been so kind.' She had been dreading feeling lonely at the end of her working day, far away from home and family, but she hadn't had a chance to, and as books had always been her friends, the odd night on her own had been welcome. But somehow, being in Ireland made putting Dermot out of her head harder than ever. She missed him dreadfully. How long did it take to get over a broken heart? At least she was busy, she had a social life and she was surviving.

'You're kind too,' said Gerald. 'And people are curious. They want to have a look at the new arrival in the area.'

After he had put the phone down, having arranged to come up to collect the manuscripts, insisting that she was going to be taken out to dinner by him and his wife, a sudden thought struck Laura. Did all the people who had been so kind to her know about her connection with Dermot? Had Gerald told them, or hinted at something? There had been that mention in the trade press but ordinary people didn't read that, did they? Or was that why they were all being so nice? Then she realised she was being neurotic. No one had mentioned his name to her. Just because he was on her mind every minute of every day, it didn't mean other people were similarly afflicted.

Although she almost craved time alone, she resolutely accepted all invitations. Later on she could decide whom she really wanted to spend time with and whom she didn't, but she was keen not to get a reputation for being unfriendly. Her heart sank a bit when she was asked to join a book group, though. She'd enjoyed running the book group attached to the bookshop, but this might have been because she was usually the one who got to choose the books.

'Oh well,' she said now to Shona, who seemed to be the social engine of the community, 'I'd love to come another time but I'm not sure I'd have time to read the book.'

'Oh God, we don't worry too much about that! At least, I don't. Just come for the crack and the cake and the wine.' She paused. 'Crack is conversation, you know, I wouldn't want you to think . . .'

Laura laughed. 'It's all right, I know that.'

'Then come along. You can keep me company if you haven't read the book. We can ask pertinent questions – or at least you can.' Shona paused again. 'You can tell I'm trying to convince you that we do actually talk about the book, at least for part of the time.'

'I wouldn't like to come if I haven't read it, but what is it?' She didn't like to say she'd read most of the books groups tended to choose. 'I used to work in a bookshop so I've read a lot.'

'That's why we want you to come!' said Shona cheerfully. 'And the book is *The Willows* by—'

Laura's heart had started to race before Shona had

345

got halfway through the title of Dermot's second book. 'I – I have read that,' she managed after a few dry-mouthed seconds. Typical. She was reminded of him at every turn.

'Oh well then, that's grand. You must come. You probably understand all that highbrow stuff. It was Jocasta's choice. She likes all that literary fiction. I prefer a good raunchy read myself.'

Laura didn't know if she wanted to laugh or cry. To hear Dermot's great work described as 'highbrow stuff' was partly satisfying: he might have caused her much heartache, but she did think it was one of the greatest books of the current time and she wanted to defend it. But could she bear to sit and listen while people declared they 'couldn't get through it' and 'felt it was a bit obscure'? She'd never chosen his work for her own book group, it was too special and personal to her. And that had been before she'd met the man and fallen in love with him.

'What night is it you meet?'

'It's the second Wednesday of the month. It's usually the first one, but we missed it. Someone had a fortieth.'

'That's tomorrow, isn't it?'

'It is so. Can you come? You can easily walk from your house, but I'll pick you up so you don't feel lonely when you arrive. I'll be with you just before eight.'

'Did I agree to that?' Laura asked her half-built kitchen a few seconds later. 'No, I didn't think I had.'

But she was glad enough to be going out by the time she had to get ready. Although she loved the book she was now working on, getting it into some sort of order was like herding cats. The main character was wonderful but she kept going off to other places in her head and it was hard to decide if these flights of fancy should just be severely cut or if they valuable insight into the protagonist's mind.

346

Shona was on her doorstep at a quarter to eight. 'Do you mind if I come in and have a look around? I've been dying of curiosity about what your man is doing to these houses.'

Glad she'd thrown all her dirty washing into the bin when she'd got ready, Laura laughed, and obliged.

Chapter Twenty-Three

'These women scare the bejaysus out of me,' said Shona as they walked up the drive to one of the big houses that Laura looked out at every day. They had views of the sea and lots of them were converted to holiday flats. This one was still a big family house. 'They all have degrees, or are going back into education or something.'

'Now you tell me! You made out they were a friendly lot who just drank wine and ate cake.'

'I know. I lied. I thought if I brought you it would give me a bit of credibility, having a clever friend.'

Laura had to laugh.

'Honestly,' Shona went on. 'They only tolerate me because the book group was my idea.'

'I'm sure that's not true.' Laura sounded convincing but she was wondering if she'd made a horrible mistake coming. Her own academic qualifications were fine but she'd always tried to keep her book group open and accessible to everyone. She hated it when people scored academic points over the people who were there because they loved reading.

A slim, elegant woman in a white linen dress opened the door. She had cork wedges on her perfectly groomed feet and her tan, be it fake or genuine, revealed not a single streak. Her hair was blonde, short and beautifully cut. The highlights could have been put in strand by strand. All this perfection was set off by the hall behind her: pale, hardwood floors, inset lighting and one stunning piece of glass at the end of the hall.

'Hello, so glad you could come.' A dazzling smile, with teeth to match, was directed at Laura. Its brilliance dimmed slightly as it moved to Shona. 'Shona, I do hope you've read the book this time. You know we made a rule, three non-reads and you're out. You're on your fifth.'

Shona tossed her head defiantly. 'Who cares? Anyway, it's you lot's fault for choosing such boring bloody books. Reading is a leisure activity not designed to improve the brain.'

'I'm Jocasta,' said the woman, ignoring this denial of a sine qua non as she would have undoubtedly phrased it, and putting a perfectly manicured hand into Laura's.

'I'm Laura. It's very kind of you to let me come.' The hand was cool and Laura was aware that hers was hot and anxious-feeling.

'Well, we are a closed group really, but when Shona explained that you're new to the area—'

'And I said I'd never make cake again,' put in Laura's champion.

'We felt it would be churlish of us not to let you come,' finished Jocasta. Then she studied the woman she'd been so generous to. 'Laura? That's a pretty name.'

'Thank you.'

'I long for something more ordinary – Jocasta is from the classical Greek.'

'So is mine, Laura that is. It means laurels.'

Jocasta laughed. 'Oh. I don't think mine means anything. But do come in. Most of the gang are here.'

They were ushered into more perfect space: cream walls, cream sofas, a cream rug on the blond floor, a massive abstract painting. Surprised, Laura noticed some wooden frames with pictures of children in them on a side table. Were they hers? If so, how did she keep all this so pristine? Maybe they never came in here.

349

Laura was introduced to the half-dozen women already there. They were all well dressed and probably went to the same hairdresser as Jocasta as their hair had that sleek every-three-weeks look. Unlike the one that Laura had run, this book group didn't seem to have the young mums who ran out of the house with baked beans on their clothes, desperate for a bit of adult conversation and having to fight to get it.

She sat down on a sofa next to one of the other women. Some dog hairs on her black trousers, brought with her from Somerby, made her suddenly yearn for it, as if it were home. She wasn't exactly untidy herself, but she felt out of place, like a pigeon in a flock of parakeets, in this elegant, magazine-like setting. She needed a bit of mess to make her truly comfortable.

There was a low glass coffee table in front of them and on it was a pile of books.

'I'm doing some decluttering,' explained Jocasta, handing round glasses with an inch of chilled white wine in the bottom. 'So do help yourselves to anything you'd like. Otherwise they'll go to the charity shop.'

Laura recognised most of the books. Not one of them would she describe as a 'good read'; all of them were a 'virtuous read': the kind of books you could boast of having read at dinner parties.

'I can never get rid of books I've enjoyed,' said one woman, picking over the selection. 'But maybe you didn't enjoy these?'

Jocasta was now handing round olives the size of bantam eggs. 'Of course I keep the serious literature, but this is just light reading.'

Laura heard Shona snort into her wine.

'I could sell the books, of course,' Jocasta was saying now as she swayed her perfect figure on to another sofa that was not only cream, but suede and pristine. 'I spend a fortune on them. I love to support writers.'

'Don't sell them to a second-hand bookshop then,' said Laura, wishing she hadn't opened her mouth before she even started. 'The authors don't make a penny and it's their intellectual property.'

'Oh.' Everyone was staring at her. She really did not want to get into a discussion about how authors were paid. 'So if you've excess books,' Laura said, 'you should give them to a hospital or something.'

'Or a charity shop?' asked one woman.

'Or that.' Laura had a feeling this wasn't the perfect solution for writers either, but she couldn't remember all the arguments that had been dinned into her by an author once when she worked at the bookshop.

There was some low-voiced chat and the books were picked over and some claimed. Eventually Jocasta took charge. 'Can I call us to order? Has everyone got a drink?'

'I'd quite like a top-up,' said Shona boldly.

'And me,' said a couple of the other women. 'We all walked here, so we don't have to worry about drinking and driving.'

You could tell, thought Laura, that Jocasta only poured very small amounts into the glasses not because she was mean, but because that was how you should pour wine.

'OK, we've all got drinks,' Jocasta expressed her dis-approval very subtly. 'Who would like to go first?' She looked round the room. 'Well, shall I? Because I chose the book?'

'Why not?' said one of the women.

Laura began to feel even more tense. Supposing they didn't like Dermot's book? It felt utterly personal to her, and she thought it would have done even if she hadn't met him – let alone all the other stuff that had gone on between them.

'OK, well, I chose it because I'd read an article about

351

the writer in the paper. And of course I read it to the end,' said Jocasta, 'because I'm one of those people who, if I start a book, have to finish it.'

'Did you not like it, then?' asked Shona. 'Because if you didn't, for once, I have to agree with you—'

'Shona?' Jocasta was disappointed more than annoyed. 'I shouldn't have to remind you. We wait until one person has finished speaking before we move on to the next.' Laura was reminded of Bill Edwards and smiled to herself.

'Sorry,' said Shona, feigning meekness.

Jocasta gave her an irritated look. She had a copy of the book in her hand and was looking at it, as if it could help her express herself. 'I thought this book was wonderfully lyrical. The characters were marvellous. The descriptions of the scenery were superb.'

Although Laura should have loved hearing Dermot's work praised like this there was something about Jocasta's enthusiasm that seemed a little forced. Jocasta looked at the woman on her left and said, 'Your turn, Fionnuala.'

Fionnula's opinions echoed Jocasta's fairly closely. She praised the writing, the characters, the scenery. It seemed to Laura that they had all missed the point; they were admiring the book from a distance, they weren't getting into it, living it and, alas, loving it. Was it their fault, or was it the book's? Laura yearned to bang the glass coffee table and demand, 'But did you like it?'

Maybe Shona was telepathic because while she didn't bang the table, she did ask the question.

'Oh of course! I loved it!' said Jocasta. 'After all it's one of Ireland's most important books – from recently, anyway.'

'Not that recent,' objected Shona. 'It seemed to me to be set in the Dark Ages, although I didn't finish it.'

'You never finish the books, Shona!' It was not only

Jocasta complaining now. 'You should have more intellectual rigour.'

'I'd rather have a life,' she said, unrepentant.

'Well,' said Jocasta, 'perhaps we can hear from Laura now? Any questions you'd like to ask? We find having someone with us who hasn't read the book can promote some interesting discussion – except Shona, of course, who's never read it!'

Shona laughed good-naturedly, immune to Jocasta's reprimands. 'I did read quite a lot of this one. I might even finish it now,' she said.

'So, Laura?'

Laura was overcome with a desire to rush out of that beautiful room and jump in the mud and then come back in and roll on the rug. Fortunately before the urge overwhelmed her completely, the 'Minute Waltz' tinkled out of someone's handbag, growing louder as the owner of the phone hunted around. While Fionnuala apologised and moved away from the group, Laura decided if she went to the loo, they'd have forgotten all about her by the time she came back.

She was directed to a downstairs cloakroom of such grandeur it made her wonder what the family bathroom or Jocasta's en suite would be like. She confirmed there were children in the house because there were gold imprints of two little sets of hands and feet, mounted and framed, decorating the walls.

As she washed her hands in the glass basin, inevitably splashing the glass tiles, she speculated that no non-organic product would ever pass Jocasta's children's lips and that Jocasta's bedside table would perfectly reflect those one read about in feminist literary magazines. There the celebrities only seemed to have fresh flowers, incense and a couple of literary novels, one of them in French, by their beds. Not for them the radio, the clock, the pile of half-read tomes, the face cream and the dusty bottle of water.

She patted her hands dry on the back of the towel, so as not to mar the perfection of the room, which in real terms was a downstairs loo, but in Jocasta's was another opportunity to reveal her perfect taste. Laura was ashamed to realise that had Jocasta raved about Dermot's work with a proper amount of passion, she wouldn't have been having these bitchy thoughts, she'd have been admiring her taste and her perfect minimalist style.

She went back into the room, hoping that Jocasta had forgotten about giving her time to ask questions about a book she knew almost by heart. Perhaps by now they'd be talking about childcare, builders and bonuses. Laura knew nothing about any of these subjects, but she didn't care about them either so she didn't need to be anxious. But they were still on the book and Shona was getting the third degree.

'What do you mean you don't understand why the father was so angry?' one of the women was demanding. 'It's an Oedipal thing. Oedipus made love to his mother and murdered his father! It's blindingly obvious!'

'You spotted that too?' Jocasta seemed delighted to find a fellow intellectual. 'I thought I was the only one. The author was drawing an exact parallel to the Oedipus myth!'

'But that's disgusting!' said Shona. 'I don't want to read books with things like that in them!'

'It's not in the book in actuality,' explained Jocasta kindly. 'It's symbolic! It's what's behind the author's thinking when he put that bit in.' Seeing Laura return to the room she said, 'I do think you should give this book a try if you have a moment. You might find what we've all had to say about it quite illuminating.' She paused. 'It's a bit of a meaty read so take it on holiday with you, when you've got a bit more time and can really concentrate.'

She meant well, Laura could see that, but she was cross with Jocasta and the others, not only for not enthusing about her favourite book, but for patronising Shona. 'Oh I have read it, years ago. And I must say I think it highly unlikely that Dermot – the writer, I mean – had even heard of Oedipus when he wrote it.'

'How can you possibly say that?' Jocasta exchanged glances with the woman who'd made the reference. They didn't want their insight questioned by Laura who was not only new to the group, but English to boot.

'Well, I can't say for definite, but he was in his early twenties when he wrote it, he hadn't been to university and came from quite an intellectual backwater. When you meet him—' She didn't know if she'd intended to reveal that she knew Dermot, to discommode Jocasta and her scary friends, or if it was an accident, but whatever, she was stuck with the result. Unless maybe she hadn't actually said that out loud? She crossed her fingers and prayed.

But she had said it out loud. Everyone started plying her with questions.

'You've met him? Do you actually know him? What's he like? He was so gorgeous as a young man, God, I'd have slept with him no matter how boring his books were.' The comments came flying at her and she took the opportunity to think up what to say when everyone fell silent, which eventually they did.

'I do know him, a bit. He attended a literary festival I helped to organise.' Talking about him made her miss him even more.

'He can't have done,' said Jocasta knowledgeably. 'He never goes out of Ireland. It's a well-known fact.'

'But he did,' said Laura.

Jocasta shook her head. 'I think you must have been mistaken. We know our Irish writers in this group and—

'Actually,' spoke up one of the women. 'There's been

355

a bit about him in the papers recently. One of them mentioned a festival. Didn't you see that one, Jocasta?'

Jocasta's eyelashes fluttered while she hunted for a reason why she hadn't been completely on top of all the Sunday papers.

'Jocasta! We usually rely on you to tell us all that's going on,' said one of the women who lived near enough to walk.

'It must have been the week when Rickie had a green fit,' Jocasta said, 'and wouldn't let us buy any Sunday papers. Trust him to make me miss out on such important news.'

'Not important, really,' said Shona. 'It's just celebrity gossip. You wouldn't mind missing out on that, would you?'

'This is literary gossip!' said Jocasta. 'It's different! It does matter!'

'It did matter to the literary festival,' said Laura, chuckling a little. 'And he did come and it caused quite a sensation in the literary world. I think he's still in America, talking about film rights.' She didn't know for sure. Eleanora had been rather vague.

'Well, I know you're wrong there,' went on Jocasta, on firmer territory now. 'There was a big feature some time ago when he said he'd never let his books be filmed. And he hasn't written anything new for years and years.' She paused. 'I looked him up on Wikipedia.'

'Not a terribly reliable source, if I may say so,' said one of the other women.

'Tell you what,' said Shona, possibly taking pity on Jocasta. 'I think it's time for a socking great bit of chocolate cake!'

Jocasta wasn't grateful. She broke into the general agreement with, 'Sorry, we don't do sugar and fat in lethal combinations in this house, although we know Shona's cake is to die for.' She smiled in a way that almost earned her a slap. 'But I have made some flapjacks with millet and just a little organic honey.'

'How do you know it's organic honey?' demanded Shona, who felt slighted in so many ways. 'Do they tell the bees not to go near flowers that have pesticides on them?'

'I don't know,' snapped Jocasta, getting up. 'I just buy it. OK!'

While she was gone the other women gathered round Laura. 'So what about the real Dermot Flynn, then? Is he anything like as wild as they all say he is?'

Laura realised it would be so much easier if she could say, 'Tell you what, girls, he was a ride!' Being unable to admit she'd slept with him – for all sorts of reasons – and tell them what a fantastic lover he'd been, she just said, 'Well, he has a great sense of humour.'

Laura didn't like being the centre of attention and cursed herself several times over for not keeping her mouth shut. And she went on being unable to keep it shut, too.

'The thing about Dermot's books,' she heard herself saying, 'is the passion. Never mind the symbolism, the beautiful writing, the prose, just think of the young man's journey. Do you want to go with him, or not? If you don't, toss the book aside and read something else.'

'I couldn't do that,' said Jocasta, who'd come back into the room with a tray of herbal teas and a cafetiere of coffee for those rash enough to ingest caffeine so near to bedtime. 'If I start a book I have to finish it. I feel it's my duty.'

'Me, I'm with Laura,' said Shona, happy to be able to associate herself with the one who knew Dermot Flynn personally. 'If I don't like a book I just read another one.'

No one else confessed to sharing this cavalier attitude to books and the subject moved on.

'So,' said Jocasta a bit later, 'do you think you could get Dermot to come and talk to us, as a group?'

'No,' Laura said bluntly. 'I'm not in touch with him any more and even if I were, that is the last thing I'd ask him to do.'

'But you could get in touch with him, via his publisher,' Jocasta persisted. 'And if you got him to go to England, you could surely get him to come a few miles up here.'

'No! He'd hate it!'

'How do you know? How well do you know him?'

She didn't really know he'd hate it. He might absolutely love being idolised by all these yummy mummies, but however much he'd love it, she wasn't going to track him down and invite him. 'Not all that well.'

'So! And he can't be that precious if you got him to attend a literary festival in England!'

There was just a hint in Jocasta's voice implying that if Laura, not a formidable opponent, had got Dermot to attend the festival, Dermot must be the sort of genial guy who'd go to a book-group meeting for the promise of a glass of wine and an organic canapé.

Laura was fairly used to this reaction by now. 'He had his own reasons for attending the festival. I can't tell you what they are' – well, she could have done but she wasn't going to – 'he's a law unto himself.'

'Still,' said Shona. 'You must be proud of yourself for doing that. It's still a great feather in your cap. And knowing him personally – it'll make you a great dinner-party favourite in these parts.'

Although it was sweet of Shona to credit her so, the thought of being a dinner-party favourite made her shiver. She got up. 'I think I'd better be going. No, you don't need to come with me, Shona, I know my way home and it's not dark or anything.'

Jocasta rose to her feet to show her out. 'I have to say, Laura, I think you're going to be a real asset to our book group. And not only that – I'm having a few friends round next week. Nothing formal, just a bite to eat and some good conversation. I'd be thrilled if you could join us.'

'When's that?'

'Next Friday?'

'Oh, that's a shame! I've arranged to go back to England to visit my parents for a long weekend. I didn't get a chance to say goodbye properly when I left, and they're anxious to know how I'm settling in.'

The thing about lying, she'd learnt, mostly from reading fiction, is to keep it as close to the truth as you possibly could. When she'd got home she went straight on to the Internet to look up flights. Then she telephoned her parents.

Laura wished she felt more enthusiastic about this visit. She loved her parents, of course she did, but she was aware she seemed like a cuckoo to them, a small, undemanding cuckoo, but still not really one of their own.

They had arranged to meet her at the airport and were there when she came through the gate, looking out for her in their matching his-and-her beige anoraks.

'Oh, it's so kind of you to come and get me!' she said, feeling a rush of love and hugging first her mother, and then her father, who patted her awkwardly.

'There's no sense in wasting money on taxis,' he said, taking her bag. 'Have you only got this?'

'Mm. I didn't want to check anything in. To save time.'

'Well, come along,' said her mother. 'We don't want our parking ticket to run out.'

As she went with her parents to the car park she realised how deflated they always made her feel. If anyone else had collected her, Monica, or Grant, say, they'd have been plying her with questions about her new life, full of enthusiasm for her great adventure, or saying how much they missed her. But no, her mother was more concerned about overstaying her time in the car park.

Always she hoped that this time it would be different, and always it was the same. However, she was pleased to be seeing them again; it saved her having to talk about Dermot to people who were only interested in her because of her tenuous connection with him. Not that it had been tenuous, but at this remove, the whole Dermot thing felt like a dream, or as if it had happened to someone else and hurt just a little bit less.

'Oh, you've changed that flowerbed!' she said as they walked up the path to the house. 'Didn't it used to have roses in it?'

'Yes, but they kept catching your father's clothes as he went through to the garage, so I put lavender there instead.'

'How lovely! You must smell it as you brush past,' Laura said.

Her father turned to her as he put the front-door key in the lock. 'Can't say I've noticed.'

Laura followed her parents into the house, trying to fight the feeling of depression she always felt when she visited them.

'I think I must have grown!' she said brightly. 'Everything seems to be smaller!'

'I don't think so, dear. Everything's the same as it was. Once you've got the house how you like it, there seems no point in changing it.' She put the kettle on. 'Would you like tea? Or shall I open the bottle of wine I bought?'

A glance at the kitchen clock told her that at Somerby the wine would have been opened at least half an hour ago. She felt horribly disloyal. These were her parents, this was the home she'd grown up in, and she was comparing it unfavourably with what was virtually a stately home. She knew that children did sometimes change when they left home and went to university, but she hated herself for doing it. On the other hand, as she warmed the pot, making tea for her parents, she wondered, if she had changed, really, or if she just had never fitted in.

'So what have you been up to, Mum?' she said, finding knives and forks so she could set the table.

'Nothing much, dear. We lead quiet lives really. You know that.'

While she put three table mats on the kitchen table she waited for her mother to ask her what she'd been up to, in return. But she didn't. Laura fetched the cruet from the sideboard in silence. Surely her mother must be a bit curious about Laura's new life? Apparently not.

'Can you call your father? It's ready and there's a television programme I want to watch later. Have you got a television now?'

At last, some expression of interest! 'Um, yes. There is one in the house I'm staying in.' She waited for a question about the house. None came. 'And I can get English channels too, but I don't watch it much. I'm not in the habit of it. Besides, I've been really busy since I moved to Ireland.'

'I never miss an edition of *Midsomer Murders* if I can help it. Oh and I like that one with the two gardening women as well.'

'I'll go and get Dad,' said Laura.

Her father was a bit more interested in her life than her mother. 'So, are you going to manage on the money?'

'Oh yes, I think so. Of course being freelance isn't as secure as having a salary—' It was out before she could stop herself. Her father pounced on it.

'Then why did you take it on? Why did you want to go to Ireland anyway?' His jaw went from side to

361

side as he chewed, adding emphasis to his disapproving tone.

Hoping (unrealistically she knew) that it was just that: her father didn't like the idea of her being so far away, she ploughed valiantly on: 'Jobs like that are quite hard to get into. In England you have to work your way up. After the literary festival, and I told you how successful that was—'

'But it didn't pay very well, did it?' persisted her father.

For some reason she didn't quite understand she hadn't told her parents about her bonus. 'I didn't do it for the money, I did it because I love working with books and writers.' Why couldn't her father ever just be happy that she was doing what she enjoyed? Why did he always have to bring money into it? It wasn't as if she ever asked them for a loan or anything. 'Anyway, I met this woman who put me in touch with my new job.' She felt too deflated to tell them about Gerald in detail.

'But why go off to Ireland?' insisted her father. 'There are plenty of jobs here.'

'But this is an opportunity to do what I've always wanted to do! Ever since I left university, I've wanted it. I'm a copy editor, and editor – a permanent one if that's the way the work goes.'

'In my day, sorry if that makes me sound like an old codger' – he didn't sound at all apologetic – 'we didn't do "what we'd always wanted". We did what would put food on the table and pay the mortgage.'

Laura sighed and put her hand on his where it lay on his rolled-up table napkin. 'I know, Dad, and I'm really grateful that you did all that so you could keep Mum and me, but I haven't got to keep anyone else except myself.'

'Forgive me for saying this, Laura,' he went on, removing his hand, 'but it strikes me that young people nowadays are all me, me, me.'

Defeated, Laura turned her attention to the shepherd's pie, which was delicious.

'I've got pineapple upside-down cake for pudding,' said her mother. 'I know that's your favourite.'

It had been her favourite when she was nine years old but she'd never felt able to tell her mother her tastes had changed.

After she and her mother had washed up, which didn't take long as her mother was a very tidy cook, they spent the evening watching television. There was a documentary on about world poverty and the arms trade. Tears she hadn't allowed herself to indulge in for a while slid silently down Laura's face. Everything came back to her in a rush. Dermot; her overwhelming love for him, not returned . . . She could hardly bear it.

'I'll just watch the news and then I'll make us all a cup of tea before bedtime,' said her father.

'Oh, we never opened that wine,' said her mother.

'Never mind. Tea's fine.'

No wonder I spent all my time reading, thought Laura when she was back in her old room.

All her old childhood favourites were there, marking the progress of her growing up. There were the pony books that she adored until she moved on to Georgette Heyer in her early teens. Then there was her D. H. Lawrence phase, Iris Murdoch, Edna O'Brien, and then Dermot's two slim volumes. She'd bought these second-hand and loved them. When she went to university she found she could study them and bought new copies. It was these copies that she had taken with when she left home. She sighed, wondering how her life would have turned out if she'd never read his books. She laughed forgivingly at her old self, and congratulated her new one. She'd come a long way!

Now, she burrowed in her bag for the book that

363

Veronica had signed for her at the festival. She'd been saving it for emergencies: a time when only a really good page-turning, romantic read would do. This definitely qualified as an emergency.

Chapter Twenty-Four

The Saturday morning routines were not altered because Laura was there. The three of them went shopping, and then went to a café for lunch. Here they each had a bowl of soup, a bread roll and a sandwich. Then Laura's father had steamed pudding with custard and her mother had a small portion of vanilla ice cream. Feeling terribly rebellious, Laura had a cappuccino.

'I never could get on with coffee,' said her mother, seeing Laura stir in some sugar. 'It gives me a headache.'

'It does make me a bit buzzy sometimes,' said Laura, 'but I thought it would make a change.'

'From what?' asked her mother, puzzled.

'I don't know really,' Laura said apologetically. 'Shall we get out the paper and start on the crossword?'

'Not till we're home,' said her father. 'I don't like the paper to get all creased.'

'Besides, it rude to read at the table,' said her mother.

Laura's flight was for Monday morning but she was seriously considering changing it to Sunday, to end the agony a bit sooner. But what reason could she possibly give?

On Sunday night she and her mother had just joined her father in the sitting room, having washed up the supper things, when there was a banging on the front door. Laura was calculating that there were over twelve hours until it was time for her to leave. She was really looking forward to the number being in single figures.

'Oh my goodness, who can that be, at this time of night?' said her mother.

'I'll go,' said Laura. 'I'm on my feet.'

'Keep the chain on,' ordered her father, getting up. 'I can't imagine who'd be knocking so loudly. If they were a neighbour, they'd just ring the bell.'

Laura, feeling she'd welcome in an army of Jehovah's Witnesses just to relieve the monotony, went into the hall, unlocked the door, leaving the chain on, as instructed, and opened it.

'Hello?' she said tentatively. 'Can I help you?'

'Is that Laura? Jesus-Kerrist-on-a-jet-ski! Am I glad to see you! I've been over half the world trying to track you down!'

Sure she was about to faint, Laura fiddled with the door chain but her sweating fingers skidded over the fitting.

'Who is it?' demanded her father, coming up behind her. 'Who are you letting into the house?'

'It's me, Dermot, you silly—'

Just then, Laura got the door open. Dermot was on the doorstep wearing his old leather jacket, a pair of filthy jeans and three days' worth of stubble.

Laura's father acted quickly and had the door shut again in seconds.

There was a roar from outside and then more banging.

'Dad, it's Dermot! He's – well, he's a friend of mine.'

'I demand to see Laura!' came Dermot's voice. 'Or I'll break the door down.'

'Better let him in, Dad. Think of the neighbours!' Laura hoped this old mantra would work as it always had before.

'Shall I call the police?' said Laura's mother, who had joined them.

'Good idea,' said her father. 'I think the man must be drunk.'

366

'I don't think so, Dad.'

'I've never dialled nine, nine, nine before,' said her mother. 'I'm not sure how it works.'

'You don't need to dial it!' insisted Laura, wrestling with her father for control of the door. 'He's not a burglar! He's someone I know!'

'He's not coming into my house!' said her father. 'Making all that noise.'

'Mum, you don't want the police round. The neighbours! What would they think? Or say?' Laura had been threatened with the wrath of the neighbours all her life. Why weren't her parents thinking about them now, when it would be quite useful?

'I'm not letting him in. He sounds quite mad to me,' said her father. 'And Irish!'

'That's racist!' said Laura, fighting harder now and getting her fingers on the door chain long enough to pull it back.

'I am Irish, and I am mad,' said Dermot unhelpfully, grinning at them and certainly looking the part. 'But I'm not drunk and I undertake not to break the furniture.'

A neighbouring front door was heard to open. Laura hissed at her mother, 'People will wonder what on earth's going on! Let him in!' As she said that, she got the door open and took hold of Dermot's sleeve. 'Get in, quickly!'

'Have you any fierce chihuahuas in there?' he asked, obviously relishing the situation.

'No!' Laura pulled him in. 'They're Dobermanns!' She shut the door and leant on it, panting for a few seconds, and then regarded her parents and Dermot, who were all looking at her. She swallowed. 'Mum, Dad, this is Dermot Flynn, the one who came to the literary festival I organised.'

Her parents stared at Dermot warily.

'Maybe we should go through to the sitting room? I'll put the kettle on,' Laura persisted, convinced that the narrow hallway was not the best place to be in the circumstances.

'How do you do, Laura's mother.' He took her hand. 'Laura's father. I'm Dermot Flynn and I've been trying to trace your daughter for some time.'

'They're Mr and Mrs Horsley,' said Laura, beginning to see the funny side but trying to hide it with irritation. 'Now do go and sit down, everyone. I'll make tea.' Her heart sang at the sight of him, even if she didn't want him to see just how pleased she was to see him. He had a lot of explaining to do.

'No!' her mother squeaked, suddenly aware she and her husband would be left with this terrifying Irishman if Laura made tea. 'I'll do it!'

'Now listen,' said her father, bracing up to Dermot and seeming to Laura suddenly very old and frail. 'I don't know—'

'I'm sure he'll explain in a minute,' said Laura, suddenly protective of her parents to whom Dermot must seem like a creature from another universe. 'If we all just sit down where it's comfortable, we can talk.'

Feeling like a corgi nipping at the heels of beasts much larger, she chivvied her father and Dermot into the sitting room and her mother into the kitchen. She virtually pushed the men into chairs and switched off the television.

'Well, Dermot,' she said into the silence, frightened that she might laugh, 'fancy meeting you here.'

'To be honest, Laura, and hoping I'm not being rude –' he glanced at Laura's father, who was looking very wary and ready to spring up at any moment, should Dermot look like doing anything unexpected ' – but I'd have preferred to meet you somewhere else.'

'Oh?' She would too, obviously, but couldn't say so.

'Yes, I've had the devil of a job finding you.'

'So, how do you two know each other?' her father asked.

'The literary festival. I did tell you,' said Laura.

'I was one of the writers,' said Dermot.

'The star writer,' said Laura, to punish him a little.

'I've never heard of you!'

'You never read novels, Dad. But he was one of my set texts at university.'

'Was I?' Dermot was very amused. 'Did you ever tell me that?'

Laura winced. That sounded so intimate – it made Dermot seem more than just a writer she'd met. She was always meeting writers when she worked at the bookshop. With luck her parents wouldn't notice.

'So why were you banging on our door in the middle of the night?' demanded her father.

'It's only half past nine,' put in Laura. Although she wanted to kill Dermot for about a hundred good reasons, she was really very pleased to see him. He had at least put a stop to the boredom.

'I was looking for Laura. I've been looking for ages – ever since I came back from America – but no one would tell me where she was. And she wouldn't return any of my calls.' He looked pointedly at her. She shrugged.

'Why do you want her?' asked her father.

'Who told you I was here?' asked Laura, suddenly intensely curious. 'No one I know knows I'm here.'

A glance at her father, and Dermot decided to ignore his question. 'I eventually tracked down Grant.'

'Grant?' said her father. 'That chap you used to work with?'

Dermot nodded. 'It's a long and complicated story. Eleanora – my agent – wouldn't tell me where she was.'

'I told her not to,' said Laura.

'Nor would Fenella and Rupert.'

'Who are all these people?' demanded her father, as if trying to pick up the plot of a long-running soap opera.

'Friends of mine,' said Laura. 'Oh good, here's Mum with the tea.'

Mrs Horsley had got out the best cups and saucers. Pouring and distributing tea took an inexorably long time, but it did mean her mother had accepted Dermot as a guest, thought Laura, which was a start. She'd have to hope her father thawed soon or they'd be in for a very tricky evening.

'So how did you get on to Grant?' Laura was touched by her friends' efforts to obey her entreaties not to give away her whereabouts, even if a part of her had secretly wished one of them might have disobeyed her.

'Via Monica's website,' said Dermot. 'She said she was sworn to secrecy but she didn't think that Grant was, and so gave me his email address.'

'Oh.' Good for Monica! She knew when a woman was lying to herself and her friends.

'Sadly for me, his email was down for a couple of days. He said he had been told not to tell me anything but that he thought I had a right to know. So he gave me your address.'

'It's all very complicated,' said Mrs Horsley, nibbling a ginger nut to aid her concentration.

'So I went there,' Dermot continued.

'Where?' asked Mr Horsley.

'To where Laura lives in Ireland.'

Some hint of what might have happened, given what had gone on earlier, occurred to Laura. She blushed retrospectively. But joy at the enormous trouble Dermot had gone to find her was starting to warm her heart like sun on the first spring day.

'I was banging on your door,' he went on, 'although to be honest, I could tell there was nobody in.'

Laura was sweating now.

'Eventually a girl came up to me and asked what I was up to. She recognised me and went mad. Flung herself at me and said, "Oh my God! We didn't believe her when she said she knew you, but she does! Fantastic!" Stuff like that.' He frowned slightly at Laura. 'I didn't realise you'd be proud enough to know me that you'd tell your new friends about it.'

'It was forced out of me,' Laura explained. 'It was at a book group. They were reading *The Willows*. They said you'd put in the Oedipal bit consciously. I said you didn't. I did not say I knew you well!'

Only Laura saw the laughing message in his eyes, referring to just how well they did know each other. 'Thank goodness for that.'

'So what else did Shona say?'

'She asked if I'd go and talk to her book group and I said hell would freeze over first.' He paused. 'Unless, of course, you'd like me to? I didn't know it was your book group too, at the time.'

Laura thought she might cry. It wasn't a declaration of love but it was a very, very kind thing to say. She shook her head.

'Anyway, after a bit more banter, I asked her if she knew where you were. She said you'd told a friend of hers that you were going to visit your parents in England.'

'So you'd left your address with your friend in Ireland?' suggested Mrs Horsley. 'How sensible.' She regarded her daughter as if surprised she had shown so much intelligence.

'No,' said Laura. 'I didn't.'

'I got back to Grant. Fortunately I had his mobile number by then.'

'He's only been here once. He's usually hopeless about remembering addresses,' Laura said.

'He remembered the name of the town,' Dermot explained. He looked at Laura's father. 'Thank God you're not ex-directory.'

'Hmm. Well, you never know when someone might

need to get in touch with you,' said Mr Horsley, as if he had foreseen this very occasion.

'So here I am. If the flights had been a bit more frequent, I'd have been here sooner.'

The clock on the mantelpiece struck ten.

'Where are you staying?' asked Mrs Horsley.

Dermot looked at Laura. 'To be frank with you, I only had one thought in my head, and that was to find Laura. I didn't think about booking anywhere to stay.'

'There are no hotels in town,' said Mr Horsley.

'It's too late to book in at a bed and breakfast,' said Mrs Horsley. 'Although I suppose I could ask Sheila if she's got vacancies, but I don't really like—'

'Couldn't he stay here?' asked Laura, fighting to keep the edge of hysteria out of her voice.

'No. The spare room is full of your stuff, Laura,' said her mother reprovingly, the silent subtext being: if you'd wanted your friend to stay you should have done something about it.

Her father said, 'We took it all out of the loft when we had the extra insulation put in.'

'Oh, for goodness' sake! He can have my bed!' said Laura. 'I'll sleep on the sofa.'

'No,' said Dermot firmly, 'I'll sleep on the sofa.'

Laura's parents exchanged worried glances. What had happened to their safe, familiar Sunday evening? Their daughter, who'd never been much trouble, even if she had been difficult about her studies, had inflicted this wild Irishman on them. What was the best way to react?

'Is there really nowhere he could stay in town?' Mrs Horsley asked her husband.

'No, dear.'

'Mum! It'll be all right.' Laura tried to be patient. She did understand her parents' anxieties. 'Really it will. It's only for one night.'

'I'll be quite happy on the sofa,' said Dermot. 'I've slept on plenty of them in my time.'

'No, you must have Laura's bed. We can't put a guest on the sofa. I'll go and find some clean sheets.'

'Really, Mrs Horsley.' Dermot was firm. 'There's no need to change the sheets just for one night. It's not worth all that washing.'

'I've only slept in them two nights,' Laura pointed out. 'They'll be fine for him.'

'Really—' her mother protested.

'Really,' Dermot repeated. 'They'll be fine.'

'Shall I make some more tea?' said Laura, feeling the argument about where Dermot should sleep and the sheets could go on all night if some kind of full stop wasn't put to it. Tea was the ultimate full stop, she felt.

'And maybe you would like some sandwiches?' asked her mother, making Laura send a wave of gratitude towards her. She wouldn't feel so grateful to Dermot if he accepted them, however. She didn't know why he'd really come to find her and she just wanted the evening to end. Perhaps everything would seem clearer in the morning.

'No thank you, Mrs Horsley, I ate some fish and chips somewhere along my route. Can't remember where.'

'If you want good fish and chips you have to go up north,' said her father, whose own family came from Lancashire.

'I'll make some more tea.' Laura disappeared into the kitchen to be joined by her mother seconds later. It was obvious her parents had no intention of retiring just yet. Usually nothing would stop their nightly routines.

'Darling, who is he?' she whispered, although it was unlikely she could be heard through two doors and quite a long corridor.

'I told you!' replied Laura, also whispering, finding mugs, the best china being still in the sitting room. 'He's

373

a writer who came to the literary festival I helped arrange. I did tell you, about the festival, I mean.'

'But why has he gone to so much trouble to find you? You're not . . .' she hesitated '. . . an "item" or anything?'

Laura put her arm round her mother and hugged her, just for using the word 'item'. 'Of course not,' she said calmly. 'I expect he just wants me to do something for him. I helped him run a writing course.'

'I don't think he would have made such an effort just for that,' said her mother, refilling the kettle. 'I think he likes you.'

These thoughts had been running through Laura's mind like a tape on fast-forward. Why had he take such pains to track her down? Could it possibly be because he did like her? But was that enough for her to risk everything for? There were still so many unanswered questions she needed to ask before she even dared to hope that. 'Well, maybe . . .'

'And I wouldn't blame you if you liked him,' she confided. 'I've always had a soft spot for wild Irishmen.'

'Mum!'

'Just as well I've got your father, isn't it? Otherwise who knows what might have happened? Shall I just put milk in here? Or bring them through with the jug on the tray?'

Laura was reeling from her mother's confession. It was not just that they shared a previously unsuspected predilection; it was the fact her mother had told her about it. 'Oh, let's just put the milk in here.'

Dermot gave up arguing about which of them would sleep in Laura's bed and which on the sofa when he realised that the sofa option involved Laura's single sleeping bag. He did not, he stated, relish sleeping like a sausage in a skin.

Laura had rearranged the cushions on the sofa for

what seemed like the hundredth time but was still not comfortable. She suspected, however, that it was not the cushions or the sofa that was making it hard to sleep, but the thought of Dermot sharing the same three-bedroom semi as her and her parents. Him turning up like that was like a miracle, or a film, or a romantic novel . . . or something.

Why had he chased her all over the British Isles? (Well, England and Ireland. Did Ireland count as the British Isles?) Surely he wouldn't have done that when presumably he could have just gone home to Bridget? Could their night of passion possibly have been more than just amazing sex for him, too?

Ever since she'd worked out, at the festival, that he'd been frantically writing, which was why he'd stopped contacting the outside world, even her, she'd wondered if their subsequent passion was just some sort of release for him, as soldiers high on adrenalin after battle need.

But surely he wouldn't have gone to all that trouble to locate her unless she was more than a woman in the right place at the right time? No. He hadn't just jumped on her, he'd made love to her, tenderly, thoughtfully, taking account of her inexperience. He'd made sure she had a really wonderful time.

She'd blocked a lot of this out of her mind since her meeting with Bridget. She'd made her brain reject the messages her heart might have given her if she'd let it. But now she allowed herself to remember the intimate details; how he'd used his skill and experience to give her pleasure. It made her sigh blissfully but it didn't help her sleep.

Then she heard a noise at the door. It could have been her father, checking up, or her mother, come down for a motherly chat. But somehow she knew it was Dermot.

'Hello?' he whispered.

'Yes?' she whispered back.

'May I come in?' he asked, still whispering.

'Yes, but don't wake my parents. Not that they're asleep, probably. They'll be worrying.'

She heard him come in and bring the door to behind him. 'Will they? Why?'

'In case you're doing what you're doing now!' She sat up, but she was still encased in the sausage skin.

'I couldn't sleep a night under the same roof as you without . . .' He paused.

Torrid and frantic thoughts of what he might be about to say made her breathing become rapid.

'What?' They were already whispering but this was hardly audible. He either heard her or guessed.

'I had to put my arms round you.'

He scooped her up and enveloped her, pinning her to him. She couldn't breathe. His shirt collar was sticking into her cheek, but she didn't care. She didn't want to breathe, really, she just wanted to go on being held by him for ever, even if his clothes dug into her.

And then she pulled back. However much she wanted to let her emotions take over, there were things she needed to know before she could give in to her feelings. She had to be able to trust him. She drew her knees up to her chest, still in the bag.

'What is it?' He frowned and then he smiled at her ruefully. 'Oh, don't tell me, I think I know. It must seem as if I've been a bit of a bastard.' He sat back and sighed.

She so wanted to forgive him everything but she had to suppress her smile at this understatement. 'Just a bit.'

He cleared his throat, got up and moved away from her. 'Can I tell you how it was from my point of view?' he said, as if asking for her permission to continue.

'Please do. I need a change of viewpoint.' Nerves were making her flippant. Whatever he had to say she needed to hear it.

He smiled slightly at this but then became serious.

'I think I fell in love with you way back in January. You were so sweet, so different, so pretty, so—'

'Enough with the flattery.'

'It's not flattery, it's the truth. And after we met I suddenly found I was able to write. You were the key. You were the reason I offered to do that writing course.'

'Oh, was I? If that was the case, why didn't you – I don't know – make any kind of move?' Her voice cracked with remembered hurt.

'There were a few reasons, really. One was that I didn't think I could do more than kiss your cheek without wanting to take you to bed and I couldn't take you to bed in those circumstances. It was too public and I needed to be really sure . . . I mean I was sure but I didn't want to risk hurting you.'

He looked at her, holding her gaze until she turned away, a wave of longing washing over her. She didn't say anything; it was important he told her everything, if she was ever to truly trust him. She nodded for him to go on.

'And back in Ireland,' he continued, 'well, I was well into a book, a book that was pouring out of me. I felt I had to finish it, or as near as damn it, and then pursue you, so I could do it properly.'

He came and sat back down beside her, taking her hand and stroking it. She didn't move any closer but she didn't take her hand away.

'Oh God, I thought I might never see you again, touch you, get the chance to tell you how much I love you, how much I need you.'

She shifted slightly in her sleeping bag, but let her hand continue to rest in his. She still had some questions she wanted answered.

'Just a few other things, if you don't mind,' she said. 'I need to know about Bridget. Why didn't you tell me you were together?'

He frowned. 'What do you mean? Bridget and I were never anything but friends, drinking companions.' He paused. 'You didn't think . . . Oh God. She means nothing to me, nothing.' He tried to pull her closer but she remained slightly distant, even though every part of her was longing for him to take her in his arms again.

After a pause he went on. 'I'm sorry I ravished you in Ireland. I was furious with the press, angry with everyone and I'd been working every hour there was, not eating properly, drinking, smoking, doing anything that would help me get a few more words down on the page. I was mad with writing – seven thousand words a day sometimes.'

'I didn't see any sign of it when I went there,' Laura said

He chuckled. 'No, I hid it all under the bed. But when I saw you, I knew I had to have you, had to put all the care and intensity I put into my work into making things all right for you.'

She blushed and smiled – he was so passionate. 'Well, you did.'

'I might have held back a bit longer if you hadn't been in a temper. There's something about a woman stamping her foot that is irresistible.'

'Hmm. You mean in a "Come here, you little fool, don't you know that I love you?" sort of way?' She felt she could dare to tease him as things started to become clearer.

'I don't know! I just knew I had to have you.'

'And you did.' He'd explained about Bridget and she did believe him but somehow she still wasn't quite satisfied; she still couldn't get rid of the feeling that he'd used her, even if it had been unintentional.

As if he'd read her mind, he said, 'Sweetheart, I didn't just want you because I wanted sex and you were there. You didn't think that, did you?' He seemed horrified by this thought. All the while his fingers were caressing hers.

'No, I didn't feel that at the time,' she replied honestly. 'But when you didn't get in touch with me afterwards—'

'But you were so cold! Running away almost before we'd had breakfast.' He paused, reluctant to reveal his gentle amusement. 'You must have sat at the airport for ages.'

'I did,' she admitted. 'It was because of Bridget.'

'I told you there was nothing between us.'

'I know, but she said—'

He interrupted her. 'What did she say?' he pressed.

'She said something that made me feel you'd . . . used me.' She couldn't look at him; all the hurt and humiliation she'd felt at the time came flooding back.

He sighed and sat back again, his hands now in a fist on his lap. 'That woman!' he said in frustration. 'But I wish to God you'd said something at the time.'

'I couldn't! I was too humiliated,' she protested.

'Well, I didn't know what had happened. One minute everything was wonderful and the next you'd become an ice maiden. I felt a bit humiliated too. I got to feeling that you'd just used me to get rid of your virginity. I tried to put you out of my mind and got back into writing. Now I can understand why—'

'Don't.' She took his hand again and held it tight. He pulled her into his arms and hugged her tightly and they stayed like that for some time until he drew away once more.

'I wanted to explain about the obsessive writing at the festival but you wouldn't give me a chance,' he said quietly.

'I couldn't bear the thought of you explaining that what we'd had was very precious but – I've read so many damn novels, I know all the expressions – but that you and Bridget were getting married or something.'

Even though she knew for certain this wasn't going to happen now, the pain it would have caused her made her flinch inwardly. 'And then there was the story.'

'What about the story?' He was confused.

'I thought it was one of the most beautiful Dear John – or maybe that should be Dear Joan – letters ever written.'

'Dear God, you're a terrible one for getting the wrong end of the stick. The story was fiction! And if it was about anyone, it was about Bridget. I never knew how she felt about me until she came up to see me after you'd left.'

Laura sighed deeply, collapsing a little with the weight of her misunderstanding. 'I just never thought you could really love me. As much as I—'

'Well, I can,' he cut in. 'And if you're not very careful I'll prove it to you.' He enveloped her again and then his mouth found hers and she heard him sigh before their lips connected. It was heavenly.

After a while, she said, 'I'm sorry, I can't let you make love to me on the sofa in my parents' house, when they're probably not even asleep.'

He was breathing hard. 'It's OK, I knew you'd feel like that. It's why I didn't get undressed. We have the rest of our lives to make love to each other. I'll go back upstairs to my room but first I need to thank you.'

'Do you? Are you grateful to me for bringing you to England and to the attention of the literary world once more? You should be! It'll make you rich and famous. Notorious maybe.' She felt she could tease him now she definitely knew he loved her.

'Well, of course I will give you a cut of my earnings – if not all my earnings – from now on in but that's not what I meant.'

'No?'

'No. You did something very much more important.'

'What? What could be more important than fame and fortune?' She spoke lightly but she really didn't know what he could be talking about.

'As I said before, you cured me of writer's block. When you came into my life I'd got jaded and cynical and you – well, you showed me that there were still sweet, pure things.' He kissed the top of her head.

Tears clogged the back of Laura's throat and she waited until they'd gone before saying, 'That makes me sound like an organic pudding, if I may say so.'

He laughed, hugging her close. 'Oh God, you're so adorable. When I'm being soppy and sentimental, you're sharp, like a drop of lemon juice.'

'OK, now I'm an organic lemon pudding.'

He suddenly paused, gazing at her, an earnest look on his face. 'Darling, have I made it clear to you how much I love you? That I want to spend the rest of my life with you?'

'Not exactly, no.' Her heart fluttered.

'Well, what do you need me to say?'

She laughed, bolder now, her heart singing with joy. How could she have forgotten how much she loved being in his company, teasing him? 'Dermot Flynn, I am not going to put words into your mouth. You have your own silver tongue to help you.'

'Laura Horsley, I do solemnly declare—'

'I think that's plagiarism.'

'Don't care. I do solemnly declare that I have never loved anyone as much as I love you. And that I will love you until the Mountains of Mourne stop going down to the sea or some other very unlikely geological event takes place. And I want to take you home to Ireland and keep you safe by my side for ever. And the little ones, when they come along. I'll keep them safe too. What do you say?'

Laura's insides were melting. 'Did you ask me a question?'

'No. I just wanted your general opinion of what I just said.'

'Apart from the plagiarism?'

'Apart from that.'

'I think they most be the most beautiful words you've ever invented.'

He seemed pleased. 'And to think I just said them off the top of my head.'

Laura put her hand up to the top of his head and pushed her fingers into his curls. 'I expect our children will have curly hair.'

'That's all right. Curly-haired children are my favourite kind.'

They had just snaked their bodies so there was as little space between them as possible when they heard movement overhead.

'You'd better go back upstairs,' said Laura. 'Otherwise we'll never be able to face my parents over the All-Bran.'

Epilogue

'Are you sure you're all right carrying that bag?' asked Dermot as they prepared to set off.

'Of course. It's only got a few things in it. You seem to have equipment for an entire Boy Scout Jamboree in that rucksack. We're only going to have tea.'

'Not at all,' he said dismissively.

They were at the farm, preparing to go for a repeat of the walk they had gone on together, back in January, when they had only just met. It was now October and the sort of autumn day that made Laura want to quote Keats: there was a hint of mist and veils of dew-spangled cobwebs on the fuchsia-filled hedgerows. Part of their picnic was apples from the tree in Dermot's garden and there was the promise of hot sun later. She had moved into Dermot's house ten days earlier, after he'd had the entire house repainted. Every morning when she woke up to hear him snoring beside her, she thought she'd die of happiness – that was if he didn't wake her first, pulling her to him and holding her tight prior to making love to her so thoroughly she was sure everyone could tell how she'd started her day just by the glow that surrounded her.

'Where are the dogs?' she said now.

'I asked the farmer to keep them in.'

'Oh, that was very kind of you. I would have coped.' Now that she and Dermot were together she felt nothing could daunt her, certainly not a few noisy collies.

'I didn't want you having to cope with anything, not today,' he said firmly.

When they had climbed over the gate, Dermot assisting Laura in a way that involved his hand on her bottom and her giggling for quite a long time, they set off walking.

After a little way, Laura said, 'I can't quite believe we're preparing for my parents to come to stay.'

'We should have that spare bedroom in a good state before they get here.'

'What I really can't believe is that you invited them.'

Dermot had behaved like a perfect gentleman the morning after he had burst into the Horsley household and by the time he and Laura left (by taxi – very extravagant) her parents had seemed quite happy that he was now taking charge of their daughter and her journey back to Ireland.

'I thought it was only fair that they should see their only child was being properly looked after,' he explained. 'And I've been thinking, we may want to sell my house.'

'But you've lived there for years?'

'I've always had a fancy to build one where you can see the sea. There's a plot up here I might persuade the farmer to sell.'

'Oh!' This sounded exciting – it was the most beautiful place. He'd obviously been giving it quite a bit of thought. And knowing how much Dermot was adored in the area, even more now he was known to be writing again, a film was to be made of *Mountain Road*, his first book, and he was bringing in more than a trickle of wealth along with his fame, she felt fairly sure the farmer would willingly sell him a field. She suspected the local planning official would also grant planning permission for it if he possibly could.

'I thought we'd have our picnic there and maybe make a few sketches of what we might want.'

It sounded like heaven and Laura was ridiculously pleased with the way he so easily and readily said 'we' these days, but she didn't comment. Anything too enthusiastic would cause Dermot to kiss her and then they might not get to their picnic destination by teatime.

They walked on in silence, Laura reliving everything that had happened since they'd last climbed the hills together and looked out over the sparkling sea. She was now working full-time as an editor, mostly at home, so she could indulge herself by cooking for Dermot when he wasn't cooking for her. They were a very modern couple. There were times when Laura still couldn't quite believe it wasn't all a dream. Then she would pinch herself and know that it was all deliciously real.

Bridget had left the village, returning to where she'd been when Laura first arrived. Although no one said anything, during the couple of times she and Dermot had gone to the pub together, she got the impression people were relieved that it was she and not Bridget who had captured the heart of their favourite bachelor.

Dermot had started a fourth book. He had turned one of the bedrooms into a study. It was a room she hadn't been in when she'd found him after he'd disappeared from the world. It was where he had been writing, writing, writing the book he had hidden under the bed that was now being fought over by several publishing houses. Now his writer's block was cured, he couldn't seem to stop, as if all the unwritten words of the previous years had been dammed up and were now flooding out of him.

When he'd finished a long stint, he'd find Laura, who was using the dining room as an office, and snatch her up wanting to make love to her. If she really had to finish a piece of work he'd go off into the kitchen and start cooking, finding recipes on the Internet and then charging off in the car, hunting for esoteric ingredients in all the neighbouring shops. Their local store was considering having a section labelled 'Dermot's Follies' in the hope that his influence might encourage others to buy shiitake mushrooms, truffle oil and capers.

'I think this is the perfect spot,' he said.

'For the picnic or the house?'

'Both.'

They stood together, arms wrapped round on another, their hands in each other's back pockets, staring out to sea.

'Imagine pulling back the curtains to that view every morning,' said Dermot.

'On a day like today it would be bliss, but what about when it was stormy and grey?'

'Then we'd pull them shut again and not get up at all.'

She tried to look disapproving but a smile kept tugging her mouth into the wrong expression. 'Let's have tea. Have you got the kettle?'

'Of course.' Dermot opened the neck of the rucksack and started pulling things out. 'Volcano kettle – you've got the *Irish Times* in your bag. Matches, you've got those too. Oh, and tea. I think you've got that. In a paper bag? Have a look.'

After a bit of rummaging, Laura found a brown paper bag with something that felt like tea in the bottom. 'Here you are.'

'Could you just check it is tea?' Dermot seemed a bit odd suddenly, edgy almost.

'I don't think it could be anything else. There's only just the cake and biscuits in here.'

'Just have a look in the bag. Here . . .' He spread a rug on to the short turf. 'Sit down first.'

Shaking her head at her loved one's madness, Laura sat on the rug.

'Now look inside the bag.'

She looked. 'It's definitely tea. There's no doubt it isn't coffee, hot chocolate or cannabis.'

Dermot collapsed down next to her and took the bag.

He peered into it, and then poked in his finger. 'Here, have another look.'

Obedient but confused, Laura looked. In among the tea leaves was a ring. Her heart missed a beat and a smile spread across her face as she put her hand in the bag and took it out. For some reason she couldn't speak; she was overcome with a rush of emotion. She studied the ring. It was a ruby, set in gold, with tiny diamonds round it. It looked old. And there was no way that this was anything other than an engagement ring.

Dermot was looking at her anxiously. 'If you don't like it, we can choose another one – together,' he said.

'I love it,' she whispered, looking up at him.

'Try it on then,' he urged.

She shook her head. 'I'm superstitious about putting rings on that finger unless . . .' She hesitated. Although she'd seen the love in his eyes, saw it every day, knew what this ring symbolised, she couldn't quite bring herself to take it all for granted.

'Here, let me.' He took hold of her left hand and then, taking the ring from her, he slid it on to her finger. It was a little large but she thought it looked lovely. Before she could admire it for long he took it off again.

He was already kneeling but he put one leg behind him so that he was on only one knee. Laura stifled a giggle. It was all so hopelessly romantic and he looked so serious.

'Laura, dear heart, love of my life, will you marry me?'

Sighing and smiling, she said, 'Well, I just might.'

'Just say yes, would you, woman!'

'Yes,' she said, her voice strong and clear.

'Yes, Dermot, I will marry you?' he said, holding her once more beringed hand tightly as if he was afraid she'd scamper off.

'Yes, Dermot, I will marry you.' But she'd hardly got out the last word before he had taken her in his arms and they were rolling on the rug together, kissing and laughing.

'Now we can tell your parents when they come to stay.' He reached across to the rucksack and produced a newspaper-covered bottle. 'Let's have a mug of champagne.'

'I thought we were going to have tea!'

'Bollocks to tea. We'll have that afterwards. Now, we're celebrating!'

Read on for an exclusive short story
by Katie Fforde . . .

Christmas Shopping
by
Katie Fforde

Christmas Shopping

Evie's overloaded trolley slid slowly but unstoppably into the trolley next to her. She'd been wishing all the way round that she'd tested it for wonkiness before she set off and should have changed it the moment she realised it wouldn't steer. Now it paid her back for her inefficiency by crashing into a trolley that seemed a dream – a perfect dinner for two: a packet of pheasant breasts, a bottle of champagne and some potted shrimps. Evie was very fond of potted shrimps. She looked up at the lucky shopper, who apparently didn't need enough food to feed a small country, just because it was Christmas. Of course, because Evie was showing the strain of the festive season in every line, wrinkle and pore, he was extremely good-looking. He had greying black hair, strong eyebrows, and beneath them dark eyes that crinkled attractively at the corners. Evie was aware her hair needed cutting, she hadn't bothered with make-up that morning and was wearing clothes she did housework in. She smiled, hoping to distract him from her looks.

'So sorry. Can't control this wretched thing. I should have changed it, but you don't quite have the heart, do you?' Then she looked at the contents of his trolley again and wished she'd just said 'sorry.' Those choice items did not indicate a man who'd appreciate small talk about shopping trolleys.

But he smiled. 'They're not very well designed, are

they?' It was only to make her feel better but she was grateful – and he had a lovely voice.

She sighed. 'No.' Then she frowned. 'I'm looking for agar agar. I've got the family for Christmas and I don't cook much as a rule.'

He glanced down at her load which she now had under control. 'You wouldn't guess that from the amount you've packed in there.'

She laughed. 'Panic buying. My sister-in-law is a vegetarian and I can't decide what to cook for her. I thought agar agar would be useful.'

'I'm sure you must have the ingredients for several recipes – a whole book, possibly.' His gaze roamed over the disparate ingredients – quinoa, bulgur wheat, various forms of tofu, and some mushrooms she'd have sworn were poisonous if they hadn't been for sale in an upmarket shop.

'That's what I thought! But as I can't decide I think I'd better have—'

'Here you are.' He put the packet on top of the other things.

'Thanks. I wish I liked cooking more. It's my turn to have them all and I dread it. Some of them are such foodies.' The pheasants and champagne caught her eye. 'Oh, you probably are too.'

'Well, I do cook, but I have no one to cook for this year. My parents are on a cruise. I'm living in the family home, looking after the cat.'

'I expect you're looking forward to a quiet Christmas. I know I would be.'

'Mm, yes, sort of. It'll be different, anyway.'

Evie looked up at him, and on impulse she said, 'Would you think I was absolutely mad if I invited you round for Christmas dinner?' Aware of his astonishment she went on. 'Of course, say no. I don't expect you to accept, but I wouldn't feel right about myself if I didn't ask you.'

394

He laughed. 'Why ever not?'

She hesitated. 'Lots of reasons. The most important to me is, if Christmas is about anything it's about welcoming strangers into your home.' Too late she wished that she'd said something different – anything but the truth really. She tried to explain further – which would probably make it worse – but what the hell. 'I'm rubbish at cooking, and cleaning and decorating the house stylishly. I never get the Christmas cards out in time and I mostly buy people things from Marks and Spencers so they can take them back. But I do feel strongly about being welcoming.' She was blushing so hard now she was challenging the cardboard Santa's that swayed above her head. 'Now you've confirmed I'm completely batty, you can move on and finish your shopping.'

He laughed again but kindly. 'Actually, I was going to offer to come round and make you a vegetarian dish. I haven't got much cooking to do at all and I like it. And you obviously have a lot.'

'Would you do that?' Gratitude almost made Evie fling her arms round his neck. Fortunately middle-class restraint saved her from herself.

'Of course. It would be a pleasure. Where do you live?'

She gulped, suddenly aware that she'd invited a complete stranger into her home. She didn't know anything about him. He could be targeting her – he could have seen her neediness and deliberately got talking to her. Then she allowed common sense into her panic-stricken brain. She would be surrounded by people on Christmas Day; she'd be perfectly safe.

'I live at the top of Stoke's Hill. One of the big houses up there.'

'Oh yes, I know. Do you live in all of it? Or has it been divided into flats?'

She smiled to hide an unexpected sigh. 'No, all of it.'

It wouldn't be for long. Once everything else had been sorted out after her parents' death, the house would go on the market. It was why everyone decided there needed to be one more family Christmas in the old home. Then it *would* be divided into flats, no doubt.

She gave him the rest of the address and they exchanged names and contact numbers. Then she finished her shopping, adding two boxes of crackers to the pile, just because they were reduced to half price. Still, crackers were always good fun even if she was the only member of the family who thought so.

She didn't tell her family that she'd invited Edward for Christmas. She hadn't really meant to lie to them, but she didn't work hard enough at finding an opportunity to do it. They were all so busy, preoccupied with deciding who should have what from the house.

Evie had two brothers, Bill and Derek, both married. Donna, the vegetarian who was causing Evie such food-stress, was married to Bill. Derek's wife was much more practical but she always made Evie feel like a bit of an idiot. It was probably because Sarah never saw Evie in her working environment, running a team of sales staff, but only when she was being domestic, and not making a good job of it.

Evie's own sister was the eldest of the family. Diane was married to a lovely man called William who always reminded Evie of a Labrador, friendly and always trying to be helpful – not always succeeding. Diana nagged him horribly, Evie felt. But then Diane nagged everyone, especially Evie.

They all had two children each, and Evie always called them the wrong names which caused huge offence although Evie had no idea why. She always got people's names wrong – as had their mother before her.

Christmas Eve went well, Evie felt. She had bought

things to add to the children's stockings and had even bought stripy socks and filled them for the adults. This had kept everyone in bed for a bit longer than usual on Christmas morning, giving Evie time to defrost croissants and make Buck's Fizz. Her sister would disapprove of champagne at breakfast, even if it was mixed with orange juice. Donna would sweetly but firmly refuse all the organic, wheat-free, stone-ground, air-dried, free-range cereals that Evie had bought on spec, and eat half a banana and some wheat germ, produced from her own bag of healthy supplies. The men would probably demand eggs and bacon and there was no telling what, if anything, the children would want for breakfast, they were probably full of chocolate already.

The present opening would go on after lunch so now, after breakfast, and with a huge effort, Evie managed to get them all to go for a walk. She didn't go with them, she wanted to fiddle with the vegetables and wonder what to cook for Donna. Donna had asked her what she was getting for Christmas dinner. Evie had said it was a surprise.

Annoyingly a fine rain descended and the walkers came back early. Evie had depended on them being out until at least midday giving her plenty of time to cook. Edward, she decided, was a figment of her imagination. She'd so wanted to meet a nice man who'd cook a vegetarian dish for her she'd created one in her head.

She didn't want sisterly help so she sent the women into the dining room to set the table and make it festive, the children into the den to watch telly – an illicit treat in the daytime for those particular ones. The men she sent down to the cellar to sort out wine. They could spend a happy time there discussing what her parents had bought over the years and if any of it was still decent.

When she heard the doorbell ring she was surprised

but delighted to find Edward on the doorstep, his arms full of carrier bags. Not that she'd thought about him all morning. She'd gone for quite long spells – as much as ten minutes at a time – without giving him a thought.

It was hard to decide if he was actually more attractive than she'd remembered him or if he just seemed more attractive because she thought she'd made him up anyway. In her head she'd just made him a keen cook and didn't allow him long legs or a quirky smile or anything else he seemed to have in reality.

'Hello! I didn't think you'd come!' she said, instantly aware it made her sound terribly needy.

'I didn't think you'd be here. I thought I'd find the house empty and shuttered, or sold and half-converted.'

They laughed awkwardly. 'Come in,' said Evie. 'Happy Christmas.'

He put down the large number of carrier bags he had with him. 'Happy Christmas.' He bent and kissed her cheek.

Evie flushed, hoping he'd just think it was slaving over a hot stove that made her so pink, and very glad she had dressed carefully for Christmas Day and was looking OK.

'Come into the kitchen. Let me get you a drink.' She didn't say, 'come quickly before the family see you,' although she wanted to.

The kitchen was fairly tidy, in that the table was only partly covered in potatoes, carrots, parsnips and sprouts, some half-made stuffing and various attempts at vegetarian options.

'Oh, so you had a go yourself then,' said Edward, seeing the soaking bulgur wheat and the tofu, still in its bag. A packet of alfalfa looked very like duck weed.

'I had to. In case.'

He didn't ask 'in case what.' 'Well, as I had the time I made a dish all ready. You just need to put it in the oven.'

Evie, who'd had her breakfast champagne without the

sobering effects of orange juice embraced him. 'You're an angel!'

Just then the eldest child came in. Luke was ten. 'Oh, Auntie Evie. Hey, everyone, Aunt Evie's got a man in the kitchen!'

Had he shouted 'fire' they would not have appeared as quickly, but as it was the kitchen was filled with people within seconds. And they were all staring. They were so used to Evie being single that the sight of her with a very attractive man in the family kitchen threw them completely.

Evie was aware she had to take charge. 'Everyone, this is Edward. I invited him for Christmas.'

'Why didn't you say anything about him coming?' asked her sister. 'Where did you meet?'

'In the supermarket,' said Edward. 'Evie was looking for agar agar.'

'What on earth is that?' asked Bill.

'A vegetarian setting agent,' murmured Donna, 'but I'm surprised you knew about it, Evie.'

'Anyway it turned out that Edward was going to be alone for Christmas Day so I invited him.'

'You'd better do the introductions,' said Diane, and Evie obliged, pleased with herself for getting all the children's names right for once.

'But which one is your husband?' asked Edward when the others had drifted away again, back to their tasks, wondering about their aunt or their sister depending on age.

Evie was confused for a moment. 'Oh, I haven't got a husband. Those men are my brothers.'

'Your brothers? That is good news. I assumed you were married.'

'Did you? Why?'

'Single women don't usually have shopping trolleys they can hardly push,' he explained.

Evie bit her lip. 'I hope you don't mind that I'm single. I would hate you to think I was trying to entrap you or anything.'

'Mind? That's the best Christmas present I've had in years.' Edward put his arm round Evie and hugged her.

'I think I should tell you,' said Luke, who had come back for a second look, 'that my Auntie Evie is a rotten cook.'

'But I'm a brilliant one, so that's all right.' He looked at Evie. 'Did you say something about a drink?'

Mr Right?

STELLA BAGWELL

MILLS & BOON®

Pure reading pleasure™

*First published in Great Britain 2008
by Harlequin Mills & Boon Limited,
Eton House, 18-24 Paradise Road, Richmond, Surrey TW9 1SR*

© Harlequin Books S.A. 2007

*Special thanks and acknowledgement are given to Stella Bagwell for
her contribution to the MONTANA series.*

ISBN: 978 0 263 86064 1

23-0808

*Harlequin Mills & Boon policy is to use papers that are
natural, renewable and recyclable products and made from
wood grown in sustainable forests. The logging and
manufacturing processes conform to the legal environmental
regulations of the country of origin.*

*Printed and bound in Spain
by Litografía Rosés S.A., Barcelona*

To my family –
the real golden nuggets in my life

STELLA BAGWELL

sold her first novel in November 1985. She still loves her job and says she isn't completely content unless she's writing. She and her husband live in Seadrift, Texas, a sleepy little fishing town located on the coastal bend, where the water, the tropical climate and the seabirds make it a lovely place to let her imagination soar and to put the stories in her head down on paper.

She and her husband have one son, Jason, who lives and teaches maths in nearby Port Lavaca.

Dear Reader,

I was thrilled when asked to do a MONTANA book, and when I learned the theme – striking it rich – I knew it was a subject that would touch everyone. After all, haven't we all wondered what it would be like to win the lottery or fall into sudden fortune? Ahh, the things we could do with all that money. Shopping till we dropped. Travelling around the world. Indulging ourselves with anything and everything we've ever wanted. Sounds good, huh? Sounds like all our problems would be solved. Or so my heroine thinks.

After scratching her way through years of poverty, Mia believes money is all she needs to fix the troubles in her life. But when a fortune suddenly befalls her, she slowly and painfully begins to see that being rich in money is not nearly as great as being rich in love.

I hope you enjoy reading how Mia finds the real treasures in her life!

God bless you with life's true riches,

Stella Bagwell

Chapter One

Was this his lucky day or what?

Using the back of his arm, Marshall Cates wiped the sweat streaming into his eyes and peered a second time at the woman sitting on a boulder some twenty feet below. From his precarious position on the rock ledge, the only view he had was of a portion of her back, the long fall of her raven-black hair and her nipped-in waist; but those tempting glimpses were enough to tell him it was *the heiress*.

For the past three weeks every male employee at Thunder Canyon Resort had been talking and fantasizing about the mystery guest. So far Marshall had only gazed at her from afar and wondered what a beautiful young woman with money to burn was doing here alone in

Thunder Canyon. True, the small western Montana town was growing in leaps and bounds and Thunder Canyon Resort, where he worked as staff doctor, was garnering a reputation for fine hospitality surrounded by scenic splendor. The clientele was becoming ritzy, flying in from all corners of the nation. Still, Marshall couldn't help but figure a woman with her apparent class would rather be vacationing on the French Riviera than in the middle of a cowman's paradise. The fact that she appeared to be here without an escort intrigued him even more.

This morning, Marshall had risen early, wondering what to do with his off-duty time. With his brothers and his buddies all tied up with other interests, he'd eventually decided to do something he loved, climbing, and had headed up one of the mountains near the resort. When he'd set out on this trek, he'd never dreamed that the chance to meet Ms. Heiress would present itself on the edge of a rocky bluff. Since he'd only ever spotted her lounging around the lodge, he hadn't figured her for a nature girl.

Quickly, he rappelled the last few feet of the layered rock until his boots hit solid ground. Once there, he gathered up his climbing equipment and left his ropes, rings and anchors in a neat pile with his backpack.

As Marshall walked over to the woman he noticed she was sitting near an opening in the trees, looking out toward the endless valley that swept away from the mountain range. The view was majestic, especially to someone who'd never seen the landscape before. But this woman didn't appear to be enjoying the scenery;

she was deep in thought. So much so that she was completely unaware of his presence.

Fearing his approach might scare her so badly she'd fall from the boulder, he stopped ten feet from her and called out.

"Hello there."

The moment she heard his voice, her head whipped around and her palms flattened against the rock in preparation to push herself to her feet. Surprise was etched upon her parted lips and wide eyes, telling him she'd definitely believed herself to be totally alone on this particular piece of mountain. She was dressed in khaki shorts that struck her mid-thigh, a pale pink T-shirt that hugged her breasts and sturdy brown hiking boots. Her hair hung like shiny satin against her shoulders.

An enchanting princess sitting on her throne, he thought, as he felt every male particle in him begin to buzz with excitement.

"Sorry if I scared you," Marshall went on before she could gather herself enough to speak. "I saw you sitting here and thought I'd say hello."

Slowly, warily, she eased her bottom back on the boulder and her dark eyes carefully monitored his movements as he came to stand a few feet beside her. Marshall wondered if he really looked that sinister. It was an odd thought for a doctor who'd taken an oath to save lives, not harm them. But Ms. Heiress didn't know him and he supposed she was wise not to trust a strange man out in the wilderness.

Finally, she returned his greeting with a faint nod of her regal head. "Hello."

Spoken quietly, that one word was clear and without a hint of accent, giving little clue as to where she might live. However, it did tell Marshall that she'd not traveled up to Thunder Canyon from a Southern state.

Giving her the sort of smile he reserved for skittish female patients, he asked, "Enjoying the warm weather?"

Actually, it had been downright hot. Not an unusual occurrence for August, but it would take a native like himself to know the nuances of Thunder Canyon climate and right at this moment he wasn't ready to let this beautiful sophisticate know he was a born-and-bred local. She might just snub her straight little nose at him and walk off, and he was too curious about the woman to take that chance.

"Very much," she quietly replied.

Marshall took two steps forward, all the while feeling her dark eyes gliding over him, weighing him as though she were trying to decide if he was worthy of conversation. The idea irked Marshall just a bit. Especially since he was accustomed to women smiling warmly at him, not studying him like a bug on a leaf.

"The view is beautiful from here," she suddenly went on. "The sky seems to go on forever and I was thinking about hanging around to see the sunset this evening, but I suppose being caught out here in the dark wouldn't be wise."

At least the woman had a little common sense to go with all that beauty, he thought, as his gaze covertly slid down a pair of long shapely legs. Her skin was slightly kissed by the sun and the warm gleam told him it would be butter smooth beneath his hand.

Trying not to dwell on that pleasant thought, he shook his head. "No. I wouldn't recommend being here on the mountains after dark. Black bears and mountain lions are spotted in this area from time to time. You wouldn't want to meet up with any of those."

Glancing at the forest surrounding them, she said, "I've noticed the warnings signs on the hiking trails and read the information posted in the lodge." She lifted one hand and shook a bracelet adorned with sleigh bells. "Just to be safe I wore a bear bracelet. I was told the sound would scare the creatures away."

"So they say." He didn't go on to tell her that as a teenager he'd had his own run-in with a black bear and that the sow had refused to back down until his brother had shot a round from his hunting rifle over the angry animal's head. Scaring the woman would hardly be the way to entice her into further conversation.

To Marshall's surprise, she suddenly climbed down from the rock and stood within an arm's length from him. The short distance was enough to give him a clear view of her face. High rounded cheekbones, a dainty dimpled chin and full lips were perfectly sculpted out of creamy skin. Her eyes, which appeared dark from a distance, were actually a blend of earthy green and brown, outlined by a thick fringe of jet-black lashes. Above them, delicate brows of the same color arched into a smooth, wide forehead.

At the moment, the corners of her pink lips were curved faintly upward and Marshall could hardly tear his gaze away.

"You've been mountain climbing?" she asked, her gaze sweeping past him to the mound of equipment he'd left beneath the rocky bluff.

"Since this morning," he answered. "I didn't make it all the way to the top, but far enough for a good workout."

Her gaze pulled back to him and he could feel it sliding over his sweaty face and down to the damp patch in the middle of his black T-shirt. Normally when a woman looked at him, Marshall didn't give it a second thought. But Ms. Heiress was studying him in a way that left him close to blushing. Something he hadn't done since his sophomore year in high school.

"I hiked up this far, but when I ran into the rock bluff I realized this would be as far as I could go," she said a bit wistfully. "Is this something you do often?"

His smile crinkled the corners of his eyes and exposed a mouthful of snow-white teeth. "You mean, find a beautiful woman up in the mountains?"

The faint flare of her nostrils said she didn't appreciate his flirty question and Marshall inwardly sighed. He should have known the woman would be cool. Rich, pampered women usually were. The words friendly and down-to-earth probably weren't in her vocabulary.

"No. I mean rock climbing," she said a bit curtly.

"Oh. Well, actually I do quite a bit of climbing and hiking. Along with biking and kayaking. Once the snow leaves the slopes, that is."

She looked faintly interested and Marshall felt momentarily encouraged. Maybe the woman was approachable after all.

"You obviously like outdoor sports," she said.

"Yeah. Skiing is my first love. I could do that every day of the year. But of course, my wallet would get pretty empty if I didn't work once in a while," he added with a grin.

Like the flip of a light switch, her back went ramrod straight and her lips compressed to a tight line. Her gaze shifted from him to a magpie squawking from a branch on a nearby spruce tree. Apparently she preferred the bird's talk to his.

After a moment, she asked in a cool tone, "Or find a willing woman to pay for your sporting games."

Stunned by this abrupt change in her, Marshall stared at her profile. She might look like an exotic princess, but that didn't mean he was going to let himself be insulted. Hadn't she ever heard of a joke?

"I beg your pardon?" he asked.

Her head swiveled back around and she stared down her straight little nose at him. "Oh, come on, I'm sure you do this all the time. Strike up innocent conversations with single women, turn on the charm and eventually get your hand in their pocketbook. Isn't that the way your game is played?"

So she thought he was after her money. Marshall was so incensed he would have very much liked to turn her over his knee and whack that pretty little bottom of hers until she apologized. But he wasn't about to use caveman tactics on a woman. She'd probably miss the point of a spanking anyway.

"Sorry, Ms.—uh—Smith, isn't it? Mia Smith?"

A mixture of surprise and suspicion suddenly crossed her face. "How do you know my name?"

"I'm Marshall Cates—the staff doctor for Thunder Canyon Resort. I've heard your name mentioned by some of the other staffers. And in case you didn't know, there are people, like me, who can make it just fine in life without a pile of riches. My salary easily takes care of my wants. I certainly don't need a woman to take care of me financially," he added coolly.

Completely stunned now, Mia stared at the man standing a few steps away. She'd assumed he was also a guest at the resort. She'd jumped to conclusions and figured he'd heard she was a single woman with money and thought she would probably be an easy prey to his good looks. To learn that he was a doctor at the resort— no doubt a well-to-do one—both rattled and embarrassed her.

Hot color washed across her face as her fingertips flew up to press against her lips. Too bad she hadn't kept them shut earlier, she thought. No telling what the man was thinking of her.

"Oh, I—I'm sorry, Dr. Cates. I don't know what else to say." Glancing away from him she let out a loud, inward groan. Why couldn't she do anything right anymore? Is that what inheriting money had done to her? Turned her into a mistrustful snob?

Drawing in a deep, bracing breath, she turned her

gaze back to him and once again felt the jolt of the man's presence. He wasn't just a good-looking guy in a pair of sweaty shorts and T-shirt. He was so masculine that she could almost feel the sexuality seeping from him. Waves of coffee-brown hair naturally streaked by the sun were tousled around his head. Eyes the color of a chocolate bar peered at her from beneath thick, hooded brows. A straight nose flared slightly over a pair of lips that at the moment were compressed into a tight, angry line. A faint shadow of evening stubble covered a strong jaw and a chin that jutted proudly forward, telling her more about his personality than his words.

At the moment he appeared to be waiting for her to explain the meaning of her insulting comments and she supposed he deserved that much from her. Yet how could she really explain without telling the man things about her that she didn't want anyone to know?

"I thought— I took it for granted that you were a guest, Dr. Cates, and I was afraid— Well, you see I've had to deal with the problem of men…approaching me for financial reasons." Her features crumpled with remorse. "I'm sorry I was so quick to misjudge you. Please accept my apology."

He continued to study her with a guarded eye and Mia realized he was weighing her words and her sincerity. She couldn't blame him for that. Even so, she didn't know why his opinion of her should matter so much. She wasn't at Thunder Canyon Resort to find herself a man, even a respectable man like Dr. Cates. In fact, she'd run almost blindly to this area of Montana, hoping that no one from her past would be able to follow. She'd come here seeking peace and privacy, nothing more.

"I'm curious, Ms. Smith. Just exactly what is it about me that made you think I was a gigolo?"

More hot color washed up her neck and over her face and her gaze dropped guiltily to the toes of her hiking boots. "There wasn't—You don't look like a gigolo, Dr. Cates. I guess it was that flirty line about finding a beautiful woman in the mountains that set my alarm bell off."

She glanced up to see the doctor folding his arms across his chest while studying her with curious amusement.

"I'm sure a woman like you runs into flirty men on a daily basis. I hope you don't insult them all the way you just did me."

So he wasn't going to make this easy for her, Mia thought. Well, it didn't matter. She had apologized to him. He could accept her offer or not. Either way, she'd probably never see the man again.

Stifling a sigh, she reached up and shoved back a strand of hair being tossed about by a lazy wind. "Look, Dr. Cates, I've apologized. There's not much more I can say."

He grinned at her in much the same way that he had earlier and, in spite of the rigid resistance she'd been trying to hold onto, she felt herself drawn to the man.

He said, "Except that you'll walk down the mountain with me."

His offhand invitation took her by surprise. Even though that flirty smile of his was aimed straight at her, she wasn't expecting him to take this meeting between them a step further. And though her first instinct was to withdraw and tell him she preferred her privacy, the feminine side of her was intrigued and flattered by his overture.

"That is," he added, "if you are ready to leave the mountain. I wouldn't want to rush you away from this spot. Not after the laboring hike it took to get up here."

The idea that he appreciated her physical effort to climb to this particular shelf of the mountain warmed her even more and she found herself smiling back at him.

"It was quite a trek for me to make it this far," she admitted. Twisting around, she bent down and picked up a small backpack lying at the base of the boulder. As she shouldered it on, she said, "But I am ready to go. The sun is beginning to dip."

"Great," he said with a smile. "Just let me get my things and we'll head down the trail together."

Mia followed him over to the rock ledge and waited while he shoved his climbing equipment into a vary large backpack. After he'd secured the straps over his shoulders, he gestured toward the direction of the trail.

"Shall we go?"

Nodding, Mia fell in step with him and was immediately staggered by his nearness. Since less than a foot separated their shoulders, she was close enough to pick up the faint spicy scent of cologne mingled with sweat, an odor that was extremely masculine, even erotic. And for the first time in ages, Mia found her senses distracted by a man.

"I guess getting outdoors is a nice break from working in an office," she commented as they picked their way down the rocky trail.

"I'd go crazy if I couldn't get out and do something physical," he told her. "But I do enjoy being a doctor."

She glanced at him from the corner of her eye. Looking at his lean body, Mia could plainly see he got plenty of strenuous exercise. His arms and legs were roped with hard muscles.

"Are you a general practitioner?"

A hint of amusement grooved his cheeks and Mia couldn't help but wonder about his odd reaction to her question. Did he think being a general practitioner was a joke? She hated to think he was one of those specialists that went around with their nose up in the air.

"No. There's not much need for one of those at the resort. I specialize in sports medicine. Twisted ankles, broken bones, strained muscles and pulled tendons. We have lots of skiers and hikers here."

For some reason, she could easily imagine him examining a blond ski bunny's strained leg. She'd bet a pile of money that the majority of his patients were female. But she wasn't about to suggest such a thing to Dr. Cates. She'd already stuck one foot in her mouth this afternoon. Mia wasn't about to try for a second.

"What about sniffles and fever? Can you treat those, too?"

He tossed her a wide grin. "Sure I can. Why? You're not feeling ill, are you?"

Her nostrils flared at his suggestive question. "I feel

very well, thank you. I was just wondering about those guests that might get colds or tummy aches."

He chuckled and Mia realized she liked the warm husky sound that rolled easily past his lips. It said he was happy with himself and his life. She was envious. Desperately envious.

"Well, wonder no more, Ms. Smith. I can do what any general practitioner can do, plus a little more."

The teeny thread of arrogance in his voice was just enough to give him an air of confidence rather than conceit. And she realized she liked that about him, liked the self-assurance he possessed. If only she could be that sure of her own abilities and decisions, she thought wistfully. Maybe then she could step out and begin to live again, instead of hiding herself here in Thunder Canyon.

"If that's the case, the resort must be getting a lot for their money."

He chuckled again. "I like to think so."

The trail suddenly turned a bit steep and treacherous, forcing them to focus on their steps rather than their conversation. But despite her best effort, Mia's boots slipped on the loose gravel.

Her arms were flailing about, snatching for any sort of bush to help her regain her balance, when she felt the doctor's arm wrap around her waist and his strong hand grip the side of her waist.

"Careful now," he said in a steadying voice. "I've got you."

Breathing deeply from the physical scramble to stay

upright, she tucked her long hair behind her ears and darted a grateful glance at his face.

"Thanks," she murmured between quick breaths. "I…almost went over head first."

Their gazes collided and Mia felt as though everything around them were slowing to a crawl. Except for her heart, which suddenly seemed to be going at breakneck speed, pumping hot blood straight to her face.

"It would be a steep tumble from here," he said, his voice husky. "I'm glad that didn't happen."

His brown eyes left hers and began to glide over her face as though they were fingers reverently touching a beautiful flower. The idea so unsettled Mia that she nervously swallowed and looked away from him.

Tall, pungent spruce along with white-barked aspen grew right to the edge of the hiking trail. The branches blocked out the sun, making it appear later in the evening than it really was and leaving Mia feeling as though the two of them were cocooned in their own little world. She wasn't ready for that much togetherness with a man who took her breath away each time she looked at him.

"Uh, we should be going," she quickly suggested. "The shadows are getting longer."

"Let me go first so I can help you down this rough patch," he told her.

To her relief he released his hold on her waist and carefully eased down the path a few feet in front of her. Once he found solid footing, he reached a hand up to her.

"Take my hand. I don't want you to fall."

She could have sat on her rump and scooted down the washed out part of the trail, but that would have been a little humiliating to do in front of a man who climbed mountains. Besides, he was only watching out for her safety, not merely trying to find an excuse to touch her, she told herself.

Leaning forward, she latched her fingers around his and with a firm grip he steadied her as she maneuvered over the last few treacherous steps.

"Thanks," she told him. "I've got to admit I was dreading going over this area again. I had to practically crawl on my way up."

He nodded. "I think this washout needs to be reported. The resort has maintenance people for repairing just this sort of thing. It might save a guest from a bad injury."

Mia suddenly realized he was still holding her hand and she was letting him.

Feeling like a naive teenager, she disengaged her fingers from his and carefully stepped around him. To her relief, he didn't try to delay her. Instead, he followed a few steps behind her.

She was trying hard to focus on the trail and the birds flittering among the limbs of the aspens, rather than the man behind her, when his voice suddenly sounded again.

"Are you a Montana native?"

His question put her on instant alert. If his questions grew too personal she didn't know how she could evade them without coming off as snobbish.

"No. Actually, I'm from Colorado."

"Oh. Then you're used to the mountains," he casually commented.

Truthfully, she'd grown up in a southern area of the state where most of the land was flat and used for farming and ranching. But that was more information than she wanted to give this man. He might inadvertently say something to other employees at the resort and if Janelle, her mother, just happened to be searching for her, the information might put the woman on her trail. And seeing Janelle right now was the very last thing Mia wanted in her life.

"Well, you could say I'm used to gazing at them from afar. I...uh, live in Denver."

He chuckled. "There're hundreds of beautiful vacation spots all over your state and you chose to come to Thunder Canyon. I'm amazed."

Put like that it did sound strange, even ridiculous. But she wasn't about to explain her motives for coming to Montana. Dr. Cates was obviously a man with wealth and prestige, maybe even a family. He would be outraged if he knew the real Mia. Mia Hanover. Not Mia Smith. That name was just as phony as the person she was trying to be.

Stifling a sigh, she said, "I'd never been up here. I wanted to see more of the state than just pictures."

Her simple excuse sounded reasonable enough. Lord only knew it was a mistake for a man to try to understand the workings of a woman's mind. Still, something about Mia Smith being here didn't feel right to him. Even so, he wasn't going to press her with any more questions. Something about the clipped edge to her words told him not to pry, at least, for right now.

"I'm glad you did. I hope you're having a nice stay," he told her. "Do you have plans to stay much longer?"

Long moments passed without any sort of reply from her and Marshall had decided she was going to ignore his question completely when she suddenly paused on the trail and looked over her shoulder at him.

"I'm...not sure. I'm taking things a day at a time."

A day at a time? Most normal folks went on vacation with a planned date of arrival and departure. They allotted themselves a certain amount of time for fun and mentally marked a day to go home. Work, school and other responsibilities demanded a timetable. But then Mia Smith wasn't like "normal folks." She was obviously rich. She didn't have responsibilities, he reminded himself. More than likely she was a lady of leisure. She didn't have to worry about getting back to a job.

She's out of your league, Marshall. You'd do well to remember that.

The tiny voice running through his head made sense. But it also irked him. He wasn't a man who always wanted to play it safe. He liked excitement and pleasure and getting to know Mia Smith would definitely give him both.

The next five minutes passed in silence as the two of them carefully made their way to the bottom shelf of the mountain. Here the ground flattened somewhat and the trail they'd been traveling split, with one path looping by the river before it headed back to the resort. The other trail was a more direct path to the ski lodge.

Shifting his backpack to a more comfortable position, Marshall paused at the intersection of trails to look at her.

"Would you like to walk down by the river?"

Her gaze skittered over his face before it finally settled on the horizon. Even before she spoke a word, Marshall could feel her putting distance between them.

"Sorry, but I have a few things I need to do back at my cabin. In fact, if you'll excuse me, I think I'll get on down the trail." She reached to briefly shake his hand. "Thank you for helping me with the trip down. Goodbye."

Before Marshall could make any sort of reply, she quickly turned and headed down the beaten path that would lead her back to the lodge.

Amused by her abrupt departure, Marshall stared after Mia Smith, while wondering where he'd gone wrong. He wasn't accustomed to women walking away from him. In fact, most of the time he had to think up some polite excuse to get rid of unwanted advances.

Mia Smith had just given him a dose of his own medicine and though the idea should have had him throwing his head back and laughing at the irony of it all, he could do nothing but stare down the trail after her and wonder if he would ever have the chance to talk with her again.

Chapter Two

Thunder Canyon Resort's infirmary was a set of rooms located on the bottom floor at the back of the massive lodge. When Caleb Douglas, wealthy businessman and cattle baron of Thunder Canyon, decided to build the resort, he'd spared no expense. The multistories of wood and glass spread across the slope of mountain like a modern-day castle. By itself, Marshall's office was large enough to hold a Saturday night dance. In fact, he'd often thought how perfect the gleaming hardwood floors would be for boot scootin' and twirling a pretty girl under his arm. Not very professional thoughts for a doctor, Marshall supposed, but then he hardly had the job of a normal doctor.

One whole wall of his office was constructed of

glass; it was an enormous window to the outside world. His desk, a huge piece of gleaming cherrywood, had been placed at the perfect angle for Marshall to view the nearby mountains and a portion of the ski slope. At this time in the summer, it wasn't rare for him to look up from his paperwork to see elk or mule deer grazing along the slopes.

Yes, it was a cushy job. One that Marshall had never dreamed of having. At least not while he'd been trudging through medical school, burning the midnight oil over anatomy books while his friends were out partying.

When Marshall had finally received his doctorate, he'd come home and taken a job at Thunder Canyon General Hospital. At the time some of his friends had wondered about his choice. They had all continually reminded him that his specialty in sports medicine could possibly open up big doors for him. Wouldn't he like to work for a major league team in baseball or the NFL where he could make piles of money?

Marshall would be the first to admit that he liked money and he'd gone into the medical profession believing it was a way to make a fortune without breaking his back. But he hadn't necessarily had his eye on a job that would take him away from his hometown.

By the time he'd finished medical school and his internship, he'd been too homesick to even consider going off to some major city on the East or West Coast to look for a job. Instead, he'd returned to Thunder Canyon, never dreaming that his hometown was about to undergo a sudden and drastic change.

A little over two years ago the discovery of gold at the Queen of Hearts mine had quickly changed the whole area. Businesses, mostly catering to tourists, were sprouting up in Thunder Canyon like daffodils in springtime. The resort, which had started out as a single lodge with a ski slope, had expanded to an upscale, year-round tourist attraction with all sorts of indoor and outdoor enticements for the young and old. And the resort was continuing to build and expand. Under the management of Marshall's longtime buddy Grant Clifton, the recreational hot spot had become a gold mine itself. And Marshall was definitely reaping part of the rewards.

This morning, as soon as he'd entered his office, his assistant Ruthann had placed a steaming cup of coffee along with a plate of buttered croissants on his desk. The woman had been a registered nurse for nearly thirty years and three years ago had just settled into retirement when her husband suddenly died of a heart attack. The tragedy had put her in financial straits and when Marshall had heard she'd needed a job, he'd decided she'd be perfect as his assistant.

Now after a year of working with her, he realized he'd been more than right about the woman. She was an excellent nurse with plenty of experience, plus he didn't have to worry about her ogling him as something to take home to meet mother. In fact, in her early fifties, Ruthann was more like a mother to him than an assistant.

"Surprise, surprise. You actually have three patients this morning," she said with dry amusement as she watched him chomp into one of the croissants. "Any clue as to when you'd like to see them?"

"Are any of them critical?" he asked, even though he knew if any patient had arrived with serious injuries, Ruthann wouldn't be standing around gabbing.

"A sprained ankle, a cut knee and a jammed finger. I think the finger case is just a ruse to see you. She's young and blond and drenched with designer perfume."

"What a suspicious mind you have, Ruthie," he scolded playfully.

Her laugh was mocking. "I see the sort of games that go on in this infirmary. Frankly, it amazes me how brazen women can be nowadays when it comes to you men."

The memory of Mia Smith's aloof, even shy behavior toward him yesterday had been something entirely different from the sort of women Ruthann was describing. Maybe that's why he couldn't get the heiress out of his mind.

"Okay, Ruthie, I'll forget my breakfast and go see if Ms. Blonde really has a finger problem."

The petite woman with short red hair and a face full of freckles snorted with playful sarcasm. "That's no way for a doctor to eat."

Grinning, he retorted, "Then why did you put it here for me?"

"Because I knew you'd sleep instead of get out of bed and make yourself breakfast."

Marshall shook a finger at her. "I'll have you know I was up early this morning. I just didn't make breakfast because I was chasing Leroy halfway down the mountain. He dug a hole last night beneath the backyard fence. Guess he was mad at me for not taking him hiking yesterday."

Marshall's Australian blue heeler was often so adept at understanding his master that it was downright eerie. No matter how he tried, Marshall couldn't fool the dog.

"You went hiking? I thought you were going to help your dad paint that workshed of his."

Shaking his head, Marshall wiped bread crumbs from his fingers and picked up the three files Ruthann had placed in front of them. Since they all belonged to current guests of the lodge, each of the manila folders held only a single sheet inside them. Being a doctor at a place where people resided for only a few days or weeks didn't allow the opportunity to make longtime patients. Temperature and blood-pressure readings didn't tell him much about a person. But that was okay with Marshall. He'd never set out to be one of those kind family doctors who knew all the townsfolk by name, made sure they kept all their routine checkups and often served as their counselor and therapist. That sort of doctoring took commitment and he was too busy enjoying himself in other ways to chain himself to an office.

"He and Mom had to do something with some friends—something about an anniversary celebration. We've planned the painting day for another time."

He rose to his feet, a signal to Ruthann that it was

time for them to get to work. As they walked to the door, he said casually, "I met the heiress yesterday."

Pausing, Ruthann twisted her head around to give him a bemused look. "The heiress," she repeated blankly. "What are you talking about?"

He rolled his eyes. Normally Ruthann was the one who kept him up on resort guests. He couldn't believe she was unaware of Mia Smith.

"*The heiress.* You know, that black-haired beauty that everyone has been talking about. The one that's always alone."

Ruthann's brows suddenly lifted with dawning. "Oh, that one. I didn't realize she was an heiress. Where'd you get that information?"

"Well, I don't know for a fact that she's an heiress. Grant was the one who insinuated that she must be from a rich family. She's been here more than two weeks now. Only a person with money to spare could afford that much time at a luxury resort. He said she rented a safety deposit box for her jewels, too."

"Grant! Isn't he supposed to be engaged to Stephanie? What's he doing gossiping about a female guest?"

Marshall sighed. Yep, Ruthann was just like a mother, he decided, maybe worse. "Don't go jumping to the wrong conclusions. I was the one asking Grant about Mia Smith."

Ruthann shot him a frown of disgust. "I should have guessed." She clucked her tongue in a disapproving way. "A grown man, a doctor at that, prying for information about a woman you don't know from Adam. Shame on you, Marshall Cates. Now what was she like?"

Marshall laughed at the nurse's abrupt turnaround on the sins of gossiping. "Cool. Very cool," he told her. "But as pretty as the rising sun. I got the sense, though, that she's like that beautiful actress, uh—" he paused as his mind searched for the name "—Greta Garbo. She wants to be alone."

Nodding shrewdly the nurse said, "In other words she didn't fall for any of your nonsense."

Reaching for the doorknob, Marshall yanked it open and taking Ruthann by the shoulder ushered her over the threshold.

"Don't count me out yet, Ruthie. Besides, for all you know the woman has been pacing her room, wondering how she can get a second chance with me."

Ruthann chuckled. "I'm sure she's tearing her hair out for an opportunity to get her hands on you."

That was the last thing Mia Smith was probably doing, Marshall thought wryly. But then he wasn't going to let her snub get to him. He'd never had to beg or cajole any woman into having a date with him and he'd be a fool to start now.

With a good-natured chuckle, he nudged Ruthann on toward the first examining room. "Let her pine. Why would I need a beautiful heiress when I have you?"

Behind the lodge, several hundred feet farther up the mountain, Mia paced through the suite of rooms she'd been living in since she'd arrived at Thunder Canyon Resort. A day ago she had considered the luxurious log cabin as a refuge. But now, after the encounter on the mountain with Dr. Marshall Cates, her peace of mind had been shattered.

She'd gone there hoping the quietness and the beauty would allow her to meditate, maybe even help her decide what to do next with her life. But then *he* showed up and her senses had been blown away by his charming smile and strong, masculine presence.

Now she was afraid to step out of her cabin and especially leery of walking down to the lodge, where the infirmary was located. The lodge meant maybe running into Dr. Cates and Mia didn't want to risk seeing him again. He was trouble. She'd felt it when she'd first looked into his eyes and felt her heart race like a wild mustang galloping across a grassy plain.

So what are you going to do, Mia? Stay in your cabin for the next month?

Groaning with self-disgust, Mia sank onto a wide window seat that looked down upon the lodge and the cluster of numerous other resort buildings, imagining what it would look like in the dead of winter. Everything would be capped with white snow and skiers would be riding the lifts and playing on the slopes.

Suddenly, her cell phone rang, the shrill sound jangling her nerves. She stared warily at the small instrument lying on an end table.

There were only a handful of people that had her number and she'd left all of them behind in Colorado. She'd told what few friends she had that she was taking an extended vacation and didn't know when she might return. As for her mother, Mia hadn't told Janelle Josephson anything. She'd simply left the woman a note telling her that she was going away for a while and to please give her the space she needed.

That had been nearly three weeks ago, and Janelle had rang Mia's cell phone every day since. And every day Mia had refused to take her call.

Mercifully, the ringing finally stopped and Mia left the window seat to look at the caller ID. Just as she expected. Janelle wouldn't give up. She wanted to be a part of her daughter's life. And as much as Mia hated to reject her, right now she couldn't even think of Janelle as her mother. As far as she was concerned her mother was dead and nothing, not even a pile of money, would ever bring her back.

There are people, like me, who make it just fine in life without a pile of riches.

Dr. Marshall Cates' words had pierced her heart like a flaming arrow and even a day later they continued to haunt her, to remind her of the awful, selfish choices she'd made in her life.

Money. She desperately wished that she'd never needed or wanted it. She wanted to take what she had of it and throw it into the nearest river. At least then maybe she would feel clean. At least then maybe she could start over. But something told her that even that drastic measure wouldn't heal the wounds she was carrying.

Angry with herself, she put down the phone, walked over to the dining table and grabbed the handbag she'd tossed there earlier. Seeking privacy didn't mean she had to totally hide from life. And if she did cross paths with Dr. Marshall Cates, she could handle it. After all, he was just a man.

A man who would look at you with disgust if he knew you'd once been Mia Hanover, a woman who'd killed her own mother.

For a brief moment, Mia shut her eyes tightly and swallowed hard as the memory of Nina Hanover's death filled her mind like a dark cloud. Her adoptive mother had been a woman who'd worked hard as a farmer's wife, who'd always tried to give Mia the best in life. She'd been a sweet, loving woman until the alcohol had taken her into its awful grip.

With a groan of anguish, Mia shook her head and hurried out of the cabin, wallowing in guilt and self-pity wasn't going to fix anything. She had to get out and get her mind on other things.

A half hour later, in downtown Thunder Canyon, she parked her rental car in front of the Clip 'N' Curl. Even though Mia had made use of the fancy beauty salon and spa located on the resort, she felt much more comfortable here in this traditional, down-home beauty parlor. Here the women dressed casually and everyone talked as though they were all family.

Since the majority of the women at the resort appeared to use the Aspenglow for their beauty treatments, Mia figured the patrons of the Clip 'N' Curl were local residents. In fact, a few days ago when she'd visited the place, she'd heard a couple of the women complaining about the traffic problems that the influx of tourists had brought to Thunder Canyon.

Since Mia was one of those tourists, she'd simply sat quietly and listened to the other customers discussing the Queen of Hearts mine and how the recent discovery of gold there had turned the town topsy-turvy. Several of the women felt that the new money was a wonderful thing for the little town, but others had spoken about how much they hated the traffic, the crowds and the loss of Thunder Canyon's quaintness.

Money. Gold. Riches. The subject seemed to follow Mia no matter where she went. If she could manage a walk-in appointment today, she hoped the shoptalk would be about something different. The last thing she wanted to think about was the money Janelle, her birth mother, had showered upon her and how drastically it had changed Mia's once simple life.

Leaving her small rental car, Mia walked into the Clip 'N' Curl and waited at the front desk. The small salon was presently undergoing major renovations. Only three stations were up and working amid the chaos of working carpenters. And today all three styling chairs were full while only three empty chairs remained in the small waiting area.

Figuring she'd never get an appointment, Mia turned to leave the shop when one of the hairdressers called out to her.

"Don't leave, honey. We'll make a place for you. Just have a seat. There's free coffee and muffins if you'd like a snack while you wait."

"Thank you. I'll be glad to wait," Mia told her, then took a seat in one of the empty plastic chairs.

As Mia reached forward and picked up one of the style magazines lying on a coffee table, the woman sitting next to her said, "Your hair looks beautiful. I hope you're not planning to cut it."

Easing back in the chair, Mia glanced over to see it was a college-aged woman who'd given her the compliment. Short, feathery spikes of chestnut hair framed a round face while a friendly smile spread a pair of wide lips.

Mia smiled back at her. "No. Just a shampoo and blow-dry. I've tried short hair before and believe me I didn't look nearly as cute as you."

The young woman let out a quiet, bubbly laugh. "Thanks for the compliment, but compared to you I'm just a plain Jane." She thrust her hand over toward Mia. "Hi, I'm Marti Newmar."

Mia shook Marti's hand and as she did she realized it had been months, maybe longer since she'd felt a real need to communicate with another woman just for the sake of talking and sharing ideas. Dear God, maybe this quaint little western town was beginning to help her heal, she thought.

"Mia Smith. Nice to meet you."

Marti's nose wrinkled at the tip as she thoughtfully studied Mia. "I think I've seen you somewhere. You live around here?"

Trying to push away the cloak of wariness she constantly wore, Mia said, "No. I'm a guest at Thunder Canyon Resort."

Marti's lips parted in an *O*, then her fingers snapped with sudden recognition. "That's it. That's where I've seen you. In the resort lounge."

Mia relaxed. She should have known this young woman had to be a local and not someone from Denver or Alamosa, Colorado, where she'd lived for most of her adult life.

"Yes, that's probably where it was," Mia agreed.

"I just started working at the coffee shop in the lounge a few days ago." She laughed. "I'm still learning how to make a latte. I grew up on a nearby ranch and the only kind of coffee my parents ever drank was the cowboy kind. You know, throw the grounds and water into a granite pot and let it boil. This fancy stuff is all new to me."

Warmed by the woman's openness, Mia smiled at her. "I'm sure you'll learn fast."

"I hope so. Grant Clifton, the guy that manages the resort, was kind enough to give me a job doing something. You see, I'm trying to get through college and the cost is just awful. I got a partial scholarship on my grades and this job should help with the rest of the expense."

Marti's situation was so familiar to Mia that she almost felt as though she were looking in a mirror. Five years ago she'd entered college with hopes of getting a degree in nursing. But at that time her father had already passed away and, using what little money she and her mother could earn at menial jobs, she'd had to settle for taking one or two classes at a time. Those years had been very rough and discouraging. It had been during those terribly lean times in her life that her priorities had gone haywire. She'd begun to think that money could fix everything that was messed up in her life. She'd been so very, very wrong.

"Whatever you do, don't give up," Mia encouraged her. "It may take you a while to find your dream, but you will."

Nodding, Marti said, "Yeah, that's what my mother keeps telling me." Tilting her head to one side, she continued to study Mia. "Have you met many people at the resort?"

The young woman's question instantly brought the image of Marshall Cates to Mia's mind.

"A few. I'm not…much of a social person."

"Hmm. Well, there're all sorts of good-looking men hanging around there." She gave Mia an impish grin. "But I only think of them as eye candy. I'm not about to let some smooth-tongued devil change my plans to become a teacher."

"I'm sure some day you'll want to marry. When the time is right for you," Mia told Marti, while wondering if that time would ever come for herself. At one time, Mia had dreamed and hoped for a family of her own. Now she would just settle for some sort of peace to come to her heart. Otherwise she'd never be able to give her love to anyone.

Marti shrugged in a ho-hum way. "I don't know. I've seen my older sister get her heartbroken over and over again." She looked at Mia. "You know Dr. Cates? The hunk that works at the resort?"

Every nerve in Mia's body suddenly went on alert. What was she going to learn about the man now?

"Vaguely," she said, not about to elaborate on the surprise encounter she'd had with the man.

Marti sighed, telling Mia that the young woman definitely considered Marshall Cates eye candy. "Gorgeous, isn't he?"

"He's, uh—a nice-looking man."

"Mmm. Well, my sister, Felicia, thought so, too. They dated for a while and she was getting wedding bells on the brain."

Mia was afraid to ask, but she did anyway. "What happened?"

Wrinkling her nose, Marti said, "She found out the good doctor wasn't about to settle for just one woman. Not when he had a flock of them waiting in line."

So the man was a playboy. That shouldn't surprise her. No matter where he was or who he was with, the man was bound to turn female heads. The best thing she could do was forget she'd ever met him. Still, she couldn't help but ask the question, "Is your sister still dating Dr. Cates?"

Marti chuckled. "No, thank goodness. She finally opened her eyes wide where Marshall Cates was concerned. She recently moved to Bozeman and got engaged to another guy."

Across the room, one of the hairdressers called out. "Marti, I'm ready for you, honey."

Smiling at Mia, the young woman hurriedly snatched up her handbag and jumped to her feet. "Nice meeting you, Mia. Maybe I'll see you at the coffee shop. Come by and say hello, okay?"

Nodding, Mia returned Marti's smile. "Sure. I'll look forward to it."

Later that afternoon, at the resort lodge, Marshall finished up the small amount of paperwork he had to do, then left Ruthann in charge of the quiet infirmary and headed down to the lounge bar for a short break.

Three couples were sitting at tables, busy talking and sipping tall, cool drinks. One older man with graying hair and a hefty paunch was sitting at the end of the bar. He appeared to be sleeping off his cocktail.

Lizbeth Stanton was tending bar this afternoon, and the pretty young woman with long auburn hair smiled when Marshall slid onto one of the stools.

"Hey, there. I was about to decide you weren't going to show up today." She glanced at the watch on her wrist. "This is late for you."

Marshall chuckled. "I'm so relieved that at least one woman around this place is interested enough to keep up with my comings and goings."

She shot him a sexy smile. "Awww. Poor Marshall," she cooed. "Had a bad day?"

With an easy grin, he raked a hand through his dark, wavy hair.

"I've never seen so many patients in one day. Several were suffering from altitude sickness and one had taken a nasty fall on a hiking trail. But they'll all be okay."

Not bothering to ask if he wanted a drink, Lizbeth

went over to a back bar and began to mix him a cherry cola. At one end of the work counter, a small stereo was emitting the twangy sounds of a popular country music tune.

"Well," Lizbeth said to him, "that *is* what you're paid for. To doctor people who have more money than sense."

Yeah, he thought, that's right. But sometimes in the darkest part of the night, when everything looks different, he wondered if he was just as shallow as some of the guests he treated. He'd not gone to school for eight years intending to doctor women who'd ripped off nail beds trying to rock climb with false fingernails. But on the other hand, Marshall was making an enormous salary and most days he hardly had to lift a hand to earn it. He'd be crazy to want anything else. Wouldn't he?

Lizbeth carried the tall glass over to the bar and placed it on a cork coaster before she pushed the frosty drink in front of him.

"Here, since you can't drink anything alcoholic on the job, maybe this will perk you up."

"Thanks, beautiful. Remind me to do something for you sometime." Giving her a wink, he took a sip of the drink, then lifted the stemmed cherry she'd placed on top and popped it into his mouth.

As he chewed the sweet treat, Lizbeth's brown eyes studied him in a calculating way. "Well, if you really mean that you could take me out to dinner tonight. I'm getting tired of taking home a sack of fast food and eating it in front of the television."

Marshall chuckled a second time. He doubted Lizbeth ever had to spend a night alone, unless she wanted it that way. Even if she was known as a big flirt, she was pretty, bubbly and enjoyable to be around, the perfect type of woman for Marshall, who didn't want any sort of clingy hands grabbing hold of him.

"If you'd really like to go out to dinner tonight, then I'm all for it."

A faint look of surprise crossed her face. "You really mean that?"

Marshall shrugged. He and Lizbeth both knew that neither of them would ever be serious about each other, but that didn't mean they couldn't enjoy an evening together. Besides, eating dinner with a warm, appreciative female was better than being snubbed by a cool, beautiful heiress.

"Sure," he answered. "Let's splurge and eat at the Gallatin Room. The grilled salmon is delicious."

Lizbeth's brown eyes were suddenly sparkling and Marshall wondered what it would take to see Mia Smith react to him in such a way.

Damn it, man, forget the woman, Marshall scolded himself. You've got plenty of female distraction around here. You don't need to get hung up on a woman who's apparently forgotten how to smile.

"Oh, this is great, Marshall! I can wear my new high heels. Just for you," she added with coy sweetness. "What time shall we meet?"

"When do you get off work?" Marshall asked.

"Six this evening. But I can ready by seven."

"Okay, I'll meet you in the lounge at seven-thirty," he told her. And by then he was going to make damn sure that the winsome Mia Smith was going to be pushed completely out of his thoughts.

Chapter Three

Mia wasn't at all sure why she'd bothered going out to eat this evening, especially at the Gallatin Room. Before she'd found Janelle, Mia had never been inside a restaurant where the tables were covered with fine linen and the food was served on fragile china. After her father, Will Hanover, had died of a lung disease, she and her mother had been lucky to splurge on burgers and fries at the local fast-food joint. The sort of life she was experiencing here at Thunder Canyon Resort was the sort she could only dream about back then.

Today at the Clip 'N' Curl, her brief visit with Marti Newmar had reminded her even more of how simple and precious those years on the farm had been with her adoptive parents. Maybe she'd not had much in the way of material things, but she'd been wrapped in the security of her family's loving arms. Mia had learned at an early age that she was adopted; yet that hadn't mattered. She'd been a happy girl until her father had died. And then things had gotten tough and she'd made all sorts of wrong choices. She'd begun to believe that money was all it would take to fix everything wrong in her life. Well, now she had it, but she was far from happy.

With a wistful sigh, she realized the Gallatin Room was the sort of restaurant that a woman should visit with her husband or lover. The small table where Mia sat near a wall of plate glass gave a magnificent view of the riding stables and several corrals of beautiful horses. Far beyond, near the valley floor, a river glistened like a ribbon of silver in the moonlight. Yet the pleasant sights couldn't hold Mia's attention. Instead she was imagining what it would be like if the handsome Dr. Cates was sitting opposite her, reaching across the fine white linen and clasping her fingers with his.

"Ms. Smith, your steak will be ready in a few minutes. Would you like more wine?"

Mia looked around to see a young waiter hovering at her elbow, willing to jump through hoops, if necessary, to please her. After the first few days at Thunder Canyon Resort, Mia had become aware that some of the male staff seemed to bend over backward in an effort to make her happy. She'd not been fooled into thinking they were at her beck and call because they liked their job. No doubt they'd heard gossip or simply assumed that she was rich. The fact that she *was* rich, only made her resent their behavior even more.

"Yes, I will take more wine, thank you," she told him.

The young man filled Mia's goblet with the dark, fruity wine she'd selected, then eased back from the table. As he moved from her sight, Mia got a glimpse of movement from the corner of her eye. Turning her head slightly to the right, she was shocked to see the handsome doctor and a sexy redhead taking their seats several tables over from hers.

Mia stared for a moment, then purposely looked away before either of them could spot her. She'd seen the redhead before, but where?

Recognition hit her almost immediately. She was the bartender here at the lounge. Mia had visited the bar on a few occasions, just to enjoy a cocktail and a change of scenery from the rooms of her cabin. The redhead had always been working behind the bar, but Mia had never seen Dr. Cates there. Were the two of them an item? It certainly appeared that way to Mia. But from what Marti Newmar had told her at the Clip 'N' Curl earlier today, the man liked women in the plural form. The bartender was probably just one in a long line waiting for a date with Dr. Smooth.

Across the room, at Marshall's table, he and Lizbeth had ordered and the waiter was pouring chilled Chablis into Lizbeth's stemmed glass when he looked slightly to the left and spotted *the* woman. She was sitting alone and, even over the heads of the other diners, Marshall couldn't mistake the black-haired beauty. It was Mia

Smith, wearing a slim pink sheath and black high heels with a strap that fastened around her ankles. Her black hair was swept tightly back from the perfect oval of her face and knotted into an intricate chignon at the back of her head. She was a picture of quiet elegance and Marshall found it hard not to stare.

"Dining here in this posh part of the resort is quite a treat for me, Marshall. You must be feeling generous," Lizbeth teased.

Jerking his head back to his date, Marshall plastered a smile on his face. Lizbeth was the sort of woman who'd be happy to let a rich man take care of her for the rest of her life. Since it wasn't going to be him, he could afford to feel generous.

"Maybe I just felt as though I had earned my paycheck today," he told her.

She laughed. "Oh, Marshall, you're so funny at times. I hope you never go serious like that brother of yours. He should have been a judge."

Marshall had three brothers. At thirty, Mitchell was four years younger than him. And then there were the twins, Matthew and Marlon, who were just twenty-one and trying to finish up their last year of college.

At one time in their young lives both Marshall and Mitchell had walked somewhat on the wild side. And while the two boys had lived on the edge, they'd both loved a passel of ladies and broken more than a few hearts. But age had slowed both of them down, Mitchell especially. He'd founded a farm and ranching equipment business and spent nearly all his time making the place turn big dollars.

"That's why Mitchell has made a big success of Cates International," Marshall said to her. "He takes his business seriously. When I'm out on the slopes skiing, he's usually at work. That's the difference between him and me."

Lizbeth playfully wrinkled her nose at him. "What's the use of money if you can't have a little fun with it?"

Marshall sipped at the beer he'd ordered, then licked the foam from his lips. He would surely like to ask Mia Smith that question, he thought. But then maybe she was having fun. Maybe being alone was how she liked things.

He looked back to the table where Mia was dining and before he could catch himself he was gazing at her again. At the moment she was eating one slow bite at a time. There was something very sensual in her movements, as though she was a woman who savored each and every taste. Marshall could only imagine what it would feel like to have those lush lips touching him.

"In case you don't know, her name is Mia Smith."

Lizbeth's comment doused him with hot embarrassment and he quickly jerked his attention back to his dining companion.

"You caught me. What can I say, Lizbeth, except that I'm sorry?"

Laughing lightly, she reached over and touched the top of his hand. "Don't bother. I know when a man considers me just a friend. It might be nice if you looked at me the way you're looking at her. But you don't."

Relief washed through him. Jealous women were

hard to handle, especially in a place that required good manners. "Thanks for understanding, Lizbeth," he said, wryly. "I guess I'm pretty transparent, huh?"

"Well, if I knew the Gettysburg address I would have had time enough to recite the whole thing while you were staring at Ms. Smith."

Shaking his head with a bit of self-disgust, he said, "I'm sorry. It's just that—well, I met her yesterday. On the mountain while I was hiking."

Intrigued by this morsel of news, Lizbeth leaned forward. "Really? Did you exchange words with the woman?"

The two of them had exchanged words, glances, even touches, but apparently none of it had affected Mia Smith the way it had Marshall. She'd walked away from him as though he were no more than a servant.

"A few."

"That's all? Just a few?"

"The lady is cool, Lizbeth. She—uh—wasn't interested in getting to know me."

Picking up her wineglass, Lizbeth laughed, which only caused the frown on Marshall's face to deepen. "That's hard to believe. I've talked with her at the bar and she seemed friendly to me."

Now it was Marshall's turn to stare with open curiosity at Lizbeth. "You know the woman?"

Shrugging, Lizbeth said, "She comes in the bar fairly often. Drinks a piña colada with only a dash of alcohol."

"Does she ever have anyone with her?"

"No. She's always alone," Lizbeth answered. "Can't

figure it, can you? The lady is beautiful. Men would swoon at her feet, but apparently she won't let them. Maybe you ought to ask her for a date. If anyone can change her tune about the opposite sex, it would be you, dear Marshall."

He chuckled with disbelief. "Me? Not hardly. I offered to buy her a drink. She pretty much gave me the cold shoulder."

"Maybe you should try again. That is—if you're really interested in the woman."

Unable to stop himself, Marshall glanced over at Mia's table. At the moment she was staring pensively out the window as though she were seeking something in the starlit sky.

"Frankly, I wish I wasn't interested. I have a feeling the lady is trouble. She doesn't come across as the other rich guests around here. She's different."

Lizbeth smiled coyly. "And maybe that's why you can't get her off your mind. Because she *is* different."

He thoughtfully studied his date. "Hmm. Maybe you're right. And maybe once I got to know her, I'd find out she's not my type at all. Then I could safely cross her off my list."

Lizbeth let out a knowing little laugh. "You'll never know until you try."

The next morning on his way to work, Marshall entered the lodge by way of the lounge and headed to the coffee shop. After the busy day in the infirmary yesterday, he wanted to pick up one of those fancy lattes and present it to Ruthann when she walked through the door. No doubt the surprise treat would make his hardworking nurse want to whip out her thermometer and take his temperature, he thought wryly.

At this early hour, the coffee shop was full of customers sitting around the group of tiny tables, reading the *Thunder Canyon Nugget* and the daily newspaper from nearby Bozeman while drinking ridiculously expensive cups of flavored java. Marshall found himself waiting at the back of a long line and wondering if he had time to deal with getting the latte for Ruthann after all, when a vaguely familiar voice spoke behind him.

"Looks like we have a long line this morning."

Turning, he was more than surprised to see Mia Smith. She was dressed casually in jeans and a white shirt with the sleeves rolled back against her tanned arms. Her black hair was loose upon her shoulders and the strands glistened attractively in the artificial lights.

The sight of her put an instant smile on his face. "Yes. Everyone must have had the same idea for coffee this morning."

Mia could feel his gaze sliding over her face and down her throat to where her shirt made a V between her breasts. The sensual gaze made her wonder if he'd looked this same way at his date last night. Then just as quickly she scolded herself for speculating about the playboy doctor. The man's private behavior was none of her business.

Even so, she couldn't stop the next words out of her mouth. "How did you like your dinner last night at the Gallatin Room?"

His brows lifted ever so slightly. "I didn't realize you saw me there."

This morning he was obviously dressed for work in a pair of dark slacks and a baby-blue button-down shirt. A red tie with a blue geometric print was knotted neatly at his throat. She could see that he'd attempted to tame the wild waves of his thick hair, but several of the locks had already fallen onto his forehead. Just one look at him was probably enough to cure most of his female patients.

"I...uh—spotted you and your date when you were arriving."

"Oh. Well, Lizbeth wasn't actually a date. I mean— she was—but we're basically just friends. Actually, she was the one who asked me out."

Mia shot him a droll look. Was this the sort of line he handed out to all unsuspecting females?

"Good for her."

The line of customers began to move forward and she tried to peer around his shoulder to gauge how much longer the wait would be, but the man held her gaze.

"I stopped here at the coffee shop this morning to pick up a latte for my nurse," he explained. "She's always treating me so I thought I'd do something for her."

Figuring his nurse was a twenty-something blonde with long eyelashes and a come-hither smile, Mia said, "Why settle for just a coffee? Perhaps you should take her to the Gallatin Room, too."

To her amazement a look of dawning swept over his face and he nodded in agreement. "You know, that's a wonderful idea. Ruthann has been a nurse for more than thirty years and she's always taking care of other people, even when she isn't on the job. Her husband died of a heart attack about three years ago and she's having a hard time making ends meet with just his social security to help her along. Dinner at the Gallatin Room would be something really special for her. Thank you, Mia, for suggesting it."

Feeling suddenly like a heel, she hoped he never guessed that her suggestion had been given in sarcasm. Damn it, why did she continually want to believe this man was only out for himself? Because Marti had described him as a ladies' man? Or because a user could always spot another user, she thought dismally.

But you're not a user, Mia. Everything you have has been given to you freely. You haven't taken anything from anybody—except your adoptive mother's life.

Trying to shut away the guilty voice inside of her, Mia gave him a hesitant smile. "I—uh—think that would be a very nice gesture for your nurse."

"Well, I'm not always as thoughtful as I should be. Blame it on my male genes."

The grin on his handsome face was as wicked as the images going through Mia's head. She'd never been around a man who continually made her feel like she needed to take deep breaths of pure oxygen. Dr. Cates was making her think things that definitely belonged behind closed doors.

Smiling in spite of herself, she said, "I'm sure your nurse will think you're very thoughtful."

At that moment a customer carrying a portable

cardboard holder filled with several cups of coffee was attempting to work his way through the crowd. As he jostled close to Mia, the doctor's hands closed around her shoulders and quickly set her out of the customer's path.

The abrupt movement brought her even closer to Marshall and he realized her thigh was pressed against his and the thrust of her breasts was almost touching his chest. His breathing slowed, while the faint scent of gardenia filled his head like a gentle breeze on a hot night.

"I—uh—thought that man's drink was going to topple right on you." Reluctantly, he eased his grip on her shoulders. "Sorry if I startled you."

He watched a pretty pink flush fill her cheeks. "I—it's okay. Better to be a little startled than scalded."

The line ahead of them moved again and Marshall quickly glanced over his shoulder to see he was next to place an order. If he was ever going to make his move on this woman he needed to do it now and fast.

"You— I noticed you were dining alone last night and I was wondering if you might like some company tonight? I'm free if you are."

Faint surprise crossed her face, an expression that puzzled Marshall. Surely a woman who looked like her was used to men asking her out to dinner.

"Actually, I don't think I could take the Gallatin Room two nights in a row. It's a little stuffy for my taste."

Hope sprang up in him like an exploding geyser and he wondered what the hell was coming over him. The world was full of pretty women and willing ones at that.

Why had getting a date with this one suddenly become so important?

"Mine, too. I only took Lizbeth there because she— Well, she enjoys that sort of thing, but she can't really afford such a splurge on her own." Another quick glance over his shoulder told him the customer was about to step away from the counter. He turned a beseeching look on Mia. "We could go downtown and maybe grab a burger or pizza. How does that sound?"

She opened her mouth as though to speak, then just as quickly her pink lips pressed thoughtfully together. Behind him, the coffee shop attendant said, "Dr. Cates, it's your turn to order now."

With his eyes riveted on Mia's face, he tossed over his shoulder, "A large latte with plenty of foam."

His dark brown eyes were pulling her in, making her forget there was a crowd of people around them. In the back of her mind, she understood he was a man who would be dangerous to any woman's heart. Yet there was something about his smile that made him impossible to resist.

"Sure," she heard herself saying. "A burger would be nice."

"Great. Where shall I pick you up? Are you staying here in the lodge?"

Not yet ready to give him that much information, she said, "I'll meet you here at the lounge."

A wide smile suddenly dimpled both cheeks and Mia felt her insides go as gooey as warm taffy.

"Great. I'll be here. Six-thirty okay?"

Why not, she thought. It wasn't like she had anything

important to do and maybe it was time she did something about this aimless path she'd been on for the past few months. "Six-thirty is fine. I'll see you then."

After he'd picked up his latte and given her a quick farewell, Mia found herself standing at the counter staring straight into Marti Newmar's smiling face.

"Hi, Mia! I didn't expect to see you here so soon. What can I get you this morning?"

"Hi yourself," Mia greeted the bubbly young woman. "I'd like a cappuccino with sugar and a pecan Danish."

Marti repeated the order to another worker who was busily preparing the drinks and rang in Mia's purchases.

While they waited on the cappuccino, Marti leaned slightly over the counter and said in a hushed voice, "Looks like Dr. Cates has his eye on you. Be careful, Mia. I wouldn't want you to end up like my sister."

Shaking her head, Mia smiled at the young woman's earnest face. "Don't worry, Marti. I'm not about to let the doctor turn my head."

"Yeah, well that's what Felicia said, too."

Thankfully, a worker set her order on the counter and Mia quickly scooped it up. Now that she'd agreed to a date with Dr. Cates, the last thing she wanted to hear were warnings about the man's character. She'd rather find out such things for herself than listen to gossip.

"I'll keep that in mind. See you later, Marti."

At the back of the lodge, in Marshall's airy office, Ruthann sipped leisurely at her latte while Marshall playfully tap-danced around her chair.

"Have you lost your mind, doc?" she asked with a

laugh. "First you surprise me with a cup of coffee that cost more than my wristwatch and now you're trying to imitate Fred Astaire. What else do you have planned for today?"

Laughing, he grabbed her swivel chair and spun her in a wild circle that had her yelling for him to stop.

"How about a date with the heiress? That's what I have planned."

She planted her feet on the hardwood floor and stared at his smug face. "Oh. So that's what this display of joy is all about. You've proved me wrong and talked the mystery beauty into a date. I should have guessed. How did you do it?"

Still smiling, he sauntered over to his desk and took a seat in his plush leather chair. "Frankly, Ruthie, I don't have a clue. I ran into her at the coffee shop and—" He stopped and held up a hand. "Wait a minute, I'd better tell you about last night first. I saw her, the mystery beauty, dining at the Gallatin Room last night."

Ruthann lowered her coffee and frowned at him. "It's a good thing we don't have any patients waiting this morning, cause I'd like to hear what you were doing having dinner in the Gallatin Room. You have so much money that you've decided to start throwing it away?"

His expression suddenly sheepish, Marshall shrugged. "I took Lizbeth out to dinner."

Ruthann groaned out loud. "Oh, Lord, Marshall, what were you thinking? She's nothing but a big flirt."

He batted a dismissive hand at her. "Never mind Lizbeth. I'm not serious about her."

Ruthann's expression turned incredulous. "And you are serious about the mystery woman?"

Marshall chuckled at his nurse's question. "Ruthie, you know me, I don't have plans to get serious about any woman. Why should I? I'm having too much fun."

She smirked. "Why indeed? Have you ever thought of children? Of someone to spend your golden days with?"

Marshall's barked laugh said he was worried about Ruthann's sanity. "Just how old do you think I am, Ruthie? I've got years ahead of me before I think about anything like a family. Right now I've got mountains to climb."

She leveled a thoughtful look at him. "And what are you going to find when you reach the top?"

Tilting the plush chair to a reclining position, he linked his hands at the back of his neck and let out a smug sigh. "The satisfaction of getting there. That's what I'll find."

"Satisfaction, huh? Well, you go on climbing, doc. I'd rather have two loving arms around me."

Chapter Four

Later that evening, before it was time to meet Marshall, Mia sat on the bed in her cabin and slowly sifted through the stack of photos in her hand. She wasn't at all sure why she'd packed the snapshots when she'd left Colorado.

Maybe she'd brought them along as a reminder of all she'd left behind. The photos were the only images she had of herself with her birth mother. They'd been taken during Mia's twenty-sixth birthday party, which had been held at Janelle's lavish home.

A frown tugged at the corners of her mouth. She still couldn't think of the mansion in Denver as her home. But for nearly two years Mia had lived there with her birth mother. During that time she'd tried to fit into Janelle's rich social life and accustom herself to the role of an heiress. All of which had been a drastic change for the young woman who until then had been struggling to work her way through school.

With a sigh, Mia stared at the snapshot in front of her. No one could mistake the identity of the tall woman with her arm draped affectionately around Mia's shoulders. She was almost the mirror image of Mia, only older. One minute Mia had been a young woman in nursing school who longed for the safe and secure home she'd had when her father had still been alive and working their potato farm, a young woman on a long and seemingly fruitless search for her birth mother. The next minute she'd not only found Janelle Josephson but she also discovered the woman was unbelievably rich. After that, Mia and her adopted mother's life had taken a drastic turn.

For years Mia had hunted her birth mother and for just as many years Nina had tried to dissuade her from the search, insisting that Mia's birth mother didn't want to be found. But Mia had felt driven to find the woman who'd signed her baby girl over to a stranger.

In the end, both Janelle and Mia had been shocked at the occurrences that had separated mother and daughter. Controlling parents had led a teenage Janelle to believe her baby was stillborn. She'd had no idea that her daughter was alive and searching for her. As for Mia, it was difficult for her to absorb the fact that she had a wealthy mother, one who seemingly loved her and was only too happy to lavish her with all the treasures and resources that money could buy.

What happens when a person goes from poverty to riches? Mia was a good example of that age-old question. Suddenly she could have any material thing she wanted, but none of it had made her happy.

For a moment the turmoil in Mia's heart brought a stinging mist to her eyes. But then she determinedly pressed her lips together and shoved the photos in the nightstand drawer.

Right now she needed to put her troubled reflections away and put on the cheeriest face she could muster. It was almost time for her to walk down to the lodge and meet Dr. Cates. And she wanted to give the jovial, flirty doctor the impression that she was just as carefree and happy as he.

Minutes later, Mia walked into the lounge and spotted her date sitting on the end of a plush leather couch. He was focusing intently on the BlackBerry in his hand and for a brief moment Mia paused to study his sexy image.

Even after she'd become an heiress, she'd never dreamed a man of his stature would show interest in her. But she realized that if the doctor knew the real truth of her past, he wouldn't be sitting here waiting to have an evening with her.

Tonight, however, she wasn't going to dwell on that, she wanted to have fun and see if she could remember how to enjoy herself on a simple date.

Mia was walking across the lounge and had almost reached the couch where he was sitting, when he happened to look up and spot her approach.

The quick leap of her heart surprised her. For so long now she'd felt numb. Incapable of feeling anything.

Smiling broadly, he rose to his feet and shoved the BlackBerry into the pocket of his blue jeans. As she walked toward him, he quickly closed the last few steps separating them.

"Hello, Ms. Smith," he said warmly.

His voice was just rough enough to be sexy and she wondered what it would sound like if he were to whisper in her ear.

Smiling in return, she thrust her hand toward his. "Please make it Mia. Calling each other Ms. and Dr. over a burger would be a little ridiculous, don't you think?"

"And shaking hands with a beautiful woman is more than ridiculous for me," he said. And before she could guess his intentions, he leaned forward and placed a gentle kiss on her cheek. "There. That's a much better greeting, don't you think?"

His dancing brown eyes held hers, and Mia realized she was far too charmed to scold him for being forward. The skin along her cheekbone tingled where his lips had touched her and she was getting that breathless feeling all over again.

Deliberately avoiding his pointed question, she said, "I hope you haven't been waiting long."

"Not more than five minutes," he answered. "Are you ready to go? Or would you like to have a drink at the bar before we leave the lodge?"

"Actually, I'm hungry. Let's save the drink for another time." If there was another time, she reminded herself. If Marti's opinion of this man was correct, he'd probably have a different woman on his arm tomorrow night.

"Great," he said. "Let's go. My Jeep is waiting outside the lodge."

Figuring his "jeep" would be one of those plush SUV's that could comfortably haul seven, she was surprised to find his vehicle was one of those compact two-seaters built high off the ground and generally used to traverse rough terrain.

After helping her negotiate the lofty step up, Marshall skirted the hood and quickly slid beneath the wheel. While he buckled his seat belt and started the engine, Mia glanced around the small interior. Behind them, a small bench seat was loaded down with a canvas backpack and a pair of boots caked with mud. An assortment of empty bottles that had one time held water and sports drinks lay on the floorboard below. In front, a small crate of CD's was wedged between the console and the dash. Hanging from the rearview mirror was a small dream catcher made of black and white feathers.

"I promise I cleaned the dog hair from your seat before I drove over here to the lodge. The rest of the mess I hope you'll forgive. I get busy doing things I enjoy and put off all the tasks I hate."

Actually she was relieved that he hadn't shown up in some sleek, spotless luxury car. This vehicle made him seem far more human and closer to the lifestyle Mia had been accustomed to before Janelle had taken her in and presented her with a treasure trove of riches.

"It's fine," she assured him as she adjusted the seat belt across her lap. "You say you have a dog?"

He shoved the floor shift into Reverse and backed out of the parking slot. "A blue heeler named Leroy. He's spoiled worse than I am."

Mia smiled faintly as she glanced over at him. "I take it you spoiled him, but who spoiled you?"

He grinned that sexy grin of his and Mia was suddenly reminded of their close quarters. If she were so minded, she could easily reach over and curl her hand over his forearm.

"My mother insists she ruined all of her boys. Much to Dad's dismay," he added with a chuckle.

Interest peaked her brows. "You have brothers?"

"Three. Mitchell. He's thirty. And the twins, Matthew and Marlon, are twenty-one."

Three brothers and a complete set of parents, Mia couldn't imagine having a more wonderful family. "Where do you fit in among the bunch?"

"I'm thirty-four, the oldest of the Cates brood. My parents live north of town, not too far out. Maybe you'd like to meet them before you leave?"

Meet his parents? No. She didn't think so. Making too many memories here might make it that much harder to leave. And she would have to leave soon, she reminded herself. She couldn't continue to hide from Janelle much longer.

"Maybe," she answered.

By now they were leaving the resort area and the Jeep was heading south on Thunder Canyon Road. Ahead of them on the far horizon, the sun was sinking, spreading a golden-pink glow over the mountain basin.

"I guess all the hoopla over the Queen of Hearts mine is what drew you to this area? Or did you choose to stay at Thunder Canyon Resort for other reasons?"

The only reason she'd ended up in Thunder Canyon was because she'd gotten lost on her way out of Bozeman. Originally she'd been intending to travel all the way into Canada. But Marshall Cates didn't need to know the story of her life.

"I thought it would be beautiful and peaceful. And when I saw your little town with its Old West storefronts and flavor, I was enchanted. I didn't know anything about gold being found in Thunder Canyon until I'd been here a few days. From what I hear, the discovery has turned the place upside down."

With a wry twist to his lips, he nodded. "I never realized money could make people go so crazy. People who've been friends around here for years are now fighting over choice lots in town. Everyone wants to get their hands on a piece of the fortune that's coming in from the crush of tourists."

I never realized money could make people go so crazy, thought Mia.

Marshall didn't know it, but he could have spoken those very words about her. For a while money had slanted her every thought and controlled every choice she'd made. Now having the stuff was more like a dirty little secret that she couldn't hide or discard.

Stifling a sigh, she said, "Well, I've overheard several

women in the Clip 'N' Curl beauty salon talking about all the changes that have come to this area. Some of them like the opportunities the gold find has brought about. Others seem pretty resentful of all the traffic as well as all the strangers clomping up and down the sidewalks of their little town. How do you feel?"

Shrugging, he glanced at her and grinned. "Personally, I don't understand these people that want to hang on to the past. Hell, before the gold rush, lots of folks around here were hurting for jobs and an income of any kind. Now most of them are doing better than anyone ever thought possible, including me. And frankly, I don't see anything wrong with a man wanting to do better for himself."

No, Mia thought, doing better for oneself was hardly a crime. Unless somewhere along the way the rush for riches harmed innocent people. The way Mia's desperate need for financial security had ultimately harmed her dear adopted mother.

"I guess it's all in the way a person sees things," she murmured thoughtfully.

He tossed her another grin. "That was put very diplomatically, Mia. Maybe you should referee some of Thunder Canyon's town hall meetings," he added teasingly. "There's been so much feuding going on that the police have to hang close just in case a fight breaks out."

"No, thank you. I'm not into politics, local or otherwise."

She'd hardly gotten the words out of her mouth when the outskirts of town appeared in the distance. In a few short minutes they were passing the town's outdoor ice rink, now a quiet arena in the summer heat; then just around the corner was the Wander-On Inn, a stately old hotel that had originally been built and operated by Lily Divine, Thunder Canyon's own lady of ill repute.

As Mia studied the landmark, Marshall said, "Lily Divine first built that old hotel. If you've read anything about Thunder Canyon's history, you probably haven't forgotten her name. She's been called everything from a wicked madam to a noble suffragette. Her great-great-granddaughter Lisa Douglas owns the Queen of Hearts mine." He shook his head as if that fact was still hard to believe. "Now there's a rags-to-riches story. A couple of years ago, the woman was as poor as dirt and then she finds out she's the owner of a lucrative gold mine. I can't imagine how that sudden catapult must have felt."

Mia could have told Marshall exactly how finding sudden fortune felt. One day she'd been wondering if she could make two meals out of a package of wieners and the next she was eating steak from a gold-rimmed plate. The drastic change in her life had sent her emotions spinning in all directions.

Careful to keep her expression smooth, she asked, "This Lisa…is she happy now?"

Something in her voice pulled Marshall's glance over to her. She looked wistful, even hopeful, and Marshall could only wonder why she would be so interested in the outcome of a person who was a total stranger to her.

"I suppose so. She married one of the Douglases, a

family that probably owns half the valley. In fact, his old man built the resort where you're staying. She'll never want for anything again."

Her lips pursed and then her gaze dropped to her lap and a curtain of black hair swung forward to hide her pained expression. "You can't be sure of that," she said quietly. "People die—things change."

"Yeah. But she'll always have the money."

Her head jerked up and she glared at him as though he'd just uttered a blasphemy. "What does that mean? You think money can take the place of a loved one? Well, it can't!"

Her voice was quivering with outrage and Marshall was befuddled as to why she'd reacted so strongly to his comment. With his right hand he reached over and gently touched her forearm. "Whoa, Mia. Don't get so bent out of shape. I just meant that she'd always have financial security. I like money just as much as the next guy, but my loved ones mean more to me than anything—even a gold mine, if I had one."

His gaze left the road long enough to see her release a long breath and her pretty features twist with regret.

"I—I'm sorry, Marshall. Having money has made me too touchy, I guess. But people say insensitive things, especially when they don't understand that we have problems, too."

He wanted to ask her what sort of problems she was talking about, but he could see she was hardly in the mood. Besides, he sensed the woman needed joy and laughter in her life and that was the very thing he wanted to give her.

"You're right, Mia. People are too quick to judge. But let's not have a philosophical discussion about human nature right now. I want to have fun with you tonight. Okay?"

She nodded jerkily and he was relieved to see a faint smile cross her face.

"Sure," she said. "I didn't mean to suddenly get so serious on you. Let's start over, shall we?"

Marshall gave her a broad smile. "Okay, we'll start over. Good evening, Mia. What would you like to eat tonight?"

"Burgers and fries. I'm sure you advise your patients not to eat such things, but maybe you can forget about the fat and calories for one night."

Glad to see she was going to follow his suggestion and lighten up, he chuckled. "Believe me, Mia, doctors don't always practice what they preach. Burgers and fries sound great to me."

At the next intersection, he made a right onto South Main. As they passed the town square with its shade trees and park benches, he said, "There's a little place right down here where I used to eat in all the time when I worked at Thunder Canyon General. They serve plain home-cooked meals and the burgers are great. You can even have a buffalo burger if you'd like."

Her nose wrinkled playfully. "I'm afraid I'm not quite that adventurous. I think I'll stick to plain ole beef."

Moments later Marshall parked the Jeep near a small bar and grill. As they walked down the rough board sidewalk, Mia noticed the front of this particular building was made to look like an Old West saloon, complete with swinging doors.

As they entered the dim interior, she could feel Marshall's hand flatten against the small of her back. And though she'd expected his touch to feel warm and strong, she'd not expected the wild zings of awareness spreading through her body.

Bending his head down to hers, he spoke close to her ear in order to be heard above the country music blaring from the jukebox in the far corner.

"We seat ourselves here at the Rusty Spur," he said. "How about a table over by the wall?"

"Fine with me," she answered.

Tonight the bar and grill appeared to be the popular place to be. Most of the round wooden tables and chairs were filled with diners and beer drinkers. Everyone was dressed casually and seemed to be laughing and talking and generally having a good time. Quite a contrast from the elegant Gallatin Room, she thought wryly.

As soon as Marshall helped her into a chair and took his own seat, a fresh-faced young waitress with a blond ponytail stopped at the side of their table to take their orders.

When Mia requested a soda to go with her food, Marshall said, "They serve beer here that's made at a nearby brewery. It's really good. Wouldn't you like to try one?"

Mia tried not to outwardly stiffen at his suggestion. She wasn't a prude, but after seeing Nina become dependant on alcohol she preferred to limit herself.

With a shake of her head, she said, "No. Soda is fine. But you please go ahead."

While Marshall gave the waitress their order, Mia looked around the L-shaped room. The ceiling was low and crisscrossed with dark wooden beams; the walls were made of tongue and groove painted a pale green. Not far from the swinging door entrance, a long bar, also fashioned from dark wood, ran for several feet. Swiveling stools with low backs of carved wooden spokes served as chairs; at the moment they were all filled with customers.

As the waitress finished scribbling onto her pad and hurried away, Mia turned her attention back to him.

"This seems to be a popular place. You say you used to eat here when you worked at Thunder Canyon General. You worked at the hospital before you took the job at the resort?"

He nodded. "I went to work there right after I finished my internship."

Mia thoughtfully studied his handsome face and realized there were more layers to the man than she'd expected to find.

"What sort of medicine did you practice there? The same thing you do at the resort?"

As Mia watched the corners of his mouth curve upward, she could feel her heart flutter like a happy little bird. Which was totally ridiculous. She'd had men smile at her before, even good-looking men. But they'd not made her blood hum with excitement the way that Marshall did.

"Mostly E.R. work."

"Did you like doing that?"

For a moment he was thoughtful, as though he'd never stopped to ask himself that question. "I suppose. There was always something different going on."

Easing back in her chair, she said knowingly, "But you like your job at the resort better."

His laugh was a mixture of amusement and disbelief. "Of course. Why wouldn't I? It's a cushy job. On most days I only see a handful of patients. I'm provided with a great nurse and the resort pays the astronomical cost of medical liability for me."

The waitress arrived with their drinks. After Mia had taken a long sip of her soda she said, "Is that what you went to medical school for? To get a job like you have at the resort? Or did you become a doctor so you could help people?"

Laughing lowly, he shook a playful finger at her. "Now, now, Ms. Smith. We weren't going to have philosophical discussions, tonight. Remember?"

Blushing faintly, she smiled. "Okay. I won't dig at that anymore. So tell me about your siblings. Do you get along with them?"

"Sure. We're all good buddies. 'Course, with Mitchell and I being closer in age, that made us a little tighter, I suppose. We love our twin brothers, too, but growing up they were just a little too young to do much with us."

"Any of them like sports as much as you?"

"Kind of, the twins are into baseball and football, sports of that sort. But Mitchell is more of a brain than an athlete. I couldn't pay him to climb a mountain with me."

"I don't blame him," Mia said. "It's dangerous stuff."

"Not if you know what you're doing." He leaned toward her, his dark brown eyes twinkling in a way that warmed her blood even more. "I could teach you."

Mia laughed and as she did she realized this was the first time since her mother had died that she'd felt this good. Before she realized what she was doing, she reached over and squeezed his hand with her fingers.

"You must be an optimist, Marshall, if you think you can teach me to climb a mountain. I'm too awkward and certainly not strong enough."

His thumb reached out and curved over hers. The touch was ridiculously intimate, but although Mia told herself to pull away, her body wouldn't obey her brain's instructions. His touch made her feel secure, even wanted. Something she hadn't felt in a long time.

"You hiked all the way up to the bluff on Hawk's Home. That's a pretty stiff climb."

His compliment put a warm blush on her cheeks. "Thank you for the confidence. But that's hiking. That's not what you do with the pulleys and ropes and such."

"I can teach you all that. In baby steps, of course."

The grin on his face deepened, showcasing his dimples. It was hard for Mia to concentrate on their conversation; her senses were spinning, her mind conjuring up all sorts of sexual images.

"I—don't know. Maybe before I leave you can take me on a baby climb."

Surprise and then pleasure swept across his face. "I'd like that, Mia. You'd be the first woman to go climbing with me."

She shot him a skeptical look. "You don't really expect me to believe that, do you?"

"Why not? Most of the women I've dated don't like to do that much outdoor strenuous stuff. A bicycle ride maybe. But not mountain climbing."

For some reason, Mia didn't want to be compared to his other dates. Nor did she want to think of him as a playboy or herself as just one of many women who'd sat across a table from him and held his hand.

Easing her fingers away from his, she said, "Shows you how much sense I have."

The grin on his lips eased to a pleased curve. "No, it means you're unique. Just like I imagined you'd be."

She was unique, all right, Mia thought wryly. If he looked for a hundred years, he wouldn't find another woman who'd turned her back on the loving mother who raised her. He wouldn't find another woman stupid enough to think that financial security would fix all the ills in her life.

Yes, Mia was unique, all right, but in all the wrong ways. Hopefully, Marshall Cates wouldn't discover any of those terrible things about her until long after she'd left Thunder Canyon.

Chapter Five

Before Mia and Marshall left the Rusty Spur, he insisted that the two of them needed dessert and asked the waitress to get them a container of Golden Nugget to go.

Later, after Marshall had paid for the meal and the two of them had left the building, she looked suspiciously at the brown paper sack in his hand.

"What is that—did you call it Golden Nugget?"

His grin mischievous, he helped her into the Jeep. "I did. They conjured up this stuff shortly after the gold strike. You'll find out what it is when we get to where we're going to eat it."

"A man of mystery," she said teasingly. "Well, I suppose I'll just have to wait for this surprise dessert."

Once he'd pulled away from the bar and grill, he

turned the vehicle toward North Main. While he negotiated the busy narrow streets, Mia realized she hadn't
felt this warm and mellow in a long time. Like their
meal, their conversation had been simple and comfortable. She was enjoying being with the man far more than
she had expected.

To Mia's surprise, Marshall drove them straight to
Thunder Canyon Road and stopped the Jeep in the large
graveled parking lot of the ice rink.

"What are we doing at an outdoor ice rink in August?"

Marshall's chuckle was suggestive enough to lift
her brows. "We're going to eat our dessert, what
else?" he asked.

Picking up the brown paper bag, he left the vehicle
and came around to help her down to the ground. As Mia
placed her hand in his she felt a rush of naughty excitement. After nearly three years of avoiding men altogether, being out with a man as sexy and sensual as
Marshall was like having a plateful of cherry pie after
a long stretch of dieting. Sinful, but delicious.

Once she was standing on the ground, he slipped his
free arm around the back of her waist and guided her
toward the rink, which was surrounded by a chain-link
fence and dimly lit by one lone lamp standing near a
small building that was used as a warming room. The
gate was unlocked and once they were inside the
compound they walked over to one of the wooden
benches looking out over the rink.

A huge cottonwood tree shaded the seat while
overhead the fluttering leaves were making soft music

in the evening breeze. In the far distance, the mountains surrounding Thunder Canyon Resort loomed like majestic sentinels robed in deep greens and purples. Mia sighed with pleasure as she sank onto the bench.

"It's pretty here. I'll bet it's really nice when the rink is frozen over and skaters are whirling about. Do you skate?" she asked.

"Sure do. Our parents taught all of us boys how to skate long before we ever went to kindergarten." He smiled fondly out at the now empty rink. "I've had some really fun times here. Even when I cracked my wrist."

He began to open the paper bag and pull out a quart-sized paper carton. When he pulled off the lid she could see it held something that looked like ice cream.

"Oh. A cracked wrist doesn't sound like fun to me."

He handed her one of the two plastic spoons.

"Several of us skaters had made a dandy whip and I was getting a heck of a ride out on the tail end. It was a blast until the g-force finally got me and I flew completely off the ice and crashed into a bench like the one we're sitting on. My wrist was in a cast for six weeks."

Mia gave him a knowing smile. "Sounds like you were a little daredevil. I'll bet you gave your mother plenty of gray hairs."

"Probably more than a few," he admitted with a wry smile. "But my parents always encouraged us to be independent and adventurous. I think it stuck on me the most."

He thrust the container toward her. "Dig in. I can't eat all this by myself."

Mia followed his example and spooned up a bite. As the ice cream melted on her tongue, she closed her eyes and savored the taste. "Mmm. You were right. This is scrumptious."

"See, the streaks of caramel are supposed to represent veins of ore and the chunks of almonds are the gold nuggets. This is definitely one good thing that came out of the Queen of Hearts striking it rich. Next to you, that is," he added with a wink.

Mia understood his words were just playful flirting, but she also considered how nice it would be—and more than flattering—for a man like him to look at her in a serious way. When her father had still been alive and her life had been fairly secure, she'd been smart enough to know that she'd never belong to the elite of the world. She didn't dream of marrying a prince or even a doctor or a lawyer. She'd always pictured herself with a farmer or, at the very most, a man who made his living working outdoors, like Lance, who'd worked as a Colorado forest ranger.

But after a tumultuous year of dating, Lance had walked away from her, she thought grimly. He'd tired of her obsessive search for her birth mother, then later he'd hated the woman she'd changed into after finding Janelle and her inheritance.

Trying to shake away that dismal thought, she lifted her gaze to Marshall and gave him a lopsided smile. "You need to remember that Golden Nugget is a permanent fixture here in Thunder Canyon. I'm not."

His spoon paused in midair as the corners of his

mouth turned downward in an exaggerated frown. "You're not leaving soon, are you?"

This past week Mia had been telling herself that it was time to go, time to get back to reality and finally make a few painful decisions concerning her relationship with Janelle. But then she'd met Marshall on the mountain and now she was foolishly looking for any reason to stay at the resort a few days longer.

Dropping her gaze to the ice-cream container wedged between their thighs, she murmured, "I don't suppose it's necessary for me to leave in the next few days. But I—really should."

The last word had hardly died on her lips when his forefinger slid beneath her chin and lifted her face up to his. The serious look she saw on his handsomely carved features jolted her; her heart pounded heavily.

"We're just now getting to know each other, Mia. I really would like you to stay longer."

His gravelly voice was a soft purr and the sound tugged at every feminine particle inside of her. "I—uh—I'll think about it."

Suddenly his head was bending toward hers and the whispered words that passed his lips skittered a warning down her spine.

"Maybe you should think about this."

Mia wasn't totally naive. She knew what was coming and knew she should jump from the bench and put a respectable distance between herself and the handsome doctor. But longing and even a bit of curiosity held her motionless as his lips descended onto hers.

Cool and sweet from the ice cream, his hard lips moved gently, coaxingly over hers. Mia's senses quickly began to tilt. In search of an anchor, her hands reached for his shoulders and she gripped the muscles as the lazy foray of his kiss went on and on.

By the time he finally lifted his head, Mia was breathless and her face was burning.

"A man isn't supposed to kiss a woman like that on their first date," she said as primly as she could, while inside she was quaking, shocked that she could feel such connection from a single kiss.

A crooked grin spread across his face and even in the semidarkness she could see that his brown eyes were shining as though he'd just conquered a dragon and laid it at her feet.

"Well, I was pretending that this was our second date. Forgive me if I was too forward."

She swallowed as emotions tangled into a ball in her throat. "You were. But that's my fault. I should have stopped you in the first place."

Before he could make any reply, she jumped from the bench and began walking around the edge of the rink. The deep reaction she'd felt to Marshall's kiss had left her almost frantic and she told herself she should have never agreed to this date in the first place. It was clear that nothing meaningful could ever happen between them. Being with him was asking for trouble.

Her mind was spinning with all sorts of agonizing thoughts when his hand came down on her shoulder and stopped her forward motion.

"Mia, wait. Don't be angry."

Quickly, she turned to face him and when she spoke Marshall was surprised to hear her voice was almost contrite. As though she were apologizing for kissing him. The idea stunned him.

"I'm not angry at you, Marshall. I—"

Before she could react, he wrapped his arms around her and pulled her close against him. "You're a beautiful woman, Mia. I've wanted to kiss you ever since I met you. There's nothing wrong in what just happened between us."

Even though it had been more like an earthquake than a kiss, Marshall thought. His head was still reeling, but he was wise enough to know that he had to play down the whole thing. She was already trying to run from him and he couldn't let that happen. One way or the other he was going to make her his woman—at least for a while.

Her fingers fluttered against his chest while farther down her thighs were brushing against his. Desire surged through him like a prairie wildfire.

"Marshall, I'm just a tourist. The most we can ever be is friends. And friends don't touch each other like this."

She started to push him away, but he held her for a moment longer. "You and I are going to be more than friends, little darlin'. You might as well take my word on that."

Frowning, she stepped out of the circle of his arms and marched back in the direction of where they'd been sitting. Marshall tempered his long strides to match hers.

"Are you this—this arrogant and cocky and overly confident with your other dates?" she demanded.

He laughed. "I don't know. My other dates have never stirred me up like this."

She shot him a glare. "Then you'd better give yourself a pill to get unstirred, doc. Because I have no intention of becoming one of your many lovers!"

By now they were back at the gate that would lead them to the parked Jeep. As her hand reached to open the latch, Marshall caught it with his.

"Whoa now, Ms. Smith. Somewhere along the way things have gotten way out of hand. I'd like to know where this 'many' came from?" he asked crossly. "How would you know how many women I've bedded?"

Her lips pressed tightly together, then she deliberately turned her head away from him. "I shouldn't have said that. I'm sorry. It's none of my business anyway."

More frustrated than he could ever remember being, Marshall raked a hand through his hair and blew out a weary breath. "Okay. I'm sorry, too. I shouldn't have thrown that taunt at you. I just—well—I like you, Mia. I really like you." His voice was a low, gentle murmur as he dared to step closer. "And I do want us to be more than friends. There's nothing wrong in being honest with you, is there?"

Her head turned back to his and he was disappointed to see that her expression was carefully guarded, as though she didn't trust him enough to allow him to see what she was actually feeling and thinking. It wasn't the first time he'd noticed the curtain she pulled across her features and he suddenly vowed to himself that he was going to learn what was behind those beautiful eyes, no matter how long it took or how painstaking the effort.

"No. I do appreciate your being up-front with me," she said finally. "I'm just trying to tell you that I'm not in the market for a brief affair."

His fingertips made gentle circles on the back of her hand. "Why? Do you have a boyfriend or fiancé waiting for you back in Denver?"

Her lips parted and she hesitated for a split second before she replied, "No. There's no significant man in my life."

Marshall didn't realize how much her answer meant to him until she said it. Relief poured through him like a warm spring rain.

"Look, Mia, I'm not asking you to have an affair with me. I'm just asking you to spend time with me and see where it takes us. That's all." Taking her hand between his, he gave her a pleading grin. "I think we can have fun together, Mia. And I have a feeling you could use a little of that."

A few stilted moments passed before she let out a soft sigh and the stiffness in her body melted away.

With a halfhearted smile, she said, "I'm sorry, Marshall. I shouldn't have overreacted the way I did."

"Forget it. I'm just as guilty." His fingertips tenderly touched her cheek. "What do you say we go finish the ice cream?"

Her quiet laugh warmed his heart.

"It's probably melted by now."

Draping his arm around her shoulders, Marshall turned her back toward the ice rink. "Then we'll drink it."

Two days later, Marshall's Thursday turned out to be a busy day at the infirmary. He'd tended everything from strained knees to poison ivy to bee stings. However, the last patient he examined didn't have the usual external problems he normally encountered. The middle-aged woman he was treating complained of stomach complications. She was dressed in casual but expensive clothes and her jewelry shouted that her bank account was overflowing. Yet Marshall didn't miss the fact that her ring finger was conspicuously empty.

"I really think it's just a virus, doctor. If you could just give me something for the pain—my stomach feels like it's clenching into a tight ball."

Stepping back from his patient, Marshall studied her face. She'd obviously had a face-lift at some point. The job wasn't a bad one, but as a doctor he could easily pick up on the telltale tightened skin. Her light blond hair had been manufactured at a beauty salon, probably to cover the gray that was beginning to frost her temples. Yet on the whole she was an attractive woman, or would be, he decided, if her eyes weren't filled with such sadness.

Is that why you went to medical school? To get a cushy job? Or did you become a doctor so you could help people?

Mia's pointed questions suddenly hit him like a brick. Normally, he wouldn't have taken the extra time to dig into this patient's problem. In the past Marshall would have simply written her a prescription to relieve her symptoms and sent her on her way. She obviously needed more help than he could give her. But now, with Mia gnawing at his conscience he felt compelled to do more for this woman.

"Ms. Phillips, I have my doubts that your stomach problem is a virus. Something like that usually lasts no longer than a couple of days and you tell me this problem has been going on for two or three weeks."

She nodded. "That's right. It started while I was still home, but I ignored it. I thought once I got here at the resort I'd feel better. You know, getting out and away from…things always makes a person forget their aches and pains."

Thoughtfully, he placed the clipboard he was holding on the edge of a cabinet counter. "Do you have a family, Ms. Phillips?"

A nervous smile played upon her carefully lined lips. "Call me, Doris, doctor. And yes, I have…a daughter. She's grown now and just married this past spring."

"That's nice. And what about your husband?"

She suddenly looked away from him and her fingers fiddled nervously with the crease of her slacks. "I'm not married anymore. We're divorced. He—uh—found someone else."

"Oh. I'm sorry. Guess that's been hard on you."

Her short laugh was brittle. "Twenty years of marriage down the drain. Yes, it's been a little worse than hard. Now my daughter is gone from the house and—and the place is really empty. I decided to come here to the resort to be around people and hopefully make new friends."

Marshall gave her shoulder an encouraging pat. "It's good that you're trying to change your life, Doris, and things will get better. In the meantime, I'm going to give you a prescription that will help ease your stomach. I have an idea that all the stress you've been through is causing the problem and I want to give you this anti-anxiety medication." He pulled a small pad from his lab coat pocket and began to scribble instructions for the pharmacist. "But I want you to come see me again before you leave. If this doesn't help, we'll take a closer look, okay?"

A bright look of relief and gratitude suddenly lit the woman's face. "Yes, doctor. Thank you so much."

Marshall left the examining room with a warm feeling of accomplishment and was still smiling when he met Ruthann at the end of the hallway.

"What's the grin all about?" the nurse asked. "Happy that you've finished the last patient for the day?"

Frowning, he thrust Doris Phillips's chart at her. "Put this away, will you? And no, I'm smiling because I think I just made someone actually feel better."

Rising on her tiptoes, Ruthann placed her palm on his forehead. "Yeah, you're a little flush. One of the patients must have passed a bug to you."

The frown on his face deepened. "Quit it, will you? I am a doctor, you know. My job is to make people feel better."

He pushed her hand away and stalked toward his

office. Ruthann hurried after him. "I was only teasing, doc," she said as he took a seat at his desk. "What's with you, anyway?"

Picking up a pen, he tapped the end against the blotter on his desk as he regarded his concerned nurse. "Nothing is wrong, Ruthie. Aren't I supposed to enjoy my job?"

"Well, yes. But I never remember you—well, you mostly get to the point and send the patients on their way. You were in there so long with Ms. Phillips I was beginning to think she'd attacked you or something."

Was that how Ruthann saw him? Effective but without compassion? Marshall realized he didn't care for that image. But then he had no one but himself to blame.

"The woman has stomach problems and I was trying to get to the root of the matter. She thought she'd picked up a virus but the real germ she's dealing with is an ex-husband."

"Oh. You got that out of her?"

It had been easy, Marshall realized, to get his patient to open up. So why wasn't it easy with Mia Smith? After their date last night, he'd realized that she truly was a mystery woman. She didn't talk about her family or her past and the shadows that he sometimes noticed clouding her eyes meant that whatever troubles life had thrown her way were still haunting her. But what were they and why did he feel this need to help her?

Seeing that this new, more compassionate side of him was putting a look of real concern on Ruthann's face, he laughed and gave her one of his usual winks.

"Ruthie, I haven't lost my touch with women yet."

Seeing him back to his normal self, Ruthie rolled her eyes with amusement. "And I'm pretty certain you never will." She walked over to a door that would take her into another room where hundreds of charts, most of them from one-time patients, were stored. "Ready to call it an evening? Dr. Baxter should be here any minute."

Dr. Baxter was the doctor who worked evenings and remained on call all night long. The man had much less to do than Marshall, but Grant insisted that medical personnel be available to the guests twenty-four hours a day—just one of the added conveniences that set Thunder Canyon Resort apart from the competition.

"Go ahead, Ruthie, I think I'll stop by the lounge and have a drink before I head home."

Her expression suddenly turned thoughtful as she walked over to his desk. "I hope you're not stopping by to see Lizbeth Stanton. That girl doesn't need any encouragement. She has her eye on you and any man that could give her a home on easy street."

Marshall dismissed Ruthann's remark by batting a hand through the air. "You're being a little too harsh on the woman, Ruthie. She's really not all that bad. She just needs to grow up a little and get her head on straight."

"Well, just as long as you're not the one doing the straightening," Ruthann said.

Laughing, Marshall turned off the banker's lamp on his desk, then rose to his feet and pulled off his lab coat. "Ruthie, I can't go around fixing all my girlfriends. Now," he said, curling an affectionate arm around her shoulders, "how would you like to go to dinner with me at the Gallatin Room some night soon?"

Ruthann practically gaped at him. "Me? With you? At the Gallatin Room?" Before Marshall could answer, she let out a loud laugh, then patted his arm in a motherly way. "I couldn't step foot in that place. Not with the clothes in my closet. But thank you for the gesture, Marshall. It's sweet of you." Leaving his side, she opened the door to the chart room. After she stepped inside, she stuck her head around the door and added, "Listen, doc, that mystery heiress you were so enchanted with the other day is the kind you need to be taking to the Gallatin Room. Why don't you ask her?"

Because something told him that Mia needed more than glitz and glamour and a meal at a ritzy restaurant.

Thankfully, Ruthann didn't expect any sort of answer from him and Marshall didn't give her one. Instead, he quickly hung his lab coat on a nearby hall tree and told his nurse goodbye for the day.

A few minutes later, Marshall entered the lounge. For an early weekday evening, the place was unusually full of guests. But he didn't pay much attention to the people relaxing on the tucked leather couches and armchairs covered in spotted cowhide. Instead, he made his way straight to the bar where Lizbeth was busily doling out mixed drinks to a group of barely legal young men.

Marshall slung his leg over a stool at the end of the bar and waited for her to finish placing a tray of drinks in front of the lively group.

"Hey, what does it take for a guy to get any service around here?" he called when she finally turned in his direction.

Smiling with apparent pleasure at seeing him, Lizbeth waved and hurried to his end of the polished bar. "Doctor, all you have to do to get a woman's attention is just throw her a grin."

Not where Mia Smith was concerned, he thought. She seemed immune to those things that normally charmed women. Looking at Lizbeth, he inclined his head toward the boisterous group of men at the other end of the bar. "You've got me confused with those young guys."

Resting her forearms on the bar, Lizbeth leaned slightly toward him and lowered her voice so that only he could hear her words. "They just think they know how to flirt with a woman, but they're still wet behind the ears. Unlike you, Dr. Cates."

Any other time Marshall would have laughed at Lizbeth's flirtatious remark, but this evening it only made him feel old and even a bit shallow. It was a hell of a thing when a man was more noted for being a playboy with the women than a doctor to the sick.

"Give me a beer, Lizbeth. Something strong and cold."

"Sure." All business now, she started to push away from the bar, but at the last moment paused and gave him a thoughtful look. "Just in case you're interested, I saw that *heiress* of yours a few moments ago walk out to the sundeck. She was carrying a book of some sort. You might still find her out there reading. Or maybe she's just pretending to read and really looking at the scenery." To make her point, Lizbeth glanced at the young men she'd just served.

Marshall's head whipped around and his gaze studied the far wall of glass that separated the lounge from the large wooden sundeck. From this vantage point, he could see several people lounging on the bent-willow lawn furniture, but Mia wasn't one of them.

Quickly, he slipped off the stool. "Forget the beer, Lizbeth. I'll catch one later."

As he strode away, he heard the bartender call after him. "Good luck."

Luck? It was going to take more than that for him to get inside Mia Smith's head and delve into her secrets, he thought as he stepped onto the sundeck. Or was it really her heart that he wanted to unlock and hold in the palm of his hands?

Chapter Six

Marshall was asking himself how a question of that sort had ever gotten into his mind when he spotted her. She was stretched out in a lounger, her long legs crossed at the knees, her shiny black hair lying in one thick, single braid against her shoulder. A book was open on her lap, but her gaze was not on the pages. Instead she was staring straight at him and the tiny smile that suddenly curved her lips hit Marshall smack in the middle of his chest.

If he'd been a smart man he would have turned and run in the opposite direction just as hard and fast as he could. But when it came to the opposite sex, Marshall was as weak as a kid in a candy shop. And Mia Smith was definitely one delectable piece of candy.

Feeling like a man possessed, he walked to her chair

and squatted on his heels near the arm so that his face would be level with hers.

"Hello, Mia."

"Hi yourself."

Her voice was soft, sweet and husky. The sound shivered over him and for one fleeting moment he felt like a humble knight kneeling to the princess fair.

"Lizbeth told me I might find you out here. Been reading?" He glanced briefly at the hardback book in her lap, then back to her face. There was a faint hint of color on her cheekbones and lips, but for the most part it was bare of makeup, giving him a hint at the natural beauty he would see if he were to wake and find her head pillowed on his shoulder.

"Trying. But the story is rather slow. And there's a bit too much distraction around the lodge," she added with a pointed smile.

"That's me. A distraction," he jokingly replied while everything inside of him wanted to reach for her hand and bring the back of it to his lips. He wanted to taste the soft skin and watch the reaction on her face.

Folding the book together, she swung her legs over the side of the lounger where he was still crouched. She was so close that the flowery scent of her perfume drifted to his nostrils and the palm of his hand itched to slide up her bare thigh.

"Are you finished with work for the day?" she asked.

He nodded, then with a nervousness that was totally foreign to him, he asked, "Do you have plans for the evening?"

Marshall's question made Mia realize just how unplanned her life was at this moment. Staying here at Thunder Canyon Resort was easy and pleasant. But she was living in limbo and sooner or later she was going to have to step over the dividing line.

A sardonic smile touched her lips. "I don't really have anyone around here to make plans with."

"You have me."

His simple words unsettled her far more than he could ever know and, to cover her discomfiture, she rose to her feet and walked over to a low balustrade that lined the edge of the sundeck.

Slanted rays of the sinking sun painted the distant bluffs and forests a golden green. Below them, guests ambled around the manicured grounds of the resort. As her senses whirled with his blatant comment, Mia carefully kept her gaze on the sights in front of her.

"That is—if you want me."

She hadn't realized he'd walked up behind her until his murmured words were spoken next to her ear. She tried not to shiver as his warm breath danced across the side of her cheek.

"I—uh—enjoyed last night," she admitted. In fact, Mia had lain awake most of the night, reliving the connection she'd felt when Marshall had kissed her. It had been more than a fiery meeting of lips. The kiss had been full of emotions so ripe with longing and sensuality that she'd felt it all the way to her heart. And that scared her.

His body eased next to hers and she felt his warm arm encircling the back of her waist.

"So did I," he said lowly.

Part of her started to melt as his fingertips slid back and forth against her forearm.

She was trying to think of any sensible thing to say when he spoke again.

"And I was wondering before I ever left my office if you'd like to have dinner with me again."

All sorts of skeptical thoughts raced through her head. What could a successful man like him find attractive about her, she asked herself. She was not a raving beauty or a sexy party girl. She wasn't even much of a conversationalist. As far as she was concerned she was totally boring. She was also a fake. How long would it take him to figure her out, she wondered dismally.

"Dinner tonight?"

He nodded and she couldn't mistake the sensual glint in his green-brown eyes. As his gaze traveled slowly over her face, the suggestive sparkle warmed her cheeks.

"Sure. Have you eaten yet?"

If Mia had had any sense at all, she would have lied and told him she'd just stuffed herself at the Grubstake, a fast-food grill located in the lounge. At least that way she'd have an excuse to politely turn him down. But the awful truth was that she didn't want to turn the man down. Being with him was too exciting, too tempting for her lonely heart to pass up.

"No. Before you walked out here I was thinking about grabbing a salad at the Grubstake."

His nose wrinkled with disapproval. "You need more than rabbit food. How about letting me grill you a steak at my place? I'm pretty handy as a chef." A corner of his lips curved up in a modest grin. "An outdoor chef, that is."

She hesitantly studied his face. "At your place?"

The grin on his face deepened, saying she had nothing to fear, and when his fingertips reached out to trace a lazy circle on her cheek, she knew she was lost.

"Yes, my place. I live here on the resort, not far from the lodge. I'd like for you to see it. And while you're there you can meet Leroy. He loves company."

Seeing his home, meeting his dog—did she really want to let herself get closer to this man? Especially when she knew she could never have a meaningful relationship with him.

"I…Marshall…"

As she began to hesitate, he wrapped his arm around hers and led her away from the balustrade toward a set of steps that would take them off the sundeck. "I'm not about to let you say no," he said. "So don't even try."

"Okay, okay," she said, laughing. "But I need to go home and change first."

He glanced pointedly at her denim shorts and pale yellow T-shirt. "Why? You look great to me and I'm the only one who's going to see you. Besides, this is going to be a casual affair."

Knowing she'd already lost, Mia groaned with surrender and allowed him to lead her around to the back of the massive ski lodge to the private parking area where his Jeep was parked.

The drive to his home took less than five minutes on a winding road that spiraled up the mountainside.

Spruce and aspen trees grew right to the edge of the road and shaded patches of delicate blue and gold wildflowers nodding in the evening breeze.

Suddenly the road widened and the Jeep leveled onto a wide driveway. Mia leaned forward at the sight of a large log structure with a steep red-metal roof nestled among several pines and cedars.

A graveled walkway lined with large white stones led up to a long, slightly elevated porch made of wooden planks. Ferns and blooming petunias grew in baskets hanging along a roof that was supported by more thick logs. Double doors made of wood and frosted glass served as an entrance to the charming structure.

"Wow, is this the sort of housing all the employees at the resort get?"

His chuckle was almost a little guilty. "No. I'm an exception. When the resort was first being constructed, this house was actually built to rent as a honeymoon suite. But for some reason that was nixed and I ended up getting it for my digs."

She glanced at him curiously as he parked the Jeep in front of the house. "Why? Because you're the resort's doctor?"

His expression a bit sheepish, he answered, "No. Grant Clifton, the manager of the resort, is a good friend of mine. We grew up together and attended the same school. It helps to have friends in high places."

Had it helped her to have a mother in high places? Mia asked herself. She'd be lying to say it hadn't. She was no longer scraping pennies to buy gas for a clunker car to carry her from a ratty apartment to the college campus, or wondering how she was going to find enough in the cabinets to cook a meal for her adoptive mother and herself. But in most ways Janelle's massive wealth had only caused Mia grief and more trouble than she could have possibly imagined. From the moment she'd found Janelle, the woman had smothered her with love and money. By themselves those two things would have been good, but along with the love and money, Janelle had also wanted to hold on to Mia and control her every step. Having spent years believing her baby girl had been stillborn, she now clung to the grown daughter that had miraculously been resurrected before her eyes.

"Well, it's a beautiful place," she finally said to him. "I'm sure you must love it here."

"It's nice" was his casual reply before he opened the door and climbed out to the ground.

After he helped her out of the vehicle and they began the short walk to the porch, Mia glanced expectantly around her. "I was expecting your dog to run out to meet us. Where is he?"

With his hand at her back, he ushered her up the three short steps to the porch.

"The backyard is fenced. That's where Leroy has to stay. Otherwise, he'd follow me down to the lodge and harass the guests."

"Oh," she said warily. "He bites?"

Marshall laughed. "No. But he'll knock you down trying to get your attention. I suppose I should send him to obedience school, but I'd miss him too much. And besides, none of us behave perfectly. Why should I expect Leroy to?

None of us behave perfectly. He couldn't have gotten that more right, Mia thought. But if he could see into her past behavior she doubted the doctor would have that same lenient compassion toward her.

Don't think about that now, Mia. Just enjoy the moment and bank this pleasant time in your memory. Once you leave Thunder Canyon and face your real life again, you're going to need it.

"We all have our bad habits," she murmured. "I'm sure Leroy is a nice boy."

Chuckling, he opened the door and ushered her over the threshold. "You've got it all wrong, Mia. I'm the nice boy around here and Leroy is the animal."

They passed through a small foyer furnished with a long pine bench and a hall tree adorned with several hats and jackets that she supposed would be needed once autumn came and the cold north winds began to blow across the mountains and plains.

"Oh, this is nice and cozy," she commented as they walked into a long living room with a wide picture window running along one wall.

Rustic pieces of furniture fashioned of varnished pine and soft butter-colored leather were grouped together so that the spectacular mountains could be viewed from any seat. Brightly colored braided rugs covered the oak flooring while the chinked log walls were covered with paintings and photos. Potted plants sat here and there around the room and from their lush appearance Mia figured he must have a green thumb along with his eye for the ladies.

"Well, I'm sure it doesn't compare to your home," he said, "but it suits me."

Pretending to study the view beyond the window, Mia looked away from him and hoped the mixed feelings swirling through her didn't show on her face.

It was true that Janelle's home was a mansion and large enough to hold several houses this size. But the last ratty apartment that she'd shared with Nina had been more of a home to her than any of those opulent rooms in Janelle's house. Funny that she could see that so clearly now when only a couple of years ago she'd believed Janelle was welcoming her into a castle in paradise. Dear God, she'd been so naive, so gullible, she thought.

"I think it's beautiful," she said, then turned to him and smiled in spite of the tears in her heart. "Where's the kitchen? I'll help you get things started."

"Whoa, slow down, pretty lady. We're going to relax and have a drink first. That is, after I change out of these work clothes. Why don't you have a seat and I'll be right back."

She was far too nervous to simply sit while she waited for him to return. Clasping her hands behind her back, she said, "I think I'll just wander around the room and see how good you are about keeping things dusted."

"Lord, I'd better hurry," he said with a laugh and quickly darted through an open doorway.

Once he was gone from the room, Mia ambled slowly along the walls, curiously inspecting the many paintings that depicted the area and the cherished photos that were carefully framed and lovingly displayed. Eventually she discovered one of four smiling boys and an adult man, all of them dark-haired and all possessing similar features. The group had to be the Cates brothers and their father.

As she quietly studied their smiling features, she felt a pang of total emptiness in her heart. If Mia had been lucky enough to have siblings, her life would have no doubt taken a different track. Certainly she wouldn't have felt such a driving need to search for her birth mother. And with a sibling to lean on, Mia mightn't have been so profoundly influenced by Janelle. But ifs didn't count. And she'd not been as blessed as Marshall Cates.

Moments later, Marshall stepped through the door and spotted Mia at the far end of the room. Just seeing her there filled him with strange emotions. He'd never invited one of his girlfriends here before and he wasn't exactly sure why he'd felt compelled to blurt the sudden invitation to Mia. Something about her seemed to make him lose all control and throw out all the dos and don'ts he carefully followed with other dates. The fear that he might be headed for a big fall niggled at the back of his mind, yet the sight of her slim, elegant body standing in his living room was somehow worth the risk.

Obviously lost in his family photos, she didn't hear him approach until he was standing directly behind her. Resting his hands lightly on her waist, he said in a teasing voice, "I see you found the Cates brood. What do you think? That we could pass for the wild bunch?"

She didn't answer immediately. Instead, she turned and gave him a smile that was wobblier than anything. The glaze of moisture in her eyes completely dismayed him.

"You have a nice-looking family, Marshall," she said huskily. "You must love them very much."

Before he could say anything, she eased out of his grasp and stepped around him. As Marshall turned to follow, he could she was wiping a finger beneath her eyes. The image hit him hard and he was stunned to discover his throat was knotted with emotion. Why would seeing a photo of his family affect her like this? he wondered. And why was her tearful reaction tearing a hole right in his chest?

Clearing his throat, he caught her by the shoulder and gently pulled her to a standstill. "Mia? Are you okay?"

She lifted her face up to his and the smile he found plastered upon her delicate features was really just a cover-up and they both knew it.

"Of course I'm okay. I...I just get silly and sentimental at times. Don't pay any attention to me. Women get emotional. You ought to know that, doc."

Of course he understood women were emotional creatures, but as far as he could remember none of his dates in the past had ever shed a tear in front of him. The women he squired were more likely to have fits of giggles, a sign he must be dating good-time girls, he thought, then immediately wondered why that fact should fill him with self-disgust.

He glanced back at the photo of his family. Then, looking questioningly to her, he asked, "Do you have siblings?"

Shaking her head, she said, "No. I'm an only child."

She tried to smile again and this time her soft lips quivered with the effort. Marshall was stunned at how much he wanted to pull her into his arms and soothe her. Not kiss or seduce her, but simply quiet her troubled heart. Something strange was definitely happening to him.

"I'm—sorry, Mia," he murmured. Then, quickly deciding he needed to put an end to the soppy moment between them, he urged her forward. "Come on," he said a bit gruffly. "Let's go have a drink and start dinner. I don't know about you, but I'm famished."

She seemed relieved that he'd suddenly changed the subject and by the time they reached the kitchen, she appeared to have pulled herself together. Marshall did his best to do the same as he went to the cabinet where the glasses were stored.

"Would you like a beer or a soda? I have a bit of everything stashed around here," he told her.

After a long pause, she answered. "I—uh, I really don't care much for alcohol."

Marshall looked over his shoulder to see she was resting her hip against the kitchen table, her long bare legs were crossed and she was studying him through lowered lashes. The provocative sight forced him to draw in a long, greedy breath of air.

"Oh. Since you visited the lounge, I didn't figure you had anything against drinking."

"I—" suddenly she straightened away from the table and glanced at a spot over his shoulder "—I have a weak cocktail on occasion. And I don't mind other people enjoying themselves. But it bothers me when it's abused."

Had she had trouble with overdrinking herself, Marshall wondered, then quickly squashed that question. She didn't seem the sort of woman to lose control over anything—even though that kiss they'd shared at the ice rink had been hot enough to sear his brain cells.

"Well, unfortunately we humans abuse a lot of things. Even food," he said.

"And people," she added in a small voice.

"Yeah, and people," he grimly agreed, then quickly shrugged a shoulder and grinned. "But we're not going to ruin our evening together by fretting over the ills of the world. Why don't I fix you a soda and I'll have a beer?"

Her smile was grateful. "Sounds good. Let me help."

Happy to change the solemn mood, Marshall gave her a glass to fill with ice then showed her where a selection of sodas was stored in the pantry. Once they had their drinks in hand, he ushered her out the back door and onto a wide deck made of redwood planks.

Almost instantly, she heard loud happy barks and turned around to see a stocky dog with a bobbed tail bounding onto the deck and straight at them.

"Leroy! Don't even think about doing your jumping act," Marshall warned the animal. "You sit and I'll introduce you to our guest."

The blue-speckled dog seemed to understand what his master was saying and Mia was instantly charmed as Leroy sat back on his haunches and whined happily up at her.

"Oh, you're gorgeous," she said to the dog, then glanced questioningly at Marshall. "Is it okay if I pet him?"

Marshall laughed. "That's what he's waiting for. But beware. He'll smother you if you let him."

Placing her soda on a small table, Mia leaned down and with both hands lovingly rubbed Leroy's head. "You're just a teddy bear," she cooed to the dog. "I'll bet you wouldn't hurt a fly."

"Maybe not a fly," Marshall said with amusement, "but he'd love to get his teeth around a rabbit or a squirrel."

Mia stroked the dog's head for a few more moments then picked up her soda. Marshall waited until she'd settled herself on one of the cushioned lawn chairs grouped on the deck before he took a seat next to her.

Leroy crawled forward to Mia's feet, then rested his muzzle on his front paws. Smiling affectionately at the dog, she said to Marshall, "I'll bet he's a lot of company for you. Have you had him long?"

"Close to two years. I got him not long before I came to work here at the resort."

Mia glanced over at him and felt her heart lurch into a rapid beat. She'd been around handsome men before, but there was some indefinable thing about Marshall that sparked every womanly cell inside of her. It was more than the nicely carved features and the ton of sex appeal; there was a happiness about him that filled her with warm sunshine, a twinkle in his dark eyes that soothed the gaping wounds inside of her. Being with him filled her with a sense of worth, something she'd not felt since her father had died years ago.

Like Marshall, Will had been a happy man with a love for life. He'd always made a point of telling Mia that she was special, that she could do or be anything she wanted. He'd made her smile and laugh and look at the world as a place to be enjoyed. When she'd lost him, she'd also lost her self-confidence and security. But she wasn't going to think about that tonight.

"When was the resort built? There's so much to it that I figured the place had been here for several years."

Marshall shook his head. "Mr. Douglas didn't start building Thunder Canyon Resort until after gold was discovered in the Queen of Hearts mine, and that was about two years ago."

"Wow. He must have lit a fire under the contractors to have gotten the place up and running in such a short time."

"Yeah, well money talks and having plenty of it makes it easier to get things done quickly. Did you know there's a golf course in the makings, too? Construction is supposed to start on it next summer. Maybe when you come back to Thunder Canyon for another vacation we can play a game together. Have you ever played?"

Golf? Mia almost wanted to laugh. As far as she was concerned that was a rich man's sport. Even when Will, her father, had still been alive, the Hanovers hadn't been well off. The potato crops he'd harvested every year had been enough to keep them comfortable but not enough for luxury. Then after Will had died, she and Nina couldn't have afforded a set of used clubs from a pawnshop, much less the fees to belong to a country club. That was the sort of life Janelle enjoyed. It was the sort of life she wanted Mia to experience. But try as she might, Mia couldn't make herself comfortable with Janelle's money or lifestyle. How could she, when everywhere she looked she saw Nina Hanover's troubled face?

"No. I— Golf was never an interest at my home." At least that was the truth, she told herself.

The crooked smile on his face melted her. "Well, that will give me a good reason to get you out on the course and teach you."

If she ever returned to Thunder Canyon, Mia thought grimly. What would he think if he knew she was only here at the resort because of a missed turn on the wrong road? That she was running from herself and hiding from her mother? God, she couldn't bear to imagine how he would look at her if he knew the truth. That her actions had caused her mother to drink and then climb behind the wheel of a car.

Trying to shake the disturbing thoughts away, she sipped her soda and glanced around the small yard fenced with chain link. On the west side three poplars shaded them from the red orb of the sinking sun. To her left, in one corner of the grassy space, a blue spruce towered high above the roof of the house. Even from a distance, the pungent scent of its needles drifted to her on the warm breeze.

Near one end of the deck was a doghouse made with traditional clapboard and shingles. Nearby, a small wading pool meant for children was full of water—for Leroy's amusement, she supposed. A few feet farther, in the middle of the yard, a black gas grill was positioned near the end of a redwood picnic table.

The only thing missing in the family-friendly setting was a colorful gym set and a couple of laughing kids playing tag and wrestling with Leroy. The dreamy picture floated through her mind and filled her heart with wistful longing. Would there ever be a place like this for her? she wondered. Would there ever be a man who could love her and want a family with her in spite of her faults?

"Mia. Are you okay?"

His voice finally penetrated her thoughts and with a mental shake of her head, she glanced at him. Apparently she'd been so lost in her daydreams that she'd not heard his earlier remarks.

"Oh. Sorry. I was just thinking…how quiet and pleasant it is here on the mountainside." Her expression turned wry. "But to be honest, this is not the bachelor pad I expected to find."

His eyes wandered over her face as he grunted with amusement. "What were you expecting? A round bed and mirrors on the ceiling?" His eyes crinkled at the corners. "Maybe I should remind you that you haven't seen my bedroom yet."

He was teasing and yet just the mention of his bedroom was enough to make Mia jump nervously to her feet and rub her sweaty palms down her hips. "Uh—maybe we should start dinner. I'm actually getting hungry."

Marshall set aside his empty beer glass, then slowly rose from the lawn chair. It was all Mia could do to stay put as he closed the short distance between them.

"Mia, Mia," he said softly as his hands slipped over the tops of her shoulders. "You really do think I eat women for breakfast, lunch and dinner, don't you?"

Embarrassed now, her gaze dropped to her feet. "Not exactly. But I'm sure you've had plenty of—female friends up here and—"

Before she could finish, his forefinger was beneath her chin, drawing her face up to his. "You're wrong, Mia. Very wrong. Yes, I've had plenty of female friends over the years. But not one of them has been here at my home. Until you, that is."

Something deep inside her began to quiver and she didn't know whether the reaction was from the touch of his hand upon her face or the surprising revelation of his words.

"Marshall, you don't have to tell me something like that. I mean— I'm not expecting special treatment from you."

Frowning now, his hand fisted and his knuckles brushed the curve of her cheekbone. Everything inside Mia wanted to close her eyes and lean into him. She wanted to taste the recklessness of his lips again, feel the strength of his arms holding her tight, crushing her body against his.

"You think I'm lying, don't you?"

Her head twisted back and forth until his fingers speared into her hair and flattened against the back of her skull. With his hands poising her face a few inches from his, everything in her went completely still. Except for her heart and that was beating as wildly as the wing of a startled bird.

"Marshall—it doesn't matter what I think."

"Doesn't it?"

She swallowed as emotions threatened to clog her throat. "Soon I'll be gone and you and I will probably never see each other again."

Even saying the words brought a wretched loneliness to the deepest part of her heart and she suddenly realized she was in deep trouble with this man. It was painfully clear that he was becoming a part of her life, a part she didn't want to end.

"Mia," he said in a gravelly whisper, "when are you going to stop thinking about *leaving* and start thinking about *staying?*"

She couldn't stop the anguished groan in her throat. "Because I— Oh, Marshall, there's nothing to keep me here."

Mia had hardly gotten the words out when she saw a wicked grin flash across his face and then his lips were hovering over hers.

"What about this?"

His murmured question wasn't meant to be answered. At least not with words.

Mia closed her eyes and waited for his kiss.

Chapter Seven

Leaves rustled as a soft breeze blew down from the mountain, carrying with it the faint scent of spruce. Birds twittered overhead and across the deck Leroy lifted his head and watched in fascination at the couple with their arms entwined, their lips locked.

As for Mia, she was hardly aware of her surroundings. Marshall's kiss was spinning her off to a place she'd never been before, a place where everything was warm and soft and safe. The wide breadth of his chest shielded her, his strong arms girded her, cradled her as though she were something very precious to him.

Back and forth his lips rocked over hers, while inside tiny explosions of pleasure fizzed her brain, transmitting streaks of hot longing throughout her body.

Her hands were clinging tightly to his shoulders and she was wondering where she was ever going to come up with enough resistance to end the kiss, when he suddenly lifted his head. As she gulped for breath, his eyes tracked a smoldering trail across her face, down her neck, then still lower to the perky jut of her breasts.

"See, you do have something to keep you here," he murmured, his voice raspy with desire. "Me. This."

Mia was smart enough to know that Marshall wasn't an old-fashioned man. He considered a kiss as nothing more than a sexual pleasure between a man and a woman, a sweet prelude for something more intimate to come. It wasn't a pledge of love or even a promise of fidelity. For him it was a carnal act, plain and simple.

With every ounce of strength she could muster, Mia gathered enough of her senses to push away from his embrace and walk across the deck. Bending her head, she stared unseeingly at the grains in the wooden planks while asking herself what she was doing here at Marshall's home. Pretending that she could have that fairy-tale life she'd once fervently dreamed of? No. She'd learned the hard way that fairy tales weren't the heavenly fantasies she'd thought them to be. The reason she was here was far more basic. Marshall made her momentarily forget, made her feel as if she'd soon discover sunshine over the very next mountain.

She was blinking at the haze of moisture collecting in her eyes when Leroy's head appeared in her line of vision. The dog must have sensed her troubled mood.

He looked up at her and whined, then promptly began to lick her ankles.

The warm, ticklish lap of the dog's tongue against her skin had Mia suddenly laughing and she squatted on her heels to stroke his head.

"You're a funny fellow," she crooned to Leroy.

Walking up behind her, Marshall put a hand beneath her elbow and eased her up to her full height. Slowly, she turned and met his somber gaze.

"I wish I could make you laugh like that," he said quietly. "It sounds nice. Really nice."

Feeling slightly embarrassed now, but not fully understanding why, she directed her gaze to the middle of his chest.

"I guess I'm not the most jovial person to be around, Marshall. I—" Pausing, she lifted her gaze back to his face. There was a smiling warmth in the brown depth of those eyes, a tenderness that she'd not expected to see and her heart winced with longing. "I really don't understand why you'd want to be around a person like me."

With a wry slant to his lips, his hand reached up and stroked gently over the shiny crown of her head then down the long length of her thick braid.

"A person like you? What does that mean? You're a beautiful, desirable woman. Any man would be crazy not to want your company."

Her nostrils gently flared as his fingers reached the end of her braid and lingered against her breast.

"Like I told you before, I'm not a party girl."

His palm flattened against her breast and Mia's pulse

quickened as heat pooled beneath it and spread to the center of her chest.

"What makes you think that's the type of girl I want?" he murmured huskily. "Maybe I'm tired of party girls."

Why did she so desperately want to believe him? Mia wondered. Why did the foolish, wishful part of her want to believe that he might actually come to care for her, when every sensible cell inside her brain understood that once her past was revealed he'd run faster than Leroy after a rabbit?

She sighed as a faint smile curved her lips. "That kiss you just gave me didn't feel like a man who was looking for a woman to share an evening of political theories. But I— I'll hang around Thunder Canyon for a while longer. Just don't expect me to fall in bed with you. That isn't going to happen."

To her surprise, a wicked grin flashed back at her. "What about jump into bed with me? Or leap? Yeah. Leap sounds better. That would get us there faster."

He was teasing and Mia was glad. It gave her a chance to step away from him and end the awkward intimacy that constantly seemed to sizzle between them.

"You're crazy," she teasingly tossed over her shoulder. "And right now I'm wondering if you actually know how to cook or if you're going to let me starve."

Chuckling, he draped his arm around the back of her waist and guided her down the steps and onto the grassy lawn.

"C'mon," he urged. "You can watch me start the grill

and then I'm going to cook you the best rib-eye steak you've ever eaten."

Once Marshall got the charcoal burning, the two of them went inside the kitchen to prepare steaks, potatoes and corn on the cob for grilling. As Mia worked alongside him at the counter, she tried to push the heated memory of their kiss aside. She tried to convince herself that being in Marshall's arms hadn't really been that nice. But she couldn't lie to herself. Not when his very nearness begged her reach out and touch him.

They ate the simple meal on the picnic table while Leroy sat near Marshall's feet and begged for scraps. By the time they pushed back their empty plates, the sun was casting long shadows across the lawn.

"There's a little sunlight left," Marshall said as the two of them sipped the last of their iced tea. "Do you have enough energy for a walk? There's a beautiful little spot I'd like to show you. It's just a short distance up the mountain."

With a hand against her midsection, she groaned. "It had better be a short distance because I'm stuffed."

He extricated his long legs from the picnic bench and rose to his feet. "I promise the exercise will be good for your digestion," he said impishly, then held his hand down to her.

She curled her fingers around his and he helped her to her feet. "What about Leroy? Can he walk with us?" she asked as he led her over to a gate where they could exit the backyard.

Since the heeler was already bounding eagerly

around their feet, Marshall didn't have the heart to order the dog back to the porch. Besides, Mia seemed to enjoy Leroy and whatever made her happy was what he wanted to give her.

Hell, if he ever admitted his sappy feelings to his brother and longtime buddies, the group of men would fall over with laughter, Marshall thought. Either that or warn him that he was in danger of losing his bachelorhood.

"If I didn't let him go, he'd probably dig out from beneath the fence," Marshall told her, then to Leroy he said, "okay, boy, you can go. But no running off and hiding in the woods or I'll leave you out for the bears to eat."

Leroy barked as though he was big enough to take on any black bear that happened to cross his path. The moment Marshall opened the gate, the dog shot through the opening like a rocket on four feet. Mia laughed as the animal raced far ahead of them.

"Boy, you've certainly got him trained."

"Yeah, he follows my directions about as well as my patients," he joked.

Marshall ushered her through the gate and onto a small trail leading out to the dirt road that ran past the house and on up the mountain.

"You mean we can walk on the road?" she asked with surprise. "We don't have to go into the woods?"

"For about a quarter of a mile we'll stick to the road," Marshall told her. "Then we'll turn into the woods. It won't be far then."

"And what will I see there?" she asked curiously.

He wagged a finger at her. "If I told you now, it wouldn't be a surprise when we got there. Don't you like surprises?"

When the surprises were nice, Mia thought. Like the ones her mother and father used to give her on her birthday: a kitten with a bow around its neck, a sweater with a fur collar and shiny pearl buttons, a small cedar chest to hold all her cherished trinkets. Yes, those had been precious surprises and gifts worth more than all the gold in the Queen of Hearts mine. She'd just been too naive to realize it at the time.

"Sometimes," she said.

They were walking close together and every few moments the swinging gait of their arms caused them to brush together. Mia made herself widen the distance between them, but Marshall countered her move by reaching for her hand and dragging her even closer to his side.

As he threaded his fingers through hers, he said with a provocative little grin, "We're not on a military hike, Mia dear, we're on an after-dinner stroll."

The feel of her palm flattened against his and their fingers locked together was all it took to send Mia's blood singing through her veins. It was crazy, she thought. They were only holding hands, yet the connection she felt was almost as if they were kissing all over again. She wanted to pull away even while she wanted to draw closer to his side.

"It's a good thing," she said in a breathy voice. "Because I need to take this uphill grade slowly."

He was teasing her about being out of breath when they suddenly heard voices, then muffled whimpers. The sounds appeared to be coming farther up the mountain from them and Mia and Marshall paused long enough to exchange watchful glances.

"That sounds like someone in distress," Marshall said. "Is that what you heard?"

Concerned now, Mia nodded. "Is it unusual for anyone else to be on this road?"

"Not really. It's on resort property and some hikers like to go up the mountain the easy way rather than the narrow trail that winds through the woods. C'mon. Let's go see if we can find them."

He tugged on her hand and the two of them hurried up the steep road. Around a sharp curve, they spotted a boy no more than eight years old with taffy-brown hair and a smattering of freckles across his nose, sitting in the ditch. Tears were streaming down his face as a young woman with a light brown ponytail was trying to untie his hiking boot.

Mia shot Marshall a glance of concern, then rushed forward. The woman looked up in surprise as Mia practically stumbled to a stop in front of them.

"Oh, thank God," the young woman said with a desperate note of urgency. "Can you help us?"

"What's happened?" Mia asked quickly as she knelt down next to the woman.

"I'm not sure how it happened. Joey and I were walking through the woods and the next thing I knew he was on the ground screaming in pain."

"I was trying to jump a stream," the boy said in tearful explanation. "The next thing I knew I landed on a rock and it rolled beneath my boot. I fell and now my leg hurts something awful."

A grubby little hand rubbed down his shin and stopped somewhere near his ankle. Mia's heart ached for the little fellow. Apparently he'd taken quite a tumble. There were deep scratches on his knees and legs. Mud and dirt was smeared on his chin and alongside his nose.

The woman said fretfully, "Wouldn't you know it, this is the one time I didn't bring my cell phone with me. And Joey is too heavy for me to carry off the mountain."

Giving the boy a soothing smile, Mia reached into a pocket on her shorts and pulled out a clean tissue. Gently, she dabbed at the tears rolling down his cheeks, then went to work wiping away a trickle of blood from his knee. "You're a brave boy. Don't cry," Mia told him, turning toward Marshall who stood behind her. "This man is a doctor," she told Joey. "He'll take good care of you."

"A doctor!" Jumping to her feet, the woman stared at Marshall in disbelief. "Really?"

Marshall thrust his hand toward her. "I'm Dr. Marshall Cates. I'm the staff doctor at Thunder Canyon Resort."

A look of relief crossed her plain features. "Oh. I'm Deanna. Deanna Griffin." She gestured down to the boy who was grimacing with pain. "And this is my son, Joey. We're not resort guests. We're staying in town at the Wander-On Inn. We just decided to drive out to the mountains and then Joey wanted to climb. I guess someone will probably charge us with trespassing."

"Don't worry about any of that," Marshall tried to assure her. "You're not going to get into trouble for being on resort property." Quickly, he broke off the conversation and kneeled down beside Mia and the boy. "Okay, Joey, can you show me where it hurts?"

The boy glanced to Mia for reassurance, then with a short nod pointed to his right ankle. "Somewhere down there. But it kinda just hurts all over. Is it broke?"

"I don't know, son. We'll have to take X-rays of your leg before we know that," Marshall told him.

Carefully, he cradled the bottom of the child's boot in both hands while anchoring his thumbs on the top. "Mia, can you loosen the laces while I keep his foot steady?" he asked.

Without hesitation she nodded, then gave the boy a conspiring wink. "Sure. We're gonna get through this together, aren't we, Joey?"

Gritting his teeth, Joey reluctantly nodded and Mia quickly went to work easing the bootlaces. Eventually she loosened them enough for Marshall to slip the shoe from the boy's foot. A thick white sock followed.

When Joey's foot was finally exposed, Marshall ran his fingers over the already bloated joint. "Mmm. The ankle is beginning to swell and turn blue. I don't feel anything broken." He glanced up at Joey's mother. "But there could be a fissure that can't be felt. We need to get him down to my office for X-rays."

Close to tears now, Deanna Griffin groaned with misgivings. Mia looked away from Joey and up to his mother. Although the woman was dressed in a decent-looking pair of Capris and a tank top, the look on her face spoke volumes to Mia. She'd seen that frantic what-am-I-going-to-do expression many times before on her own face. The fear in Deanna Griffin's eyes said she saw a mound of cost suddenly thrown at her, a cost she couldn't meet.

"Look, Dr. Cates, I think—maybe—I'd better have you take Joey to the county hospital. I'm not insured and, well, I hate to sound ungrateful but I don't think I can afford your services. At the hospital…"

The deep grimace on Marshall's face was enough to cause the woman to pause. "Ms. Griffin, this isn't about money," he said with rough impatience. "This is about your son's leg!"

Stunned by Marshall's attitude toward the woman, Mia touched him on the shoulder to get his attention. "Marshall, could I speak with you a moment? Alone?" she asked pointedly.

He hesitated for only a moment, then, leaving Joey, he followed Mia several feet away from the mother and son.

"What is it?" he asked before she could say anything.

Her lips pursed at his impatience. She was seeing a different side of this man and she wasn't at all sure she liked it.

Tossing back her tousled hair, she lifted her chin to a challenging slant. "For your information, Marshall, not all people are blessed with plenty of money like you. She's probably barely able to make ends meet and I doubt there's a man around to help her in any way. Now you bark at her as though she's an unfeeling mother!"

A look of impatience came over his face. "Unfeeling! Mia, I was trying to tell the woman not to worry—that money isn't the issue here."

Stepping closer, she tapped a finger against the middle of his chest. "You still don't get it. Money *is* an issue with her. She doesn't have it. And medical care—the kind you provide—ain't cheap! Now do you get the picture?"

Frustration marked his features as he glanced over his shoulder at Joey then lowered his head to Mia's. "This woman is a stranger to you. How could you possibly know anything about her situation?"

Because she'd been there, Mia thought grimly. In that same dark, terrifying place with nowhere to turn and no one to help. Mia understood how humiliating and humble it felt to have to throw herself on the mercy of a total stranger. But she couldn't tell Marshall Cates about that part of her life. He wouldn't understand. No more than he could empathize with Ms. Griffin.

"It's…easy. I—I'm a woman and I can…just tell these things. And if she needs financial help, I'll be glad to pay for Joey's care."

Shaking his head with dismay, he raked a hand through his hair. "Mia, look. It's very generous of you to make the offer. But even if the kid has to spend time in the hospital, I have connections—I can make sure the bills are taken care of. Does that make you feel better?"

"Much better." Rising on tiptoe, she kissed his cheek, then hurriedly stepped past him and over to Joey's mother.

The woman turned a harried look on Mia. "Dr. Cates

is right. Joey's leg is the first concern here. It's just that I have to be…uh, practical. And—"

"You don't have to explain, Ms. Griffin," Mia swiftly interrupted. "And there's nothing to worry about. Marshall meant to say that Joey will be treated and you're not to worry about the cost."

Her eyes blurred with grateful tears, Ms. Griffin reached out and gave Mia a tight hug. "I don't know what to say," she murmured. "Except thank you."

Mia was about to tell the woman that no thanks were necessary when Marshall approached the two women. "I think the best way to handle this is for me to jog back down the mountain and get the Jeep," he told Mia. "Can you wait here with Ms. Griffin and her son?"

"I'd be glad to."

His nod was grateful and as he turned to go, Mia thought she spotted a flicker of surprise in his eyes. As though he'd expected her to come up with some sort of excuse to quickly extricate herself from these people's problems. But Mia had learned that when a person cried out for help, someone needed to be there for them. This was one tiny way of making up for her mistakes.

"Good. I'll be back in a few minutes. In the meantime, make sure Joey doesn't try to move or stand. If he does he could hurt himself even more."

"We'll make sure he stays put," Mia assured him.

Two hours later Mia and Marshall were sitting on the deck behind his house, drinking coffee and watching the stars come out.

Only minutes earlier on the lodge steps, they had

waved goodbye to Joey and his mother. Thankfully, the boy's ankle had only been badly sprained. Marshall had ordered ice packs for the swelling and had made a point of giving Ms. Griffin samples of pain medicine rather than writing her a prescription.

"I'm sorry that we didn't make it to the special place I wanted to show you," he said to Mia. "We'll have to try again another day."

The two of them were sitting on a cushioned glider and every now and then Marshall would use the toe of his shoe to keep the seat rocking. The lazy movement, along with Marshall's nearness had lulled her to a dreamy state of mind and for the first time since Lance had left her, she felt herself drawing closer and closer to a man.

"I'm just glad we happened to run in to Joey and Deanna. The boy would have probably panicked if she'd left him there to go after their vehicle."

"Hmm. Well, I'm just glad the boy didn't have a broken bone. He was lucky." Marshall leaned forward and placed his coffee cup on the floor, then squared around to face Mia. "Now that things have quieted down, I want to compliment you on the way you handled Joey. A real nurse couldn't have done it any better. Where did that come from? Have you cared for children before?"

Mia very nearly laughed. The number of children she'd babysat to make extra money was too high to count. But heiresses didn't do those menial types of jobs, so she simply said, "I like children. I guess it's just a natural thing."

"I wouldn't say that," he argued. "When we walked up on them, his mother was getting nowhere at quieting him down."

She looked away from him and up at the blanket of stars twinkling across the endless Montana sky. There was so much she wished she could say to Marshall; so much she'd like to share with him, if only he would understand.

"That's nothing unusual. Most kids respond better to someone other than a relative. And I... Actually, at one time I was studying to become a nurse."

She glanced over to see he was staring at her in total surprise. What now?

"A nurse! Really?"

She swiftly sipped at her coffee to cover her nervousness. She didn't know why she'd blurted that bit of information about herself. "Yes. I'm very serious."

"You said you were studying. What happened? Why did you stop?"

What could she say, other than finding a rich mother had suddenly put a stop to all the goals and dreams she'd set for herself. Somehow she'd allowed Janelle to slowly take over her life, to push her into believing that being rich was all that was required for happiness.

Bitterness rose in her throat, but Mia did her best to swallow it down before she answered. "I guess in the long run you could say I stopped because I was weak. Too weak to fight my mother. You see, she, uh—she didn't want me doing something as blue-collar as being a nurse. To her a nurse does nothing more than hand out pills and empty bedpans."

Even though it was dark, there was enough light coming from the kitchen window for her to see that his brown eyes were searching her face as though she were a different woman than the one who'd first sat down beside him. As she sat there waiting for him to speak, she felt totally exposed and fearful that he was seeing the real Mia. Mia Hanover.

"I'm sorry she feels that way. I have a feeling you'd make a great nurse."

A nervous laugh escaped her lips and she quickly turned her head away from him. When she spoke her voice was wistful. "I wouldn't know about that, but I do think I would enjoy caring for people who...need me."

A few silent moments passed and then she felt him shifting on the seat and his arm settling around her shoulders.

"What about your father, Mia? Doesn't he have any say about this?"

This is the sort of thing that happened, she thought, when she let one little thing about herself slip. It always led to more questions. Questions that she didn't know how to answer without exposing her dirty secrets; questions that were too painful to contemplate.

Her next words were pushed through a tight throat. "My father died a long time ago."

"Oh, that's too bad, Mia. I can't imagine not having my father around. He's like an old tree trunk. I know I can lean on him if things ever get bad." His hand gently kneaded her shoulder. "Guess you have to do all your leaning on your mother."

Janelle wasn't the type, Mia thought. She wanted to lead her daughter rather than support her. Besides, she wasn't a mother to Mia. Not as Nina had been a mother. Nina was the one who'd bathed, diapered and fed Mia as a baby. She was the one who'd taken on multiple jobs; scraped and sacrificed to make sure Mia had a roof over her head and food to eat.

"I try not to do much leaning," she said. Then, with a smile she was hardly feeling, she quickly turned to him. "Let's not talk about such serious things, Marshall. You haven't offered me dessert yet. Do you have anything sweet hidden in your kitchen?"

"Sorry. The only thing I have is a package of cookies that has to be at least two months old."

Mia wrinkled her nose. "We could drive into the Rusty Spur and share a carton of Golden Nugget," she suggested.

The last thing Marshall wanted to do was leave this quiet porch where Mia was practically sitting in his lap. From the moment they'd sat down together on the glider, the warmth of her body had been tempting him; the scent of her soft skin and silky hair cocooned him in a sensual fog. For the past half hour his mind and certain parts of his body had been zeroed in on making love to her. The idea of having her in his bed, her naked curves just waiting to be explored, was enough to leave his stomach clenched with need. It was all he'd been able to think about. Until she'd shocked him with that bit about nursing school.

Marshall had gotten the sense that she'd not intended to give him that information about herself, but now that she had, he only wanted more. He was beginning to see that there were layers to this woman he'd not even begun to see and he wanted to peel them away almost as much as he wanted to peel away her clothing.

But tonight was too soon to push her. She'd agreed to stay on at the resort for a while longer. For now Marshall had to be content with that.

Stifling a wistful sigh, he rose from the glider and offered a hand down to her. "Whatever my lady wants, I'm here to give."

Chapter Eight

The next evening, after Marshall had gotten off duty, he was walking through the lounge searching for any sight of Mia when his cell phone rang.

Flipping the instrument open, he was surprised to see it was his brother Mitchell calling. Quickly, he pushed the talk button as he continued to amble through the several couches and armchairs grouped in front of the massive fireplace.

"Hey, Mitch, what's going on?"

"What the hell do you mean, what's going on? We're all over here at the Hitching Post. Have you forgotten that it's our night to meet?"

Pausing at one of the empty cowhide-covered chairs, Marshall sank onto the padded arm. His brother's question had literally stunned him. How could he have forgotten boy's night out? For years now, Marshall, Mitchell, Grant and Russ and Dax had all gotten together once a month at the Hitching Post to drink beer, play pool and sit down to a game of poker. It was their time together, to relax and forget about any problems they might have. Just the idea that he'd been concentrating on Mia instead of his normal routine was enough to worry him.

"I suppose I had forgotten. Are you guys already gathered up?"

"Hell, yes. We were waiting on you to start the poker game, but the rest of the guys gave up and decided to play pool. What's the matter, did you have some sort of emergency this evening?"

"I'm still here at the lodge, I just stayed late to do a bit of paperwork." And to wait around and see if Mia made an appearance at the lounge, he thought wryly. Last night after they'd eaten ice cream, he'd dropped her off at her cabin and given her a chaste good-night kiss. He'd not wanted to press his luck and ask her for another date tonight, but he'd damned well wanted to. Dear Lord, if he'd missed boy's night out because of a date, the guys would never let him live it down. "Just hold my place, Mitch. I'll be there in a few minutes."

Friday night at the Hitching Post was always a rowdy affair with drinking, loud laughter and even louder music. The popular nightspot located on the southwestern edge of town was Thunder Canyon's version of an

Old West saloon, complete with live country bands on Friday and Saturday nights and hardwood floors with plenty of space for boot stompin' and two-steppin'. A restaurant serving everything from steaks to burgers was situated on one side of the building, while on the opposite side was the original bar that had once graced Lily Divine's sporting house. And over the back bar, above the numerous bottles of spirits and rows of shot glasses, hung a painting of Thunder Canyon's most infamous lady.

Marshall, along with every guy who'd ever visited the Hitching Post, had often gazed at the nearly naked Lily and wondered if she'd really been as bawdy and decadent as the good folks of the town had depicted her to be back in the 1880s. There were always two sides to every story and he figured the truth of Lily's past would never be understood. The beautiful madam was a mystery. Just like Mia Smith, he thought, as he skirted the edge of the crowded dance floor and shouldered his way toward the bar. She was another beautiful mystery that he seriously wanted to unravel.

After wedging his way past the crowd packed around the busy bar, Marshall spotted his brother standing near one of the several pool tables located just off the dance floor.

He worked his way toward his brother while the band's rendition of a popular country tune rattled the rafters and forced people to communicate with hand signals rather than conversation. For one brief second, as he waited for a big burly cowboy to step aside,

Marshall longed for the quiet sanctuary of his back porch, the glider and his arm around Mia.

Hell, what was coming over him, Marshall wondered as he finally reached the pool table where his brother and friends were racking balls for a new game. He'd always loved the nightlife, the louder and wilder, the better. The Hitching Post had given him some damn good memories and getting together with his brother and buddies was a tradition since their high school days. This was his idea of the good life and he didn't want to change a damn thing about it.

"Hey, buddy, you finally made it," Grant Clifton called to him from the opposite end of the table. "Want to play this game?"

Russ Chilton, the rancher of the group, took the pool stick he'd been leaning on and offered it to Marshall. "Go ahead. I've already lost one game to the stud down there." He motioned his head toward Grant. "Why don't you see if you can wipe that smug smile off his face?"

"Aw, Russ, the smile on Grant's face doesn't have anything to do with beating you at pool." Dax Traub, spoke up over another blast of loud music. "The man is in love. Real, true love."

Marshall looked across the table at Dax, who owned a motorcycle shop in the old part of town. The remarks he'd made about Grant's love life had held more than a hint of cynicism, but that was to be expected from Dax. He was six foot of brooding sarcasm since his marriage to Allaire had hit the skids.

"How do you know so much about Grant's love life?"

Marshall asked at the same time as he signaled to a nearby waitress.

Dax jerked his thumb toward Grant. "The big manager of Thunder Canyon Resort has been telling us all about his upcoming wedding to his cowgirl. I've advised him to take her spurs off first, though. Otherwise she might trip on her way down the aisle."

By now the waitress had reached Marshall. He quickly ordered a beer, then turned and walked to where Grant was resting a hip against the edge of the pool table.

"Sounds like Dax is giving you a hard time about becoming a husband," Marshall said with faint amusement.

Grinning, Grant tossed his pool stick to Dax. The other man quickly positioned himself over the table and busted the triangle of balls.

With the game going again, Grant moved a few steps away from the table and Marshall followed.

"I wouldn't expect anything else from Dax. He's jaded."

Marshall blew out a lungful of air. Even though he'd known that Grant was engaged, the idea that his old buddy would soon be married shook him in a way he'd never expected. Grant's bachelor days were coming to an end.

Marshall glanced shrewdly at his longtime friend. "Maybe Dax is concerned that you'll end up getting hurt—like him. But I'll have to say you don't look like a worried man."

Grant chuckled. "Worried. Why should I be? I'm

marrying the woman I want to spend the rest of my life with. I couldn't be happier."

Marshall slapped a hand on Grant's shoulder. "If you're happy, then I'm happy for you."

"Thanks. Maybe you can deliver our children when they come," Grant added jokingly.

With a wry shake of his head, Marshall said, "I'm a sports doctor, Grant. Remember? I don't do babies."

Grant's calculating laugh was loud enough to be heard above the music. "Maybe not in the delivery room. But you might just make a few—if you meet the right woman."

Marshall didn't think he'd ever seen his longtime friend so buoyant and happy. Nor had he ever heard him talk so openly about love and kids, subjects that normally would have made both men squirm. Now Marshall could merely look at him and wonder.

Glancing toward the other members of their group, Marshall said, "You know me, Grant, I'm never really looking for the *right* woman. But I—I'm half afraid that I may have found her anyway."

The waitress arrived with his beer and he tossed a few bills onto the serving tray before she hurried off to deliver more drinks.

As he gratefully sipped the dark draft beer, Grant edged closer. "What do you mean? I didn't realize you'd been seeing one certain woman."

Feeling more than a little foolish, Marshall shrugged. "I hadn't been. But then I ran into Mia and we—uh— we've gone out a few times." He glanced at Grant and appreciated the fact that his friend wasn't grinning like a possum. "This is probably going to sound crazy, Grant, but I think I'm falling for this girl."

Grant's dark brows lifted with surprise. "Mia? Do I know this woman?"

"You should. Her name is Mia Smith. She's one of the high-toned guests at the resort. I remember you said she rented a safety deposit box for her jewelry."

Grant's lips formed a silent *O*. "Yeah, I remember now. The mystery heiress that all the staff was chattering about when she first arrived. You've been seeing her?"

Marshall nodded. "Believe me, Grant, I never thought she'd give me the time of day. Now that she has I—well, all I want is to be with her. And if I'm not with her I'm thinking about her. Does that sound like love to you?"

Frowning, Grant said, "Marshall, from what I've heard about Mia Smith, she keeps to herself. No one around the resort knows where she came from or anything else about her. Do you?"

What little Marshall knew about Mia was hardly enough to fit in his eye, yet he'd learned enough to tell him she was a good, decent person and that being with her made him happy. Wasn't that really all that mattered, he asked himself. To Grant he admitted, "I've learned a little about her, but not as much as I'd like to."

Slapping a comforting hand on Marshall's shoulder, Grant said, "Well, I wouldn't worry about it, ole buddy. You're probably just infatuated with her because she's a mystery. Once you give yourself time to really get to know the woman, your feelings might change completely."

After a long gulp of beer, Marshall glanced out at the crowded dance floor. For the life of him he couldn't imagine Mia laughing and kicking up her heels like the women here at the Hitching Post were doing tonight. She'd said she wasn't a party girl, but Marshall instinctively felt there was more to her reserved mind-set than what she was telling him.

"You may be right, Grant. The only thing I'm sure about now is that I'm going to keep seeing her—until she leaves the resort."

Several loud shouts suddenly sounded from the pool table and both men returned to the group of friends just in time to see Dax send the last ball on the table rolling into a corner pocket.

Looking for anything to get his mind off Mia, Marshall said, "Give me that cue, Russ. Somebody needs to knock Dax off his throne."

More than an hour later and after several games at the pool table, the five guys found seats and ordered pitchers of beer.

As for Marshall, he tried to keep up with the bits and pieces of conversation flowing back and forth across the table, but all the while he was wondering what sort of believable excuse he could come up with to leave the party early.

He could always pull out his cell phone and pretend he had an emergency message from the resort. But with Grant being the manager, he'd eventually find out the truth and then his departure would need even more explanation. Damn it, why couldn't he just sit back and enjoy himself like he usually did at these gatherings?

The next thing Marshall knew, Dax was waving a hand in front of his face. "Hey, buddy, are you with us?"

Realizing he'd been caught daydreaming, Marshall placed his beer mug on the table and glanced around the table. "I'm here," he answered a bit sharply. "I was just thinking about a patient," he lied. "Did you ask me something?"

"Yeah, we want to know about your date with Lizbeth Stanton. What was that all about?"

Grimacing, Marshall asked, "How did you know about that?"

Russ laughed. "Since when did anything stay a secret around Thunder Canyon? You ought to know Dax hears a stream of gossip in his motorcycle shop."

Marshall shrugged. "Well, there wasn't anything to it. She asked me out to dinner and I accepted. No big deal. She's really more of a friend than anything."

"Sexy as hell, though, don't you think?" Dax tossed a wink at him. "And she's just your style—a big flirt."

Marshall was about to tell him to go jump off a cliff when he spotted Mitchell staring at him like a hound dog with perked ears.

"You say Lizbeth asked you out?" his brother asked. "Not the other way around?"

"That's right," Marshall answered. "But like I said, the two of us are just friends. In fact, while we were having dinner she encouraged me to go after Mia Smith."

"I see."

Marshall thoughtfully watched his brother tip the pitcher of beer over his near-empty glass. If he didn't know better, his brother seemed unduly interested in Lizbeth Stanton, but that idea was ludicrous, he thought. Mitchell was the serious one. Flirty, flighty Lizbeth would be the last woman to fit his needs.

"Oh, so you've already moved on to this Mia now?" Dax asked. "Maybe we should be asking about her instead of Lizbeth."

Rising to his feet, Marshall pulled several bills from his trouser pocket and tossed them onto the table to pay for his portion of the beer.

"Sorry guys. I've had a long day and there's a patient I want to check on before it gets too late."

"A patient! Are you kidding?" Grant exclaimed. "Since when did you ever worry about a patient after working hours?"

Since he'd met Mia, Marshall silently answered. Aloud, he said, "There's a first time for everything, guys."

He walked away, leaving every man at the table staring after him.

The next morning Mia had just stepped out of the shower and was toweling dry when she heard a knock on the door of her cabin.

Puzzled that anyone would be trying to contact her, she quickly pulled on a blue satin robe and knotted the sash at her waist as she hurried to the living area.

Even though the resort was basically safe and away from the dangers that lurked in city living, she still opted to use the peephole before simply pulling the door open to a stranger. But to her surprise the visitor wasn't a stranger. It was Marshall, dressed in a green short-sleeved shirt and faded blue jeans. The tan cowboy boots on his feet reminded her that even though the man was a doctor, he still had a bit of Montana in him. And it was that rough edge that made him just too darn sexy for a woman's peace of mind.

Her pulse fluttering wildly, she thrust strands of wet hair off her face and pulled open the door to find him smiling back at her.

"Good morning, beautiful," he said softly.

The sweet, sensual greeting knocked her senses for a loop. Embarrassed that he'd caught her in such a disheveled state, she clutched the folds of her robe chastely together at the base of her throat.

"Hello yourself," she replied while her mind spun with questions. What was he doing here at her cabin so early in the morning? And why did the sight of him make her heart sing? She was clearly losing control with him—and herself.

"Uh—I know it's early. I tried to call, but there was no answer." His dark gaze left her face to travel downward to where her puckered nipples were outlined by the satin, then farther down to where the edges of the fabric parted against one naked thigh. "I guess you were in the shower—or something."

Just before Mia had stepped into the shower she'd heard her cell phone ringing, but even though she'd given her number to Marshall the other night after they'd dealt with Joey's sprained ankle, she'd figured the only person who would be calling so early was Janelle. And Mia was still far from ready to talk to the woman.

"Yes, I was in the shower," she repeated as though she didn't have an ounce of brain cells. Then, realizing she couldn't keep him standing on the small porch, she pushed the door a bit wider. "Would you like to come in?"

The grooves in his cheeks deepened as he stepped across the threshold and past her. "I thought you'd never ask," he said as he glanced thoughtfully around the small but luxuriously fitted cabin.

Her hands shaking, she shut the door behind them and then adjusted the front of her robe to a more modest position.

"This is quite a surprise," she said. "I wouldn't have expected you to be up so early on a Saturday morning. Would you like coffee?"

She moved around him and into the kitchen. Thankfully she'd turned on the coffeemaker before she'd stepped into the shower and now the brew was ready to drink.

"I'd love a coffee," he said as he followed her behind an L-shaped bar and into the small kitchen area. "And this might surprise you, but I'm not one to lay in bed on my days off. There's too much to enjoy and life's too short to sleep it away."

Grateful that the task of finding cups and pouring the coffee gave her a moment to collect herself, she said in a teasing voice, "Oh. Well, I figured with your nightlife you'd need the rest."

He chuckled. "Nightlife? Now who's been talking

about me? I don't have that much of a nightlife. Even though I was out last night—at the Hitching Post with my brother and friends."

Turning, she handed him one of the mugs. Their fingers met and at the same time their gazes clashed. For a brief moment Mia's breath stopped, as arcs of sizzling awareness seemed to zip back and forth between them.

"Friends?"

She realized the question was personal, that it was the same as saying *I'm interested in you,* but she couldn't stop herself. If he'd been out with another woman last night, then his showing up here this morning wouldn't be anything for her heart to sing about. Maybe it wasn't anything to sing about anyway. But she couldn't seem to get her heart to go quiet. Instead it was thumping and jumping joyously around in her chest.

"My old high school buddies." A corner of his mouth slanted upward. "Guys—just in case you're wondering."

Feeling a blush coming on, she lifted the cup to her lips and sipped while she waited for the heat in her cheeks to subside.

"I guess it's time to confess that I have heard gossip about you."

One of his dark brows arched with amused speculation. "Really? Where?"

She lowered the cup and tried to keep her voice casual. "The Clip 'N' Curl."

Marshall laughed. "The beauty salon in town? Mia, you're *supposed* to hear gossip at a beauty salon. Something would be wrong if you didn't."

She did her best to chuckle along with him. Yet these past few days she'd not been able to completely dismiss what Marti had revealed about her sister and Marshall.

"This particular person I met there seemed to know you quite well. Or, at least, her sister did."

His amusement turned to outright interest. "You don't say. Well, who was this person?"

"Marti Newmar. She works at the coffee bar in the lounge."

Sudden dawning crossed his face and then he glanced down at the cup in his hand, but not before Mia glimpsed something like regret in his eyes.

"Hmm. Marti. Yes, I'm acquainted with her. And yes, I dated her older sister, Felicia. It was nothing serious, though, and she's gone on to other things. In fact, I don't even think she lives here anymore."

He sounded so casual, almost too casual. And a prick of warning sent a cool shiver down her spine. If he was that flippant about his past girlfriends, then who was to say he'd be any different with her?

But you don't want him to be serious about you, Mia. You're a fake, a phony. Even if he did grow to love you, the truth would end everything. No, a mild flirtation is as far as this thing with Marshall could ever go.

Sighing, she leaned against the bar and stared across the expanse of living room. "Marti seems to think that her sister was in love with you."

She could hear his boots shifting slightly, but she didn't turn to look at him. If she saw another dismissive look on his face she didn't think she could bear it.

"I couldn't help that, Mia. Felicia was—she wasn't my type. I'm at fault for dating her in the first place."

"Why wasn't she your type?" Mia asked stiffly. "Because she was poor?"

"Poor? You think that's why I ended things with her?"

There was such indignation in his voice that she glanced over her shoulder at him. He was glowering at her and she knew she'd hit a nerve, but at this moment she didn't care. Maybe it was time Dr. Playboy was questioned about his dating ethics.

"I don't know," she said. "From the way Marti describes her home and family, it doesn't match up to yours."

"Well, the Newmars' financial situation had nothing to do with anything," he countered. "Felicia was— naive. That was the whole problem."

Mia's lips twisted. She'd been naive before, too. She'd been foolish to believe that Lance had loved her enough to stick with her through the good and the bad. But even worse, it had been silly, perhaps even child-like, to believe that Janelle and her stacks of money could buy happiness.

"Why?" she asked, her voice brittle. "For believing a guy like you could care about a girl like her?"

He groaned. "Why are you trying to make me look like a cad?"

With a shake of her head, she said, "I'm not trying to do anything. Maybe you've already done it to yourself."

There was a pregnant pause and then she heard a rough sigh escape him.

"Look, Mia, you're probably right in thinking that I

hurt Felicia. I'm sure I did. But I didn't do it intention-
ally. I never led her on or tried to make her believe she
was *the* special woman in my life. She was simply a
pretty girl, a fun date. But she obviously wanted more
than I was prepared to give. When I finally saw where
her feelings were headed, I quickly ended things. If that
makes me an unfeeling bastard, then I guess I'm guilty."

Feeling a bit raw without even knowing why, she
said, "Forget it, Marshall. I shouldn't have brought the
matter up anyway. You and I are just friends. And your
past dating habits are no concern of mine. No more
than mine are yours."

Chapter Nine

Before Marshall could say any more on the subject of Felicia Newmar or any other women he'd dated, Mia turned toward him and gestured to one of the tall bar stools pushed up against the varnished pine counter.

"Have a seat," she invited.

He pulled out one of the bar stools and slung a long leg over the padded seat. Mia placed her coffee mug on the bar, then carefully climbed onto the stool next to him. As he sipped at his coffee, she pulled a wide-tooth comb from the pocket of her robe and began to smooth the wet tangles away from her face.

As Marshall watched her deal with the mass of black hair tousled around her head, he couldn't help but wonder why she'd confronted him about an old girlfriend and why he'd felt so compelled to defend himself. Before Mia, he'd not really cared what anyone thought of his dating habits. If a heart got broken here and there, he'd justified his part in the malady by telling himself the woman had learned a lesson about men, albeit the hard way. But now, to even think of breaking Mia's heart troubled him deeply. Dear God, what was she doing? Taking a freewheeling bachelor and turning him into a conscientious but boring gentleman?

"I thought you might like to know that I stopped by the Wander-On Inn last night and checked on Joey," he commented. "His ankle is coming along nicely."

She looked at him with surprise. "You mean you interrupted your night on the town to check on a patient?"

A wry smile twisted his lips. "You see, I'm not all bad, as you seem to think."

"I never thought you were *all* bad."

Their gazes clashed and her eyes darted nervously away from him. He watched her put down the comb and pick up her coffee.

"I would offer to make you breakfast," she said after a moment, "but I don't have any food in the house. I'm afraid I've been doing too much eating out, letting others do the cooking."

"Don't worry about it. I actually stopped by to invite you out, anyway. I thought we could grab some breakfast at the Grubstake and then do a bit of climbing."

Her gaze swung back to him. "Climbing? As in mountain climbing?"

He grinned at her wariness. "Sure. You're up to it, aren't you?"

Even though he had mentioned the two of them going climbing together before, Mia had never believed he'd actually get around to asking her. Taking an inexperienced person on such a strenuous trek would be like taking a toddler on a shopping excursion.

"I don't know." She licked her lips as she weighed his invitation. Mia Smith, the heiress who wanted to stay hidden from the world, knew it would be wise to politely decline and send him on his way. But she was getting so weary of being that woman, so tired of pretending. And more importantly, it didn't matter to her what this man's motives to spend time with her were; being with Marshall simply made her feel good. And right now she needed that very much.

She said, "You've surprised me."

"Good. A man shouldn't be predictable." His eyes sparkled with all sorts of innuendos. "At least, not to a beautiful woman."

Her nostrils flared as her pulse fluttered. It would be so much easier if she could forget the taste of his lips, forget the feel of his strong arms wrapped around her, but she couldn't and now as she looked at him her senses buzzed with erotic memories. This was probably how Marti's sister had felt, she thought, charmed, helpless, ready to give the man anything he wanted.

"I'll go climbing with you. Just as long as you don't try to take me up something like Pike's Peak."

Marshall chuckled. "The highest mountain in

Montana is Granite Peak and it's many miles east of here. We'll go up a baby mountain here on the resort. Promise." He used his forefinger to make a cross against his chest, then leaning toward her, he wound a strand of wet hair around the same finger. "You ought to know I wouldn't hurt a hair on your head."

Even though Mia desperately needed to draw in a deep breath, the air lodged in her throat. "I'm—um. It's not my hair that I'm concerned about. It's my bones."

A deep chuckle rumbled up from his chest and his finger left her hair to slide down the stretch of thigh exposed by the part in her robe. "I'm a sports doctor, remember? I can fix broken bones."

Yeah, but what about broken hearts? Don't think about it, Mia. Just go. Have fun. Forget.

Carefully, she caught his wayward hand and placed it safely on his knee. "All right, doc," she conceded. "You've talked me into it. What time did you want to go?"

His smile was a picture of pure triumph. "Great! I'm ready right now."

Mia glanced pointedly down at her robe. "Well, I'm not. You're going to have to give me time to get dressed. What should I wear?"

"You might want to settle on loose-fitting shorts. It's going to be a warm, sunny day."

Mia quickly slipped off the bar stool. "Give me five minutes," she told him.

Just as she was walking across the living room, her cell phone began to ring. Mia glanced at the small table where the device was lying and felt her spirits sink. Janelle had been ringing and ringing, no doubt determined to make Mia pick up and talk to her. So far, she'd not found the courage or determination to confront her mother.

"Go ahead," Marshall spoke up from his seat at the bar. "I'm not in that big of a hurry. Answer your phone."

Knowing it would look odd if she didn't acknowledge the ringing, Mia picked up the phone and flipped it open. The caller ID flashed the name Janelle Josephson and her heart sunk all the way to her toes.

Snapping the phone shut, she said, "I— It's nothing important. I'll return the call later."

The ringing stopped and Marshall watched her place the phone back on the table. Her features, which only a moment ago had been smiling, had rapidly gone pensive, then guarded. Who could the caller be, he wondered. A family member? A lover? All along he'd sensed that something was going on with Mia Smith, something that she wanted to keep hidden.

He figured the answer could be found if he sifted through the call history information on her telephone. A name. A number. Someone from her past was obviously still reaching out to her. He desperately wanted to know, but he couldn't push her. He had to be patient and wait to see if she would ever feel close enough to confide in him.

"Are you sure? We have all day for climbing," he tried to assure her.

Suddenly she snatched the instrument up from the table again and this time slipped it into the pocket on her robe. "It's nothing important, Marshall," she said in a firm voice, then whirled and started out of the room. "Just let me change and we'll be on our way."

Marshall was still thinking about her odd behavior when she emerged from the bedroom a few minutes later wearing a pair of black khaki shorts and a white tank top. A white scarf secured her wet hair into a ponytail at the nape of her neck.

Even with a bare minimum of makeup her face was lovely, but at the moment it wasn't her features that had snared his attention. With a will all their own, his eyes slid an appreciative gaze down her long, shapely legs and ended as her trim ankles disappeared into a pair of heavy brown hiking boots. The sight of all that honey-tanned skin was enough to distract him from the earlier phone call and he put it entirely out of his mind as he slid from the bar stool and walked over to her.

"Ready to go?" he asked.

Nodding, she patted the back pockets of her jeans. "I think I've taken everything I needed from my handbag." She glanced eagerly up at him. "Is Leroy going to come with us?"

Laughing, he placed a hand at the small of her back and guided her toward the door. "Not this time. I want to devote all my attention to you, dear Mia."

After a quick breakfast of hotcakes, they left the Grubstake and climbed into Marshall's Jeep for a short drive to the north edge of the resort. Before they reached the base of the mountain, a meadow carpeted with pink and yellow wildflowers came into view and Mia gasped with delight.

The idea scared him, but the feeling was so thrilling that he couldn't stop. Couldn't look back.

"Marshall, I didn't know how much I wanted this— you—until tonight. But when you kissed me out in your parents' yard…I don't know. Everything felt different— right. Does that make sense?"

At this moment nothing made sense to Marshall except the extraordinary need to kiss her, hold her, feel his body sliding into hers.

"Making sense doesn't matter," he said thickly. "You and me together—that's all that matters."

Rolling her onto her back, Marshall used the next few minutes to make a feast of the mounds and hollows of her body and each nibble, each tempting slide of his tongue sent shivers of longing down Mia's spine. In a matter of moments she forgot everything except the desire that was surging higher and higher, begging her body to connect with his.

When she began to moan and writhe beneath him, he eased back enough to slip the scanty piece of lace from her hips. The black triangle of hair springing from the juncture of her thighs beckoned his fingers. For a moment he teased the soft curls and then, lifting his gaze to hers, he stroked lower. Her eyes widened with surprise, then closed completely as he gently, coaxingly touched the intimate folds between her thighs.

"Marshall, Marshall," she said on a thick, guttural groan. "Don't torment me like this. I need—"

The rest of her words stopped on a gasp as one finger slipped into the moist heat of her body. Stock still, she

"Oh, how beautiful! Can't we stop here for a few minutes, Marshall?"

An indulgent smile curved his lips. "We'll make a visit here on the way back," he promised. "I'm afraid if I let you wander out in all those flowers now, I'll never get you up the mountain."

She sighed as she gave the splendorous sight one last glance before she turned her gaze on his profile. "You're probably right, doc. Most women tend to prefer picking flowers to climbing rocks. But I'm game and I'll try to keep up."

Reaching across the small console, he picked up her hand and gently squeezed. "You're a good sport, Mia. I like that about you. Believe it or not, you're the only woman who's been brave enough to go climbing with me."

His admission warmed her heart, even though she told herself it shouldn't mean anything.

"Maybe you mean the only woman *crazy* enough to go climbing with you," she said with a wry smile.

His fingers tightened around hers. "You're not crazy, Mia. You're an adventuress. I knew that when I first saw you sitting on that boulder on the side of the mountain. A weaker woman wouldn't have even attempted that much of a climb. You not only made it, but you made it alone. I was impressed."

Mia's lashes fluttered downward to partially hide her mixed emotions. He'd called her an adventuress and that much was true. Even before she'd graduated high school, she'd set off on a quest to find her real mother. In spite of having limited funds, even more limited means of searching and her adopted mother's disapproval, she'd been determined, almost relentless in reaching her goal. She'd been brave enough to make calls to total strangers and badger those persons holding the key to private records. Yet once she'd actually found Janelle, her bravery and independent nature had melted. She'd allowed the woman and her money to very nearly swallow her up. It had taken Mia months and months to realize that her weakness had not only caused her to lose Nina and Lance, it had also caused her to lose herself.

Lifting her head, she did her best to push the dark thoughts from her mind. "You didn't give me any impression that you felt that way," she replied.

"I didn't know you well enough. And you weren't exactly inviting me to strike up a personal conversation."

No, she thought miserably, when she'd first arrived at Thunder Canyon Resort, she'd gone out of her way to keep every encounter with staff and guests to a totally impersonal level. It was easier to maintain her guise as Mia Smith that way. But now Marshall was digging at the doors she was hiding herself behind and every moment she was with him she had to fight to keep from flinging them open and letting Mia Hanover pour out. The only thing stopping her was knowing the deluge of truth would end their relationship.

"So," she said carefully, "do you think you know me now?"

To her surprise, he lifted her fingers to his lips. "Not as much as I'd like to, but enough to make me want you beside me."

No one had to tell her that Marshall Cates was a dangerous flirt, a smooth charmer. Yet none of that seemed to matter whenever he touched her or flashed her one of his sultry grins. Mia realized she was losing herself to him and there didn't seem to be any will inside her to stop the fall.

Moments later, he steered the Jeep onto a dim, washed-out road that led up the base of the mountain. When the going finally became too rough for the vehicle to handle, he steered it off the path and parked beneath a huge pine.

She helped Marshall unload the climbing equipment from the back of the Jeep, then stood to one side and watched as he strapped on a heavy backpack.

"What about me?" she asked. "Do I need to carry something?"

"You can be in charge of our water. Since I only brought two bottles, they shouldn't be too heavy."

"Two bottles? The day feels like it's going to be hot. Won't we be needing more water than that?"

He glanced at her as he adjusted the pack to a more comfortable position on his shoulders. "You're right, but trying to carry too much of it will only weigh us down. I've brought a filtration device along, too. And once we climb higher, there are several falls and pools where we can get water."

She looked at him with fascination. "There are pools of water up on the mountain?"

"Several," he answered as he took her by the arm and urged her away from the Jeep. "And one of them will make your flowered meadow look humdrum."

"I'll believe that when I see it," she said with a laugh.

The day was bright and sunny, the breeze warm and gentle. The first two hundred feet of their climb were strenuous but fairly easy to maneuver with plenty of hand- and footholds. Thankfully Mia was accustomed to jogging in the high altitude of Denver, so her breathing was no more labored than Marshall's as they levered and worked their way upward. During the slow climb he'd made sure to stop at frequent intervals to give her some lessons on the basic techniques. Apparently his instructions had been a big help to her, because each time he'd glanced over his shoulder to make sure she was keeping up and each time she'd surprised him by being right on his heels.

Eventually he paused long enough for her to join him on a small rock ledge. "I think it's time I made our trail a little more difficult," he said. "This is no challenge for you."

Groaning, she shrugged off the small pack she was carrying and dug inside for one of the water bottles. "C'mon, Marshall, give me a break. I'm already covered with sweat."

While she took a long drink from the bottle, a cunning grin flashed across his tanned face. "You haven't done any real climbing yet. We're going to get out the anchors and ropes and make our way up that bluff."

Mia's gaze followed the direction of his index finger. When she spotted the bluff he was talking about, her jaw dropped. The red layers of rock appeared to be shaved off evenly without even the smallest of ledges to give a climber a toehold.

"You're crazy!" she squeaked. "I can't make it up there! Just look at my boots, they don't have spikes!"

"Neither do mine. In fact, I wore these old cowboy boots today and they're slick on the bottom and hell to climb in."

Mia rolled her eyes. "Then why did you wear them?"

"For a challenge. And to put me on an even keel with you."

She let out another groan. "And here I was patting myself on the back for keeping up with you. I didn't have a clue that you'd handicapped yourself."

Chuckling, he reached out and cupped the side of her face with his palm. "You're doing great, honey. I'm proud of you."

Shaken by the sweet sensation of his touch, she handed the water to him, then turned away to gaze out at the quaint town of Thunder Canyon spread beneath the endless stretch of blue Montana sky. Months ago, after Lance had walked away and her mother had died, she'd believed that no spot on earth would feel like home again. But this place was beginning to tug at her heart.

Or was it the man standing beside her?

"Maybe you'd better wait until we tackle the bluff before you say that," she told him.

He moved closer and Mia's eyelids drifted down as the back of his hand moved against her bare arm.

"You're going to make it," he murmured. "We'll make it together."

Together. It was difficult for Mia to remember back to a time when she'd thought of herself as a part of a team. She had a few female friends back in Denver, but they were Janelle's sort, spoiled and out of touch with the real world. They'd readily accepted her into their circle and all of them were basically nice to her, but she'd never felt a connection with any of them and she'd quickly come to the conclusion that she didn't want an idle life without goals or dreams. As for the young men who'd tried to court her, she'd felt frozen by their flippant attitude toward life and money and family.

"Mia? You've grown awfully quiet. Are you all right?"

She glanced over her shoulder and up at him. The look of concern on his face warmed her and made her wonder what it would be like if he really did care about her, even love her.

"I was just thinking," she said, then before she could stop herself, she twined her arm through his. "Tell me about your friends, Marshall. The guys you went out with last night. Are they—special to you?"

A look of real fondness swept over his features. "Very special. We all grew up together—went to high school together and even now we make sure we all get together at least once a month. 'Course, I call Mitch my brother and my friend. He's four years younger than me and a hell of a lot smarter. He owns and runs Cates International in Thunder Canyon."

"That's some sort of business?"

"Farming equipment." His expression turned wry. "Not everyone around here has a gold mine where they can harvest nuggets."

"Is your brother married?"

Marshall's laugh was robust to say the least. "No. He's as serious as a judge. I'm not sure any woman could deal with him."

"What about your friends? Do they have families?"

He thought for a moment. "Not exactly. Dax used to be married to Allaire, but their marriage didn't last. Now he runs a motorcycle shop down in the old part of town. Then there's Grant, I think I told you about him. He manages the resort. He's a workaholic, but he's finally managed to get himself engaged to the woman who runs his ranch, Clifton's Pride. Russ has a ranch outside of town. He's from the old school—hates everything the gold rush has brought to Thunder Canyon. He used to be married a long time ago and has a kid—a son—but he never sees him."

Mia frowned. "How sad."

"Yeah. I think his ex didn't want the connection— I'm not sure. Russ doesn't talk about that part of his life. Anyway, he's definitely single and I don't see him changing."

"So that's all of them? Your friends, I mean."

"No. There's also Dax's brother, DJ, but he took off to Atlanta and has been living down there for a while. He owns a bunch of barbecue places and we've been trying to talk him into coming back to Thunder Canyon. What with the gold boom, a barbecue joint around here ought to do handsprings."

Mia smiled wistfully. "You're lucky to have friends and especially lucky that you've stayed together for so long."

"I'm sure you must have good friends, too." He

grinned impishly. "I'll bet you were the prom queen or the cheerleading captain—someone that all the girls envied."

Mia had to stop herself from snorting out a laugh. She'd been tall, skinny and gawky. Her clothes and shoes had mostly come from thrift stores and her hair had been worn with thick bangs and chopped off straight at the bottom because that was the only way her mother could cut it. A visit to the beauty salon had been out of the question. Necessities came first and there was rarely a dollar left over for luxuries. No, none of the girls she'd gone to school with had envied Mia Hanover.

Now Mia probably had more money than all of those young women put together. But it meant nothing. She'd give every penny of it away to go back to being that poor Mia whose mother was still alive and cutting hair with not much skill, but a whole lot of love.

Blinking at the mist of tears that had gathered in her eyes, Mia quickly looked away from him and adjusted the pack on her back. "We'd better be going, don't you think?"

The abrupt change in her took Marshall by complete surprise. Moments ago she'd seemed eager to hear about his friends and then when he'd barely mentioned hers, she'd dropped a curtain and went off to someplace he wasn't invited.

For a moment he considered taking her by the shoulders and asking her point blank about her life, her past. But so far the day had gone so well that he didn't want to push his luck. There would come a time for him to gently pry at her closed doors and when that time arrived he would know it. Right now he was going to be content with her company.

For the next hour, as the two of them slowly made their way up the rough crags of the mountainside, Marshall tried to forget about the empty look he'd seen on Mia's face when he'd suggested she'd been a star attraction in high school. He didn't like to think that her past had been less than happy, but he wasn't blind. In a sense she was like Doris Phillips, who'd come to his office for help. She was putting on a brave pretense at happiness, but underneath her smiles there was a wealth of pain.

But what had caused it? Marshall wondered, as he hammered an anchor in between two slabs of rock. A man? With Mia's striking looks he'd be a fool to think a man hadn't been a serious part of her life at some point. Hell, for all he knew she could already have been married and divorced. That notion left such a bitter taste in Marshall's mouth that he felt almost sick.

With the last anchor in place, Marshall attached a strong rappelling rope and slipped it through a ring on his belt. In less than a minute, he'd swung himself down to the narrow ledge of rock where Mia was patiently waiting.

"I really think I've lost my mind. Are you sure I can do this, Marshall?"

Her question came as he girded a belt around her hips, then tested the buckle with a hard tug to make sure it was secure.

Straightening to his full height, he forced himself to rest his hands on his own hips rather than the sweet tempting curve of her behind. "We'll take the easiest route. Just remember everything I've taught you. And once you begin climbing, don't start staring down at the floor of the canyon. You might get vertigo and then we'd be in a hell of a mess."

"I don't get vertigo," she said with a frown. "See, I'm looking down now and nothing—"

Before she could get the remainder of her words out, she felt as though the top half of her was swaying forward. Frantic that she was about to tumble head over heels down the mountainside, she snatched a death grip on Marshall's arm.

He reacted instantly by snaring her with both arms and wrapping her tightly against his chest.

"Mia! Why did you do that?" he gently scolded as he cradled the top of her head beneath his chin. "If you'd lost your balance I might not have been able to catch you!"

Shivering with delayed fright, Mia clung to him and pressed her cheek against the rock hard safety of his chest. "I—I'm sorry, Marshall. I thought— I didn't think it would bother me. I've never been affected by heights before."

And Marshall had never been so affected by a woman before. It didn't matter that the two of them were precariously perched on a small shelf of mountain or that jagged edges of rocks were stabbing him in the back. All he could think about was covering her mouth with his; letting his hands explore the warm curves pressed against him.

"Oh, honey, don't scare me that way." Anguish jerked

his head back and forth as unbearable images flashed through his head. "If you'd fallen, I would have had to jump after you."

Slowly her head tilted upward until her troubled gaze met his. "Don't say such things, Marshall. I'm—I'm not worth trying to save, much less dying for."

Softly, he pushed away the black strands of hair sticking to her damp cheek. "Why not? I wouldn't be worth much without you."

To Marshall's surprise tears suddenly gathered in her eyes and he could feel her trembling start anew, as though his words scared her even more than her near fall.

"Don't say something that serious, Marshall, unless you really mean it."

It suddenly struck him that he'd never been more serious. Losing Mia for any reason was something he couldn't contemplate.

"I couldn't be more serious, Mia."

Disbelief flashed across her face, but Marshall didn't give her time to respond. Instead he gathered her chin between his thumb and forefinger, then lowered his head to hers.

"Don't argue with me, Mia," he murmured huskily. "Don't say anything. Just let me kiss you."

He could see questions shouting in her eyes, but her lips were silent, waiting to meet his. He groaned as a need he didn't quite understand twisted deep in his gut, then his eyes closed and his lips fastened hungrily over hers.

Chapter Ten

Two hours later, after climbing nearly to the timber-line of the mountain, then descending back to their starting point, Mia and Marshall returned to the Jeep and were now traversing the rough track of road that would eventually carry them back to the resort.

Mia was hot, tired and thirsty. Her knees were scraped raw and she'd cut a painful gash in her palm, but those problems were minor discomforts compared to her spinning thoughts.

The kiss Marshall had given her on the rock ledge had frightened her with its intensity and she was still wondering what had been behind it and his suggestive words. He couldn't be getting serious about her. They'd only known each other a few days. On top of that, he wasn't a man who wanted to get serious about any woman. And even if he were, she was carrying a trunk full of baggage. All he had to do was open the lid to see she wasn't the sort of woman he'd want to gather to his heart.

"Are you too tired to stop by the meadow?"

Marshall's voice interrupted her burdened thoughts and she glanced over to see he'd taken his eyes off the road and was directing them at her. Just looking at him pierced her with a longing that continued to stun her. She'd never expected to feel so much desire for any man. Even Lance, whom she'd believed that she'd once loved, had never elicited the hungry need she felt for Marshall. What did it all mean? And where could it possibly lead her, except straight to a crushed heart?

"I'm tired, but I did want to take a closer look at the flowers."

The corners of his lips turned softly upward. "Good," he said. "There's something I want to talk with you about before we get back to the resort."

Her brows lifted with curiosity, but she didn't have time to ask him to explain further. By now the road had leveled and they were quickly approaching the flower-filled meadow.

Moments later Marshall parked the Jeep along the side of the road. As she waited for him to skirt around the vehicle to help her out, she made a feeble attempt to smooth her mussed hair. She was trying to do something about the dirt and blood caked on her palm when he jerked open the door.

"What's the matter?" he asked as she quickly closed her hand away from his sight.

"Uh—nothing. I just gouged my hand a little on a rock. I'll clean it up later, when I get back to my cabin."

With a frown of concern, he gestured for her to give him her hand. "I'm the doctor around here, remember. Let me see."

Mia was reluctant to let him treat her, even for a basic scratch. Something had happened to her when he'd kissed her up there on the mountain ledge. It was like he'd woken her sleeping libido and turned it into a hungry tigress. Letting him touch her, for any reason, was enough to send her up in flames. But she could hardly explain any of that, so there was nothing left for her to do but place her hand upon his palm.

"Mia!" he exclaimed as he gently probed at the deep gash. "Why didn't you tell me you'd hurt yourself? This is going to have to be cleaned. Otherwise the dirt might cause infection. It might even need a stitch or two. And you're going to need a tetanus shot. We need to go to the office where I have the equipment to deal with this."

With a nervous laugh, she swung her legs over the side of the bucket seat and pulled her hand from his grip. His gaze dropped instantly to her raw knees and he shook his head with misgiving.

"You look like you've met up with a grizzly bear and lost the fight. I'm sorry, Mia. When I asked you out this morning it wasn't with the intention of getting you hurt."

"I'm not hurt, doc. Just scraped a little. Now help me

out. You can take care of my wounds later. After I take a look at the flowers."

Seeing he wasn't going to deter her, he took a firm hold on her arm and helped her to the ground.

"Don't even think about trying to get away from me," he told her as he guided her into the deep grass of the meadow. "I don't want any more cuts and bruises on you."

The two of them walked several yards into the quiet meadow before they found a seat on a fallen log bleached white by years of harsh elements.

Mia sighed with pleasure as she looked around at the thousands of tiny pink and yellow blooms carpeting the surface of the meadow. "It's like a fairy-tale world," she said in a hushed voice. "I don't think I've ever seen anything so pretty."

"I have."

"You mean the pool of water you showed me up on the mountain? Well, it was beautiful," she admitted with another sigh. "But not as much as this."

Without warning, his hand came against her face and he turned her head so that she was facing him. Her heart jolted at the tender glow she found in his brown eyes.

"I'm not talking about the pool on the mountain," he murmured. "I'm talking about this."

His fingers brushed against her face, as though her cheek was a rose too delicate to touch. Mia couldn't stop the strong leap of her heart or the blush that crawled up her throat and onto her face.

"You're a terrible flatterer, Dr. Cates. I never know what will come out of your mouth."

The faint grin on his face was both wry and wistful. "I never know myself. Sometimes I get into trouble for saying what I'm thinking. And right now I'm thinking I'd like to lay you down in all these flowers and make love to you."

His admission shattered Mia's composure and for a moment all she could do was stare at him. Then suddenly she realized she had to get away from him, before she fell into his arms like a complete fool.

Quickly, she started to push herself up from the log, but he caught her by the arm and tugged her back beside him.

"We'd better go. Now!" she blurted sharply.

"Calm down, Mia. I'm not going to act on my words. I was simply telling you what I felt. Surely it isn't a surprise to you that I want to make love to you."

Mia slowly breathed in and out as she tried to still the rapid beating of her heart. She could have told him that it wasn't him she was afraid of, but rather herself. Yet to do that would only reveal that she was falling for him, that she wanted the very same thing he wanted—to make love to him in a bed of flowers.

Bending her head, she said in a thick voice, "You're right, Marshall. I'm not some innocent young woman. I'm twenty-six years old and I—I've had a man in my life. We were close for a long while—very close. And I...don't want to give myself to anyone like that again."

She looked up to see his brown eyes searching her face and she felt a little more of her resistance slip, a little more of the hidden Mia screaming to come to the surface.

"What happened? He wouldn't make a commitment?"

No, he'd gotten tired of her obsessive hunt for her mother, Mia thought. Tired of her putting their relationship on hold while she'd pored over names and telephone numbers, searched through stacks of birth records and driven miles to strange places with the mere hope that she'd find a lead. By the time she'd actually found Janelle and fell into her newfound fortune, her relationship with Lance had suffered greatly. Yet she'd thought, hoped, that having financial security would change everything for the better and that she and Lance could finally be happy, marry and start a family. But the money had only caused more of a wall between them. He'd walked away, but not before accusing her of being selfish and unfeeling. Dear God, he'd been right, she thought sickly. And that was the hardest part she'd had to live with.

Bitterness coated her tongue when she answered, "He made a commitment, but then…changed his mind."

Silence settled around them until the raucous screech of a hawk lifted Mia's gaze toward the blue sky. The predator was circling, searching for a weak and easy prey to wrap his talons around. Only the strong survived in this world, she thought sadly. And she wasn't strong. She'd been weak and needy enough to allow Janelle to get her hooks in her, to draw her away from Nina, the only mother she'd ever known.

"I'm sorry you had to go through that, Mia. But I can tell you why it happened."

Her nerves went on sudden alert as she dared to look at him. Did he know? Had he guessed at the terrible mistakes she'd made?

"You can?" she asked in a strained voice.

His smile was gentle, almost loving, and her hammering heart quieted to a hard but steady pound.

"Sure I can. Call it what you want. Fate or the hand of God. That thing you had with the other guy ended because you were supposed to wind up here—with me."

Hopeless tears poured into her heart until she was sure it was going to burst, but she carefully hid the pain behind a wan smile.

"Marshall, you're just so…"

When she couldn't finish, Marshall did it for her. "Sweet? Romantic? Yeah, I know," he said, his eyes twinkling. "I just can't help myself."

Sighing, she slipped off the log and bent down to pick a handful of delicate wildflowers. Marshall watched as she lifted the blossoms to her nose and wondered why the more he learned about her, the more he was growing to love her.

Love. Was that what it was? This endless need to see her face, hear her voice, have her beside him? He'd never felt like this before. Never felt so protective of a woman, so mindful of her feelings. He wanted more than just sex from her. He wanted to cradle her in his arms, wipe away the sadness from her eyes and cherish her for the rest of his life. If that was love then he'd fallen like a rock tossed into a river.

"My parents are having a little farewell dinner for my twin brothers this weekend," he said suddenly. "I'd like you to go with me."

She turned to stare at him and he could see doubts

running rampant over her face. He wanted to reassure her with promises that he'd never hurt her, but he figured anything he might say right now would ring hollow. He was going to have to earn her trust. Show her that he wasn't the same sort of man that had changed his mind and walked away from her.

"Where is this dinner going to be?" she asked finally.

"At my parents' home."

As she chewed thoughtfully on her bottom lip, Marshall rose to his feet and laid a hand on her shoulder.

"Don't worry, Mia, it'll be a casual affair. And my parents are nice, laid-back people. You'll like them." He squeezed her shoulder. "And I know they'll like you."

Her eyes drifted up to his. "I'm not sure it would be a good idea."

"It would mean a lot to me," he said softly. "A whole lot."

She drew in a shaky breath and then a wobbly smile slowly spread across her lips. "All right, Marshall."

Leaning his head back, he gave a loud yip of joy.

That Saturday, as Marshall drove the two of them to the Cates homestead on the west edge of town, Mia continued to ask herself what in heck had possessed her to agree to this outing. Meeting a guy's parents was a serious thing. Or, at least, it was where she came from. She wasn't sure that Marshall meant anything significant by his invitation. But if by some odd chance he did, then she was digging herself into a deeper grave. She couldn't continue to let Marshall believe she was simply a rich young woman who'd been raised in a nice, wealthy family. Yet to confess would only mean the end of their time together. And her hungry heart just wasn't ready for that yet.

The Cates home was a brick two-story structure set on five acres of a gently sloping property dotted with large shade trees. A wooden rail fence cordoned off a large front yard landscaped with beds of blooming perennials and neatly clipped shrubs. A concrete drive led up to a double garage. Presently the garage was closed and Marshall parked his Jeep next to a white pickup truck with logos on the doors that read Cates Construction—Built to Your Needs.

As Marshall helped her out of the vehicle Mia stared at the professionally done sign. "I thought you said your brother's business was called Cates International. That says Construction."

"That's another Cates," he said with a laugh. "The pa of the herd. Dad's been in the building business since he was a very young guy. Started out with his dad—my grandfather. Before the gold strike most of their business was over in the Bozeman area. The economy in Thunder Canyon was so slow that the city did well to build picnic tables for the town square. But now Dad and his employees can't keep up with all the contracts being thrown at them from a number of townsfolk. He thinks it's great, but Mom isn't so happy. For years now she's been planning for them to take a trip from coast to coast, but that's been postponed until Cates Construction catches up or the town goes bust."

"Marshall, quit dallying around and come in! We've all been waiting for you!"

Mia looked over her shoulder to see a middle-aged woman with chin-length pale blond hair standing on the small square of sheltered concrete that served as the front porch. She was dressed casually in tan slacks and a white sleeveless blouse. The warm smile on her face made Mia feel instantly welcome.

"Coming, Mom!" he yelled, then wrapping an arm around the back of Mia's waist, he urged her toward a wide sidewalk that bordered the front of the large house.

"You're a true doctor, son. Always late," Edie Cates fondly teased as Marshall guided Mia up the steps.

"I like to keep with tradition," he joked back, then quickly thrust Mia forward. "Mom, this is Mia Smith. She's a guest at the resort. And, Mia, this is my mother, Edie, the beautiful female of the bunch."

"The *only* female of the bunch," Edie said with a laugh.

"It's very nice to meet you, Mrs. Cates."

Expecting the woman to shake hands, Mia was surprised when she slung an arm around her shoulders and began leading her toward the door. "It's Edie, my dear. Don't make me feel any older than I already do with that *Mrs.* stuff. And I'll call you Mia, if that's okay with you."

"Of course," Mia told her. "And thank you for having me as a guest tonight."

"It's our pleasure," she said. She opened the door and ushered Mia inside while leaving Marshall to follow. "None of our sons have been brave enough to bring a girl home to meet us until now. Marshall has definitely treated his parents by inviting you."

Mia tossed a look of surprise at Marshall, but he merely winked and grinned.

Edie ushered them through a small foyer, a formal sitting room, then on to a den where the rest of the Cates family was congregated in front of a large television. A major league baseball game was playing on the screen, but the sound was turned low, telling Mia that the four other Cates men had been doing more talking than watching.

Over the next few minutes Mia met Marshall's father, Frank, a tall, well-built man with salt and pepper hair and a jovial attitude that reminded her of Marshall. Mitchell, the second oldest son, was an attractive man with the same dark coloring as his brothers, but very quiet. Especially when she compared him to Matthew and Marlon, the young twins, who were continually telling animated stories and swapping playful swings at each other.

After all the introductions were over, Edie passed around soft drinks and Marshall directed Mia to take a seat at the end of a long couch. If anyone noticed that he tucked her into the crook of his arm, they didn't let on, but Mia was riveted by the warmth of his torso pressed against her side, the weight of his hand lingering on her upper arm.

He was treating her as though she were someone special in his life and he wanted his family to know it. The idea was a thrilling one to Mia. Even though she knew this time with him couldn't last forever, she decided that this evening she was going to relish it. After all, leaving Thunder Canyon would come soon enough.

After a few minutes of light conversation and much bantering between the four brothers, Edie rose from her husband's side and announced she was heading to the kitchen to check on dinner. Wanting to feel useful, Mia instantly rose to her feet and offered to help.

"I can manage, Mia," Edie said. "But I'd love the company."

With a smile for Marshall, Mia quickly eased out of his gentle clasp and followed the woman out of the room and down a short hallway.

"Mmm, something smells delicious," she exclaimed as the two women pushed through a swinging door into the large, brightly lit kitchen.

"Lasagna. I hope you like Italian food. All the boys love it. Frank prefers steak, but since this is the twins' last night at home, he wants them to be treated."

"I love pasta of any sort," Mia told her as she watched the other woman open the oven door on a gas range and peer into the hot cavern.

"I do, too. And it shows in all the wrong places." Chuckling, she patted one shapely hip.

"I think you look beautiful," Mia said sincerely. "And you certainly don't look like you've had four children." Nor did she look as though she'd had the nips and tucks from a plastic surgeon that Janelle and thousands of other women chose to have in order to appear youthful.

Edie removed the large glass casserole dish full of bubbling lasagna and carefully placed it on the top of the stove. "You're very kind, dear. And very pretty. I can see why you caught Marshall's attention."

Feeling more than awkward, Mia let the woman's comment slide. "Is there anything I can do to help? Make a salad? Ice glasses?"

With a knowing chuckle, Edie glanced at her. "Don't want to talk about that, huh? Well, don't worry, I'm not a nosy mother. Now that the boys are grown, I stay out of their private lives unless I'm asked advice." She moved on down the counter and began to pull silverware from a drawer. "It's better that way. Otherwise they resent the interference." She laughed. "'Course there are times I'd like to tell them plenty."

Mia joined her at the cabinet counter. "I wish my mother were so understanding."

Edie glanced up from counting a handful of forks. "Does she live close to you?"

In the same house, but Mia wasn't going to admit that. It made her sound like a child who was now all grown up but too indolent to leave home. When actually the circumstances of living with Janelle were nothing close to that. Mia had fought against moving into the Josephson mansion. She'd wanted to keep her independence and privacy. But Janelle had played on Mia's soft heart by pointing out that she'd gone for twenty-five years believing her baby had died, surely living in the same house with her was not too much to ask. Not wanting to hurt her mother any more than she'd already been hurt, Mia had agreed and moved into the stately house. Ultimately that move had been a mistake, one that she was still paying for.

"Yes. And she can be very controlling. That's one of

the reasons I've been vacationing here in Thunder Canyon," she admitted before she could stop herself. "Sometimes a person needs a little breathing room." She slanted a regretful glance at Marshall's mother. "That sounds pretty awful, doesn't it?"

Her expression empathetic, Edie reached over and touched Mia's arm. "No. It sounds perfectly human to me." She smiled warmly and with an ease that totally charmed Mia, she quickly changed the subject by pointing to a cabinet above her head. "Now if you'd like to ice the glasses, you'll find them there. Looks like there're seven of us tonight. A nice lucky number."

Midway through dinner it struck Mia that the Cates were the sort of family she'd always dreamed of being a part of. Marshall and his siblings were close enough to bicker and tease without fearing that their love for each other could ever be shaken. They had parents that still adored each other after decades of marriage. Obviously Edie and Frank had raised their four boys with love and that love had stood as an anchor for them as they'd grown into men. If either parent was the controlling, smothering sort, it wasn't evident to Mia. Of course, with a guest present, she assumed that everyone was probably on his or her best behavior. Still, as far as she could see, there were no taut undercurrents or furtive glances of impatience between family members. All Mia could see was genuine affection and it filled her heart with golden warmth, like a treasure chest spilling over with incomparable riches.

As the group dined on plates of lasagna accompanied by hunks of garlic bread, Mia drank in the easy ambiance like sips of wine to be savored. With Marshall at her side showering her with attention and affectionate glances, it was easy to let herself dream that she was home and she was loved.

"Did you make any extra lasagna, Mom?" Marlon asked as the meal began to wind down. "You know Matthew and I will need something to eat once we get to the dorm."

The roll of Edie's eyes was tempered with an indulgent smile. "I'm sure there's not a place on campus that sells food," she teased. "That's why I made an extra pan. When you get to your dorm room just make sure you keep it in the refrigerator. You can't leave it sitting out, then rake off the mold expecting it to be good."

Mia looked at Matthew, who was sitting directly across the table from her. Marlon was striving for a career in business agriculture while Matthew was working his way toward a law degree. Both twins appeared eager to head back to school, although she could sense they were going to miss being home. "When will you two be leaving?" she asked.

"In the morning," Marlon spoke up before his twin could answer. "As soon as I can kick Matthew out of bed."

"Hah!" Matthew tossed at his brother. "I'll be the one doing the kicking. You don't even have your bags packed."

Marlon shot him a droll look. "That's because I'm not the dandy you are. I don't need trunks of clothing or hours to pack it. Five minutes to fill a duffle bag will be enough for me."

From the end of the table, Frank chuckled. "Well, I know one thing," he said to the twins. "Both of you are going to miss having your mom do your laundry and cooking."

Edie smiled at her two youngest sons, then settled a privately shared gaze on her husband. "Oh, Frank, you know I've spoiled the twins the same way I have you and Marshall and Mitchell. And just like you three, they take it all for granted. Once they get back to college, they'll forget all about their ole mom and everything I've done for them."

Both twins groaned with loud protest and everyone around the table began to laugh. Except Mia. She wasn't hearing the laughter or seeing the teasing faces. She was suddenly back in Denver and Nina Hanover was begging her to come home, which at that time had been a little apartment in Colorado Springs. Nina, a little drunk and full of a whole lot of pain, had accused Mia of forgetting her mother, the mother that had raised her from a newborn, the mother that had worked and sacrificed to keep a roof over Mia's head and food on their table.

The memories were suddenly too much for Mia to bear and, as tears began to blur her vision, she frantically realized she had to get away from the dinner table before she broke down completely.

"Please excuse me," she mumbled, then before Marshall or the rest of the family could respond in any way, she scraped back her chair and rushed from the room.

Chapter Eleven

Mia's abrupt departure from the dining room halted all laughter and Marshall stared in stunned silence at his parents and brothers.

"What happened?" Mitchell was the first one to ask. "Did somebody say something wrong?"

Edie looked across the table at Marshall who was already tossing down his napkin and rising to his feet. "Son, you'd better go see about her. I got a glance at Mia's face as she turned away from the table and I thought she looked sick. Dear heaven, I hope my cooking hasn't upset her stomach."

Marshall headed out of the dining room. "Don't worry, Mom," he tossed over his shoulder. "I don't think it's anything like that. The rest of you finish dinner and I'll go check on her."

After checking the guest bathroom and finding the door open and the light off, Marshall hurried to the den. When he didn't spot her there, he stepped through a sliding back door and onto a small patio. During dinner, the sun had fallen and now golden-pink rays were slanted across the backyard.

At first glance he didn't notice the still figure standing with her back to him in the shadow of a poplar tree. But as he turned to step back into the house, a flash of her coral-colored blouse caught his eye.

Quickly, he made his way across the yard to where she was staring out at the ridge of nearby mountains. If she was aware of his approach, she didn't show it, even when he came up behind her and gently placed his hands on her shoulders.

Through the thin fabric of her blouse, he could feel her trembling and concern threaded his softly spoken words. "Mia. What are you doing out here? Everyone is worried."

Several moments passed and then she reached up and wiped at her eyes. The realization that she'd been crying hit him hard.

"I'm…sorry, Marshall," she said in a raw, husky voice. "I—didn't mean to upset your family. They've all been so wonderful to me. Too wonderful."

The painful cracks in her voice struck Marshall right in the heart and he slowly turned her to face him. Tears rimmed her beautiful eyes and spilled onto her cheeks. Marshall wiped them away with the palm of his hand.

"If everything is so wonderful then why are you out here crying?"

Bending her head, Mia stared at Marshall's boots. She'd gone and done it now, she realized. There was no way she could easily explain away her behavior. Not without giving away the past she desperately wanted to keep hidden. But he was expecting an explanation and she was so sick of the deception she'd been playing.

"I—uh—guess I just got swamped with memories, Marshall. Your family is so nice and I guess it hit me all over again that mine is gone."

"Gone?" he repeated blankly. "I remember you saying your father died long ago. Are you telling me that your mother has passed away, too?"

She lifted her gaze and the concern she saw in Marshall's eyes gave her the strength to release the words bottled in her throat. "Yes. About a year ago. She—uh—was killed in an auto accident. And I—I've been having a hard time dealing with—the whole thing. I miss her terribly. Her death—" She paused, swallowed, then tried to keep her voice from breaking. "Her death has left a hole in me, Marshall, and I—just don't know how to fill it back up."

With a gentle shake of his head, he said, "I'm so sorry, sweetheart. I know that doesn't mean much, but I really don't know what else to say. If I told you that I understand what you're going through, I'd be lying. I've been blessed. I don't know what it's like to lose a loved one."

She blinked furiously at the fresh tears that threatened to spill onto her cheeks. "My parents were like yours, Marshall. They loved each other very much and they loved me—maybe more than I realized—until they were gone. It troubles me that I didn't appreciate them as much as I should have."

He reached out and smoothed a hand over the crown of her head. The soothing touch caused Mia's eyelashes to flutter down and rest against her cheeks. If only she could always have him by her side, she thought longingly. To soothe her when she hurt, to laugh with her when she was happy, to simply love her for who and what she was.

"We're all guilty of that, Mia. I hate to admit it but there have been plenty of times that I've taken my family for granted and forgotten to show them how much they mean to me. Fortunately they know that I love them anyway. I'm sure your parents knew that you loved them, too."

Over the past months Mia didn't think her heart could hurt anymore than it already had, but the pain ripping through the middle of her chest was so deep it practically stole her breath.

"I hope so," she choked out. "But it's different for me, Marshall. My family…well, I wasn't raised up like you."

"I never expected that you were," he countered. "Dad has always made a nice living for his wife and children, but I'm sure it can't compare to your family's wealth."

She shook her head viciously back and forth and the truth, or at least part of it, demanded to be let out. "No—

you have it all wrong, Marshall. I wasn't born into wealth. Will, my father, raised potatoes and alfalfa hay and Nina, my mother, was a simple housewife. We lived in a modest farmhouse outside of the little town of Alamosa down in southern Colorado. We weren't rich—just rich in love. It's—" she paused long enough to draw in a deep breath and lift a beseeching gaze up to his "—it's taken me a long time to realize that, Marshall. Too long."

Marshall would be lying if he said that her admission hadn't taken him by surprise. Learning she wasn't a born heiress was the last thing he'd expected to hear. But her stunning declaration couldn't compare to the emotions piercing him from all directions. He'd never imagined that he could feel someone else's pain this deeply. It had emanated from her like a tangible thing and wrapped around his heart like an iron vice. And like a flash of lightning, Marshall suddenly realized he was just now learning what it truly meant to be a doctor to the needy and a man to the woman he loved.

"Oh, Mia. I'm glad you told me. And if you think it could make me care about you less, then you've got it all wrong. I don't care that you weren't born into wealth. None of that matters. All I want is for us to be together."

He *cared* about her? Dear God, maybe it didn't matter to him that she'd come from a modest background, Mia thought. But he couldn't begin to imagine the whole story. And he wouldn't be nearly so understanding if he found out she'd caused her mother to turn into a drunk driver. Nina Hanover had turned to a bottle of vodka to drown out her sorrows. First to forget that she'd lost her husband, then more heavily because her daughter had deserted her for a pile of riches. Or at least, that's the way it had seemed to Nina. Actually, Mia hadn't ignored her mother because she'd stopped loving her. She'd simply grown weary of dealing with Nina's drinking and whining and pleading. It had been easy to let Janelle shield her from all of that and give her a quiet haven away from Nina's emotional problems. But Mia couldn't forsake Nina entirely and one day she'd agreed to meet her for lunch. She'd had plans of talking her mother into entering rehab and finding the help she needed. But Nina had ended any and all of Mia's hope when she'd climbed behind the wheel of a car and crashed on her way to meet Mia.

"Marshall, I…" The rest of her confession lodged in her throat like pieces of poisoned bread. She couldn't tell him the rest. Not tonight. Maybe she was wrong, even greedy for not telling him everything. But she wanted this fairy-tale time with Marshall to keep going for as long as possible. "Thank you for understanding," she finally whispered.

For long, expectant moments, his dark gaze gently skimmed her tear-stained face and then suddenly his head was bending down toward hers, blocking out the last bit of twilight.

When his lips settled over hers, she didn't even try to resist. The taste of his tender kiss was the very thing she needed to soothe her aching heart and before Mia realized what she was doing, she rose up on tiptoes and curled her arms around his neck.

Marshall was about to place his hands on her hips and draw her even tighter against him, but thankfully, before their embrace could turn into something more passionate, he caught the sound of footfall quickly approaching from behind.

With supreme effort, he quickly lifted his head and turned to see his mother watching them with a frown of concern.

"Sorry, I didn't mean to intrude," she quickly apologized. "We were all getting a little worried about Mia. Is everything all right?"

Clearing his throat, Marshall arched a questioning brow down at Mia. Of course *everything* wasn't okay with Mia, he realized sadly. It was going to take her a long time to recover from the recent loss of her mother. But at least for the moment her tears had dried and a wan smile was curving the corners of her lips.

Mia stepped toward Marshall's mother. "I'm fine, really, Edie. And I'm so sorry that I ruined the last of your dinner. Please forgive me. I guess—I got a little too emotional thinking about my own family."

Edie closed the short distance between them and wrapped Mia's hand in a warm clasp between the two of hers. "Don't bother yourself one minute over it. You didn't ruin anything. We've loved having you. Would you like to come back in now and have coffee? I'm afraid that the twins have already dug into the brownies, but there're plenty left."

Mia glanced back at Marshall and all he could think about was taking up their kiss exactly where they'd left off.

"I think Mia's had enough of the rowdy Cates brothers for one night," he told his mother. "If you and Dad won't mind, I'm going to take her home."

Edie's understanding smile encompassed both Mia and her son. "Of course we won't mind. As long as you two promise to come again soon."

"You can bet on it," Marshall told her, then bent and placed a kiss on his mother's cheek. "Tell everyone goodbye for us, will you?"

"Sure."

Edie turned and disappeared through the patio doors. Marshall took Mia by the arm and led her around the house to where his Jeep was parked.

Before he opened the door to help her in, he gathered her back into his arms. Then resting his forehead against hers, he whispered, "I hope you don't mind that we're leaving. Do you?"

The suggestive tone in his voice set her heart thumping with anticipation. "No. I'm ready to go if you are."

He placed a quick, but promising kiss on her lips. "I couldn't be more ready."

Once they were in the Jeep driving back to the resort, Mia stared, dazed, out at the darkened landscape. Marshall had said he cared about her. He couldn't *love* her, she mentally argued. Could he? Especially now that he knew she wasn't a born-and-bred heiress.

She didn't realize he'd passed her cabin and had

driven them on up the mountain to his house until the vehicle came to a final halt and she looked around her at the encroaching pine forest.

"This isn't my cabin, it's yours," she stated lamely. "What are we doing here?"

He shoved the gearshift into first and pulled the key from the ignition. "I didn't think you needed to be alone right now. And I wasn't sure you'd invite me in if we stopped at your place."

Her heart melting at the tender look on his face, she reached over and touched his hand with hers. "I was going to invite you in. But this is just as good."

Leaning toward her, he slipped a hand behind her neck and pulled her face toward his. His lips were warm and searching, inviting her to forget everything but him.

Mia was about to wriggle closer when Leroy's loud barks caused her to flinch away from him.

"Oh. Leroy scared me!" she exclaimed.

"Damn dog," Marshall muttered. "He has no timing at all."

"Yes, but he's a sweetheart," Mia crooned as she looked toward the front-yard gate. The dog was reared up on his hind legs, pawing eagerly at the wooden post where the latch was located.

Mia laughed and Marshall shot her a droll look. "Hey, beautiful, you're confused. I'm supposed to be the sweetheart around here. Not Leroy."

She was still laughing as they crossed the yard and entered the house with a happy Leroy trotting behind them. But the moment he shut the door and drew her into his arms, he swallowed up her chuckles with a kiss hot enough to curl her toes.

"I think Leroy is watching," she whispered when he finally lifted his lips a fraction from hers.

"Not for long."

She was trying to guess his intentions when he suddenly bent and scooped her up in his arms.

"Marshall!" she squeaked. "You're going to drop me!"

"Then you'd better hang on," he warned with a chuckle.

Flinging her arms around his neck, she clung to him tightly as he began to walk out of the living room. When his route took them down a narrow hallway it was obvious he was headed to a bedroom and she wasn't so naive that she had to ask why. For the past few days, she'd felt the two of them drawing closer and closer, ultimately leading them onto this path and this very moment.

Seconds later, Marshall entered a room, kicked the door shut behind them, then set her on the floor. Black shadows filled the corners and shrouded most of the furniture, while faint shafts of light sifted through the windows and slashed across part of the bed and the upper half of his face. The illumination was enough to give Mia a glimpse of his heated gaze and it arced into her like a sizzling arrow.

Her heart was suddenly pounding, pushing heated blood to every inch of her body as his hands came up to cradle her face.

"You can tell me you're not ready for this, you know," he whispered gently. "But I hope you are."

He was giving her the opportunity to walk away from

him and the intimacy he was offering. He was giving her a moment to analyze her feelings and consider the consequences of making love with him. But Mia didn't need the extra moment to question the rightness or wrongness of being here. She was sick of analyzing and agonizing over every decision she made, tired of guarding her true feelings. She wanted to be a woman again and for tonight that was enough to justify stepping into his arms.

Slipping her arms around his waist, she rested her chin in the middle of his chest and tilted her face up to his. "I want you, Marshall. Here with you is the only place I want to be."

Groaning with a mixture of relief and need, he skimmed his hands down the sides of her arms. "I want you, too, baby. So much."

Her breath caught as his head slowly lowered down to hers and then she forgot all about breathing as his lips settled over hers and his hands clasped her waist and drew her against the length of his body.

Like a desert wildfire, his kiss raged through her body, turning her insides to molten mush. His tongue pushed its way past her pulsing lips and then she was lost, groaning with abandoned pleasure as he explored the dark cavern of her mouth, the rough edges of her teeth.

In a matter of moments a tight ache started somewhere deep within her and began to spiral outward and upward until she was twisting and clinging, fighting to find the relief his body would give her.

Fueled by her heated response, Marshall continued

to kiss her as his hands quickly went to work releasing the buttons on her blouse and finding his way to the warm flesh beneath. Her skin was smooth beneath his fingers. He couldn't touch her enough as his hands slid upward, along the bumps of her ribs, then around to her spine where they climbed until his thumbs snared in the fastener on her bra.

With deft movements he unhooked a pair of eyelets and the garment fell apart, the loosened tails dangling against her back. He broke the kiss and their gazes locked as he slowly pushed the blouse from her shoulders, then slipped the straps of her bra down her arms.

Beneath the trail of his fingers, he could feel goose bumps breaking out along her skin, telling him just how much he was affecting her. As for him, he felt like an awkward teenager, touching a woman for the first time. His heart was pounding. Blood was rushing to his head, fogging his senses, filling his loins to the aching point. He'd never wanted so much. Needed so much.

He was asking himself what it could mean when the bra fell away from her breasts and the perfectly rounded orbs were exposed to his gaze. The lovely sight of puckered rose-brown nipples momentarily froze him and then slowly, seductively, he raked the pads of his thumbs across the delicate nubs.

Almost instantly Mia's head fell back. A moan vibrated in her throat. Bending his head, Marshall slid parted lips along the arch of her neck, over the angle of her shoulder, then lower until he was tasting the incredibly soft slope of her breasts.

When his mouth finally fastened over one taut nipple, Mia was panting, thrusting her fingers against his scalp, urging him.

When he finally lifted his head, he was shaking from the inside out and wondering if he was in some glorious dream that would end at any moment. But Mia's warm flesh brushing against his was enough to remind him that she was real and waiting to become his woman, his lover. The implication brought a tremble to his hands as he reached to undo the front of her jeans.

"Let me do this," she whispered as his fingers fumbled with the button at her waist. "It will be faster."

Not in any condition to argue with her, Marshall eased away from her and while he struggled to fling aside his own shirt and jeans, he darted hungry glances at Mia until she finally pushed the denim off her hips.

With his own clothes out of the way, he stood watching as she stepped from the pool of fabric. The sight of her plump breasts and tiny waist, the curves of her hips and the long firm muscles of her thighs just waiting for him to touch and taste was enough to leave him just short of speechless.

"Mia. Oh, Mia," he whispered.

Stepping forward he lifted her onto the queen-sized bed, then followed her onto the down comforter. As he enfolded her in his arms, she pressed her cheek against his and the sweetness of her gesture pierced his heart, filling it with something warm, something that had nothing to do with sex and everything to do with love.

waited, barely breathing as he stroked and explored that secret part of her. But after a few short moments the teasing rhythm of his movements was too much for her to bear.

Crying out with a mixture of intense pleasure and pain, she reached for the boxers riding low on his hips and, hooking her thumbs in the waistband, pulled them down around his thighs.

"Make love to me, Marshall. *Please.*"

The urgency of her whispered plea was like throwing accelerant on an already raging fire. On the verge of losing all control, Marshall forced himself to move away from her and over to a chest of drawers where he fished out a small packet and quickly tore it open.

When he returned to her, Mia hardly had time to notice that he'd been dealing with protection. All at once his knee was parting her thighs and his hands were slipping beneath her buttocks, lifting her up to meet the thrust of his arousal.

A sudden rush of fiery sensations brought a keening moan to the back of Mia's throat and, seeking any sort of anchor she could find, her fingers latched a tight grip around his upper arms. Bending forward, he began to move inside her and when she slowly began to move with him, he brought his lips to hers and growled out her name.

"Mia. Mia. Touch me. Love me."

Happy to comply with his sweet request, she swept her palms over the hard muscles of his chest, down his ribs and abdomen, then back up until her fingertips lingered at his hard nipples.

With each bold foray of her hands, she heard his

breath catch, felt his thrusts quicken. Frantic to keep pace with him, she wrapped her legs around his and clung to his sweat-drenched shoulders.

At some point the room around her spun away, leaving a black velvety place where only she and Marshall existed. With each rapid plunge, he drove her to a higher ledge, where her heart was hammering out of control, her lungs burning with each raspy breath.

They took the climb together, racing frantically toward the peak of the mountain where a crescent moon poured silver dust and lit their pathway to the stars.

She was straining, her body screaming for relief, when Marshall's lips came down over hers to swallow up her cries and nudge them both over the last precipice of their journey. He drove into her like a man possessed, his hands and hips gripping her to him as he spilled his very heart into her.

His throaty groan of release launched Mia even higher and, like a rocket gathering steam, she shot straight through a bright, molten star. She cried his name as lights glittered behind her tightly closed eyelids. And then she was drifting, glowing, falling back to earth on a cloud of emotions.

When Marshall's senses finally returned, he was still breathing raggedly and sweat was rolling into his eyes and down his face. Beneath him Mia's body was damp and lax, her face covered with a tangle of black hair.

With a groan that sounded like it belonged to someone else, Marshall rolled to her side and reached to push the veil of hair away from her cheek. As his fingers brushed against her neck, he could feel her pulse hammering and he bent and pressed a kiss to the throb of her heartbeat.

"I'm not sure I'm alive," he murmured. "Are we in heaven?"

The corners of his lips tilted into dreamy smile. "I think I just went there."

Slipping a hand over her belly, he latched onto her hip bone, then rolled her onto her side and against the length of his body. After cuddling her head in the crook of his shoulder, he pillowed his jaw against the crown of her hair and closed his eyes in exhausted contentment.

For the first time in Marshall's life words seemed inadequate to describe what he'd just experienced. Joy was swimming around inside him, warming him like bright sunshine. Maybe that made him a sappy fool. But he didn't care.

"I knew it would be good with us," he murmured, then silently cursed himself for emitting such a stupid remark. Hell, good was a long way from portraying the connection he'd felt to Mia. Why couldn't he tell her that? Because he was a chicken, he realized. Because even though she'd made love with him, his hold on her was still too fragile. Any remark suggesting a future together would send her running.

"Mmm. How did you know that? Experience?"

Sliding a finger beneath her chin, he tilted her face up to his, but the darkness of the room hid her expression. He touched the pad of his forefinger to the middle of her lips.

"Oh, Mia, I thought I knew what being with a woman was all about. But making love with you—" He shook his head, then chuckled with wry disbelief. "It felt like the first time. No—not the first time. The *only* time."

Her heart wincing with regret, she lifted her fingers to his face and slid them along the length of his jawline. "You'll feel differently about that in the light of day. Especially if you see me when I first wake up," she tried to tease.

His arms moved around her back and hugged her even closer. "I hope that means you're going to stay here with me tonight."

She was wondering how to best answer that question when his arms tightened around her even more.

"Don't bother answering," he said, "because I'm not going to let you out of this bed for any reason. Except breakfast, maybe."

She tried not to let the possessive tone in his voice thrill her, but it did. Everything about the man thrilled her. And tonight she needed to be close to him, needed to let herself believe that she could be loved.

Bringing her lips up to his, she kissed him softly, temptingly. "Will you be doing the cooking?"

His sexy chuckle fanned across her face and curled her toes.

"Just tell me what you want."

Chapter Twelve

When Mia woke the next morning, she was momentarily startled by the strange room, but as she sat up in Marshall's bed, everything about the night before came rushing back to her. And the memories were enough to send a scarlet wave of heat across her face.

Oh, my, oh, my. She glanced at the empty spot where Marshall had lain beside her. Never had she behaved with such abandon. She'd responded to Marshall as though he'd been her lover for years rather than hours. Nothing had inhibited her. Nothing had stopped her from showing him how much she wanted him.

Well, she could be thankful she hadn't made a slip of the tongue and confessed that she loved him, she thought dryly, as she climbed from the bed and snatched up her clothing from the floor. At least she'd still have a shred of pride to hang on to whenever he eventually sent her packing.

Minutes later, after a quick shower in the private bath of his bedroom, she jerked on her jeans and blouse and hurried out to the kitchen. Marshall spotted her just as he was ending a call on his cell phone.

He snapped the instrument shut and hurried over to place a quick kiss on her lips.

"Good morning," she murmured shyly, then glanced at the phone he was dropping into pants pocket. It was six o'clock. She wouldn't expect him to be getting calls at this early hour. "Is anything wrong?"

He grimaced. "Afraid so. One of the guests is having some sort of chest pains. He thinks he pulled a muscle while rowing on the river yesterday. His wife is afraid it's his heart. I'm going to check him out. You can't be too careful with something like this." He glanced regretfully down at her. "There goes our breakfast for now. But I did have a chance to make coffee before the call came through. Why don't you have some and I'll be back as soon as I can. If I don't have a line of patients waiting on me, we could go to the Grubstake later for breakfast."

Mia quickly shook her head. "Don't worry about me. Go. Tend to your patient. That's the most important thing. I'll walk home to my cabin after I have a cup of coffee," she assured him.

Relief washed across his face. "You're too understanding, Mia." He planted another brief kiss on her lips, then turning to go, he tossed over his shoulder. "I'll see you later. This evening. Promise."

She waved him out the kitchen door and seconds later she heard the Jeep drive away.

Later that morning, after Marshall had determined that his early bird patient was suffering from a pulled ligament rather than a heart attack, he wrote the man instructions for care at home, along with a prescription for inflammation. The couple was just leaving his office when Ruthann arrived for work.

The redheaded nurse stared at Marshall as though the sight of him had sent her into shock. "What are you doing here?"

Marshall shot her a droll look. "I'm the doctor around here, Ruthie, remember? Marshall Cates, M.D."

Rolling her eyes at him, she marched over to his desk and dropped a white sack full of sugary doughnuts and cream-filled pastries. "Shouldn't you add BS to that?"

He followed after her and snatched up the sack. As he pulled out a doughnut, he asked, "What does that mean?"

Ruthann banged the heel of her palm against the side of her head. "Do I have to spell it out for you? It's something you shovel out of the barn and you're full of it."

He bit off half the doughnut and swallowed it down after a few short chews. "Hell! That's not what I mean! Why are you insulting me by implying that I work banker's hours? I am a doctor," he reminded her pointedly. "I do have emergency calls."

Her brows shot up. "I thought you regulated those to Dr. Baxter."

"Not anymore."

"Since when?" she countered.

Frowning, he dropped into his desk chair and pulled another pastry from the sack. "Since a few days ago," he answered with a tinge of annoyance. "Since I decided I needed to do more around here to earn my pay."

Ruthann slapped a palm against her forehead and sank into a chair angled toward the front of Marshall's desk. "My God, let me sit down! I think I'm hallucinating—I think I'm actually seeing a doctor with a conscience."

He leveled a gaze at her. "Sometimes it stuns me that you can be such a mean woman."

She started to laugh and then another thought must have struck her because she frowned at him in confusion. "What was the emergency that called you out of your bed this morning?"

"Chest pains. But it was nothing serious. The patient and his wife were very relieved. And grateful. Made me feel good to help them. Even if I did have to miss cooking breakfast."

This time Ruthann did laugh, although the sound was more like a snort.

"Yeah. Sure, Marshall. You slave over the stove every morning, then eat a sack of pastries after you get to work."

Dusting the powdered sugar from his hands, he leaned back in the cushioned leather chair. He was exhausted. But it was the most pleasant sort of exhaustion he'd ever felt in his life. Mia had kissed him, touched him, whispered to him, turned him inside out with her lovemaking. He felt like a new and different man. And suddenly all the things he'd considered unimportant in life were now shouting at him to take a second look.

"Ruthie, do you think I'd make a good father?"

The startled nurse scooted to the edge of her chair. "Did you get drunk last night?"

Only on love, he thought. It was crazy. Foolish. He'd never imagined that the bug would bite him. He'd thought he was immune. But he felt like a grinning idiot and it was downright glorious.

"No. And I asked you a perfectly logical question," he shot at her.

She drew in a long breath and slowly released it. "Don't you think you ought to be a husband first?"

He pondered her question as he reached for another doughnut. "Yeah. That would be the way to do it, wouldn't it? A husband and then a father. Yeah. I could do it. Just follow after my dad."

"Well, I have to admit that Frank Cates is probably the best example of both. But as for you—you're thirty-four years old. You've gone through women like a stack of cotton socks. No," she said with a shake of her head, "if you had a wife you'd only end up breaking her heart and then I'd really hate you."

"I wouldn't do any such thing," he countered.

She snatched up the bakery sack before he could reach for the last pastry. "You're not only crazy this morning, you're eating like a hog. Why in heck are you so hungry?"

A wicked grin spread across his face. "Exercise, Ruthie. You ought to try it some time."

With a roll of her eyes, she left the room, carrying the last sugary treat with her.

Later that day, Mia sat on the porch of her cabin, trying to read, trying to forget the endless times Janelle had rung her cell phone today and, even more, trying to come to terms with the fact that she'd fallen in love with Marshall.

An objective friend would probably tell her that she was simply still glowing after a night of good sex. But Mia didn't have a close friend here on the resort to confide in. And even if she did, she wouldn't go along with that reasoning. Yes, being in Marshall's arms had given her a glimpse of ecstasy, but it hadn't just been sex. Not with her half of the partnership. The only reason she'd allowed him to carry her to his bed was the love that had been growing in her heart, building until she'd been unable to shut it down or hide it away.

Now what was she going to do about it? she wondered miserably.

Fool! There's nothing you can do about it. Marshall believes you're a sweet girl who unfortunately lost her parents. Once he gets the real picture of who you are, he'll turn his back and walk away.

Painful emotions knotted her throat and misted her eyes, making it impossible to read the open book on her lap. She was trying to compose herself and will the attack of hopelessness away when the sound of an approaching vehicle caught her attention and she looked up to see Marshall's Jeep braking to a halt next to her rental car.

Desperate to hide her turmoil from his perceptive gaze, she quickly dashed the back of her hand against her eyes and rose to her feet. By the time he'd jogged up on the porch to join her, she'd managed to plaster a bright smile on her face.

"Hello, doc."

His lips tilted into a sexy grin, he slid his arms around her and locked his hands at the back of her waist.

Mia's heart fluttered with happiness as he brought a soft, sweet kiss to her lips.

"Hello, beautiful," he murmured.

"My, that's a special greeting."

The grin on his lips deepened. "You're a special girl. My girl," he added softly.

Her heart winced at the sincerity in his voice. The idea that he was actually starting to care for her only made matters a thousand times worse. It would be wrong to lead him into a relationship that could go nowhere. Yet she wanted him so. Needed him so. Oh, God, help me, she silently prayed.

Dropping her gaze away from his twinkling eyes, she buried her cheek against the middle of his chest. "How did your emergency go this morning? I hope everything turned out okay."

"It did." He rubbed his chin against the top of her head. "The guy's heart checked out perfectly fine. He had a pulled ligament."

"That's good."

"Yeah. I'm just sorry it interrupted our breakfast together. That's one reason why I'm here. I thought I'd make up for it by taking you to the Grubstake for a quick bite. And then…"

His suggestive pause had her tilting her head back to look up at him. The sultry squint of his eyes told her he'd already planned a repeat of last night and Mia realized if she wanted to avoid an even bigger heartache, she'd turn tail and run. But she couldn't. Not when everything inside her was hungering to be back in his arms.

"Then what?" she softly prompted.

"We're going on a bike ride."

Her eyes widened. "A bike ride! Where?"

He chuckled at the surprise sweeping across her face. "Up the mountain from my house. Where we found Joey and his mother. I never got to show you my special spot up there. Are you up for it?"

At this moment she felt certain she could run for miles. As long as he was by her side.

Smiling, she eased out of his arms and picked up the book she'd left laying in her lawn chair. "Just let me change into some jeans. The last time I went up a mountain with you my knees were ground into hamburger meat."

Laughing, he followed her into the cabin.

Two hours later, after eating hearty sandwiches and fries at the Grubstake, Mia and Marshall rode up the mountain, two miles past the spot where they'd found Joey, then left their bikes at the side of the road to walk into the woods.

When they first ventured into the thick forest of tall aspens and fir trees, Mia expected a long steep hike over treacherous boulders, but it turned out to be more of an easy stroll along a lightly beaten path.

"Do other resort guests know about this place of yours?" she asked as she closely followed him through a stand of aspens.

"I doubt anyone else has ever found it. I've never seen anyone else climbing up this far."

"Hmm. Well, no one else is a mountain goat like you are," she teased.

"Just wait. You'll see that this trip was worth it."

Moments later they rounded another stand of trees and suddenly an open area appeared before them and Mia gasped with shocked pleasure.

There before them were slabs of red rock towering at least fifty feet above their heads. Water was spilling over the top of the ledge, falling and tinkling against the rocks until it reached a natural pool edged with tall reeds and blooming water lilies. The spot was so incredibly beautiful that it seemed more fairy tale than real.

Mia's first instinct was to rush forward to get an even closer look, but before either of them took a step, Marshall grabbed her arm and silently pointed to a mule deer with a fawn at its side slipping quietly from the trees and over to the pool's edge.

As mother and baby drank, Mia looked up at Marshall and smiled gratefully. "Thank you for bringing me here," she silently mouthed up at him, so as not to give away their presence and startle the animals.

Marshall responded by bending his head and pressing his lips to hers. The kiss was full of tenderness and something else that Mia had never felt before. It tugged at her heart and filled her chest with such emotion that she could scarcely breathe.

When he finally lifted his head, they both turned their heads to see that the doe and fawn had disappeared. Marshall slipped his arm against her back and urged her toward the waterfall.

"Come on," he said quietly. "Let me show you where I come when I really want to think."

When they returned to Marshall's log house later that evening it was no surprise to Mia that the two of them ended up in his bed. Nor was it a surprise that their lovemaking was even more earthshaking for her than it had been the night before. Her heart was well and truly entangled with the man and each time she'd given her body to him, her very soul had gone with it.

This morning after cooking her a leisurely breakfast, he'd dropped her off at her cabin on his way to work. He'd kissed her goodbye with the promise of calling her later in the day to talk over plans of getting together tonight.

Since that time, Mia had been prowling around her cabin, unable to relax, unable to concentrate on anything except this impossible situation she'd fallen into.

Situation. No, it was far worse than a situation. It was a complete and utter disaster. This thing between them was snowballing, racing along so quickly that she didn't know how to put on the brakes, much less stop it. But stop it she had to. Now. Tonight. Before Marshall found out she was really Nina Hanover.

The ring of her cell phone interrupted her pacing and for a moment she simply stared in dread at the instrument. If Marshall was calling what was she going to say? Just enough to put him off without alerting him that something was wrong? Yes, she thought, frantically. If she had tonight alone, then maybe she could figure out how she was going to deal with him tomorrow.

For once she wished that the caller actually was Janelle. But the ID number glaring up at her was Marshall's and she was forced to answer. Otherwise, he'd wind up on her porch and she wouldn't be able to find the resistance to stay out of his arms.

Swallowing hard, she pushed the talk button and spoke. "Hi, Marshall."

"Hi, darlin'. I'm five minutes away from leaving the office. Tell me where you'd like to eat dinner. How about driving over to Bozeman? I doubt you've been off the resort since you first arrived."

It was true. Once Mia had decided to temporarily settle at Thunder Canyon Resort, she'd ventured no farther than town. She'd not wanted to show her face on any of the major cities along the interstate, just in case Janelle had private investigators out looking for her. And there was little doubt in Mia's mind that the woman had been searching for her. Since finding Mia's note explaining that she was taking an extended trip to give herself time to think, Janelle had probably whipped into action, doling out money to anyone who'd make a concentrated effort to find her runaway daughter.

"Uh—no, I haven't been to Bozeman." Her voice sounded strained even to her own ears, but she couldn't help it. Her heart was breaking and all she really wanted to do was throw down the phone and sob until she couldn't shed another tear.

"Is something wrong, Mia? You sound strange."

She swallowed again as her throat clogged with a ball of guilt and regret. "I—well, actually there is something wrong. My head. I—developed a migraine this afternoon. And it's really cracking. I don't think I can make it out of bed."

"Mia, honey! You should have called my office earlier! I can prescribe you something for the pain or if necessary give you an injection. Just hold on. I'll be there in five minutes."

"No!" she blurted, then realizing how frantic that sounded, she added, "I mean, there's no need for you to come over. I took something a few minutes ago and I'm going to try to sleep."

Several moments passed before he finally replied. Mia got the feeling that this sudden change in plans had really taken him aback. Well, it had done more than that to her. The pain that had started in her chest was now radiating through her whole body, leaving her numb and dazed. If there was some sort of painkiller that could wipe out this love she felt for him, then she desperately needed it.

"All right, Mia. But I'd feel much better if you'd let me examine you."

"Don't be silly, Marshall. It's just a headache. I'll be fine tomorrow. I'll call you then."

She could hear him drawing in a rough breath. The sound brought tears to her eyes and she swiftly squeezed them shut.

"I—I was really planning on us being together tonight," he said softly. "The house is going to be damn hollow without you."

She was choking, dying from the bitter loss washing over her. "I'm—sorry, Marshall," she spoke through a veil of tears. "I didn't want the evening to end like this, either."

"You can't help it if you're sick, honey. Try to get some sleep and I'll check on you in the morning."

Relieved that he'd accepted her excuse, Mia quickly told him goodbye. But once she'd pushed the button to end the call, she broke into racking sobs that continued until she'd cried herself to sleep on the sofa.

When Mia woke the next morning, her heart was so heavy she could hardly push herself into the kitchen to make coffee. For all she noticed, the bright sunshine pounding against the windowpanes of the cabin might as well have been fierce raindrops. The first real joy she'd found since Nina passed away was over. The first real love she'd ever felt for a man couldn't be continued. She couldn't hold on to the happiness that love should bring to a young woman's life. And all because she'd made horrible choices in the past. Choices that painted her as a selfish gold-digger and someone that a good man like Marshall could never love.

After a quick cup of coffee, Mia decided the best thing she could do this morning would be to leave the cabin and go for a walk in the forest. That way when Marshall called or dropped by to check on her, she'd be gone. It was a cowardly way for her to behave, but she wasn't sure she could face him just yet without breaking down in tears.

She had changed into clean jeans and a white peasant blouse and was walking swiftly away from the cabin when she heard a vehicle approaching her from behind.

Her whole body heavy with dread, she turned to see Marshall's Jeep bearing down on her. He skidded to a stop beside her and hopped out with the athletic ease she'd come to associate with him.

"Good morning," she greeted, tilting her chin, bracing herself for what had to be.

"Good morning, yourself," he said, his stunned gaze whipping over her face. "What are you doing out here? I thought you were sick?"

Her heart was pounding so hard she thought she might lose her coffee right there in front of him. "I—was going out for a little hike this morning."

"After being bedridden with a migraine? Don't you think that's a little much?"

Of course he would view it that way. He was a doctor. Oh, God, help her, she prayed.

Clearing her throat, she glanced away from him and continued to pray for strength. "Okay, Marshall. I confess. I didn't really have a headache last night. I...knew if I didn't tell you something like that...you would…well, the two of us would end up in bed together again."

Looking even more stunned, he closed the distance between them and put a hand on her arm. The contact sent shivers of excitement and aching regret through her rigid body.

Bemused, he shook his head. "I don't understand, Mia. I thought you *wanted* us to be together—to make love."

Tightening her jaw to prevent her lips from trembling, she said, "I did. But I've been thinking it all through. And I— Well, this thing between us is going too fast. Way too fast." She forced herself to look at him and quickly wished she hadn't. Pain was clouding his brown eyes and the idea that she'd put it there made her even sicker. "I believe that we…need to cool things between us for a while."

He sucked in a deep breath then slowly blew it out and as he did, his eyes narrowed to two angry slits. "Why don't you just come out and say what you really mean, Mia. You jumped into bed with me. You've had your fun. And now you want out. Well, it looks like I was wrong about you. Dead wrong."

She froze inside. "What do you mean?" she asked tightly.

His face like a piece of granite, he said, "I didn't believe you were just one of those rich little teases out for your own enjoyment. I thought you were different— sincere. But it looks like the joke is on me, isn't it? I've got to admit, Mia, you really had me fooled. I thought— Oh, to hell with what I thought. You obviously don't give a damn what I think anyway!"

He turned and climbed back into his Jeep and though everything inside Mia was screaming at her to call him back, to explain that she hadn't been teasing him, using him, all she could do was stand there, her gaze frozen on the vehicle as he drove away.

Once his Jeep rounded a stand of trees and disappeared from view, finality set in and washed over her heart like a crushing wave. Everything between them was over. She'd accomplished what she'd set out to do. Now all she had to do was get over the only love of her life.

Chapter Thirteen

Two days later the weather turned wet and unusually cool for late August. For the most part, the guests at the resort were whiling away their time with indoor games and rounds of warm drinks from the bar and the coffee shop.

Marshall's patients had dwindled down to none and by late afternoon, he told Ruthie to close up shop and let the answering service deal with any oncoming calls. The idle day was driving him crazy. With too much time to dwell on Mia, his office felt like a cage.

He left the building by way of the back entrance and once in his Jeep, automatically turned the vehicle toward his home. But halfway there, he muttered a disgusted curse and made a U-turn in the middle of the dirt road.

There was no use in going home. The place was hauntingly empty without Mia.

That's what you get, Marshall, for letting the woman get close, for letting her into your home as though she were someone who'd be around for the rest of your life.

The accusing voice in his head was right. He'd been a fool to think an heiress would fit into his life on a permanent basis. What the hell had he been thinking? He hadn't been thinking. He'd been feeling. Only feeling.

Moments later, he passed the turn off to Mia's cabin and continued barreling on out of the resort. He'd not tried to contact her since their brief encounter the other morning. He wasn't a glutton for self-punishment and though he'd finally let his guard down and allowed a woman to get under his skin, that didn't mean he was a naive fool. She'd made it clear that she wanted to end things between them. There wasn't any sense in going back for more pain, to give her another chance to pour salt into his wounds.

By the time he reached town, he realized his misery was leading him to the one person he could really talk to. At this hour of the day, his brother Mitchell would be at work, but he wouldn't mind if Marshall showed up unexpectedly. With all of the Cates, family always came first.

Cates International, Mitchell's successful company, was located on the edge of town. The large metal warehouse's light green exterior was trimmed in a darker green and surrounded by a huge paved parking lot that was partially filled with displays of planting and harvesting equipment.

A fancy showroom was attached to one side of the building, along with Mitch's luxurious office, but Marshall ignored the double glass door entrance gilded with gold lettering and walked on to a simple side door that accessed the warehouse. If he wasn't swamped with customers, Mitch would most likely be inside, tinkering around in his workshop.

Having guessed correctly, Marshall found his brother working at a computer and from the look of deep concentration on his face he was in his creative mood.

Walking around the desk, Marshall stood behind his brother and peered over his shoulder. "Is that some new design you're drafting, or are you just trying to draw an ice cream cone?"

His concentration broken, Mitchell looked over his shoulder. "Hey, brother. What's up?"

Unable to summon a smile to his face, Marshall shrugged. "Nothing. The weather has everybody on the resort playing safely inside. I don't have a thing to do. And I thought…I'd come out and see what you're up to."

Mitchell pointed to the small object on the computer screen. "Nothing much, just working on a little toy that might eventually make me millions."

"What the hell is that? Looks like a dunce cap for a mouse."

Mitchell grimaced. "That's why you're the doctor and I'm the inventor. I'm trying to come up with a seed broadcaster that will work on a smaller implement but cover more ground. It would save hours of labor and gallons of diesel for farmers."

"Good luck. It might be nice to have one millionaire in the family," he said dryly.

Mitchell turned off the computer and rose to his feet, motioning for Marshall to follow him over to a little nook in the room where a coffee machine was located.

"You look like you need something to perk you up, big brother. I don't think I've ever seen you looking so grim."

Mitchell poured two cups full of coffee and handed one of them to Marshall. "I'd offer you a sandwich to go with it, but the crew ate them all."

"No matter. I'm not hungry," Marshall told him. "And I should leave. I'm interrupting your work."

Shaking his head, Mitchell walked over to a comfortable couch. After taking a seat, he patted the empty cushion next to him. "I needed a break anyway. Come on. Sit. I can see something is on your mind. Tell me about it."

Raking a weary hand through his windblown hair, Marshall took a seat. "I always thought the big brother was supposed to be the listener. I'm the big brother."

Mitchell grinned at that observation. "Then who's supposed to listen to you?"

Marshall lifted his gaze to the ceiling far above them. His brother was smart, successful and smart enough to avoid the snaring arms of a woman. Too bad he hadn't been more like Mitchell, he thought. Instead, he'd gone through women like a stack of cotton socks. Just as Ruthie had said. Only this time, the tables had turned and he was the one doing the hurting. Maybe he deserved this misery.

"I don't know. Dad, I suppose. But I can't talk to him

about this. He'd only remind me that I'd wasted years of my life regarding women as playthings when I should have been looking for a wife."

Sudden dawning crossed Mitchell's face. "Ah. A woman. So that's what this mopey look of yours is all about. I should have known. So the heiress has dumped you already?"

Marshall glared at him. "You don't have to be so flip about it."

This time Mitchell frowned. "Well, what do you expect, brother? The woman isn't your style. I don't know why you're bothering with her anyway."

His jaw tightened and then he answered in a low voice, "Maybe because I loved her. Because I...still love her."

Mitchell was suddenly regarding him in a different light. "I've never heard you talk this way. You're scaring me."

"I'm scaring myself. Especially now that Mia doesn't want to see me anymore."

"Why?"

Bending his head, Marshall stared at the concrete floor. "How the hell should I know! One day she was all warm and loving and the next she says she thinks we should cool it. I can't figure what's going on with her."

Mitchell studied him thoughtfully. "Hmm. Well, she seemed nice enough at the family dinner. A little introverted, but nice."

His heart was suddenly aching as he recalled the tears on Mia's face as she'd talked about losing her mother. He'd wanted so much to help her and he'd thought loving her would give her the support she needed. He'd been wrong. Painfully wrong. "She has reason to be. She's lost her family—her mother more recently."

Mitchell blew out a long breath. "Forget her, Marshall. She's trouble. You don't need a woman carrying around a trunk of emotional issues. Put Mia Smith out of your mind and find someone new."

Marshall groaned with frustration. "I don't want another woman, Mitch. I want Mia. That's the whole problem."

Mitchell laid a comforting hand on his brother's shoulder. "If that's the way you feel, then my advice is to go confront her. Make her tell you what's wrong."

Marshall regarded his brother for a long thoughtful moment before he finally gave him a jerky nod. "You're right. If Mia wants to dump me, she's going to have to tell me why."

At the same time Marshall was visiting with his brother, Mia had finally ventured out of the cabin and walked over to the lodge. The cold weather had made the past two days even gloomier for her and though she didn't want to risk running into Marshall, she couldn't continue to hide in her cabin. She had two choices, she thought grimly, face him with the truth or leave Thunder Canyon once and for all. Either way, she was bound to lose him.

Thankfully, there was a cheery fire burning in the enormous rock fireplace in the lounge and several guests were sitting around reading, talking and playing board games. Mia purchased a cup of hot cocoa from the coffee shop and carried it over to one of the couches facing the crackling flames.

She'd just made herself comfortable and was sipping at her drink when she looked around to see Lizbeth Stanton, the lounge bartender, easing down on the cushion next to her.

"Hi," she said. "Mind if I sit down?"

Since the woman was already sitting, the question seemed inane. Mia shrugged, while wondering what could have prompted Lizbeth to join her. Even though she was acquainted with the sexy bartender and had chatted with her during her stay here at the resort, the two of them weren't what you'd called bosom buddies.

"Not at all. Are you on a break from the bar?"

Lizbeth shook her head. "No. I don't go on for another thirty minutes. I saw you sitting here and thought I'd stop by. I—uh, there's something I've been wanting to say to you and you're probably going to take offense at my being so frank, but I don't know of any other way to approach you about this."

Piqued with curiosity now, Mia turned slightly toward the bartender. "Oh?"

Frowning prettily, the auburn-haired siren folded her arms against her breasts. "Yeah. I think you're making a big mistake. No, more like a *huge* mistake. Marshall is a great guy. Everyone around Thunder Canyon will tell you so. I don't know what your game is, but he doesn't deserve to be dumped."

Mia stiffened. Is that what all of Marshall's friends here on the resort were thinking? God, she couldn't bear it. "Where did you hear such a thing—that I dumped Marshall?"

"That's not important. News travels fast here on the resort. Although all of his friends didn't have to ask what happened. They can see he's miserable thanks to you." Her accusing gaze was practically boring into Mia's eyes. "It's beyond me how any woman could throw away a man like Marshall. But you seem to be doing it quite easily."

Mia drew in a bracing breath and tried to remember she was supposed to be an heiress with class and manners. She couldn't fire back at the bartender. She couldn't scream out that good men like her father died and left grieving widows and lost daughters. That there were no guarantees for lasting love.

"Look, Lizbeth, I think you're making a mistake by putting Marshall, or any man for that matter, on a pedestal. They're fallible. They don't always stick around. Or haven't you noticed?"

Lizbeth sneered. "What's the matter with you anyway? Are you jealous because Marshall dated me first?"

As Mia looked at her in stunned disbelief, she suddenly realized that her stay here at Thunder Canyon Resort was well and truly over. Tonight she would pack and in the morning she would put Marshall and his friends behind her.

"No. Marshall doesn't belong to me."

Lizbeth rolled her eyes. "Can't you see that Marshall is crazy about you?"

Maybe he was in love with her right now, Mia

thought painfully. But if he ever met Mia Hanover that love would dissolve like a sugar cube tossed into a cup of hot coffee. Swallowing away the burning tears in her throat, Mia muttered, "Marshall never has been a one-woman man. I think you know that, Lizbeth. Most love doesn't last forever and a woman needs to learn to lean on herself and cope with life on her own."

Pity suddenly filled Lizbeth's eyes. "You know, I think I'm actually starting to feel sorry for you. You're lacking something in here."

Lizbeth pressed fingertips to her heart and it was all Mia could do to keep from bursting into tears. Apparently this woman hadn't watched her father die. Hadn't watched her mother fall apart and turn to alcohol because she'd lost the love of her life. Mia wasn't blind or crazy; she understood that Lizbeth saw her as a hardhearted woman.

Oh, if only that were true, Mia thought. If only her heart were made of steel, or anything that couldn't ache. Then walking away from Marshall wouldn't be tearing her apart.

Rising to her feet, she stared down at Lizbeth. "You're probably right," she said coldly. "You're a far better woman to nurse Marshall's wounds. Maybe with all your virtues you'll be able to persuade him to walk down the aisle with you!"

By the time Mia reached the last words her voice had risen to a trembling shriek. She sensed the guests around them were all turning their heads to take notice, but for once she didn't care. She raced out of the lounge and didn't stop running until she was completely away from the lodge and halfway to her cabin.

Two hours later, her bed was covered with open suitcases and she was blindly but methodically filling them with all her belongings.

The tears that had threatened to pour from her during her confrontation with Lizbeth had flowed like a river once she'd reached her cabin, but now they were dried tracks upon her cheeks. She felt dead inside.

She was pulling the zipper closed on a leather duffle bag when a knock sounded on the front door of the cabin. Frozen by the unexpected sound, she stared at the open door of her bedroom. Could that be Lizbeth wanting to go another round? If so, she was going to use a few choice words to send the woman on her way.

Leaving the bag, she walked out to the living room and peered through the peephole on the door. The moment she spotted Marshall standing on the other side, her heart stopped as though all the blood had drained from it.

He must have heard her approaching footsteps because he suddenly shouted through the door, "Mia, it's me. Let me in. I'm not going away until you do."

Marshall. In her wildest dreams she'd never expected him to speak to her again. Why was he here? To tell her that he didn't appreciate everyone on the resort knowing that she'd embarrassed and demeaned him?

Her hand trembling almost violently, she pushed back the bolt and opened the door. He didn't bother with a greeting or invitation. Instead, he strode across the threshold and came to a stop in the middle of the room.

Mia shut the door behind her and forced herself to turn and face him. He was dressed casually in jeans and boots and a navy-blue hooded sweatshirt. His cheeks were burnished to a ruddy color from the cool wind and his coffee-brown hair was tousled across his forehead. He looked so handsome, so endearing that it was all she could do to keep from running to him and flinging herself against his broad chest.

"I—" She swallowed hard and tried again. "I—never expected to see you here."

Anguish twisted his lips. "What were you thinking, Mia? That I'd simply keep my distance? Let everything between us end as though it had never happened at all?"

Fear rippled through her, making her insides quiver. She turned her back to him and bit down hard on her lip. "It would have been better if you had," she whispered starkly. "I'm a person that you need to forget, Marshall. I'm—no good. Not for you."

"What are you talking about?" he muttered roughly.

"Haven't you talked to Lizbeth?"

He walked up behind her but stopped short of putting his hands on her shoulders.

"No. What about Lizbeth? Has she been saying things about me to you?"

Mia bent her head, then shook it. "Don't worry. Only that you're Dr. Perfect and I'm stupid for throwing you away."

Moments passed in silence and to Mia's complete horror she felt more tears rush to her eyes. Dear God, where was this endless waterworks coming from? Why couldn't she gather herself together and stop her tears once and for all?

"Is that what you're doing?" he asked quietly. "Throwing me away?"

She squeezed her eyes, yet she couldn't hide the raw emotion in her voice. "No," she whispered. "I—I'm leaving…for your own sake."

Quickly, before he could stop her, she stepped around him and raced to the bedroom. Once there, she frantically began slinging the last of her clothes into an open suitcase.

Marshall hurried after her. "Mia? What—"

Glancing to see he'd followed her into the bedroom, she cried at him, "Don't try to stop me, Marshall! Don't ask me anything! It's useless. Totally useless!"

She was lashing out at him like a frightened kitten; hissing and pawing, when all she really wanted was to curl up in his arms.

Sensing that nothing was really as it had first seemed, Marshall went to her and folded his fingers around her shoulders. "Nothing is useless. Not when you love someone, Mia. And I love you. Don't you understand? Don't you care?"

I love you. How many times had she dreamed of hearing Marshall say those words to her? Too many. And now she had to rip them all away, to smear and mar the most precious thing he could possibly give her.

"I care. More than you could ever dream, Marshall. But—"

His hands came up to tenderly cup her tear-stained face and as the warmth of his fingers flooded through her, she suddenly realized she couldn't pretend anymore. Not with him. Not with anyone.

"Then what is it? Tell me," he softly urged.

She drew in a shaky breath, but it did little to brace her composure.

"I'm a phony, Marshall. I'm not really Mia Smith. I'm Mia Hanover. I—I've been using the name Smith in order to keep someone from trailing me."

Stunned, he dropped his hands from her face and she used the opportunity to turn away from his searching gaze.

"Someone," he repeated blankly. "Someone like a man? A lover? A stalker?"

With a shake of her head, she slowing began folding the last pieces of clothing lying atop the mounded suitcase.

"No, the only man I've ever been seriously involved with was so disgusted with me he left—walked away. He didn't care enough to come after me and try again. This person is a woman. She's—uh—my birth mother. Her name is Janelle Josephson."

Marshall looked confused. "You said your mother was killed in a car accident."

"That's right. Nina Hanover. She was my adoptive mother. She's the one who raised me since I was a baby, the one who nurtured me as I grew up, sacrificed to give me food, clothing and a roof over my head." Groaning with pain, she squeezed the fragile silk blouse in her hands. "You see, Marshall, when my father—my adoptive father—died, I was about to enter college. Up until then my family—my *life*—had been so nice. My parents loved me and although we didn't have lots of money, I had all the necessities. Daddy saw to that. But then he developed lung cancer and it seemed to take him almost overnight. Mom—Nina—was devastated. For more than twenty years, he'd been her whole life, the only man she'd ever loved. Losing him so suddenly broke her, Marshall. She couldn't deal with the grief and at some point—I can't even remember exactly when—she started drinking."

Marshall's head swung back and forth with complete dismay. "Oh, Mia. I'm so sorry."

"You won't say that. Not when I tell you the rest."

Putting a hand on her arm, he slowly turned her back to him. "Mia, nothing you say will change my love for you. Believe that."

As she met his loving gaze a sob choked her to the point that she could scarcely get any words past her throat. "You don't understand, Marshall. I caused my mother's death! I caused Nina to get behind the wheel of her car and drive. She was driving to see me—to meet with me because…because I'd been avoiding her—moving on with a life away from her."

Marshall didn't make any sort of reply. Instead he cleared an area on the side of the bed and sat Mia down, easing himself down next to her. "I want you to slow down, Mia," he said gently. "Tell me what happened from the very start."

She wiped a shaky hand over her face and sniffed back her tears. "Maybe I'd better go back to after my father died. That's when everything started going downhill."

Nodding, he reached for her hand and clasped it tightly. "Your father died and your mother started to drink. Did she become an alcoholic then?"

Mia considered his question for a moment, then shook her head. "No. I don't think she was dependent on the stuff at that time. She didn't have the opportunity to drink too much, she was always working. But no matter how many jobs she had, we could barely afford rent and utilities."

"What about the farm? You didn't try to keep it?"

Regret twisted her features. "We were forced to sell it to pay off the astronomical medical bills. There wasn't much left after that and it went quickly. During that time I began to think that if Mom and I only had money it would fix everything. It would make her happy. She wouldn't have to work all the time and it would give us both security and all the things we needed. She wouldn't want to drink anymore and everything would be wonderful again. I thought it was the answer for everything. And then I began to wonder about my real mother. I kept thinking that if I could only find her she might want to help me."

The desperate picture she was painting struck Marshall like the blade of a knife. It was so far removed from the born-into-riches-heiress he'd first believed her to be and he could only wonder at the suffering she'd gone through.

"You didn't know the circumstances of your birth?"

Shaking her head, she looked down at his hand closed tightly over hers. "No. Not a clue. Nina didn't know, either. And she didn't want me to know. She feared that if I did find my birth mother I might learn something that would haunt me for the rest of my life.

But I wouldn't listen. The image of finding my birth mother had become a beautiful dream to me. One that I wasn't about to let go."

"How on earth did you find her? Adoption information is carefully guarded."

"It took years. I used the Internet and newspapers to ask questions and put out information. I met with any- and everyone associated with my parents back around the time I was born and tried to gather any sort of leads from what they recalled about my adoption."

"Were any of them able to help you?"

"In a roundabout way," Mia answered. "One man who'd lived next to our farm, but later moved from the area, remembered that my parents had traveled up to Denver to get me. And he thought that was where the adoption had taken place. With that information, it was logical to assume the records would be there and I was determined to get my hands on them somehow. But that was like butting my head against a brick wall. I begged, cajoled, even tried to con my way into getting a glimpse at my adoption papers. Security eventually threatened to have me arrested if I didn't quit badgering the filing clerks. Then I finally happened on to a young woman working in the capital building in another department who empathized with my predicament. She was also adopted and she understood this driving need I had to know about my family. She managed to acquire a copy of my papers and mail them to me. After that it was fairly easy to trace Janelle's maiden name of Laughlin to her married name of Janelle Josephson."

Marshall tried to imagine what it would be like not knowing the woman who'd given birth to him, not knowing why she'd given him away. The anguish would haunt him, eat at him until he would probably do just as Mia had done. He would search for her and the answers he hungered for.

"That must have been like finding a rainbow in a hurricane," he murmured.

Mia nodded grimly. "Literally. Complete with the pot of gold beneath it. Janelle had come from a very rich family. Her father was a real-estate mogul in and around Denver. They were worth millions and too prominent a part of the community to allow their teenage daughter to raise a child out of wedlock. They tried to pressure her into an abortion but Janelle fought them all the way. Finally they appeared to give in to letting her have the baby, just as long as she would agree to stay with relatives living in another state until I was born."

"Sounds like a pair of real loving parents," Marshall said sarcastically. "She must have been underage and unable to reach out to anyone else for help. So how did they talk her into putting you up for adoption?"

"They didn't. After she gave birth they told her that I'd been stillborn and they didn't want her to go through the trauma of seeing me. They even held a mock funeral to make things look real to Janelle."

"Incredible," he muttered with amazement. "So what happened when she discovered that you were really alive and a grown woman?"

Mia closed her eyes and drew in a ragged breath.

"She was shocked, but ecstatic. She immediately took me into her home and began lavishing me with everything, clinging to me as though she couldn't bear for me to get out of her sight."

"What about her husband? What did he think about all this? And her parents—your grandparents—are they still around?"

"Her father died a few years after I was born. Later on, Janelle's mother became debilitated from a stroke and she now resides in a nursing home. As for her husband, he died a few years ago of a heart attack and since then Janelle has remained a widow."

Frowning now with confusion, Marshall studied her rueful expression. "So you came along and filled Janelle's life up again. That's good. Good for both of you. Wasn't it? *Isn't* it?"

"In many ways, yes. But on the other hand there was Nina—the only mother I'd ever known. It wasn't long before the two women were pushing and pulling me between them. Janelle was offering me a secure home, riches beyond my wildest imaginings. Nina accused me of turning my back on her and ignoring her because she was poor." Her pleading eyes lifted to Marshall's. "That wasn't true, Marshall. But I'm sure it must have seemed that way to Mom."

His hand left hers and lifted to gently touch her cheek. "What was the truth, Mia?"

"The truth?" She let out a mocking laugh. "God, Marshall, I've tried to hide and pretend for so long now I often have to ask myself who I am and what I'm supposed to be doing. But the truth was that I grew to care about Janelle. How could I not? She loves me and she wants to care for me. Nina loved me, too, but the more I tried to reason with her the more she wanted to drink. She began to cling and whine and tell me that it was all my fault that she couldn't leave the bottle alone. She kept insisting that if I'd come home to her she'd get sober and stay that way."

Marshall's head swung back and forth. "You didn't believe her, did you?"

"Not really," Mia said sadly. "But I didn't want to give up on her completely. I gave her money. Helped her buy a nice home and a car. I thought lifting her out of poverty would help her see that she had every reason to quit drinking. It didn't. She wanted me to come home. One day I agreed to meet with her for lunch—to talk things over and try to reassure her that I would always love her no matter where I lived. I had hopes that I could talk her into entering rehab." She looked away from him and when she spoke again her voice was as hollow as a drained barrel. "She crashed her car on the way to meet me. Later, the toxicology report in the autopsy revealed that she was driving drunk. So now you know. I killed my mother…she died trying to… reach me."

Her chin suddenly dropped to her chest and silent sobs shook her shoulders. Crushed by the sight of her pain, Marshall moved closer and put his arm around her.

"Mia, don't keep punishing yourself like this. Nina's death wasn't your fault."

Mia lifted her head and stared at him in stunned fascination. "You mean—you don't think I'm a greedy gold digger? That I caused my own mother to kill herself?"

Her questions amazed him. "Is that what you've been afraid of all this time? That if I knew about your past that I wouldn't want anything to do with you? Oh, Mia, can't you see that you didn't cause Nina's death? She was the one who chose to drink. She was the one who climbed behind the wheel."

A sob caught in her throat. "Yes. But I made her unhappy. Because I started making a new life with Janelle."

Groaning, he slipped a hand behind the back of her head and pulled her forward until her cheek was resting against his shoulder. "I've gathered enough from all you've told me that Nina chose to be unhappy long before you found Janelle. She had issues that you weren't qualified to deal with, Mia. She needed professional help. Alcoholism is a horrible disease—you couldn't have cured her just by staying away from Janelle."

Sobbing now with relief, Mia held on to him tightly. "I came here to Thunder Canyon to hide from Janelle. In lots of ways I guess I thought of her as a coconspirator in Nina's death and I resented the love she was trying to give me. I suppose it made me feel even guiltier about Nina. But now I can see that I was wrong about that, too." Lifting her face up to his, she tried to smile. "You've opened my eyes, Marshall. In so many ways."

"I think you should call Janelle. I'm sure she's worried sick about you." He stroked her long black hair with slow, steady movements. "And now that your eyes are open, I hope you can now see that I love you. More than anything, Mia."

She groaned with disbelief. "I don't know why. I'm a bundle of trouble."

"A beautiful bundle," he crooned. He brought his lips over hers in a long, tender kiss. Once it ended, he looked at her pointedly, expectantly. "This means you're going to stay here in Thunder Canyon, doesn't it? With me?"

Slowly, thoughtfully, she eased out of his arms and he watched with a sense of dread as she folded the last of her clothes and placed them in the open suitcase.

"I've got to leave, Marshall. There're so many unsettled things in my life that I need to deal with right now. It wouldn't be right for me to make promises to you. Not when I need to straighten up my head and my heart." With a tiny flame of hope flickering in her eyes, she glanced at him. "Can you understand that, Marshall? Really understand?"

Rising to his feet, he placed his hands on her shoulders and gave her an affectionate squeeze. "A month ago I probably wouldn't have been able to appreciate what you're feeling. I was so full of myself that I never stopped to really look at my patient's needs or count the blessings that I'd been given. You've changed me, Mia. I'd rather you stay here and not leave my sight." A wry smile touched his lips. "But you've already had enough people pulling and pushing you. I don't want you here with me because you're under duress. If you come back to me I want it to be because you love me, because it's where you want to be."

Turning toward him, she pressed her cheek gratefully against his heart. "Thank you, Marshall, for understanding."

Chapter Fourteen

A week later, in a small cemetery on the outskirts of Alamosa, Colorado, Mia carried bunches of yellow and bronze chrysanthemums as she worked her way to the small patch of ground where her parents lay in rest.

A cool wind was blowing across the graveyard, but a bright sun was shining overhead, glinting off the double granite headstone shared by her parents.

Bending on one knee, Mia brushed away the fallen autumn leaves, then carefully propped the bright cheerful mums against the sparkly black rock. After a moment, she spoke to her mother.

"It's me, Mom. I've come back. Finally. I realize I'm too late to feel your arms wrap around me or to tell you how very much I love you. But I pray that you can somehow hear me now, that you understand I never, ever once stopped loving you.

"After Daddy died we went through so much together. So many hard times. So much sadness. I didn't know how to help you deal with your disease and you didn't know how to fight your way out of it. In the end I guess we were both guilty of not trying hard enough. But I'm positive you've gone on to a better place. And now when I think of you, Mom, I'm going to think of all the good and happy times we had together. I'm going to smile and remember how lucky I was that you chose me to be your daughter."

With a whispered goodbye, Mia rose to her full height and wiped away the single tear on her cheek.

The walk back to her car was short, yet as she lifted her gaze toward the sky, she was certain it had become brighter and there in the vivid blue she could almost envision Nina's smiling face.

Sweet release poured over her like warm sunshine as she pulled a cell phone from her coat pocket and punched in Janelle's number.

Several days later, Marshall was in his office, using the last of his lunch break to make a long distance call to his old friend DJ Traub down in Georgia. For weeks now he'd been trying to talk the other man into coming home once and for all. And today, for the first time, Marshall caught a hint that DJ was seriously considering a return to Montana.

As their conversation reached the end, Marshall made one last pitch to his friend. "All right, buddy, I hope we see you soon. Everybody here misses you. And Thunder Canyon could use some of that good barbecue. There's plenty of space for a Rib Shack here on the resort. Get yourself on a plane and get back here, DJ. No excuses."

Marshall added a quick goodbye and was hanging up the phone when Ruthann paused at the corner of his desk.

"Who was that? I thought I heard you say something about barbecue," she said nosily.

"Sure did. That was DJ Traub. Remember him?"

The nurse thoughtfully tapped a finger against her chin. "I think I do. He's Dax's brother, isn't he?"

"You're right."

"And isn't he the one who made all that money with some sort of barbecue sauce?"

Marshall smiled. "Give the woman a prize. Right on both counts. Besides the sauce he now has a chain of restaurants called DJ's Rib Shack. I'm trying to talk him into putting one here on the resort."

"Oh, now that would be my style of eating," Ruthann told him. "Elbows on the table, paper towels for napkins. The next time you talk to him, tell him he's got one waiting customer for sure."

"I'll be happy to." Marshall reached around to his hip and pulled out his billfold. As he pulled out several large bills and tossed them toward his nurse, he said, "There. Go buy yourself a fancy dress. You and I are going to the Gallatin Room tonight. I promised and now I'm following through. And I don't want to hear any arguments from you, Ruthie."

Frowning, she picked up the bills, counted them, then shook her head in dismay. "I'm not about to waste this money. Like I just told you, I'm not fancy. You need to save this—" she waved the money at him "—and take the heiress to the Gallatin Room."

A shadow crossed Marshall's face. "Have you forgotten, Ruthie? Mia isn't here at the resort anymore."

Her expression was suddenly apologetic as she sunk into one of the chairs in front of Marshall's desk. "I'm sorry, Marshall. I guess I got so used to you talking about the woman that I forgot she isn't here anymore. Have you heard from her since she left?"

Picking up a pen, he doodled senselessly on a prescription pad. "No. Not yet. But I will. At least, I'm praying that I will."

The nurse studied his glum face. "You got it bad for her, huh?"

He drew in a long breath and released it. For days now, he'd been trying to convince himself that Mia loved him, that one of these days he would look up and see her smiling face. But as each day slipped by without her, he was beginning to worry that she had moved on to a life without him.

"I love her very much, Ruthie. She's changed me. Now I can see that life isn't just a game to be enjoyed. It's a precious gift."

Her expression perceptive, Ruthann leaned forward and touched his hand. "I can see the change in you, Marshall. I'd almost bet that when the snow comes this winter you'll be spending more time here in your office than out on the slopes."

A sheepish smile crossed his face. "I guess I did do a lot of playing last year. It annoyed the hell out of me when I'd have to come in and tend to a patient. I was a real dedicated doctor," he said with sarcasm, then shook his head with a hefty measure of self-disgust. "You know, Ruthie, when the Queen of Hearts struck it rich and the town started going crazy making money, I thought it was the best thing that could have ever happened to this place. I still do think it's helped many people, but it wasn't the right thing for me. I got this cushy job and forgot why I'd become a doctor in the first place."

Ruthann tossed him a look that said she'd watched the circle he'd made and she couldn't be happier that he was back to treating his patients with real care and concern.

"Even if the heiress never comes back, she's been good for you, Marshall. You're back to being a doctor I'm proud to work for."

He wasn't going to even contemplate the idea that Mia would never come back. She had to. She'd become everything to him. "Oh, hell, Ruthie, you're getting maudlin on me now. Get out of here. Go buy that dress. I'm picking you up at seven. So be ready."

The nurse started to toss the money at him, but he grabbed her hand and folded it over the wad of bills.

"Don't argue, Ruthie," he said firmly. "Just do as I say."

"But, Marshall—"

A knock on the office door caused both doctor and nurse to pause and exchange a look of surprise.

"A patient probably took a wrong turn and can't find the exit out of here," Ruthie finally said. "I'll go see."

While Ruthann went to the door, Marshall closed the last chart he'd been updating and flipped off the lamp on his desk.

Rising from the chair, he glanced over to see his nurse was still speaking to someone on the other side of the door. It never failed that a patient would show up when the clinic was closing, but Marshall no longer minded being detained. Not if he could truly help someone.

"There's no need to dawdle around, Ruthie. If someone is sick or injured take the person back to an examining room. I'll be right there."

Ruthann tossed over her shoulder, "This is a patient I'm certain you'll want to see. I'll put her in examining room one."

"Fine. I'll be right there."

Picking up his stethoscope, he hung it around his neck and quickly strode out of his office. When he started down the hallway toward the examination rooms, Ruthann was nowhere in sight. Figuring she'd stayed with the patient, he rapped lightly on the first door he came to and stepped inside.

The moment he spotted Mia sitting on the end of the examining table, he stopped in his tracks and simply stared at her.

Smiling broadly, she said, "I hope you can fix me, doc. I'm really hurting."

"Mia!"

Her name was all he could manage to get out as he rushed forward and enfolded her in his arms.

Mia held him tightly and as the warmth of his body seeped into hers, she knew without a doubt that she had finally come home.

"There's no other place I could be. Except here with you."

Thrilled by her words, he eased his head back far enough to search her smiling face. "You look happy, Mia. Really happy. Are you?"

Her hand lifted to his face and he turned his lips into her palm and pressed a kiss on the soft skin.

"Thanks to you, Marshall. If you hadn't made me face my past I think I would still be running, hiding, trying to forget all the mistakes I have made. Facing them has been more therapeutic than you could ever imagine. Or maybe you can," she added, her eyes twinkling. "You're a doctor. A very special one, too."

He rubbed his cheek next to hers and she closed her eyes and savored the sense of contentment sweeping through her.

"What about your mother—Janelle? I hope you're getting things settled with her."

"Very much so. I think she finally understands that she doesn't have to make demands or smother me to have my love. I've assured her that I'll see her on a regular basis and she can contact me anytime on the phone."

"If you'll answer it, that is," he said wryly.

Her blush was compounded with a guilty smile. "I confess. I had reached the point where I couldn't deal with her, Marshall. But then I met you and fell in love and everything started changing. When I finally saw that you could actually love me for the person I really was—that gave me the courage and strength to face my problems. *You* did all that for me."

His hands cradled the sides of her face as his gaze delved deeply into hers. "Did I hear right? You—fell in love with me?"

The shy smile on her face turned seductive and with a groan of desire, she rested her forehead against his. "I tried hard not to. But you're irresistible, Dr. Cates. Now you're stuck with me. I'm making my home here in Thunder Canyon. And I'm going back to school to finish my nursing studies—especially in counseling. Eventually, I'd like to use my inheritance to create The Nina Hanover Center, a place where women experiencing grief and emotional problems can come to get the help they need. What do you think about that?"

Smiling broadly, he closed the last small space between their lips. "I think it's the grandest thing I've heard since gold was found in the Queen of Hearts. And I just happen to know a good doctor with plenty of strings to help you. We'll build that center together, honey."

Mia's heart sang as she curled her arms around his neck and met the sweet promise of his kiss.

When he finally lifted his head, he shouted with sheer joy and plucked her down from the examining table. "C'mon! Let's go find Ruthie. I promised to take her to dinner tonight at the Gallatin Room. I've got to tell her it's going to be a threesome now." He tugged her toward the door, but before he jerked it open, he snapped his fingers with afterthought. "Hell, let's make it more than a threesome! I'm going to call my family and friends. We'll make tonight a big celebration."

Laughing, Mia followed him down the hallway and knew in her heart that life with Marshall would always be a celebration.

* * * * *

Next month, don't miss Her Best Man
by reader favourite Crystal Green

The third book in the new Special Edition continuity MONTANA

Years ago, DJ Traub left home to escape a broken heart. Now he's back and he's got a second chance with the woman he's never stopped wanting…

*On sale September 2008,
wherever Mills & Boon® books are sold.*

The Baby Bind
by Nikki Benjamin

After unsuccessful attempts at conceiving left her marriage in tatters, Charlotte Fagan had one last hope – to adopt a child. For the application to be approved, she and her estranged husband Sean would have to pretend to still be together. He agreed to go along with the plan – on one condition...

From the First Kiss
by Jessica Bird

From day one, Alex Moorehouse loved architect Cassandra Cutler – but she'd said "I do" to his best friend, Reese. Then Reese got caught in a storm at sea...and drowned. Cass was rebuilding Alex's B&B, but perhaps there was scope for them to build a future...

Finding His Way Home
by Barbara Gale

Years ago, heiress Valetta Faraday had fled her privileged California upbringing and forged a new path as a reporter in New York state. But now Linc Cameron was on a mission to bring her back. Would the pretty widow persuade the LA playboy to share her small-town life instead?

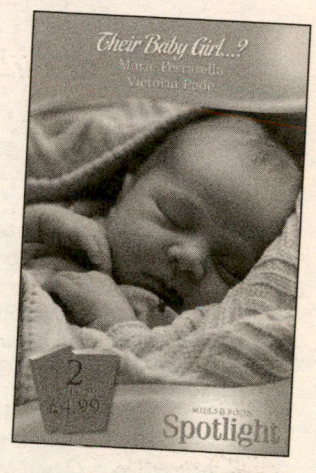

Queens of Romance

Uncertain Summer

Serena gave up hope of getting married when her fiancé
jilted her. Then Gijs suggested that she marry him instead.
She liked Gijs very much, and she knew he was fond of her –
that seemed as good a basis as any for marriage. But it
turned out Gijs was in love…

Small Slice of Summer

Letitia Marsden had decided that men were not to be trusted,
until she met Doctor Jason Mourik van Nie. This time, Letitia
vowed, there would be a happy ending. Then Jason got the
wrong idea about one of her male friends. Surely a simple
misunderstanding couldn't stand in the way of true love?

Available 1st August 2008

Collect all 10 superb books in the collection!

M&B

This proud man must learn to love again

Linda Lael Miller

Miller

The Millionaire's Pride

Successful, rich widower Rance McKettrick is determined that nothing is going to get in the way of his new start in life.

But after meeting the sweet, beautiful Echo Wells, Rance finds her straightforward honesty is challenging everything he thought he knew about himself. Both Rance and Echo must come to grips with who they really are to find a once-in-a-lifetime happiness.

Available 18th July 2008

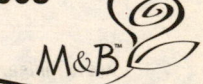

M&B

Would she surrender to the sheikh?

Possessed by the Sheikh by **Penny Jordan**

After being stranded in the desert, Katrina was rescued by a sheikh and taken back to his luxury camp. The sheikh thought Katrina little more than a whore. And then he discovered that she was a virgin… Now he must marry her!

Prince of the Desert by **Penny Jordan**

One hot night in the kingdom of Zuran has left Gwynneth fevered and unsure. Gwynneth doesn't realise she shared a bed with Sheikh Tariq bin Salud – and he is determined to claim her virginity…

Available 18th July 2008

From the Number One *New York Times* bestselling author NORA ROBERTS

Stars
Containing the classic novels
Hidden Star and *Captive Star*
Available 5th September 2008

Treasures
Containing *Secret Star*, the exciting final part in *The Stars of Mirtha* trilogy, plus a special bonus novel, *Treasures Lost, Treasures Found*
Available 7th November 2008

Don't miss these two sparkling treasures!

Queens of Romance

Bedding His Virgin Mistress

Ricardo Salvatore planned to take over Carly's company, so why not have her as well? But Ricardo was stunned when in the heat of passion he learned of Carly's innocence…

Expecting the Playboy's Heir

American billionaire and heir to an earldom, Silas Carter is one of the world's most eligible men. Beautiful Julia Fellowes is perfect wife material. And she's pregnant!

Blackmailing the Society Bride

When millionaire banker Marcus Canning decides it's time to get an heir, debt-ridden Lucy becomes a convenient wife. Their sexual chemistry is purely a bonus…

Available 5th September 2008

Collect all 10 superb books in the collection!

M&B

Celebrate 100 years of pure reading pleasure with Mills & Boon®

To mark our centenary, each month we're publishing a special 100th Birthday Edition. These celebratory editions are packed with extra features and include a FREE bonus story.

Plus, you have the chance to enter a fabulous monthly prize draw. See 100th Birthday Edition books for details.

Now that's worth celebrating!

July 2008

**The Man Who Had Everything
by Christine Rimmer**
Includes FREE bonus story *Marrying Molly*

August 2008

Their Miracle Baby by Caroline Anderson
Includes FREE bonus story *Making Memories*

September 2008

Crazy About Her Spanish Boss by Rebecca Winters
Includes FREE bonus story
Rafael's Convenient Proposal

Look for Mills & Boon® 100th Birthday Editions at
your favourite bookseller or visit
www.millsandboon.co.uk

FREE

4 BOOKS AND A SURPRISE GIFT!

We would like to take this opportunity to thank you for reading this Mills & Boon® book by offering you the chance to take FOUR more specially selected titles from the Special Edition series absolutely FREE! We're also making this offer to introduce you to the benefits of the Mills & Boon® Book Club™—

- ★ **FREE home delivery**
- ★ **FREE gifts and competitions**
- ★ **FREE monthly Newsletter**
- ★ **Books available before they're in the shops**
- ★ **Exclusive Mills & Boon Book Club offers**

Accepting these FREE books and gift places you under no obligation to buy; you may cancel at any time, even after receiving your free shipment. Simply complete your details below and return the entire page to the address below. You don't even need a stamp!

YES! Please send me 4 free Special Edition books and a surprise gift. I understand that unless you hear from me, I will receive 6 superb new titles every month for just £3.15 each, postage and packing free. I am under no obligation to purchase any books and may cancel my subscription at any time. The free books and gift will be mine to keep in any case.

E8ZEE

Ms/Mrs/Miss/Mr..Initials ....
BLOCK CAPITALS PLEASE

Surname ....

Address ....

....

....Postcode ....

Send this whole page to:
The Mills & Boon Book Club, FREEPOST CN81, Croydon, CR9 3WZ